DATE DUE

AG 10 '06	JUL 2 - 2015	
SE 06 06	AUG 5 - 2015	
SE 21 '06	4/18/16	
JA 15 '07		
12/13/06		
JA 3/06		
FE 1 07		
MR 29 07		
APR 2 - 2011		
APR 17 2011		
SEP 10 2012		

Amethyst

Also by Lauraine Snelling in Large Print:

Blessing in Disguise
Dakota Dream
Dakota Dawn
Dakota Dusk
The Healing Quilt
Ruby
Pearl
Opal
A New Day Rising
A Land to Call Home
The Reapers' Song
Tender Mercies
An Untamed Land

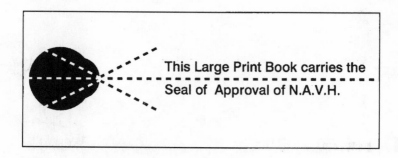

Amethyst

Lauraine Snelling

Thorndike Press • Waterville, Maine

Copyright © 2005 Lauraine Snelling

Dakotah Treasures #4

Published in 2006 by arrangement with Bethany House Publishers.

Thorndike Press® Large Print Christian Fiction.

The tree indicium is a trademark of Thorndike Press.

The text of this Large Print edition is unabridged.
Other aspects of the book may vary from the original edition.

Set in 16 pt. Plantin by Al Chase.

Printed in the United States on permanent paper.

Library of Congress Cataloging-in-Publication Data

Snelling, Lauraine.
　　Amethyst / by Lauraine Snelling.
　　　　p. cm. — (Thorndike Press large print Christian fiction.)
　　Originally published: Minneapolis, Minn. : Bethany House, c2005. (Dakotah treasures ; 4)
　　ISBN 0-7862-8682-2 (lg. print : hc : alk. paper)
　　ISBN 1-59415-136-9 (lg. print : sc : alk. paper)
　　1. Women pioneers — Fiction.　2. Medora (N.D.) — Fiction.　3. Large type books.　I. Title.　II. Thorndike Press large print Christian fiction series.
PS3569.N39A84 2006
813'.54—dc22　　　　　　　　　　　　　　2006008068

Dedication

To Jeanne and Bill, Mona and Eileen,
who gave me space and a place to write
faster than I ever have before.
What blessings you all are.

Acknowledgments

This book wasn't planned as part of the Dakotah Treasures series in the beginning, but when I ran out of book for Opal before I ran out of story, I asked my friends at Bethany House if we could add one more book. I danced for joy when they said yes, so thanks, Carol Johnson, David Horton, and all others involved in that decision. I wanted to find out what happened next as much as our readers did.

Kathleen, Chelley, Mona, Eileen, Woodeene, Nanci, thanks for brainstorming, for asking questions, reading again and again, helping me figure out these characters and get enough conflict. Sharon Asmus, you are always a delight to work with, the speed with which you get back to me is amazing. Do you read in your sleep? Deidre, agent and friend, what a journey we are on. Thanks for your wisdom and encouragement.

My perpetual thanks to all the readers who write and ask for more. I am so blessed. I'm glad these books mean so much to you and that you take time out of your busy schedules to let me know your thoughts.

To God be the glory, great things He has done.

CHAPTER ONE

Eastern Pennsylvania, Fall 1886

Her father's words itched worse than a bur in her camisole.

"Go find Joel." He'd said those words more than once or even twice. Every time he got to feeling poorly, he'd point his bony finger at her and utter those same words. What did he think she was — a gypsy who could look in tea leaves or a crystal ball and find out where the boy had disappeared to? What possibly irked her the most was that "feeling poorly" meant he'd had one — or many — too many drinks and would come home feeling right sorry for himself. And convinced he was dying.

More than once Amethyst Colleen O'Shaunasy, called Colleen because her father had thought her mother's naming her after a pinky-purple rock was the height of stupidity, wished she could join the temperance movement. If there were some way she could destroy the local tavern, she would. Or at least shut it down. But there was far too much work to be done on the farm if she wished to keep a roof over their heads and food on the table to go gallivanting off to join a women's movement. Not that all the hard work would help her any.

"Did you hear me, girl?"

"Aye, Pa, I heard you. But no one knows —"

"That's what ya allus say. Ya ain't got the brains God gave a goose. Find 'im before I die, or you won't even have this house to live in. Ya know a woman can't inherit land. I'm just lookin' out for yer own good."

Like you have all these years chasing away any beau who came calling? Her father didn't think she knew of his perfidy, but she'd found out, thanks to the local gossip. He wanted her home to take care of her ailing mother and him. Not that he worried much about any ailing female, unless she collapsed in the field, as her mother had. An affront to his dignity that was.

"If you have any suggestions as to how I should go about finding Joel, I'd be most grateful if you would share them with me." Of all the five siblings, only her brother Patrick had managed to live long enough to sire any children, and then only one son, Joel, who was seven the last time they saw him, more than five months earlier. After his father's death in an accident, his mother, who'd been suffering from consumption, took the boy off, and they both disappeared. Eventually they'd heard that Melody's body was found in a river to the west, but there was no sign of the boy.

"Write to her kin and ask if they know where the boy might be. Maybe he is with them."

"Do you know their names?"

"Surely your ma wrote that down in the Bible. Daft woman was at least good about keeping records like that."

Colleen narrowed her eyes. Never did he have a good word to say about her mother. Not that he ever had a good word to say about anyone, but still, she'd borne his children and his ire and worked herself to death.

If her father had worked as hard as he drove his wife, the farm most likely would have supported them quite well, but he'd always found something to be ailing about that needed a drink or two to alleviate.

"I've looked in her Bible. There are no records within its pages."

"There's the big one, the family one what's been passed down the generations. Where did it get to?" He reared up in his chair and stared around the room as if the book might come leaping out of a corner or off a shelf.

"Didn't you give it to Patrick when Mother passed on?" Colleen moved the coffeepot to the hotter part of the stove. She'd have a cup of coffee before heading out to do the evening chores. After milking in the morning, she'd finished digging the potatoes and stored them away in the cellar, along with the other root crops, all in their bins and covered, some with straw and others, like the carrots, with sand.

"Do I got to do all yer thinkin' fer ya? Didja ask those folks what took over his farm?"

"Why, no. I never thought of that." She glared at him. "Of course I asked them." *But perhaps I will do so again.* The Bible was too large for easy travel.

The next afternoon she took time out from banking the house for the winter with used straw from the cow barn, made sure her skirt wore no traces of her morning activities, that her russet hair was corralled in a topknot, and strode down the road. Across the field would have been a mite faster, but the road seemed more proper. She took along a jar of her special raspberry syrup as a calling gift.

"How nice of you to come calling," Sally

12

said with a smile at her arrival and invited her in.

While the coffee heated, they chatted about the lovely fall weather they'd been having. Their conversation meandered to the Women's Missionary Society that Sally had gotten involved in at the church. Colleen had always wished she could, but her father considered anything beyond Sunday attendance frivolous. Her interest perked up again when the discussion went on to the crops left in the garden.

"My Judd always takes care of the harvesting." Sally turned from lifting the coffeepot and refilled their coffee cups. "Did you dry any cut corn this year?"

Colleen shook her head. "Just beans." Other than the corn for the chickens and the cows, which now resided in the corncrib, ready to be used for shelled feed during the winter.

"I'll send some on home with you, then. Nothing like dried corn cooked in cream. I add a bit of onion too, for extra flavor."

"That would be right nice." Colleen took all her resolve in hand and said, "When your husband first moved here, I asked him if he'd found our family Bible anywhere." While she spoke, she sketched the size of it with her hands. "Have you found anything since then?"

"Not that I know of, but there are some things up in the attic that I've not gotten around to sorting. We could have a look-see if you want."

"That would be most obliging of you. If you have a lamp, I'll do the crawling up the ladder."

"We'll both go, and thataway I'll know what all is up there."

As soon as they both stood upright in the attic, they raised the lamp high, then crossed to a pile of boxes pushed into a back corner, a broken rocking chair, and a chest of drawers, minus one.

"Well, I never. My Judd could fix these right up. He's real good at fixing things."

I would have thought my brother was too. Strange the things that end up in attics. Colleen pulled out the top drawer — empty. The second drawer was missing, and the third held baby clothes, wrapped carefully in a knit blanket that the moths had turned into shreds.

"Oh, how sad." Sally lifted the things out and, after dusting the top of the chest, laid them there.

"They only had the one child." Colleen caught her breath. "My mother made many of those."

"Do you want them?" Sally sent her guest a gracious smile.

Colleen thought a moment. She remembered her mother sewing some of the gowns and shirts by lamplight, her stitches so fine as to be nearly invisible. But wouldn't it be better for the dear little garments to be used? After all, her childbearing years were about past, and with no man in her life other than her father, she would never need them. The thought made her heart clench. *But I want children to love and a man who loves me and to whom I can be devoted.*

She stroked the tucks in one little gown. One piece — would it hurt to keep one piece in memory of her mother?

Sally took the initiative and handed the perfect little gown to Colleen. "You take this one. I'll take the rest down and wash them all. Will be a few months yet before I need them, but I will think of your generosity when I dress my baby."

"Thank you." Colleen took the garment and, folding it carefully, placed it in her apron pocket. When she tugged at the bottom drawer, it refused to open. She pulled again, but only a squawk rewarded her efforts. The women each took a handle and pulled firmly to gain only an inch. "Again." This time the drawer gave up the battle with a groan, and therein lay the family Bible. "Ah." Using both hands, Colleen lifted the heavy book out and set it on top of the chest as Sally removed the clothing bundle.

Both women sneezed at the dust generated by moving things around.

"I can tell you I am going to give this attic a thorough cleaning. Don't know why I put off coming up here."

"A companion always makes one braver."

"True."

Colleen held the lamp closer to the pages as she opened the cover. Sure enough, Mother had recorded all the information she needed, even to the town Melody had come from. "Do you mind if I —"

"You needn't ask. This Bible is yours. Let's take it downstairs and dust it off."

"Thank you." Such simple words for the feelings welling up like an artesian spring. She now had the Bible, part of her mother, part and parcel of the family.

After staying long enough to be polite, she took the tiny dress and the heavy book back with her to the homeplace. The chill in the air told her that her father had left sometime earlier, most likely as soon as she walked down the road. And there was no doubt in her mind where she would find him, if she cared to go looking. She checked the tin where she kept her egg and cream money. Empty!

No more! From now on she would keep the money she earned someplace safe, where his marauding fingers would not find it.

That night, after her father returned home and fell asleep, Colleen sat at the worn kitchen table composing a letter to Melody's parents, pleading with them to give her any information they had learned about the boy named Joel, her nephew. Her father's heir.

Dear Mrs. Fisher,

I am sorry for waiting so long to write to you, but I had no idea how to contact you. Melody did not leave your address, and I just found the family Bible in the attic of their house, which is now owned by another. I hope this letter finds you well, although I am sure you are still grieving for your daughter. She was a good wife to my brother and a friend to me. Joel was the child of my heart and greatly loved.

I know a long time has passed, but my father is insistent that we find Joel, as there are no other male heirs in our family and my father is afraid he will die before seeing Joel again. I cannot begin to tell you how grateful we would be for any bit of information. Is he living with you or do you know where he is? I know that Melody took Joel to see someone in a small town in Dubuque Valley, Pennsylvania. If I don't hear from you, I plan to go there and make some discreet inquiries.

I hope that all is well with you and yours, although I understand that the sorrow of losing your daughter never goes away.

I thank you in advance for any help you could offer.

I remain respectfully yours,
Amethyst Colleen O'Shaunasy.

Colleen addressed an envelope, folded the letter, and inserted it, sealing the missive with a drop of wax from the candle she kept for that purpose. She'd walk into Smithville, the closest village, in the morning to mail it. Her father didn't allow the horses to be used for transportation when feet were available. Unless they were his feet.

She pulled out the pins and let her hair,

which was constantly fighting to fall free, tumble around her shoulders. The required one hundred strokes a night gave a sheen to the russet fall that glimmered in the lamplight. Her mother had always said her two best features were her hair and her eyes. The rest of her left a lot to be desired, as far as she was concerned. She had a jaw strong enough to outclamp a bulldog and a forehead broad enough to write on, and while most women were curvy, she had looked once in the mirror and thought she saw a broom with hair.

"Ah, Mother, why did you go off and leave me like this?" She continued with the regular strokes, thinking back to her sister-in-law. Melody had been so lovely when she and Patrick were married, and while the boy had been born a bit early, if one bothered to count, he'd been a precious baby. Since their house was right across the field, Colleen had spent as much time there as she could.

When she reached a hundred strokes, she tied her hair back in a club with a bit of cotton ripped from a larger piece, blew out the lamp, and slipped underneath the covers. The moonlit shadows of the red oak branches danced on the floor, the limbs themselves brushing the house boards with familiar taps and sighs, as if seeking entrance.

Her father's snoring from the room below her grated her nerves like the washboard grated the skin off her knuckles. What if she were to find Joel and bring him back here? What kind of example would her father set for a young boy?

"Ishda." She muttered one of her mother's favorite sayings. *Mother, I miss you so.*

CHAPTER TWO

November

"There's a letter for you."

Colleen turned at the announcement from the man behind the counter, her hat not quite following. Between hat and hair, remaining properly attired was often a test of her persistence. Because it was market day, when all the farmers brought their goods to Smithville to sell, her father had driven the wagon, filled with her wares, to town. Renowned for her cottage cheese that always sold out first, Colleen had also brought freshly churned butter, buttermilk, and eggs, not to mention her piccalilli. She'd made extra jars because people liked it so much. At the end of the day, with a tidy sum in her reticule and her father at his favorite hangout, she'd gone into the mercantile, giving the owner her list of needed supplies and taking time to peruse the calicos and woolens. She needed a new winter skirt and a dress without holes. No matter that she could mend with the best of them,

21

patches on patches it was. She pushed at her hat, knowing she needed to reset the hatpins, but that was not something a woman did in public. Raising her arms above her head that way was just not seemly.

Who would be writing to her?

"Thank you." She took the letter and stared at the return address. An answer to her letter of nearly a month ago. She'd given up on receiving a reply, placating her father with the old adage, "No news is good news." Although, as he'd pointed out, along with several comments about her stupidity, that didn't seem to apply here.

Rather than spending the time reading under the man's watchful eye, she placed the letter in her reticule and continued her shopping. Once behind the laden shelves, she reached up and reset her hatpins, hoping to restrict the swirl of russet hair. She had enough cash on hand to pay her past-due bill and for the supplies she'd purchased, but if she bought dress goods, she'd have nothing to hide away in case of an emergency. Her father had raided the last hoard, as he had earlier ones.

Sometimes she wished he'd go back to making moonshine. They'd had extra cash then. But even that had proved too laborious for him, so now he just reminisced about those days. The heart had indeed gone out of him when Patrick died, not that he'd ever been what one would call a hard worker.

With a shake of her head and a grimace at the hat shifting again, she left the dress goods section and returned to the counter to pay for her purchases.

"You want I should load these in the wagon for you?"

"Yes, please."

"You have any of your goods between now and next market day, you know I would be happy to sell them here."

"Well, thank you." In the past she had traded butter and eggs for the things she needed. "I'll keep that in mind."

She thanked him again when the staples of flour, sugar, coffee, and other things she couldn't produce on the farm were loaded into the wagon. Glancing up the street to the saloon, she hoped to see her father waiting on the front porch. No such luck.

Muttering under her breath, she untied the team, backed them up, and drove around the block so she could stop with the seat of the wagon in direct line with the steps from the saloon. Then, proper or not, she climbed out of the wagon, using the spokes of the wheel for steps, tied the nearest horse to the hitching rail, and mounted the stairs. Stopping at the door, she peered inside. *Lord above, how I hate going in here.*

"Could you please bring him out, Mr. Peters?" When there was no response, she raised her voice and repeated her request. No answer. *Couldn't you have a bit of mercy on me?* She glanced skyward. "Sorry for any disrespect." Blowing out a heavy sigh, she pushed open the door and stood blinking in the dim light, waiting for her eyes to adjust.

Her father even had his own table. And right now he lay cheek down, snoring loud enough to scare the rats that sometimes scavenged for bits of food dropped from the tables. The thought of seeing one again made her shudder. But they weren't as prevalent in the daylight hours, so she sucked in a restorative breath, coughed on the fumes that permeated the place, and crossed the room. How would she get him out to the wagon if he was passed out?

"Father." She tapped his shoulder. No response. Just like from the owner of this place, wherever he was. She shook her father, none too gently.

"Go 'way." His mutter sent the alcohol fumes right up her nose.

Her eyes watered and she fought the urge to gag. Why did men do this to themselves? "Pa, either you come with me now, or you'll be finding your own way home. I am finished here for the day." *And I have enough work to do at home to fill two days with some left over.*

"Minute."

She had to lean over to understand him because his lips and cheek were mashing the wood of the tabletop. Colleen took a step back with a finger to her hat. Never before had she had the courage to leave him. But the thought of sitting under a shade tree and waiting for him to stagger out gave her the desire to pick up the bottle sitting on his table and tap him on the head with it.

Aghast at the thought, she shook him again, more firmly this time. "Pa, it is time to go home. You said you would meet me at the mercantile." Why even talk? He wasn't listening.

The back door opened, and the proprietor pushed his way in, dragging a dolly loaded with crates. "Sorry, Miss O'Shaunasy, I had to pick up my freight or someone might have lightened my load, if you get my drift. I'll haul his carcass out to the wagon for you. Don't know what you'll do when you get home though."

"I'll let him sleep it off in the wagon, that's what. How can you allow him to drink this much?"

"Man pays his money, I ain't his keeper."

"What if he has no money?" She addressed his back as he slung the old man over his shoulders like a sack of wheat and hauled him out to the back of the wagon, where he dumped him on the goods already loaded.

"I use ta run a tab, but not no longer. Not for him."

"Thank God for small favors."

Peters dusted his hands off. "If I was you, I'd hide my money real good."

"Thank you for the advice." She mounted the wheel, eyed the line to the hitching rail, and sighed, a shoulder-drooping, toenail-curling sigh.

"I'll get that for ya."

"Thank you so very much." When he knotted the line back to the harness, she picked up the reins and slapped the team lightly along with a "giddup." The horses, long used to finding their own way home, ignored her orders and, nodding, each picked up one hoof at a time, making sure it was set again before picking up another.

Feeling Mr. Peters staring at her from the doorway, she slapped the reins again, with

26

considerably more force, along with a sharp "giddup" to match. The shock made both horses throw their heads up and jerk forward. Her hat skewed toward the back of her head, and her posterior slid to the rear of the seat, making her grateful for the backboard so that she didn't go head over teakettle into the wagon bed. Now, that would have caused some stir.

By reflex she jerked back on the reins, the horses stopped, and there she was. *Lord, let me hide myself in thee.* She glanced back over her shoulder to make certain she still had her father in the wagon but wasn't sure if she was grateful that he'd slept through it all or not. Feet braced against the footboard, she slapped the reins again, this time holding them firmly to make sure the horses would walk not leap. They seemed to get the idea, as they walked out with quick feet. After she ripped the hat from her head and tucked it under her skirt so it wouldn't blow away, she slapped the reins again, and they picked up an easy trot.

Lowering clouds in the west, the direction they were headed, made her groan. All she needed to do was let the bags of flour and sugar get wet. She clucked the horses faster and drove them into the barn just as the errant sprinkles turned into a downpour.

Obeying her father's orders to never leave the team in harness, even though he often did it himself, she unhooked the traces from the doubletree and, after leading the horses into their stall, unharnessed them. "You ungrateful wretches," she muttered as the darker of the two bays swung his haunches out enough to pin her against the sideboards. "Get over." She slapped him on the rump with one of the leathers. "You kick me and, so help me, I'll shoot you myself. Horsemeat must not be much different than beef." He straightened out and let her pass, his twitching tail saying that he'd just as soon plant a hoof on her foot as not.

She hung the harnesses on the wall pegs, dumped a small amount of oats in each feedbox, gathered the smaller packages, and made her way to the house. By the time she stopped on the porch to catch her breath, her hair was drenched, her clothes were soaked through to her skin, and her felt hat was squashed beyond rehabilitating.

Lord, what did I do to deserve this? She dropped the packages on the table, wishing for a cup of hot coffee and knowing that she'd have to start the stove first. Which to do? Change clothes so she didn't catch her death, or start the fire so she could warm up both body and coffeepot?

The gray-and-white-striped cat with the white bib and paws rubbed against her skirt, then sat down to lick the moisture off her fur.

"If you're hungry, go catch a mouse. It's a long time till supper." Colleen, against all she knew to be proper, dropped her skirt and petticoat by the stove so she could hang them up to dry. Her blouse joined the skirt in a heap, and she debated about her chemise and bloomers. But fearing the arrival of her father or some passing stranger, she hauled herself upstairs to her room, where she stripped down to bare skin and rubbed her body with a coarse towel until she felt warmer. If only she could crawl in bed to warm up. Were her mother here, she would have had the stove lighted and something hot forthwith. She might have even brought a cup up to her daughter's room, not that Colleen could remember such a time, other than when she'd had the measles.

Colleen sank down on the edge of the bed, feeling as if the roof of the house were pressing down on her. That and the black sky. *How can I bear this? Yet how can I not? I mean, what choices do I have?* Crawl in bed and let the animals suffer? *You could crawl in bed to get warm. But if I fall asleep, then what?* She shivered in the draft from the window, even though the sash was down. Wrapping the towel around her wet hair, she drew dry underthings from the drawers, her working shift from its peg on the low side of the steeply roofed room, and finished dressing. She added a sweater and warm woolen stockings her mother had knit for good measure.

Downstairs she fetched a pot of chicken soup from the larder and, after adding wood to the coals in the firebox, set the pot on the front burner. Because she'd not eaten since breakfast, she sliced bread and buttered it on both sides before laying it in one of the cast-iron frying pans that hung from a rack behind the stove. She set it right behind the soup kettle to speed the toasting.

Looking out the window, she saw the barn door was still closed. Rain pummeled the ground. The cow would most likely be in her stanchion, waiting for grain and milking. Colleen stirred the soup and turned the two slices of bread, pushing the frying pan back off the hottest part. Dark as the day had become, she lit a kerosene lamp and set it in the middle of the table.

"My letter." She dug it from her reticule, only slightly damp, and laid it on the table. Whenever mail came to the house, her father always read it first — slowly, since reading wasn't one of his strong suits. Today she would slice open the envelope, pull out the paper, unfold it, and read it — all by herself and first.

To prolong the pleasure she flipped the bread out onto a plate, dished up her soup and slid the kettle back, poured herself a cup of coffee, and set her things on the table. The pure pleasure of the quiet room, the hiss and crackle of the fire, the steaming coffeepot, and the purring cat made her sigh. If only her mother were here to enjoy this special moment with her. What more could she ask?

She salted her soup, staring at the envelope lying on the table. Good news or bad news. She ate a bite of bread, followed by a spoon of soup. The heat radiated from the stove, warming her back. She rotated her shoulders in delight.

Picking up the envelope, she slid the blade of the knife under the flap and popped open the blob of wax seal. Appreciating each move she made, she finally had the letter free and ready to read. Another slurp and bite prolonged the pleasure.

Dear Miss O'Shaunasy,
    I cannot begin to tell you how grateful I was to read your letter of

October 7. Yes, the loss of our daughter has been a trial, but as ill as she was, we were not surprised to hear of her passing. What surprised and shocked us was the inference that she may have taken her own life. I will never believe that. There must have been an accident or some nefarious event, but that we will never know.

We, my husband and I, would love to be certain of the whereabouts of our grandson, Joel. Were we able, we would go searching ourselves. As far as we know, Joel has gone west with a man named Jacob Chandler. He and Melody were childhood friends. Not long ago we received a letter from his parents and understand that he and Joel are living on a ranch in the badlands of Dakotah Territory, near a town called Medora. While we could not locate the town on any maps, we have learned there is a train station there. It is near the western edge of the territory.

We are pleased to know that Joel has a place to come back to and a purpose. Perhaps Mr. Chandler, whom I believe is a reverend, or was, will be willing to bring Joel back. The Chandlers have a farm not far from our own.

Please keep in contact with us, and we wish you God's blessing and speed in your mission.

Sincerely,
Mrs. Alma Fisher

Colleen read the letter again. Surely there was some kind of mystery going on here. Why had Melody left Joel with a man not a relative? What had happened to her in those last moments of her life? She had not been well for a long time, but after an attack of the influenza last year and the death of her husband, she had really gone downhill.

How can I leave the farm and go searching for the boy? Who would care for the livestock — and my father? Winter would be the best time to go because there was no fieldwork and the cow would be drying up around Christmas. But the heifer was due in January.

Colleen finished her soup and bread, poured herself another cup of coffee to sip while she put things away, and wiped off the crumbs. She cradled the hot mug in her hands as she stared out the window. The rain clouds looked to have taken up residency right over the farm. She should have thrown a horse blanket over her father. All she needed was to have him

33

down with the grippe or worse.

Fetching a wool blanket from the linen shelf, she donned her chores coat and a broad-brimmed hat, took the milk pail from the springhouse, and headed for the barn. The cow wouldn't mind being milked a bit early, and if she waited longer, she'd have to light a lantern. One more thing to fuss with.

She finished the chores and tried to wake her father, who was snoring under the blanket she'd spread over him, but when that effort failed, she let the horses out to pasture and headed for the springhouse. She carried the milk bucket in one hand, eggs nested in straw in a basket in the other. As soon as it turned cold enough, they needed to butcher the two hogs she'd kept for fattening. How could she leave before then?

Lord above, if I am to go, who will do the work around here?

CHAPTER THREE

"You left me in the barn!"

Colleen jerked upright in bed. "What? Who?" She put her hand to her chest to still her thundering heart. The wraith in the doorway staggered slightly. "Pa?"

"Who else would you go leaving in the barn? Like to catch my death out there."

"I tried to wake you, but you wouldn't wake. I almost left you at the saloon."

"You left me out there in the cold."

"I put a blanket over you. You were hot enough to set the hay on fire anyway."

"You goin' ter fix me supper?"

She felt her jaw drop. The nerve of him. "If you are hungry, there is bread and cheese. Help yourself." *I am not getting up now to fix a meal you were too drunk to eat before.*

"Yer mother —"

Colleen closed her eyes. "I am not my mother. I am not your wife. I am your daughter, and I am not getting up." Where she found the courage to make such a statement was beyond her. "I had to go into that place looking for you. Thankfully, Mr. Peters had the decency to haul you out to the wagon, rather than just throwing you out the door when it came closing time. You are too heavy for me to lift — there's no way I could have dragged you into the house."

He turned from the doorway and muttered his way back down the stairs. She waited to hear if he went to the kitchen, but the bedsprings creaked, and she knew he'd gone to bed.

You shouldn't treat your father that way. The Good Book says to show respect to your parents. That is a sign of godliness.

Had I gone down, he'd have fallen asleep in the chair before the food was ready. Lord, you know I have honored him all these years. I can honor the man but not his drinking. Great God, what do I do?

Let me.

She lay still, waiting for more. Two words. *Let me.* "But how? I can pray for him. I have. Is that what you mean?" She slipped back into sleep, the puzzlement still there when she woke in the darkest dark, before the line of dawn penciled the horizon or brightened the sky to cobalt. The rooster called up the sun and her. Dressing quickly in the chill, she looked outside for her first of the day checks. All appeared as she'd left it, albeit considerably wetter. Was it still raining when her father woke her? She didn't remember the song of the eaves, when water cascaded down the roof and dripped to the line of gravel below.

She checked on him, though his snoring had announced his presence when she was still upstairs. At least he'd had the sense to crawl under the covers, even though he'd not undressed — one sleeved arm testified to that.

Let me. She thought again to the words. Now, *let it be* she understood. And *let it lie* or *let it down* — what she often had to do with her dresses when one hem wore to tatters. She'd let out the hem, trim off the raggedy threads, sew a seam around the bottom, and then hem it back up. One could make a dress appear almost new again with such doings. Her mother had many tricks like that for stretching and reusing everything. "Waste not, want not" had been another of her favorite sayings.

While she pondered, Colleen started the fire, set the coffeepot to cooking, stirred cornmeal into cold water so it wouldn't go lumpy, and set it on the back of the stove to heat, giving it a good stir every once in a while. By the time she finished milking the cow, the mush would be ready to eat.

When she picked up the bucket out in the springhouse, she checked the pans from the night's milking. A thick layer of cream floated on top. She'd bring some in with her. Her father loved cream on his mush. And brown sugar. Far as he was concerned, skim milk was good only for hog slop.

He was sitting at the table working on his first cup of coffee when she walked back in the door. "Mornin'."

"Good morning to you too. Breakfast will be ready in three shakes of a lamb's tail."

"I stirred the mush."

She glanced over her shoulder at him. He was in mighty good humor for someone who'd been yelling at her in the middle of the night.

"You bring in all the supplies by yourself?" He held up his coffee cup, and she refilled it.

"No, it had started to rain, so I left everything in the wagon." *Including you.* She sliced bread and brought the jam and butter out from the larder to set on the table, then poured the cream from the crock into a pitcher. When she dished up the mush and sat down, he folded his hands, bowed his head, said grace, and started in to eat.

"Musta been right tired last night. Still

had my boots on this mornin'."

Colleen poured some of the cream into her coffee and stirred in a bit of sugar. She wasn't going to comment on that. "We better be thinking on butchering soon."

"Art's goin' to bring over his two hogs at the first heavy frost. We'll do 'em together. His missus and the biggest boy'll come too."

"When did you talk to him?"

Her father frowned, his eyes wrinkling in puzzlement. "Don't rightly know, but he said so." He nodded. "You done good yesterday?"

"Yes, I did. Nothing left to bring home again. Could have sold more butter and eggs. With two cows milking next year, we should do right well. Think I'll let more of the hens set come spring."

"Got more of that mush?"

She refilled his bowl and sat back down. "I got a letter yesterday, an answer from Melody's folks. You want to read it?"

"A'course."

She fetched the letter and watched as he picked up his knife to slide under the dab of wax, then realized it was already open. He glanced up at her, but she only smiled back. *You were in no shape to read anything. I can't believe this. It looks to me like you*

39

don't remember a thing that happened. Not waking up in the barn, nothing. Lord, if this is what you meant by let me, *I give you all the thanks and praise.*

When he finished reading, he looked up. "You got to go find 'im."

"Who will take care of the livestock while I'm gone? And what will I use for a train ticket?" The two questions sounded insurmountable to her. Like a rocky cliff face on a mountain she'd seen in a picture once.

"I ain't helpless, ya know. I was milkin' cows afore I went to school. And I kin cook if need be. You jest find us that boy."

"How will I pay for the ticket?"

"You got money from yesterday."

"I paid our bill at the store and bought winter supplies. Paid for them too. Don't owe a dime now." She said the last with a bit of pride. She hated owing anyone. Didn't seem to bother her father none though. And she hadn't lied to him either — about the money she now had hidden where he'd never find it.

"Well, if that don't beat all. What an idjit thing to do. Crawford don't mind none. Just means we keep comin' back." He thought a moment. "We could sell the heifer, I s'pose."

"I'm counting on her milk to tide us over

when the cow is dry. Then I can sell cottage cheese and butter all through the year. Been thinking on making soft cheese too."

"Got to get that boy back here. How much is a ticket?"

"I have no idea." She looked at him over the cup rim.

"You ask at the station. See about if children are cheaper. Only need one way for him." He twisted from side to side. She knew what was coming. "I sure got a hitch in my side. Think I better be layin' down fer a spell. Otherwise I'd take one of the horses and ride on back into town."

Knowing where he'd end up, she didn't say anything, not that she had any words that would make a difference anyway. *If you hadn't stole the money from the sugar tin, there might have been enough for the train tickets.* But what good would bringing that up do? The money was gone, and now he'd have to figure a way to get money for the tickets if he wanted her to go that badly.

A week later the weather changed, and the Soderbergs arrived with most of their family and their hired man just after the rooster's first crow to begin the day's labors. Colleen had laid the fires under the scalding tank the night before and had lit them first thing after she woke up. She breathed a sigh of relief when she saw all the helpers. How she and three men were going to butcher four hogs in one day had been beyond her.

"Gerry Lynn stayed home to get the little young'uns off to school, and then she'll be right on over." Mrs. Soderberg climbed down from the wagon and hefted two baskets of food out of the back, giving her two little ones instructions to stay away from the fire and out of the way of the menfolk.

"Can I help you?" Colleen hustled out to the wagon, where she saw two more baskets, several crocks, and a meat grinder. "My, you did come prepared."

"Wasn't sure what all you had." She set her baskets on the kitchen table. "I sure do miss your ma. Life just ain't been the same since she died."

Colleen swallowed the tears that snuck up on her whenever someone mentioned her mother. "Me too. Never a day goes by that I don't think on something she'd say."

"She knew her Bible. That was for sure. Better'n the preacher knows his, I'm thinkin', at times. But don't you go tellin' him I said that."

"I never would." Colleen opened the oven door to check on her baking beans. She'd started them the day before, as soon as they decided to butcher. Baked bread and pies all day too. Took a lot of cooking to feed hungry working men. Her father sprang out of bed when he heard the wagons driving in, grabbing bread and cheese as he went. Never matter that Colleen had been up for hours.

Colleen kept the scrapers and knives sharpened as they killed one hog at a time, dunking it to scald in the hot water before laying the carcass up on a trestle table and scraping off all the coarse hair. Hanging and gutting followed, and then the carcass was sawed down the backbone and the halves left hanging until the cutting table was cleared of the one before.

The job Colleen hated the most was cleaning out the intestines and then washing them in salt water so as to be ready for stuffing. While she washed, Mrs. Soderberg kept the grinder going, using up every bit of meat. The haunches and rib meat were set in salt water, preliminary to smoking for ham and bacon.

By the end of the day all four hogs were finished, and so were the workers. Colleen waved good-bye from the porch, arched her back, and kneaded the aches away with her balled fists. What a job that had been. She returned to the kitchen, where two pigs' heads simmered in her largest pot. When the meat fell off the bones, she would set the kettle to cool and bone it out in the morning. Bay leaf, cloves, and other pickling spices kept together in a cheesecloth bag scented the room, all the flavorings needed for headcheese. Scrubbed pigs' feet simmered in another kettle. Once cooked, she would remove the hoofs, add vinegar, a bit of sugar, and her secret spice and, after draining the feet, put them in the crock and cover with just enough liquid, then weight them down with a plate. Since Mrs. Soderberg hadn't wanted the feet from their hogs, Colleen would take some to town at the next market day. Pickled pigs' feet were especially prized by the local German population.

She heard the cow beller from the barn. Had her father not gone out to milk? She wiped her hands on her apron and went in search of him. Not in the bedroom, nor in his chair. "Pa?" No answer. Slipping her arms into her chores coat, she checked the springhouse. The bucket waited patiently, as did the egg basket. Muttering under her breath, she grabbed the two handles and headed for the barn.

She found him sound asleep in the haymow. How long had he been here?

When had she seen him last? She knew of but had ignored the flask she'd seen passed around as the day's work had lengthened. As if the women were supposed to be dumb and blind as well as keeping on without even a cup of coffee.

"Pa." She pushed at him with the handle of the hand-carved pitchfork. While many farmers used the new iron forks, the three-pronged one he'd carved who knew how many years ago still suited them. A ready excuse for not spending money they didn't have on a newfangled fork.

She prodded him again, less gently this time.

He sputtered and opened his eyes, then rose up on his elbows, shaking his head. "What in —" Glaring at her, he wiped his mouth with the back of his hand. "Can't a man rest in peace after a day like we just been through?"

"You'll rest in peace all right. I thought you'd gone out to milk and do the chores so I could finish up with the hogs."

"Now, Colleen, you jist don't know how weary a man can get, hefting those hogs, scrapin' and cuttin'. Why, my back . . ."

Colleen shook her head. "I just hope you were there until the end and didn't leave your work for the others." The humiliation of it made her face grow hot.

"Held on to the last, I did." He flopped back. "Jist give me a minute or two more, and I'll . . ."

Colleen forked hay down for the cow and climbed back down the ladder. "You can catch your death up there for all I care. I'm not coming back for you." She milked the cow, threw oats to the chickens, and rubbed two dried ears of corn together so the hens had an extra treat of shelled corn. She'd noticed that when her father fed the hens, he just threw the corncobs on the floor for them to fight over.

For supper she warmed up what was left of the baked beans and the stew, sliced herself a piece of bread, and instead of eating at the table, sank down into the rocking chair she'd pulled closer to the stove. She set her plate on the reservoir and sipped at her tea. While it was a good thing the temperature was dropping so that none of the meat spoiled, the warmth from the drink felt mighty good down in her belly.

Should she go get her pa or let him sleep out in the barn? *You could at least go throw a horse blanket over him. If he gets chilly enough, he'll come inside.* The argument in her head raged all through her meal. He wouldn't freeze to death in the haymow.

Knowing him, he'd burrow down into the hay without even waking. He'd done so before.

"Oh, Ma, if only you were still here. Not that I'd want you to leave your heavenly home and return, but . . ." *What can I do about my father?* The *let me* floated through her mind again. *Hmm.*

CHAPTER FOUR

Trains tore along at an unbelievable rate.

Colleen felt as though she needed to hang on to the seat around every corner, and when they crossed a trestle with the river far below, she closed her eyes and covered her mouth to still the shriek she felt rising. The fastest she'd ever traveled was a slow gallop, and that wasn't even halfway from town to home.

"How you doing, ma'am?" The conductor stopped beside her, a gentle smile easily showing the carved commas that ridged his dark cheeks. Corkscrews of silver peeked from under the band of his hat.

"I . . . ah . . . fine." She knew her eyes were round as sugar cookies. "Really." She sucked in a deep breath. "I'm fine."

"Sho you are." He nodded, his eyes twinkling. "It get easier. Just remember to hang on to the seat backs when you walk the aisles."

Since she had taken a seat right behind the ladies' necessary, she hadn't had to walk far. And the walls were close together.

"Thank you."

"When we be out of de mountains, it gets easier."

She nodded. He might think it easier, but thoughts were relative. She watched him move down the aisle, swaying with the rocking of the train. Rigid as an oak plank would be more the way she described her own movements.

Rigid was a word she often used to describe her father — especially his opinions. She thought back to their discussion. With December already here, she'd suggested she go west in the spring, but he was adamant — she needed to find Joel now and bring him home in time for Christmas. When she reminded him she needed money for a ticket, he rode into town and returned twenty dollars richer.

She never asked where he got the money. That along with what she'd hoarded in a flat tin stuffed in her mattress allowed her to buy a round-trip ticket to Medora in Dakotah Territory. She would buy Joel's ticket after she found him. All she knew was that Medora was located somewhere west of Fargo, which was west of St. Paul in Minnesota. She had found them on a map she studied at the schoolhouse.

She closed her eyes and leaned back

against the seat. The night before she left for Harrisburg to catch the train, she'd taken the family Bible up to her room and, with a lamp on the bedside table, opened it to read the family history on her mother's side. Only her father's parents were included from his side. Beside each of her children's names her mother had written in her pains-takingly precise hand, *Deceased* and the date. Except for Colleen's and Patrick's. And now Patrick was gone too.

"Ah, Mother, so much death in your life. I don't know how you managed." Leaving the front pages, she thumbed through the Bible, stopping here and there to read pas-sages or to admire the pictures. Her mother's family must have had money to own a Bible like this one. Pictures, maps, fancy capital letters at the chapter heads. She read bits and pieces and, in flipping pages, found a lock of hair in a bit of tissue. Whose? She held the tissue to the light, but the ink on it had faded so as to be illegible. Several ribbons marked pages, and she read carefully to see what had caught a reader's fancy some time before. Psalm 23, Psalm 139, Jesus' Sermon on the Mount, Paul's letter to the Philippians. She turned the last page, and the light caught two round ridges in the back cover. She smoothed the circles with the tip of her finger, figuring something round had indented the heavy paper lining the leather cover.

Something round and hard lay under the backing. Using a darning needle from her sewing basket, she lifted the paper with great care. How had no one else found this? Did no one ever read the Bible? She pulled out a paper-wrapped packet and laid it on the table, folding back one side of the paper to expose half of two gold coins. As if lifting the Holy Grail, she folded back the remaining paper to reveal two twenty-dollar gold pieces. Her breath caught in her throat. Who? Why? She picked up one of the coins and bit down on it. Her slight teeth marks proved what she thought. Gold, real gold.

When she lifted both coins from the paper, she saw the writing underneath. *For you, my daughter, for when you are desperate. Your loving mother.* Colleen lifted the paper closer to the light. It was indeed her own mother's handwriting. When had she come upon such largess or, most likely, how had she scrimped and hoarded to amass such a fortune?

One thing for certain, her father had never searched the family Bible. And while he confessed to being a believer, one would not discern such faith by his actions.

Colleen had taken the Bible with her and sewed the coins into the hem of her heavy black wool coat. The coat was so heavy that the extra weight would not be noticed if someone picked it up. The same coat was now her blanket on this journey west.

She kept herself from fingering the coins for fear of drawing attention to them. What wealth. More than enough to buy a ticket back for Joel, for she doubted that her father would find the money to buy the boy a ticket and send it to her in Medora.

Once the they left the mountains, the trip was indeed more comfortable, just as the conductor had assured her. She looked with delight out the windows at the passing scenery — bare trees, lakes rimmed with ice, sleeping fields and smoke rising from chimneys on farms and in villages. Since she had never traveled farther from her home than Smithville, where she sold her wares and attended church, the expanse of the country was a constant awe to her.

The power and heat of the steel plants in Pittsburgh hinted at the fires of hell. The black soot that hung in the air assured her of it. How could people live and work in such a place? Changing trains set her heart to pounding while the smoke brought on a coughing fit. When she was finally on the correct train heading west — she'd checked her ticket several times and asked the conductor to make sure she was on the right train — she could breathe freely again. Rationing the food she'd brought in her basket made her stomach growl in resentment, but the fear of running out of money before she returned home made her drink more coffee from the pot on the heating stove in the middle of the car.

She knit her way through the tenements of Chicago, anything to distract her from the squalor she'd read about but could barely believe even when she saw it: a woman in rags standing on an iron stair of the third floor of a brick building, smoking a cigarillo, a small boy at her feet, with not enough railing to keep the child from falling to his death. A line of raggedy clothing looped from the railing, behind which the woman stood talking to another.

A woman smoking. *Ishda.* Colleen wanted to scream out the window. *Take care of that child; you are fortunate to have one.* But if the window did indeed open, she'd not let the frigid air in. Snow on roofs and icicles hanging spoke to the cold. The stockyards had seemed to go on for miles, myriads of cattle, some with horns, some not, in a patchwork of corrals with a stench strong enough to permeate the train.

At the train station she ordered a bowl of soup at the counter that served lines of travelers. Shaking her head over the exorbitant price, she took her plate with bowl and a slice of bread over to one of the tables. A man stepped back and bumped her arm, sloshing her soup.

"Oh, excuse me, ma'am." He eyed her hat, which was, as usual, fighting the battle to be free of her hatpins, and smiled. "I hope that wasn't so hot as to burn you."

"No, no. Not at all." She set her plate on the table and used the napkin to mop her gloved thumb. "Just messy."

"I am sorry." He tipped his hat and strode off. Other than the conductor, he was the first person to speak to her in three days.

She ate her hearty bean soup, the smell of ham and beans reminding her of the smokehouse at home. Was her father keeping the fires stoked? Had he fed the livestock? Of course he had. While he was inclined to laziness, he would not hurt the animals that provided their livelihood — would he? A pang of homesickness caused her to choke on her soup. Tears burned behind her eyes, so she had to blow her nose in one of the handkerchiefs she'd hemmed herself. How quickly would she be able to reach Medora, find Joel, and head back home? She listened to the voice announcing the trains that were loading and departing. When she heard the voice call for Minneapolis/St. Paul, she quickly finished her soup and tucked the bread into her carpetbag to eat later.

Waiting in line to board, she watched the people around her. Reverend Landers at home had reminded her to watch out for thieves and pickpockets who preyed on travelers. In front of her the conductor assisted a white-haired lady with a cane up the steps, then a black-shawled woman with a young boy at her side. At least Colleen wasn't the only woman traveling alone.

Once they were all seated and the train huffed and snorted its way out of the station, Colleen shook her head at all the streets with square little houses, many not nearly as big as her own. At least her house had an upper floor, while many of these did not.

The conductor came by and checked the tickets. As he moved down the aisle, the white-haired woman, whose black felt hat with a matching feather stayed in place, leaned across the armrest and waved to catch Colleen's attention.

"Will you be getting off in St. Paul?"

Colleen shook her head. "I'm going to Medora in Dakotah Territory."

"Oh, good. Since I am traveling clear to Seattle to visit my son, we have many miles ahead of us. Perhaps you wouldn't mind humoring an old lady and taking time to chat. I have found that I make good friends when traveling like this."

"You travel often?"

"This is my third trip west. My son wants me to move out there, but I would hate to leave Chicago."

"Leaving home is difficult." And that might be the biggest understatement she'd ever offered. The thought of her kitchen, warm with the fragrance of baking bread or ginger cookies, filled her with memories. "I've never gone more than a few miles from home before."

"Oh, dear, this must be quite an adventure for you. Will you be visiting family?"

Colleen thought to the time ahead. *If I can find him.* "Hopefully." She could see the curiosity fairly bristle the hat feather that curved over the back of the woman's head. The hat remained firmly seated on an upswept coil, much like her own, only without the least trace of a propensity for escaping. Black jet gleamed on the collar and lapels of the fitted black traveling jacket. She was sure the skirt and jacket were made of wool serge, at far greater cost than anything she would even dream of owning.

"My name is Mrs. John Grant, but I prefer Agnes among friends. What is yours?"

Colleen almost said Colleen, but paused. "Amethyst Colleen O'Shaunasy. Miss." From now on, for this brief portion of her life, she would be the woman her mother named her to be. *At least I would like to be called Amethyst, but I'm sure it is going to take some time to get used to the new name. Amethyst.* Formally Miss Amethyst O'Shaunasy. That did sound rather grand.

"Amethyst, what a lovely name. And you must be Irish by the sound of it, although I'm not surprised with all that luscious red hair and milky skin."

Colleen, er, Amethyst put a hand to the side of her stubborn hair. Red? She'd thought it russet, not the true red of a real Irish colleen. Like she was a sepia painting instead of the real thing.

"Why, thank you." Compliments had been about as scarce as hen's teeth in her life, another saying of her mother's. Questions buzzed within like the bees when she disturbed a hive. She could feel the heat of embarrassment climbing her neck. While this wasn't a real lie, it most surely felt like one. What would her father say if he could hear her introduce herself like this? And her mother? Were the angels applauding her?

"So tell me why you are going to Medora. That place has been booming. An article I read in the paper said it was almost like the gold rush back in '49. I was but a girl, but my father took me out to see the wagon trains heading west. I often wondered if there were any people left back east of Chicago, since so many were traveling westward."

My, Mrs. Grant did love to chat. "I'm looking for my nephew." Best to keep the details to herself — at least that's what had been drummed into her since childhood. Although she'd often wondered what secrets her family had that were different than the others in Smithville Parish.

"Oh, really. Did he come west to work for Marquis de Mores?"

Amethyst considered whether or not to speak of the details. Mrs. Grant seemed truly interested, and Amethyst was enjoying the conversation. . . . Why not, she'd never see the woman again. "Hardly. He's only eight. You see, my sister-in-law, my dead brother's wife, left their son off with someone we didn't know, who took Joel west. My father insists that since the boy is his only living heir, he should come back to the home farm."

"Your father?"

"Yes."

"Well, aren't you a living relative?"

"Since women are not allowed to own land, he wants Joel back."

"Pardon me, I wouldn't want to gainsay your father, but times and laws are changing. I own property in Chicago, and I also own the farm of my grandfather. I bought it from a — and I quote — 'legal heir' who was letting it run to ruin. My second son is in charge of the farming; my eldest son is a lawyer. It is my third son whom I'm going to visit."

"Have you no daughters?"

"Alas, not that survived infancy. But I am blessed with daughters-in-law, one of whom usually travels with me, but this time she is indisposed." She leaned closer with a chuckle. "What an idiotic term for pregnant. They say men usually have a case of the wanderlust, but in our family, it is I."

Amethyst could not help but smile back. Never had she met someone like this Mrs. Grant. But then, never before had she done many of the things she was now doing.

"Go ahead. I can tell you are dying to ask me something."

"Your husband, is he . . . I mean . . . ?"

"Mr. Grant died, I believe from overwork, some ten years ago. But he had the wisdom and foresight to make certain that I would inherit all of our businesses and assets. Some of our friends were shocked, but our sons feel as I do. If a woman has the intelligence and the education, she should be allowed to do whatever she is able. And we women are far smarter, wiser, and more capable than most men give us credit for."

Amethyst thought back to how hard she worked on the farm and how she sold the surplus, yet her father had the final say in all things. She was no more than a hired hand, one who received no pay.

Mrs. Grant smiled sweetly, as if the words she'd uttered were not even seditious. "Don't you agree with me? You look like an extremely capable woman, and if you've had any schooling . . ." She paused, waiting for an answer.

"Thanks to my mother, who insisted — against my father's wishes — I attended our local schoolhouse through the eighth grade. He thought six years of not helping all day, every day, were enough." Actually, he'd resented any of his children going to school at all but knew his sons had to have schooling if they were to better themselves and, hopefully, help provide for their pa.

"Ah, your mother is a wise woman."

"Was. She died five years ago, and there isn't a day goes by that I don't think of her, her sayings, how hard she worked and yet managed to have a song and a smile." Amethyst thought to the coins in her hem, the Bible that weighted her carpetbag, and the small gown, so lovingly stitched and embroidered. "So many gifts she managed to give me."

"And do you take after her?"

Amethyst thought for a bit. "You know, I never thought about it, but I guess that I do."

"Why don't you come sit over here by me, and it will be easier for us to visit? I knew there was a reason I chose these double seats."

Surprising herself, Amethyst pulled her carpetbags out from under the seat and, one at a time, shoved them under the other. By the time she finished, her hat hung down over her ear and her hair had won and cascaded down her back. She rolled her eyes, settling herself in the seat.

"I should just braid it and wrap the braids around my head, but —"

Mrs. Grant cocked her head like a bright-eyed chickadee. "No, the way you wear it suits you. It would be a shame for all of you to be so confined."

"Pardon me?"

"Ah, my dear, in your hair I see the spirit inside you that wants to break free."

Amethyst stared at her, for once not even bothering to try to save her hat. Instead, she pulled out the pin and, with hat in hand, wove the long hatpin back into the felt. She shook her head, then using her fingers, since she refused to be digging in her case for her brush and comb, twisted her hair and pinned it again on top of her head.

"I once saw a beautiful woman, Chinese I imagine, who wore her long hair in a coil held in place by two ebony sticks. I always wished I could find sticks like that, for she looked so regal. Instead, I use combs." Mrs. Grant touched an ivory comb that peeked out from under the pert hat. "Hmm. I think I have extras." With a lift of her eyebrows and a widening of her eyes, she turned and opened the clasp on a leather case beside her on the seat. Humming a little tune, she sorted through things, using her fingers for her eyes. "Here we go." She pulled a drawstring pouch from the case, opened the neck, and retrieved two amber-colored combs. "These will look quite lovely in your hair."

"But I can't, I mean . . ." Amethyst pushed her spine tight against the seat back. "You can't just give things to a stranger like this."

"Whyever not?" Mrs. Grant looked from the combs to Amethyst and back. "Of course, if you don't like them . . ."

"No, that's not it at all. They are beautiful, but . . ." *Snatch them, clutch them,* the voice in her head screamed at her.

"Ah." Mrs. Grant pursed her lips and gave an emphatic nod that set the feather bobbing. "Now, let me see if I understand this. I have two combs that are not being used, and if the truth be told, I have many more at home. I want to give them to a friend of mine, and for some reason known only to her, she is looking at me as if I offered her a live mouse."

Amethyst rolled her lips to keep from chuckling out loud. Mice were the last thing she'd thought of. The desire of owning something so lovely made her mouth dry. Whoever had made the combs had carved a design into the bar of the comb. Her fingers ached to feel the cool comb in the palm of her hand. "If there were something I could do in exchange."

"Why, you've been doing something for me ever since we left the station."

"What?"

"Helping me enjoy my journey." She reached over and took Amethyst's hand in her own and placed the combs in the palm. "There now. They are yours, and we'll hear no more about it."

"Thank you." Amethyst gazed at the treasures in her hand. A lovely color, like apple cider that had been sitting for a time and its bubbles were just beginning to rise. She held the combs closer to the window to see the engraving. Simple, like the fronds of the ferns that grew in the deep shade of the trees down by the creek.

"Do you know how to use them?"

"Not really." *How backward she must think me. Father God, you have given me a gift in this woman, and I promise to learn from her all that I can.*

"Like this. You hold the comb so the curved side is out, then set it against the hair. If you set it with the hair, it will fall out and be totally useless."

Amethyst twisted her hair in a rope, rolled it around her hand, and tucked the end under the coil, then settled one of the combs into the side. When it slipped, she did it again, and this time it held. She set the other one on the left side and tipped her head gently from side to side. Her hair didn't shift.

She tucked the three hairpins she'd been so careful not to lose into her reticule. "At home I wore a scarf tied round my head to keep my hair back when I was working." She didn't say that she'd found her hat in a box someone sent to the church for the minister's family. Mrs. Landers had insisted she take it, for no proper woman went without a hat.

Not that she'd ever been proper.

The next day they had several hours to wait in St. Paul for their westbound train, so Mrs. Grant insisted that they have a meal in the restaurant at the station.

"But I . . . I cannot do that."

"Ah, but you don't understand. You have become my traveling companion, and I might need your assistance, so you must humor an old lady and join her for dinner." Agnes locked her arm through Amethyst's and guided her in the direction of tables covered in white cloths and a man who snapped to attention when he saw Mrs. Grant.

"We'd like a table for two — and not by the kitchen."

65

"Yes, madam." He turned and led the way to a table that had a padded bench on one side and a chair on the other. "Will this be acceptable?"

Mrs. Grant smiled at her companion. "Will this suit?"

Amethyst wet her lips. "Of course." If only her father could see her now.

Several hours later, with the train rocking its way across western Minnesota, Amethyst found herself swallowing and swallowing again. Bile rose in the back of her throat, and her stomach roiled like the creek in spring freshet.

"Are you feeling all right?"

"I'll be fine, thank you."

"How long since you had eaten?"

"I had some bread with me."

"Perhaps the beef was too rich."

"Perhaps." A shiver started at her feet and worked its way upward. She pulled her coat around her, even though they weren't that far from the potbellied stove and the air was not cold. Her stomach cramped and, before she could clamp her hand over her mouth, erupted. She twisted her head so that the vomit missed Mrs. Grant, but the stink and the mess of it made Amethyst want to die. What would her benefactress think now?

CHAPTER FIVE

Surely death would be better than this.

The train rocking made even opening her eyes a risky business.

"Amethyst, dear, do you think you can drink some water?" Mrs. Grant leaned forward from the facing seat and wiped the perspiration from Amethyst's face. The cool cloth brought only momentary relief.

Amethyst thought to shake her head but, having suffered the consequences of responding to a query like that once before, chose to try to speak instead. Her "No, thank you" came out as an indecipherable croak.

She heard two people talking but couldn't focus enough to understand what they were saying. Never in her life had she been so sick. *Ah, Ma, how I need you.* Her belly cramped again, but there was nothing to come up. *Lord God, please take me home. I cannot endure this.* She fell back in the deep pit of near unconsciousness, Mrs. Grant's conversation just at the edge of her awareness.

"You are going to have to take her off at Fargo, Mrs. Grant. If she is contagious, all the other passengers are in danger."

"If I find a place to take care of her, will the train wait for me?"

"You'd have to catch tomorrow's train, ma'am."

"I see. She is far too weak to walk. Is there someone who will assist us?"

"Once we arrive in Fargo, I'll talk to the ticket agent and see if he can find a wagon or a buggy. The doctor has some beds at his house. Perhaps he will take her in. There are hotels too and several boardinghouses. One of them might be able to help you." He stopped for a moment. "She isn't really your traveling companion, is she?"

"Not really. We struck up a conversation and went together for dinner in St. Paul. She fell sick not long after that."

"So you have no responsibility for her, then?"

"No, none other than that of Christian charity. I cannot just leave her."

"Others might. You are a gracious woman. As soon as I find some help, I'll let you know."

"Have you by any chance checked to see if there is a doctor on board?"

"Yes. There's none on this trip. Not so

many people travel in the winter, you know."

"All right, then. Well, thank you."

Amethyst opened her eyes to see Mrs. Grant sponging her face again.

"We'll be getting off in Fargo, Amethyst dear, so that we can find medical attention for you."

Amethyst blinked and shook her head the slightest. "N-no." Her throat burned as though she'd swallowed a live coal. Her head throbbed, keeping time with the clacking wheels.

"Do not fear. I'm not going to leave you."

"W-wa-ter."

"Of course, but just a sip." Mrs. Grant held a cup to her charge's lips, but when the liquid dribbled down the side of her face, she slid an arm behind Amethyst's neck and propped her with one arm, tipping the cup with her other hand. The train lurched and liquid spilled again, but Amethyst got enough in her mouth to swallow.

"M-more?"

They repeated the routine again and were a bit more successful. The cool liquid eased the fire in her throat, and Amethyst managed the barest hint of a smile.

The conductor stopped at Mrs. Grant's seat. "Fargo is just ahead. I'll get the others off and then find someone and come back for you."

"Thank you so much."

He walked on through the car and headed out the door at the end.

Amethyst tried to rouse when she felt strong arms lift her from the train seat. What was going on? Where were they taking her? She ordered her mouth to ask questions, but her tongue failed, and only guttural sounds came out.

"You'll be fine, miss." The male voice echoed as much in the rumble of his chest as in her hearing.

She'd be fine. *What is wrong with me? I'm going to . . . to . . .* She couldn't even remember the place she was bound for. Why not take her home? Where was she?

Cold bit her nose and cheeks. Bright sunlight closed her eyes. Strong arms, like bands, held her tight, and then her benefactor set her on the seat of a buggy. In spite of her desire to stay upright, she slipped sideways until she fell against a soft cushion. Mrs. Grant wrapped her arms around her.

"Thank you, sir. You have been most kind."

The buggy swayed as the driver mounted the front seat and clucked his team forward. "I'll take you to the doctor's, unless there is somewhere else you'd like to go."

"No, that is all I can think to do."

Some time later Amethyst swallowed warm broth that was spooned to her mouth. The bed was warm and not rocking, with space for her to stretch out and turn her face into a pillow beneath her head. She continued swallowing until the broth was taken away, and she heard a strange woman murmuring to her that they'd get her into something more comfortable and she could rest easy now.

When she woke again, a lamp beside the bed shone on a woman sound asleep in the chair. A white apron covered her dress, and she wore a shawl around her shoulders. Amethyst tried to be quiet, but her slightest move roused the woman caring for her.

"Ah, there you are." The woman laid a hand against Amethyst's cheek. "I think you're on the mend. Let me fetch some more broth, since you've kept down what I've given you. Doctor says to give you as much as you can tolerate."

"Where am I?" Finally, words made it from her mind to her mouth and were spoken aloud. She could even hear them.

"Why, you're in Fargo at Doctor Sampson's. I'm Alvia, the doctor's missus and the main nurse. He's out on a call and won't be back until that baby is born. So I'll leave you for a minute and fetch the broth."

Amethyst forced her mind to remember. *Who was it who had taken care of her on the train? Ah, Mrs. Grant.* "Mrs. Grant?"

"She's gone to the hotel. She said to let her know as soon as you woke up, but I think we'll wait until morning. You've been here two days."

"Thank you." Two days? What all had she missed? Amethyst tried to remember something that might have happened, but she wasn't sure.

The nurse had to waken her again when she returned with the broth. "Here we go, dearie. You just swallow now, and this will be gone in no time. Perhaps you'd like an egg for breakfast in a few hours, and then we'll give you a good bath. Amazing how much better you'll feel."

Like a small child being fed, Amethyst opened her mouth every time the spoon reached her lips. Never had she been so weak she couldn't at least feed herself. Gratitude brimmed over, and a tear trickled down her cheek, followed by another.

"Is there something else I can do for you? Do you hurt anywhere?"

Amethyst shook her head, but the tears continued.

When Amethyst finished the broth, Mrs. Sampson dipped a cloth in a basin of water she'd brought. "Here now, this will make you feel better." She gently washed her patient's face and hands, then patted them dry with a soft cloth. "I have some cream here that will help too." She smoothed a creamy liquid over Amethyst's face and rubbed it into her hands.

"Roses. In the winter?"

"Yes, I add rose petals. Sick folk need something soothing that smells good."

"Yes. Thank you."

"You are most welcome. I think I'll go on to bed now, but there is a bell here for you to ring if you need anything."

Amethyst nodded, her eyelids so heavy she just gave up and drifted back to sleep.

When she woke again many hours must have passed because now Mrs. Grant had taken the chair, moved it over closer to the window, and sat reading. Amethyst watched the woman who'd been her savior, watched the sunbeams play with the fine strands of white hair until her whole head appeared to be afire, glinting like sun on snow, making her smile. She must have shifted, because Mrs. Grant looked up, marked her place in the book, and set it aside.

"You are looking far better than when we left the train. Welcome back."

"How will I ever thank you?" Ah, finally she could give voice without sounding like a frog croaking from a pond.

"Just by getting well. Would you like a drink?"

"Yes, please." At that moment she realized thirst rampaged through her like marauding foxes. She drank from the cup that Mrs. Grant held, was even able to hold up her own head, although the action made her pant with the effort.

"I'm going for Mrs. Sampson. She said to let her know when you awoke and she'd bring in breakfast."

"Thank you." Was that actually hunger she felt growling in her middle?

Between the two women, Amethyst was fed, bathed, and clothed in a clean night-dress that felt heavenly against skin that had indeed been soothed by the cream they'd rubbed over her entire body.

"I smell like a flower garden." She lifted her hand to her face and sniffed. "Do you by any chance have a receipt for your cream? How I would love to make something like this." *Back when I am home again and can use some ingredients from my garden.*

"I will write it up for you. I get the glycerin over at the apothecary. My mother used goose fat for her skin, but this is much more soothing. You can put mint in it too, or sometimes I've used lavender. That makes a real nice lotion."

Mrs. Grant rubbed the leftovers into the backs of her own hands. "Have you ever thought of making this to sell?"

"Oh no. I just make enough for my patients. That little bit of extra caring helps them get better more quickly. I use the mint for men. They don't take to smelling like a flower garden. It helps when someone is in bed so long they get bedsores."

"I think you should make it to sell. I know many women who would purchase a lotion like this." Mrs. Grant sniffed the back of her hand again. "Delightful."

The next day Mrs. Grant was again sitting by the bed. "Would you like me to read to you?"

"Oh, would you? No one's read to me since Ma did when I was a little girl. How she found time to read to us, I'll never know. Mostly it was in the winter around the fire, when Pa was gone." She didn't add that her pa had frequented the saloon more often than was good for him, or for them either, for that matter. She thought back to her home, wondering if he was taking proper care of the livestock. You couldn't be ailing when the animals needed to be fed.

"I'm reading from Hawthorne. Do you mind if I don't go back and start at the beginning?" The older woman held up her book so Amethyst could see its cover.

"No, not at all." But no matter how hard she tried to stay awake, she lasted for only a couple of pages.

The next day Amethyst was the one in the chair by the window, feeling the sun on her back, the draft on the floor around her ankles, and the joy of being strong enough to feed herself. She glanced up when the door opened and the doctor walked in.

"Good afternoon, Miss O'Shaunasy. It appears to me that you've been a fine patient."

"Your wife is a fine nurse."

"Yes, she is. Knows enough to be a doctor in her own right." He listened to her heart and lungs and took both her hands in his. "Squeeze."

She squeezed as hard as she could, but even she could tell it was rather a puny effort. "At least I can sit in a chair now. I never thought of sitting in a chair as taking effort. I've always been grateful for a moment or two to sit down."

"Mind if I ask you some questions?"

She shook her head. "Not at all."

"Were you feeling sick earlier that day?"

"No, I was fine. We left our train, had a meal at the station, and boarded our westbound train. All of a sudden I could feel some cramping in my belly, and then everything came up. Don't know what I would have done without Mrs. Grant."

"The conductor would most likely have put you off at the next stop."

"Oh, my land. God certainly has taken good care of me. When do you think I'll be able to continue my journey? I was supposed to be home again in time for Christmas."

The doctor stroked his gray-shot beard between fingers and thumb. "Heard tell there are intermittent blizzards and heavy snows across the west. It's already the nineteenth. Medora is only a day from here if there aren't any problems. Winter isn't a good time to cross the prairies."

I tried to tell my father that, but walls are more biddable than he is when he gets a wild idea. "I see. Well, I just need to find my nephew and get back on the return train."

Considering how difficult this trip had been so far, anything would be easier.

Three days later, still needing frequent rests, she and Mrs. Grant stood at the door waiting for the buggy to arrive. "Mrs. Sampson, I don't have much, but I will send you money as soon as I am able. You need to tell me how much I owe."

"Why, don't you worry, dearie, the bill has been paid." Mrs. Sampson patted her hand and handed her a paper box. "Here are some sandwiches and cookies to tide you over."

"But I . . ." Amethyst turned to look at Mrs. Grant.

"Never you mind. It's my money, and I can spend it the way I want. I have no one but God himself to hold me accountable, and that's the way I like it." She turned to Mrs. Sampson. "I'd like you to consider selling your lotion. We could take that receipt and turn it into a thriving business. My husband always said I had a nose for new things and the good sense to invest wisely. I'd be honored to be your partner in this endeavor."

"Why, I . . . I can't believe this."

"You think on it, and I'll write to you. Perhaps I'll stop by when I'm heading back east."

Amethyst almost collapsed when they found their seats on the train. "I'm weak as a kitten. Hard to believe."

"You could have died, you were that sick." Mrs. Grant settled her bags underneath the seat and leaned back with a sigh. "Now, that was most certainly an interesting interlude." She dug in her reticule and pulled out the paper the doctor's wife had given her. "Such simple ingredients, but that is often the case. The most simple are the most effective." She bent over and opened her carpetbag to pull out a medicine bottle with a cork stopper. "I would use little pots. Make a pretty label. Alvia's Lotion."

"How could she make enough to sell in stores?"

"We'd start small. I'm sure I can find some company to manufacture the product in Chicago when we're ready for that." She uncorked the stopper and sniffed, then with a smile stoppered it again and put it back in her bag. "We could probably make a whole line of ladies' sundries. Have you heard of the lead poisoning that happens when women use that awful white powder on their hair and faces?"

Amethyst didn't mention that where she came from no one put anything on their faces except for some melted fat on chapped lips and hands in the winter. "No, I'd not heard of that."

"I read about it in the newspaper. What women will do to be beautiful." She shuddered. "I'm glad I never did more than pinch my cheeks and bite my lips to make them pink. Mr. Grant always said he didn't have much patience for such folderol. 'Women are more beautiful as God made them,' he used to say."

"He sounds like a wise man."

"A prudent one. Secretly I wondered if he just didn't want me spending his hard-earned money on such things." Her chuckle made the feather on her hat bob.

When they left Dickinson for the final leg of their journey, Mrs. Grant leaned forward and took Amethyst's hands. "I wish I could convince you to come west with me. I'd like my son to meet you, and I will so miss your company."

"Some company I've been, getting sick like that and now falling asleep at the drop of a hat. I would like to pay you back some for all I've cost you."

"You keep your money. You might need it worse than I do before you get home. And besides, I might want you to come help with this new company we'll be forming. Three heads are better than two."

"You really think Mrs. Sampson will go along with your ideas?"

"I pray so. I need to convince her she could use the money to help her patients. Such a dear lady." Mrs. Grant handed Amethyst her calling card. "I've written my Chicago address on the back, but I most likely will get a letter off to you that will be at your home before you are."

"No, no. Please wait. My pa opens all the mail, and —"

"I see. Well, I wish I were going to be in Chicago when you go through there again. You and your nephew could come visit me for a few days." She squeezed Amethyst's hands and let them go, sitting perfectly straight on the edge of her seat. "You promise to write to me?"

"Yes, I promise." The thought of getting off in a strange town, knowing no one and not even where she was going, made Amethyst feel like throwing up again.

When she stood on the platform watching the train chug on west, she blew out the breath she must have been holding. Her white breath reminded her how cold it was. Although there was no snow falling, the clouds above her looked pregnant. *Lord, what do I do now?*

CHAPTER SIX

Amethyst stared down the track one more time. Loneliness echoed like the wind that tugged at her skirts.

"Ma'am, you better get on in here out of that cold." The voice came from behind her.

Amethyst turned with a nod. She picked up her carpetbags and headed for the station door being held open by the man who had called her. His green eyeshade proclaimed him the telegraph operator as well as the stationmaster.

"Thank you." She stamped the snow off her feet on the mat and glanced around the very utilitarian room, the main focus right now being the cast-iron stove with a kettle boiling on top. The steam caused her stomach to rumble in anticipation. Right now, beef soup smelled more like perfume to her than simple food. Ever since she'd started on the road to recovery, she'd felt hungry every time she turned around. "My, that smells good."

"Where you going?" The man inserted

another chunk of wood in the door with red glowing glass, closed the door, and gave the kettle a stir. He turned to look at her, waiting for an answer.

"Here. Medora, I mean. I'm searching for my nephew."

"Plenty of folks lookin' for someone come through here. As if we know where all those who want to start new lives either went or live." He shook his head. "Best tell me about him."

"His name is Joel O'Shaunasy. He's eight years old and came west with a man named Jacob Chandler. I have information that they live near here somewhere." Her stomach rumbled loud enough for him to hear.

"How long since you ate? You're welcome to some soup here. It's nothing fancy but it's filling." He indicated the steaming kettle.

"I . . . I don't want to put you out."

"Look, out here someone comes in hungry, we feed them. Thirsty, we got good water. So I got an extra bowl and spoon, and you can just help yourself." He limped over to the counter and brought out the mentioned bowl and spoon. "My wife sent over a loaf of bread, if that sounds good to you too?" He cocked his head, waiting for her to swallow her pride and answer.

"Can I pay you?"

"For what? Being neighborly. Ain't no charge for that, far as I know. Besides, we can sit and visit a mite while we eat. Gets some lonesome in here after the train's gone by, 'specially with weather like this."

Amethyst moved her bags over to the bench seat and crossed to take the two bowls. "I'll fill these while you slice the bread, and I do thank you. If everyone in Medora is as kind as you are, this town must have an excellent reputation." She filled the bowls with beef chunks and vegetable soup and set them on the bench seats, then sat down. Waiting for him to bring the bread so they could have grace left her salivating.

He handed her a thick slice of bread, straddled the bench, and bowed his head. "For this thy bounty we give thee our most hearty thanks. Amen." He nodded to the repast. "Dig in."

Amethyst did just that, holding the bowl close to her chin so that she wouldn't drip down the front of her garments. While she'd unbuttoned her coat, ten feet from the stove the room was chilly, with drafts along the floor enough to make her grateful for her woolen stockings and quilted petticoat. "My, you must thank your wife. This is delicious."

"Can't go wrong with good beef, beans, a few carrots, and whatever else she has to hand. At home she makes the best dumplings, but I go for the plain fare here. Now, let me think on the boy you are looking for." He sopped the last of his soup with the crust of his bread and squinted his eyes while finishing chewing. "Last summer a man and a boy came here looking for work and a place to live. Adams over at the general store sent them on out with Ward Robertson. He's gone now, but —"

"You mean Mr. Chandler has left and gone on to somewhere else?"

"No. Robertson was killed by a freak ricocheting bullet in a shootout last summer. Terrible thing. He was a good man. Left a wife and five girls. Terrible doings."

Amethyst waited. "So Mr. Chandler is still around here?"

"Far as I know he's still helping out at the Robertsons'. Unless he rode out instead of taking the train. The boy comes to town with the other children to school. He turned into a right good little cowhand, so I heard. Opal Torvald made sure of that. She was teaching the father too, but that boy really took to it."

"So is he here in town at the school-house?"

"Don't rightly know. We had a bad snow last few days and looks to be coming back. Times like this the ranch kids stay to home."

Amethyst fought to keep herself in her seat and not scream at the man to hurry up and tell her how to get out there. "How far is it to the Robertsons'?"

"Oh, somewhere 'bout a mile or two, but you'll need a horse and sleigh. You'd be better going out to Miz Hegland's boardinghouse if you need a place to stay. Perhaps if Carl ain't too busy and the weather holds, he could take you on out to the ranch."

"I see." Oh, why couldn't this be easy? "When is the next train east?"

"Sometime tomorrow. All depends on the weather. Had one train sit here in the station till they could clear the tracks. Been a bad year for blizzards already, and I fear we got more to come. All the signs point to a bad one." He picked up their bowls. "You want some more soup?"

"No, thank you. But please be sure to tell your wife thank you. If you could give me directions to the boardinghouse, I will be on my way."

" 'Tain't hard to find. You head on south over the railroad tracks. The snow's froze hard enough to walk on, and you'll see their house off to your left. Snugged right up against the hill. Two story with a porch across the front. All the others round there are only one level. But you get confused, you could stop at any house and ask for directions."

Just then the door blew open, and a man stepped in, putting his shoulder against the door to slam it shut. "Colder'n a witch's . . ." He paused when he saw a woman sitting on the bench. "Sorry, ma'am. I thought Owens was here by his lonesome."

"Howdy, Jake. What can I do for you?"

"Jest hoped you had a coffeepot on." He patted his chest. "Got a little somethin' here to put in it." Jake wore a coat of pelts, dusted with white, and a broad-brimmed black felt hat. For some reason the grin he sent her made Amethyst want to take a few steps back. As the man rubbed his hands together in the heat of the stove, she caught a whiff of something so rank that her eyebrows shot up. She drew a handkerchief from her sleeve, ostensibly to wipe her nose, but in reality to cover the odor.

"Sorry, but I'm plumb out of coffee. Perhaps Adams has a pot on."

"Better head on home, then. Thanks for the warm-up." The man named Jake turned and headed back out the door.

If he was typical of the people living in Medora . . . Amethyst thought longingly of home, but the stationmaster had been most cordial, and she hoped Mrs. Hegland would be too. *If I can find the place.*

"If it'd been anyone else, I'd have asked him to take you out there, but I trust Jake Maunders about as far as I can throw a buffalo." He stared at her long enough for her feet to want to shift and her hands to wring. "I hate to send you out in this weather."

"But the sun tried to break through."

"That's 'cause you're looking south, and the bad weather comes from the north, right down off the Arctic, and blasts on through here. There's nothing to stop it." He shook his head. "And I know Miz McGeeney don't have no room, nor are there any beds over at the dormitory, but then, they don't take women anyway."

He appeared to be muttering to himself, so Amethyst picked up her bags and started for the door. "Thank you for the soup. I'll be fine."

He followed her to the door. Once outside he pointed to the south. "See that house over there, the big one? That's the boardinghouse."

"All right. That doesn't look too far." *Not*

if I'd not been sick. Should she ask him to find her a conveyance? But surely he'd have suggested one if one were available. If only she didn't have the carpetbags to carry too. "Thank you again."

She started off bravely but hadn't gotten across the train tracks before she had to stop to rest. She looked over her shoulder to see black clouds hovering beyond the top of the cliff behind the town. Surely that hill protected the town of Medora. Off to her left she saw a three-story building with a tall brick smokestack. Perhaps that was the slaughtering enterprise Mrs. Grant had spoken of. Amethyst took the scarf from around her neck and tied it over hat and head, tucking the ends into the front of her coat. She raised the collar to protect her neck and started out again. The north wind at her back pushed her enough to make the walk somewhat easier, but the cold seared the inside of her nose and down into her chest. She stopped again and adjusted her scarf to cover her face up to her eyes.

Her stops grew closer together, and each one took longer for her to get moving again. She passed several small houses, one with smoke coming from the chimney, one looking silent as death. A dog barked, but even the animal was wise enough not to venture out.

Glancing back, she thought the clouds looked closer and the town not far enough away. She plowed onward, the crust of ice on the snow enough to hold her weight. The outline of the house blurred, and she stopped to break the ice from her scarf where her breath had frozen. Too exhausted to utter the words, her mind kept up the refrain, *Help me, oh, Lord God. Be my strength and my shield*. The snow smacked her on the head as she sank down.

"Get up!" She heard the voice and, using every remaining bit of strength, stumbled to her feet. Four feet, ten feet, she staggered on, her bags forgotten where she'd dropped them.

A dog barked, then set up a frantic howl.

Was that voices she heard or the wind playing tricks with her mind? She slipped on the ice and crashed to the ground again. *Lord, my help, my salvation. I cannot rise again*.

A dog whined, and a warm tongue licked her face. He wriggled close to her and howled again. The mournful sound sent fear up her spine. Was she to die here? No, just rest a moment. Just a moment. That's all she needed.

The heat of the dog's body penetrated her coat, and she wrapped both arms around the animal, clinging to the heat, the whimpering creature.

"Get up!" That voice again.

But I cannot. I cannot breathe. I cannot.

The dog tugged on her coat, taking his warmth away. She pushed herself to her knees. Were it not for her skirts strangling her, she would crawl. The dog returned and stood beside her. She braced her hand on his back and inch by inch got one foot underneath her and then the other. Now bracing both hands on his back, she heaved herself upright and staggered forward. The dog whined just ahead of her, encouraging her.

When he barked again, this time with joy, Amethyst ceased her slow forward motion.

"Brownie!" The voice sounded fairly close.

Amethyst brushed the ice away from her face again so she could see. Snow swirled around her, but out of it loomed a real person. "Help." Did she only think the word, or did she really say it?

"Oh, Brownie, good dog. Here, let me help you."

Amethyst collapsed into the woman's arms.

CHAPTER SEVEN

"Are you sure you want to do this?"

"Yes, General, I've been thinking of it for some time. This just makes it certain now." Major Jeremiah McHenry motioned to the black patch covering his missing left eye. Better a missing eye than missing in action. That along with what seemed to be becoming a permanent limp from a bullet to the thigh would cut short his military career. He didn't mention his stumbling over everything or that he couldn't even get his foot in the stirrup right.

"So what do you plan to do?"

"You mean with all the wealth I'll be receiving in my pension?" Actually, along with what he'd saved through the years, he had a pretty good nest egg. Jeremiah smiled on the inside, but smiles had long before taken leave of absence from his face. Fighting the Apache in the arid Arizona Territory stole the hearts of many and the minds of some. While they'd finally shipped Geronimo off to Florida, Jeremiah had been assigned to remain with the troops at Fort Bowie.

"I wish it were more. You've earned it."
The general leaned back in his leather chair.
"You didn't answer my question. Are you
heading home?"

"No, I'm heading back to the badlands of
Dakotah Territory. Those buttes and cliffs
— never could get them out of my mind.
There's no one that important left at home
in Kentucky, so I plan to find me a stream,
build a log house nearby, run a few head of
cattle, and take up with the friends I made
there." *Find me a woman like Ruby and
perhaps even have me a family of my own.*
Some dreams one kept to himself.

"You taking Kentucky?"

McHenry nodded. "He's lame in the
shoulder and me in the thigh. We're a
couple old war horses put out to pasture."

"I could transfer you to Fort Beaufort."

"Why are you so insistent on hanging on
to me?"

"Good men like you are getting harder to
find." The general pushed a decanter across
his desk. "Pour yourself another." He
steepled his fingers, wrists against his chest.
"I will be reassigned soon, and I want you
on my staff. You could enjoy the winter
here, which is really Arizona's best season,
recuperate from your wounds with light
duty, and I will give you the promotion you

so richly deserve when I am reassigned. I'm hoping for Washington."

"If that is your dream, sir, I hope you are posted there. My dream lies in the wild and beautiful badlands, where the eagles cry, the fish leap from the river, and the people care for one another." He thought to some of the ruffians he'd met there and added, "Most of them anyway."

"But you're a soldier."

"According to those papers I signed, I *was* a soldier."

"I will tear them up if you give me the word."

"General, I know you are an honorable man, and I trust you would not do such a heinous thing." McHenry sipped the whiskey he'd poured. He'd most likely never have such quality again, but then, he used hard liquor only medicinally anyway. He was sure Jake Maunders or Williams still had access to rotgut if he ever wanted to burn his innards out. Staring over the rim of the glass and into the flame of the lamp, he saw a campfire with Rand Harrison on the other side. Some of the other cowboys lying around, telling stories late at night, swapping lies as they joked. The fire threw dancing shadows up on walls of red ochre and pale cream sandstone with dark gray capstone. Though after Ruby Torvald arrived in Little Missouri, he and Rand had not been so friendly, more like bull elks in rut. Of course, courting the same woman can do that to a friendship. But that was long gone. Rand had married the spitfire, and McHenry wished them every blessing, periodically even corresponding with them.

"The only place I've seen to rival a Dakotah sunset is right here in Arizona Territory. Someday this country will be covered with ranches too. But give me the grasslands of the prairie over the cactus anytime. You ever need a place to put your thoughts back in perspective, come to Medora and see me. I'll take you hunting."

The next day when the train stopped at Bowie, McHenry loaded his horse, some feed for the animal and food for himself, a water barrel, a trunk that contained all he owned, and himself onto a railroad car bound east to Kansas City. There he would board a northbound train for Chicago, then west to Dakotah. Rather a long way around, but he'd see a lot of country.

In spite of the cold he sat in the doorway, Indian fashion, a heavy woolen Navajo blanket over his shoulders, and watched the miles slide by. Mountains, deserts, plains covered with snow, the sun so bright on it, he had to tip his hat near to his nose to shield his one good eye. Rivers frozen, rivers flowing sky blue beside white-covered banks threaded with red willow, spirals of smoke marking the houses, barns snug against the season. He saw cattle drifting before the wind and deer eating the tender tips of branches. When the light was right, he read his Bible, starting with Genesis and on through the Old Testament. He figured he'd get through the New Testament before spring. When the conductor asked him why he didn't come to the passenger cars to get warmed up, he shook his head.

"Horse has to put up with the cold, so guess I can too." But he accepted the hot coffee and the visit. From Chicago west, it was one holdup after another. The wind whistled through the cracks between the exterior boards, but the load of hay he bought in Chicago insulated him and Kentucky from the worst of the cold. That and their heavy blankets. The pot of coals burning in an old washtub provided enough heat to keep them from freezing. Every time he tripped on something, he reminded himself that his vision would adjust eventually.

He and Kentucky had moved into a local

livery for two days to wait out the blizzard that struck Fargo. By the time the train headed west, he could hear the buttes and spires calling his name. But when the conductor called out, "Dickinson," Jeremiah opened the door in spite of the cold wind and rode in the doorway the remaining miles, watching for landmarks to tell him where they were and how far he had yet to get home. The letter he'd written to tell Rand Harrison he was on the way still lay in the trunk. He figured he'd get there about the same time as the letter would have anyway.

The journey had washed the twenty-five years of army life and all the fighting clean out of him, so when he led Kentucky off the train on December 24, 1886, he felt reborn. A new man with a new life, or at least he hoped so until he tripped over the ramp, saved from falling only by his grip on Kentucky's halter rope.

"Well, Captain McHenry, fancy seeing you walk off that car." The Medora stationmaster stared in wonder.

"The name's plain Jeremiah McHenry, and by the looks of the weather" — he inclined his head towards his horse — "we better get us a place here in town for a night or two."

"Very wise. Another hour or so and it won't be fit for man nor beast."

"Paddock still own the livery?"

Owens nodded. "He'll be right glad to see you. They moved over here across the river after de Mores got going good." He looked off to the buttes behind the town. "Welcome home, Ca— McHenry. We're glad to have you back."

"I'll pick up my trunk later. You want me to haul it inside?"

"No, I'll take care of that. What you going to do with that hay?"

"Pitch it out when I find a sledge to haul it. Railroad said no hurry."

"Where you going to live?"

"Gotta go looking for a place to build me a house, but for now thought maybe the cantonment."

"Cattle company took that over. You might try out to Heglands'. That big house over there." He pointed across the railroad tracks.

"Thanks. Maybe Harrison will have some work for me till I find a place." *At least I hope so. Spending the winter over at the barracks still might work if there's room. Only God knows the next step, and He's not telling.*

CHAPTER EIGHT

Amethyst's teeth chattered so loud she could hardly hear what the woman said.

"Th-thank y-you." She forced the words between stiff lips. With her feet in a tub of lukewarm water, someone rubbing her arms and shoulders through a heated blanket, and the stove bathing her in warmth, she knew she was still alive. Returning to life from so close to death hurt more than one would think. Some demon was stabbing her feet with the sharpest of needles, and her throat burned in spite of the warm drink they'd forced on her. The woman said it was from breathing such cold air. Her jaw ached from clenching it to try to keep her teeth from falling out.

"Thank our good Lord for our dog, Brownie. He insisted he had to go out and went tearing across the snow like he was chased by a wolf. When he found you, he set to barking, and we knew something or someone was in trouble. Although last time it was a small cat he brought home. Carried that little cat in his mouth as gentle as its mother would."

Amethyst glanced down at the dog now sound asleep in front of the stove. He'd saved her life. God was looking out for her. No doubt about it. She coughed and flinched at the same time.

"Have some more of this tea. The honey in it should help soothe your throat. Are you feeling any warmer?"

Amethyst nodded. This time she could hold the cup to her mouth herself. Before, her hands shook so much, the warm liquid splashed out. She wasn't sure if she was warming from the outside in or the inside out, but the two seemed to have met in the middle.

"I am Pearl Hegland. Were you coming to stay at my boardinghouse?"

Amethyst nodded. "The stationmaster sent me here."

"He should have found someone to drive you, with the storm coming on like that."

"I would have made it just fine, but I got sick on the train and spent several days at a doctor's house in Fargo. Guess I haven't gotten my full strength back." *Please, heavenly Father, protect me from sickness again. I'm already so far behind schedule that Pa must be worrying himself sick.*

"And your name?"

Amethyst shook her head slightly, feeling the rasp of the blanket against her hair that now hung around her shoulders. "I'm sorry. I am Amethyst Colleen O'Shaunasy from Pennsylvania. My father refused to call me Amethyst, said it was a foolish name, but when I left home I decided to no longer use Colleen and took up Amethyst as my name. Sometimes I forget to answer when someone calls me that, however." *Amethyst — Colleen — use whichever you want, but you are babbling like your pa when he's had too much to drink.*

"Well, Miss O'Shaunasy, I'm sure you are exhausted after your ordeal. What a strange welcome you've had to Medora. I have a room upstairs that is vacant. Would that suit you? I can help you up the stairs, since near freezing like that makes one terribly weak." Pearl knelt down and tenderly lifted one of Amethyst's feet from the water, inspecting it carefully. "I don't see any white spots. You are very fortunate. The white indicates frostbite. Let me see your hands."

Amethyst felt herself slumping more and more into the chair, melting from the glorious heat. While she tried to pay attention, she felt as if she were looking at her hostess from the wrong end of a spyglass. Her voice came and went as if a door opened and closed on the sound.

After carefully inspecting each finger, Pearl rubbed Amethyst's hands gently between her own. "There's a white spot on your little finger, but it's not very big. God was indeed watching out for you."

"Indeed." Amethyst turned at the sound of a child crying.

"That's the baby waking from a nap. Let's get you tucked in upstairs so I can go take care of him."

Amethyst wanted to say, "Take care of the baby first," but the words wouldn't move past the fog insidiously taking over her mind. She knew Mrs. Hegland helped her to stand and waited a moment for her to regain her equilibrium. She recognized they were climbing stairs, but the moment she collapsed on the bed, she knew only warmth and softness as she floated away.

Amethyst awoke sometime in the night to feel a cool hand on her brow and the covers tucked more securely around her.

"Thanks be to God, there's no fever."

"If she recovers without it going into her lungs, she'll be one blessed woman." The man's voice faded in and out.

No fever. Thank you. . . .

The next time she woke to see a little girl

dressed in a pink pinafore over her dress and holding a rag doll by one arm. One finger in her mouth, she stood watching Amethyst. Being stared at in such a concerted manner made her want to make sure she still had nose and chin. But before she could marshal her thoughts to say something, the little one turned around and made her way down the stairs.

"Ma. Ma, awake. Come see."

Amethyst smiled and glanced toward the window. It might as well be night, so dark was the snow pelting the pane. Now that she was awake, she realized the roaring in her dream was not a train but the wind making every effort to tear down the walls and ravage the occupants.

Stretching her arms above her head, she debated whether to snuggle back down under the quilts or to get up. When her body suggested she'd better take care of some long-delayed functions, she sat up and swung her feet to the braided rug on the floor. Having taken care of the necessary things, she set about to find her clothing. Her carpetbags — had anyone thought to go look for them? Otherwise, all she had were the clothes she'd been wearing and this borrowed nightdress. *The Bible. I have to have my Bible*. Most probably the weight of that huge family Bible had been one of the things that had worn her out so quickly. That and having been so terribly ill not more than a few days earlier. Thank God she had sewn the two gold pieces into the hem of her coat.

She smiled as her gaze roved the room. It was square with two long windows, one on each outer wall, with the four-poster set crosswise of the corner between the windows. The lace curtains would surely billow when the windows were open in the summer. Right now the wind would tear the lace right off the rods. A braided rug for under her feet, a washstand to the right of the bed, pegs on a board along the forget-me-not papered wall to hold her clothes. A kerosene lamp ready for lighting took up one end of a chest of drawers, where her meager belongings wouldn't fill even one drawer. White painted woodwork, everything so new, clean, and comfortable.

She'd never been in such a room in her entire life. Her room at home had a single bed, nails for her clothes, again so few needed, and a wooden box that held the lamp. She'd had the bare necessities, but then, what did it matter? She stayed in her room only long enough to sleep and dress.

Amethyst closed her eyes against tears that threatened. If only Ma had seen such

"Yes, when the weather breaks. This has been the worst year for blizzards since I've been here. And we're still only in December."

Amethyst leaned back against her pillows. "That was a delicious breakfast, but I don't think you need to carry trays up and down those stairs for me. I will join you for dinner and supper." She barely trapped a yawn. "Goodness me."

"Please excuse my manners. Here I go on rattling about us when I want to know about you. What brought you to Medora?"

"I am looking for my nephew." Amethyst missed the next yawn, it came so fast. "Pardon me, I'm the one whose manners are delinquent."

"I thought you might be exhausted today from the ordeal you had yesterday. Your nephew?"

Amethyst nodded, and another yawn kept her from answering.

"Oh, mercy me, I forgot to tell you the good news. Carl found two carpetbags on his way home yesterday. Might they be yours?"

"Yes. That is good news."

"I hung your things near the stove to dry. Snow had seeped into the bags, but your beautiful Bible escaped any damage. I can

beauty, how she would have loved it. But then, perhaps her mother had. Some things she said through the years made her daughter realize that her mother had given up much to marry the man who had worked her to death.

"Miss O'Shaunasy?" The voice came from the stairs. "I'm bringing you a breakfast tray. I'm sure you must be famished by now."

Amethyst scrambled back into the warmth of the bed and smoothed the crazy quilt over her outstretched legs. A tray in bed. What luxury. And she felt well enough to enjoy it. "You shouldn't have. I could have come downstairs." She smiled at the woman who wore a high-necked dress with the lace tickling her earlobes, her silver blond hair bundled in a crocheted snood.

"Well, I wasn't sure how you would be feeling. Staying in bed for the day surely wouldn't hurt anything." Pearl set an inlaid wood tray on the bed. "I thought mush would go down easily if your throat is still sore. I poured cream over it and added brown sugar. There's bread and jam. If you've never had Juneberry jam, it is a specialty of this area. I brought coffee, but if you would rather have tea, I can bring that up."

"No, this is just fine." Amethyst felt her insides rumble at the smell of the food. "I think I am indeed very hungry." She picked up the bread and took a bite. "Ah, what a treat."

"You might want to eat the mush while it is hot. I ground up the oats myself."

Amethyst did just as suggested and took a spoonful, then another, smiling around her mouthful. After swallowing, she set her spoon back on the tray.

"Is it not to your liking?"

"I want to know what you did to make this cereal so good."

"Well, you eat and I'll tell you."

Amethyst indicated the foot of the bed. "Can you sit down for a few minutes? I imagine you've been going at a dead run ever since your feet hit the floor this morning."

Pearl sat with a slight sigh. "Not as much as usual. With the storm still brewing, the men can't get out to work, and my husband, Carl, is doing chores around here. We didn't have to be up so early and could eat a bit later. Also, you are our only guest right now, so I am having an easy day. Carl and my daughter, Carly, are doing something mysterious, and since it is the day before Christmas, I was told not to ask questions."

Perhaps that was the man's voice Amethyst thought she might have heard during the night. She ate her way to the bottom of the bowl, just listening. "And the mush?"

"Oh, that's right. I toast the oats just slightly before I grind them. I set the coffee grinder on coarse, and after the oats are ground, I put them to cooking throughout the night. You know, on the back of the stove. That means part of the breakfast ready when we get up."

"You keep the stove going all night?"

"We have to. When it gets so terribly cold like right now, Carl gets up during the night and restokes the fires several times. I am so blessed. He lets me sleep."

"And you have how many children?"

"Two. Carly was your visitor." Pearl leaned against the post at the foot of the bed and turned with one knee up on the quilt. "Christmas will be different this year. With a storm like this, no one will be able to make it to town for church. Our church meets in the schoolhouse, but some of our people come from miles out in the country. Last Sunday it was announced that if it was snowing, there would be no Christmas Eve service, which means no program, and the children have been working so hard on it."

"Will they have it later, then?"

bring them up for you any time." She smiled when Amethyst yawned again, this time behind her hand. "I have a suggestion: you let yourself take a nap and come down whenever you feel like it. How does that sound?"

"It sounds like I am being cosseted." *And I am used to being the one doing the cosseting.* "Thank you . . . for everything."

"Good. You rest now. We eat dinner promptly at twelve, since Carl usually comes in to eat."

"What does your husband do?" Amethyst fought to keep her eyes open and be polite.

"He is a carpenter and a furniture maker par excellence. He has a workshop out back. When you come down, I'll show you the desk he made for me when I was still teaching." She paused at the door. "And tonight we'll light our Christmas tree."

"Good." *Good grief. Is it really Christmas? If Pa is worried, there is no way I can help him this time.*

The wind had picked up again when she awoke, alternately howling, whistling, and whispering like a child wanting his own way. It cajoled, pleaded, and then screamed again in fury — perhaps more like a certain father whose moods she knew far too well.

What if I never go back?

The thought made her sit straight up in bed. Of course she was going back. She would find Joel, and the two of them would become good friends again on the journey home. She remembered carrying him in a sling while she took care of his mother during one of Melody's bad spells. She had taught him to read — he was such a bright little boy — and had read to him when she could squeeze out the time. He helped her feed the chickens when the rooster was almost as tall as he was, and one day she found him standing between the front legs of one of the workhorses, arms around the stout legs, swinging back and forth and singing.

The horse never moved, quite unlike her heart, which did a panic dance as she went to retrieve him, gently talking to the horse so the animal did not get frightened. But then, Joel had always gotten along well with the animals, even with the sow that could have gobbled him easily but instead let him ride on her slightly arched back. Except when she had piglets. Then everyone treated her very carefully and knew enough to jump quick. Mama sows looked after their own with a vengeance.

"But how to find him in this wild

country?" She shook her head. *What if he is living far away from town?* From the little she saw, Medora could be quite sizable, larger than Smithville. At least it had a train station. Many of those she'd passed while looking out the train window had nothing but an arm for a mail sack, perhaps a water tower to fill the train boiler, and a platform of sorts to unload things from the train. Both the land and the sky seemed to go on forever, although it must be a friendlier land in the spring with growing grass — and someone had mentioned wild flowers. What would spring be like in this wild country?

She resolutely threw back the covers and sat up, swinging her feet to the floor. Her two carpetbags sat by the wall, where pegs lined a board. Her dark skirt and both waists she'd sewn after a particularly good market day hung from hooks, a towel hung on a peg beside them, and a washcloth took up another. Pearl had been there and hung up Amethyst's meager wardrobe while she had slept. Amethyst could hear a child's high voice from downstairs and the rumble of a man's. Someone laughed. Then quiet reigned.

Had they left? The notes from a piano drifted up the stairs — her favorite Christmas hymn, "Lo, How a Rose E'er

Blooming." Even here so far away from home and civilization, that rose would bloom again and always bloom. Amethyst hurried into her clothes and, after brushing her hair, twisted the long strands and swept them in a knot on top of her head. She found only one amber comb on the dresser top.

Tears burned her nose and eyes. The precious gift from Mrs. Grant, the only combs she'd ever had, and one was gone. She picked up the remaining one and ran her fingertip over the carving. Lost in the snow. So cold, so weary. *You nearly lost your life in that snow. You shouldn't be grieving about a comb. Be grateful for your life,* she reminded herself. Someday perhaps she could purchase another. But that wasn't the point. A pair of such beauty would always remind her of the special friend she had met on the train.

You might have lost the comb, but you will always have those memories in your heart.

"Amethyst Colleen O'Shaunasy, listen to that still small voice. Wipe your eyes, fix your hair, and go down those stairs to join the family for the evening. Hiding up here is not only churlish but cowardly." Her hand wobbled as she inserted the comb. Digging in her carpetbag, she found her hairpins and used them to tuck up the sides. She smoothed the front of her gored wool skirt and made sure all the buttons were in place on her waist, including those at the wrists. The mutton sleeves should have been ironed, but that was the least of her worries. *I wonder what Pa is doing this night. Has he made any preparation for Christmas? Tomorrow I must write to him.*

With one hand on the rail, she walked down the stairs, her heart pounding as if she'd chased the cows all the way to the barn from the far pasture. She wasn't sure if it was the exertion of getting ready or the trepidation of meeting all the family and other boarders, if there were any by now.

She followed the notes into the front room, pausing in the doorway.

"See, Ma." The little girl was leaning against the piano bench where her mother sat, bringing forth bits of heaven from her fingers rippling up and down the ivory keys.

Pearl brought the song to a close and turned to smile at Amethyst. "Welcome. I'm glad you feel up to joining us. Come in and meet everyone." She stood and came over to take her guest's arm. "We have a perfect chair for you right here by the fire. Supper will be ready shortly." She turned to one of the men. "Carl, if you could do the introductions, I need to check on the stove."

"Miss O'Shaunasy, I am Carl Hegland."

"I'm pleased to meet you." Amethyst managed a smile. She felt that she should curtsy. She'd met more strangers since she got on that train than in the whole of her life. Should she extend her hand? With a slight hesitation she did just that, to have her hand overwhelmed by her host. For that brief instant, the calluses of a man who created beauty with his hands and wood rubbed against her own. She looked into dark eyes that smiled back at her. A man sure of himself, whose Norwegian accent added another depth of quiet charm. Like his wife, he had a gift for making her feel welcome.

"And this is our other guest, Major Jeremiah McHenry. He used to be stationed here." Hegland motioned to a man who, even by the way he stood, said military.

Amethyst smiled and nodded, her hand extended. To her shock and surprise, he bowed slightly over her hand, his grasp sending a warmth flowing up her arm. He smiled, reminding her slightly of pictures she'd seen of General Robert E. Lee, though without the full head of silver hair.

Major McHenry wore silver sideburns, while the rest of his ear-length hair was touched by a first fall frost. The eye patch made him look even more distinguished.

"I'm pleased to meet you, Miss O'Shaunasy, but I need to make a correction here. I am no longer a major. I have retired, and now I'm plain Jeremiah McHenry."

In spite of the black patch over his left eye, the smile he gave her fell into well-used crinkles around both eyes and mouth.

"I see." *But there is no chance you could ever be plain anything. Don't be a ninny. You must have something more appropriate to say.* But in spite of her efforts, her tongue remained glued to the roof of her mouth. She slowly withdrew her hand from his, wanting nothing more than to flee back up the stairs.

CHAPTER NINE

"And where are you from, Miss O'Shaunasy?" McHenry leaned forward in his chair.

"Pennsylvania. Near . . ." There was no sense giving the name of her little village. It was so small no one had ever heard of it. "And you?"

"I was last stationed in Arizona. But my family home is in Kentucky. My favorite post was here in the badlands, so when I retired, I came back."

"I see." Surely she could be more creative than that. But Amethyst realized she'd never really talked with a man she hadn't known since childhood. If someone came to the farm, her father did all of the talking. And when she took things to town, she visited with the women who bought her wares. At church on Sunday she'd dutifully followed her mother as she chatted with the other women, the men usually gathering a ways away.

Amethyst held herself stiffly, passing the bowls and platters back to Pearl, who was dishing up Carly's plate along with her own. "My, this looks so delicious." She feasted on the smells of roast goose, ham, mashed potatoes, gravy, and rolls still warm from the oven. To sit here and be waited upon — she half expected her mother to show up and ask what was wrong with her feet that she didn't get up and help.

But when she'd offered, Pearl had declined, saying she was a guest and recovering from a terrible ordeal.

"Ma? Tree?"

"Yes, we'll light the tree after supper." Pearl smiled at the look on Amethyst's face. "We made candles especially for the tree. Carl made us holders, so after supper we will light the candles. Have you ever done that?"

Amethyst shook her head. She'd read about such a tradition, but at home if they cut a tree from the woods and brought it in to decorate, that was a miracle in itself. Pa didn't hold much with such foolishness, or so he said. They'd not had a tree or even much of a celebration since her mother died. Melody had invited them to their house until Patrick died. So many deaths in her family.

"And what brings you to Dakotah Territory in the middle of winter like this?"

The major's question caught her with food in her mouth. She finished chewing and wiped her lips with a napkin. Should she tell them? Why not? "I've come searching for my nephew."

"Oh, really?" Carl Hegland looked up from spreading jam on his roll. "What is his name?"

"He is Joel O'Shaunasy. He was seven when I last saw him. He came west with a man named Jacob Chandler."

Pearl turned to her husband. "Sounds like our Mr. Chandler. He's working out at Robertsons'."

"He's a fine man, that Jacob Chandler. He used to be a minister. Hope he'll be doing more of that for us out here." Carl rocked back on the chair legs, caught the look from his wife, and let the chair legs settle down on the floor where they belonged.

"A lot of people have moved in since I left," Jeremiah commented. "Thought I was coming back to Little Missouri, but Medora's a real town now."

"Thanks to de Mores and his big dreams of icing the freight cars to carry hanging beeves back to the big cities, where they need the meat, and of underselling the big packing houses. He's earned himself some

118

enemies." Carl turned his head. "That the baby crying?"

"I'll get him. Carly, you may come help me."

"Why don't I clear the table?" Amethyst stood before Pearl could turn down her offer and picked up her plate and the child's.

The men talked while she carried the plates and serving dishes to the kitchen to set on the table. Three kinds of pie waited there. Amethyst rubbed her midsection. Full as she was already, the pie didn't even look appetizing. She moved the coffeepot to the hotter part of the stove after checking the firebox. Even if it wasn't her kitchen, it felt good to be in one. Never would she have thought she'd feel that way. She glanced around at the white cupboards lining the light blue walls. Yellow-and-white-checked curtains matched the tablecloth. One door led to the pantry, where the temperature dropped due to the pie safe in the window. Should she whip the cream? Instead, she set a pan on the stove, filled it with hot water from the reservoir, and shaved soap into the water from the bar she found on a shelf behind the stove. After scraping the plates, she set them in the dishpan.

"You didn't need to do all that." Pearl, baby on her shoulder, returned to the kitchen. "But I appreciate it. I need to feed this young man, and then I'll serve the pie."

"The coffee is heating. How about if I pour the men some and promise them pie later? You feed the baby, and maybe Carly would like to help me by drying the silverware?" Amethyst smiled down at the little girl who peeked out from behind her mother's skirt.

Carly nodded, eyes wide.

"You be careful, then," her mother admonished.

"Carly, you can use the bench. We'll put a towel down on it." Amethyst motioned toward a bench pushed under the edge of the table. "You have the most practical kitchen I have ever seen."

"My Carl watched me work and then figured out how to make things easier for me, what with cooking for guests so often."

"He did wonders for a kitchen." Amethyst thought of her kitchen at home. Almost everything was done on the old oak table. While there were shelves in the pantry, there were not nearly enough in the kitchen itself. When she got home, she aimed to remedy that. Pa wasn't the only one who could saw a board or drive a nail.

The steam coming from the coffeepot spout said it was hot enough, so she looked around for towels to fold as potholders. Instead she saw squares of gingham, several layers thick, hanging by loops from hooks on the wall. "That what you use for holding hot things?" Amethyst inclined her head.

"Yes. Aprons and towels were never thick enough. I got tired of burning my hands, so I made those." Pearl sat in a rocking chair near the stove, baby nursing sounds coming from under a flannel blanket she'd thrown over her shoulder.

"How old is the baby?"

"He's almost seven months old, growing faster than a thistle in summer." She lifted the blanket to check on her son.

Carly leaned against her mother's knee. "Tree?"

"Soon."

"I'll pour the coffee." Amethyst took the pot and headed for the dining room. She poured coffee for each of the men. "You're welcome," she answered to their thanks and returned to the kitchen. What was it about that man? Most probably he still wore the air of command of an officer. In fact, he seemed to fill the room. But the twinkle in his one eye belied the idea that he was suffering from his wounds, though the limp and the flinch she'd caught when he wasn't looking told her otherwise. He was a gifted storyteller, although her mother had always drilled into her that you do not ever listen to another's conversations. But without any effort she could hear him talking at the dining room table. It wasn't that she had her ear to a crack in the door, something she and Patrick had done as children.

The thought of Patrick whisked her back to Pennsylvania. What was the weather like there? Most likely there was snow on the ground, but not like here with the fences covered with snowdrifts.

"Miss." A small hand tugged at her skirt.

"Yes, Carly?" Amethyst looked around. Here she was, daydreaming in the midst of washing dishes. "Sorry." She quickly lifted the silverware from the rinsing pan and set it all on the towel on the bench.

The little girl pointed to the silver, dried and on the table. "Spoons?"

"You are a good dryer, Carly."

"Yes."

"Say thank you," her mother prompted.

"Tank you." She turned to her mother.

Amethyst chuckled. Ah, how she had missed Joel. She hadn't realized how much until now that there was a real chance she would see him in the next day or so. Then they could buy his ticket and return to the East — and home.

Pearl fastened her bodice and set her son on her lap, rubbing his back. A hefty burp made Carly giggle and run to her mother's knee to pat her brother's back.

"Such a good helper you are." Amethyst turned to Pearl. "What do you do with the dishwater?"

"In the summer I water my garden with it. Now I just throw it out the back door. We'll use the rinse water for the next washing."

"Just like home."

"Tell me about your home."

Amethyst shuddered from the icy blast when she threw the water out the back door. She wiped out the pan and hung it on a hook behind the stove. "We live on a small farm a couple of miles from Smithville. The farm used to be larger, but Pa gave part of the land to my brother Patrick, and now someone else lives there. Pa sold it after Patrick died and his wife disappeared."

"You never mention your mother."

"She died five years ago." *Of overwork and mistreatment. She died far before her time.*

"I'm sorry to hear that. You must miss her greatly."

"Every day. So I take care of the farm and my father."

"Is he not well?"

Amethyst wanted to turn and run. *He's as well as he wants to be. He likes his liquor a little too well. He's well-versed in getting out of work.* Instead of answering, she shrugged.

Pearl laid her son on a pad on the floor with some toys and retied her apron. "Carly, please play with Joseph. There's a good girl." Turning to Amethyst she continued, "I'll whip the cream, and you cut the pie and put the slices on the plates."

"Shall I ask them what kind they want?"

"No, we'll have the pumpkin now, the apple later tonight, and keep the mincemeat in case someone comes by. Usually we would have church tonight but not with this weather. Nor most likely tomorrow either. In years past on Christmas Day our friends and neighbors took out their sleighs and went house to house visiting one another. Ah, the songs of the bells, the laughter. I love Christmas in Medora. Actually, I just love living in Medora and the Dakotah Territory."

"You came from somewhere else?"

"Oh yes. From Chicago. One day I'll tell you the tale." She whipped even harder to get the cream to stiffen. "Whew, this reminds me of why we don't have whipped cream very often."

"Let me help." Amethyst reached for the bowl and the egg beater. Finally the cream began to stiffen, and within a minute they added the sugar and a dash of powdered vanilla.

Pearl plopped a spoonful on each pie wedge and nodded to the coffeepot. "We better bring that too."

A short while later the family, with the exception of Joseph, who'd fallen asleep and been put to bed, gathered in the front parlor. Pearl sat down at the piano and let her fingers wander over the keyboard until she segued into "O Tannenbaum." Carly stared at her father as he lit the candles on the tree that stood proudly in front of the window. It was decked with carved wooden ornaments, popcorn chains, and dainty crocheted bells, wreaths, and snowflakes starched to hold rigid shapes.

Amethyst felt just like the little girl. Never had she seen such a lovely tree or floated on such thrilling music. While there was a piano in the church at home, those who played it never showed the skill and love of music that poured forth in this room.

"Ooh." Carly turned to smile at Amethyst. "Pretty."

"Pretty is right."

One by one Carl lit each of the candles

fastened to the branches of the tree. He nodded to Jeremiah McHenry. "Would you read the Christmas story to us? The Bible is open to the correct page."

"Of course." McHenry picked up the Bible and leaned closer to the kerosene lamp. " 'And it came to pass in those days, that there went out a decree from Caesar Augustus, that all the world should be taxed. . . . And Joseph also went up from Galilee, out of the city of Nazareth, into Judea, unto the city of David, which is called Bethlehem. . . .' "

The words flowed over Amethyst, bathing her in memories of when she was a child and Pa would read aloud. Even though he wasn't the best reader, he had memorized the words and brought the Christmas story alive. Those were the years before he needed so much outside help to get through the days. When had he started drinking? Most likely the years he made moonshine, but then, maybe he made moonshine because he wanted a cheap drink.

Had he run out of firewood? She'd made sure plenty was split and stacked before she left. But she hadn't planned on being gone so long.

" 'For unto you is born this day in the city

of David a Saviour, which is Christ the Lord.' " McHenry's voice sent shivers up her back.

She'd been sore afraid when she was so sick on the train. Thank God for Mrs. Grant. She fulfilled a female version of the good Samaritan.

All the while McHenry read the age-old story, Pearl played softly, rippling from one Christmas carol to another.

When they were finished, one would have thought they'd spent hours rehearsing. Both she and Carly applauded. Carl joined in.

"That was mighty fine," he said. "Thanks to both of you. Now we better blow out these candles before they catch the tree on fire. You want to help me, Carly?"

The little girl slid off her chair and ran to his arms to be lifted up to blow out the higher ones. Her pa pinched each candle-wick after she blew it out to make sure there would be no spark.

"I've never seen such a lovely tree before," Amethyst whispered, as if speaking aloud would break the feeling of peace that had settled in the room.

With the quiet, one could hear the wind outside, but even it sounded less fierce than earlier, as though the birth of the Christ child calmed even the mighty storm, as only Jesus' words could do.

"I thought we might sing the carols, but I think instead we'll have our dessert and sing tomorrow in place of church. How does that sound?"

"Lovely." Amethyst trapped a yawn before it embarrassed her. Perhaps she would see Joel tomorrow. What a Christmas present that would be.

CHAPTER TEN

After more pie and coffee Jeremiah excused himself. "Thank you for the delicious meal and perfect evening."

"You are welcome." Pearl nodded and smiled. "We're glad you are here with us for Christmas."

"I'll bid you all good night, then." McHenry stood and headed for the stairs. *Be careful,* he reminded himself. But even so his boot caught on the first tread, and he pitched forward.

"Oh, sir," Amethyst said from right behind him. "Can I help you?"

"No! I'm fine," he barked, as if ordering a platoon of new recruits who didn't know right from left. *Tell her you're sorry, man.* He glanced back to see a look of — was it fright or just shock on her face? She took a step backward, her face flushing.

He straightened his shoulders. "Pardon me. Oh, er . . . I'm sorry." *Sorry is right. You are one sorry excuse for a gentleman, Jeremiah McHenry.* He ignored the inner reprimand and continued up the stairs, forcing himself to slow down and make sure he raised each foot plenty high enough. To cover his embarrassment, he admired the turned spindles of the stairs and the carved railing. While others would have just had a smoothed rail or board, this work of art felt like satin to the fingers, and the wood glowed with the finish. *If I ever have a two-story house that needs a staircase, I know who to go to. In fact, think I'll ask him to make me some chairs and a table. Maybe a rocking chair — a leather rocking chair. If he started now, he might have them done by the time I have a place to put them.*

Jeremiah thought back to the homeplace where he grew up. Surely there was extra furniture there if he wanted to write and ask for some. Not that he would. His sister would demand he come back for a visit and then would insist he stay.

The idea of living under all the strictures of civilization made him shudder. Give him the badlands of Dakotah Territory any day. A low log house just like Rand's would be more than adequate. Although he might have to go back east to find a wife. There were few women out here. Carl had told him about the death of Ward Robertson. Might Mrs. Robertson be interested in marrying again? His memory of her was of a rather comely hen with all her female chicks around her. After chastising himself for thinking about her ranch in conjunction with her good cooking, he shook his head. How would he adjust to living around civilians again? He'd left that kind of life a boy, and now he was an old man. Some days, when the pain was bad, feeling older than others. Or when he tripped again.

Shame Miss O'Shaunasy wasn't planning on staying. Where had that thought come from? Not that she'd ever speak to him again after his oafish behavior. And the others had heard it too. What must they think of him? He shook his head as he slid between the sheets, warmed by two rocks near where his feet would be. His years in Arizona had made him forget Dakotah winters. That was one good thing about the southern territory — warm winters. However, the summers there were killers.

Remember to tell Mrs. Hegland thank you for that extra courtesy in the morning and apologize, he reminded himself as he drifted off to sleep without writing in his journal, something he had been faithful about for the last years.

His throbbing leg woke him long before he wanted to wake. He rubbed his thigh, the hole where the bullet entered still tender to the touch. The cratered flesh and accompanying scar were not a pretty sight. He left the warmth of his bed and dug his flask out of his carpetbag. A couple of good swallows would ease the pain rather quickly and help him get back to sleep.

Though he did fall asleep again, he was up long before dawn and writing in his journal by lamplight. He left off to watch as light streaked a thin line on the horizon, chased the cobalt away, blew out the stars, and woke up the rooster, who even in winter took seriously his job of announcing the sun. After painting the clouds in pinks, the heavenly artist added reds and oranges, outlined in gold, and soon a rim showed above the dark horizon. Like a prairie dog first testing the breeze, then showing his head, the sun popped up, and the land dazzled a welcome diamond-dusted white.

"Ahh," Jeremiah breathed in delight. "I am home. Storms or not, Dakotah does sunrises and sunsets like no other place on earth." He thought a moment. "Not that I've seen too much of the earth, but at least of what I have seen of this country."

He heard the clank of stove lids, the murmur of voices, one female, one male. Glancing at his pocket watch, Jeremiah realized he was missing something. Reveille, that's what it was — the bugler announcing the new day with the clear notes of reveille. The rooster came in a close second. Jeremiah noted in his journal that he would most likely find more than the bugle to miss about his army life, which had been most of his life — from age seventeen until less than a month ago.

The back door slammed. *Carl must be going out to milk. I need to get out there and take care of Kentucky. If I leave him in that stall without walking around, he might get permanently stove-up. Maybe for his sake I should have waited out the winter in a warmer climate, as the general said. Possibly for both our sakes,* he thought as he put his weight on the bad leg while putting on his pants. But rarely one for looking back, McHenry finished dressing and headed down the stairs. He'd lived his life with his mother's motto, "You do the best you can and let God handle the rest." *Lord, please give me the words I need.*

"Well, good morning, Mr. McHenry." Pearl finished tying her apron as she spoke.

"Good morning, Mrs. Hegland. Please forgive my churlish behavior last night. I don't see right —" He gestured to his eye patch.

"I understand. You're forgiven."

133

He breathed a sigh of relief.

She continued, "And I'll tell the others."

"Merry Christmas, Mrs. Hegland." His words were more heartfelt for her graciousness. "And thank you for opening your home to me. I cannot begin to tell you how I enjoyed the room, the bed, including the hot rocks, the quiet —"

"You didn't hear the baby in the night? I didn't want him to disturb our guests."

"I heard him and lay there thinking how long it had been since I'd heard a baby cry in the night. What a warm sound of a home and love within it."

"Perhaps you'll have one of your own one day."

"I doubt it. Getting kinda late in life to have a baby." He sighed. Was that another thing to miss? "Better get on out and take care of my horse. I've got hay at the station that we can bring out here if I can use the sledge. If you have one, that is."

"Oh yes. Carl outfitted our wagon with runners for the winter. Hay is going to be at a premium if the weather doesn't let up some." She took out crockery bowls and wooden spoons as she talked. "Breakfast will be ready in about an hour. Thank God the blizzard blew itself out."

"Ma?"

"Excuse me, Mr. McHenry. Yes, Carly?"

McHenry shrugged into his sheepskin coat, a remnant of his years stationed here in Dakotah Territory, and after watching the doorsill, he shut the door securely behind him. As soon as he stepped past the shelter of the back porch, the cold attacked with his first breath like broken glass slashing and burning its way down his lungs.

He flipped the end of his scarf over his lower face and pulled his broad-brimmed felt hat down more securely on his head. Even with no wind to speak of, the cold penetrated the wool of his pants and long johns, reminding him he didn't want to stay out in this weather any longer than necessary. Even though the sun was shining, it held little warmth for the land. He followed the path of Carl's boot prints and entered the barn through the smaller door in the shed side of the hip-roofed structure. Barns smelled like no other place on earth: oats, corn, hay dust, horse, cow, and dung. He sniffed again. Surely there was a pig here somewhere, and the chicken house took up a good part of the other shed side. With one more sniff, he was a boy on his way to milk the two cows and feed the rest of the stock. As the eldest, much of the chores had fallen to him until his brother grew old enough to take over while he helped his father with the fieldwork. To think that he'd dreamed of the glory of army life, barely passing his seventeenth birthday before enlisting, so afraid was he that the war would be over before he got in.

"Morning. Merry Christmas." Carl looked out from around the hind legs of the cow was he milking.

"Merry Christmas to you too. All right if I walk Kentucky around inside here? He's not up to plowing through snowbanks yet."

"Of course. There's oats in the bin and hay in the mow. Help yourself."

"I'll fork some down for your team too, and the cows."

"Thanks."

McHenry climbed the ladder, wincing each time his full weight hit the bad leg. Stairs and ladders weren't the easiest for him at the moment, but inhaling the fragrance of hay took his mind from the pain. And he didn't trip — one more thing to be grateful for. He found the fork stabbed into the stack and pitched enough to feed the animals. If this was all the hay Carl had, unless spring came real early, he was liable to be in trouble.

Unwrapping the scarf from around his

neck, he stuffed it into his pocket. Pitching hay warmed one right up, like chopping wood. He'd noticed Carl had a nice wood-shed with cut wood stacked around the three walls. The other building must be his workshop.

Jeremiah fed the animals hay and dumped a small amount of oats in the grain box in the manger. "Don't need you getting fat, old son, what with nothing to do here." He pulled off the blanket and gave Kentucky a good brushing, threw the blanket back on, and backed him out of the stall. They walked up and down the aisle behind the cows and around the open center of the barn, Kentucky following him like a dog on a leash. After putting the horse back, he dipped water out of a barrel, breaking through the ice crust, and gave him a drink, then did the same for the Heglands' two horses and the cows. "What are you feeding the pigs?"

"I have a bucket up to the house. Keep it on the porch mostly, so it will have to thaw some. I throw a little grain and water too." Carl stood up from the last cow and poured the frothing milk into a milk can, keeping out a bit to pour in a flat pan for the begging cats. "They don't give much these days but enough to keep us going. Pearl sends what she can in to the store. Winter can get kind of tough."

"I'll help you carry that."

"Oh, I got the sled right outside the door. Need to build a well house this year. Right into that hill east of the house will be a good site. Can run a pipe from the pump."

"Looks like you've done real well for yourself."

"Been working for de Mores long hours. It's good pay, long as we can build. That man has more ideas than a sheep has ticks. Shame he's not here right now so you could meet him. You and he got a lot in common, both having been in the military."

"All those brick buildings there to the west of town are his?"

"Cattle yards, abattoir, railroad siding, icehouse. He ships butchered beef halves and some sheep in ice-cooled cars to the big cities back east. He's even brought salmon from the West Coast clear to Chicago and points east."

"So he doesn't live here year-round, then?"

"He mostly does. His family comes out for the summer and returns to New York for the winter. He's got so many people working for him. . . ." Carl shook his head. "He owns Medora, in a way."

"He hiring any?" Jeremiah shut the barn door behind them, making sure the wooden handle was secure, and followed the sled to the house, remembering to cover his face this time.

"Not that I'm aware of. Things kind of shut down for the winter, you know." Both men stamped the snow off their boots after lifting the can up the stairs and into the warmth of the kitchen.

"I've heard rumors that he's not well liked."

"Don't bother me none. I just do my work and go on about my own business. He thinks he's always right and everyone should know it. Not much patience."

"Sounds like some of the generals I've known."

"Sometimes when folks got a lot of money, they lord it over the rest of us. He's French, you know."

"If you two will wash up, breakfast is ready." Pearl nodded to a pan of water warming on the stove.

"Pa?" Carly stood in front of her father. "Yes?"

"Tree." Her mouth was as round as her eyes. She pointed to her chest.

"Gifts for you? Really? How do you know?"

"Ma say."

"Said," Pearl corrected from the stove where she was stirring redeye gravy. "We just need to put the things on the table."

"Come, Carly, let's get you up in your chair." Carl smiled at his wife and took his daughter's hand.

Jeremiah glanced over his shoulder from wiping his hands to see Miss O'Shaunasy carrying platters of food in to the table. "Merry Christmas."

She nodded. "Merry Christmas to you." Her tone was guarded.

Well, he could understand that. Still . . . He sat across from Miss O'Shaunasy again and thought back to his years in Little Missouri and the women he'd known here. Belle — now, that was one *not* quiet woman — Daisy, Cimarron, and then there was Ruby. He bowed his head for Carl to say grace, another nicety that didn't happen much in the mess line or when he ate with the other officers. Grace was one of those things that came west with the women. Not that it should be that way, but from what he'd observed, it seemed to be.

Now, why was that? He read his Bible fairly frequently, well, at least when he was in camp and for sure on Sundays. All the while he passed the platter and bowls and answered questions and said please and thank you, his mind played with what was really a new thought to him. When there was a worship service around, he went and worshiped. That brought up another thought. He'd attended the worship services in Dove House after it lost its tarnished reputation and truly became Dove House, a fine boardinghouse and a good place to eat, but Ruby brought that all about. The three other women who lived in Little Missouri, those not at Dove House, did nothing to make their men be civilized, but then, what could one do with the likes of Jake Maunders and Williams?

He turned to Pearl. "That was a fine breakfast. I haven't had two such fine meals in a long time, and it's been too long since I was in a real home with ladies in attendance. You cannot begin to know what life was like in Arizona Territory."

"Why, thank you, sir. You're going to find a lot of changes since we are Medora now and not Little Missouri, although there are still a few living over there."

"What are you going to do?" Carl leaned back in his chair and nodded to Jeremiah.

"For starters, I'd like you to build me some furniture — a table and chairs and a big rocking chair with leather seat and back. I've always wanted a chair of my own."

"But you don't have a house."

"I will soon as I can get back on the land and check out a few places. I remember a likely spot up the river beyond Rand's. If no one is building there, I'll stake a claim, build me a log cabin, and settle in. I'd like to run a few beeves, get myself a dog, and not chase any more Indians or renegades for the rest of my life."

"You don't want to be closer to town?"

"Why?"

"I don't picture you as a hermit." Pearl stopped her table-clearing. Amethyst could already be heard in the kitchen washing dishes.

"Don't plan to be. But a good horse can get me to town when I want. Other than beef and sheep, is anyone supplying meat for those who can't go hunt?"

"Opal brings us a deer once in a while. She brought us the geese we had last night. A man north of town raises a few extra hogs. That's where we get our pork. Atticus was a big help. He and his brother would bring us fish, help Pearl with the garden, and such."

"Ruby wrote to me about that. What a shame. He was one good worker, honest as the day is long."

"So you kept in touch some?"

"She was more faithful than I. While I'm

not surprised that Opal is out hunting, it's hard to believe she is old enough to do all that she does."

"More coffee?"

Carl raised his cup. "You got any of those sandbakkels left?"

"You just had breakfast."

"I know, but I got a hankering for some of your cookies." He turned to Jeremiah. "She only bakes these at Christmastime. She also makes cinnamon rolls that melt in your mouth."

"Hush, you're embarrassing me." Pearl laid a hand on her husband's shoulder as she leaned over to refill his cup.

Jeremiah watched the little byplay, an arrow of jealousy piercing his heart. *I want that — my wife's hand on my shoulder, loving by teasing. I don't want to take it from them. I just want it too. Lord, is there a woman for me in your scheme of things? Is that why there was no room at the other places in town, so I could get a glimpse and grow a hunger?*

After breakfast they adjourned to the parlor, where the gifts under the tree were passed out by a beaming Carly.

"That one is for you." Pearl pointed to a package with a red bow.

"Me?" Carly looked over her shoulder

once more as she squatted in front of the gift. She touched the bow with a reverent finger. "Pretty."

"See, you slide the bow off like this." Carl put his hands over hers and did as he said. Then they slid her finger under the pasted paper at the bottom. Carefully, so as not to waste the precious paper, Carly worked at each spot of paste until she had the paper free. She stared into the box, her eyes wide.

"For me?"

"Yes."

She lifted out a doll with a carved wooden head, arms, and feet and dressed in a red calico dress with a white apron. A matching sunbonnet was tied in a bow under the chin.

Jeremiah studied the doll, which was dressed down to leather shoes. "Did you carve the head?"

"Yes. First time I've tried a doll." Carl set the box on the floor next to his daughter, who sank down at his feet and traced her doll's face in between hugs. "Carly, why don't you go get the other box?"

"You want to bring it here, and we can open it?" Pearl asked.

Carly nodded, picked up the package, and carried it to her mother. She set it in her lap and beamed up at her.

They went through the same slow process

as before until finally the gift was revealed.

"For me?" Carly held up a wooden rattle, carved so intricately that a wooden ball rattled around the ribs to make noise.

"No. That's for Joseph." Pearl held out her hand. Carly giggled as she shook the rattle by the rounded handle and laid it in her mother's palm.

"You take that box to Miss O'Shaunasy, Carly."

"But —"

Jeremiah saw the consternation on her face. He knew what she felt like. Here they were giving out gifts, and he'd not brought anything. He was sure she hadn't either.

She unwrapped a cable-knit scarf, dyed a soft yellow.

"How beautiful. Thank you."

Carly brought the next gift to him and held it out without getting too close. "Here."

"For me?"

She nodded soberly.

"Thank you."

"Open."

"Yes, ma'am." Inside Jeremiah found a scarf too, knit in natural black wool.

"I figure no one can have too many scarves out here." Pearl rocked gently, her son sound asleep on her shoulder.

After they opened the rest of their presents, the sound of sleigh bells brought Carly to the window where the sun beamed in. "Comp'ny."

Brownie barked from the front porch as Carl went to the door. "Hey, Charlie, come on in. Got someone here who'd like to see you." He turned and smiled at Jeremiah, beckoning him to the door.

"We'll be back later — just checking to make sure everyone's all right."

Jeremiah stepped out on the porch. "Hey, Charlie, things changed somewhat since I've been here."

"Cap'n McHenry, you made it through all those Indian wars. Welcome home."

"Told you I'd be back. And it's just Jeremiah McHenry now. I don't want any more titles, nothing to do with the military. That's finished."

"You mind if I tell the others?"

"Not at all." He waved as Charlie clucked his team and headed on out again. "Merry Christmas."

He stepped back in the house. "My word, but it's cold out there. After living in the desert of Arizona, this is going to take some getting used to."

"Rule number one: Don't go out without a coat on." Carl turned to his wife. "You

146

think we could get another cup of coffee to warm this man up?"

"I'll get it." Amethyst stood before Pearl had time to move. "You stay there with the baby."

Shame she isn't planning on staying around here, McHenry thought again as he sat back down. *Real shame.*

CHAPTER ELEVEN

When can we go?

Amethyst went through all the polite motions, when all she could think of was the coming meeting with Joel. Perhaps tomorrow they would be on their way east. Surely he didn't have a lot to pack. The weather was clear. Mr. Hegland did have a sleigh, did he not? She sought to recall what he'd said.

She knew for certain she would not try to walk to the Robertson ranch, not after the experience she'd had two days earlier. Even now she knew if she lay down, she'd be asleep again before her head hit the pillow. She'd never needed so much sleep in her entire life.

Summoning all her courage, she turned to Pearl, who sat in the rocker nursing the baby. "Could I ask a favor?"

"Of course." Pearl looked up with a smile. "What can I do for you?"

"It's not you. I mean, do you suppose it would be possible for Mr. Hegland to hitch up the team and drive me out to the Robertson place? I don't believe I dare try walking that far yet."

"Besides which you don't know the way, and storms can blow in here within an hour. We've seen the temperature drop twenty degrees in less time than that. No, you certainly can't walk out there — I will ask him when he comes back in. He and Mr. McHenry are out pumping water to fill the stock barrels while the weather is decent."

Amethyst well knew that, holiday or not, the animals had to be cared for. And caring for the animals back home in the winter was far easier than here. "Do you think he would have time?"

"We'll ask him when he comes in."

Amethyst knew she had to be content with that. "Thank you." But knowledge was one thing and making her insides mind was an entirely different thing. Her stomach clenched into a knot, and her mouth was so dry she could barely swallow. Joel was so close and yet so far away.

"This is a hard Christmas for Cora Robertson. Her husband, Ward, was shot and died last summer."

"How awful." And for poor Joel with his mother gone. *I have to know how he is faring.*

Carly stopped in front of Amethyst, the

new doll clutched to her side, no one-arm dragging with this one. "Read?"

"I don't have a book." The urge to sweep the child up and hug her nearly swept Amethyst off her feet. There had been so few children in her life, and sometimes the wanting one of her own ached worse than an infected tooth. Joel had been like her own, and he'd been jerked away. *Sometimes you don't realize how much you love someone until they are gone,* she thought. At least that had been so for her.

"Carly, go get your book off the shelf. That is, if you don't mind reading to her. She loves stories."

"Not at all, unless there is something I could be helping you with in here."

"No. The ham is in the oven, you've already peeled the potatoes, the cabbage is ready to boil, the carrots too. I'm going to put this child to bed and come join you." Smiling down at the yawning baby boy filling her arms and lap, she said, "Right, Joseph? Your tummy is full, and now you're ready to sleep." She nestled the baby tight against her side and stood. "Why don't you two go into the parlor, and I'll bring in tea and cookies. How would that be?"

I want a baby like that. The thought hit like a sledgehammer to her heart. *An auntie but never a mother.* Amethyst could hear Carly in the parlor when a book hit the floor. "I'll go help her." *Lord, I want to see Joel — you know how badly. If we could leave tomorrow, I might still have enough money to buy his ticket and pay for my stay here. We'll need to eat on the train too.* Her thoughts followed her into the parlor.

"Can I help you?" she asked, kneeling by the little girl.

Carly handed her the doll, as if bestowing a great privilege. "Here." She turned back to putting the fallen books on the shelf, her brow wrinkled in concentration, handling the books with great care. When all were neatly aligned, she dusted her hands off on her pinafore and brought the book she'd selected to Amethyst. "Sit there." She pointed to the rocking chair.

Amethyst got the point. She was to sit in the chair and hold Carly on her lap. That was just the way it was done. Once they were settled, with the doll on Carly's lap and the book open to the bookmark, the little girl looked up at the woman holding her.

"Here." She pointed to the top of the left-hand page.

"Carly, you didn't say please," Pearl said from the arched doorway.

"Pease."

151

Amethyst nodded. Joel was the last child she'd read to. Ever since he left, she'd not read aloud, knowing that it put her pa a bit on the defensive, as if she were lording her superior reading ability over him. But when she'd read to Joel, Pa had been right there to listen and enjoy. Men were certainly strange creatures. At least the ones that she knew.

The story of *Alice's Adventures in Wonderland* unfolded as she read.

"Do you know that you have a lovely reading voice?" Pearl commented as she set the tea tray on the low table. "I've been enjoying the story as much as Carly."

"Thank you. I love to read, but I never have time anymore." Amethyst didn't add about her pa.

"I'll pour the tea, and then we can visit. Carly, you come sit over here so you don't spill."

When Carly slid off her lap, immediately Amethyst felt less, as if something precious had been taken away. *Now, don't you go getting all teary-eyed over this. You will be traveling home with Joel soon, and you can read to him all the way.* Somehow her orders to herself didn't really make her feel better.

Mr. Hegland didn't harness up the team until after dinner. If Amethyst weren't still recovering, she'd not have eaten a bite, just pushed the food around on her plate. But she knew she needed the nourishment, and she didn't want to hurt Pearl's feelings. Besides, the meal was delicious. She'd never made candied carrots like the ones served and asked for the receipt.

Some time later, after Carl helped Amethyst into the sleigh, Pearl handed her a basket. "Now, make sure you stay tucked under the robe with your scarf over your face. Please deliver this to Cora Robertson. Mr. McHenry and I will hold the fort, but" — she turned to her husband — "don't be too long. You know there'll be company coming later." She handed Amethyst a hot rock wrapped in flannel. "Put this at your feet."

Bundled into the sleigh, Amethyst did as she was told. Even so, as soon as the horses trotted out, harness bells jingling a merry tune, the wind bit her nose and made her eyes water. Hearing other bells, she turned to see a wagon box on skids coming toward them from town.

Mr. Hegland waved the occupants on to his house. "We'll be back shortly. Pearl has the coffeepot on."

"Merry Christmas" floated back to them as they headed south.

"The Little Missouri River is off to our right, bordered by the cottonwood trees. It's frozen solid now. If we were going to Rand Harrison's ranch, we'd drive up the river. It's a lot closer that way. Ruby, Rand, and Opal are really good friends of ours. Ruby and Opal are sisters, and they owned a hotel called Dove House until it burned down. Ruby married Rand Harrison, a local rancher." The sleigh headed up a hill, the horses tossing their heads and continuing their spirited gait.

Amethyst couldn't believe the beauty of the country — the snow-laden trees, the red-and-orange cliffs so bright against the white snow they glowed, naked tree limbs that appeared black against the dazzling white.

Carl Hegland pointed to deer nibbling on tree branches, cattle sheltering under pine and grazing on the branch tips like their wild relatives. "That's the Robertsons' ranch house ahead on the left. You can see the smoke rising." He pointed off to the right. "You continue that way to Rand Harrison's ranch. He's the last outpost between here and points south. Marquis de Mores was running a stage and hauling line down to Deadwood from here. Come spring there should be a lot of travel out this way."

"He, the marquis, I mean, has brought a lot of change to this area, hasn't he?"

"He's a dreamer, all right. If only all his schemes would work out as well as he plans."

"They aren't?"

"Well, the big eastern packing houses are trying to force him out by making it real hard for him to sell the beef he ships. They want all the beef shipped on the hoof and let them do the slaughtering."

"I see. But as a carpenter, I'm sure all this building has been good for you."

"That it has."

A low house with a porch across the front came into view as they topped a small rise. Several outbuildings were set back from the main house, one of them flanked by a corral with only the post tops and the highest rail showing.

A young girl stepped out the front door and waved.

Is this where I find Joel? Amethyst clenched her gloved hands under the robe. *Please, Lord, let him be here.*

"Merry Christmas, Mr. Hegland." The girl ignored the shoveled steps and leaped to the smooth pathway. Someone had been out shoveling this morning. The porch was swept bare, and a path led to the hitching rail, welcoming visitors.

"Merry Christmas, Ada Mae. I brought you a guest."

"Really?" She smiled at Amethyst. "Mother will be delighted. Come in, come in." She knotted a tie rope to the hitching rail, stroking the horses' noses as she did. A cloud of vapor from their breathing made her step back. "Do you have blankets for them?"

"Right here." Carl Hegland reached behind Amethyst and lifted out two heavy blankets and threw them over his team. Then he helped his guest from the sleigh bed. "We won't be able to stay long. Can't leave the team out here — too cold."

Amethyst nodded and took the path to the front porch. "I am Miss O'Shaunasy," she answered in response to Ada Mae's greeting.

"I'm glad to meet you. Come right in." She opened the door and stepped back for the guest to enter. "Ma, we have a visitor." She raised her voice to be heard over the laughter of a group of people gathered around the fireplace.

"I'll be right there."

"Let me take your coat."

"Auntie Colleen!" Joel broke away from the group and came running across the

156

room to throw his arms around Amethyst.

She hugged him back. "Ah, Joel, you've grown a foot since I last saw you." She rested her cheek on the top of his head. "I thought you fell off the face of the earth." Stepping back slightly, she cupped his cheeks in her hands and gazed into his eyes. "I cannot begin to tell you how much I've missed you."

"Me too. How's Grandfather?"

"Fine when I left."

"Is he coming out west too?"

"No, he's waiting for you back to the farm."

"Oh." Now it was his turn to take a step back. Impossibly long eyelashes hid his gaze for a moment. He took her hand and led her nearer to the fire where a man stepped forward.

"Hello, Miss O'Shaunasy. I am Jacob Chandler . . . Joel's father." He held out his hand.

Amethyst stared from man to boy and back again. The only real difference between the two was height and age. Their blue eyes crinkled the same way, a lock of dark blond hair fell across both foreheads from the same cowlick, dimples matched in their cheeks.

"I-I think I better sit down." Amethyst

put a hand to her throat, where a pulse threatened to rip through her skin. *But what about Patrick?* her mind screamed. *He was your father. I was there the day you were born. Your name is O'Shaunasy!*

Someone brought her a chair, and she sat gingerly on the edge, but all she wanted to do was collapse in a bundle of tears.

"I know this is a shock," Mr. Chandler said, his eyes gentle. "Can I get you something to drink? Coffee? Water?"

She shook her head, thoughts dipping and swirling through her head like bats on a feeding frenzy. *What will Pa say to this? How will I ever tell him?*

CHAPTER TWELVE

"I'm sorry for the shock this is causing you, but I can see there is no doubt in your mind that Joel is my son."

"Yes, I mean, no. . . ." Amethyst wished someone would throw her a life preserver before the riptide carried her farther out to sea.

After several false starts, the truth hit her. Melody had been pregnant — no wonder the wedding had been so rushed. Did Patrick know? Ideas careened in her head, waves attacking from every direction.

When Mr. Hegland said it was time to head home, she mumbled her good-byes, grateful to be leaving.

Over and over as she tried to fall asleep that night, she replayed the scene in the Robertsons' home. She heard the words again and saw the look of compassion in the man's eyes. Joel and his father were two peas in a pod. The boy never had resembled Patrick, whom his own father had dubbed as "black Irish" with his black curly hair and flashing dark eyes, but they had thought perhaps Joel's light hair came from Melody's side of the family.

She'd never asked questions but instead was always grateful for the baby who brought such delight into her life. The baby grew into a little boy and spent a lot of time with his aunt Colleen because his mother was often sickly. She didn't correct that either, did not tell him she was now going by Amethyst. It would be Colleen again when she returned home, dreaming for the rest of her life of her brief foray into being Amethyst.

She stared at the ceiling, visions of home flashing across her mind: the house that needed painting, her kitchen with the gray cat in front of the stove, the cellar of food she'd prepared, her milk cows — the heifer would have calved by now — the cottage cheese she sold to those in town, her own special receipt for piccalilli. How she wished she had brought a jar along to share with Pearl.

She dozed for a bit but suddenly sat straight up. What would her pa say when she came home without Joel? How would she tell him that Joel was not his grandson? He'd ask a million questions, and the only answer was that Joel was very obviously Mr.

Chandler's son. Then he'd rant and rave like it was all her fault. *Lord, what am I going to do? You knew of this, and yet you let me come way out here. That awful train ride, so sick I was, and now here I am. Surely you brought me here for a reason. You never do anything without a reason. You brought Abram out of Haran to the land you had for him. You brought the Israelites out of Egypt. You brought Colleen out of Pennsylvania. You let me use my real name. An amethyst is a stone of value and beauty.*

I have a plan for you, a plan for good and not for evil. The words floated through her mind, chasing the others before it like a dog herding cattle.

Oh, Lord, what is your plan? The wind whistled at a crack in the window casing, pleading for entry. She heard someone get up and put more wood into the stoves, closing the lids and returning to bed. *Lord God, I believe you. If you sent your Son to die for us, and I know that you did, why would you ever let me go?* She took in a deep breath and sighed it out. *I suppose I'm to wait for an answer.* The pastor at their church had once referred to God's waiting room. She never had cared much for waiting for anything — the cow to calve, the seeds to sprout, the rain to stop or start. She sighed again. Her eyes grew heavy and she rolled over, pulled the covers up to her ears, and fell into a deep sleep.

"So what will you do now?" Pearl and Amethyst were alone in the house, savoring a cup of coffee with some cookies.

"I don't know. If I go home without Joel, Pa will never get over it." *And never let me forget it, as if I deliberately kept Joel from him.*

"You're welcome to stay here, you know."

"Thank you, but there is no way I can afford that." Amethyst still had not even asked what the daily rate was for room and board.

"I've been needing help with things here for some time. Opal comes in and helps me two days a week in exchange for school lessons, but in the spring Carl is planning to add four more rooms, and I have been dreaming of teaching piano lessons. As you might have guessed, out here we have a scarcity of the finer things of life like music. Rand plays a guitar, I play the piano, someone usually plays bass on a washtub, but I so miss the beauty of real music, hymns, and the great composers. We have a sing-along here every so often; in fact, one will be this afternoon. Since we missed out on church services for Christmas, we'll have an evening of carols and cookies. I couldn't pay you much beyond room and board, at least for the winter, but come spring, when they start building again, we'll have a full house. By next winter we could run heat up to the attic and turn that into a real nice room for you."

Amethyst listened with intensity. She was being offered a way of escape. "I . . . I will have to give this some thought." She sipped her coffee, reveling in the joy of sitting here snug and warm while the sun sparkled on the snow, even though it held no warmth. Here, it was satisfying to have no one reminding her of the chores to be done, whining how miserable he felt, and then making excuses to go to town where the saloon always welcomed him. What he was using to pay the tab was beyond her. What would happen to her when Pa died? The farm would not be hers. And now there was no Joel to keep the farm together for, to watch growing up into a man — unless she stayed here.

"Not that I'd expect you to stay with us too long. There are a lot of men out here looking for a wife and few women available."

Not sure what to say, Amethyst bit into another cookie.

Carly left off playing with her dolls and came to stand by her mother. "Cookie?"

"Say please."

"Cookie, pease." Carly deliberated over the three kinds on the plate before choosing a star-shaped sugar cookie. "Baby?"

"No, he's too little for cookies, but you are a good sister to think of him." Pearl dropped a kiss on Carly's head, then laid her cheek on her daughter's fine hair.

An ache filled Amethyst's heart. *I am not Joel's aunt.* The thought smacked her in her middle. *If I go back to Pa, I will never see Joel again, never watch him grow taller, never again hear him say "Auntie Colleen."*

If she stayed, would he still call her Auntie?

You could ask him to. The gentle voice seemed to acquiesce with her staying.

Father God, is this what you had in mind for me? She wasn't sure if she heard the whisper of wood falling in the stove or a heavenly chuckle, but the sensation of goodwill and approval that rose from her toes to her head made her warm all over, in spite of the draft that blew through with the opening of the back door.

"Coffee hot?" Carl asked as he and

McHenry came in.

"Will be in a minute."

"I'll get it. You just sit there with Carly," Amethyst said. She made sure she had no crumbs on her skirt, then headed for the kitchen to put more wood in the stove and pull the coffeepot to the front. "Do you take cream or sugar?"

Both men shook their heads. Carl walked over and checked the woodbox. "Better bring in a couple of armloads." As if connected at the hip, both men returned to the back porch and stacked their arms full of split wood to dump in the box.

Is this the way of all men out here, or are these men something special?

"So you picked up the harmonica while you were in Arizona?" Carl brushed the woodchips off his shirt. "You have it with you?"

"I do. I practiced for miles on the train. Kentucky seems to think I do all right. There was a man at Fort Bowie, he could make that little bitty instrument sing to break your heart. He'd play sometimes in the evening, and pretty soon there'd be a gathering outside his quarters of folks who'd been out strolling after the heat of the day. In the desert it can get right cool when the sun goes down, especially up in the

165

mountains, where we were."

"I used to pick at an old dulcimer out in our barn at home." Amethyst surprised both the men and herself with the comment.

"Ah, that takes me home. Nothing like the sound of a dulcimer. My mother played a hammered dulcimer, not as easy to pack around as a pickin' one." McHenry leaned against the doorjamb and crossed both arms over his chest. "You think you could still play one?"

"I don't suppose. I never had enough time to get real good at it." She set two cups on saucers on the tray and arranged a plate of cookies. "Would you prefer the dining room or the parlor?"

"If we can get my wife to play the piano, we'll take the parlor."

"Pa, tree?"

"Tonight, if we have enough candles."

"Do."

"How do you know?"

"Ma said."

Carl swung his daughter up under his arm. "Sack of potatoes. Anyone for a sack of potatoes?" He and the giggling Carly led the way to the parlor.

But before Amethyst could pick up the tray, McHenry did just that. "After you."

You'd think I've been standing over a hot

166

stove, Amethyst thought as she kept her fingers from burning themselves on her cheeks. "Thank you." Never had a man treated her with such politeness, and yet that was the way Carl Hegland treated his wife too. What must it be like to be treated that way every day?

The alternative, what she was used to, played out in her mind as she led the way to the parlor and cleared several books off the low table in front of the sofa. She could hear her father yelling at her for not bringing the boy back with her, going off to town in a huff, after which he would come home drunk and fall in bed to sleep it off. Sometimes in the summer he'd slept in the wagon, home only because the horses knew where they lived. What if that happened in the winter with no one there to look out for him?

But the saloonkeeper said he wasn't giving her pa any more on the tab. And where would her father get any cash? Where did he get the cash for her train fare? All the while the thoughts chased themselves through her head, she smiled and nodded, passed out the coffee, made sure everyone had cookies.

And yet it had seemed earlier that God was encouraging her to stay here in Medora.

Harness bells played their joyful song outside, and Carly ran to the window. "Comp'ny."

Carl went to the door. "The Robertsons." He opened it and snatched a coat off the coatrack before stepping out into the cold. "If you can stay for the singing, let's put your team in the barn. All the rest of you, come on in."

Pearl quit playing and joined her daughter at the door, welcoming the guests. "Come in, come in. Daisy and Charlie will likely be along in a bit."

Cora Robertson herded her girls before her, each bringing a basket and laughing as they came. Amid the flurry of greetings and divesting of wraps, Joel circled around and came to stand by Amethyst.

He looked up at her, blue eyes serious. "Can I still call you Auntie Colleen?"

"Oh, Joel, there is nothing I would like more." She laid her hands on his shoulders, then hugged him. "Thank you."

"You aren't going back there, are you?"

"Why, that is my home."

"But Grandfather will be mad at you, and it's not your fault."

Out of the mouths of babes. She made herself smile. "That's not for you to worry about. I get along."

"I know, but I think you should stay here. You could learn to ride and rope like Pa and I did."

Amethyst glanced up to see Mr. McHenry watching them. He smiled when he caught her eye. And nodded. She started to smile back but turned away. The way he'd barked at her still rankled. Even so, she could feel him watching her. It felt good.

Pearl pointed the way to the bedroom where the guests could lay their coats on the bed. The girls chattered and laughed with Pearl while Mrs. Robertson took Amethyst's hand.

"I fear we weren't very welcoming at our house yesterday. You hardly got in the door and were hit in the face with such distressing news. I wish I could do something to help you after coming so far as you did on an errand of mercy."

"Thank you, but I know there's really nothing that can be done." *Other than telling Pa.* "The West certainly seems to have done good things for Joel. He left us a little child, and here he is half grown up."

"You should see him on a horse and throwing that rope. He took to ranching like a duck to water."

I'm glad Joel's so happy out here, I really am.

So buck up and act that way. Don't be sniveling around, feeling sorry for yourself. The voice sounded amazingly like her mother's. If anyone knew about not feeling sorry for herself, it was her mother. Another of her sayings flitted through Amethyst's mind: "You made your bed, so you got to lie in it."

But I didn't make my bed, this bed. Pa sent me out here and expects me to come back — with Joel. So do I honor my father and do what he expects — or at least return home — or . . . ? She glanced over to see Joel watching her. *Would it make a difference in his life if I stayed here? It would surely make a difference in mine. If only I could be certain this is God's will for me.*

Pearl sat down at the piano, and from her fingers flowed music that made Amethyst catch her breath.

She smiled as the Robertson girls and Joel found places on the floor, the older girl cuddling Carly. All the grown-ups sat on the seats but surged up again at the sound of harness bells, and when the guests entered, Amethyst was introduced to Charlie, his wife, Daisy, and their child, who ran to join the others. More bells.

"Opal," Carly sang out from her place at the window, then ran to the door.

170

Carl stepped out to welcome and show the way to the barn. "Good thing we got plenty of tie-up spaces out there."

A young woman laughed up at him. "Just think, the blizzards are over, at least for today. Everything outside is so sparkly and glorious." Opal scraped her boots and took off her coat as she came through the door. "Merry Christmas, everybody." She handed a basket to Pearl. "Ruby sent this. She said to tell all of you Merry Christmas. She and Mary are doing well, just not up to the outside cold yet. Rand stayed home with her and Per, and Linc says Little Squirrel is much improved. So that's all my news."

Pearl took the basket. "Opal Torvald, meet Amethyst O'Shaunasy, our new boarder."

"Pleased to meet you. Welcome to God's country." Opal's smile made Amethyst smile back.

"We have a surprise for you." Pearl hugged the basket tighter.

"Really? What?"

"Not what, but who." Pearl raised her voice to be heard above the chatter. "You can come out now."

Jeremiah McHenry stepped into the parlor from behind the doorway with a smile wide as all outdoors.

"Captain McHenry." Opal flew into his arms and hugged him, laughing and sniffing. When he let her go, she stepped back and wiped her eyes. "Or should I say Major? You came home." She gave him a slanted look. "To stay, right?"

"To stay, but I am no longer major — it's just McHenry."

"But you made it to Major. Congratulations."

"Advancements happen fast during wartime, and it was indeed war in Arizona." He took in a deep breath. "But I am retired and, with that, renouncing the rank along with the army." He bowed slightly. "Jeremiah McHenry at your service." He lowered his voice. "And I do like seeing you in female attire."

Everyone laughed as Opal's cheeks reddened. "Just shows I can dress up if I have to." She glanced down at her skirt, then held it out to the sides. "Straight from New York — they said that sapphire matches the color of my eyes." The sapphire blue gown, nipping in at the waist with an overskirt gathering up into a small bustle, set off her golden hair and fair complexion. Dark pearlized buttons trailed from the high neck to the point at the waist and lined the cuffs on the long sleeves.

"Yes, it does." The masculine voice from the doorway stopped her like she'd run into a wall of ice.

The young woman's cheeks flamed, but she straightened her shoulders back, and her forthright chin dipped slightly to the side. Haughty, regal. "Thank you, Mr. Chandler." Her voice froze the word *mister.*

Oh my, thought Amethyst, *just what is going on here?* She glanced up to catch Pearl's laughing gaze and raised eyebrow, as though they shared a private joke. *Will someone please tell me the punch line?* The way Opal threw herself into McHenry's arms had made her think there might be a romantic connection, but there was great disparity in their ages. And now Mr. Chandler. The fleeting look she'd caught in his eyes made her wonder again. Not that she was much good at recognizing romance.

"Sit beside me, Opal." Joel patted the floor.

"No, she needs to sit on the sofa." McHenry indicated the place beside where he had been sitting. He gave her a knowing look. "Like a proper young lady." He took her arm and guided her to the place.

Ignoring the look from Mr. Chandler, she laughed up at McHenry. "Mustn't mess my dress, eh? You sound just like Ruby."

"And we all know that Ruby knows what's proper."

Opal leaned closer to the man. "And we all know that her little sister has a perpetual war with proper."

Carl and two more people entered just behind Mr. Chandler, and more introductions set Amethyst's head in a spin. How to remember all the names? Everyone was so friendly, welcoming her like a long-lost relative.

Pearl's fingers rippling over the keys brought an end to the greetings as voice after voice picked up on the words of "Silent Night," then flowed into "It Came Upon a Midnight Clear" and "Away in a Manger." The harmony sounded like a heavenly chorus. When McHenry's mouth organ soared on the high notes of "Joy to the World," the voices faded away, leaving the piano and mouth organ to finish their duet.

Amethyst sniffed back the tears of joy at such beauty. Never had she heard anything like it.

After everyone had enjoyed the variety of desserts set out on the table and headed out the door, laughing their good-byes, Joel stopped beside his aunt. "You won't leave without telling me good-bye, will you?"

Amethyst cupped his cheeks with her

hands and looked right into his eyes. The words that came from her mouth surprised her and delighted him. "I'm not leaving."

Joel threw his arms around her waist. "Auntie Colleen, I'm so happy."

"Me too." She glanced up from Joel's hug to see McHenry watching them. Had he heard her announcement?

CHAPTER THIRTEEN

"Ah, Ruby, I'm so sorry you weren't there. I've never heard singing like that."

"That's all right, dear, there'll be more singing. I'm just so glad Cap— Mr. McHenry is back." Ruby shook her head. "Fiddle. I'll never be able to address him without his rank. That's just who he was."

"Was is right. He said he retired from the army, and his rank retired with him." Opal sat cross-legged at the foot of Ruby and Rand's bed with Ruby nursing her baby and Rand sitting in the rocker, pipe smoke circling his head. "We sure missed you, but everyone said to tell you congratulations and they'd be by to see the baby when she gets a bit older." Opal cocked her head. "Seems like I got home just in time." The wind had picked up and now whined at the eaves of the low log house that had started as a log cabin and grown as needed. Both front and back walls were shaded by porches that stretched from one end to the other. Now the back porch that faced into the trees at the base of a bluff was stacked to the roof with firewood. Rand had taken no chances, believing all the natural signs of a hard winter ahead.

"Shame Atticus didn't stay long enough to attend tonight and get to see everyone." Rand rested one ankle on his other knee, his feet clad in two pairs of wool socks knit by his wife.

Opal blinked back the tears that caught her by surprise. She thought she was done crying about Atticus leaving — again. While she'd been thrilled to see him, and knowing he was well again was such a relief, he seemed to have no qualms about leaving her again. And he'd almost not stopped by to see her. That thought dried her tears. What kind of a friend would just go on by and not stop? And yet he'd said he was coming back. She glanced up from playing with the yarn ties on the quilt. "What?"

Ruby smiled at her. "You took off somewhere, and we were just waiting."

"Sorry." The thought that she'd said she'd be waiting for him nagged at her. Did she want to marry Atticus? After all, she volunteered. He didn't ask her. And marriage, well, marriage was forever.

Her thoughts veered back to the singing at the Heglands', reminding her of the look in Mr. Chandler's eyes when he saw her all dressed up like that. She could still feel the heat start about her collarbone and work upward.

"You know, sometimes dressing up like that isn't so bad."

"I'll bet you caught McHenry by surprise." Rand laid his pipe down in the ashtray. "He left here when you were still a girl, and you walked in there a very fashionable young woman."

"He was rather shocked, but when I ran and threw myself into his arms, he didn't mind." She glanced up at Ruby from under her eyelashes. "He's still as handsome as ever, even with the eye patch."

"Eye patch!" Ruby sat up straighter.

Opal nodded. "He lost an eye in this last campaign, took a bullet in his leg, and still limps. He said Kentucky took an arrow in the shoulder, and he's still limping too. 'Two old war horses put out to pasture.' That's what he said."

"Well, he won't find pasture here for a few months, let me tell you. That wind is sounding worse by the minute." Rand rose to look out the window. "Nothing but whirling snow. Sure glad I got all those posts redone, so our ropes aren't buried." He and Beans had nailed taller posts to those already planted. "Snow doesn't usu-

ally get that deep up here by the house."
Earlier in the fall they had dug holes for
posts and strung rope to the springhouse,
the barn, and on to the bunkhouse and the
soddy where Linc and Little Squirrel lived.
During the winter the ranch hands took
turns out on the prairie at the line shacks,
which were set up to keep the cattle from
drifting before the wind out on the open
prairies. Otherwise the hands lived in the
bunkhouse but took their meals at the main
house along with the family.

Opal caught a yawn. "Guess I better go
on to bed. You want me to put more wood
in the stove first?"

"Thanks, but I'll take care of that." Rand
stood and stretched. "Might be a good thing
we put in supplies and plenty of wood at the
bunkhouse. I told the guys if a bad blizzard
hits to just stay inside."

"The same for Linc and Little Squirrel.
Sure hope she is feeling a whole lot better.
Did he come up tonight to talk with you?"
Opal had stopped in the doorway. With the
term of their baby coming closer, Little
Squirrel had fallen terribly sick and had not
recovered yet.

Rand shook his head as he answered.
"Nope. But he'd have let us know if there
was a change for the worse. Not much else

we can do but wait it out."

Once in bed Opal managed to thank God for taking care of them all. Still praying, she tucked the covers over her head, leaving only her nose showing, and fell asleep to the roar of the howling wind.

She woke sometime in the night hours to hear the wind trying to tear the roof off, some blasts making the house shudder. The room was so cold, she pulled the coyote pelt blanket up, covered her head with the quilt, and went back to sleep.

Snow had blown into drifts that covered the front windows when, after pulling her clothes on under the covers, she rushed out to the kitchen in the morning, boots in hand, trusting that Rand would have the fire burning. Even though he'd kept the stove hot all night, the water bucket on the stand against the wall had frozen several inches down. He was pouring hot water from the reservoir on it to melt it enough so they had water for breakfast.

"Good morning." He gave up and set the water bucket on the end of the stove. "Melt quicker that way."

"What about the livestock?"

"No way we can go out there. We'd get blown clear out of the territory." He fed the flames and set the lids back in place. "I got the other stove going, but move ten feet from the fire and you'll get frostbite. We took Per in with us during the night. Figured if you got too cold, you'd come too."

"Those coyote skins helped keep me warm. Get a whole blanket of them, and I'll never be cold." Opal pulled on her boots and buttoned her sheepskin vest. "Did Ruby say what to make for breakfast?"

"Can't get out to the springhouse for eggs, so we'll have mush. We got plenty of ham in here too. Going to have to bake bread today."

"You think it will rise, cold as it is?"

"If you leave it set on the reservoir or the oven door."

Opal set about starting breakfast; cooking for so few would seem strange. "The men are all right?"

"They'll have to shovel to get out, but other than getting bored, they'll be fine. Good thing we added more stovepipe to the soddy."

"There's Per."

"I'll get him. We better think of setting up a bed in here for Ruby and the baby. Might move all the beds in here and close off the back of the house. Had to do that one other year." He shook his head as he left the room.

Opal knew what he was thinking. Back then he'd not had a wife and children, one a newborn baby.

Per had a runny nose and coughed when Opal took him from his father. "I'll dress him."

"Opa, hungry."

"I know. It'll be ready in a minute." She stood him on a chair near the stove with the oven door open to send out extra heat. Stripping off his nightdress, she unbuttoned his long johns and stripped those off too. He'd wet during the night, so she'd need to wash clothes. Suddenly the day loomed overwhelming.

"One thing at a time," Rand counseled as he pushed the kettle to the back of the stove. He laid ham slices in the frying pan before pouring himself a cup of coffee. "You want some?"

"No, thanks." Opal finished washing Per and dressed him in clean, dry clothes, including a sweater and woolen stockings. She set him on her lap to pull his shoes on, but they wouldn't go.

He whimpered and pulled his foot back, looking up at her over his shoulder. His eyes looked as crusty as his nose.

"Too tight with all that stocking in there, eh?"

"Put his shoes on, then pull the wool stockings over them. From the look of him, he won't be running around much on the floor anyway." Rand chucked his son under the chin and headed back to the bedroom. Even with the vent in the wall for the heat to float through, the bedroom was not warm.

He brought Ruby and the baby back out, wrapped in quilts, and, pulling the rocker close to the fire, set them in it.

"Sorry to be so weak yet. I thought I'd be feeling fine by now." Ruby set the baby to her breast and covered her with a flannel blanket.

"Is she warm enough?" Opal asked, setting Per on his stool on a chair pulled up to the table.

"She's fine, but from the looks of him, Per isn't."

"I know." Opal handed the little guy a crust of hard bread to gnaw on while she finished making breakfast.

"Jelly."

"Coming."

With the rest of the breakfast on the table, she and Rand sat down and he said grace, thanking God for keeping them safe and snug in this strong house. "And, Lord, protect our cattle and our livestock, the men in the line shacks, all our friends, and the folks around here. You can see through the blizzard, and if you choose, you can calm the wind. We thank you for this meal and for Opal, who is taking over so capably. Amen."

"Thank you." She dished up the bowl of mush for Per, drizzled honey on the cereal, and checked the cream. It had thawed enough to pour, so she gave it a stir and poured some on his cereal.

Per pushed the bowl away. "No." He coughed again and rubbed his nose.

"You have to eat." Opal reached for his bread and smeared more jam on it before giving it back to him. She glanced to Ruby. "Should I feed him?"

"If you can." Ruby laid her hand on her son's forehead. "Warm."

Opal studied the pale skin and bright red circles on his cheeks. He really did look miserable. She stood and picked him up, then sat back down with him on her lap. Kissing the top of his head, she dipped a spoonful and held it to his lips. Like a little bird, he opened wide and the mush disappeared. "Good boy, Per. Let Opal help you."

"Ja, Opa."

After eating about a third of the bowl, he shook his head and turned his face into her shoulder. "No mo." He turned to look at his mother. "Ma?" And held out his arms.

"Trade you." Ruby nodded to the babe in her arms.

"All right." Opal stood, Per on her hip. After wiping his nose again, she set him on the table, took the baby, and Per crawled into his mother's arms. Opal's stomach rumbled. Here she'd fed the others but not had a bite yet herself. But glancing down at the little bundle wrapped so snugly and sound asleep in the crook of her arm, she felt a grin stretch her cheeks. "For a human baby, she's not bad."

"Opal Marie Torvald!" Ruby faked a glare at her sister. "What a thing to say."

"Well, if she was a calf or colt, and it was summer, she'd be running across the pasture by now, following her mother, all spindly legs and fluffy coat. She'd even know how to get her own food, just bop her mother's udder."

Rand rocked his chair onto the back legs, picking up the game. "Of course, we wouldn't have branded her yet, but . . ."

Ruby shook her head. "You two." She kissed Per and wiped his nose again. "Blow, Per."

He looked up at her and coughed, then sneezed instead.

"Well, that worked about the same." Ruby wiped his nose and face and glanced up at Opal. "You did save some of that goose fat, didn't you?"

"Yes, there was plenty after I made the gravy. I poured it into the crock." Goose grease had many uses, one of which was for healing chapped skin. Bear grease was best for waterproofing boots, chaps, and even leather jackets. Rand had learned that from the Indians. Opal handed him the baby and fetched the crock.

Per turned his face away when Ruby dipped some up with her finger, but she persisted until his nose, cheeks, and mouth wore a patina of the fat. After rubbing the last of it into the backs of her hands, Ruby put both arms around her son and rocked back and forth.

Opal added more wood to the fire. "If we're to have bread today, I better get going on it." She cleared the table and put the dishes into the steaming dishpan. This wasn't what she'd planned for today, but the book she'd been reading would have to wait.

"Why don't you forget the bread and make biscuits," Ruby suggested.

"All right." Opal felt a surge of relief.

Rand stood with his daughter in his arm and carried her over to the cradle he'd moved near the back of the stove. Ghost, their mottled gray-and-black cow dog, looked up from her nest, yawned, and went back to sleep. Laying the baby on her tummy in the cradle, Rand covered her with the baby quilt Ruby had made and checked the woodbox. "I'll fill both of these and stack some more inside the door so it warms up. There's snow on everything out there."

"You're not going out to the barn, are you?" Ruby yawned, her jaw cracking.

"No. Once I get the wood in, Opal and I are going to bring our bed in here where it is warmer. You and Per both look ready for a nap. Then we'll bring Per's bed in, and Opal can bunk with him. I'm going to close off the back of the house by hanging the buffalo robe over that doorway." He indicated the hall entry. "Next time I build a house, the fireplace is going on an inside wall so the heat can go both ways. That hole in the wall works fine except when the cold gets as bad as this." He shook his head. "Some different having a family in here instead of a bunch of ranch hands."

"What a good idea, not that you are planning on building a new house any time soon." Ruby felt Per's forehead again and shook her head. "You better take some of those willow twigs I brought in and steep them for a tea. Rand, we still have some of the whiskey, don't we?"

Opal knew that honey and whiskey added to the willow-bark tea was good for coughs, and from the sound of Per, she'd better get it made sooner rather than later.

Some time later with the back rooms blocked off, Opal could feel a difference in the heat. Between the fireplace and the kitchen stove, the room felt almost warm, although with the beds in place, there wasn't a lot of room for walking around. Ruby and the children slept through the clink of stove lids that made noise no matter how hard Opal tried to add wood silently. The wind seemed to have let up, or else she'd just grown so used to it that she ignored the howling and shrieking.

Rand brought in more wood, lining it up against the wall next to the back door. "I think this is the worst I've seen since I moved here." He spoke in low tones so as not to disturb those sleeping.

Opal had a boiler steaming with diapers that she'd need to hang to dry. While Ruby had strung the winter clothesline on the back porch, they now needed one in the kitchen.

Rand took his hammer and a thin rope to the buffalo-hide drape. "I'll stretch this in our bedroom. The diapers can freeze dry there so we still have room to move around in here."

Opal kneaded her back with her fists. Making biscuits, cooking, scrubbing diapers on the scrub board, then rinsing and wringing them as dry as possible — no wonder Ruby was tired by the end of the day. *I'd rather do roundup and branding anytime than this. And what's happening with the cattle and the horses?* She knew Rand was thinking much the same but was being very careful about what he said so as not to distress his wife. Ruby needed all her energy to take care of the baby and get well herself.

By evening, with the storm still raging, Opal thought to read awhile.

Rand stoked the fires and lay down with a sigh. "Wake me when you go to bed, all right?"

"Sure." But it wasn't two minutes later that Mary started to fuss, and that woke Per, who started to cry, and that set him to coughing.

"Is there any more of that tea?" Ruby asked.

"Yes, I'll get it." Opal had poured the remainder into a small jar and set it on the warming shelf of the stove. She closed her book and heaved herself to her feet to fetch

189

the medicine and a spoon.

Per turned his head away when she tried to spoon it into his mouth. "Ma."

"Come on, Per, be a good boy." He shook his head. She whipped the spoon back just in time to keep him from spilling it.

"Do we have any clean diapers?" Ruby asked.

"A few. The others will be dry by morning."

"Better bring some in and dry them above the stove." Ruby sounded as weary as Opal felt. "I'm sorry I'm not more help."

"We're doin' fine." Rand jumped out of their bed, shoved his feet into his leather moccasins, and headed for the cold part of the house. He brought back an armful of frozen stiff diapers and leaned them on the backs of chairs. "Guess we could dry them with an iron if we had to."

Opal looked at the solid standing squares of white flannel. "New kind of table decorations?"

"No, we invited diapers for dinner." Rand winked at her.

"Soon they'll be melting with joy." She tried to keep a straight face, but glancing at Ruby did her in. She wore a Lord-deliver-me kind of look.

Opal felt a giggle coming on, the kind that

happens when you are so tired you can't see straight.

But Per started coughing again, so hard his whole body shook.

"I'll hold him. You bring the medicine." Rand picked up his son and wrapped both arms around him, one around his middle, the other his head. "Now."

"Rand, be careful." Ruby waved her free hand.

He nodded to her and then to Opal.

Lord, help us. Opal shot her plea heavenward, as she'd been doing all afternoon.

Per screamed, but he swallowed the two spoonfuls.

"Thank you, Lord." Rand's heartfelt prayer covered it for all three of them.

The night ahead, their second with the storm raging, loomed long and dark.

CHAPTER FOURTEEN

"I'd just as soon you stayed up here in the main house. You know what the last blizzard was like." Cora Robertson looked over her shoulder to the man shrugging into his heavy wool coat.

"We have the ropes strung. I'm closer to the barn from the soddy."

"I know, but . . ." She shook her head. "I just got me a feeling. We have plenty of beds. You and Joel can take my bed, and I'll sleep with one of the girls. Sometimes when it's real bad cold we bring the beds or pallets into the kitchen and sleep by the stove."

"It gets that cold?"

"It can. One year the water bucket froze not ten feet from the stove. We wore our coats and hats in the house, mittens too."

Jacob let out a sigh and gave a slight nod. "Do I need to go get anything from the soddy?"

"Not that I know of." A smile lightened the seriousness of her face. "Glad you changed your mind."

"Me too, Pa." Joel unwound his muffler

and hung it back on the peg by the door, followed by his coat.

"Think I'll bring in more wood." Jacob glanced at the full woodbox. "Stack it by the door?"

"We never can have too much dry wood." Cora Robertson pulled the coffeepot to the front of the stove. "Give everybody a hot drink before we go to bed. We got plenty of hot rocks too and a bed warmer." She pointed to a round shallow pan with a lid and a long handle. "Fill that with coals and slide it around under the covers." A shadow crossed her face, like a cloud hiding the sun. She turned to fetch a gingerbread cake from the larder.

Jacob tucked his chin into his collar, the muffler he'd received for a Christmas present wrapped around his hat and the lower part of his face. He brought in five loads of wood, with Joel opening and closing the door for him to keep as much of the cold outside as possible. Even here on the sheltered side of the house, the wind drove the snow in what looked to be an impenetrable wall. The roar of it sounded like a train passing overhead. His nose burned in spite of the scarf.

Once inside again he pushed a rolled-up rug tight against the door to keep out the wind and blowing snow. The windows were all frost-covered, as bad inside as out. Dark had fallen by three o'clock, not that there'd been much daylight. While he and Joel had slept in the soddy last night, he was grateful he'd not insisted they set out again. Besides, this way there was someone else in the house to help keep the fires burning.

When he crawled into bed with a hot rock at his feet and the warming pan had proved its worth, he wished he'd brought his Bible from the soddy. *Lord God, thou who seest all, protect us by the power of your mighty hand. Thank you for this snug house to keep us from the storm. Please take care of Opal and her family.*

"Pa?"

"Yes."

"Do you mind if I call her Auntie Colleen like I always have?"

"Not at all." Jacob still thrilled every time his son referred to him as Pa. Since they'd known of each other less than a year, there had been a lot of adjustments to be made. When he left his parish in Pennsylvania and fled west with his newfound son at his side, they'd not talked much. They'd not liked each other too well at first, but their new life had been good for both of them. And God put them here at the Robertsons' at a time when they were sorely needed after Ward Robertson's death.

"Good. I'm glad she's staying. You'll like her when you get to know her."

"I'm sure I will." Talk about a surprise — Miss O'Shaunasy showing up like that to claim his son for her nephew. *"Oh, what a tangled web we weave, when first we practice to deceive!"* The couplet floated through his mind. One of these days Joel was going to start asking some rather embarrassing questions, and he needed to be ready with some honest answers. Ah, the consequences of a thoughtless night of passion. Well, not thoughtless. Before it happened, he'd thought of nothing else. Then he spent the rest of his years after Melody disappeared trying to ignore what he'd done.

Lord God, I know Melody is with you. How desperate she was and in such terrible pain. I cannot blame her for what she did, and I thank you that she had the presence of mind to bring this boy to me first. I never thought I would say that, but then, I do not pretend to understand your ways. Bless us, Father, in Jesus' name. Amen. He rolled onto his side, listening to the wind and straining to hear the gentle breaths of his son beside him. How was Joel feeling

195

this first Christmas without his mother? He had grown up so much, but he never mentioned her.

He woke some time later and, pulling his pants on over his long johns, headed for the kitchen to stoke the stoves again. He'd just finished turning down the dampers so that the wood would burn more slowly when Mrs. Robertson joined him.

"You didn't need to get up," he whispered.

"I wasn't sure if I heard you out here or if it was the storm. Thank you." She walked before him back to the cold bedrooms.

Grateful for his son's warmth, Jacob crawled back under the covers. *Lord, please wake me again. This was just the right time.*

The next time he woke, he fed the fires again and decided to stay up. He checked the shelves, and sure enough, the Robertson family Bible held a place of honor. After lighting a kerosene lamp, he pulled a rocker close to the kitchen stove, opened the oven, put his feet up on the door, and basked in the warmth. Even hot as his feet soon were, the cold drafts on the back of his neck made him fetch his muffler and throw it over his shoulders. He turned to the Gospels, reading the miracles that Jesus performed, and then stopped at the verse, "Greater works than these will you do because I go to the Father." *He made the blind see, the lame walk, drove out demons, and yet He says greater works are we to do. Lord, what am I missing here? You say all things come by faith.* He flipped to another passage. "If ye have faith as a grain of mustard seed, ye shall say to this mountain, remove hence to yonder place; and it shall remove; and nothing shall be impossible unto you." *Heavenly Father, I want to take you at your word. I want that kind of faith, but where do I find it?* He leaned his head against the back of the rocker. *I'm sure, like everything, it grows, so I ask for faith seeds. I feel you are calling me, that you brought me here to Medora for a reason. Well, for many reasons, most likely. If I am to pastor this group of people, I need more — more knowledge, more wisdom, and most of all, more faith. I ran before. I will not run again.*

The picture of Opal in her glorious blue gown flashed before his eyes. How that sight had set his heart to hammering. *But I cannot hurry time either. Rand made it clear I can say nothing to her of how I feel until she turns sixteen, a full year from May.* Plenty of time to learn discipline — and to love her more each day. He refused to allow thoughts of her not loving him back to take up residence in his mind. *If she is to be my wife, I have to leave it all in your hands. I want to trust you.* In spite of Atticus. He'd overheard her telling one of the girls that she'd told her friend Atticus she would be here when he returned.

Nothing like a little competition.

Why couldn't I have fallen in love with Edith? She so obviously was willing for me to court her. He had told Mrs. Robertson that he had no romantic feelings for Edith and didn't want to hurt her feelings any more than he already had. He knew the girl had been sent off to help her older sister as a means to make things easier on her in the long run.

So he had to wait for Opal to grow up.

"You didn't stay out here all night?" Mrs. Robertson entered the room, tying on her apron.

"No, not at all, but the last time I added wood to the stove, I thought I could use the time more wisely than sleeping it away."

"Ah yes. Any time spent in the Word is more valuable than sleeping. That's what saved my life after Ward was killed. I'd sit here just like you are and find the comfort our Father promises. I memorized Psalm 91 so that I would always remember I am safe in the shadow of His wings. He orders our footsteps. He decides how many days we have on this earth. My job is to give Him praise and glory."

"And to love one another. Thank you for the reminder."

"That too."

"You have shown that love to Joel and me, making us part of your family. I'll never be able to thank you enough."

"Hard as you work is more than sufficient thanks. I was hoping to be able to pay you wages by now, but with this storm — blizzards and cold like this are hard on range cattle. I thank God I listened to Rand and sold off the steers rather than keeping some of them another year."

"He's a wise man and listens to God's prompting." Jacob recognized wisdom when he saw it.

Mrs. Robertson poured the coffee into the pot, then added water and two whole eggs in the shells.

"Why do you add the eggs?"

"So we have something to eat along with our coffee. They'll be done when the coffee is."

"I see. My mother used to throw in eggshells when she took the boiling coffee off the stove. Said it made the grounds settle."

"I've heard that." Cora set a frying pan on

the stove and, taking a pan of cornmeal cooked the night before and left to set in loaf pans, removed a loaf and sliced it to fry. With a dollop of bacon grease from the canister on the warming shelf, she moved the frying pan to the hotter part of the stove and laid the slices of mush in the pan to sizzle and snap.

"As soon as it dies down some, I'll get on out to the barn with water for the animals."

"The animals are not nearly as important as your life."

The words lay there, an edict or a challenge. Jacob watched Mrs. Robertson go about her cooking as if the matter were settled.

"I can't see letting them die for lack of water." He smiled when she poured him a cup of coffee and handed him a shelled boiled egg in a bowl. "Thanks." *Surely I can get to the barn and back with the rope. Please, Lord, calm these winds as you did on the sea.*

"Ma, Emily won't let me wear her sweater. Mine's too small, and she has two." Ada Mae made a beeline for the stove front.

"You girls settle your own differences." Mrs. Robertson turned the browning cornmeal slices. "Breakfast is nearly ready."

"I'll get Joel up." Jacob heaved himself to his feet. Why did he feel as though the fate of all the Robertson livestock rested on his shoulders? How did one find prayer time with all these children running in and out? Not that the older girls could be called children anymore. And the arguing — could they never get along? He closed the door behind him and entered the room where Joel hardly made a mound under the covers.

"Breakfast, son." He shook the boy's shoulder.

"All right."

Jacob tucked Joel's pants and shirt under the covers. "You're going to want to dress where you are. The girls are all in by the stove." He'd heard the sound of their feet padding toward the kitchen. They'd most likely dressed under the covers too. He sat on the edge of the bed, waiting. His breath hung in a white cloud.

"Blizzard still blowing?" His son's voice came from the depths of the bed, where the bumping of the covers showed he was doing what his father said.

"Yes."

"Second day."

"I know."

Joel's head popped out of the covers. "It's cold in here."

"I know." Jacob could feel the cold penetrating his woolen shirt, right through his woolen long johns. Now he understood why men wore sheepskin vests in this part of the country, or those made of deer hide with the hair left on. He'd read of people wearing buffalo, elk, or deer robes, since most of the cattle hides were tanned to be used for shoes, chaps, and harness and tack repairs. He had two down at the barn that he wished he'd brought up to the house so they could be put to good use — like covering the window.

Winter in Pennsylvania had not prepared him for weather like this — that was for sure.

After breakfast he brought in more wood and emptied the slop pail off the back porch. Filling the boiler, a tub, and the big kettles with snow, he hauled them back inside to set on the stove to melt.

"That should give us plenty of water." Mrs. Robertson nodded. "Thank you."

"We'll do extra in case we get a break and can take it to the barn."

"Mr. Chandler . . ."

"I know. I just want to be prepared for when God answers our prayers."

She huffed a sigh but said no more about that. She turned to her daughters. "Once you girls have finished the dishes, bring your schoolbooks in here by the stove."

"But, Ma, there's no school now anyway." Emily's eyes widened in horror.

"This way you'll get ahead. Bring your knitting too. Virginia, you can help with the mending. That basket has plumb gotten away from me. Seems to me that if you have time to get in arguments, you have too much time on your hands."

"But Joel's books are down at the soddy."

"You can share yours."

Joel looked to his father, who just nodded. Giving Jacob a disgusted look, Joel set aside the piece of wood and knife Mrs. Robertson had given him for Christmas. She'd said Mr. Robertson got a whole lot of pleasure out of carving and perhaps Joel might too. So far he'd made a pile of woodchips.

When the wind failed to mitigate its howling, Jacob caught himself pacing from the window to the door to the stove and back.

"You planning on wearing out your boots or the floor first?"

"Sorry. Guess I know what a caged lion feels like about now. What did Ward do when a blizzard hit?"

"He always worked on things that needed fixing here at the house. Like that chair leg."

She nodded to one of the chairs that was missing a rung. "I should have warned you." She laid the shirt she was mending in her lap. "He slept or whittled, or we played games. When the schoolwork is finished, we'll get out the cards."

"I see." Jacob set the chair up on the table so he could see better. He'd never repaired a chair before, but now was as good a time as any to start. The rung had shattered when someone stood on it to reach something out of the cupboard.

The saw was down at the barn, as was the plane. He picked up the smallest chunk of wood and started paring it down.

"Ma, my ears hurt from all that noise." Ada Mae clapped her hands over her ears.

"Some people go out of their mind from the howling wind. I read that in one of the books." Emily glared at her sister, then hissed, "Could be you."

"Emily, there'll be no more of that. You apologize, and you will do the dishes after dinner."

"But it's not my turn."

"It is now."

Jacob heard her mutter, "You always take Ada Mae's side," as she stomped down the hall. He could understand how people went insane if the wind howled like this day after day. The girls' arguing set his teeth on edge. He'd never lived in a house with this many females in one place. He glanced around the kitchen area. In this small space.

Lord, please give us a break. Would his and Opal's children squabble like these girls? *Please, Lord, I pray not.*

"Mr. Chandler. Mr. Chandler."

Was it the wind or someone calling him?

Cora Robertson shook his shoulder — hard.

"What?" Jacob rolled over, instantly awake.

"The front window blew out. Snow is drifting in."

"Gather up whatever you can to cover it. I'll be right there." Having slept in his clothes since the last time he stoked the fire, he headed for the kitchen with Joel following behind. In the flickering lamplight, the two-foot drift gleamed white.

"Put your coat on." He had to yell over the howl of the wind. The temperature had dropped in the room as if he'd stepped outside.

Mrs. Robertson, her nightdress and robe billowing around her, dropped the quilt she had brought in and went for her coat and muffler. Her girls were pacing the cabin, uncertain about how to help.

"Where's a hammer?"

"Out in the woodshed with the other tools."

"Any nails?"

"No."

His nose and cheeks burned already. The hatchet was on the back porch. He crossed to the back door and tugged. It didn't move.

"Is it frozen?" Mrs. Robertson and the girls had returned from the bedrooms with a feather bed and a straw-stuffed pallet. "You won't make it to the woodshed."

"The hatchet's on the porch."

He slammed his shoulder against the door, then kicked along the bottom. *Lord, open the door; calm the wind.* "Is the fire still burning?"

"Yes, the snow is sizzling when it hits the stove."

He jerked again, and this time the door gave way, almost knocking him off his feet. He flipped his muffler over his face and kicked the snow buildup out of the doorway.

"Can you see?"

"Hold the lamp to the window and close the door behind me." They shut it behind him, leaving him seeing only swirling snow until he saw the glow from the window off to his left. Scooping the snow off the woodbox, he dug out the hatchet and forced his way back into the house. With the door shut again, half the wind howl stayed outside. Mrs. Robertson held the pallet against the window frame.

"This should work. I sent Joel and the girls back to bed."

"Nails, what can I use for nails?" He turned to the woodbox and pulled out a chunk, splitting off narrow pieces. Taking the time to sharpen each one, he finally had several to peg the pad into the window frame.

The wind pushed against the mattress, but the pegs held.

"I should do this from the outside."

"In the morning. This takes care of the worst." She stepped back. "Don't know what I'd have done without you here. Thank you, Lord God, for your providence."

"Amen to that." Jacob added more wood to the fire. "You go on back to bed. I'll stay out here and keep this roaring."

"Dawn isn't that far away. I'd never sleep now." She looked toward the window. "I'll just clean up this snow. Blew the window right out. I'd never have believed it if I didn't see it with my own eyes."

Jacob made a face. "I asked the Lord to give us a break, but this certainly wasn't what I had in mind." He rubbed his hand, which hurt like fire.

CHAPTER FIFTEEN

"How do people endure storms like this?" Amethyst asked with a shiver.

"The term is *blizzard*. They come roaring down from the Arctic, and there are no mountains or even trees to stop them. I've heard that the high plains, like where we are, get more blizzards than any other place on earth." Pearl set the stove lids back in place and dusted off her hands.

Amethyst finished rolling and cutting the cookies while they visited. "Does the snow often cover your windows?"

"No, only when drifting. Sometimes we've had to shovel our way out the door, but usually the porches protect us. That's why, when Carl built this house, he put the front door to the west and the back door to the east. We've never had one storm right after the other like this year."

Amethyst sprinkled sugar on the cookies she'd laid in the pan. The letter she'd written to her father still lay on the table by the door. No one had been to town in the three days since Christmas — thanks to the blizzard. With the noise of the storm, she had no idea if the train even made it through.

Some time later the men came in from the workshop, which was located about a hundred feet from the house. McHenry had gone out to help Carl put together a hutch he was building for the Chateau, as everyone referred to the de Mores home. While much of their furniture came on the train from the East, de Mores had drawn the plans and hired Carl to build the piece over the winter.

"Good thing I put that building so close to the house," Carl said as he brushed the snow off his coat and hat before hanging them on the pegs along the wall. "Without the rope we still might not have made it back from there."

"I'd forgotten how bad the blizzards can be here." McHenry hung up his things. "Or else thought I was exaggerating when I remembered."

Amethyst put the dinner on the table because, as usual, the baby wanted to be fed whenever the others sat down to eat. How did Pearl manage without help? She sat down so Carl could say grace, and as soon as the amen was said, she began passing the bowls. Good thing the cellar was under the house instead of in a separate building so there was plenty of food. What did folks do who weren't prepared like this house?

Her already high estimation of Carl went up a notch or two further.

After the dinner dishes were done and the children napping, Amethyst rinsed the diapers she'd washed and then hung them on the line Carl had strung on the swept-off porch.

"It's time to sit down and enjoy a bit of quiet," Pearl said when Amethyst returned with bright red cheeks and a shiver.

She hung up her coat and scarf and stamped the snow off her shoes. "The diapers froze about as fast as I hung them up." She held her hands over the stove and rubbed them together. Her finger ached something fierce from the frostbite that had happened when she collapsed in the snow that day on her way to the boarding-house.

"I made tea if that sounds good to you too. Do you take milk or sugar?"

"I've had tea, but I've never used milk before. I sweetened things with honey when I could."

The two women took their tea into the parlor, where Carl had started a fire in the

211

stove. The tree stood in the window, without candles now, a silent witness to the best Christmas Amethyst could remember. No one got drunk, her father hadn't been whining, and she knew her mother had celebrated the Savior's birth with Him and all the angels.

"Your home is so lovely." Amethyst smoothed the covering on the horsehair sofa. "What brought you to Medora?"

"I was running away from my father. He wanted me to marry his bookkeeper, who had five children. But the man was so dull, I left. Actually, I got myself hired as the schoolteacher in a town called Little Missouri, about as far away from Chicago as I could go at the time. My father was not happy." She rolled her eyes, making Amethyst smile. "He threatened to come out and haul me back, but by then I was living at Dove House, which Ruby Harrison owned, and was teaching school in the room they used for card playing at night. We had some grand times in that big hotel."

"Is that the one that burned?"

"Yes, to the ground. Struck by lightning." Pearl talked as she poured out the tea and passed a cup to Amethyst.

"Your father tried to marry you off, and mine ran off any suitors so I would be there to take care of him."

"Was he ill?"

Amethyst thought a moment. "He called it 'feeling poorly,' then made a trip to town for the cure to be had at the saloon."

"Ah, I see. And your mother died when? You said five years ago?"

Amethyst nodded. "She was the one who made sure all five of us got at least a grammar school education. She came from a good family, but I never learned much about them. Pa resented her mentioning them much."

"Interesting that we have a lot in common, you and I. My mother died when I was twelve, and my father remarried a year later. I only began to really appreciate my stepmother as I grew older and even more so when I ran away. I have a brother, a step-brother, and a stepsister, none of whom I have seen for going on four years now. I do write to my stepmother to keep up with the news.

"I had an accident when I was little and was burned — that's what this scar is." Pearl touched her neck where her high-collared gown and the lace ruching hid the dark wrinkled scar. "I always thought everyone was looking at that. But now I just cover it as much as I can and forget about it." She sipped her tea. "I started teaching school once I was graduated from Mrs. Eldrige's Finishing School. I loved teaching at the settlement house for children who were immigrants or just terribly poor. I was able to give them the ability to read, write, and do their arithmetic so they could grow up and be better off than their parents."

"Traveling on the train through Chicago, I thought it looked like a lot of poor people lived there."

"The train goes through the worst part. There are lovely parks, and I loved the lake. Lake Michigan is the northern border of Chicago. It's big enough to seem like the sea." She reached for the teapot. "More?"

"Please. I lived on the same farm all my life and thought I would inherit it since my brothers all died."

"How sad. So after your mother died, you did most everything?"

"Pa helped some." She thought back to the butchering day. Some was almost an exaggeration. Glancing over at the piano, she smiled. "You play so beautifully. Sounded like heaven when everyone sang the other night. My mother taught me to sew. If you have any flannel, I would love to sew a new dress for Carly. I never got to sew for a little girl before, but I used to sew shirts for Joel."

"Why, that would be lovely. We'll look in the sewing room tomorrow." Pearl poured the last of the tea. "I have a favor to ask."

"Of course."

"Would you be offended if I shared some of my far too many clothes with you? I know they would have to be altered, but I want you to be warm enough. Between us we could redo them."

Amethyst felt a burning at the back of her eyes. "You are already so good to me, but if that would make you happy, I would not be averse to receiving such largess. I am most grateful."

"I think we should do tea like this every afternoon. Thank you for all you've done to make my life easier here."

But I've done so little, Amethyst thought as she gathered up the tea things and made sure there were no crumbs on the floor. *I don't have to milk the cow and feed the chickens or anything.*

That evening they gathered around the stove, and Pearl opened a book. "I'm sorry to keep reading from the middle like this, but you are welcome to go back and read the first part if you want." She found the place where she'd stopped and continued the story of *Robinson Crusoe*. Carly sat in her father's lap, and the baby slept in the cradle that rocked gently, thanks to Carl's foot.

Amethyst let her knitting fall into her lap as she thought of the years earlier when her mother had snatched a few minutes to read to her. While the words poured beauty through her mind, her heart ached for the woman who had taught her so much. *Sometimes, Ma, I miss you so badly I can feel my heart crack*. Only her mother had loved her the way a person ought to be loved. *But, then, that's the way we should all love one another*. That thought brought her upright, and she picked up the knitting needles again. She wound the yarn between her fingers so the tension was just right, and the knitting needle song accompanied the story. Her father probably needed new stockings by now.

Feeling someone watching her, she looked up to catch the studied gaze of Jeremiah McHenry. A slight smile creased his cheeks when he saw she was aware of his attention, slow, like he saw something he liked. She ducked her head and dropped a stitch. *Pay attention,* she ordered herself, ignoring the fact that she never paid attention to her knitting, she just let her fingers do what they knew best. With an effort she kept from touching her hair to make sure it remained properly in place. Good thing her

216

hands were already busy.

Heat started below her neck and worked its way upward. She glanced up from under her eyelashes. He was still watching her. *Don't you know that's not polite?* She dropped another stitch and had to rip out a good part of a row. She had a hard time paying attention to the story, what with the man across from her and the needles and yarn that had a mind of their own.

Jeremiah loved to watch a woman knit. How she could manage to knit at the same time as listen to the story was beyond him. He'd seen some women walk along a road, knitting and talking with a companion. They never tripped, they laughed in the right places, and whatever they were knitting grew accordingly. Miss O'Shaunasy was probably like that. Not like him, who tripped even when watching carefully. She didn't have much to say, but when she did speak, her voice had a cadence that pleased the ear. She didn't laugh much either, but she had chuckled with Carly once, and the sound made him want to make her laugh more. From the bit he'd overheard earlier, he had an idea she'd not had much to laugh about in her life.

He thought back to life at Fort Bowie and

compared it to now. There the sun blazed the moisture out of any living thing, while here a blizzard fought to freeze all living creatures to death. There the hills hid marauding Indians who'd just as soon kill anyone in blue as breathe. Here there were two women bent on providing comfort, entertainment, and good food, instead of lonely soldiers who often drank too much and lived in dread of the next campaign.

He brought his thoughts back to the room and the warmth both physical and mental, in spite of the storm doing its best to blow them and their houses off the face of the earth.

He woke sometime during the night to silence. *Please, God, let it stay that way.* He went back to sleep and woke to the rattling of stove lids and the low murmur of the Heglands talking softly so as not to awaken their guests. Darkness still reigned, but when he scraped the frost off the window, he could see a lightening of the eastern sky and several stars overhead. He heard the back door slam and saw a lantern throwing circles of bouncing light as Carl made his way to the barn. While they'd taken water to the animals yesterday, they'd not been able to let them drink their fill. Today they would. Hard to believe this was the second blizzard since Christmas.

Jeremiah pulled on his clothes and sat down to lace up his boots. No telling how long they had to get the stock watered and fed. He couldn't see the northern sky from his window, and the dark clouds wouldn't show until daylight anyway if they were brooding.

Both Miss O'Shaunasy and Mrs. Hegland wore full aprons over their clothes and were dipping hot water out of the reservoir to pour over snow in buckets, boilers, and washtubs. Every container that could melt snow covered the stove.

"Good morning, Mr. McHenry. I hope our banging around didn't wake you."

"No, the silence did sometime during the night." He shook his head. "Who'd think silence would wake one."

Miss O'Shaunasy glanced over her shoulder. "Strange, wasn't it?"

He nodded and smiled, hoping he could bring her to smile back. She had a lovely smile when playing with Carly, but so far she'd kept it from him. "If you have buckets of hot water ready to go, I'll take two out."

"Good, take those." Pearl pointed at two. "When the sun comes up, Carl will try to thaw out the pump, but in the meantime we can get all the animals a drink this way."

Jeremiah shrugged into his coat and wrapped the muffler around his neck.

"Take that other hat of Carl's. It will keep you warmer than yours."

He did as she suggested. Flat-brimmed hats were great for protection from the sun and rain but did nothing for cold such as this. After both men had made three trips, they sat down at the table set for breakfast.

"I know what I'm building next," Carl said after saying grace.

"What?"

"A house for the pump. I wanted to do it last summer but never had time." Carl passed the platters of ham and eggs around the table.

"I'm hoping to build a house. Will you be for hire?"

"You get the logs together, and we'll all come out and put it up in a day, just like a barn raising."

"Do you know where you plan to build?" Pearl asked.

"Out on Pinewood Creek. That's one bend upriver from Rand's place. The bottom there isn't as large as where he is, but I'm not planning on putting up a lot of buildings. Just a house, barn, and corral. Perhaps a smokehouse." He glanced up to see Miss O'Shaunasy watching him. He smiled when he caught her eye, and she ducked her chin, but not before a slight smile teased the corners of her mouth.

The jingling of harness bells caught their attention. Carl pushed back his chair and went to the front door. But when he pulled it in to open it, snow covered the opening chest high. "Morning, Charlie, come on around to the back door," he hollered over the top of it. "Haven't had time to shovel here."

"Will do."

Carl slammed the door before the snow wall fell in on him. "First time that's happened."

"I'll clear it off after breakfast," McHenry said. "Then I think I'll ride out and see how Rand and his family are doing."

"You might do better if you skied. You know how?"

"Never learned. Though Opal did. I remember how that girl can do about anything she sets her mind to."

"She's becoming a young woman now, as you saw when she came to visit in her sapphire gown. When she was sent back to New York last summer after the drifter tried to attack her, she returned with two trunks of gowns for all occasions, along with all the

221

shoes and hats one could dream of." Pearl smiled. "I love watching her grow up."

"Drifter? What happened?" Jeremiah asked.

Carl turned to Jeremiah. "Long story, but she and Atticus beat him off."

Pearl shook her head. "Ended in the tragedy of Ward Robinson being killed. Just awful, the whole thing."

After a knock on the back door, Charlie was inside and stamping snow off his boots. "Near to blind you out there, the sun off that snow."

"Come and have a cup of coffee with us. There's more ham and eggs if you'd like."

"No, thanks, I already had breakfast. Just checking to see that everyone is all right."

"You going on out to Harrisons'?" McHenry asked.

"Plannin' on it. You want to come?"

"Sit down and have a cup of coffee while I finish here."

Amethyst rose and fetched another cup and saucer. "You sure you won't take a piece of this ham?"

"You twisted my arm." Charlie hung his coat on the peg and took the chair offered him.

"How are things at your house?" Carl nodded his thanks at the refill Amethyst poured into his cup.

"All right now that I got water and feed to the stock. Won't nobody be getting much milk after the cows went without water for two days."

"Yeah, we lost some of the chickens in the last one. Should have let them out of the chicken house, loose in the barn. You'd have thought enough snow seeped in to give them enough to drink. Everyone's healthy though?"

"Other than baby Thomas — he has a runny nose. Daisy spends most of her waking hours wiping it." He nodded his thanks when Amethyst set a plate with cookies in front of him. "Ingermeir's soddy got buried under the snow. He might have to put an extension on his stovepipe to keep his fire burnin'. You could drive a sleigh right over the top of his house if you didn't see the stovepipe. Helped him dig out some."

While the men discussed the weather, Amethyst took the baby so that Pearl could eat. She sat the squirming little boy on her lap and patted his back until a solid burp made Carly smile.

"Baby."

"He sure did burp. You want to help me change him?"

Carly nodded and, after a glance at her

mother, slid from her chair.

"Wipe your hands and face."

Carly looked from her hands to her mother, then licked the jam off one finger. "Done."

"The washcloth is on the bar on the reservoir. Use it."

Amethyst laid the baby on the padded flannel quilt on the low chest. The stack of folded diapers on the shelf above it was diminishing rapidly. Time to wash diapers, baby soakers, and gowns.

She heard the men prepare to leave as she pulled the woolen knit soakers back up. Instead of knitting socks for her father, perhaps she should make more soakers for this little one. Had she known she would be staying, she would have packed differently, that was for sure. Although she had brought so few clothes, that wasn't the issue. And she didn't need household things, since there were plenty here. But she would have brought her sewing things: needles, thread, scissors, a darning egg, pins.

"Me hold him?" Carly looked up at Amethyst, her eyes pleading.

Oh dear. Amethyst kept a smile in place while she thought. "I know, let's go sit in the rocker and you can climb up on my lap to hold the baby."

"Good." The little girl ran to the rocker, her eyes dancing. "Me rock baby."

Holding the child on her hip, Amethyst sat down carefully, then gave Carly a hand to scramble into her lap. With the little girl settled, she positioned the thin arms and sat Joseph on Carly's lap. "Now hold him but don't squeeze him."

Carly gazed at the face of her baby brother. "Sleepy."

"Babies sleep a lot so they can grow faster."

"Me bigger."

"Yes, you are growing like a weed." Pearl knelt in front of the rocker and smoothed her daughter's hair back. "Looks like we need to braid your hair."

Carly shook her head.

"Yes, after we put Joseph to bed." Pearl reached for the infant. "I'll put him in his bed now."

Another nod from Carly. "So grow big, huh?" She slid to the floor as soon as her mother took the baby. "Cookie?"

Amethyst stood. "I'll get you a cookie."

After handing Carly her cookie, she tested the water in the boiler. "Do you need this, Mr. Hegland, or can I use it for washing diapers?"

"You go ahead. I'll bring in more snow to melt."

Amethyst took the bar of soap and scraped curls off it with a knife into the steaming water. After adding the diapers, she put the cover back on the boiler and moved it closer to the heat to set it boiling. After scraping soap into the dishpan, she finished clearing the table. Pearl reentered the kitchen and headed for the dishes.

"No, you sit there and enjoy your coffee, Pearl. I'm taking care of this."

"You'll spoil me."

"I doubt it. I don't know how you've managed with all this by yourself."

"We haven't had many guests here since the summer, when we could have had men sleeping in the barn since so many needed rooms. Some slept in tents and then ate supper here every night. Opal has been a big help, but until the weather lets up, she'll be staying home."

"What are you planning on for dinner?" Amethyst asked.

"The goose carcasses from Christmas are in the window box in the pantry. I was thinking of making soup from them. Then for supper we'll bake that venison haunch, and we can make hash or stew from the remainders. At least this cold weather guarantees we'll have no worries about anything going bad."

After Mr. Hegland headed out with buckets of hot water to thaw out the pump — he would add snow to cool it down so as not to crack the metal pump — Pearl joined Amethyst doing the dishes. "Thank you for taking over for me like that. Carl and I never have time to talk during the day."

"You are welcome."

"I've been thinking."

"Yes?"

"Mr. McHenry really is a fine gentleman, isn't he?"

"Seems so."

"I would imagine he will be looking for a wife now that he is building a home."

Amethyst shrugged. Not after the way he barked at her, sounding just like her Pa. Of course, any man would be frustrated at stumbling on the stairs like that.

CHAPTER SIXTEEN

If I don't get outside pretty soon, I am going to go stir crazy, Opal thought.

"Opa." Per raised his arms to be picked up again. No matter how sick he felt, he wanted Opal to carry him.

Just go to sleep, and maybe you'll feel better. But Opal picked him up and held him on her hip as she stared out the small space where she'd scraped the ice off the inside of the window. The sun glinted off the snow so brightly that even the window frost looked to have rainbows frozen in it.

"Look, Per, see how pretty." She pointed to the colors in the frost.

"No." He scrubbed his face across her shoulder, smearing snot and tears on her shirt. But when she tried to wipe his nose, he reared back, nearly pitching himself from her arms. "N-o-o! No mo. Ma?" His cries set him to coughing again, a deep cough that sounded like he was coughing up his lungs. He coughed until he gagged and threw up.

If Opal had thought the snot on her shirt

bad, this even smelled sick. "Per. Ugh." She set him down in the rocking chair and patted his back. "Let me get cleaned up."

"What happened?" Ruby returned from changing the baby.

"This." Opal pointed to the mess on her shirt.

"Well, wash it off."

"I will, and then I'm going to the soddy to see how Little Squirrel is feeling." And to check on Bay and the other horses and to slide down a drift or two. Anything to get out of this house and away from a sick and screaming child.

"Good. Although Linc said she is much better."

"With all these socks I can hardly get my boots on." She slammed her heel against the wood floor. "I can't wait until spring."

"Opa! Go, pease." Per raised his arms and flipped himself over to dismount from the chair.

"No. You're sick. You have to stay inside." She knew she sounded snappy, and the look on his face made her feel like she'd kicked a puppy.

"Opal, you could be kinder than that."

I've been about as kind as I can be. "You know he's too sick to go outside in this cold."

"Of course, but . . ." Ruby picked up her son and kissed his cheek. "You stay here with Ma and Mary." The look she sent Opal conveyed her disgust.

"N-o-o. Go with Opa!" He scrunched up his face and cried the most pitiful cry, which led to more coughing and made Opal feel one inch high.

"I'll be back soon, Per." She pulled a knitted hat down over her ears and wrapped a muffler around her neck. "Takes so long to get ready that it'll be time for dinner before I get out the door." She pulled on knit mittens and then a pair of sheepskin ones with the wool inside. "I feel like a walking clothespress."

"Take this to Little Squirrel." Ruby handed her a basket with a loaf of bread, a jar of jam, butter, and cheese. She screwed down the lid on a jar of soup and tucked that in the middle. "Tell her I hope she can make it here for breakfast tomorrow but only if the weather holds."

"Linc isn't going out to stay at the line shack, is he?"

"Not until she is all better. The others will just have to make do. And Rand didn't want Mrs. Robertson left without a man around, so Mr. Chandler won't be going out either."

"Leave it to Rand." While Opal had volunteered to go man or, in her case, woman one of the line shacks, Rand had let her know in no uncertain terms that it was man's work and no woman would be out there on his behalf. If Ruby hadn't had a new baby, he most likely would have taken a turn by now too.

Opal stepped out the door and slitted her eyes against the piercing bright white. Her nose immediately began to run, and when she took in a breath of air, it felt like knives slicing inside her chest.

As she approached the soddy, Opal called, "Little Squirrel, I've come to visit."

The door creaked opened, and Little Squirrel beckoned her inside. "Come now."

"You sure look better than the last time I saw you." Opal handed her the basket and shut the door behind herself. After the brightness of the outside, the only thing she could see was the red fire in the fireplace. She blinked and let her eyes adjust. Even so, the soddy was so dim she could hardly see. "Don't you have a kerosene lamp?"

Little Squirrel nodded. "Save for night."

"Oh." Opal studied the Indian woman. She looked to be all belly hung on a post. "How are you feeling?"

"Better. How Ruby and baby?"

"Good. Per is sick, but he must be getting

better. He hollered, which made him cough, when I was leaving. He wanted to come along."

"Per always want to go."

"I know. Ruby told me to ask if you have enough food in case another blizzard hits. The way they've been coming, we can expect more."

"Enough. Meat and beans good."

"Wish I could go hunting."

"None left."

"What do you mean?" Opal let her long scarf hang free.

"Snow hard on cattle, deer. Rabbit die too."

"How do you know?"

"One time, when girl, in winter like this many die."

Opal shivered. *Please, Lord, keep everyone safe.* Here she'd been grumbling about being stuck in the house, while people might be dying. What if they had run out of wood, or food?

"Listen, bells." Little Squirrel went to the window and pulled back the skin that they'd draped there to help keep out the cold. "Charlie."

"I better go see what's been going on. Do you think you'll be to the house for supper tonight?"

Little Squirrel shook her head. "Better here." She rubbed the shelf that her rounded belly made. "Baby come soon."

"Tonight?"

"No, but soon."

"You'll send Linc for Ruby?"

Little Squirrel shrugged. "We see." She patted Opal's shoulder. "We good. No worry."

"Yeah, well, you said that before, and then you got really sick. I was so afraid you were going to die."

"Not my time. Great Spirit give strength."

Opal never knew if Little Squirrel was referring to the Great Spirit of her people or to the Holy Ghost part of the God she knew. God was God, was He not? She gave Little Squirrel a hug and headed back outside, covering her face with the muffler as she stepped into the sun. For a moment she closed her eyes and raised her face to the golden light. Even though there was no warmth to speak of, the light kissing her face reminded her of one of the promises she'd read in the family Bible the night before. *"Whosoever shall call upon the name of the Lord shall be saved."* And they had called, and He had kept them all safe.

She waved at Charlie as he knotted his

team's tie rope over the hitching rail that was nearly buried under the snow. "Hey, Charlie, you checking on everyone?"

"Sure enough. And so far so good."

She paused as another tree cracked from the cold. Between lightning in the summer and the cold this winter, there would be plenty of dead trees for firewood.

"Rand around?"

"No. He and Linc went out with supplies to the line shacks."

Ruby let Ghost out, and she ran up to Charlie, yipping her delight at a visitor. "Good morning," Ruby called. "Come on in. The coffee will be hot in a few minutes."

"Be right there."

Sound carried in the stillness, unlike anything Opal had experienced before. If she could pucker up enough to whistle without freezing her lips, she figured the Robertsons would know it was her. And their house was over a mile away with two hills in between.

She filled the woodbox before brushing the woodchips off her coat. They'd sure made a dent in the wood stacked on the porch. Perhaps she should dig out the toboggan and haul a few loads from the stacks lining the springhouse. *After Charlie leaves, I'll do that.*

"Hey there, you can come do the same at

234

our house if you like." Charlie nodded toward the woodbox. "Good thing I listened to Rand and split that extra cord. Can't believe how much wood we've gone through."

"We closed off the back of the house and lived here in the kitchen for a couple of days." Ruby set a plate of gingerbread on the table. "Would you like applesauce on that?"

"Of course."

"Our cream is frozen, so I can't offer you that."

"But you didn't lose any livestock?"

"Not here on the homeplace. Rand hasn't said anything about the range cattle, but I can tell he's worried." Ruby looked to Opal. "Would you please check on Per? He finally fell asleep after I gave him more cough medicine and rocked him."

Opal pulled her boots off at the jack by the door and padded down the hall. She could hear Per's breathing. It sounded like the leaky bellows the blacksmith used to have. Poor little guy. *Lord, please clear his throat and chest*. His cough made her own chest hurt.

She slid her feet into the fur-lined moccasins Little Squirrel had made for her in the fall. They were far warmer than her boots.

She'd rubbed enough bear grease into her boots that they were waterproof, but the smell if they warmed up was a bit hard to take.

When Per whimpered and opened his eyes, she picked him and his quilt up and carried him in to his mother, who smiled her thanks.

Least I did something right, she thought as she rubbed her hands over the heat of the kitchen stove and joined Charlie and Ruby at the table.

"If the weather holds through Sunday, we can have a service at the schoolhouse. Maybe Jacob Chandler will lead it and give the sermon."

"He's agreed to be our pastor?"

"Not sure of that, but he seems to be leaning that way. Can't say I feel bad giving up my Scripture reading."

"You've done well, and we all appreciate it."

"Who'd have thought that an old barkeep like me would be reading the Holy Word on Sunday mornings? My mother must be dancing on the heavenly clouds." He looked over to Opal and shook his head. "I remember the first time I laid eyes on the two of you there in the storeroom of Dove House. Ruby had you tucked behind her, ready to take on the world. Old Per died a happy man, knowing his two daughters were there to see him off."

"I wish I had known him for longer than a couple of hours." Opal reached for a piece of gingerbread and bit into it. "And Captain McHenry brought me a horse to ride. I thought that was the greatest thing anyone could do."

"When I think on it, Ruby, you brought the greatest change when you came and took on Dove House. Look how blessed we all are. Married now, with families and a growing town."

"Makes me wonder how Belle is. She's the only one who missed out." Opal licked her finger and picked up gingerbread crumbs with the tip, then set them on her tongue.

"Opal."

"Oh." She flinched. "Sorry." Ruby fully expected good manners at all times. Even when no one else was around.

Charlie pushed back his chair. "Well, thanks for the warm-up and the coffee. I better be gettin' on back. Left McHenry off at the Robertsons', so I'll pick him up on the way home. He said to tell you he'd be out to visit one day soon. He was planning on coming out here, but they got to talking.

He's thinking about settling south of here where that good bottom borders the river."

"Another neighbor. What is this land coming to?" Ruby widened her eyes as though she didn't really believe it. Per lay against her chest, his head tucked under her chin, eyes trying to close but for the valiant effort he made to keep them open. He seemed to be breathing more easily. At least Opal couldn't hear him wheezing from across the room.

"Greet everyone from us, and we'll sure be looking forward to church. Tell Captain McHenry . . ." She paused when Charlie cleared his throat. "Oh, that's right. *Mr.* McHenry."

"I wish I could go with you," Opal whispered as she saw him out. "I'd love to see someone else. Being cooped up in the house and listening to that wind howl is enough to drive anyone right around the bend."

"Heard tell of an old woman up north wandering out in the middle of the blizzard. Her husband said it drove her right crazy, and they haven't found any sign of her yet." Charlie shook his head. "These blizzards ain't something to joke about, that's for sure."

Opal shuddered. "I think I can understand that now." Add in a sick little boy and

238

a new baby, and the situation worsened. She'd rather be out herding cattle any day — even in the rain.

You should be grateful you got outside and saw some new faces. That little voice inside could sure be obnoxious sometimes.

That night the blizzard returned with banshee winds and cold that drove through the walls.

"We better move the beds back in here," Rand said, watching the deerskin he'd hung over the window sway in the draft. With that accomplished, they crawled in bed — Per next to Opal and Mary with her mother and father.

Opal shuddered when the house did. Surely this was worse than before. Even with Per coughing in his sleep, she finally fell asleep, thankful for the coyote pelts that warmed them. It felt as if she'd just closed her eyes when Ghost, who slept on a blanket behind the stove, barked and scrabbled her way to the door. At the dog's insistent barking, Rand rose and opened the door but heard nothing other than the wind. "Must be wolves," he muttered as he shut the door and crawled back in bed.

Opal lay straining to hear the wolves howl, but the wind drowned out everything.

Ghost returned to her blanket, and Opal could hear her turn around trying to get her bed just right. The dog had just settled down again when she flew from her bed, her barking shrill and deafening. When Rand didn't get up immediately, she ran and tugged on his covers.

"All right. What is it?" Rand opened the door just in time for Linc, with Little Squirrel in his arms, to stagger in.

"Help."

Rand caught Little Squirrel in his own arms as Linc collapsed on the floor.

Ruby hurried to light the lamp while Rand turned to lay Little Squirrel down.

"Here." Opal threw back the covers and lifted sleeping Per out of her bed, taking him over to the other one. When she turned, she covered her mouth with her hand. "Rand, there's blood."

"Roof fell in." Linc pushed himself to his feet, blood dripping from a gash on his forehead.

"Here, let me —"

"No!" He pushed her hand away. "Beam fell on us. Help. Baby."

As Rand laid Little Squirrel in the bed, her back arched, legs thrashed, and a keening cry broke from her throat.

Please, God. Please, God, matched the

pounding of Opal's heart.

"Ruby, there's more blood." Opal sank down by the side of her bed and stroked Little Squirrel's hand. "All down Rand's leg."

Ruby knelt on the other side of the bed. "Rand, put more wood in the stove. We'll need hot water and —" She stopped when Little Squirrel convulsed again, her moan guttural. A huge gush of blood puddled on the sheet, and the baby slid from her body. "Oh, dear God." Ruby laid the inert form on Little Squirrel's chest.

"Little Squirrel." Linc clutched his wife's hand and held it to his cheek, his lips moving.

She sighed and was gone.

"N-o-o!" He cupped her face in his hands, then laid his cheek against her forehead, his tears mingling with the blood from his wound and dripping on her face. "No, don't go. Please, please, don't go."

Opal watched through a veil of tears, but when the sobs shook her body, she came around the end of the bed and threw herself into Ruby's arms. Rand stood behind them, his hand on Ruby's shoulder, tears flowing. "Dear God, please help us all."

CHAPTER SEVENTEEN

The chinook wind arrived sometime between midnight and sunrise on March 5, 1887.

Jacob heard it in his sleep and woke to the music of water dripping off the icicles that hung from the roof of the line shack. He stared out the one window of the ten-by-twelve, tar paper-covered shack. Far as he was concerned, he'd gotten the best of this duty because Rand wanted a man at the Robertson place during the worst of the winter, no matter what Cora Robertson said about the matter, and Jacob was elected. Or appointed, as the case may be. He'd not been offered a choice. Until this stint. He'd finally insisted on manning a line shack, since the winter had let up some. And Linc had asked to work somewhere else.

Beans had told him about the warm chinook wind that would blow in one day, but when blizzard after blizzard came instead, Jacob had begun to think Beans was pulling his leg. Everyone said this was the worst winter they'd had since the white men came and recorded things like weather and grass-hopper swarms and range fires, all of which had happened in the months since he'd come west.

He heated up the beans and coffee from the day before and ate looking out the window until he thought of sitting outside on the stoop. The sun shone so warm he shucked his jacket and lifted his face to the heat-filled rays. Now, how could this be? One day the wind was doing its best to rip his coat off his back, and the next the sun threatened to raise a sweat. If only Opal were here to enjoy the sun with him. The thought was no surprise. No matter how hard he tried to keep his thoughts in line, they strayed to that golden-haired, steel-willed young woman whom he couldn't court until she turned sixteen, fourteen months away. He had promised to not even mention love until then. What a hard — nay, near-impossible — bargain he had agreed to. How could he stop his eyes from wooing her or trying to comfort her? Watching Little Squirrel and the baby die was more than she could bear — seeing her looking like an injured puppy about broke his heart.

The line shack and the fierce weather had been good hideouts. *But, Lord, am I running again?* It seemed so to him. Yet he'd felt God telling him to come out — out here, where he had to listen. The icicle music caught his attention.

From what Beans had said, this warmth didn't necessarily mean spring was here to stay. "Lord, we've got such capricious weather in this part of your creation. But let me tell you, the sun shining like this makes praising you far easier than the blizzards did." He'd tried to describe the wind in a letter he wrote to Mr. Dumfarthing but figured he failed miserably. He never would have believed the wind himself had he not fallen asleep to the frenzy of it more nights than he cared to count.

The pack of letters he'd written in the hours alone in the shack had grown considerably. Letters were a good antidote to the lunacy that wind and cold induced. Many times he'd been writing bundled in quilts and elk hide next to the stove, since five feet away water froze.

He thought about the letters he'd written to Opal. Would that someday he would be able to give them to her, for they described the state of his heart far better than his stuttering spoken words would. Why was it that he could preach in front of a congregation, but the thought of explaining his feelings to a certain young woman turned him into a mass of quivering jelly? His words of comfort had sounded preachy even to him. He'd written a letter to Joel, telling him all of his story to be read someday when he'd be old enough to understand. Jacob knew his family would be glad to receive the letters he wrote them.

He tossed the dregs of coffee grounds from his cup into the snowbank and returned to the dim interior of the shack. Best get to riding the line, although he'd not seen sign of any live cattle for days.

At midmorning he saw another rider coming toward him, recognizing it was Chaps by the high-peaked hat he wore. It reminded Jacob of a mountain he'd seen in a picture once, one steep peak with a rounded shoulder. As he drew closer, they both waved.

"Ya better get on back before the crust thaws and the horses sink in to their bellies," Chaps called across the glistening snow. "Cattle won't be movin' much either. If there are any left."

"So what do we do?"

"Make early morning trips while the snow is still froze from the night."

"I see."

"We'll most likely get another storm or

two. Rand usually pulls us in when the chinook comes, but this has been one strange winter." Chaps reined his horse around. "See ya."

Jacob waved and did the same. He was near the shack when the snow crust gave way and his horse lurched forward. The gelding reared back on his haunches and fought the entrapping snow and ice. Dismounting, Jacob tried to lead the horse forward. After a few leaps and bucks the animal stood belly deep, his sides heaving.

"Lord God, what do I do?" Jacob walked around the horse, catching his own breath and letting the animal rest. He measured the distance from the horse to the shed. A hundred yards, perhaps. He knelt down and pulled the strap to the cinch loose, but the snow under the horse's belly held the cinch in place so he couldn't pull the saddle off. Picking up the reins, he walked ahead of the horse and helped pull him out. One foot at a time, move a horse length, and rest. When they hit a patch where the snow was only a couple feet deep, the horse walked on out and into the shed. Jacob threw him some of the fast-dwindling stock of hay and hauled the saddle into the shack.

"Thank you, Lord, we got that close before the problem. Sure hope Chaps got back without this happening to him." He'd gotten so used to talking aloud, just to hear a voice, that he laughed when he hauled in more wood and dug in the banked stove for some live coals. Taking his knife, he shaved curls of wood off a pitchy piece he kept for this purpose and within moments was blowing on the smoking coals until an orange flame burst into sight. The steady drip of snow melting off the roof kept his thoughts company. *Please, Lord, comfort Linc.* Jacob thought back to the wedding just before Christmas. Little Squirrel had come so close to dying then.

That night he ran out of kerosene for his lamp, so using light from the stove, he set about getting ready for bed. For a change his breath didn't show as fog right near the stove, as it had for the last weeks.

Within two days bare dirt showed in the places where the wind had blown some of the snow away before the chinook. Watching spring come in with warm winds, gentle songs, and flying birds that dripped pearls of sound encouraged him to leave his jacket behind as he took out the ax to split more wood. What he didn't use could be kept for next year. Before long his arm and shoulder muscles screamed at the effort of lifting the heavy ax again and yet again, so he switched to hauling and stacking. When he fell into bed that night, he thanked his Father for the blisters on his hands despite his leather gloves, the pull of tight muscles, and the joy of breathing air that didn't sear his lungs. And a few hours without trying to figure out God's purposes and plans. Sometimes the only answer was, "I will praise the Lord."

A horse and rider coming across the melting snow caught his attention the next day.

"Git packed up," Beans ordered as he drew near. "Time to go on home."

"None too soon. I've run out of butts to split. The coffee's hot."

"Good." Beans stepped to the ground. "I brought you some cookies, compliments of Mrs. Harrison. She said she thought you line guys might be hankerin' for something sweet."

"Anything besides beans will be a treat."

"Usually we trap rabbits or bring down some grouse when we're out here, but I ain't seen hide nor hair of game of any kind."

"What about the cattle?"

Beans shook his head. "Worse'n bad. Carcasses stacked in the draws like cordwood. Some carcasses up in the cotton-wood trees even. They was eatin' the tops and got trapped. Never seen the like in all my born days. The wolves and coyotes are so fat, they can hardly waddle." He poured himself a cup of coffee and watched as Jacob gathered his things, rolling his clothes in the bedroll and stuffing his papers and books into his saddlebags.

"Leave what food's left in the tins so the mice don't get it." Beans took a cookie from the bag, and it disappeared in two bites. "That woman sure can cook." He took another cookie. "Let's get outta here."

"What about Chaps?"

"I stopped there first."

Jacob threw his saddlebags over his shoulder and tucked his bedroll under his arm. Stopping in the middle of the room, he turned in a circle, studying to make sure everything was back in place and he was leaving nothing behind. He rattled the grate one more time to shake the coals loose. He should take out the ashes.

"Come on. I want to be back in time for dinner."

"Coming." Jacob shut the door behind him, making sure it was snug. Then he dropped the hook into the bent nail to latch the door and headed for the shed.

"Pa!" Joel leaped from the porch of the Robertson house and came charging across the mud to reach him.

"Hello to you too." Jacob leaned down, grasped his son's outstretched hands, and swung the boy up behind him.

"So how you been?"

"Good. School started again. Mister Finch said he isn't coming back in the fall."

"Really?" At the soddy they dismounted, and Jacob flipped the reins over the hitching rail.

"Said he ain't never seen such a winter, and he don't never want to see one again."

"Ain't? Did he really say he *ain't* never seen such a winter?"

Joel thought for a moment, then shook his head. A grin tickled his cheekbones. "Prob'ly not." He took the bedroll after Jacob untied the latigos, holding it behind the saddle.

How's Opal? Jacob wanted desperately to ask the question. "Careful, don't drop all the stuff I have in there." He untied his saddlebags and his scabbard. Not that he'd needed it or the rifle in it. There was nothing out on the range to shoot. They pushed open the wooden door, and the odor of packed dirt greeted them. Jacob had forgotten the smell after living out on the open prairie like he had the last weeks. He set a chair in front of the door to keep it open and let the room air out. The woodbox yawned empty, and the hay-filled ticks on the wooden beds needed plumping.

"Mrs. Robertson said to tell you to come on up to the house for dinner. She has plenty of leftovers. We ate about an hour ago."

"How about you put my horse away, and I'll get a fire started. When the sun goes down, it can turn mighty cold."

"Sure. I'll bring my bedroll down after supper. You going back up on the line?"

"No. Beans says we're done for this year. What has gone on while I've been up there?"

"Well, school, chores . . . Ada Mae brought home a lamb, a bummer someone gave her. We keep it in the house 'cause it's too little to go in the barn yet. We're feeding it with a bottle."

"You mean the sheep are already having their lambs during this cold and miserable weather?"

"I guess so. I don't know anything about sheep, but we have one."

Jacob lifted the lids off the stove and set them to the side. The ashes needed to be hauled out. "You take care of the horse and come on back. We need the woodbox filled and a bucket of water brought in."

Joel flipped the reins around the horse's neck and mounted with a bit of difficulty since his legs weren't anywhere near as long as his father's. He turned the horse away and trotted off to the barn.

Jacob watched his son handle a horse as if he'd been doing so all his life instead of less than a year. He'd stretched not only in height since they arrived but in experience. The only one he knew who worked harder on learning and perfecting ranching skills was Opal, and she'd done her best to teach them and the Robertson girls how to ride, rope, and round up cattle since Ward Robertson died in the shootout. *Opal, when will I see you?*

Loading his arm with cut wood, Jacob returned to the soddy, blinking in the dimness. He dumped the wood in the box and picked out a piece with plenty of oozed pitch. Using a bit of dried pine needles for fire starter, he shaved off slivers to lay over the broken needles, and then picking the flint and a granite rock from the shelf, he held the two pieces together right near the starter and struck to get a spark. The third one continued to glow, and a minute spiral of smoke rose. Blowing gently, he encouraged the spark to spread and smiled when a flame licked the pitch and burst into flame. Bit by bit he added larger pieces, and once the fire was consuming them all, he set the lids back in place and adjusted the damper to full open. It would take some doing to get this small house warm.

At least he had kerosene for the lamp again, even if the chimney did need washing. Ah, the things one took for granted.

"Welcome home, Mr. Chandler." Cora Robertson looked up from the batter she was beating in a large crockery bowl. Dough dots marred the white apron that covered her from neck to foot, and when she brushed back a lock of hair falling from the knot she always wore on the back of her head, flour dusted her cheek.

"Thank you." Jacob inhaled. "I don't know how you do it, but this house always smells of good food and a warm welcome."

"See my lamb?" Ada Mae held up the wooly creature with pipe-stem legs, black face, and a long tail.

"I sure do. I thought sheep had short tails."

"We have to dock it, but I can't bear to do

that." Ada Mae cuddled the creature under her chin.

"Cut it off?"

"Yes, and the sooner the better." Mrs. Robertson pulled a full plate out of the oven. "Before it gets a lot of feeling in the tail. Take your place there. Ada Mae, put that lamb down and get Mr. Chandler some bread and butter. Coffee will be ready in a minute."

Jacob sat down as instructed and admired the plate put before him. "Sure beats beans."

"Had you run out of food?"

"Nope, still had beans, flour, lard, and cornmeal." He picked up the piece of bread Ada Mae set in front of him and smiled as he sniffed that too. "I did learn how not to burn cornmeal cakes in the frying pan."

"Uff da. I'm sorry about that. Should have tried harder to get more supplies up there."

"What? And lose someone's life in the process? No. I managed, and I know Chaps did too. But I tell you, this was the most unusual winter I ever spent." *And the worst.*

"You can say that again, for all of us."

"Where are Emily and Virginia?"

"They stopped by the Heglands. Pearl is teaching them to play the piano."

"I didn't want to learn. I'd rather play the guitar like Rand." Ada Mae turned to Joel. "You done your homework yet?"

He shook his head. "I hate memorizing poems."

"Me too."

"So get on it and get it done." Cora rolled her eyes. "You'd think they had to learn the complete works of Shakespeare."

"You could always memorize Bible verses. The psalms are ancient Hebrew poems," Jacob commented.

"Ma made us do that during the blizzards." Ada Mae brought a book out and laid it on the table.

"Not there. You'll get flour on it."

"Sorry." Ada Mae sat down and opened the book at the marker. "Do you want to do 'The Song of Hiawatha' or 'Paul Revere's Ride'?"

Joel heaved a sigh. "I'd rather rope a steer any day."

"Too bad. Begin."

Jacob watched his son close his eyes, scrunch up his face, and swallow hard. "Surely it can't be that bad." He fought to keep a straight face. "Come on. . . . 'Listen my children and you shall hear / Of the midnight ride of Paul Revere, / On the eighteenth of April, in seventy-five; / Hardly a man is now alive / Who remembers that famous day and year . . .' "

The three of them chanted their way through that famous ride. " 'One if by land, and two if by sea . . .' " When one stumbled, the others kept going, and they finished with a flourish.

Joel looked to his father, admiration shining in his eyes. "You knew the whole thing."

"I learned it long, long ago. Things like that stay with you." Jacob finished off his plate. "Thank you, Mrs. Robertson. I cannot begin to tell you how much I appreciate your good cooking."

"Can I get you anything else?"

"Not if I want to do justice to supper." He turned to Joel and Ada Mae. "I'll go on down to the barn and feed so you two can get through 'Hiawatha' too. Be ready to recite when I get back."

Jacob shrugged into his coat again. "Do I need to milk the cow too?"

"No," Cora said, "she dried up during the blizzards. We are rationing the hay so the cow doesn't lose her calf. It's thanks to Mr. McHenry that we have any at all. He brought out a load on the train for his horse." Her eyes darkened. "So much loss around here."

"I know." Jacob pulled on his gloves. "Joel, you need to bring in water."

Joel nodded. "Right now?"

"After 'Hiawatha.' "

Both Joel and Ada Mae groaned, setting Cora to laughing.

What was Opal doing now? Strange how being closer to the Harrison ranch brought her to mind so much more often. As if he hadn't been thinking about her half the time anyway.

But most important, was there a way he could help her in her sorrow?

It might be easier when the ground thawed enough so they could dig the graves and have the funerals.

CHAPTER EIGHTEEN

"I don't want to go."

"Neither do I, but for Linc's sake, we need to do this." Ruby sighed. "I'm sorry, Opal, this is a terrible time for all of us."

Opal tried to fight the tears, but as usual, her efforts failed. She didn't bother mopping the stream running down her face. "How can this help him?"

"You ask such hard questions. But something about a funeral helps with the grieving. All of us together calling on our heavenly Father to bring us and Linc comfort. This is the final act one can do for someone they love."

"Some of the Indian tribes burn their dead or put them up in trees."

"But Linc asked for a funeral."

"Do you believe Little Squirrel believed in Jesus?" Opal sniffed and finally wiped her eyes.

"Yes."

"So she's in heaven now?"

"I believe so."

"And the baby."

"Oh yes. God makes special provisions for babies." Ruby glanced down at her infant daughter nursing under the blanket. She looked up to Opal. "I know you don't understand, and I have to tell you, I don't either. All this death around us doesn't make any sense, but I believe that God makes sense and He has not left us. He loves us and is right here, crying with us."

Opal snorted. "But He could have fixed it. All He needed to do was make the blizzards stop."

"I know." Ruby held Mary to her shoulder and patted her back. "But some things we have to take on faith, no matter how hard that faith is to come by." She sighed. "This is one of those times."

"I don't think he'll stay here — Linc, I mean." *Not God. Do I believe you are still here? Yes, and I know you are listening. But . . .* Sometimes she wished He couldn't read her thoughts. Like now, when she wanted to scream at Him and say bad things. And climb up in His lap and be held close no matter how mad she was.

"It's too much."

The men had built a fire to melt the ground enough to dig the grave. Even so, they still had to use pickaxes to break

259

through the frozen ground. Rand and Linc had built the box that now sat beside the hole.

Jacob stood at the head of the grave, his Bible open, looking as sad as the rest of them. When silence fell, he raised his voice. "Dear friends, family, for we are all God's family, let us pray. Father in heaven, look down on us with compassion, for times are hard, and this is the hardest. We give thee Little Squirrel and her baby, and we thank thee for the time she was with us here on earth. We thank thee for keeping her safe. Thou sayest that our days are numbered, but thou knowest even the numbers of the hairs on our heads. We matter to thee — thou hast called us by name. Bring comfort to Linc and be thou his staff and his guide. Amen."

He looked out to them all. "The Bible says there is a time for everything under heaven. A time to be born and a time to die, a time to weep and a time to sing. It also says that weeping tarries for the night, but joy cometh with the morning." He bent down and picked up some of the earth. "Ashes to ashes, dust to dust. Little Squirrel and your child, we commit you to the earth from which you will be raised again on that last day.

"Join me in the prayer our Lord taught us. Our Father . . ."

The mourners joined in, some voices wavering, some with tears, but all growing stronger as they prayed together. Four men lowered the box into the hole, and Linc tossed in a handful of dirt.

"You are all welcome to come to our house for dinner." Pearl nodded to those gathered. Jeremiah McHenry drew his harmonica from his pocket and played the opening bars of "Amazing Grace." The notes rose clear like an offering to heaven, and the mourners' voices joined in.

As they walked away, Opal wanted to plug her ears against the thuds of dirt on the lid of that box.

Jacob walked beside her, stopping only when someone thanked him for such a good service.

Opal slowed down. She wasn't waiting for him, not really, but somehow she felt better when he was there, as though he took part of the load away that was trying to drive her right into the ground.

The next morning Linc and his bedroll were gone from the bunkhouse. No one had heard him leave. On a piece of wood, he'd written in charcoal, *Thank You.*

★ ★ ★

Two days later the nightmare woke her again, but this time since the sky was lightening toward day, Opal dressed and headed down to the corral. According to the verse Mr. Chandler read about time, mourning should be over and a new day of joy rising. If that was so, why was it so hard for her to pick up her feet? *Put this behind you and think of something else.* No matter how many times she told herself that, it wasn't getting any easier. Out in the pasture she whistled for Bay, and when the old mare nuzzled her shoulder, Opal swung aboard and rode her to the barn. *Think on something else.*

"Is Atticus still in Oregon or on his way back to Ohio, old girl?"

Bay's ears swiveled to listen. When Opal dismounted inside the barn, the horse shook all over.

"No idea, huh? You'd think he could let me know how he's doing." Opal used the currycomb on Bay's mane and tail. Talking to the horse made more sense than talking to herself. She got about the same number of answers.

You know he can't write very well.

"Whose side are you on?" Now she was arguing with herself. He could ask someone to write for him. Even she snorted at the absurdity of Atticus asking for help. That would be about as likely as Rand moving to New York.

New York. The Brandons. Would they come to visit this summer? They'd said they would if it could be worked out. Wouldn't it be wonderful if Mr. Roosevelt was in the area at the same time and Bernie Brandon could meet him or go hunting with him? Her thoughts took off on all kinds of possibilities.

Bay flicked her ears and turned to look over her shoulder.

Opal stopped with the currycomb and rubbed the old mare's ears and down her neck. "You are so thin, girl. A walking rack of bones." Even though she'd snuck some of the chickens' grain for her horse, there was no hay left — not even any of what McHenry had brought them. Would the grass come back soon enough to keep the rest of the stock from starving to death?

She leaned against the horse. "What else can I feed you?"

Rand and the men had been cutting cottonwood trees and dragging them closer to the barn for the cattle that had hung around the homeplace instead of dying out on the plains. With the snow melting so swiftly, the carnage left by the blizzards became more obvious every day. Dead animals stacked in the draws, scattered across the land, food for the scavengers and death to the ranchers. Rand had returned from town where he'd talked with some of the other ranchers, the look in his eyes so close to defeat that even Ruby had nothing to say. She just hugged him.

He had yet to talk about what he'd learned, at least to Opal. Every time the men came in from range riding, they just shook their heads.

For the first time in her life, Opal did not want to go riding. Grateful that Bay had made it through the winter, she went back to brushing the long rough coat.

That night around the supper table, she asked, "Can't you go on the train and buy grain or hay somewhere else and bring it back?" She knew the answer before she asked the question. Where would they get the money to do such a venture? They'd need everything they had to make it through till fall. Maybe she and Ruby could sell the jewels their pa had left them.

She tuned back into the conversation. "No fall roundup?"

"Not for sure yet, but if the steers recover, they'd have to gain twice as much as usual.

The cattle brought in from Texas and points east fared the worst. I'm hearing eighty and ninety percent loss."

She was afraid to ask but did. "Was ours that bad?"

"No, because we sold that lot of steers in the fall. Thank God for leading us to do that. I shipped some that I would have kept over another year. They were a bit small, but they're not coyote food out on the prairie. I have no idea how many we have left, other than that fifty head or so around here. And some of the brands aren't ours."

"No one's seen the horse herds either." Chaps took another swig of coffee. "They should be moseying back north sometime soon." His unspoken "if they come" lay there as loud as if he'd shouted it. Every fall the ranchers let most of their remudas loose to fend for themselves over the winter, keeping only enough horses to pull the sleighs, provide rides to town, and to round up the wild bunch. The horses banded together and drifted in search of feed, pawing down to the dried grass under the snow. But this year the range had been overgrazed and, with the drought, winter feed was scarce to none.

"Going to be a lot of dead trees this summer, the way the animals stripped off all the bark." Beans tipped back his chair. "We ain't seen the worst of this yet."

Opal pushed back her chair and headed for her room. She couldn't let them see her cry again. All she'd done lately was cry. *Why, God? Why all this destruction? All the cattle dying. Little Squirrel and the baby. You could have changed the weather. You calmed the wind for the disciples.*

Don't think about it.

She threw herself on the coyote pelt quilt, the deep fur against her cheek. *Why not calm the wind and lessen the cold here?*

Perhaps they should head west like Atticus. She cried until the tears dried, blew her nose, and then meandered back to the table. The men had gone to the bunkhouse, and Rand sat in his rocking chair near the lamp with his Bible on his lap.

Opal sat on the stool at his feet. "Will we make it?"

"Are you asking if we'll be leaving like so many of the others?"

"Guess I am."

He shook his head. "No. We'll stay. The grass will come back, the cows will have calves again; our bull might be one of my better investments. We may not have any money coming in to speak of, but we will have food on the table and a roof over our heads. I imagine this will be the end of the abattoir, so we'll go back to shipping cattle to Chicago on the train. Shame de Mores is going to lose it all. He had good ideas."

"And the horses?"

"We'll have to wait and see." He shook his head slightly. "I'm afraid there won't be many to train and fewer to buy."

"I figured that."

"I don't want you out riding the range."

Opal stared down at her boots. While the mud was drying somewhat, she still managed to find some to slop in. When she looked up at Rand, he shook his head. A sigh escaped the clamp her teeth had on her lip.

"Besides, Bay isn't strong enough."

"I could ride one of the team."

Again Rand shook his head. "Opal, you don't need to see the carnage. I heard you crying in the night."

She made a face and stared off to the pines on the ridge south of the house. She'd awakened to the sound of sobbing and then realized it was her sobs. The clouds that stood on her shoulders pressed her into the ground, wore black linings with no touch of light or silver, ever since she'd started toward Pearl's and seen the heap of decaying cattle carcasses that half filled the draw, their long horns locked among the tree branches, their bloated bodies with the hides sloughing way. The smell made her gag, and the sight of buzzards ripping at the bodies was branded on her inner eyes. Instead of going on, she'd turned and come home, still white and green from throwing up when the wind wrapped the smell around her and wouldn't let loose.

"I'm not doing my share, and with Linc gone . . ."

"What do you think we're doing?" Rand frowned.

She half shrugged.

"In the last two days we've pulled three live animals out of the mud, rounded up ten more that might not make it. Thanks be to God that the grass is growing, but it can't come up fast enough. We've stripped the trees of branches, the sagebrush is grazed down to the ground, and . . ." He spun around at the thunderclap that rocked their ears. A roar like ten freight trains bearing down on them made him mount up and ride back around the barn. The river ice was breaking up.

"Get back to the house!"

She could barely hear his shout over the roaring and grinding. She raced up the slight rise and, once beyond the barn, looked back to see the iced-over river bucking and surging with huge chunks of ice piling, then tilting and disappearing under the surge. Dead cattle floated on the ice, spun in the frothing water, flipped up, and went under. Water covered the ice along the shore and flowed out onto the bottom land, splintering trees, always with the roar, be it of agony or a cry for freedom from winter's solid lock.

Rand nudged his horse to a gallop to herd the cattle in the bottom away from the flooding water.

Opal stood watching, unaware of the tears pouring down her cheeks. All that death now choking the river that usually brought life. Most years the spring breakup was a celebration, but this year's was an ear-pounding dirge. She turned at the hand on her shoulder. Ruby stood just behind her, Per on her hip and leaning against her shoulder.

Together, tears streaming down their cheeks, arms around each other's waists, the sisters held each other up.

" 'The Lord gave, and the Lord hath taken away: blessed be the name of the Lord.' " Ruby muttered the verse over and over until Opal wanted to clap her hands over her ears and scream at her to stop.

"If He loves us so much, why does He keep taking away?" The cry wrenched from her heart, leaving a gaping hole.

"No matter what, He is right here with us. He promised, and our Lord God never breaks a promise." Ruby rocked her son, who had started to whimper, a small cry turning into the cough that had never left him. " 'Yea, though I walk through the valley of the shadow of death, thou art with me. . . .' "

The valley of death. The ridges of death and a prairie that stank of death to high heaven. Opal reached over to take Per. "I'll get his medicine." What she really wanted to do was start running and not stop until there was clean air, clean grass with cattle grazing, and clean rivers flowing with spring runoff, not winter death and coughing children with runny noses.

Maybe Atticus chose the wiser move by heading west. Surely a place where the winters weren't so terrible was better than here in the Little Missouri River Valley. Whatever had she seen in the badlands anyway?

CHAPTER NINETEEN

April

Hanging the wash out on the clotheslines made her feel that winter was indeed past.

"Amethyst?"

She turned at Pearl's call. "Out here."

"Is Carly with you?"

"No." Amethyst dropped the clothespins back in the basket and turned toward the house. "She was playing with her baby on the back porch." Where could the little girl have gone? Out to her father's workshop. She picked up her skirts and ran toward the shop.

"Here she is," Carl called from the door of his shop. "She can play in here for now."

Ah, such welcome words. Amethyst patted her heart back into its normal pace and returned to finish hanging up the diapers. The sheets were most likely dry now with this warm wind blowing. If March came in like a lion, which it had, it certainly went out like a lamb, leaving room for burgeoning April.

You haven't written to your father. That inner voice could be a nag at any time, but on a day like this, it seemed particularly offensive.

I wrote once.

I know, but that's not enough.

I don't know what to say.

Just say what is true.

What? That I'm never going back there? That I am happy here, working for someone else, which he always said was a fate worse than death. She stopped shaking out the diapers, twisted to get most of the water out, and took a moment to look around. The bluffs across the river and to the north glowed red and rust with a line of gray, as if a giant painter were trying out new colors. The tops of the cottonwoods along the river sported apple green fuzz, and the willows waved wands of yellow green that glistened in the sun. Puff clouds, white as the flapping diapers, set off a blue so dense that only God could dream up the color.

Carl had identified the birdsong that made her smile as a meadowlark. A pair of them dueled back and forth, each trying to out-concert the other. Darting swallows attached daubs of mud to the eaves of the barn, building their houses new every year. Sparrows flitted in the brush that backed the barn going up the hill, and two jays fought over a hole in a dead tree.

When spring came to the badlands, it didn't wait around on polite but rolled in on laughter and singing.

Amethyst checked on the sheets — dry, as she'd surmised, and smelling of new life and clean. As she took them down and folded them, she watched huge Vs of ducks quack their way overhead, heading north to their nesting grounds. The haunting songs of the geese took her heart with them. Where did they go so high and free in the blue expanse of sky that went on forever? The hills and forests of Pennsylvania didn't begin to prepare one for the Dakotah sky that arched in a celestial bowl overhead.

Amethyst folded the last of the sheets, her mind going back to a time she and her brother Patrick lay in the spring green grass and watched the clouds sailing on invisible courses overhead, shaping and reshaping into figures of fairy-tale proportions. They'd tried to outdo each other in the stories they created until Pa came looking for them, chivying them back to endless work.

Carrying the basket under her arm and on her hip, she returned to the tubs simmering over fires in the yard. Washing all the bedding, the curtains, towels, and winter long johns worked better outside. She stirred the caldron of work clothes bubbling in the soapy water and added another bucket of fresh water to the rinse.

Carl had built a bench to hold the tub with the scrub board where Pearl labored, rubbing her husband's work pants up and down on the rippled board, soaping the stains and rubbing some more. She wiped a lock of hair from her forehead with the back of her hand and went back to the scrubbing.

"Why don't you let me do that?" Amethyst set her basket down and dipped shirts out of the rinse water into another tub on the bench where she could wring them out. She and Pearl worked together on wringing out the sheets and heavy things, each taking an end of the garment or sheet and turning in the opposite direction.

"I will. At least we're not hanging things on bushes like years ago. Or pounding the clothes on rocks at the river."

"You didn't really wash that way?" Amethyst stared at her friend.

"Not I, but those before me did. They had a scrubbing board at Dove House, and Daisy did most of the washing. Cimarron was and still is a beautiful seamstress, and keeping white tablecloths on the dining room tables kept Daisy at the ironing board a good part of the time. We held school in one room and used the dining room on Sunday mornings for worship. Then afterward everyone stayed for hot rolls and coffee. Ruby did her best to provide comfort and culture in a hamlet — not big enough to be called a village as far as I was concerned — that really didn't want or appreciate her efforts. Little Missouri had a sordid reputation, still has for that matter. Marquis de Mores started Medora, named after his wife, and wouldn't allow drinking and gambling into town."

"Life here must have been a shock for you after living in Chicago." Amethyst poured the water from her wringing back in the rinse tub steaming over the fire and added more wood to both fires. Then she used a sturdy stick to stir the clothes in the soapy water. She walked over to the bench and nudged Pearl to the side. "My turn. You rinse and wring."

"It was a shock but refreshing too. And after I met Carl — I can tell you, my father had no good things to say about that."

"But you married him anyway." Soap, shove, and rub. The rhythm was easy, but the lye soap ate at the skin on one's hands.

"I've never once regretted it." Pearl gave the shirt she was wringing out an extra twist.

"Carl knew how to laugh, and he loved books and music." She paused for a moment, staring into space. "I am so blessed." A smile curved her cheeks. "Perhaps there's a fine man for you here, just like there was for me."

Amethyst ignored the last comment. "What about your father?"

"Oh, he came out here to get me, but I was in love with Carl by then and had no intentions of returning to Chicago. Carl and Rand stood up to him, wouldn't let him take me back."

"My land, but you were a brave one." Amethyst could feel a trickle of perspiration down her back. Scrubbing dirty winter clothes on a scrub board was about as warming as chopping wood. She'd done her share of both.

"What about you? You traveled farther than I did, with only a glimmer of where you were going and no guarantee your nephew would be here — in the middle of the worst winter ever." Pearl dropped the last of the washed things into the rinse water, then added more men's pants to the wash water and pushed them all under with the stirring stick. She studied the brew for a moment before carving more soap into the pot.

"My father said I had to do it — had to

come for Joel. And it was all for nothing."
She lifted her face to the sun and caught a
view of the buttes across the river. "Well, as
far as Pa's concerned, that is." She puffed
out her cheeks on a sigh. *I have to write to
him again.* Guilt was as bad a burden as icy
snow. Both left you feeling weighted down
and wanting to give up.

"He's not written to you?"

"No. I'm sure he's waiting to hear me say
I'm on my way back to the farm, groveling
and pleading for his permission to live there
again." She shook her head. Just the
thought gave her the shivers.

She'd given up that day in the blizzard,
and God had sent an angel to rescue her.
He'd sent His Son to rescue her from guilt.
She understood that much from her years of
sitting in church on Sunday mornings.
Albeit she understood more about hell and
the dangers thereof than of heaven and a
God who loved her. But who else had sent
the angel to save her if not He?

Two meadowlarks dipped and trilled
overhead. Other birds sang from the
thicket. Every day she heard new birdsongs.
Water ran off the hill and joined that from
the spring, gurgling and dancing to the river
that still raged but now without ice floes.
Carcasses of cattle could be seen floating,

along with trees and brush. Overhead, ducks and geese heading northward all sang wild songs of their own.

"This is my favorite season, when winter is banished with its howling wind and spring returns with songs from brush and sky and land. The peeper frogs that sing in the evening always make me know that spring is here." Pearl handed Amethyst the legs of a man's pants, and they began twisting again.

"I better go check on the bread," Amethyst said when the pants were dry as possible. "Can I bring you anything?"

"A glass of buttermilk would be a fine treat."

"That it would if we had any. When is the cow due to calve?"

"Mid-April, so it won't be long." Pearl looked around to check on her daughter. "Cookies would be good."

Amethyst headed for the back door. She'd set the bread to rising between starting the fires for the wash water and cooking breakfast.

She punched the dough back down and set it to rise again in a patch of sunshine with a cloth over the bowl, checked on the beans baking in the oven, and looked in the cookie jar to find only three cookies left. Another job needing doing. At breakfast Pearl and

Carl had discussed digging up the garden. The men had pulled the straw and manure banking away from the house and scattered it on top of the snow that had still covered the garden spot, and now it needed to be dug in and the peas and potatoes planted. Pearl had started some seeds in the house to get a head start on the garden.

With the cookies in a napkin, she returned to the outside, giving Carl one, then Carly, and the last to Pearl.

"Are we out?"

"Yes. I should have baked last night."

"There is no law that says the cookie jar must always be full." Pearl broke her cookie in half and insisted Amethyst take a share.

"The bread won't be ready for dinner, so perhaps I should make biscuits."

"Or corn bread. Once the ground dries out enough so we can take the wagon out, we'll go get staples at the store in town." With the melting of the snow, Carl had taken the runners off the wagon and set the wheels back on, but as the frost melted out of the ground, the prairie turned into a quagmire that trapped wagon wheels and sometimes the horses.

"Ma?" Carly joined them. "Baby crying."

"I know. I heard him. Thank you." Pearl had set Joseph in a basket in the shade of the shop, and he had been sleeping peacefully. "You didn't wake him, did you?"

The little girl shook her head. "Hungry."

"You had a cookie."

"More?"

"Sorry, all gone."

Pearl glanced up to check the sun's position. "Dinner will be soon."

The warm wind tossed the clothes on the lines and tugged at skirts and aprons. In spite of hairpins and her remaining comb, Amethyst had to stop often to repin the hair that insisted on partying with the wind. *Tomorrow I'm going to braid it,* she promised herself. *This is silly.* Back home she had frequently worn a triangle of cloth over it, but the feel of the sun and the wind was like a tonic after being housebound for so long.

"Comp'ny," Carly sang out.

Pearl shaded her eyes with her hand, the better to see the rider heading their way. "Oh no." Her groan made Amethyst look up. The man wearing a cape of skins looked vaguely familiar, seeming to dwarf the pony he rode.

"Why the groan?"

"Jake Maunders. You can always recognize him by his smell. That and the hides he wears."

Since he was downwind of them, his odor

didn't precede him, but Amethyst recognized him as he drew closer. "He came into the station when I was trying to decide what to do. The stationmaster said had it been anyone else, he'd have asked him to bring me here."

"Wise man. Jake is one of the best guides for hunting and fishing, but his morals leave something to be desired. I wouldn't trust him any farther than I could throw him and his horse."

The man stopped his horse and crossed his arms on the saddle horn. "Fine day, ain't it, ladies?"

"What do you want, Mr. Maunders?" Pearl continued dipping clothes from the boiling water.

"Just tryin' to be neighborly." He nodded to Amethyst. "And greet our newcomer here." He paused as if waiting to be introduced. He tipped his felt hat, a feather in the band. "Howdy, miss. Jake Maunders is my name."

"Don't say anything," Pearl muttered under her breath.

"You in need of fresh meat? I got here a string of grouse."

"Thank you, but we have sufficient."

"No charge. Call it my welcome gift." He rode closer and held out the birds, their feet tied together with a leather string.

Pearl sighed and shook her head. "Thank you." She took the birds and stepped back. "We'll enjoy these."

He tipped his hat again. "I'll be seein' you."

Amethyst caught a whiff of rank skins, stale booze, and unwashed human. It reminded her of her father. A shudder started inside her, and she breathed through her mouth. As if she would ever be interested in a man like him.

CHAPTER TWENTY

"Now that the winter's broken, we — I mean the folks around here — would be pleased if you would lead the service on Sunday." Charlie looked up from the hat brim he'd been mangling.

I've done two funerals and a wedding, so I guess the secret that I'm a pastor is pretty much out of the bag. It would be churlish to refuse his request. *But how can I lead the service when . . . how can I not?* Jacob did his best to keep his face neutral. *Lord God, is this from you, or am I running ahead again or behind?*

In order to serve here, would he have to tell them everything? True, he'd told Rand about his less than perfect past, but that was some different than confessing to an entire group of people.

But I've been forgiven! So why do I feel like a pile left by one of the cows? He thought to the Scripture he'd read after another night of nightmare attacks. If he'd had more self-control, if he'd loved enough to wait, if he'd not run. *You know better than* *to be assailed and defeated by **ifs**.* He tried to talk sternly to himself, but he could chalk up another in the failure column. *The verse. Hang on to the verse. "There is therefore now no condemnation to them which are in Christ Jesus."* He repeated it to himself again. If there is no condemnation to those in Christ, why did he feel so condemned? Some days he rose above it, and others, like now . . .

He sighed. "I don't have time to prepare a sermon." What a flimsy excuse. "But I could use one written from before . . . I mean, from a long time ago."

"Jacob, we are so hungry for the Word of God to be taught and preached . . ." Charlie paused. "You know I been leading the services. We sort of take turns reading the Scripture and singing and praying, but other than reading aloud, I got nothin' to offer. We need a pastor here, especially now when everyone is so dunked in despair after this winter."

Including me. I need to write to Melody's folks. . . . All the letters I wrote up at the line shack, I didn't include one to them. They deserve to know that Joel is doing great out here. And about the aunt who came to get him.

"Look, Charlie, I'll lead this service, and

then we need to call a meeting to officially form a congregation and see if everyone would like me to become their pastor."

"We got no money to pay you."

"Did I say anything about pay?" *I owe some people here such a debt, I'll never get it paid off.*

"No, but thought I should make that clear." Charlie nodded. "All right, I'll head on out and let everyone know. Church at ten . . ." He paused again and looked Jacob in the eye. "If that's all right with you."

"Whatever you've done in the past is all right with me."

"Good. Ten it is. After church everyone will most likely be invited to Heglands' — they've got the biggest house — for coffee and dinner. Everybody brings what they have and we share. Then if you felt like giving a lesson, we'd most appreciate it. Something encouraging would be real good."

He'd said that word again. If people were really feeling down because of the horrible winter, they seemed to have handled it fairly well. *Or, like you, they wear good masks when out in public.*

I'll get to see Opal. The thought flashed across his mind like a meteor in the night sky. His heart picked up and then thumped again. *Lord, give me strength to stay away from her.*

"I'll make sure the fire is started to warm the place up some. Usually the singers get together before the service and practice a bit, so we have some special music."

"I see."

"Miz Hegland plays the piano. It's thanks to her pa that we have a piano at the schoolhouse. Rand plays the guitar, Opal has the voice of an angel, and Daisy and Cimarron do harmony. The whole group sings real fine."

"I'm glad to hear that." His mind, which refused to be controlled today, thought back to his church in Pennsylvania, a congregation some fifty years old. How different his life had been there compared to here in the badlands. His biggest problem had been staying ahead of the matchmaking mammas. Talk about life changing in an instant.

"Well, I better get on my high horse. Thanks, Jacob . . . er, Pastor Chandler." Charlie stuck out his hand.

"Just Jacob." He watched as Charlie swung aboard his horse and headed for the house. Now he could go back to returning the wagon box to the summer wheels and refitting the rims. Hard to believe the wooden wheels shrank over the winter, cold and wet as it had been. What he'd give for a good blacksmith.

Once the children returned from school, he'd have them bring more wood to the circle, where they'd heat the rim, set it back on the wood wheel, and dunk the whole thing in the cow trough. Good thing Mr. Robertson had the basic metal-working tools set up in the shed by the barn. Talk about a man of all trades.

After doing as much prep work on the wagon as possible, Jacob went to work on the woodpile. Splitting wood gave one plenty of thinking time. Which sermon to use? He'd not brought many with him. What had happened to the things he'd left behind? Perhaps he'd ask Mr. Dumfarthing to inquire into that the next time he wrote.

And what about Joel? Other than the funeral, this would be his first time preaching in front of his son.

Encouragement. Charlie said everyone needed encouragement. What was more encouraging than knowing that God loved them, that He would never change that love, and that He loved no matter what? Not like man's love, putting conditions on, loving someone if they felt like it.

You say you love Opal. Is that love un-

conditional? What if she never loved him back? *Slam* and *crack* — he swung so hard, the ax head buried itself in the chopping block. The two split pieces leaped apart and did flips before hitting the ground. That was the question of course. What if she truly loved Atticus? And Atticus came back for her?

He set another chunk on the block and slammed the ax home. What if Opal was not the woman God had in mind for him? He'd been so certain she was when he talked with Rand early in December and he'd agreed not to say anything to her until after her sixteenth birthday, a year from next month. Then he'd been a ranch hand; now he might be a preacher again. Would Opal want to be a preacher's wife?

"Goodness, Mr. Chandler, you trying to chop enough for next winter too?" Cora Robertson stopped on the back porch.

Jacob wiped his forehead with the sleeve of his shirt. "Hello, Mrs. Robertson. Do you need something?"

"Not at the moment. You just looked like you were fighting a battle or something."

"I started out planning a sermon and got carried away, I guess."

"Well, if you were thinking hellfire and brimstone, I wouldn't be surprised. Coffee

288

will be hot in a minute or two. You want a break?"

"Thanks." He glanced around at the split wood. They'd need to haul in dry trees pretty soon, and from what he'd seen, there wouldn't be a lack of firewood this year. He'd better sharpen up the crosscut saws, and his ax needed a new edge too.

Sunday morning dawned with enough butterflies flitting in Jacob's middle to lift him off the ground. He bypassed breakfast and headed out to walk to the schoolhouse, leaving the horses for the others. Though the ground was drying out now, the wagon would still sink up to the hubs if they tried to use it. He buttoned his black wool coat up to the neck until walking fast warmed him enough to unwind his scarf.

"I have good news for you." He shouted his opening line to the crows flapping and cawing overhead. If anyone heard him, they'd think him nuts. He toned his voice down so that he could hear the meadowlarks trilling in the sun. How the music of spring contrasted with the howling of winter. Frost still shimmered in the shade, retreating from the beaming sun. "O Lord, let our hearts be open like the budding flowers, let us be free from the sorrows of the winter, and let us sing like the birds. Give me the words you want spoken so that we can praise you and draw closer always to your mighty heart."

"Good morning, Charlie." Jacob stopped at the doorway of the schoolhouse.

"Morning to you. Fire took the chill off the room, but I'm thinking on a glorious day like today we won't need it."

"I think you're right. Perhaps we could rearrange the room a bit, move the teacher's desk back against the wall?"

"Of course."

"What do people sit on?"

"Children sit on the floor. Folks use the desks, and we got some benches out in the shed. I'll bring them in. We make do."

While the musicians warmed up inside, Jacob mingled with the folks who arrived by foot and horseback, welcoming them all and meeting some for the first time. He heard laments of the dead cattle, despair at the losses, and talk of moving on. With the abattoir not reopening since there were no cattle to slaughter, building had halted, and there would be no jobs.

"Boom or bust. Ain't that the way."

"But the land is still here. . . ."

Charlie rang the school bell right at ten

o'clock, and folks filed inside. He waited until they'd settled, then raised his hands for quiet. "Welcome, everyone. Today we will be led in worship by Jacob Chandler, a real pastor for a change." He beckoned Jacob to the center. "Thank you for sharing with us."

"You are welcome to our Father's house." Jacob smiled at those gathered. "Our first hymn for this morning is 'Holy, Holy, Holy.' "

Pearl played the introduction, and the service commenced. When the choir — if five people could be called a choir — rose, Jacob glanced over to see that Opal remained sitting beside Ruby. Was she sick? One look at her face told him something was definitely wrong. Was she still struggling with all the death and destruction?

Trying to put Opal out of his mind was about as effective as telling the blizzard to stop.

Jacob stood before the gathering and bowed his head. "Let us pray." When the rustling ceased, he began. "Father in heaven, we come before thee a broken and frightened people. We need to know that thou dost love us . . . and deeply. We need thy comfort and sustaining might. I thank thee that thou art right here in our midst

291

and thou knowest our hearts and minds. Hold us in thy mighty right hand. Amen."

Jacob held up his worn Bible. "Do you believe this is the Word of God?" Several nodded; others looked confused. "The reason I ask is because I want to read you some passages that tell us how much our Father loves us, but if you don't believe this book is His Word, then the words may sound nice, but they will mean nothing. So let me ask again. Do you believe this book is the Word of God?" He waited for a heartbeat before several people said, "Yes," others nodded, and someone said, "Of course," with a snort.

"Then listen to what God is telling you, for this book is His love letter to us, and these are His words to us. John 3:16. 'For God so loved the world, that he gave his only begotten Son, that whosoever believeth in him should not perish, but have everlasting life.' And in First John we read, 'That which we have seen and heard declare we unto you, that ye also may have fellowship with us: and truly our fellowship is with the Father, and with his Son Jesus Christ. And these things write we unto you, that your joy may be full.' "

Jacob closed his Bible. "He loves us so much that He sent His Son to die for us.

'Greater love hath no man than this, that a man lay down his life for his friends.' Jesus did that for us. 'Yea, though I walk through the valley of the shadow of death, I will fear no evil: for thou art with me.' He is right here, walking with us through the carnage of this horrible winter where, though your cattle died, He kept us safe. He has brought us out on the other side, and He will bless us. Know that our heavenly Father loves you, and next to that, nothing else matters." He stared deep into the eyes of the people in front of him, some filled with tears, others that looked away. But one pair of eyes glared at him. "Prove it" was written all over her face. *Lord God, help Opal.* "Amen."

CHAPTER TWENTY-ONE

During his years in Arizona Territory, Jeremiah had forgotten what spring was like in the badlands.

Even with snowbanks still covering most of the gullies and north faces, blades of green reached for the sun, and water gurgled from under the snow in a pell-mell race to the lowlands and the river. But as the snow melted, the horrible truth became known. The gullies were full of even more dead cattle that had sought shelter and been covered with snow.

He'd planned on stopping to see Cora Robertson but rode out to the Harrison ranch instead, feeling heavier by the minute.

"Welcome. Come on in." Rand stood in the open doorway before Jeremiah could dismount.

McHenry flipped the horse's reins over the hitching rail and followed his friend inside, kicking the mud off his boots before he crossed the threshold. He'd not ridden Kentucky yet but had led him around the

Hegland place to loosen him up. He figured the mud could cause problems for his horse's shoulder so was grateful when Carl offered the loan of one of his team.

"Your horse still laid up?" Rand motioned his friend to one of the chairs at the table.

"Gettin' better. Have to admit, though, he might never be able to ride out again. But then, long hours in the saddle aren't too appealing to me either. Your men out on the range?"

"Somewhat, but it's pretty wet and muddy yet. The few animals we've seen alive are racks of bones. Never thought to see critters lookin' so bad. Where you headed?"

"Thought to go upriver a piece to Pinewood Creek, see how that bottom lays to build on. But the river is so high, I'd have to ride up on the buttes, so guess I'll wait a bit."

"We're adding on to the corral if you want to come on out and help. Ruby and Opal went over to Cora's for some gab and quilting."

"Opal is quilting? Now, that's a hard one to believe."

"Ruby hoped getting her out of the house would help. She's having a right hard time of all this."

"I figured something was wrong when she wouldn't sing at church."

"She says there's no music left." Rand rubbed his chin. "I wish it wasn't this bad too, but . . ." His sigh brought Ghost to his side. "Like Ruby says, 'The Lord giveth and the Lord taketh away, blessed be the name of the Lord.' The land will come back, and we'll grow more steers. It just takes time."

"And money. I'd thought to buy a few cows once I get the house underway."

"Some of the ranchers are selling out. You might attend the Cattlemen's Association meeting and talk to a few of them. Probably get stock cheap."

McHenry nodded. "Thanks for the information. Carl's holed up in his shop, Charlie and Jed took off, and I thought maybe you'd like to go hunting."

"Ducks and geese are flying but haven't seen any deer. The antelope must have headed south before the wind. Elk are getting scarce. Beans said the snow buried the rabbits and grouse. Found birds frozen in the trees. Going to take some time for the land to come back after this winter."

"Let's go on over to those beaver ponds on Wolf Creek. Waterfowl always land there."

Rand slapped his hands on the table.

"Good idea." The two headed out the door to mount up.

McHenry turned to say something to Rand, and his foot missed the stirrup. He muttered as the horse spooked and shifted several feet away from him.

"You all right?"

"Yeah, I will be. This eye has —" He cut himself off. *Stop whining and just pay attention.* How he missed Kentucky.

Within minutes the two men rode off, Rand ordering Ghost to stay home. The mottled cow dog sank down on the porch, resting her muzzle on her front paws, a perfect picture of dejection.

The sun was sliding toward the horizon when they returned, feather blankets nearly hiding their mounts. They'd tied duck and geese feet together and draped the strings of fowl over the horses' withers and haunches.

"Should have taken a wagon along," Rand said as he dismounted in front of his house.

"Or made a travois." McHenry shook his head at the sheer volume of their hunt. "Good thing we have lots of friends to give these to. Take what you want, and I'll deliver the rest."

"I'll have one of the men take some over

to Robertsons'. You can't carry them all."
He grinned up at Jeremiah. "You always
were the lucky one, hunting or fishing."

"Luck. Come on, man, admit it. I didn't
waste a shell."

"Not hard when they're that close together." Rand pulled several strings of birds
off his horse and laid them on the porch,
where Ghost gave them a thorough sniff
test.

"Thanks, Rand, I needed this."

"Come on out anytime. I can always put
you to work here."

"Thanks, but I better start felling trees.
Thinking on going upriver to the pines and
when the water drops, float the trees down.
You want to come?"

"Hate to leave right now, but one of the
men could go with you."

"I'd only be gone a couple of days."

"Anytime."

Jeremiah rode on back to the boardinghouse and dropped off four geese and four
ducks before going on to give away the
others.

"Thank you, McHenry," Cimarron said
with a wide smile. "You come bearing gifts
just like you always did."

"Haven't been hunting like that since I
left here. You don't see migrating flocks like

that in Arizona Territory. But the jackrabbits were big enough to feed a whole platoon."

"Bring me more of the geese, and I'll start a feather bed for your new house."

"What a fine idea. Here I've been thinking on building materials and not given a thought to furnishings, other than have Carl build me a table and a rocking chair. Going to put me a rocking chair on the porch and while away the days."

Cimarron nearly choked on her laugh. "If you can't find enough to keep busy, I can guarantee that Rand or Opal or someone will find plenty for you to do."

"Not to change the subject, but you ever heard from Belle?"

"No. After Dove House burned and she realized she lost her investment, she hotfooted it back to Deadwood and crossed us all off her list. Opal asks after her sometimes."

"Might go on down to Deadwood and see how she fares." He nodded slowly. *Now would be a good time, before I get to building my house. If I can stand to ride that long.*

"Oh, knowing Belle, she's faring just fine. Come on over for supper one of these nights, and we can catch up on old times."

She hoisted the strings of geese. "Thanks." She smiled up at him. "Be sure to greet her from all of us when you go."

Jeremiah rode on back to Heglands' and put his horse away. Kentucky nickered a welcome. "Well, I didn't get to the Robertsons', but I sure had a most pleasant day." He stroked Kentucky's nose and rubbed his ears. "Old son, I sure hope we can get you back in shape for riding." He kneaded his own back and rubbed his leg. "You ride a heap more easily than that one."

He headed for the house, forcing his bad leg to match stride with the good one. "Evening, Miss O'Shaunasy." He stopped to watch her plucking the goose feathers and stuffing them in a bag.

"Mr. McHenry." Her nod scarcely moved her head.

He waited a moment, then asked a question that had been nagging at the back of his mind. "Did I do something to offend you?"

She glanced up, her eyes wide. "No. Why?" The shake of her head caused the knot of russet hair to loosen.

Because I watch you smile, and even though you aren't a chatterer, you carry on a conversation with others yet clam right up when I come around. He couldn't tell her that. "Oh, nothing. Just wondered."

"Supper will be ready soon."

"Good. I better go on and wash up then." He touched the brim of his hat with one finger and made sure he didn't flinch as he climbed the three treads to the porch. Bum leg.

After they filled their supper plates, the conversation resumed.

"That Jake Maunders came by again," Pearl said.

McHenry wiped his mouth with his napkin. "He's come before?"

"I think he's hoping to impress Miss O'Shaunasy."

Amethyst shook her head, a shudder saying all he needed to know.

"Why didn't you tell me?" Carl asked, his tone firm.

"Please, I don't want to cause trouble."

"No trouble, Miss O'Shaunasy. We'll take care of him," McHenry promised.

Carl nodded. "You had quite a hunt."

"We did. If you want more let me know." McHenry turned to Pearl. "I've decided to ride down to Deadwood. Should be gone a week or so."

"De Mores had a stagecoach and hauling route down that way for a short time. He might have made it if he'd gotten the mail contract." Carl took another bite of meat. "Nothing worked right for him. Downright shame."

"Would you like to take food supplies along?" Pearl asked. "I can pack some things."

"Thank you." Jeremiah glanced at Amethyst, waiting until she looked up. "Thank you both for such a delicious meal. I'll miss your cooking."

CHAPTER TWENTY-TWO

The quilters' conversation chattered around her like a creek tumbling over rocks, sometimes music, sometimes a torrent. Opal heard none of it. While she felt Ruby's gaze linger on her every so often, she ignored it. She left off her stitching and sat on the floor to play with Per.

"Opa?" He stood next to her and patted her cheek.

Opal nodded, then reached into her pocket to pull out a rag to wipe his nose. "Wait."

He jerked back and stared at her out of wounded eyes.

"Come on, Per, blow." He turned his face away, whimpering like an abused puppy.

You look like I feel. Opal wished she could whimper and have someone wrap his arms around her as she did Per. Atticus. But with each day his face faded like a stain washed out of a garment. His voice, too, seemed to be receding to the point that at times she wondered if she had made him up. He'd never returned to Medora at

Christmastime. She'd dreamed it all.

"Mr. Chandler will be in to eat dinner with us. It's a shame we didn't invite Rand too." Cora Robertson pushed her chair back from the quilting frame that took up a corner of the room. "Virginia wanted to stay home and help us today, but they have so much work to make up at school after all those days they missed this winter." She opened her oven door, and the fragrance of baking pie, of cinnamon and apples, filled the room. "Used the last of the apples. They still cook up good even if they're shriveled to nubbins."

"I made applesauce out of the last of ours." Ruby cut her thread and smoothed out the section she'd been stitching. "I forget how comforting quilting can be."

Opal choked back a rude noise. Forcing herself to take such minute and even stitches made her shoulders, elbow, wrist, and fingers ache. She'd rather do a full day of roundup. *Don't think about it. No roundup this year. Don't think about it!*

"Opa." Per climbed into the haven made by her legs crossed Indian fashion. Today she'd worn her britches, hoping that would make her feel like her real self and not like something slimy one found under a rock. If the rock hadn't already smashed it. She rested her cheek on top of Per's head as he leaned against her chest and rocked them both.

It was another example of God's not listening. She'd prayed, and she knew Ruby and Rand had too, that God would heal Per, would bring back the sunny little boy who loved nothing more than running rather than walking, laughing rather than talking, rolling on the floor with Ghost licking his face and making him giggle. This pale shadow who coughed and sat without moving — who was he?

"Opal, would you please set the table?" Cora Robertson set her pies on the counter and returned to the stove to stir the pot of stew she'd had simmering all morning.

"Of course." Standing from cross-legged was usually easy, but with Per clutching her shoulders, she grabbed at a chair, one hand securely clutching his bottom, his legs wrapped around her waist. He'd been carried more since he got sick than in his whole first year of life.

"You want to give him to me?" Ruby asked.

"No. We're fine." Opal realized she was getting pretty good at working with one hand.

Per looked up at her with sad eyes. "Hungry."

"I know. We'll eat soon."

"Now?"

"Soon."

"Why don't you set him on that chair, and he can start with bread and jam." Cora patted his head as she walked by.

Opal pulled out the chair. "Come on, Per, you have to let go."

"No."

"Bread and jam." Bribery.

He shook his head, rubbing his face and runny nose into her shirtfront. "Opa."

"No bread, then." Per loved bread and jam above all else.

He loosened his grip and let her lower him to the chair seat. She took the towel Cora offered her and tied it around his waist and to the chair. Cora handed him a quarter of a slice of bread with wild strawberry jam spread on it. She set a plate with the other three pieces in front of him.

Freed of her burden, or at least one of them, Opal put plates, silverware, and coffee cups at the rest of the places. She could hear boots stamping off mud on the back porch. The house seemed so empty without the girls and Joel here. They'd all worked so hard last summer to learn to handle cattle, and now there were none to rope or drive bellering into the corral.

Pounding her fists against the wall only made her hands hurt. It did nothing to lift the weight or bring life back to her heart. Sometimes she wished she'd died in the winter too.

But not often and not for long. Those thoughts had darted past like small birds after a raiding crow. She'd not dared to admit to such thoughts to anyone.

"Howdy, Miss Torvald." Jacob Chandler smiled at her as he hung his hat on the wall peg.

She ignored the quiver in her middle that happened every time she saw him or heard his voice. There was something about the man that managed to get to her. "Howdy," she answered back. Ruby had always insisted on good manners, and ignoring his greeting was not good manners. He smoothed back the lock of blond hair that fell over his forehead as soon as the restraining hat left. Just like his son. Joel had learned roping skills faster than anyone she ever knew, but then, he'd worked at them about as hard as she had when she had first moved to the ranch.

"Dinner is ready." Cora set a large bowl of stew at one end of the table. "Opal, would you bring the bread plate, please?"

"Mo bread?" Per quit licking his fingers

307

long enough to ask.

"In a minute," Opal replied.

"Mr. Chandler, would you say the grace, please?" Cora asked after they'd all taken their places.

"Of course. Father God, we come to you with thanksgiving for the food you have provided and for the hands that prepared it. Bless this house, those who dwell here, and those who visit. In the name of your precious son, Jesus. Amen."

Opal kept herself from shaking her head. Nope, no thanksgiving. And the God he prayed to did what all the men in her life had done — they left. And when they left, they left things in a mess.

Opal Torvald, that's what your pa did, but Mr. Brandon took good care of his family and of you. Besides, look at Rand. He's not leaving.

But Atticus did, and I loved him. I loved my pa too, and what good did it do me? And Linc. All the while she passed the plates that Cora filled, her thoughts ran after one another. A miracle she could hear anything else, her mind was screaming so loud.

"Opal."

She blinked and turned to face Ruby. From the frown that etched her forehead,

308

she must have said something more than once.

"Sorry. What did you say?"

"I asked if you would pass the butter."

"Sure." She glanced up to find Mr. Chandler watching her. What kind of look was that in his eyes? Her neck warmed up.

"I was sorry you couldn't sing on Sunday, Miss Torvald," he said.

"Nothing to sing about." The words slipped out before she could stop them.

She knew Ruby was glaring at her again. She could feel it in her bones, no need to look. But she did and sure enough.

"Ah, I see."

Do you really? She looked down the table to where Mr. Chandler sat — where Ward Robertson used to sit. The look of compassion in his deep blue eyes made her eyes smart and tears plug her nose. *You will not cry!* She pinched the skin on her wrist to keep the tears at bay. Beside her Per coughed, and she dug out the handkerchief to wipe his nose. Baby Mary could be heard stirring in her basket.

Opal sniffed and stared at the ceiling, then at Per as he tried to wiggle away from having his nose wiped. "Blow, Per, it will be easier."

"Poor little guy," Cora said. "Good thing

spring is here so the sun can drive out the winter ills."

Opal felt like shaking her head. What good would the sun do?

"It was that way with Ada Mae. She'd get all plugged up in the winter, coughing and hacking, but when spring came, she'd be running outside and pretty soon no longer feeling peaked. I'd dose her with castor oil and molasses too. Helped every time."

"Castor oil? Really?" Ruby rose and took Per on her lap.

"And molasses. The darker the better. Give him a tablespoon — no, he's small, make it a teaspoon every day for a week. You'll see a difference."

Opal pushed chunks of potato around on her plate. Food just didn't taste good anymore, but when Ruby cleared her throat, she knew she better not leave any. She ate the last bite and stood to clear the table since everyone else was finished.

"Thank you, Opal, such a nice thing to do." Cora handed up her plate.

"You're welcome." Anything was better than sitting still. Since her mind wouldn't pay attention to the conversation, moving was far preferable.

"Any chance you'd like to give a refresher course in roping and throwing, Miss

Torvald?" Mr. Chandler asked. "I tried working with that rope the other day, and all it did was twist."

"Why?"

"Because I need some more coaching?"

"Why bother? There's not enough animals out there to need branding or castrating or anything. They're all dead."

"Opal." Ruby's eyebrows drew sharply together.

"Rand said there would be no roundup." Opal fought to keep her tone low. If she raised her voice, she might start screaming, and once she started, she might never stop.

"Opal!"

"Yes, ma'am." Ruby just didn't understand. She wasn't the one who cared for the cattle. Rand was. And she was. The black cloud clamped back down, and she fought to even be able to breathe. "Excuse me." She headed for the door.

Once she was off the porch, the tears came and with them great gulping sobs, another thing she had feared. She broke into a run and, arms pumping, headed beyond the house to the rise. A familiar stench came on the breeze, further clogging her throat and nose. She reached an oak tree and leaned against the trunk, gasping and choking. Pain speared her lungs and cramped her side.

Her dinner came up, and after it left, she stood with her eyes closed, swallowing against the bitter gall.

"Miss Torvald."

"Go away." How dare he follow her? She brushed back the strands that insisted they should not be confined to the braid she wore.

"I thought maybe you needed someone to talk to."

She shook her head.

"Sometimes talking things out stops all the shouting going on in your head."

"How — ?" She cut off the question.

"How do I know there are voices screaming at you and arguing back and forth till you feel like a battlefield?" He chuckled softly. "Because I've been there too. I suspect most everyone gets there at one time or another."

"Not Ruby!" *Not my perfect sister who trusts God for everything. I don't even like God.*

"Oh, I'd bet if you could talk with her without getting mad, she'd admit to feeling like that."

"Go away."

"I thought we were friends."

"I did too." She spun around and stabbed him through squinted eyes. "But you've

312

been about as friendly lately as a porcupine caught in a trap." She waited for an answer and heard only a sigh.

"I-I'm sorry. I've had some things to work out."

"Doesn't matter."

"Yes, it does." His voice came gentle, tip-toed into her heart, and planted a little seed of peace.

"You said that God loves us."

"In my sermon?"

She nodded and dug in her pocket, but her handkerchief was soiled from Per. She wiped her sleeve across her eyes. "I don't believe it."

"Why?"

Opal rolled her lips and blinked several times. *I will not cry any more!* "How can you look at all that has gone on and say God loves us? Ruby does the same. Can't you see?" She swept a wide arc with her arm. "All the dead cows, the dead ranches. People died too — Little Squirrel and the baby. If God did this, how can you say He loves us?" Her voice dropped, and one tear forced past her control and slid down her cheek. She dashed it away with the back of her hand. "If that is what His love looks like, He can keep it."

"You ask hard questions."

"I never thought love smelled like dead critters." She shuddered.

"The Old Testament speaks of animal sacrifices God required to atone for the sins of the people. The animals were burned on altars, and the blood was sprinkled to purify. These burnt offerings were called a pleasing aroma to God. I've often thought the area of the temple where they did this must have smelled pretty strong. Burned meat isn't pleasing to my nose."

"I never thought about that." Opal squatted down and picked a blade of grass, thin, new grown, not the rich green it would become. "But that's not answering my question."

"I know." He shrugged. "The answer I had to come to, and have to return to over and over when terrible things happen, is that God knows everything, and He has said He will be with us in times of trouble."

"But He could take it away — like the storms this winter. He could have stopped them."

"Yes, He could have."

She glanced over her shoulder. "Then why didn't He?"

"I don't know. But in order to get strong, you have to push against things stronger than you are. Bad things happen in this world because Adam and Eve sinned and were thrown out of the Garden of Eden. Ever since then, humans and the whole world have suffered. But God says He will walk beside us and get us through it all. All the struggle helps us and our faith grow stronger."

"And you believe that?"

"That's what faith is. Believing that God's word is true."

Opal shredded the bit of grass and dropped it on the ground. "Well, I think . . ." She paused and shook her head. "I don't know what I think." She stood. "I better get back and help with the dishes. The others will be home soon."

"Do you miss school?"

"Not usually. Pearl is a great teacher." She started down the hill, and Jacob fell in beside her. She glanced up at him. "Thanks."

"That's what friends are for."

"Atticus and I used to talk about most anything." She shook her head slowly. "And look what happened to him."

"Makes no sense, does it?"

"Nope."

"Opal, I hope the music comes back for you soon."

She nodded. "Me too."

CHAPTER TWENTY-THREE

Amethyst stared at the flask on the table McHenry was using as a desk.

He's a drinking man. Why did the thought make her want to sweep it away? After all, it was no business of hers. All she had to do was clean his room. She turned her back and pulled the sheet and one quilt tight. They'd put away the heavier woolen quilts of winter. She plumped the pillows, checked the chamber pot, cleaned and dusted the flat surfaces. Without picking up the flask.

She could hear her father's voice. *"There's nothing wrong with a good belt once in a while."* But for him the good belt was never enough, and once in a while came far too often. Along with a sodden ride home and time to sleep it off. He'd called it medicinal.

She noticed that McHenry limped sometimes. Was that in the flask medicinal for him? If so, then it was no business of hers. Not that what he did was ever any business of hers.

She thought back to the night before. The two of them had remained sitting in the parlor for some time after the Heglands had gone on to bed. She'd finally gotten up the courage to ask him a question.

"What was it like in Arizona Territory?"

He had smiled and nodded, a faraway look drifting into his eyes. "About as different from here as could ever be. Have you seen pictures of cactuses?"

"In a book one time. I think there are many kinds."

"That is true. Some are huge, like the saguaros that can weigh several tons, and some are much smaller, like the cholla that look soft and fluffy but will fill your or your horse's legs with spines if you even go near them. They earned the name jumping cholla because the spines seem to jump out at anything that nears them. The desert can be a fierce and unforgiving land in the summer, yet a place of incredible beauty in the spring when it blooms."

"It is not all sand?" She thought to a picture she'd seen of the Sahara Desert in Africa.

"Oh no. There are rocks and gullies, mountains and arroyos, where the water can run deep and swift — they call them flash floods. If it rains in the mountains, water can come roaring down rapidly. People need to stay out of the low places. The land isn't good for much unless you're by a river and can get water. There's not even enough grass in most places to raise cattle, just sagebrush and creosote bush, which burns hotter'n any regular wood." He paused and let his eye drift closed, nodding a bit. "But you watch, settlers will come more and more for the fine winters. After we captured Geronimo and I lost my eye and Kentucky and I were both wounded in an ambush, I lost my taste for military life. There's something about Geronimo. . . . It was kind of like capturing a wild and proud stallion and breaking him to the plow." He half snorted. "Poor analogy, but . . ." He paused, lost in thought.

Amethyst had watched the lamplight play over the planes of his face, corrugating his cheekbones, squaring his jaw, tossing lights into his silvered hair. The black patch seemed to fit, as if he'd worn it forever instead of only a few months. While it might look daring on some, on him it added to the sense of tired. Weary. Worn down.

"I always loved the badlands. It's good to be home." He opened his eye and smiled at her. "You're a quiet and gentle presence; do you know that?"

Amethyst shrugged, ducking her chin. She was quiet because she had nothing to say. Her father would not call her gentle, not after she had left him in the wagon in the barn overnight. "Worthless" was the only word she'd ever heard — from men anyway. How to tell this man that he was the first to ever talk with her like this.

"Can I get you anything before . . ." She couldn't mention bed. That would be improper.

"No, I'm fine. Thank you for your time. I'm sure you're tired after all the work you've done today." He smiled, the movement of his mouth causing deep brackets in his cheeks. "I'd like it if you told me something about yourself."

"There's nothing to tell. I lived on my father's farm all my life. He sent me here to bring Joel back because he thought Joel was his grandson. He wanted him to live on the land he would inherit." Was there a touch of bitterness in her tone? She hoped not.

"Where?"

"Eastern Pennsylvania."

"And I take it Joel is not your nephew?"

"I always thought he was." A sigh caught her unaware. *Now I have no one.* The thought brought on another sigh. *You haven't written to your father again.* That thought plagued her every day as if it were a vengeful creature out to make her miserable. *All I want to do is forget. Forget all the work I did for a place that would never be mine, no matter how often I wished it so. Forget the man who, even though he is my father, thinks me worth less than the dog that lived under our porch. So, Father, how are you faring on your own? And since I am not there, who are you browbeating now, as you did my mother before me?*

Just write the letter and get it off your conscience. The voice of reason was never as strident as the one seeking her misery.

Amethyst had listened to Jacob Chandler's preaching on Sunday. He'd said God the Father loved all of His children, which must include her. Hard to think of a loving heavenly Father when the one who, as he said, provided all her needs was no earthly good.

She glanced up from studying her chapped fingers when she felt Jeremiah's gaze upon her.

"So what will you do?"

"I'm not going back." There. She'd declared her intentions aloud again. Mrs.

Grant had said she had a good head, the first compliment from anyone other than her mother, and she'd believed her. Working here for Pearl was nowhere near as arduous as doing both the man's work and the woman's work on her father's farm. And Pearl so often expressed her gratitude.

"I know Pearl is grateful for your help here. I've heard her say so."

Was she just being polite? Amethyst often wondered. Pearl wore graciousness like a fine knit shawl and shared it with all around her. Especially with Amethyst. Never before had she heard "please" or "thank you" spoken with a smile rather than a grudge.

Amethyst gathered the compliments and stored them against a day when she might indeed be forced to return to her father's house.

Getting to her feet, she had been surprised to see him stand also. "I bid you good night, then, and thank you for a pleasant evening."

He had sketched a bow and nodded. "We must do this again."

He had acted the perfect gentleman that night, had been rude only that one time. But now the flask. What was she to make of it all? Well, it was no business of hers.

★ ★ ★

Several mornings later she woke long before the rooster. She lit her kerosene lamp, took out paper and pencil that she'd borrowed from Pearl some time earlier, and sat down to write to her father.

Dear Pa,

She printed in slightly large block letters so that he could read it more easily.

Since I have not heard from you, I think that you may not have received my earlier letter. I have news for you that will not make you pleased. Upon arriving in Medora, I learned that Joel is truly not your grandson. I do not know all the particulars, but he is with his real father. One only need to see them together to know this is so. He and his pa live at the Robertson ranch, and his father is becoming the pastor for the church here.

I am doing housework at the boardinghouse where I first came to stay. I do not plan to return to Pennsylvania. I like it here in the West.

I was very ill on the trip here, and a wonderful woman named Mrs. Grant

322

from Chicago made sure I received medical treatment, or I might not be here now.

I hope all is well with you.

Your daughter,
Amethyst Colleen O'Shaunasy

She thought of writing *loving daughter* but was not able to force the pen into the proper configuration. She addressed the envelope, including a return address in case he ever wanted to contact her, and placed her folded letter inside. Tomorrow she would walk into town and mail this letter, to finally get it off her conscience. She had thought about asking him to send her a box of her things but knew that would be useless.

At the rooster crowing she made her way downstairs, dipped warm water from the reservoir, and returned to her room to wash and dress.

Back down in the kitchen she sliced the cornmeal mush in preparation for frying, having set it the night before with bits of venison sausage worked into it. The hens were laying better again, so they could have fried eggs too; such a treat after the oatmeal, cornmeal mush, and pancakes they'd been having for breakfast. Surely Pearl wouldn't mind if she let several of the broody hens hatch their eggs to replace the hens lost in the winter and to have young fryers to eat. If the Heglands could afford another cow, she would love to begin making cottage cheese to sell at the store in town, and perhaps they could build up a milk route, something she'd thought of doing at home — or rather, in Pennsylvania. No longer would she refer to that place as home.

"Good morning, Amethyst. You are up early." Pearl set Joseph in the high chair his father had made for him so he could sit at the table.

"You've already fed him?"

"Yes, the little piglet nursed twice during the night." Pearl hid her yawn behind her hand. "Carl is already out in the shop. One certainly can't sleep through a fussing child, at least not this one. I saw light under your door in the wee hours. Are you all right?"

"Never better. I finally wrote to my father again after putting it off so long. This time I said I was not returning to Pennsylvania."

"Congratulations."

"If you don't mind, I'll walk in to town this morning to mail the letter and anything you want to send. Then I can stop by the general store. I'd like to sew Carly a new pinafore and some shifts for summer."

"How nice. I'll give you the money for

sewing supplies and the cotton. I'll make a list of things we need. I think you should take the horse and wagon."

"I don't want to get stuck. I'd rather walk. I have a question."

Pearl smiled and nodded. "Go ahead." She smiled even more broadly after Amethyst laid out her dreams to sell cottage cheese again and maybe even deliver milk. "Wonderful. I'll ask Carl."

Later, as Amethyst served breakfast, she caught Mr. McHenry watching her. The heat started right about her heart, and she hoped it didn't shine like a beacon on her face. She'd been surprised at how pleased she'd been to see him on his return from Deadwood.

"Would you care for more?" she asked.

"No, thank you."

She held the platter for Mr. Hegland. "And you, sir?"

"Thank you." Carl waited while she slid several slices onto his plate. "Amethyst, I would appreciate it if you did not call me sir."

"Yes, sir." She smiled at him with a slight shrug. "It just comes out." That annoying heat, again setting her cheeks afire.

Pearl laughed, which set Carly to giggling, and soon they were all chuckling. "Please, Amethyst, we are not laughing at you."

"I know, but it is so good to hear and see laughter in a house." Amethyst picked up a cloth to wipe the syrup from Carly's hands and face. "There you go, little one." She swooped her up and planted a kiss on the little cheek before setting her on the floor. *I shall make her a rag ball from the bits and pieces left over. If I could find a jingle bell to put in it, that would make her smile more.*

Sometime later when she handed her letter in at the post office, she almost looked up to see what took the weight off her shoulders.

"Here is some mail that has come in. Would you be willing to drop this off at the Blacks' on your way home?"

"Of course." Home, on her way home. Another bit to take in and let it warm her heart.

She chose a calico with flowers on a green background that wouldn't show the dirt too much for Carly's pinafore and a red-and-white gingham for the little girl's shifts. With a clean waist, that would do for church. For herself, she fingered a fine white lawn with sprigs of green leaf that would look lovely in a high-necked blouse

326

with leg-of-mutton sleeves and lace set in tucks down the front and gathered around the neck and cuffs. Never had she worn such a fine garment. But she'd seen other women dressed in similar fashion. *Be satisfied with the dresses Pearl has given you,* she told herself, glancing down at the green cotton skirt she'd altered to fit her.

Would Mr. McHenry — ? She cut off *that* thought with a snort. No matter what she wore, no man would look at her that way. Her father had told her so often enough. *"Colleen, you are good enough to cook and plow, but don't get any highfalutin ideas out of your station. God put you where you are for a reason."* And while Mr. McHenry said nice things to her, he had a temper and he drank. Mix the two together, and she well knew what could happen. She wanted no part of it. As if he cared anyway.

Amethyst, no longer Colleen, fingered the half-inch lace one more time and carried it with her other choices up to the counter to be cut. One yard for now for Carly. One day the fine lawn for herself.

CHAPTER TWENTY-FOUR

Whoever heard of playing a harmonica in church?

Jeremiah shook his head at Rand's suggestion. "If you say so," he answered, chuckling inside. If his mother could only see him now. All those years she'd wanted him to sing in the choir and he had run the other way like the Indians he chased for so long. Now, here in this end-of-the-world town, he was joining the choir, on a mouth organ no less. Surely God had a marvelous sense of humor.

Of course, when you thought of it, his mother had most likely gathered her friends around, and they were all looking down laughing.

"I'll need more practice time than that brief bit you all do on Sunday morning."

"Come on out on Saturday, spend the day, and we'll work it in. Maybe we'll get Opal singing again that way." Rand rubbed a raw place on his jaw, a close encounter with an angry mama. The few cows that were calving he'd kept close to home to be there if any needed help. While the cow needed help, she'd not been a bit polite about accepting it.

"Good. How many calves do you have?"

"Ten."

McHenry swallowed. *God above, help my friend.* "More still to come?" The two men were riding the range, taking it slow and easy so that Kentucky wouldn't wear out. The Dresden blue sky wore whipped-cream clouds kissed by the golden sun — a spring day all the more glorious after the terrible winter. A song sparrow invited a mate to come see the territory he'd picked out. The earliest butterflies tasted from gold flower to blue, a smorgasbord of choices.

"Hope so. We found a few wandering the plain a couple days ago. The steers seemed to have fared better than the cows."

"Sure. They were only eatin' for one."

"How many logs you got cut? Enough to start the walls?"

"Not really. And I've not got the logs rounded up in one place yet." McHenry crossed his arms on the saddle horn. It seemed strange, after all his years riding a military saddle, to be using a western saddle, but the heavy pommel and horn were necessary for roping and the daily business of ranching. He intended to do it right — ranching, that is.

Right now the twenty head he'd bought, from someone who wanted out, grazed with Rand's herd. Jeremiah hadn't a cow in the bunch, and the steers looked like moving bones with skin on. Their horns weighed more than the rest of the body.

"You going to file on the land around your house?"

"Ruby's been after me to do that. Just seems to stick in my craw. The land should be free for all to use, just the way God made it. The Indians have the right attitude there. You use and take what you need and leave plenty for the next that come along." Rand blew out a sigh. "I know times are changing, but the thought of fences all over these plains makes me want to choke."

"De Mores had a bad time with the ones he put up, but you already have that one plot fenced."

"Right. And if I plant grain, I'll have to fence to keep the cattle out rather than in."

"You seriously thinking of seeding? Oats or wheat?" Jeremiah looked up when he heard a hawk scree, the sound so wild and free his heart leaped as if to join the dark wings lifting the bird on the air currents. He'd been reading a book by Theodore Roosevelt about his times here on the prairie, hunting and ranching both. The man had a love of the western lands, that was for sure, along with a keen eye.

"You know when Roosevelt is coming back?"

"Nope. He was just here for the cattlemen's meeting — that one in Miles City."

"Why didn't you go?"

"Didn't want to be away. And besides, it's bad enough seeing what happened here, let alone listening to the horror stories from the big ranchers." Rand nudged his horse forward and shook out his rope. The two men had been riding the prairie, searching out living stock, pulling some from mudholes, putting a bullet in the head of one too far gone, ending its misery.

McHenry followed suit, not yet seeing what Rand had seen. Times like this he wanted to rip the patch from his face and have the sight of both eyes again. He'd been known as an eagle eye, the greatest compliment anyone could give him, and look at him now. One-eyed, a gimpy leg that clung to its pain, and the stamina of a girl in a tight corset.

Rand pointed to a recently dead cow lying in the mud of a water hole. She'd been too weak to pull her feet out of the mud. A calf tottered along the edge, bawling for her to come and feed him.

"We'll take him on home with us." He settled the loop over the baby's head and stepped to the ground, Buck taking up the slack, as any well-trained cow horse would.

"Your cow has enough milk for hers, the house, and this one?" McHenry nudged Kentucky over to give the bawling calf some shade. The sun shone hot as if to make up for lost time.

"I think so. You want him in front of you?"

"Sure, why not?"

Rand threw the calf on its side, tied front legs together and then the rear, then hoisted the struggling baby up to his chest and up to McHenry's arms. "This'll give Opal something to care for. Now, if we could trap some wild horses, maybe she'd come back to herself."

"You're that worried about her?" McHenry settled the calf in the saddle in front of him and stroked the mottled hide. "Hey, little one, easy now. We'll get you fed."

"I am." Rand swung back on Buck and re-coiled his rope. "Let's head on home. Tomorrow, if you want to come along and file on that piece you decided on, we'll take the train to Dickinson and get the deed done. I'll ask Cora Robertson if she wants to go too. Might as well make a day of it."

"What about Charlie, Carl, and the others?"

Rand shrugged. "Near as they are to town, I think it's different. We're looking at a quarter to half a section. Should think more, but I'm hoping the range can stay free. I thought to have Opal file on a piece too, but —"

"Where?"

"Next to me." Rand shrugged and stood in his stirrups, peering off to the east. "Someone's coming."

"Opal?"

"No, I think it's Beans. I told Opal not to come out here. Seeing all the carcasses is just too much for her."

"Opal is stronger than you think."

Rand shot him a warning look over his shoulder.

Okay, my friend, I won't go there, but women are stronger than you think, and Opal is one of the stronger. He wasn't sure how he knew this, but he did. When she first came to Little Missouri she learned to fish faster than anyone he'd seen, gave her all to learn to ride, getting back on when she fell off, listening to what he taught her, and making herself do it. Opal had more spunk than three ordinary kids. And a sense of humor that took life on the chin and came back punching.

The calf bawled and bopped him in the sore thigh with his head.

Jeremiah grunted and wished he'd slung the animal the opposite direction.

Beans waved to them before they were close enough to shout.

Rand nudged his horse to a lope, leaving McHenry and his burden to catch up at their own pace. When he caught up to them, Rand turned in the saddle. "How about you take the calf back to the barn and give him to Opal. I'm going to help round up the bunch Beans found. Tell Ruby I'll be late for supper."

"Will do." How strange not to be the one giving the orders. Not that Rand ordered, but he was obviously the one in charge. As he should be. Jeremiah felt a warmth run down his pant leg. He looked down to see that the calf had let loose, and the odor was less than pleasant. He waved Rand and Beans off and stroked Kentucky's sweat-dotted shoulder. "Just us, old son, and we can take our time."

"Opal, you there? I brought you a

present," he called from the hitching rail some time later.

Opal came through the door, no bounce in her step and a smile that didn't quite make it. "Hey, Mr. McHenry."

"You want to heat some milk and bring it on down to the barn? Teaching this little feller to use a bucket is going to take some doin'."

"The cow died?"

"In a water hole. Poor beast was too weak to pull her feet out of the mud. This young'un was bawling fit to be tied."

She glanced at his pant leg, then raised an eyebrow, a slight hint of the girl he remembered in her eyes.

"Yeah, his mother didn't have time to teach him good manners."

"I'll get some milk." She waved as she headed back into the house.

Down at the barn McHenry dismounted, giving a grunt of pain when he put the weight on his right leg. He'd been too long in the saddle without a break, and now he was paying for it. Shame he'd not brought his medicinal flask along. A good pull or two and the whiskey dulled the knives ripping into his thigh muscles. When he got moving again, he lifted the calf down and carried it into the barn, where he found an empty box stall. He braced the calf while he fumbled for the latch, swung the door open, and laid the critter down with a grunt.

The baby bawled and thrashed his tied legs, struggling to get up in spite of the leather strings on his legs.

McHenry knelt and untied the knots, then rocked back on his heels as the calf aimed a kick at him and wobbled to his feet. The little one stood spraddle-legged to catch his breath, then tottered forward to inspect his surroundings, his plaintive calls for his mother echoing in the empty barn.

Opal eased her way in the door a few minutes later, a bucket with warmed milk in hand. She looked up at McHenry leaning against the stall half wall. "You know how to teach a calf to drink from a bucket?"

He shook his head. "The ones I knew all used their mother."

"All right, then, let's get a rope around his neck. I'll braid him a halter or fashion a collar later, but for now you hold him, and I'll see if I can get him sucking my fingers. Then I'll lower my fingers into the bucket, and he's supposed to start drinking."

"Supposed to?"

"That's the theory. Some learn faster than others."

"Sort of like people, eh?"

"Right."

Together they trapped the calf in the corner, and while McHenry held him there, she fetched the bucket and stroked the calf's head and neck. "Easy now, baby, let's get some milk into you, and then you can fuss all you want." She stuck her fingers down in the milk, then held them in front of his nose. He reared back, but when she did it again, he sniffed, and when she eased her fingers into his mouth, he sucked. Keeping her fingers in his mouth, she lowered them into the bucket. He jerked back, almost knocking the bucket out of her hands, the milk sloshing.

McHenry grabbed for a more secure hold, winced when his weight landed full on his right leg, and muttered something that he apologized to Opal for.

"That's all right. We'll get this yet. Thought to use the milking stanchion, but his head is so small he'd probably pull right out." She stood up and took a quieting breath. "Here we go, young sprout. Let's try again. You'd think we were trying to kill you rather than feed you, the way you're acting." She dipped her fingers again, got him sucking them, then slowly lowered her fingers to the milk in the bucket. This time he followed her down and kept on sucking. His tail twitched like a metronome as he sucked and swallowed. He bopped the bucket, as calves do to get their mother to let down her milk. If Opal had not had lightning reflexes, she'd have had a milk bath. But with some fancy grappling, she managed to keep the bucket from flying away.

"You are good, my friend." McHenry grinned at her. "Again?"

"Again. He's learning." Dip fingers, get him sucking, lower fingers, and sure enough, he drank again. Down to the last drop. Milk dripped from his mottled red-and-white muzzle as McHenry let him go and Opal set the bucket on the hard-packed dirt floor. The calf stuck his head back in the bucket, then bumped it over.

"And that's your opinion on an empty bucket, eh, Sprout?" Opal actually smiled.

"Sprout? That's his name already?"

"Sounds like a good one to me. Now to keep him alive without the scours."

"Scours?"

Opal picked up the bucket and exited the stall. "The runs. Calves sometimes have a problem going from nursing the cow to bucket feeding. If we had a cow that had lost her calf, we'd see if we could get her to accept this one. You can skin the dead calf and wrap the hide around the orphan. The cow smells it and thinks it is her own. I don't think we have any nurse cows this year."

McHenry locked the stall door behind him and rested his crossed arms on the top. "He's a cute little thing. Been through a lot already. Anything else we can do for him?"

"He's too young to graze yet. If I had some straw, I'd throw it in here for him to lie on, but there's no straw. No grass tall enough to cut either. Hmm, I wonder if Carl has some sawdust I could use."

"I have some up where I've cut the trees but not enough to make a difference. I'll check with Carl."

"Thanks. You want to water Kentucky and turn him out in the corral?" She half smiled at McHenry. "You are staying for supper, aren't you?"

"Is that an invitation?"

"If you need one. Ruby would skin you alive if you left without eating."

"Since I need my skin, I'll stay." He glanced down at his manure-spattered leg. "I smell rather ripe."

"You can wash that off at the pump. I'll pump; you wash." There it was again, just a hint of the girl who used to follow him, peppering him with questions about the West, about riding, fishing, the river. She had a sense of curiosity about anything and everything.

"Good." He stopped at Kentucky's side and began unlacing the cinch strap. "Opal?"

"Yeah."

"It's going to get better, I promise you." He turned to catch a glistening in her blue eyes, then pulled his saddle off and, with a grunt, slung it over the corral rail.

"I'll take Kentucky to the trough." She flipped the horse's reins loose from the rail and led him to the spring-fed water trough. "Not much, you know, but you feel pretty dry." She stroked his shoulder. "That calf sure made a mess of you. I'll clean you up after dinner." After Kentucky took a few swallows, she pulled him away and led him to the entrance of the corral, where McHenry had pulled open the gate.

Once inside the corral, she slipped off his bridle and let him rub his forehead against her upper arm. "Good fella." Slapping his neck, she stepped back and strode on out of the corral. Kentucky shook all over, snorting at the same time.

"You sure know your horses, young lady. Not too many people have taken care of him, mostly just me."

"No matter that dent in his shoulder, he's still a beauty. I remember that first Fourth of July celebration when you raced him. He's some runner."

"No more, but I might use him as a stud if I can find any mares. Be a good cross with range stock." McHenry coughed. "Forgive me. I forget you are a young lady whose ears should not be soiled with such earthy talk."

"Oh, for —" She glanced over her shoulder and he grinned at her. "You can treat me like a young lady when I'm dressed more like one, which is not often."

"That evening at Pearl's I could hardly believe it was you in that sapphire gown and your hair up. I wanted to go looking for the real Opal." They stopped at the pump and made sure his pant leg and boot were washed until the water ran clear.

"Opa!" Per met them on the back porch where a gate had been closed so he couldn't take off on his own. He raised his arms, and she swung him up on her hip. He stared at the visitor, one finger in his mouth.

"Per, this is Cap— ah, Mr. McHenry. He's a friend of ours from a long time ago."

"Pa?"

"He's out on the range."

She nodded her thanks as McHenry held the door open for her.

When they stepped into the kitchen, Ruby turned from the stove and smiled at them both. "Welcome. Make yourself at home." She nodded toward the table. "Have a seat."

"Rand said to tell you that he and Beans would not make it back for supper."

"I'm not surprised. Thanks for passing on the message."

McHenry took a seat and glanced around the room. *This is what I want,* he thought. *I want what Rand has. A home with a wife and children. Lord, this is it. Not that I want his, for that is indeed coveting, but near as like it as you can manage.*

"Did you see Belle when you went to Deadwood?" Ruby asked after they were settled at the table.

Jeremiah nodded without looking up. "I did."

"She's well?"

"Seems so. But she made it real clear she wasn't happy to see me or anyone from up here."

"That's too bad," Ruby said.

"Yes it is, and she looked pretty worn. Life's not been easy for her. Not that she'd ever admit it."

CHAPTER TWENTY-FIVE

From blizzard to burning hot and not much in between.

Jacob wiped the sweat pouring from his brow and wished he could do the same for the trickles down his back. Chopping wood did that to one, especially on a day like today. The bitterness of winter made spring even more of a delight to the senses. Since he had already repaired the wagon for haying season, sunk a new post in the corral, and replaced the shingles on the barn roof, he figured cutting wood would always be a priority. He was down to the last tree trunk that had been dragged in for firewood. Rand had told him of downed trees near the ranch, so one of these days he'd go out and begin stripping off the branches.

Opal was coming over this afternoon on her way back from the Heglands to give them all a refresher course in roping. While he'd asked for it for all of them, he meant it for himself. Ever since their talk, he'd been praying for her, that she would see God's hand in all things and would trust that He would work good out of everything.

"I don't know how you do it, Lord," he said, swinging the ax down hard, "but I've seen you in action so many times that now I believe. 'And we know that all things work together for good to them that love God, to them who are the called according to *his* purpose.' " Sometimes it was good to declare the promises out loud.

You have to be looking to see me in action.

"I know. Please open my eyes that I may see. And, Lord, come to Opal in a special way. You know that I promised Rand I would not court her or let my feelings be known. Show me how to do that. Staying away hurt her, being with her — you know how I have to stay on guard in order to keep my pledge. And I will. I will not allow my desires to bring suffering again. God, give me strength." He slammed the ax again, the shriek and slam of wood splitting, the thunk as the ax hit the block, all of it making a special kind of music, the bass beat of life.

"Jacob?" Cora no longer called him Mr. Chandler, which pleased him.

"Coming."

"You don't need to come now, but when you do, please bring in a load?"

"I will."

"I'll have fresh coffee on pretty soon, and the bread just came out of the oven."

Such temptations. Jacob went back to his wood splitting and praying. The two seemed to go hand in hand.

"Lord, if I haven't thanked you enough for your provisions for Joel and me in bringing us to this place, I'm thanking you again. Your Word says that you provide beyond our wildest dreams. And you even have a church here for me, one that needs a shepherd, and you prepared me to be that shepherd. You are bountiful beyond description, mighty God, king of kings." He planted the ax down into the block and stacked his arm full of split wood. One of these days he planned to make a wheelbarrow so he could get wood to the house more easily, as could Joel, since the chore of filling the woodbox both morning and evening had fallen to him.

"I feel I should be out riding the range with Rand and the others," he said after accepting his full coffee cup.

"Well, Rand said that with McHenry he had plenty of help, so I'd let it go at that. There's enough work around here to keep three men and a boy busy, let alone one man, one boy, and a bunch of females."

"That bunch of females, as you call yourselves, seem to accomplish about anything that needs doing. I'll get to digging up the garden tomorrow."

"Girls can dig and turn dirt over also. Many a garden I've dug up."

Jacob smiled, thinking back to the mothers of marriageable daughters who had lived in his parish in Pennsylvania. Soiling their hands with garden work was not permissible. They would have worn gloves had they been forced into such servile labor. But then, most of his church members had lived in the town, a town that had pretensions of cityhood. Or at least dreamed of such. Now, cooking, baking, stitching, and sewing were much practiced, as were the wiles of snagging a good husband.

Things were certainly different out here.

Living here took a certain kind of ruggedness. Pearl, who came from a fairly wealthy family in Chicago, now ran the boardinghouse. And look how Medora de Mores rode out hunting with the men and was known as an excellent shot.

"Where did you live before you came here?" he asked, buttering the crunchy heel of the bread loaf.

"Ward and I came west from Missouri when our girls were young. Ada Mae was born here. We were some of the first settlers after the hunters and trappers. We liked the thought of living on the Little Missouri River, and when Ward came to check things out and saw the badlands, he lost his heart to the land. All he could see was grass so deep that cattle would surely fatten, and there was land for the taking. So he returned home, loaded us up in two wagons, and west we came. We had ten head of cattle, a milk cow, and a crate of chickens. That first year we lived in a dugout, what is now the cellar, then he cut trees for our house and the barn the next year. His brother came with us, but he didn't care for the winters, so after three years he headed back home."

"You've done all this work yourselves?"

"My Ward was the workingest man you ever did see. But he didn't like his daughters doing a man's job, so they excel in things of the house and garden. Now, thanks to you and Opal, they know how to work cattle too."

"Will you stay?"

She tipped her head slightly to the side. "Why, Jacob, where would I go? I have all that I need right here. And my Ward is buried out there under that big oak tree. Someday they'll plant me right beside him where I belong." Her eyes glistened and her voice thickened. "Not a day goes by I don't think on him and miss him."

"You always are so composed, I thought . . ."

"That I'm not grieving?"

He nodded. "I suppose."

"Oh, I could get married again if I chose. There are many men that have been around here, but when you've had the best . . ." Her voice caught. "I'll see my daughters grown and married, and I'll have grandbabies to enjoy. You watch, this land will come back. Might be a long time, but it will." She reached over and patted his hand. "And God sent me you to help through this hardest part." Leaning closer, as though she wanted to share a secret, she continued, "And I trust my heavenly Father to always provide what I need."

"Thank you for telling me this. If I am to be the pastor for the church here, I need to get to know the people who will be the church."

"True, and when you want to be doing that, you go ahead and go."

"I have a favor to ask." He took a deep breath.

"Of course."

"I haven't told you what it is yet." Her smile made him think of his mother. "Would you pray for me? I mean, for me as the pastor of a church again. You know that I told God I wasn't going to do this again, and yet here I am."

"I promise to do so every day, and I already have been. All the women will pray for you, and I know some of the men will too. I want our church to be known as a praying church that loves one another. Like the church in Acts. I love the verse that says the people were awed at how they loved one another, and they were drawn to the church because of that. Wouldn't that be an amazing thing?"

Jacob stared at her. "I think I better study on Acts, then." *Could we have a New Testament church here in the middle of nowhere?* He'd begun to think of Medora as miles from everywhere. The sound of horses' hooves and laughter floated through the open front door.

"The girls are home. And Joel." She patted Jacob's hand. "Don't you go worrying about all this. God will do what God will do. He promised. We just need to ask big."

"You are so wise."

"Thank you."

"Ma!" Ada Mae burst through the door. "Someone put a mouse in Mr. Finch's desk, and he made us all stay after school." Pigtails flying, she threw her arms around her mother and giggled into her shoulder. "You should have seen him."

"I do hope it wasn't you." Cora hugged her daughter.

"No." Ada Mae looked up, the dusting of freckles across her nose bright against her winter-pale skin. "I can't catch a mouse."

"Which is a good thing." Virginia followed her sister in, setting their saddlebags on the chair. "Hey, Mr. Chandler."

"It wasn't Joel, was it?"

"No. I don't know who did it, but Mr. Finch was really mad. Wait until Opal hears this."

"Who's putting away the horses?" Cora asked.

"Joel."

"You know better than to let him always do that. You girls take turns."

"Take turns what?" Emily strolled in, untying her sunbonnet as she came. The others wore theirs on strings down their backs.

"With the horses."

"He offered."

"That's because he is a gentleman."

Ada Mae snorted at that and rolled her eyes.

"You girls go change your clothes and come have coffee and warm bread. I thought Opal was coming home with you."

"She had something else to finish at Mrs. Hegland's, so she'll be along soon." Virginia, the dreamer of the girls, smiled sweetly at Jacob. At fifteen, she was becoming a true prairie rose, with milky skin and pink cheeks. This would be her last year at the school, and since there was no higher school nearer than Dickinson, she would graduate in May.

Jacob leaned back in his chair, disappointment chewing at the edges of his mind. While he enjoyed the arrival of the schoolchildren, he'd been looking forward to watching Opal as she caught up on the news from school. Though she'd disliked Mr. Finch, Jacob figured she must like learning when she continued working for Mrs. Hegland to pay for school lessons.

Emily turned to her mother. "Do you think I could take piano lessons more often than once a week if I could figure a way to pay for them?"

"I don't know why not. Have you talked to Pearl about it?"

"Not yet. Hey, Opal told me that she might not be working there any longer."

Jacob sat closer to the table and leaned his

elbows on it. Disappointment took another bite. What was Opal planning now?

Joel came in the back door as Opal came in the front. He'd stopped by the soddy where he and Jacob lived and had changed out of his school clothes already. He hung his hat on the wall peg and came toward the table.

"Hey, Opal."

Jacob studied his son. Did he grow another two inches overnight? His pants were too short again, and his wrists were showing bone below his shirt cuffs. Granted these were his old clothes, but still he seemed to be shooting up fast.

While Opal smiled at their mouse story, she didn't break into laughter as she would have in the fall. Opal had always laughed so easily, her merry eyes inviting everyone to join her. Had she been there, she might have been the one to put the mouse in the desk. But not this Opal.

"You all ready for a roping review?" Opal asked, shaking her head for a "no thanks" when Cora offered her coffee and warm bread with jam.

"In a minute." Ada Mae charged off down the hall.

"Pa," Joel said, standing by his father's shoulder, "Auntie Colleen said to greet you.

I'm glad she's not going back to Pennsylvania."

"Yes." Jacob nodded. "That was a wise move."

"She would be a good ma." Joel took his chair and bit into the slice of bread sitting in front of his place.

Jacob stared at his son. Where had that come from? If he didn't know better, he'd think perhaps Joel was hinting, playing matchmaker. He glanced up to catch a gleam in Mrs. Robertson's eye. She'd heard. He shook his head, one side of his mouth trying to pull the other into a full smile.

If Joel still missed his mother, he'd never said so. But then, they never talked about the trip west or what went on in their former lives. That seemed to be a pattern with the people who landed in Medora, as if their lives began when they put down roots here in the badlands.

Did this mean his son was growing up? Other than eyelashes long as a jackrabbit's, he was all gangly boy with freckles and a gap between his two front teeth that made it easy to whistle. At nearly nine years old, he already showed evidence of gaining the Chandler height. Looking at him was like seeing his younger brother, Rob, when he was this age. Everyone had said that he and Rob looked enough alike to be twins.

Jacob pushed back his chair. "I'll be down at the barn when you're all ready."

Before long they all trailed down to the barn, where he had their ropes set out on the corral posts and the milk cow loose in the enclosure. While she would most likely take offense at being roped and try to kick him when he milked her, there were no cattle close enough to the homeplace to use.

"Ma said not to forget our chores." Ada Mae rolled her eyes. "She says that every day."

"All right, everyone, shake out your rope and let's begin." Opal stood in the middle of the corral, the milk cow at the far side, watching them all carefully.

Virginia, Ada Mae, Joel, and Jacob formed a circle and did as she said.

"Now, one at a time, drop the loop over the snubbing post. Joel, you go first."

Joel's loop swirled and floated over the post as if nothing else could be done. It took Virginia two tries, but she managed. Ada Mae's slipped off the first time but settled the second.

Jacob watched the others, his hand tightening, as did his stomach. Why? He could preach on Sunday morning, conduct weddings, baptisms, and funerals, visit the sick and dying, but right now he might as well be dying. His hand shook.

"Mr. Chandler." Opal nodded. "Your turn."

I know. Does she think I'm blind or something? All right, hand, rope, mind, let's all get along. God, I really don't want to make a fool of myself.

"Go, Pa, you can do it."

Jacob looked over to see his son nodding and smiling, the wide kind of smile that said "I'm cheering for you." He shook out his rope, spun the loop, and let it fly — to drop over the post on the first try.

"Very good, Mr. Chandler." Opal's smile almost reached her eyes.

Joel jumped and clapped. "You did it. See, you did it!"

Jacob walked forward and lifted his rope from the snubbing post, coiling it back in his hand. Now, if only he could rope her heart like he had this post. "Thank you, Miss Torvald." He kept his gaze on his rope, knowing his eyes would say too much.

CHAPTER TWENTY-SIX

Today they were raising McHenry's house. What a way to celebrate May.

Amethyst stared out the still-dark kitchen window. The sky lightened as she watched, and the rooster gave his first creaky crow. He tried again and by the third effort burst forth a full cock-a-doodle-do. With that, the sun painted the high clouds in shades of vermilion, streaks of persimmon, and patches of deep purple. She wished she were up on the butte to see the thin curve of live gold on the horizon. They had done just that a week ago and waited until the sun broke the bounds of night and threw itself into the heavens.

She'd heard the men leave some time ago to be out at the site at the first hint of light. The women would bring the food in wagons later. The kitchen was already ripe with the aroma of the beans that had baked through the night, rising bread, and browning bacon. She'd not seen a house-raising before, so this promised a new adventure. She could already see the cabin in her mind, since McHenry had described it to her so clearly one evening when they visited on the porch until the mosquitoes drove them inside.

How she loved to listen to his stories, the sound of his voice, his laugh.

"Good morning." Pearl entered the kitchen, as usual tying her apron on as she came. "I laid out a dress that I know I will never get back into because I refuse to any longer be laced into a corset. Having babies is detrimental to a slim waist. It should fit you with a bit of altering."

"But I — you have given me so much." Amethyst ducked her chin and nibbled her lip. She knew that with few boarders, the house was not paying for itself.

"Never enough for all you have done for us. And since I have no money for wages, this way I feel I am meeting my obligations somewhat." She patted Amethyst's shoulder as she walked by. "Besides, you are bringing in money for us with the sale of your cottage cheese. Mrs. Paddock was asking about more after church on Sunday." Pearl shook her head. "If we could find another milk cow, I would buy it, as you suggested, but Carl says we can have no more cows than we can cut enough hay for, so I shall be content with two."

Amethyst thought to the cheese she had ripening in the press Carl made for her. Wait until they tasted that. The chickens were growing fat on the whey; if only they had a sow with piglets to use up the rest.

"Ma?" Carly wandered into the room, rubbing sleep from her eyes, her nightshift dragging on the floor.

Pearl picked her up and hugged her close, rocking from foot to foot in a way the little girl loved. "How's Ma's big girl this morning?" They waltzed over to the window and watched the swallows swoop to pick up mud from along the pump and build their houses under the eaves of the barn.

"Birds. Pretty." Carly leaned her head against her mother's shoulder.

Lord, will there ever be a baby in my life? Amethyst thought of the little gown she'd kept from those her mother had made. Was she foolish to have saved it? Would she ever have a chance to use it? Much as she loved living and working here at the Heglands' boardinghouse, she dreamed of a man of her own, a home of her own, and children.

She'd even written down the names for her children: David, Darius for a girl, Stephen, and Melinda. That last name she'd heard one night in a story Pearl was reading aloud.

Lord, you are so good to me to bring me

here. She could never thank Him enough. While she often prayed for her father, with the passage of the months she doubted he'd come looking for her. He would have done that immediately. Or so she reasoned. She no longer woke with nightmares of him walking off the train and showing up to drag her home.

"You seem preoccupied this morning." Pearl set Carly in her chair and kissed the top of her daughter's head.

Amethyst felt the heat start in her chest and flare upward. Here she was daydreaming when she should be preparing breakfast. *Ach. Such laziness.* She gave the porridge a good stir and held a spoonful up to see if it was done. With a nod, she filled two of the bowls on the warming shelf and dolloped one spoonful for Carly in another. She set the bowls on the table and heard a familiar "da-da-da" from the bedroom. Joseph had progressed to recognizable sounds, and he entertained both himself and them with his chuckles and finger plays and sounds.

"You want me to get him?"

"No." Pearl pointed to a chair. "You sit down, and I will fetch him. If I gave you a chance, you would spoil me so rotten I'd never do a thing."

"Not much chance of that," Amethyst muttered under her breath as she did as she was told.

"And what time did you get up?" Pearl cocked her head and an eyebrow to make Amethyst shrug, then followed the sounds to her son, who crowed in delight as soon as he saw her.

Morning sounds at the boardinghouse spoke peace and delight every day.

They'd just finished cleaning up when a "Halloo" called Amethyst to the back porch.

Cimarron and Daisy and their children laughed from the light wagon pulled by a single horse. "Good morning. We're on our way out to McHenry's and brought you some mail. Came yesterday, but I didn't have time to run it over."

Amethyst walked out to get the mail and admire the doll one little child showed her. "Thanks. We'll be leaving soon too, but we're not loaded yet."

"Charlie took the coffeepot with him but forgot the coffee, so I figured we better get on out there and get the coffee brewing."

"Good idea. We'll see you in a bit."

"Hup." Cimarron pulled on the reins to back the horse and turned to leave, the children laughing and waving good-bye.

Amethyst glanced up as a meadowlark spilled joy from overhead. *Ah, what a glorious day.* On the porch she glanced at the two letters in her hand. Her father's spidery handwriting leaped up at her. Her heart skipped a beat, then fell, as if coated in lead.

"What happened?" Pearl rushed toward her. "You're white as a sheet."

Amethyst handed her one letter and held her own between two fingers. "My father."

Pearl sucked in a deep breath. "I see." Bit by bit through the months, she'd pulled information from Amethyst about her family and life in Pennsylvania. "Okay, I'll pour you a cup of coffee and you sit out on the porch, if you want to be by yourself, and read your letter. I'll go ahead and finish packing the food."

Amethyst nodded. She glanced toward the stove, so tempted to drop the letter in the fire and pretend she'd never received it. But that was the coward's way. Instead, she did just as suggested and retired to the porch. Slitting open the envelope, she dragged a piece of paper out and unfolded it. She closed her eyes. *Please, Lord, help me to bear this.*

She read the first two lines, and a smile tickled her cheeks. The next line brought on a chuckle and the last a full-throated, belly-bobbing laugh. She read the missive again and kept on laughing.

Pearl burst through the door. "What is it? Are you all right?"

Amethyst shook her head, nodded, and laughed some more, handing Pearl the letter at the same time.

"He's married?" Pearl read it aloud.

"Dear Daughter,
Thank you for yer letter of April. I am sorry Joel is not my grandson. I am married. Beulah takes good care of me.

The best,
Yer Pa

P.S. Send back train ticket."

"Beulah takes good care of him. God give her strength." Amethyst tipped her head back and chuckled again. "That poor, poor woman."

"This means you don't have to worry about him anymore." Pearl handed the letter back. "You won't send him the ticket, will you?"

"Good heavens, not in this life." Amethyst thought to the return ticket she had safely tucked away in the back of the family Bible. If she ever needed money, she could get some by cashing in the ticket. And she still had the gold pieces her mother had left for her should an emergency occur.

She planted her hands on her knees and pushed herself to her feet. "Let's get on out to the raising before it is all done. You do know how to get there?"

"Carl said he'd tie flags on bushes for us to find the way."

"I'll harness the horses and bring the wagon up." Amethyst stared at the envelope in her hand. *Burn it. What a waste of good paper. Tear it up in tiny pieces and burn it. Waste not, want not.* Ignoring the clamor in her mind, she marched into the house, set the stove lid aside, ripped the letter, envelope, and all into tiny bits, and watched them flare into flames before even reaching the coals. She set the lid back in place, dusted off her hands, and headed outside to the applause made by Pearl's clapping hands.

Sunbonnets shading their faces, they followed the flags and, as they neared McHenry's site, heard the sound of laughter, the thudding of axes, the shouting orders, and children calling to one another in a game. They smelled the smoke of a campfire and the fragrance of boiling coffee.

"I thought you'd never get here." Opal trotted over to tie the horses to a hitching post in the shade of a wide sheltering oak tree.

Amethyst sat for a moment and looked around. "What a lovely place for a house." Protected by the hills on either side, the house would face west to the river and to the buttes on the opposite side. Tall cottonwood trees shaded the house that now had log walls chest high. As two men kept the next log from rolling back down the ramp, two others pulled on the hoisting rope and dropped the notched log into place. The thud echoed in the valley.

The children, along with the young girls minding them, clapped and cheered. The men wiped sweat from their foreheads with the backs of their hands and moved the ramp logs around to the next side.

Off to another side others were building the trusses to support the roof.

Amethyst's gaze unerringly found Jeremiah McHenry. He was adzing a log to flatten the top and bottom so it fit more tightly. His shirt sleeves were rolled up, sweat darkening the shirt, and when he stopped for a breather, he pushed the brim of his hat back with one finger. As she'd heard someone say once, he was a fine figure of a man in spite of the black patch over his eye.

She turned to see Pearl watching her, a knowing smile curving her lips.

The flush Amethyst so despised roared up her neck and turned her face to fire. Was it that obvious? How could she not have come to care for him — no other man in her entire life had asked for her opinion or thanked her for every little service or told her stories into the late evening — in spite of the red warning flags of flask and temper?

She shook her head both inside and out. She knew what kind of woman he wanted, one like Pearl or Ruby, who would know how to dress in stylish clothes, carry on a conversation, use the correct fork, and look fine on her man's arm. Both Rand Harrison and Carl Hegland stood straighter and walked with pride when their wives laid a hand on their arms and smiled into their eyes.

Instead of joining with the women who were sewing curtains for the windows and stitching a quilt for his new bed, Amethyst made sure the tables were ready for the food they kept in the shade and covered against the flies. She carried the water bucket around and filled the dipper for each of the men to drink, laughing when they sloshed water over their faces.

"Summer sure came by today," Charlie said. "Thanks for the water. We'll stop for dinner when the sun is straight up."

"We'll be ready."

She let her sunbonnet shade her face when she served McHenry and nodded when he said, "Thank you." Did he suspect how she felt?

At the cut of an expletive she turned, her water bucket sloshing on her skirt. She'd recognize his voice anywhere. McHenry was picking himself off the ground, muttering under his breath, yet she could still hear him. He'd never used that kind of language around her.

"You all right?" Rand stopped on his way over to help when McHenry motioned him away.

"I'm fine." His growl belied the words.

He tripped again. She'd known it immediately. That he tripped and misjudged distances so often made it no easier. She could understand that. *But he gets so angry*. She watched as he turned away, drew something from his shirt pocket, and tipped his head back. The sun glinted on the silver flask.

He must have struck his bad leg in the fall. *Lord, what do I do? I can understand why he does this, but I can't stand the idea of being around a drinker who swears.* She turned away, still wanting to go help him. Ach, such doings.

CHAPTER TWENTY-SEVEN

June slipped into July, and no matter how hard Opal worked, the darkness only lightened once in a while, usually when she was playing with Sprout. Otherwise it never left.

She'd overheard Rand and Ruby talking about her one night.

"I don't know what to do," Ruby had said.

"Nor I."

If I knew what to do, I would do it.

"The laughter she always brought just isn't here, and if I scold her one more time, I think I shall banish myself to the woodshed. Scolding doesn't help, praying hasn't helped, trying to get her to talk — that's as hopeless as trying to wash skunk stink off Ghost."

"I found her weeping out by her tree a day or so ago. I didn't even let her know I was there. It about broke my heart."

Leaning her forehead against the wall, Opal thought to her tree, an ancient oak with one branch as big as some other trees running parallel to the ground before curving upward. Opal often lay along that branch and stared into the leaves and branches above her. Bits of blue sky, the sun gilding the leaves, the breeze forming and reforming the patterns of light and shadow. One afternoon she'd fallen asleep there and awoke as she hit the ground. The branch wasn't that wide.

Every time she closed her eyes, she saw rotting carcasses, many now stripped of hide and flesh, ribs arcing white, silent testimonials to the animals that lived and breathed and wandered the wide prairie in search of the perfect grazing spot.

Rand's entire herd numbered eighty-five with only fourteen calves, six of them heifers. Several of their twenty cows had lost their calves. They had twenty head of heifers of breeding age, so next year they might have forty calves. If they all made it through the winter. If the winter were not so severe. If, if, if. None of which had to do with how hard they worked, other than having put enough hay by and planted oats and wheat, as Rand had done, so they would have grain to eat and feed.

Her mind sorted through the numbers like the Chinese man she'd once seen using an abacus, the beads clicking faster than the ear could hear.

And not only the cattle dead. Little Squirrel and the baby too. Linc gone, his absence at the table a continual reminder — they'd become like family in the time they'd been with them. There'd been another funeral when they found what was left of a woman who had wandered off. If she had to say one more good-bye, Opal was sure she'd cry herself into a puddle to be sucked up by the thirsty ground.

What concerned her the most? Rand and Ruby acted as if nothing was wrong. They said God would provide. Like He'd provided fodder for the cattle this winter? Sometimes she wasn't sure who she was angrier at, them or God. And Jacob — standing up there talking about how God loved them and ordered that they love one another.

This was home, but what if they couldn't stay here? So many others had left. Empty soddies, empty ranch houses, empty buildings in Medora, empty prairies. But for the bones. Rand said they would go out and pick up the bones after the sun and the weather, along with the critters and birds, finished cleaning the carcasses. Someone was foolish enough to pay for the bones to be ground up for fertilizer.

Rand was grateful. For the privilege of

picking up bones? Another one of those incomprehensible things. Life was incomprehensible. Sleeping seemed the only antidote, but when she slept so much, how come she never woke up rested?

Soon the all-day haying would start, and the women would work from before dawn cooking for the crew and into the night canning if something was ready. Most of the garden would be ready in August, but the Juneberries, strawberries, and chokecherries were ready in July. She wandered down to the barn and let Sprout out of his stall. Rand wanted her to let him run with the herd, but she knew something would get him. He had no fierce longhorn mother to protect him. She let him through the gate and into the pasture, where she sat down and let him graze around her.

His horns showed a couple of inches now, so if he rubbed his head against her, which he loved to do, sometimes it hurt. Like now. "Ouch, you can't do that." She pushed him away. He thought she was playing and pushed back.

"You need another young steer to battle with. Not me." Instead, she scratched under his chin and along his throat, which was guaranteed to make his long eyelashes droop and to make him stretch his muzzle out even more.

Roundup had consisted of castrating and branding their far-too-few calves, including ten for the Robertsons. They'd moved steers that wore other brands to their rightful places, and she assumed other ranchers did the same. Some steers no longer had owners in the area. Rand kept a tally of those he kept so that he could pay the owners if he could find them.

She pulled a long stem of grass and chewed the tender end. Sprout lay down beside her. "If you're done grazing, better come on back to the corral. I hear Ruby calling." She got to her feet, and when she walked off, Sprout hoisted his hindquarters, then the front, stretched, tail twisting above his back, and trotted after her, bawling as if she'd forsaken him.

Beans leaned on the top rail of the gate, shaking his head. "You spoiled him so bad he don't know he's a steer. Acts more like a dog."

Opal shrugged. "One of these days he'll figure it out."

"Ruby wants you up to the house."

"Yeah." She lowered the top two bars of the gate, and Sprout hopped over the lowest. "Back to the corral for you, Sprout."

Beans replaced the bars and slapped the

calf on the rump. He kicked up his heels and galloped after Opal, who rarely even smiled at his antics.

"Mr. Chandler is coming to supper, so I thought you might want to change."

Opal looked down at her britches. She'd put them on clean this morning. She looked to Ruby. "Why?"

Ruby rolled her eyes. "Because we are having company, and I want you to dress like the female you are."

Opal shrugged, but her jaw tightened. "He's seen me in britches before and didn't seem to mind."

"Opal, for once just do as I ask."

"You act like I never do what you want." Opal tried to keep her voice from rising, but it had a mind of its own.

"Be quiet. You'll wake Mary."

A cry from the bedroom said that already happened.

Ruby threw her dishcloth down on the table. "Now see what you did. I just got her to sleep and thought I'd have a few moments of peace and quiet." She turned so fast her skirt swirled, and she stomped down the hall.

Opal slammed the door on her way out. *Wear a dress. Put up your hair. Be quiet.*

Be more lively. There was no way pleasing Ruby. Most likely she was pregnant again, cranky as she was. As if they needed another baby around.

"Opa!" Per banged at the screen door. "Opa, out!"

"Go away."

"Opa, out!" He banged harder and started to whimper.

And if he started crying, then that would be all her fault too.

I should have gone with Atticus whether he wanted me along or not. It wasn't the first time this thought had crossed her mind. What would life be like if . . . ? Sometimes, when she was just about asleep, her mind would float back to before the day she left school and went swimming in the river, before the drifter came. Life had been perfect then. But evil came by and perfect died. She let Per out on the porch, sat back down, and wrapped her arms around her knees. The spot darkened by her tears spread.

"Opa?" Per leaned against her shoulder. When she didn't respond, he walked around her knee and patted her cheek with his soft baby hand. Opal took him in her arms, settled him in her lap, and used his head where he lay against her chest to dry her tears. *How can I be cruel even to you, who is so loving? God, I don't understand what is going on.*

After a while Ghost came and sat beside them, begging for attention. Per leaned over and dug his fingers into her fur. "Opa, see Go."

"I know. Ghost is here too. We could have a party."

"Pawty?"

"Close — party." She kept one arm around Per and laid the other over the cow dog, who quickly dried Opal's tears with her tongue and then made sure Per got his share of attention. The little boy giggled, the dog wriggled, and Opal let herself smile. *I want to be happy again. I want to be me again. I don't like this person I've become — not at all. I should at least be grateful Per is finally well.*

"Pa?"

"Gone."

The men were taking turns riding the range and helping finish the house out at McHenry's. Today Rand and Joe had gone to the building. Joe had been stringing fence around the seeded fields to keep out the cattle, not that there were that many to keep out.

"I better go help too, I guess." Opal stood

and picked up Per.

"Ride horse?"

"Nope, not today." Opal shut the gate behind herself, leaving Per on the porch.

Opal did put on a skirt before Jacob rode up to the house. Rand and Joe arrived at the same time, and Chaps took their horses down to the barn to take off the saddles and let them into the pasture. Beans came up from milking and stopped to strain the milk in the springhouse.

Opal finished setting the table as the men came in together.

"Sure smells good in here." Rand hung his hat on the tree by the door and combed his hair back with the palms of his hands. "Jacob, make yourself at home."

Opal turned to greet him and stopped, caught by the funny feeling in her middle and the look in his eyes, which might have been the cause of the strange sensation. She'd felt it around him before, before he started ignoring her. But he'd said he wouldn't do that again, that they were friends.

"Miss Torvald." He nodded.

"Mr. Chandler." *Call me Opal, for pity's sake*. But that might upset Rand, and it was bad enough having Ruby unhappy with her so much of the time, let alone both of them.

"If you men would get washed up, we can go ahead and eat," Ruby said. "Opal, please wash Per's hands and get him in his chair."

Opal nodded. Anything to get over this feeling that something was alive and fluttering in her middle. "Come on, Per."

As soon as they were all seated, Rand bowed his head for grace. "Heavenly Father, we thank you for all you have provided for us, for home, health, food on our table, and friends and family to enjoy it. All this reminds us of how much you love us. In Jesus' name, amen."

" 'Men," said Per.

Opal glanced up to catch Mr. Chandler grinning at Per. When he smiled at her that feeling returned. She picked up the platter and passed the meat around. If she didn't look at him, perhaps it would go away.

He seemed to be watching her all through the meal. She watched Per, answered Rand's question about Sprout, and mopped up where Per spilled his gravy. While he tried to feed himself, some times were messier than others. Ruby had just sat down to finally eat when Mary left off cooing and decided it was time to be fed.

"Opal, would you please make sure everyone has what they need?" Ruby said under her breath. At Opal's nod, she continued, "If you will excuse me . . ." Ever gracious, she stood and smiled at those around the table. "Duty calls."

Rand shook his head. "I think babies have a sense of whenever their mother tries to eat. They always demand to be fed then, company or not."

Opal grabbed Per's hand before he dumped his spoonful of food down for Ghost, who always sat right by his chair. "You eat that."

He looked over the chair arm. "Go."

"No, it's not for Ghost." Opal looked up at the sound of Mr. Chandler chuckling.

He grinned at her. "Keeps you busy, doesn't he?"

"Me and three or four others. Ghost grabbed the back of his shift and kept him from a tumble down the stairs yesterday. He gets to running and can't stop. How come Joel didn't come with you?"

"He and Ada Mae are working on something."

"Speaking of school, did you hear that Mr. Finch is not planning to return in August?"

"Yes. I've sent in my application to take over."

Opal stared at him. "You'd teach school here?"

"If they hire me. I don't have a teaching certificate, but I have sufficient schooling and have applied. Mrs. Hegland said there should be no problem."

"Who'll help out at the Robertsons?"

"I will. That way Joel and I can continue to live there. Although, with the exodus around here, there are houses available in town now."

When did all this come about? He talked as if it were public knowledge. Mr. Chandler as the teacher. "So, will you . . . I mean . . ." She caught the plate that Per was sliding over the edge. How did Ruby manage to talk and watch him at the same time? "Oh, would all of you care for coffee?"

Opal scooped Per out of his chair and took him over to the washbasin, then fetched the coffeepot. As she refilled the men's cups she wondered if he would be both teacher and minister, along with working at Robertsons'. He was going to be one busy man. What would it be like to have your pa be the teacher? She felt a bit sad for Joel. Now he wouldn't dare put critters in the teacher's desk.

After supper Rand and Mr. Chandler moved out to the front porch. Ruby returned to the kitchen after putting Mary down and picked up the dishcloth to wipe the table.

"You go on out. I'll finish in here," Opal said.

"You sure?" Ruby asked and at Opal's nod, she smiled. "Thank you."

A while later Opal pushed open the screen door. "I was wondering if you would like coffee out here." She noted the empty chairs. "Where did they go?"

"For a bit of a walk. I'll let you know when they come back." Ruby sat rocking Per. "We'll eat the pie then."

Opal nodded. *Well, obviously he didn't come to see me. So why did I have to dress up?* Now, why did that thought bother her?

CHAPTER TWENTY-EIGHT

"What did you want to talk to me about?" Rand asked.

Jacob puffed out a sigh. "I'm worried about Opal."

"We all are. She's so grown up on one hand and so young on another." Rand stopped to stare across the now placid summer river to the buttes with Pinnacle Peak glowing red in the last throes of the sunset. "All she can see is the death." His arm arced to include the land around him. "She can't see the life coming back, can't trust that God always brings life back."

"You have to live through death first before you can believe life will return."

"I know. You've been there."

Jacob nodded, his hands shoved in his back pockets. "Rand, I don't know what to do." The words nearly snagged on the rock in his throat, but he pushed them on by. Was it sheer desperation or the force of love?

He could feel Rand studying him as he sighed, and he wished he were on that butte across the river.

"About what?"

"Opal." A silence allowed for the croak of a bullfrog down in the cattails. "I . . . I did what I promised but . . . I don't know how to say this."

"Take your time. There is no hurry."

"Well, after you told me to wait until she's sixteen, I did what I've done before. I ran away. Running away didn't help. She thought I didn't want to be her friend any longer. That isn't what I meant. But it's hard to trust my actions when I failed so terribly before." Jacob stuffed his hands in his back pockets. "When I see the sadness in her eyes . . ."

Rand sighed, a quiet sound, gentle like the breeze that brought the scent of growing grass and evening. "I know. Life sure isn't easy. So what do you think now?"

"I think I need to let Opal know that I am her friend and will always be her friend. And pray that God will give me wisdom and strength."

"I'd say that makes good sense." Rand cleared his throat and paused. "I've even wondered if letting her know that you care for her might help her out of this."

"Really?" Jacob could feel his heart leap. "Let me know what you decide. I promise, no matter what, to take it slow and easy." He half chuckled. "After all, the thought of becoming a pastor's wife might scare her out of the sadness and into pure terror."

Rand took a turn at chuckling. "You're a good man, Jacob. Can you stay for another cup of coffee?"

"I better say good night and head on home. Where are we cutting first?"

"The lower section here, then the field at Robertsons', then the buttes. McHenry is going to help too, and we might do his before the buttes, depends on the weather."

"And you want me to do the mowing?"

"You're better at it than the rest of us. I'm always amazed at the way God brings the right people to a place at the right time." Rand stared upward where the first stars pricked holes in the deepening blue. "Nights like this, there is nowhere else I'd rather live on this earth."

"I wondered during the winter. I heard this was the worst ever, but that wind . . ." Jacob shook his head. "I understand folks leaving, but it sure seems a shame to walk away from all the hard work they put in."

"Yep." Rand turned back toward the house where a lamp glowed in the window. "See that light?"

"Sure."

"Ruby always makes sure there is a lamp in the window to guide us travelers home. I see that light, and I know she's waitin' for me. Nothin' better in this life, unless it is maybe holding your new baby for the first time."

Jacob closed his eyes. *Lord, let this be part of my life. To you be the glory.* The two men strolled back up to the house, the night a gentle lover kissing their shoulders.

"Can you stay for pie and coffee?" Ruby asked when they reached the front of the house.

"Thank you, but I better be on my way. Is Opal still up?"

"She's out on the back porch."

Jacob thought a second. "I'll go say good night, and I'll be here ready to cut as soon as the dew leaves."

"We'll see you tomorrow, then." Ruby kept her rocking chair in motion, the child at her shoulder soundly sleeping.

"Yes." Jacob untied his horse and led him around the end of the house. If he hadn't known she was there, he'd not have seen her. But something inside him knew even before his eyes.

"Opal — er, Miss Torvald."

"Here." He could hear a smile in her voice. "Miss Torvald? Hmm. That sounds

384

so formal, Mr. Chandler. Or should I call you Reverend Chandler?"

Was that a mocking tone he heard now? It would be easier to tell if he could see her face. But all he could see was the white glow of her waist.

"My friends call me Jacob."

The rocking chair squeaked a private song.

"Funny, my friends call me Opal."

"Good night, Opal." He swung aboard his horse and turned to leave. "See you tomorrow."

"Good night, Jacob."

The sound of his name from her lips lent wings to his heart as he let his horse slow-jog home. He knew the horse could see better than he could. There was that trust thing again. He thought about his sermon for Sunday. Perhaps trust was a good topic for all of them — to know that perfect love from the heavenly Father and to trust Him to live up to His promises. Did one ever learn those lessons perfectly? Cutting hay would give him plenty of time for thinking.

It was perfect haying weather. Jacob pushed the lever on the cycle mower to lower the cutting bar, hupped the team, and started out, the clacking cutting blades laying the thick grass back over the bar in a steady stream. The team plodded around the field, now rounding the corners as the cut swath broadened. Midmorning Ada Mae and Joel came running across the field to bring him a jug of water and two slices of bread with meat in between.

Jacob stopped the team, raised the sickle bar, and motioned for them to come around on the offside. "Thank you. I'm about as dry as thistledown." Looping the reins over one of the handles, he stepped from the machine, stretching muscles already weary from staying in one position.

"Mrs. Harrison said you would be," Ada Mae said, holding out the water jug.

Joel eyed the rows. "Real straight, huh, Pa?"

"I try to be. The grass is looking real good. So what have you been doing?" He took the jug from Ada Mae and drank, the cold water easing his throat.

Joel rolled his eyes. "Stacking wood. Everywhere I go, I stack wood."

"You could be splitting wood by now." Jacob took a longer glug of water, letting some dribble down his chin. While the sun felt good in the earlier morning, by now, as it climbed higher, he'd call it hot. As he'd said, it was perfect haying weather as long as the rain stayed away. They needed lots of dry weather to let it dry, rake and turn it, and then haul it to the barns and stacks. After this last winter he didn't think one could ever put up too much. The sandwich disappeared in four bites.

"We're going to pick strawberries after dinner, Pa. Opal knows where a patch is ripe."

"Good for you."

When he finished eating, Jacob fetched the oil can from behind the metal seat and squirted drops of oil into the gearbox and along the cycle. "Watch what I'm doing, and next time you can do it." With Joel watching carefully, he finished the job. "The oil helps keep the parts that move against each other from wearing out so quickly."

"How much oil?"

"A couple of squirts. You don't want to waste it, but machinery always needs oil to run well. Like horses need feed and water. One thing machinery doesn't need is to rest like horses do. This afternoon I'll take out a different team." He set the can back in its place and looked at his son and Ada Mae. "So Opal is taking you two out strawberry picking?"

"Yep. Mrs. Harrison said we can have

strawberry shortcake if we find enough."

He'd not asked about Opal, just gone about his business but hoped he would see her. Dinnertime couldn't come soon enough. He drained the water jug and handed it back. "Thanks again and tell Mrs. Harrison thank you too." He watched the children run back across the field before he climbed back aboard the mower and let down the sickle bar again. Good thing he had an extra set of blades all sharpened and ready to go.

With everything running smoothly again, he let his thoughts play. Every time Joel called him Pa, his heart chuckled. What a difference this year from last. Back then Joel was surly, and he wasn't much better himself. He'd been no more prepared to be a father than Joel had been ready to accept him as such. It hadn't helped when Joel took to riding and roping like he was born to it, and his pa had two left hands and a rope that twisted out of sheer spite. Some sight that must have been. As Opal said, it was all in the wrist.

When the sun hit straight up, he drove the team back to the barn, let them loose in the corral, and joined the others at the washing bench.

"Watching you mow is like watching an

artist at work." Rand dried his face with one of the towels.

"Thank you. That grass is near to perfect. Thicker than last year."

"I spread manure from the barn out there and on the garden. We'll see how the grain field does."

"Looks good so far. I read about a ride-on plow too. You got a lot done for using a hand plow."

"Yes, and to think that some have farmed with no horses, just one man pulling the plow and another man or woman on the handles keeping that plowshare digging in." Rand shook his head. "I'd much rather ride a horse than dig behind one."

"You read about the Bonanza farms in the Red River Valley?" McHenry asked.

"Where's the Red River Valley?" Jacob asked.

"Eastern edge of Dakotah Territory. I got the mower from a place in Fargo. That's part of the Red River Valley." Rand flipped the towel over one of the nails pounded into the springhouse wall for that purpose.

McHenry shook his head. "We should have talked about this sooner. You got the mower, so I'll get the plow. All I could think on was getting that house going."

"You want to do that, I won't argue." The

three walked together up to the house. "Might be good if one of the rest of us took lessons from Jacob here on the mower, the upkeep and all. I tried sharpening those blades. It's downright easy to put a nick in them on the grinding wheel. Sure wish Linc was here. He was a good one on the repairs. Had an eye for that kind of thing."

Jacob automatically searched for Opal as soon as he walked in the house.

She turned from serving the meat onto a platter and sent him a smile, not quite the old Opal kind but better than being ignored.

"Pa!" Per banged his spoon on the table, his face lighting with a smile that made Jacob grin back.

One day. Someday.

"So how's the house coming?" Ruby asked McHenry after all the food was on the table and grace said.

"I'm still splitting shakes. Got more than half the roof on." McHenry buttered his slice of bread and raised it in appreciation. "You'll have to teach me how to make bread. I do biscuits all right but not bread."

"I'd be glad to."

"I was lucky. I had Beans to do the cooking." Rand passed the bowl of dandelion greens to McHenry.

"You know, Joel could learn to split

shakes. I did it when I was his age." Jacob smiled at his son.

"What about me?" Ada Mae sat up straighter.

"You sure your mother doesn't need you at home?"

Ada Mae made a face. "She's got Emily and Virginia. Joel and I picked all the dandelion greens and stacked wood. We'll do the same at our house tomorrow, most likely."

Jacob watched Opal taking care of Per while she ate, not taking part in the conversation. Not like his Opal at all. *What can I do? Lord, what? How can I help her?*

Per chattered away, only some of his noises real words, but he seemed to think they should all understand him. Opal made sure he ate, didn't throw half his food down for Ghost, and kept him from flying out of his chair.

The next morning Jacob woke earlier than ever, dressed, and left the soddy where he and Joel lived. He saddled a horse and rode up the road and followed a cut up to the eastern butte to watch the sunrise. Breaking over the lip of the butte just as the sun creased the horizon, he stopped and dismounted, letting his horse graze while he admired the heavenly artist at work. "Lord, such magnificence. I will exalt your name and sing your praises throughout the earth. You are my God, and I praise you." He sank to the ground, resting his arms on his raised knees, hearing the horse crunching the grass, the bit clanking, a snort.

Dew glittered as the sunbeams struck each drop of water, meadowlarks sang their morning arias, and Jacob breathed in new life. Did Opal ever see this, living in the valley? He glanced over his shoulder to the treetops sticking above the butte lip, the greens of the grasses and prairie plants so many shades of green he couldn't believe his eyes. Off across the prairie, the grass bent before the slight wind in shimmering grass waves. All around him, low to the ground, were blue blossoms, a field of reflected sky in miniature.

He mounted his horse, saluted the sun now fully climbing the sky bridge, and rode back down to the Robertson ranch. Time to get Joel up so he could milk the cow, unless Ada Mae had already done so.

Tomorrow, he promised himself. *Tomorrow I will bring Opal up there.* "Thank you, Father. You answered my prayer."

CHAPTER TWENTY-NINE

"You want me to do what?" Opal stood on the back porch looking down at Jacob.

"Ride up to the butte for the sunrise. I've already asked Ada Mae and Joel if they want to come." Jacob tipped his hat back on his head.

She shrugged. "I guess so. But I need to be back to help get breakfast on the table." Her heart giggled for the joy of riding somewhere, anywhere, early in the morning.

"Good. Be at Robertsons' early enough to get up there. You know where we held the cattle last year before that branch took me off the horse? That's where I was this morning."

"Should I bring anything?"

"No, we'll come right down so I can eat and get started mowing again. I figure I should be done with the field here by today, if all goes well. I'll take the mower over home tonight."

"Where are Ada Mae and Joel?"

"Out with McHenry. He's teaching them to split shakes for the roof of his house and barn. Mrs. Robertson sent along a dinner basket for all of them."

"I need to go get Per out of trouble again." She'd heard Ruby scolding him. Maybe it wasn't just her. Per seemed to get his share of scolding too. Looked like she'd been right. Ruby must be in the family way again. She turned to watch Jacob stride down to the barn where he would check over the mower, fix any broken blades, oil it well, harness up the alternate team, and head on out. The other men were out raking and turning the first day's cutting. By the day after tomorrow they'd be making haystacks.

She returned to the kitchen, where Ruby was washing dishes and Per was sitting in the rocking chair, whimpering. "So what did you do now, little guy?"

"He tried to pull the tablecloth off the table and got bopped on the head with a cup and saucer." Ruby shook her head, then stretched her neck from one side to the other. She sighed when they heard Mary set up a squall. Mary went from placid to shrieking in two seconds, as if once she woke up and realized she was hungry, her mother better be there immediately. At least she'd slept through dinner today.

Opal picked Per up and took him to the

rocker outside so that Ruby could nurse Mary sitting in the other rocker. "Come on, let's rock."

" 'Ock?"

So you can fall asleep and take a nap, and we can all have some peace. Earlier he'd pulled Ghost's ears until she yipped, and he'd been scolded for that. "Poor Per."

"Po Pa." He'd yet to learn how to say Per, although he had Pa down well. *R*s were hard for him to pronounce. As soon as they sat down, he leaned against Opal and stuck his thumb and first finger into his mouth. She pushed the rocker with one foot and relaxed with the rhythm.

"Opa?"

She stroked the hair back from his forehead. "What?" She laid her cheek against the top of his head.

"Opa." His voice slurred as he mumbled a few other syllables.

It took so little to help him go to sleep. She rocked a few minutes more, then slid her other arm under his bottom and stood. She paused a moment to watch his face, but he was sound asleep. After putting him in his bed, she left the room, closing the door behind her. Returning to the kitchen, which included the whole west side of the house, kitchen and parlor all in one big room, she saw that Ruby and Mary were sound asleep in the inside rocker.

Gently taking Mary from Ruby's arms, Opal nodded at Ruby's start. "I'm going to put her to bed, and you are going to put you to bed."

"But I . . ."

The circles under Ruby's eyes made Opal shake her head. "You nothing. I can do what needs to be done." *Even though I'd rather go weed the garden than bake for the crew.*

Later that evening she looked up from the book she was reading. "Mr. Chandler invited me to go along with him and Joel and Ada Mae for a ride up to the butte to watch the sunrise in the morning."

"Should be beautiful." Ruby rubbed her forehead. "I think I'll go on to bed."

"I'll be along soon." Rand looked up from the leather bridle he was braiding. He had three long strips of tanned cowhide nailed to one end of a board and laid one over the other just like Ruby used to braid her sister's hair.

"What are you making?"

"A new headstall. We need a couple new bridles. Think I'll do this as a hackamore."

"I noticed the harness is getting pretty

worn in a couple of places."

"You'd have thought I'd get all that kind of thing caught up in the winter, especially as housebound as we were this year."

"Yes, but we spent half our time hauling wood and melting water."

"True."

Ask him. No, don't be nosy. She marked her place with her finger. "Rand, is Ruby in the family way again?"

He looked up from his braiding. "If she is, she hasn't told me."

"She's so crabby. Both times she was that way before, she was like this."

"Might just be tired from having Mary and nursing her." He paused to think. "She's worried about you."

"Me? Why?"

"The two of you wear matching circles under your eyes. You've been sad for so long now."

Opal swallowed hard. This wasn't the way she wanted the conversation to go. *What's there to be happy about?* But she didn't say it. "Think I'll go on to bed if I'm going to go sunrise-seeing."

"Good night."

Wouldn't Ruby know if she was pregnant again? She thought about that as she undressed and crawled under the sheet. The summer quilt now lay folded at the end of her bed, and her coyote quilt lay across the chest Rand had made for her to replace the trunks destroyed when Dove House burned. The lace curtains at her windows fluttered in the night breeze. She lay on her back and locked her hands behind her head. The feel of her braid reminded her that she'd not done her one hundred brush strokes for her hair every night for quite some time. Tonight she'd not even taken time to unbraid it and rebraid it loose for the night. She'd not read her Bible for some time either. Too tired. Just too tired. If Ruby felt as tired as she did, no wonder she was crabby.

Which brought up another thought. Was she crabby too? Is that what Rand meant?

How come Jacob was suddenly being so friendly again? Especially after acting like a stranger and not a friend. And Atticus. Where was he, and what was he doing? She rolled over on her side and sucked in a deep breath, then let it all out. There was more to life that was confusing than that made sense.

Night still reigned when she woke. What would Bay think of being whistled to in the darkness like this? She slid into her clothes, unbraided, brushed, and re-braided her hair. She didn't need light to do any of that. Carrying her boots, she tip-toed down the hall to the kitchen. She needed to hurry. The eastern sky was beginning to lighten.

Within moments she was loping Bay up the road, not even bothering with a saddle. The cool wind in her hair, the cloppity-clop of hooves, Bay snorting, pulling against the reins — it all felt good.

"I think you've missed being ridden as much as I've missed riding." She patted her horse's shoulder, wanting to hug it and the trees now coming alive from the shadows. The others met her at the road.

"Good morning." She pulled the snorting Bay down to a walk.

"We better hurry, or we'll miss it." Jacob grinned at her, touching the brim of his hat.

"Our cat had kittens last night," Ada Mae announced, "in Virginia's bed. She was some upset."

Opal glanced over her shoulder. Ada Mae rode behind her, with Joel bringing up the rear. Jacob led the way up the cut. Strange for him to be leading the way. She was always the leader on horseback. But now he looked at home in the saddle, no longer a beginning rider. She smiled to herself. All three of them rode like the wranglers they'd become.

Bay dug in as the cut steepened, and Opal leaned forward to help her. She probably should have saddled up, but feeling the warmth of the horse's hide through her pants, the ripple of muscles, the wonderful fragrance of horse still made her want to laugh out loud. Why had she waited so long?

Because Rand had told her not to ride out and see all the dead cattle.

So why didn't I at least ride around the pasture? Because. Because. Because if I couldn't ride where I wanted to, I didn't want to ride at all. The thought burst on her brain as Bay crested the butte. *Talk about dumb. What was the matter with me?*

The other two came right behind her, and they lined up facing east as Jacob was. The horses were breathing hard, and one coughed, making Ada Mae giggle.

Opal breathed in the splendor of the rising day. Moment by moment the clouds brightened from purple gray to fire flung with abandon across the skies. The glowing brass rim emerged above the line where land met sky, and then rose in the daytime arc of warmth and life.

"Ohh." Opal looked to Jacob, then back

to the spectacle. "Thank you."

"I didn't do it."

"No, but you brought me here."

"God flung out this gift for us to enjoy."

"True." *And He keeps on doing it.* The thought made her lay back against Bay's warm back. *Even if I don't appreciate it.*

"Pa, can Ada Mae and me ride over to that tree?"

"If you want." Jacob dismounted.

Opal swung her left leg over Bay's rump and slid to the ground, sending tingles up her feet. She rested her cheek against Bay's neck. "Thanks, old girl," she whispered. *I think I might want to live again.*

"Over here." Jacob crossed his ankles and sank to the ground, patting a place beside him. His horse began grazing as if they'd done this every day.

Opal sat down where he indicated and propped her elbows on her knees. "I'd forgotten."

"Easy to do."

"Everything looked so dark."

"That's why we have the sunrise, and the Son, S-o-n, too. See the grass bending before the wind?"

She nodded. "I saw waves like that on the Atlantic Ocean when the Brandons took us out there. Never ending."

401

"I never knew grass could look so alive until I came out here. And the dew — just think, the garden of Eden, the whole world really, was watered by dew before the Fall."

"Really?" She looked up to see him looking at her rather than the dew. That strange feeling started in her middle again. Like butterflies cavorting in the sunshine.

"Now look at this." He pointed to the carpet of blue they sat upon. "Out there where the grass flows, you wouldn't see these, but right here there are so many they all blend together. See, they are just opening to the sun."

Opening to the sun. She liked the sound of that. They could hear Ada Mae and Joel laughing as they trotted back. A crow scolded them for invading his territory. A male grouse called from the thicket, and another rooster answered the challenge. Dueling roosters.

She fingered the little flowers, picking one and holding it to her nose. Not much fragrance. Not like the strawberries she and the others picked, but such a rich color.

"Thank you, Jacob." His name felt comfortable on her tongue. She smiled into his eyes. "Now we better get back."

"I know, but we'll do this again."

"Yes." *But it won't be the same. Nothing*

on the prairie stays the same.

"Come on, Pa, we're hungry."

"And I have to help Ruby." *Or she'll yell at me again. I'm going to ask her today.*

Jacob stood and reached out a hand. She placed hers in it and allowed him to pull her to her feet. At Bay's side he cupped his hands to help her mount. She knew and he knew that she could swing up using a hank of mane. So why did this feel so good?

CHAPTER THIRTY

Amethyst caught herself listening for his horse to return.

"Amethyst, could you please change Joseph? I'm up to my elbows in dough," Pearl called from the kitchen.

"Right away."

Taking care of either of the children was always a pleasure to her. Pretending added to it. She laid the baby on the small quilt with Carly standing at her side. "Would you please bring me a diaper?"

Carly nodded, her smile bright. For one so small, she was already the little mother, coming to tell Pearl when Joseph needed something. She would play with him, shaking the rattle, picking up the cloth ball that Amethyst had made, giving it back to him and repeating the game endlessly.

Amethyst held the wet diaper in place until the new one arrived. One did not trust little boys without a diaper. Pulling the woolen knit soaker back in place she picked him up and blew on his round little belly. Both baby and Carly laughed along with

Amethyst. She looked up to see Carl standing in the door.

Carly ran and clasped her father around the knee, then sat on his foot, and he hobbled along with her. "Something is on my foot, and it is oh so heavy." The joy on Carly's upturned face twisted something inside Amethyst.

Her pa had never played with any of the children. Instead, he yelled at her mother to "keep them brats quiet." And all of them had died but her. She snuggled Joseph for the moment he allowed and put him down on the floor again, smiling at the beeline he made on his hands and knees for his pa. Sometimes he walked, but not when he was in a hurry. This one let nothing stand between him and what he wanted. Carly looked over her shoulder and laughed up at her father.

"See Joey, Pa."

"I see him." Carl swept Carly up on his arm and bent over to scoop up his son. With a child in each arm, he headed for the kitchen, where Pearl could be heard banging pots around.

Amethyst folded up the small quilt they used for changing the baby on, picked up the wet diaper, and carried it to the pail where they soaked the dirty diapers until they could wash them. Tomorrow would be washday, mostly of baby things.

She washed her hands after putting things away and glanced around the room to make sure all was in order. Keeping things neat in this house was so easy with cupboards and shelves everywhere. Every day she thanked God for allowing her to work in such a lovely home with people who cared about her and she them.

Not that all their guests lived with the same kind of order, however. According to Pearl some were out-and-out slobs.

Neatness wasn't the biggest problem. Lack of guests loomed larger. Jeremiah McHenry still kept a room there, even though he spent some nights out at his house without a whole roof. He said he always came back when he needed real food.

"You've made it hard for me to be content with my own cooking," he had teased Amethyst one evening. That was after he downed his second piece of blueberry pie with whipped cream.

Amethyst climbed the stairs to make sure the guest bedrooms were in order, the lamps full of kerosene, the pillows plumped, and a light quilt folded across the foot of the bed, in case a night turned chilly. She went on to her own room to comb her hair, making sure the knot stayed on top of her head where it belonged. Joseph loved to tangle his little fingers in her hair and giggled when it fell down.

She studied herself in the mirror. "Your father probably wouldn't even recognize you," she told the reflection. She no longer looked like a walking broom. Her form and face had shape, although the latter was hidden mostly by the full covering aprons she wore over her simple skirts and waists. No longer did she own only one good outfit and one for everyday. All the clothes Pearl had given her to alter now fit her shorter height. Some she'd had to alter again, letting them out at the hips and bosom.

She swirled her hair around her fingers on top of her head, inserted hairpins, and finished with the comb Mrs. Grant had given her. "Please, Lord, take care of Mrs. Grant, and if it be your will, I'd love to see her again." She uttered the prayer every time she worked the comb into her hair. She still felt bad that the matching one had been lost in the snow.

Back downstairs she could hear laughing from the kitchen. This house was so blessed with laughter — Carly's high and giggly, Mr. Hegland's deep and resonant like his voice, Pearl's so refined and yet so infectious.

"Amethyst, come on in here. We have something to show you."

"I'm coming." She straightened an antimacassar on one of the chairs and followed the laughter to the kitchen.

She stopped in the doorway. A rocking chair with carved arms and split-cowhide back and seat stood in the middle of the room. "Is that the one for Mr. McHenry?"

"That it is. Looks big enough to be a throne, far as I can see." Pearl smiled at her husband. "You outdid yourself."

"I am rather pleased with it. This chair will make our friend most comfortable when sitting by the fire on a winter's night. I won't take it out there, though, until he has the roof on his house. Think I'll go on out tomorrow and see if we can't finish it off."

"When will they be here to hay our field?" Pearl stroked the arm of the chair. "Such a fine finish."

"Not sure. I'll ask Rand. They finished up at McHenry's, I think."

Amethyst crossed the room and ran her hand over the smooth wood. She knew Mr. Hegland had spent hours on the chair, more so than for the more simple tables and chairs that he made on a regular basis. Not that he'd had any orders for a long time, other than the pieces for McHenry. Not with so many leaving the badlands. She'd seen too many empty houses, soddies, and places where she had been told tents stood last summer when Medora was a bustling town with building going up everywhere and men working for the marquis at all his enterprises.

"It's beautiful."

"Thank you, Amethyst. Is there any of that cake left that we had at noon? I've a hankering for something sweet."

"With coffee?"

"You read my mind."

"You'll spoil your supper." Pearl grabbed Joseph back from chewing on the woodbox.

"As if that could happen." Carl winked at his wife. "You'll have a piece with me?"

"Cake, Pa. Me too." Carly added her voice.

"See what you started."

"You can share mine, pet." He went to sit at the table and patted his knee. "Come sit here, and we'll have coffee."

Carly ran across the room and climbed up onto her father's knee. "Coffee."

"She hasn't a big vocabulary yet, but she sure says that word clearly." Pearl took out the cake pan from the breadbox Carl had made for her and cut pieces for each of them. "You'll have some too, won't you, Amethyst?"

I think you forget that I am the help and not family. But she didn't mention that, instead having resolved to enjoy every minute of her stay with the Heglands in case something happened and she had to leave.

The next morning after the westbound train had left, Amethyst heard a wagon drive up to the front door.

"Halloo, the boardinghouse." She recognized the voice of Mr. Owens, the stationmaster. Strange that he would be bringing them a guest. He never left the telegraph unattended. She hurried to the door, wiping her hands on her apron. "We're here."

Amethyst stopped and caught her hand to her throat. "Mrs. Grant."

"One and the same. I decided to stop here on my way home. Hadn't planned on spending the winter in Washington Territory, but with the weather so bad between there and Chicago, and it was such a beautiful spring . . . I guess I overstayed."

Mr. Owens helped her down from the wagon and then carried her two trunks up to the porch. "Shall I leave these here?"

"Yes, that will be fine." Amethyst felt like

a little girl staring at her Christmas present, afraid to open it. "I've prayed for you every time I used the comb in my hair, and I always asked that God would let me see you again."

"Here I am. Is there a room for me to stay here?" She gave Amethyst a hug and, with her cool, sweet-smelling hands on both sides of her face, looked deep into her eyes. "You look wonderful, my dear. This Medora seems to agree with you."

"It is working here that is so good."

"You didn't go back to Pennsylvania."

"It is a long story. Come in, come in. Can I get you a cup of tea?" She took Mrs. Grant's arm and led her into the parlor. "Pearl, Mrs. Hegland, is out on the back porch with the children. It is cooler out there. Would you like to see your room first or join her on the porch?"

"The room can wait. I want to meet the one who has helped my Pennsylvania rose burst into bloom."

Amethyst felt the heat rise to her face. "How did you know I was still here?"

"I asked that nice Mr. Owens. He said you came just before a blizzard and never left. You know how curious I am, so you must tell me the whole story."

"Come, let me introduce you. Pearl was

411

from Chicago too." Amethyst led her guest out to the back porch where Joseph sprawled sound asleep on a settee and Pearl and Carly rocked in a chair while Pearl read to her daughter.

"We have a guest," Amethyst called as she ushered Mrs. Grant out the door.

"Oh my. How did all this happen and I didn't hear a thing?" Pearl laid the book down and turned to greet their visitor. After the introductions she continued, "Why, Mrs. Grant, how wonderful to see you. And such a surprise. Amethyst has told me all about you, how you cared for her when she became ill on the trip here."

"I couldn't go by without checking on her."

"Please sit down." Pearl set Carly off her lap and started to rise.

"No, you sit right there with that darling little girl, and I'll sit here. Amethyst will bring us all tea, and we shall have a wonderful visit together."

Amethyst found herself blinking back tears at the warmth in Mrs. Grant's voice and eyes. It really hadn't been a dream, then. She'd wondered at times if she made it all up or the trip west had been a story she heard someone else tell. How could she be so fortunate to have two such women as her friends? She, who'd never had friends before other than family, and those so briefly.

By the time she'd answered all of Mrs. Grant's questions, refilled the teapot several times, and heard about the older woman's adventures in the wilds of Washington Territory, she needed to be starting supper. So the three women moved their conversation into the kitchen and kept on talking.

"I wrote to the doctor's wife in Fargo, and she finally answered me about making more of her soaps and lotions to sell in Chicago. While she will make them at first, I believe we will find someone in Chicago to produce them. I have a friend who has promised to call on the buyers for Macy's and the other stores."

"What an excellent idea."

"I believe it is important for women to create businesses of their own and to put to work other women who need positions in order to assist their families. This way we all benefit."

"I read something in *Godey's* about lotions and soaps being made in Paris. There is no reason we cannot make such things here in our country." Pearl wiped the breadcrust crumbs off Joseph's face and set him down again to play with Carly.

While they talked, Amethyst did more listening as she went about setting the table and finishing preparing supper.

Mr. McHenry returned to stay for the night and was introduced. Carl finished in his workroom and came in, heading to his room to wash up.

They all moved to the dining room, and Amethyst served the first course, leaf lettuce she'd picked in the garden just before supper and sprinkled with vinegar. After bringing in the roasted grouse Opal had brought them the day before, along with new potatoes, gravy, and green beans, she sat down at the table with the others.

"If you could stay long enough, I would be honored to take you for a ride out into the badlands," Jeremiah offered.

"On a horse?" Mrs. Grant raised her eyebrows.

"If you'd like, but I was thinking of using one of the wagons." McHenry looked a bit taken aback.

"Do you have a sidesaddle anywhere around here?"

"I'm sure I could find one."

"Then when would you like to go?"

Amethyst and Pearl looked at each other and both hid their smiles behind their napkins.

McHenry turned to Pearl. "We could make it an outing if you like. Take the buckboard and picnic baskets and eat down by the river. We should invite Opal too. She'd help us catch enough fish to serve everyone."

"Who all are you thinking of inviting?"

"I don't know. This charming lady just got the ideas rolling."

"If we wait until Saturday, the day after tomorrow, we would have time to invite everyone."

"I'll take the invitations around in the morning. There's a good fishing hole about two miles north of the railroad, and the road out there is fairly good. That will give Mrs. Grant some views of the badlands that will take her breath away." Jeremiah bowed slightly in their visitor's direction.

"Ah, now you want me breathless, is that it? Not good for an old lady, you know."

Amethyst coughed behind her hand. *Old lady? Not likely. And I will get to see the badlands too.* She didn't realize until right then that she'd wanted to see more. That she wanted to see more of all the wonders around, if she was with Jeremiah McHenry.

Mrs. Grant turned to Pearl. "You're sure this is not putting you out any?"

"I think it is a wonderful idea. Some of the

families might not come because of haying, but I know you'll enjoy the ones who make it. If I know the men around here, they'll hay all morning and join us in the late afternoon."

"I'll tell Rand to bring his guitar." McHenry turned to Mrs. Grant. "You ever danced under the stars with the good earth as the floor and sister moon lighting your steps?"

"No, I can't say that I have, but I'm always ready for a new adventure."

Amethyst smiled to herself. Leave it to Mrs. Grant. But inside she shut the lid on a thought too ugly to admit.

CHAPTER THIRTY-ONE

"A party! We're going to have a party," Ada Mae sang as she jumped on the load of hay.

"Fishing! We're going fishing." Joel bounced extra hard.

"Dancing. There'll be dancing." Emily closed her eyes and almost slipped off the edge of the hay load.

"Watch it up there," Beans warned as he forked up a load of hay.

Opal grinned at the antics of the younger ones. There hadn't been any parties since just after Christmas and right before the blizzards started in earnest. And McHenry had said there would be dancing. She looked across the field to where Jacob was working on the mower by the barn. What would it be like to dance with him again?

"Opal, quit daydreaming and keep them horses movin." Beans' shout brought her back with a start. She flapped the reins and turned at a shriek from Emily.

"Snake."

Opal started back, but Joel beat her to it and flipped the critter off the load. Snakes and mice hid under the rows of hay and sometimes got tossed up on the load. "Was it a rattler?"

"Don't know." Joel kept on trudging, now using a carved wooden pitchfork to distribute the load. "But it's gone now."

Opal shook her head. Last summer he'd been one scared little boy, and this year, what a difference. Now he teased Ada Mae, while she gave as good as she got. It reminded Opal of the Brandons, which made her sad. They'd received a letter the day before stating that none of the Brandons would be able to come this year. They had decided to take the entire family to Europe instead. Bernie had written a note saying he would rather come to the ranch, but they didn't let him choose.

With the hayrack loaded, Opal drove the team up to the stack where she could admire Jacob's new invention. Since the Robertsons didn't have a haymow in their barn, he had rigged ropes along the floor from the rack in front of the wagon. At the appointed place for the stack, they attached the ends of the ropes to a doubletree harnessed to another team. The team started forward, and the load of hay was pulled off the hay wagon and made a stack of its own. They'd pitch hay from the other wagon to build the stack higher, but this saved time and the arms of those pitching the hay. As Rand had said, Jacob was the most inventive man around.

The ride-on plow that McHenry ordered had arrived the day before. If only they'd had that in the spring when they were breaking the sod on the field to sow the grain.

When the dinner bell clanged at noon, Opal gladly unharnessed the team and followed the others to the wash bench. Tomorrow they would work in the morning and go downriver in the afternoon. There hadn't been time for play since haying started, for all the men were desperate to cut enough to keep their animals alive if they had another winter like the last one.

Ruby was already frying chicken to take for tomorrow's supper.

"As soon as I'm done with this, I'm going hunting," Opal said. "Fried grouse is good as fried chicken any day."

"What'd you say?" Rand gave her a nudge in the side.

"I need to bag some grouse for the party."

"Sounds like a good idea to me." Rand shook his head. "I was hoping to get a deer, but the only one I saw was a doe with two fawns, so I gave that idea up. Game is scarce."

"The birds have come back. Grouse on a spit over the fire would be good. Mrs. Grant has probably never had that."

"Opal Torvald, I am so glad to hear that tone in your voice again that I could —" Rand cut off his sentence as his voice roughened.

Opal looked up to see — was that the sheen of tears in his eyes? Her nose clogged instantly. How come she could cry at a mouse squeak? The cloud was gone, but now the tears were like spring rain, watering the earth to bring up the grass and flowers. No longer hail and fog.

"Different, huh?"

"I'd say so. I'm thanking God every day for this." He laid his hands on her shoulders. "You scared us."

"You? It scared me." She paused, glanced around to see that the others had all gone into the house to eat. "Rand, how could you ignore all the cattle dying? You acted like it wasn't important, like . . . oh well." She shrugged, indicating how she saw him responding.

"I didn't ignore it. It near to tore me apart inside. Seemed I was screaming to the Lord the whole time." He tipped her chin up with a loving finger. "But, Opal darlin', I believe with everything that I am that God is in charge, and He knows what He is doing. Remember when Jacob preached about how much God loves us?"

She nodded.

"Well, I believe that. I know He can restore all our losses. Go read Deuteronomy 30. Powerful promises there. I read that over and over during the winter. The darker things get, the more I have to depend on His Word."

Opal sniffed and rolled her eyes, still feeling the moisture gather. "Thanks for telling me."

"You're most welcome." He put an arm around her waist as she did his, and the two walked side by side to the house.

Another lesson, huh, God? And I flunked. She looked at Rand. *But I'm learning.*

That night she read Deuteronomy 30 as he'd suggested. And reread it. All were promises to Israel, and if she understood what Rand had said, all were promises for them too. *"The Lord, thy God shall bless thee . . ." I must love the Lord my God with all my heart and keep His commandments . . . that I may live. Lord, I do want to live again. I want to be like Rand.* The phrase "the Lord, thy God" beat over and over in her brain.

★ ★ ★

Everyone stopped work at noon on Saturday, ate, and headed for the river. Wagon after wagon pulled up, the drivers unharnessing their horses and hobbling or long-lining them in the rich grass. The children scattered to gather wood. Opal, Joel, and Ada Mae took their corks out of their pockets, cut willow sticks, tied the string to them, and caught enough grasshoppers in a handkerchief to start fishing.

"First fish gets a prize," Opal sang out as she tossed her cork and baited hook out into the eddy.

"Ouch." Ada Mae sucked on her finger.

"You're supposed to stick the hook in the grasshopper, not your hand." Joel gave a jerk on his line, and his hook came up empty. "Would you look at that." He shook his head at Opal's laugh and baited his hook again.

Opal caught herself looking around for Linc and Little Squirrel. They should be jerking fish right out of the water with Linc's teasing, his warm laughter inviting them all to laugh. She sighed. So much gone.

Some time later they trooped back to the party, all of them hauling lines of fish. The men had two fires going, one with the coals low and three racks of grouse sizzling away. Obviously Opal hadn't been the only one hunting in the twilight.

"We caught them. Who's cleaning them?" Opal, Joel, and Ada Mae held their strings up.

"We'll clean," Cora Robertson called, sharpening a narrow-bladed knife on a whetstone. "Just lay them on that log."

Opal looked around. Jacob hadn't arrived yet. He wasn't still mowing, was he? She turned at the sound of horses' hooves. Mr. McHenry rode beside a woman riding side-saddle, her dark green skirt swooping down over her stirrup. But instead of a fancy hat or bowler like Opal had seen in New York, she wore someone's flat felt hat that shaded her face. That must be Mrs. Grant, Miss O'Shaunasy's friend from Chicago. If it hadn't been for her white hair when she tipped her hat back, one would have thought her a young woman.

"Everyone, I want you to meet Mrs. Grant. She stopped her trip back to Chicago to visit us here in Medora. This party is in her honor, and it is nothing short of a miracle that all of you left off haying to join us. I suggest that Rand over there bring out his guitar, and I've got my trusty mouth organ, so let the dancing begin."

McHenry dismounted and assisted the woman down from her horse.

"To think I went riding in the badlands." Mrs. Grant reached up and patted his cheek, then took his arm. "I want to meet all of my dear Amethyst's friends." She reached out and slid her arm through Amethyst's. "Let us begin."

Opal watched as they made their way from group to group.

"You going swimming?" Joel asked.

Opal shook her head. Ever since last summer and her encounter with the drifter, she'd not gone swimming. "You all go ahead. I need to find out what happened to your pa."

"He said he'd be late."

"Why?"

Joel shrugged. "Don't know. See ya."

"Opa?"

Opal stooped down and grabbed Per in both arms. "Did you go into the water?"

"Wet."

"You sure are. And you smell like the river."

"Go mo."

Opal looked around to find Ruby. She was sitting in the shade of a cottonwood visiting with several of the women and Mrs. Grant. "Who was watching you?"

Per looked around as if searching for someone. "Pa."

Was Rand supposed to be watching his son and got involved in talking with the men and forgot? Opal swung Per up on her shoulders and went to find out. "Ugh. You're dripping down my back."

He clamped one fist into her hair and waved his other arm.

"Per, sit still."

"Per!" Rand's voice rang across the clearing.

"He's over here." Opal waved her arm so he could see her. Per had gotten away from him. At one time or another, Per managed to get away from most everyone, which was why the porches at the ranch had sturdy gates.

Rand whooshed out a breath. "Scared me outta a month of Sundays." He reached for his son. "I swear I'm going to tie a rope around your middle and the other end around my wrist."

"I'll take him. Did you know he'd been in the water?"

"Yes, I was with him. We started back, I got to talking with Charlie, and when I looked down, Per was gone. Thank the good Lord he went hunting for you."

"You going to start the music pretty soon?"

"Right away."

"Think I'll go change into a skirt, then." Somehow dancing in britches just didn't seem appropriate. She left Per with his mother, fetched her skirt out of the wagon, and headed for some brush to hide behind to change. When she emerged, she saw Jacob riding into camp.

Instantly the sun seemed brighter and the birdsong sweeter. The breeze tickled the wisps of hair that refused to stay in her braid and curved around her cheek instead. As if drawn by a fine thread, his gaze found hers and a smile sketched commas around his mouth. Opal rolled her britches up and stuffed them in the corner of the wagon while Rand lifted his guitar from under the seat.

"Ready to dance?"

"Do ducks swim?"

"That's my girl." They headed for the flat area where people were gathering.

Rand plucked the strings, tuning his guitar, and McHenry blew a few notes on his harmonica. Opal turned at the sound of someone else tuning strings.

Jacob stood frowning at the fiddle in his hands, sawing one note after another and tightening the pegs. When he glanced up, he grinned at her.

"I didn't know you played the fiddle."

"Had to do something through all those blizzards. Mrs. Robertson had this, and I'd played some years ago. Had a good time practicing."

"And no one told me."

"Made them promise not to. Just in case I couldn't manage it." He put the fiddle to his shoulder and bowed across all the strings. "There, we all match."

But now I can't dance with you. The thought made her nibble her bottom lip. *Stop it, you ninny. He can take a break like Rand does to dance with Ruby. Besides, there are plenty of men here. And since when do you like to dance that much anyway?*

Per giggled all the way through the time she waltzed him around the circle. Joel blushed redder than his neckerchief when she made him dance with her, his father grinning over the bowing of the fiddle. She danced the polka with Beans and the Texas Star with Jeremiah McHenry.

"You sure made a fine picture with Mrs. Grant."

When he met her again, he answered, "She's a fine woman."

Back around and together. "Did you get the roof on?"

"Not yet."

"We made him enough shingles." Joel was her next partner as the square dance continued. "Ada Mae and me are pretty good splitters."

"You and Ada Mae are good at whatever you decide to do."

It wasn't exertion that made the boy's face red this time. Any little compliment would do.

They finished that dance, and the music slowed for a waltz. The mouth organ sang the melody above the chords of the guitar, then Rand took a turn fingering the melody.

Opal looked around to see no one fiddling.

Jacob appeared at her elbow. "May I have this dance?"

At the look in his eyes, she swallowed her smart reply and just nodded. Butterflies exploded in her middle as her feet matched the pattern with his. The music swirled them around, her hand held firmly in his, his shoulder corded beneath her fingers.

Her heart kept on singing after the music stopped.

"Thank you."

Think of something to say. "You play real well."

"Joel wants to learn too." He squeezed her hand and let it go. "I need to get back up there so Rand can dance with Ruby."

"Sure." Lonely made her hand want to reach for his. Instead, she went to find Ruby and take Mary. "Go dance with your husband."

Ruby kissed her cheek. "Thank you. I will."

"That was the grandest party ever," Mrs. Grant said as they rode home in the wagon.

"Far different from the Chicago variety." Pearl looked up from her seat in the wagon bed behind Carl and Mrs. Grant.

"I got bored with those long ago. Your McHenry is quite the gentleman. It's not hard to picture him in full dress uniform commanding his men."

"He didn't even keep his uniforms. Said he wanted nothing more than to have a home here in the badlands." Pearl shook her head. "I think you shocked him when you asked for a sidesaddle."

"Men need to be shocked. It's good for them. My John never knew what to expect. It made our life interesting — that was for sure. Of course, I have shocked my share of people in my time. If I were younger, I'd want to live in this country too." She turned farther so she could see Amethyst, who had Carly snuggled in her lap. "You made a

429

good choice, Amethyst dear, to stay here, but I still want you to come to Chicago with me."

"We'll see."

"You're not thinking of leaving me, are you?"

Amethyst smiled at the shock in Pearl's voice. How good it felt to be wanted. How much she had wanted Mr. McHenry to ask her to dance. She sighed. But he didn't. Why was she surprised? Other than those pleasant evenings when they visited in the parlor, he never saw her for anything other than the one who cooked and served.

Maid material, not wife material. Could she stay here in Medora and see him at church and socials and not care? The ugly thought came again, and this time she gave it a name before slamming it away. Jealousy — plain and simple. But oh, so painful.

CHAPTER THIRTY-TWO

Shame that Mrs. Grant wasn't a bit younger.

Jeremiah stared into the purpling dusk. While his porch still lacked a roof, a chair tipped back against the solid wall gave him the view he'd dreamed of. A U-shaped bend in the river, cottonwoods sheltering the banks, and the buttes fading to bands of gray beyond the far shore. His cattle grazed on the bottom land where the hay had already been cut and stacked like bread loaves near the future barn site. Two deer wandered down to the river's edge to drink, alert to every movement.

Flycatchers dipped and dove; bats joined them in their nightly forage for flying insects.

He thought back to the celebration, the ride to show Mrs. Grant the phantasmal shapes of the land, the colors, the wildness. What an entertaining companion.

A companion. That's what he wanted and needed. All his life he'd been a loner, rising through the ranks of the army through sheer force and tenacity beyond a bulldog. He could get along with anyone — coerce or cajole or flat-out scare men into doing their duty or even the impossible. He had his house, his land, a few cattle, and silence. He could get a dog, hire a hand. The chair creaking sounded loud in the stillness. But he wanted his companion to be female, and he wanted to be married. Was that asking too much? Being around the other couples made him realize what he was missing.

He rubbed his thigh to ease the ache. Sometimes, like tonight, when he'd been on his feet most of the day, the ache became only a small part of the unheard scream from muscles that refused to return to their earlier strength. He got up, fetched his flask, and took a swig. The last swallow. He had no more. He'd planned on stopping by Williams' to buy a bottle, but in all the business of haying and with the picnic, he'd forgotten. Until now.

He'd tried willow-bark tea, chewing willow bark — vile stuff — and laudanum, but none worked as well as whiskey. Or at least were as pleasurable.

He thought of riding into town and claiming his still-paid-for room at the boardinghouse. He could stop by and refill his flask on the way. Instead, he grunted himself upright and went on into the house to light a lamp and read. Anything to get his mind off the pain. But with no glass in the windows and no screen doors, the mosquitoes serenading him and feasting on all visible skin made him blow out the light and crawl into the pallet on the floor. He'd not had time to string the ropes for a bed yet, or fill a tick with hay, or sew a seam for that matter.

It promised to be a long night.

In the brief moments just before he fell asleep, he saw Miss O'Shaunasy on the backs of his eyelids. Amethyst. Amethyst, ah, that was better.

They finished up the haying with only one rainstorm to slow them down but with stacks for everyone. Then the rains came and soaked the earth, sending the water to bring the prairie grass sprouting back up again to refill what they'd taken.

His roof let in nary a drop.

He kept a store to suffer the nights no more. Since his field had been hayed off, the plow took up his days. He broke an acre of sod to start with, then another, the furrows turning over straight and smooth. He'd leave it to deteriorate during the fall and winter, then after another plowing in the spring, the land would be ready for seeding. Finished with his own sod breaking, he did the same for Rand, a good thing since he was using Rand's team to plow with. He learned to sharpen the plowshare and keep the rows straight.

A farmer is what I'm becoming. I thought to range cattle and ship fat steers in the fall. Roundup time had seemed more like a huge party than grinding work. When he wasn't plowing to pay back all the debts he felt he owed for his neighbors' help, he was cutting trees so he could get a barn up to shelter Kentucky during the winter. The big horse was not used to ranging like the local ponies.

More than once he stopped by Williams'.

"Come for supper tonight," Pearl invited one day when he'd dropped by.

"Thanks. Where's Miss O'Shaunasy? I haven't seen her lately." He held his coffee cup up for a refill.

"She left for Chicago yesterday."

"Chicago?"

"Yes. Mrs. Grant invited her, encouraged her actually, to go and help start up a new business, and since we have so few guests here, she felt she was an imposition and left." Pearl swallowed and sniffed. "The house is so empty without her."

"I can't believe she left." Shock never had felt good, but this news hit like a fist in the belly.

"Me neither." Pearl sank down in a chair, propping her elbows on the table. "I tried to convince her to stay, but this was a really good offer."

McHenry drained his coffee. "I didn't see that coming." He set the cup back in the saucer with a clink and rose. "I'll see you in the morning, then."

"That will be fine."

"I'll bring a wagon by so we can load up the furniture. Carl said he's finished."

"I'll tell him."

Jeremiah left, shaking his head. *Why would she do that? I thought she liked it here.* He rode on toward home, stopping by the Harrison ranch on his way. He found Rand down at the barn trimming horse hooves.

"Did you know Miss O'Shaunasy left with Mrs. Grant for Chicago?"

"Nope, can't say as I did. Sorry to hear that." Rand ran the rasp around the hoof again and sighted down it to make sure the hoof was level.

"Now, why would she go and do that?"

Rand set the foot down and stood. "Jeremiah, are you blind in both eyes or what?"

"What?"

"The woman loves you, and you paid her no more attention than a serving maid. What do you expect?"

"Ah, come on."

"Suit yourself. You had fine wife material there, and you failed to see it."

McHenry plunked down on a bench. Surely Rand was talking through his hat. Surely.

CHAPTER THIRTY-THREE

Dear Jacob,

Thank you for your letter. I am sorry to have taken so long to respond, but I have been somewhat under the weather. Please do not think that I want to blame you for my meager life, but our discussions, when we were together, had a way of making me want to get moving again, to strike you for your obstreperous behavior, if nothing else. How you did manage to rile me, and I fought so hard at that time to keep you from being aware of the struggles deep in my heart, but you ferreted them out. Ah, the deceptions we play.

I have a tremendous favor to ask of you. I would so appreciate seeing you again before I leave this earthly realm that no longer holds much joy for me. Thanks to you, I am sure of my heavenly abode and look forward to leaving this crust of a body behind and taking on that new one that Christ has promised. Would you be willing to use the ticket I have enclosed for a trip back here? I know that is a terrible imposition, but I have some things I would like to discuss with you face-to-face.

Please send me a telegram as to your arrival time if you feel that you can manage to do this. I remain your faithful friend, hoping against hope that I will see you soon.

Evan Dumfarthing

Jacob laid the letter on the table and rubbed his forehead. Yesterday he had received a letter saying he had the teaching job here in Medora and today this. School should be starting in three weeks, so he needed to leave immediately if he were to go.

Lord, how can I not go? The thought of that interminable ride back across the country did nothing to make him excited. And he needed to get ready to open the school. Having never taught, he figured some preparation was needed. Some! Ha! That same letter had said boxes of textbooks would be on the way. Mrs. Hegland informed him that she and Mrs. de Mores had provided most of the schoolbooks up until now, including those in the meager library. She had already requested another shipment from Chicago.

He needed to ask if it was all right for Joel to stay here without him. Unless he were to take Joel to visit his grandparents. The recent letter from Melody's parents assured him they would be happy and grateful to see them anytime.

Pray first. That's what he'd preached last Sunday. The need for and the power of prayer. He closed his eyes, resting his forehead on his clasped hands. "Father, I do not want to run before you, nor do I want to lag behind. I want to rest and walk in your perfect will, the path you have chosen for me. Mr. Dumfarthing would not ask this favor were it not important to him. The ticket is here, but what about Joel? Should I take him to see his grandparents? And if I do, what do I use to pay for his ticket?" He waited, trying to listen as he'd reminded himself so often. Talking to God was easy; quieting his mind to listen, that took a struggle.

After a bit he closed his Bible with the letter folded in it and made his way up to the house. He could hear Ada Mae and Joel arguing out by the woodpile. But instead of investigating, he climbed the steps and went inside.

"Hello, Jacob. I'm surprised to see you

at this time of day."

"I had a letter waiting when I went to town. There was no mail for you."

"Not unusual." Cora pulled the coffeepot to the front of the stove. "Coffee will be hot in a minute. How does corn bread with molasses over it sound?"

"Wonderful." He twisted his hat brim between his hands.

"All right. Sit down and tell me what is bothering you." She set the plate of corn bread and the syrup pitcher in front of him.

"You remember I told you about a man in my former parish named Evan Dumfarthing?"

"The old man?"

"Yes. Well, the letter is from him, and he has requested that I come back there to meet with him. He thinks he is dying, and he could well be. I believe I should go, but —"

"But what? Do you need money for the ticket?"

"No. He sent the ticket. It is Joel I'm concerned about."

"What's to be concerned? He will stay right here where he belongs. That need not be a concern for you." She poured a cup of coffee and set that in front of him.

"I wish I could afford the ticket and the time to take him to see his grandparents while I am there, but —"

"I don't want to go back there."

Jacob turned to see his son standing just inside the doorway. "Listening to other people's conversation is not polite."

"Sorry, but I want to stay here. Please?"

"I need to be the one deciding that. I'll be out to talk with you in a few minutes."

Joel mumbled something and let the door slam behind him, a punctuation mark to what he'd said.

Cora laughed. "Guess he was clear about what he wanted."

"I don't blame him. There are few good memories for him there, and here he is happy all the time." They heard a crash and an angry shout from the direction of the woodpile. "Well, most of the time."

Cora half shrugged and hoisted her coffee cup. "To a good trip for you."

"Guess I'll ride on out to tell Rand I'm leaving."

"Rand?" Cora's eyebrows arched, her eyes twinkling.

He pushed his empty plate away and stood, his neck feeling warm. "Thank you."

He rode on over to the Harrisons', mentally figuring out what all he would need to take along. If only the textbooks would come before he left so he could review his

Latin and higher mathematics while on the train.

He dismounted at the hitching bar and climbed the front steps. A knock on the door brought no answer. Ghost hadn't even been there to announce him. The dog was probably off with the men working the cattle somewhere. He knocked again. With still no answer, he wandered on around the house to see if anyone was in the backyard. Not there either, nor at the barn, but he could hear laughing down at the river. He mounted again and rode out to find Ruby weaving baskets of cattails and Opal out on a log fishing.

"Welcome. We'll be frying fish soon." Ruby waved at him.

"Is Rand here?"

"No. They're out on the range. Opal is teaching Per to fish" — she rolled her eyes — "or play in the mud, which is more his speed."

A little boy's laugh said that whatever they were doing, he was having a good time.

"Thought I'd come by and tell Rand that I'm leaving for Pennsylvania on tomorrow's train. My friend Mr. Dumfarthing has requested that I pay him a visit and sent a ticket along with his plea."

"Well, I hope you have a good trip."

"Thank you." He dropped his horse's reins so it was ground-tied like most cattle horses and walked on out to the riverbank. He watched as Opal flipped a fish out of the water and kept an eye on Per, who scooped up mud and let it run through his fingers, giggling all the while. The log she sat on kept him out of the river proper.

"Opal?"

"Jacob. How good to see you." She grinned at him over her shoulder, unhooked the fish, strung the forked stick through his gill, and set it back in the water. "Can you stay for supper? We have potatoes baking in the ashes and will be frying fish shortly."

"It sounds good, but I have a lot to do tonight. I'm leaving for Pennsylvania as soon as I can. I may be gone for two weeks. I'm hoping less, since I'll be teaching school here in three weeks."

"Oh, Jacob, that's wonderful. The school, I mean, not your being gone. Is Joel going with you?" She glanced down to see Per rubbing mud into her rolled-up pant leg. "Ugh."

"No. He's staying with the Robertsons." *I'll miss you. Please miss me.* "I'll write to you."

"You'll be back before I could send a letter to you, unless I write it right now and make sure it is on the same train." Opal rolled her lips to hide a smile.

He knew that action. He cocked an eyebrow and grinned at her. "You might want to watch out for that little feller."

She looked down to see Per now smearing the mud in his hair and on his cheeks. "Oh, goodness sakes. Ruby will have my hide." She swooped him up and dunked him in the riverside. "You are one filthy little boy, but the mosquitoes won't bother you."

Per clapped his hands. "Opa! Mo." His squeal made them both laugh.

She dug her stick of fish from the riverbank and handed it to Jacob. "Here, take this to the Robertsons for supper. And tell Joel he can come fish anytime." A shadow creased her forehead. "I hope you have a good trip and come home safe."

Ah, that's what he'd been hoping for. She *would* miss him.

He touched his hat brim and turned to leave before his eyes could give him away. As he mounted after saying good-bye to Ruby and reining his horse around, he heard Opal's call.

"God bless."

Ah, thank you, Lord. Every day my Opal is more back to herself. Nudging his horse to a lope, he realized what he'd thought. *My Opal. Lord willing indeed.*

Four days later he knocked on Mr. Dumfarthing's heavy front door.

"Oh, Reverend Chandler. Himself has been waiting for you." Mrs. Howard, the housekeeper, reached out to take his hand and bring him in. "He will be so glad to see you."

"How is he?"

"Truly failing." She drew herself somewhat straighter, more like the woman he remembered, and sniffed. When that was insufficient, she dabbed at the edge of her eye with a hanky she took from her apron pocket. "Forgive me. This is so hard, watching him go by inches."

"I would have come sooner had he asked." Jacob set his carpetbag at the base of the coat tree.

"Let me take that and put it in your room for later. I'll take you to see him now before he hears us talking and yells." A trace of her former smile touched her lips.

If Mr. Dumfarthing had aged as much as his housekeeper had, Jacob knew he'd be in for a shock.

The body in the bed barely raised the covers. But the windows were open and the sun danced in with dust motes floating in the slight breeze.

"I don't want to wake him."

"If I don't, he will have my head." She patted Jacob's arm. "Every minute is precious now." She crossed to the bed and touched the old man's shoulder. "Reverend Chandler is here."

The old eyes fluttered open, and a smile that looked more like a grimace folded parched skin so thin that the bones showed through. Mr. Dumfarthing extended a quivering hand.

Jacob knelt beside the bed and took the old man's cold hand in his own, hoping to impart strength and warmth with his grip. "Good to see you, sir." *But not like this. Oh, Lord, treat my friend gently.*

"I've been waiting for you."

"I see."

"Get him a chair." A trace of the old imperious tone laced the request.

Jacob chuckled. "I can get my own. And if you'd like, I could help you to sit in the sun with me. Might feel good on your old bones."

"Old bones, eh." Dumfarthing made a sound that might have been a chuckle but sounded more like he was choking. "Thank you. You always were trying to get me out of bed. I'm not sure that is a possibility any longer." He motioned to the pillows. "Just help me lean up against these, if you will."

Together Jacob and Mrs. Howard stacked the pillows behind him and helped the frail frame settle back with a sigh.

"Have you had dinner yet?" she asked.

"No, I came directly from the train."

"I'll fix up trays for you both. That might be best."

"Thank you." Jacob smiled at her and turned back to his friend to see that his eyes were closed again and his breathing more labored. That little effort had tired him. Jacob sat with his hands clasped, elbows on his knees. *Lord, please give him the strength that he needs. At least he has gained more time and more assurance since I badgered him out of bed and back into living.*

"Ah, forgive me. I seem to wander in and out of sleep without much warning."

"I'm in no hurry."

"But I am. I haven't long, and we have much to do."

"We do?"

"Yes. See that portfolio on the desk?"

Jacob nodded.

"Bring that to me, will you, please?"

"Of course." Jacob retrieved the leatherbound packet and laid it on the edge of the bed. "Do you need more light?"

"No, I know what is in there. I want you

447

to read it so we can talk about it and make sure all will be well."

"I see." Jacob didn't know what else to say. Actually, he didn't see or understand anything at the moment. He picked up the binder and opened the cover. "This is your will."

"Very good observation." The dry wit still lived.

"But why should I read your will?"

"Please, just do as I ask." Dumfarthing tried to clear his throat but had to cough instead. The rattle made Jacob flinch.

"I have made the usual bequests. Mrs. Howard will be taken care of for life. Since I have no living children and my one living brother has plenty of his own wealth, I have designated a large sum to the church here." He raised his hand and a glint came back to his eye. "You need not take credit for that, although had you not bullied me back to life then, I would not be here now." He paused. "You gave an old man a new lease on life, but it seems that lease has run out now."

"I'm glad I was here."

"I wish you were still here, but I have made peace with God about many things. Young men make foolish mistakes, but God willing, they learn from them and go on to walk the path He ordained for them."

"Speaking of young men in a generic sense."

"Of course." Again the dry chuckle that sounded like a death rattle.

Jacob read further. "You can't do this."

"It's my money."

"But . . ."

"I have prayed long and hard over this. The church here in town will have the interest from the investments I have designated for them. It should help them for years to come. If I give more, they will come to depend on that and not understand the benefit of paying their own tithes. Then they will not reap the harvest God has promised to those who bring in their full tithe." He paused to catch his breath. His eyes closed and his breathing slowed.

Jacob studied the face that bore only a resemblance to the man he left more than a year earlier. A skull with skin still stretched on it. The shock of white hair standing every which way, so unlike the careful grooming he'd known Mr. Dumfarthing to expect. He needed a shave. Perhaps he could shave him after they finished talking.

He continued reading while he waited.

With a snort Mr. Dumfarthing woke again. "As I was saying, money needs to be used wisely, and I have been praying for the wisdom God has promised as to the way ahead. Mrs. Howard will have the use of this house as long as she desires; then it is to be sold and the money distributed to the libraries here in town and the surrounding area. The remainder of the money is to go to you, and I count on you to use it wisely for yourself, your church, and your school. You did get the teaching position, did you not?"

Jacob nodded. "I heard the day before I received your letter."

"I want you to take a portion of money with you. You'll find that in the brown leather envelope. The remainder I suggest you leave in the hands of my solicitor. He will make sure you receive monthly dividends. Or would you rather have them quarterly?"

"Ah . . ."

"I see. I believe the minister of a church should receive money on a monthly basis, so that is how it will be, then. Do you have any questions?"

"Ah . . ." Jacob tried to clear his throat. *Please, Lord, give me the right words.* "All I can think to say is thank you. Are you sure you understand what you are doing?"

"Believe me, son, I understand. I thank our God every day for you, and I have prayed that you will fulfill God's will for your life as

450

you helped me to finish out mine."

"But I did — I have done so little."

"That depends on whose viewpoint you are seeing." Again that dry chuckle. He sighed. "I have more for you to do for me if you will."

"Anything."

"I would like you to conduct my funeral. I have written all the instructions there. You can read them later. I spoke with our minister, and he is in full agreement that you will do the service. He will take care of whatever arrangements are needed. He knows my wishes."

"I see."

"Now, I know Mrs. Howard has fixed us something to eat, and when I ring that bell, she will come right in. Before that, do you have any questions?"

Jacob shook his head. "Not at the moment, but I'm sure some will come." *How will I come back in time to do his funeral? Lord, I don't want to say good-bye.*

Mr. Dumfarthing reached for the bell and knocked it over. "Can't even ring the bell right. Lord God, it is time."

Jacob picked up the bell and rang it.

The door opened, and Mrs. Howard wheeled in a tea cart with plates and service for two.

"I'm sure you are famished by now, Reverend Chandler, but he made me promise not to bother you until he rang the bell."

As she spoke, she bustled about the cloth-draped serving cart, making sure each plate was just so. "Would you like me to help you?" she asked Mr. Dumfarthing.

"No, I think not. Just a bit of that pudding and a drink of water."

"I brought fresh." She poured him a glass and snaked an arm behind his shoulders so he could sit enough to drink. Glancing to Jacob she asked. "Will you say the blessing, please?"

After he said grace, she nodded. "Would you like me to help you with the pudding?"

"No. Jacob will." Mr. Dumfarthing lay back as if drinking took all the energy he had. "In a bit. You go on ahead and eat and let me rest for a minute." He paused without opening his eyes. "You might finish reading all that legal mumbo jumbo so if you have more questions, I can answer them."

"As you wish."

A snort let him know that the old man wasn't really sleeping.

After he finished eating, he took the papers to the window and let the sun warm his shoulders as he read them again. This was too much to believe. *Lord, I know you said you'd provide, but this is beyond my understanding. I don't deserve such munificence.*

A gentle chuckle wafted in with the breeze.

"Any questions?"

Jacob returned to his seat. "Not a question, but I'm needing some clarification."

"All right."

"So if I need money to build the church, I just write to you —"

"To my solicitor. I won't be here. I'm changing my address."

Jacob's grin turned to a chuckle. "I see."

"So I write to whomever and tell him what I need, and he will send that amount of money?"

"Yes. Above and beyond your monthly stipend."

That's far more than a stipend. He still couldn't comprehend that he would receive that amount each month.

"You know I'll be paid by the territory of Dakotah for my teaching."

"So?"

Jacob shrugged. "Just thought I'd mention it."

"It will most likely be too late this fall to start the church building, but first thing

453

come spring you can get to it. I'll see if I can talk my Father into easing up on you folks this winter."

Jacob nearly dropped his coffee cup. He stared at the skeleton in the bed and caught a wink from one bright eye. Mr. Dumfarthing snorted, then chuckled, and finally broke out in a full laugh.

Jacob shook his head. "I can just see you standing before the heavenly throne, negotiating with the Most High God."

"He said ask."

"I know." *But what I'm asking, He probably has a better answer for.* How he had missed their chats and verbal duels. All because he had run, and yet, look at all the good God was working out for him.

When he heard the old man snoring, he rose and left the room. Mrs. Howard waited right outside the door. "If you could show me where my things are . . . ?"

"Of course. Then I'll take out the dinner things. He should sleep for a while now. This has been more effort than he's used to. Each day he's fading more." She stepped back and let him precede her into a bedroom with a four-poster bed as big as the soddy back home. "I took the liberty of hanging up your coat. I brushed it out good."

"Thank you." Jacob crossed to the padded bench at the foot of the bed and removed his Bible from his carpetbag. "I'll just go sit with him, if you don't mind."

"Not at all."

"I see he needs shaving. I could do that for him."

"We'll see."

Jacob watched Mr. Dumfarthing sleep, wondering at times if he would awaken when the breaths seemed farther apart.

"Jacob."

"I'm here."

"Good." He reached out and Jacob took his hand.

"If you feel up to it, I could shave you."

"Perhaps later." He paused, the pauses growing longer. "About your housing."

"Yes."

"Have you found a wife yet?"

"I hope so." What did that have to do with a house? But he waited, knowing there was a purpose.

"The young woman, Opal, that you mentioned in your letters?"

"God willing." Jacob went on to explain Rand's request.

"A wise man, that Rand. And a good friend?"

"I do believe so. He's one of God's gifts to

me and the whole community."

"Good. I want you to buy a ranch, since you said Joel loves ranching, and it sounds like Opal does too." He paused and lifted one eyebrow. "Again, contact *our* solicitor . . ."

Jacob caught the emphasis on *our*. It sounded like theirs would be a long-term relationship. He took Dumfarthing's hand in his again. "Sir, I cannot begin to thank you. Are you sure?"

Again the chuckle or at least an attempt at one. "Just use it all to God's glory. I trust you to do that."

"Yes, sir." *Please, God, that I can and will.*

Throughout the evening the old man sank lower and lower, his lucid times farther apart, his breathing more faint. He passed on to glory just after the clock bonged midnight. Jacob watched, fighting tears as he knelt by the bed. "Good-bye, my friend. Godspeed."

Mrs. Howard wiped away her tears. "He was a good man."

"Only Evan Dumfarthing could have planned and executed his death like this."

"I told you he was waiting for you."

"Now I understand what you meant."

The next day Jacob met with the solicitor and came away more in awe of what he'd been given than ever. Meeting with the pastor proved that Mr. Dumfarthing had indeed laid out all his wishes, and they would be followed.

"I'm going to miss him," Reverend Goldsmith said. "We had some fine discussions. He spoke very highly of you."

"I'm glad you took the time to get to know him."

"It started as a command performance." His blue eyes twinkled over round ruddy cheeks.

Jacob smiled and nodded. "I'm sure that it did. So we can have the funeral the day after tomorrow?"

"Yes, I've already set things in motion." He handed Jacob his copy, in Mr. Dumfarthing's handwriting, of the order of service.

Jacob read down and broke into a chuckle. Beside the word *Eulogy,* his old friend had written, *Keep it short*. The same instructions applied next to the word *Homily*. Jacob looked up. "Mrs. Howard said she is preparing things at the house."

"Our women will bring food in spite of his directive, so tell her to go easy."

Jacob raised his eyebrows.

"I know. She doesn't listen any better than he did." Reverend Goldsmith leaned back in his chair. "You have any questions or suggestions for the funeral?"

"Not that I can think of. He laid things out about as well as any man could." He rose to his feet and extended his hand. "Thank you."

The funeral went according to plan, but Jacob doubted Mr. Dumfarthing had any idea how many people would attend the funeral. People filled the church wall to wall and outside down the front steps. According to his wishes, the casket was closed, but people passed by it anyway, laying a flower or patting the wood. Many continued on out to the cemetery, wiping tears as the box was lowered into the ground.

"A perfect day," Mrs. Howard said that evening after Jacob had helped her put things back to rights. "Just the way he planned it." She sighed. "He misjudged the number of people we needed to feed, though. Good thing the ladies of the community brought things by."

"Reverend Goldsmith knew better. He seems like a good pastor for the church here."

"He is." She looked over at Jacob leaning

back in the leather armchair that had been Mr. Dumfarthing's favorite. "But we sure missed you after you left."

"That was a terrible thing I did." Jacob reminded himself yet again that he'd been forgiven for his actions.

"Mr. Dumfarthing looked forward to your letters. I'm glad you wrote and told him about life in the badlands. He read everything he could find about the area."

Jacob nodded. "He was an amazing man, and I will be eternally grateful, as will my friends out west who will benefit from his largess."

"Me too." She caught a yawn. "I will bid you good night, then. Is there anything you need?"

"No. Rest well — you've earned it."

She sniffed and blinked several times. "I won't hear his bell ever again." As she left the room, he heard her sniff again.

The next day he boarded the train and headed west. *Home, I'm going home. I can't wait to tell everyone this story.*

"Thank you, Lord, for the I gifts I am bringing." *I never had time to write to Opal.* He took in a deep breath. *But now I can prepare a place for her, God willing.*

CHAPTER THIRTY-FOUR

August 14, 1887

Dear Miss O'Shaunasy,

I know you didn't give me permission to write to you, but you left so suddenly that I was not the only one caught by surprise. I asked for your address from Mrs. Hegland, and while she was hesitant to share it with me, I persevered until she acquiesced. I'm certain she will be writing to you soon also, for she says she misses you greatly, as does Carly.

I am not attempting to make you feel guilty but just informing you as to our feelings here in Medora.

I am moved into my house at last. The roof is all finished, and just today I nailed the last shingle on the porch roof. I am hoping to find my windows tomorrow at the station when the train arrives from Dickinson.

Jacob received a summons from a friend back east, and he'll be leaving tomorrow on the train. That, too, was a bit of a surprise. It seems there are surprises all over the place. Now that the haying is completed, Joel and the girls are taking the wagons out to pick up bones — a rather gruesome task but another example of some good coming from such tragedy. Fertilizer companies are paying by the pound for bones to grind into fertilizer. Then I am certain they will try to sell the fertilizer back to the farmers and ranchers. There is some degree of irony there, don't you think?

There is plenty of grass for the cattle this year, as there are so few cattle grazing. No one else has left lately, so perhaps the ranchers who remain will eventually regain their livelihood. Rand predicts that cattle ranching will never again reach the epic proportions it did before the winter of '87. We shall see. I purchased another lot of fifty head, so I now own nearly a hundred.

I would be very happy if you would take up correspondence with a lonely man out here on the prairie.

Yours truly,
Jeremiah McHenry

Amethyst read the letter again. He wrote

to her. He actually took pen in hand and sent her a letter.

"Amethyst, dear . . ." Mrs. Grant paused in the doorway. "I have arranged a fitting for you. Mrs. Beaumont has made room in her busy schedule to sew a couple of new gowns for you." Mrs. Grant paused again. "Was your letter good news?"

Amethyst nodded. "From Mr. McHenry. He asked me to correspond with him. To quote him, he said he's 'a lonely man out here on the prairie.' "

"Jeremiah McHenry said that?"

Amethyst nodded. "He did. In the beginning he accused me of leaving abruptly." She set the dainty chintz rocking chair in her room to rocking. She had never seen such opulence until she walked in with Mrs. Grant and was shown to this room as though she were a beloved guest, not one of the serving women. But as Mrs. Grant reminded her whenever necessary, she was now a business partner, not a servant.

To think she, Amethyst Colleen O'Shaunasy, was the one being waited on. It made her most uncomfortable.

"Which means you didn't get his permission."

Amethyst's eyes widened. "What?"

Mrs. Grant crossed the room and sat on

the padded settee that matched the rocking chair. "My dear, you have to understand both the military and the masculine mind. A man like that is used to giving orders and having people in his command ask his permission before doing something."

"I wasn't in his command."

"No, but he was certainly taking you for granted. You made sure he had plenty to eat and drink and provided conversation when he so desired. True?"

"True." Amethyst felt her hair slipping. And Joseph hadn't been the one to cause it this time. He would grow up without her to watch. And Carly. Ach, how she missed them. "He mentioned Carly, saying that they all missed me."

"What a devious man." Mrs. Grant shook her head, wagging one finger. She huffed a sigh and laid her hands back in her lap. "Now we must continue our plans for our business. The room for you to experiment with the receipt Mrs. Sampson sent us, along with her samples, is nearly ready. We need to order whatever other supplies you need" — she looked from under her eyebrows — "or if you even dream of needing something, you must put it on the list. While you are doing that, I will see to the legalities of organizing our enterprise. However, Mr. Arthur, my solicitor, will be arriving in about half an hour, and I would like for you to meet him."

"If you think so." Amethyst felt that a whirlwind had snatched her up from Medora and deposited her in Chicago, into a house she'd not known enough to dream of and into a life she still needed getting used to. So many things Mrs. Grant, the whirlwind who was at it again, took for granted.

Riding in a wagon with iron-rimmed wheels plodding across the prairie did not compare to driving to the house in a phaeton with a fringe along the roof. But the wind blowing free and clean across the badlands had no parallel with the heavy air of city streets that stank of decay and too many people.

What would her father say if he could see her now? The thought made her shudder. On those rare occasions when she did think of him, she prayed he treated his new wife better than he had her mother and her.

Here it was only August twentieth, and she'd already had tours of the house, the neighborhood, the city. She'd worshiped in a church that made her eyes pop out, and shopped — or rather Mrs. Grant shopped while she gawked — in stores that carried things she'd never heard of. She brought herself back to the room when Mrs. Grant laid a hand on her shoulder.

She removed a pair of hair combs from her pocket. "I brought you these because I know you lost one of the others. For the dinner I'm arranging for some people who will be interested in our line of products, we'll have my maid, Alyce, do your hair. She will be delighted to work with such glorious tresses."

"Glorious tresses?" Amethyst put a hand to her slightly off-sided knot.

"Yes, of course." She patted Amethyst's shoulder. "You will look lovely. And you have added only enough weight so that most women are going to think your tiny waist is the result of a tight corset."

Terror struck. "I don't have to wear a corset, do I? I cannot bear to be hemmed in."

"While it is the mode, I will not force you into the strictures of society." She leaned forward and lowered her voice. "Don't tell anyone, but that is why I run away so often. We will have to make many trips to Fargo to work with our partner there." Mrs. Grant rose and immediately became the lady of refinement and grace. "I hear the door. Let us go down and see what Mr. Arthur can make of this."

Throughout the meeting Amethyst sat back and watched her friend at work. She alternately ordered and acquiesced, explained and listened. Selling her cottage cheese to the townspeople of Medora was far more simple and yet the same. One had something to sell that others wanted, and one received money for doing the best she could with what she had. Mrs. Alvia Sampson in Fargo saw that her patients healed faster after she applied her lotions and salves. Mrs. Grant knew that women in the city would want the same lotions and salves to help them be more beautiful.

She'd heard stories of women using white face powder and the powder making them sick, even to dying. Was it so deathly important to be in the latest fashion?

"That will be all, then — for today. Thank you for coming on such short notice."

"You are indeed welcome. I shall get these papers back for your signature as soon as possible."

"Tomorrow?" Mrs. Grant's right eyebrow arched.

He sighed and nodded. "Tomorrow. Late."

Mrs. Grant held out her hand to shake his. "I knew I could count on you."

"I am pleased to meet you, Miss

466

O'Shaunasy. Welcome to Chicago and the world of Mrs. Grant." He picked up his papers, bowed slightly, and left the room to be escorted out by the housekeeper.

"So what do you think?" Mrs. Grant asked.

"I think I have no idea what all went on, but selling cottage cheese was far easier."

"True. You took your wares right to the buyer. Here we will be sending our product to stores that will sell our product to their shoppers. We need to go shopping ourselves and watch other women shop. See what they choose and perhaps even ask them why."

"We?"

"I think so."

Fittings were far different than sewing, trying on, and sewing again. Amethyst stood still as ordered, turned when instructed, and gratefully stepped out of the half-made garment when the woman said she was finished. The watered silk felt delicious on her skin. The brocade was too heavy for now but would be warm enough in the winter.

Would Chicago have blizzards like Medora? Not according to one of the help she'd asked the question.

At night she thought of the new cabin

built out at the U bend in the river and of Jeremiah McHenry. She remembered Carly sitting on her lap and Joseph giggling when her hair tumbled down. She could hear Pearl playing the piano, and she'd not seen birds in the city other than chipping sparrows and pigeons. There were no meadowlarks on the morning wind nor eagles and hawks in full wing, black against the sun or sky so blue it looked to go on forever.

The sky wasn't prairie blue in Chicago even on a sunny day.

But no matter how busy she kept herself during the day and how resolutely she refused to allow herself to think of him, at night she saw a certain one-eyed rancher. Heard him.

He refused to be banished from her heart.

CHAPTER THIRTY-FIVE

Late August

"He's married!" Opal waved the sheet of paper.

"Who's married?" Ruby grabbed Mary before she could crawl out to the porch.

"Atticus! Can you believe that?" Opal planted her fists on her hips, the paper crumpled in one hand. "He said he was coming back!" *For me. I thought he loved me. That I loved him.* "What kind of a skunk is he?"

"All right. Let's start over." Ruby bounced Mary to calm her tears for having been thwarted from crawling out onto the porch after her brother. "You have a letter from Atticus?"

"No. I have a letter from Atticus's *wife* telling me they are *married!* It's a very short letter."

"I'm sure it is. At least he found someone to write for him."

"Ruby!"

"Sorry."

"Opa?"

"Men!"

"Opa! Come." Per looked up at her from his lock around her knee.

"Don't grow up to be a man, all right, little guy?" She grabbed him up and set him on her shoulders. "What do you want me to see?"

He pointed toward the river. "Pa come." He jerked on her braid. "Go, Opa."

"Ouch. No, I'm not playing horse for you. And that hurt." She swung him back to the ground. "Stay on the porch."

"Opa, go."

"No, stay on the porch." She reached over and latched the gate. What kind of a friend did something like that to a friend? She smoothed the crumpled paper and read it again.

Dear Opal,

Dear, my foot.

My name is Winifred and my husband, Atticus Grady, asked me to write this for him.

The big coward.

We were married a fortnight ago and are happy living on our farm here in Oregon. Atticus said he wishes you every blessing.

Right, except part of my blessing was supposed to be him.

Your friend,
Atticus

Some friend.
But he didn't have to write to you at all. The voice inside made her stamp her foot. She caught it on a root and hobbled until the sting left.

"Atticus is a rat! Atticus Grady is a low-bellied snake!"

"What are you screamin' for?" Beans sat on his horse behind her as she stood shouting into the trees that climbed the ridge behind the house.

"Men are the worst vermin on earth!"

"Thanks a heap." He crossed his arms on the saddle horn. "To what do we owe that honor?"

"Atticus had his *wife* write and tell me he was married."

"I'd say that was right kind of him. Least-ways this don't leave you hangin' around waitin' on him to come back."

She glared at him. "Leave it to a man to say something like that."

"You din't love him nohow. He was just your friend. Not that friends ain't important."

"How can you say that?" The shock of what he said dropped her mouth open. "I told him I'd go with him last Christmas, but he said no. That he'd come back. I figured he meant when we were both older."

"I'd guess he done you a favor."

Opal raised her hands toward the heavens. "Will someone around here please make sense?"

"I been watchin' the way you and Jacob don't look at each other."

"What does that mean? Jacob's my friend too. Is he going to go off and marry someone else? What's the matter with me?"

Beans shook his head, real slowlike and with a funny grin. "Honey, you're gonna find out it ain't nothin' that's wrong with you that a few months won't take care of."

Opal cocked her head, leading with her chin as usual. "You are making exactly no sense."

"Be that as it may, I better go let this horse get to grazin', so he can go again tomorrow." He reined the horse around and rode down to the barn to unsaddle.

Opal stared after him. Somehow she had a feeling she'd just heard wisdom, but for the life of her, she couldn't figure it out. She thought of ripping up the letter but instead folded it and stuffed it into her pocket. She'd better get to the milking. And gather the eggs. These were chores she never minded.

The day after her lessons with Pearl, she cleaned several rooms for her, filled the woodbox, and helped her with the last of the cucumbers she was putting up in crocks. Dill pickles were mighty fine in the winter.

"I miss Amethyst so much," Pearl said. "She was the biggest help, but beyond that, she was my friend. I thought she'd stay here until some man came along and married her."

"I was hoping Mr. McHenry would be the one."

"So was she, but after that party, she kind of gave up."

Opal spread a layer of horseradish leaves across the layer of cucumbers. "She was going to teach me to make piccalilli."

"Me too, but she left her receipt. I just haven't had time. And since she left, we have too much milk, and people are asking for cottage cheese, and I don't have time to make it. Daisy is helping me with that, but she isn't Amethyst."

"You think she'd like to hear from me?"

"Of course she would. I think she's so homesick for us out here that she'd be on that train before you could blink if she thought it was the right thing to do." Pearl paused and thought a moment. "But I could be wrong. Maybe she's fallen in love with living in a grand house with servants and all."

"Did you tell her about the cottage cheese and piccalilli?"

"No. I don't want her to feel bad. She has to learn about making lotions, and I do know living in Chicago can be real entertaining."

Opal shook her head. "Amethyst isn't cut out for city living."

"Not to change the subject, but do you have your homework assignments?"

"Yes, ma'am. And I better be going. Oh, I forgot to tell you. I got a letter from a woman named Winifred who is now married to Atticus."

"Well, I'll be. Good of him to let you know."

"That's what Beans said."

"You don't seem too sad about it."

"No. It just made me mad for a while. But I hope he is happy out there in Oregon."

"Opal honey, I think you are indeed growing up." Pearl glanced down to where Carly had hold of Opal's knee. "Hey, Carly, you going to keep her here?"

"Per does the same thing. But guess when you're their size, knees are a good thing." She bent down and picked Carly up. "I gotta go. You take care of Joseph now."

Carly shook her head.

"Why not?"

"Joey bites."

"I see." Opal inspected the place Carly showed her on her arm. Sure enough — four red marks.

"Owie."

"I see." Opal kissed her cheek and set her back down. "I need to be going. Bye."

Carly waved. "Bye. Come back soon."

"Hey, new words." She grinned at Pearl. "She's talking more than Per already."

"Girls always learn to talk faster. And according to Carl, we keep on talking." Pearl moved Joseph away from the woodbox again. "He uses that for a teething ring." She handed him a hard-baked crust of bread. "Try this. It tastes better."

Opal heard the train whistle as she rode on home. *I wonder when Jacob will be*

475

back. "Come on, Bay, let's pick it up. I got work to do."

Even though it wasn't September yet, there was already the feeling of fall in the air. Beans said the signs predicted another hard winter, and this time they were taking no chances. Hopefully the bull had caught all the cows and the heifers that were old enough, and they would have a good calf crop in the spring.

As Rand said, *"There is always next year."*

Opal still had a hard time when she saw the bleached bones of a cow on the prairie or in the draws. But they had picked up so many wagonloads of bones and hauled them to the train station, they'd managed to fill an entire boxcar.

Pearl had assigned her to read Exodus and Leviticus. Her goal was to read through the entire Bible this year as part of her schoolwork. Then she and Pearl would talk about it. Bible history, now, that was an unusual class to take for school. While the other kids weren't back to school yet, she'd started early because Pearl needed help.

"Opa!" Per banged on the gate of the porch and yelled at her.

She waved back and rode on up to the house. "You want a ride, little guy?"

"Ride." He rattled the gate again.

She dismounted and went to pick him up. "I'm taking Per," she called out to let Ruby know.

"Mange takk."

He waved his arms and leaned toward Bay. She held him out, and Bay sniffed the boy's hands, making him chuckle. Swinging him up in the saddle, she mounted and settled him in front of her. "I'm sure you'd rather go on a long ride than just down to the barn."

"Go, Opa."

She nudged Bay to a lope, and Per's laughter made her laugh too.

That night when she settled in to do her homework, half listening to Ruby and Rand talking, she heard a horse loping up to the house. Ghost barked, announcing a visitor.

"Who could that be at this time of night?" Rand went to the door. "Jacob, welcome home."

Opal felt like jumping up and running to the door. Jacob was home! She had so much to tell him. But when she thought about it for a moment, she figured she might not want to tell him about Atticus. He might not think it funny that Winifred wrote her a letter. But then again, maybe he would.

"Good evening. It sure feels good to be back on this side of the world." Jacob removed his hat as he came through the door. "Mrs. Harrison, Opal."

"How was your trip?" Ruby asked, laying down her sewing.

"Not what I expected. But I was there in time to talk with Mr. Dumfarthing before he died. We had a good visit, and then he died that night. Mrs. Howard, his housekeeper, said he'd been waiting for me."

"That sounds like what our father did. Waited until Opal and I arrived, talked with us awhile, and then died that night. Isn't it amazing people can do things like that?"

"I'm not surprised with Mr. Dumfarthing. I'm sure he's straightened out any mismanagement in heaven already. But I am grateful beyond measure for his friendship, and Rand, that is what I must talk with you about. I'll bring this up at church on Sunday, but I wanted your opinion first."

"Here or privately?"

"Actually, this is fine, but I'd appreciate if you didn't discuss it with anyone else until I can think about it more. I have to get ready to open the school in less than a week."

"Of course. What is it?"

Opal closed her book. This sounded far more fascinating than classical history.

"Mr. Dumfarthing left money in his will for us to build a church here in Medora and to better support the school. He was a strong believer in good education, both temporal and spiritual. There is money to pay my salary, and there will be money to pay for any of the children who want to go on to further schooling."

"Thank you, heavenly Father." Ruby and Opal exchanged looks of wonder.

"Are you serious?" Rand asked.

"I am. I couldn't believe it when I read the will. He made sure I read it with him there so he could answer any questions. He knows what a hard time we had here last winter and said if I wanted to use part of this money to help some who were desperate, to go ahead. He sent money home with me. Then he died. He had planned the funeral, everything down to the last dish to be served at the house after he was buried. The church was full. He left a solid legacy for them also."

"Was he richer than Rockefeller?" Rand shook his head. "Jacob, you're not making this up, are you?"

"No. There's more that we can talk about later, but this is the gist of it."

"I'll put the coffee on." Ruby started to get up.

Opal beat her to it. "I'll take care of that." Build a church, add to the school? Who had money like that and could give it away? Even the Brandons, who'd seemed rich to her, didn't have that kind of money. Or at least she didn't think they did.

"Is there enough gingerbread for us all to have some?" Ruby asked.

Opal checked the pan. "If I cut small pieces."

"Good."

Opal took out plates and forks and the vanilla sauce to be warmed up. Would Jacob continue to work for the Robertsons? How could he do it all and teach school too? Plus build a church.

"I figured it is too late to start building the church now. It would take some time to order the wood — from where?"

"Dickinson. Perhaps some things from Fargo. We'll have to look into it. I know McHenry had to order some of his windows from Fargo. They came in on the train. We got the wood for the school from Dickinson. Other than what we cut ourselves."

Opal listened to Jacob talk. Lately she'd noticed that he had a real good voice to listen to. And he wasn't hard on the eyes either.

CHAPTER THIRTY-SIX

September

"I thought you'd be happy out here with your house and all." Rand shook his head. "You look like you lost your last friend."

"Funny thing. I thought I would be too, but then I got used to having women around at the boardinghouse, and now I want . . ." Jeremiah paused and stared into the fire. "I think I made the biggest mistake of my life."

"For one who never seems to make a mistake, it must be a big one." Rand looked at his friend over the lip of the coffee cup. "I'm here if you need an ear."

"I know. Remember when you met Ruby?"

"Of course. She near to ran me out of town. No matter what I did, it riled her up."

McHenry chuckled. "She was a feisty one."

"Still is."

"You are one lucky man."

"Not luck at all. God's providence. He brought that woman into my life and then

481

gave me a good shake now and then to keep me on the right track. For a while, I thought she was sweet on you. That's when you came close to — well, let's say things turned out all right in the end."

"No, not yet."

"Not for you, eh?"

"Nope. I thought to pretty much live out my life in the army, perhaps retire someday, but not so soon. Yet I have, and I'm here where I always dreamed of being. I have my ranch started, and I'm lonely as all get out." There, he'd said it. Lonely. Like a solitary bull elk who is driven out of the herd and roams alone.

"You need a wife."

"I know. That's where I went wrong."

"Miss O'Shaunasy was sweet on you."

"As I said, that's where I went wrong. Didn't realize it until she left."

"Isn't there some saying about absence making the heart grow fonder?"

McHenry nodded. "You want another cup of coffee? Don't have anything stronger to put in it."

"What happened?"

"I realized that if I didn't get a handle on it, I was on the way to becoming a drunk. Can't have that."

"Good for you."

A silence stretched, the log in the stove snapping and popping, the heat feeling good as the night had turned chilly. McHenry looked around the room. "Pretty plain for a home. Needs a woman's touch."

"They did a good job, all of them. Made you curtains, that rag rug in front of the fire. Wasn't there a quilt for your bed too? And that chair you're sitting in — that's a real work of art."

"I know. Carl is a fine furniture maker." Jeremiah tossed the dregs of his cup into the fireplace to sizzle on the burning log. "I've been writing to Miss O'Shaunasy."

"That's a start."

"She's busy there. She and Mrs. Grant are getting some business going, making soaps and lotions. They're working with a woman in Fargo too."

"As Opal said, Amethyst isn't a city person."

"Then why'd she leave?"

"Because she was invited? How would I know?"

McHenry stood, one arm resting on the mantel above the fireplace, staring into the fire. "You got any advice?"

"Go get her."

"What if I get all the way there and she won't come back with me?"

"Well, do I have to tell you everything? Surely you know how to court a good woman."

"I don't know if I do."

"It's just like planning a campaign."

"How so?"

"I don't know." Rand laughed. "But it sure sounded good." He stood and set his cup on the table. "I need to get on home. This being out late makes Ruby a bit nervous. Afraid something might happen to me."

"Thanks, Rand."

"You're welcome. Come on by the house and talk to Ruby, if it would help. She'd have some good ideas for courting Miss O'Shaunasy."

"What if she turns me down?"

"Ruby?"

"No — Miss O'Shaunasy."

"Then you plan a new campaign. That's how you caught Geronimo, wasn't it? Same thing."

Jeremiah walked Rand to the door. "That harvest moon ought to light your way home."

"True, and Ruby will have a lamp in the window for a welcome."

Two days later Jeremiah McHenry

boarded the train heading east.

Ten days later he stepped off the train back home — alone.

"What happened?" Rand asked when Jeremiah rode up to the ranch house on his way home.

"You know how you said to plan a campaign?"

Rand nodded.

"I did. The frontal assault didn't work."

"You're not giving up, are you?"

"No. Just planning a new strategy."

September 14, 1887
Dear Miss O'Shaunasy,

The train ride home was uneventful, the best way for any traveling. I've had many rides that were not uneventful. Thank you for attending the opera with me. What a fortunate man I am to have two such lovely women to show me about. How different it would be to live on a lake like Michigan, especially for me after my years in the desert. The wind sure can blow there.

We all have been cutting plenty of firewood. We harvested Rand's fields of oats and wheat. He got a pretty good harvest for a first time like that. Beans says we are going to have another hard winter, the animals all have extra thick coats already. Amazing how God provides for His creatures, isn't it?

I am reading Shakespeare's tragedies right now. I never had much time for reading before, so I am enjoying the evenings, although they would be more enjoyable if I had company here. I do hope you will write back soon and tell me how things are progressing in Chicago.

Respectfully yours,
Jeremiah McHenry

He drew a little picture of a cottontail nibbling grass on the bottom of the letter and took it into town the next day to mail it.

September 26, 1887
Dear Mr. McHenry,

Thank you for coming to visit. I, too, enjoyed the opera. The music helped me imagine what heaven must sound like. I never knew there were so many different kinds of instruments, and when the woman hit her high notes, it sent shivers up my arms. The carriage ride along the lake made me realize how large this lake is. More like a sea, since you can't see the other side.

We have made a new fragrance for Christmas with the scent of cinnamon. What do you think?

Your friend,
Miss O'Shaunasy

October 8, 1887
Dear Miss O'Shaunasy,

I think cinnamon smells wonderful. When I think of Christmas, I remember the pine tree my father used to bring into the house. We had branches of holly with red berries, if the birds didn't get them all as soon as they turned color.

Mr. Chandler is a popular teacher with the children. I've not heard of any toads or snakes in his desk drawer. The children delighted in plaguing Mr. Finch. I didn't blame them a bit. He didn't fit well here at all.

Carly said to tell you to come back home again soon. She misses you. So do others, including me.

We will be building a church here come spring. Mr. Chandler has a benefactor who donated the money. Isn't it amazing how God accomplishes that which He sets out to do?

Yours always,
Jeremiah McHenry

He drew a flying goose on this one.

P.S. The waterfowl are flying south. They are so numerous, they darken the sky. What a sight to behold. JM.

Amethyst reread Jeremiah's latest letter and smiled at the chipmunk with full cheeks in the lower corner. Who would have thought that Mr. McHenry was a man of so many talents? She'd seen chipmunks just like that in the woodpile at Pearl's. No matter how hard she worked, she still thought of Medora as home. Taking out pen and paper, she set about answering the letter from Pearl and then the one from McHenry. Just today she'd received another one from Joel.

October 12, 1887
Dear Aunt Colleen,
We have three boxes of new books at school. They arrived today. Pa says I must call him Mr. Chandler at school just like all the others. It seems strange to do that. I was wondering, do you think you could come home for Christmas? I will be Joseph in the Christmas pageant, and I wish you could be here.

I have a real horse of my own now. Pa bought it for me. His name is Big Red. He has a blaze down his face. I would call him Blaze, but Pa says we don't want to confuse him, since there's already a horse named Blaze here. Ada Mae rides with me, and now that Virginia is no longer going to school, Emily has the other horse. Pa takes one and goes earlier than we do. We could take a wagon, but soon the snow will come, and we will turn the wagons into sleighs again.

Please come home to see us.

Your friend,
Joel Chandler

Amethyst wiped her eyes. *Come home to see us.* He must have forgotten how long the train ride was. But she could do that. She had more than enough money now to buy a train ticket, and she still had her two gold pieces. She had cashed in the ticket that her father bought. If she stopped to think about it, she was on her way to being wealthy, according to the standards she used to have. If she were to go back to Medora, she would stay at Pearl's and bring presents for everyone. Should she tell Mr. McHenry that she was thinking of coming?

CHAPTER THIRTY-SEVEN

Making different lotions wasn't much different than baking different kinds of cakes.

The light that poured into her mixing room, as she finally decided to call it — laboratory sounded too formal — made it a joy to work in there. Using rose petals, lavender, bee balm, mint, and other fragrant flowers either singly or together, along with the ingredients in Mrs. Sampson's receipt and others she read about and had Mrs. Grant order, Amethyst experimented with many combinations. She often forgot meals and needed to be reminded to sleep. With no one demanding anything of her, she played with her bowls and ingredients, added orange or lemon peel and spices such as cinnamon and ginger. Whenever she found something she really liked, she asked the servants to test her lotions to see which they preferred. Some of her creations ended in a jar in the kitchen to be used up so that she didn't waste anything, and the servants had softer, smoother skin as a result. When she read in an herbal book about the healing properties of a strange-looking plant called aloe vera, she ordered that and squeezed the clear gel contained in the succulent leaves into her potions. When it took away the pain of a burn one cook suffered, she bought more plants and added it to a special lotion with mint and lavender and called it her healing lotion. Witch hazel joined her bottles of ingredients for the same reason.

Mrs. Grant invited her friends to sample the lotions that she and Amethyst liked best, and soon more and more people were inquiring when and where they could buy some. Amethyst delighted in their enthusiasm.

One evening, after a pleasant social at which she had explained to a group of businesswomen what she was doing and then had invited everyone to try two fragrances — lavender and bee-balm mint — that she and Mrs. Grant had chosen to produce for their first release, she sat down and answered the letters she'd received from her friends in Medora. The number of those who had written surprised her.

October 24, 1887
Dear Joel,

Thank you for writing to me. I am glad school is going well. I knew Mr.

Chandler would be a better teacher than Mr. Finch. It must be a bit difficult when the teacher is your own pa. How good that the school has new books and that you like to read and study. I remember reading to you when you were little. Now you can read to me. Give everyone my best wishes.

Love,
Your aunt Colleen

October 24, 1887
Dear Pearl,

Your letters are so dear to me. I miss all of you more than I can say. Since you know what life is like here in Chicago, you understand what a shock it is to me and how I have struggled to fit in. Mrs. Grant is so good to me. We have two stores now that plan to sell our goods. Mrs. Grant says women are going to love our lotions and soaps, and has big plans for our company. She is like a whirlwind that never stops.

How I would love to show you my mixing room. When you enter, it is like walking into a flower garden filled with the most wonderful fragrances. I am learning to add color with some dyes that don't have a bad effect on skin.

The pink is especially nice, but it is the fragrances that I love the most.

I never dreamed I would be able to do things like speaking to a group of people or discussing orders and packaging with the buyers from the stores. While Mrs. Grant is in charge of that part of the business, she wants me to understand and take part in all aspects. She has found the most charming bottles for our lotions, and she says it won't be long before we need help to prepare the lotions and fill the bottles. I will send you some as soon as I can.

Please tell everyone that I think often of my friends in Medora and I miss you all. I hope Mr. Hegland has found more buyers for his furniture. He should talk again with Mrs. Grant. She would find enough buyers to keep him busy from morning until night. He'd have to hire help. Please write whenever you can; I so enjoy your letters. Give Carly and Joseph hugs and kisses from me.

> With a heart full of love,
> Your friend,
> Amethyst

October 24, 1887
Dear Mr. McHenry,

I am sorry it has taken me so long to answer your last letter, but I do appreciate hearing about your ranch and the seasons changing in Medora. There aren't too many trees to see turning reds and gold here. But out in the backyard the gardener still has roses in bloom, and fall flowers are in their glory.

Our business is growing. We now have two fragrances of lotion, two of soaps, and our own special wrapping and labels. Mrs. Grant says that I am a natural businesswoman, but sometimes I would like to bake in the kitchen instead.

Amethyst stared at what she had written. Why was it so much easier to answer other letters than his? Leaning back in her chair, she closed her eyes for a moment and remembered his visit. Such a surprise when the maid informed her she had a gentleman caller waiting in the parlor. . . .

"What is his name?"

"I don't know, Miss O'Shaunasy. He just said he was a friend of yours and wanted to surprise you."

Amethyst started to ask her another question but instead stopped briefly in front of the mirror to make sure her hair had stayed where it belonged and no crumbs from breakfast remained on her face. Then she made her way down the stairs to the parlor.

"Why, Mr. McHenry."

"I wanted to surprise you." The sun glinting through the stained-glass panes of the front windows painted him in a rosy sheen. But his smile held — held what? A hint of insecurity? Surely not Major Jeremiah McHenry, albeit retired.

"That you accomplished." She motioned to the sofa. "Please have a seat, and I'll order coffee." Realizing the leaping of her heart might show in her eyes, she smiled again and reached to pull the bell rope. When she turned around, he was still standing, holding a package rather stiffly. Oh, of course, he would never sit until she did. The thought that she was no longer the servant twitched the corners of her mouth. She seated herself, grateful she wore a rich green gown with mother-of-pearl buttons down the tucked bodice rather than her working clothes.

"You look lovely." He sat on the edge of the chair and handed her the package. "I thought this might remind you of home."

As if I need further reminders. Just having

him here made her ache to see Pearl and her little ones, Joel, and the others. One thing she was learning was how to keep all her emotions from showing on her face. "Thank you." She unwrapped the embossed paper carefully to find a suede-bound book inside. When she opened the page, a dried bluebell greeted her.

"From your place?" She remembered a swath of bluebells on the rise behind his cabin.

"Yes."

"How can I help you, miss?" the maid in her dark dress with white mobcap and apron asked from the doorway.

"Coffee, please, and a plate of those lemon cookies, thank you."

"Right away, miss." She left without a sound.

Amethyst glanced up to catch a questioning look that McHenry immediately erased. She rolled her lips slightly to keep from smiling. Today the shoe was on the other foot, and she was enjoying every minute of it. "Tell me. What is the news from Medora?"

"Jacob Chandler returned from his visit to Pennsylvania to visit a friend who was dying. Mr. Dumfarthing left money in his will to build a church in Medora and to pay

Reverend Chandler's salary."

"Really. How remarkable."

"Indeed. Caught everyone, including Jacob, by surprise. The meeting to confirm our acceptance, ah, you would have enjoyed it. They've chosen a place for the new church at the bottom of the bluffs on the northeast corner of town, just a couple of blocks from the Catholic church. We're talking of using local rock for the exterior walls. Will make it look like part of the land."

"Will there be a steeple and bell?"

"Of course. And Jacob suggested the altar window be stained glass in memory of Evan Dumfarthing. Carl Hegland will make the altar, and he plans to carve the front doors."

"It will be beautiful. What a change from using the schoolhouse."

"Mr. Dumfarthing donated money for books and supplies for the school too. And money for expenses if any of the area children choose to go on to school."

"Bless that man." She smiled up at the maid who returned with a silver tray. "Thank you, Susan. Would you please invite Mrs. Grant to join us for coffee?"

"Of course. I'll bring another cup."

"Do you still drink it black, or would you care for cream or sugar?"

"Black, thank you."

"How is Joel?" She lifted the ornate silver coffeepot, filled his cup, and passed it to him.

"He's another beneficiary of Mr. Dumfarthing's generosity. Thank you." He took the cup and saucer, just touching her fingers as he did so.

She kept the jolt from showing on her face — or hands that wanted to shake. "Really?"

"Reverend Chandler is to purchase a ranch to live on so that Joel can still enjoy the life he loves." He leaned forward slightly. "From what I've observed, I think the ranch is for Opal too."

Amethyst smiled. "Love is blossoming?" *Please, Lord, let Opal be happy again.* "And how is Opal faring?"

"She is pretty much back to her old self. I think having Sprout to baby helped. You should see him. He follows her around like a dog, and last time I was there, Rand had fashioned a harness for him, and he was pulling a little wagon with Per riding it. Opal had a halter on the calf. That was a sight to see."

Amethyst was still chuckling when Mrs. Grant crossed the room, hand outstretched to greet the visitor. "Mr. McHenry, what a treat to see you again. You have no idea how many people I have regaled about my adventure in the badlands."

He stood to greet her and sat again after she sat and waved him to his chair. "Thank you, dear, for inviting me. I was up to my elbows in more samples of glassware for our lotions." She sat and accepted the coffee Amethyst prepared and handed to her. "Oh, good, there were still lemon cookies." She passed the plate to McHenry. "Have another. Has Amethyst told you about our business?"

"No. I'm afraid I've been catching her up on the news from home."

Home, no, not anymore. This is my home now. While she'd told herself this many times, saying it still caused her heart to catch.

They visited for some time until McHenry announced, "I need to be going. I have an appointment this afternoon."

"Surely you can stay for dinner?" Mrs. Grant said.

"No, I'm afraid not, but I would be honored if I could escort you both to the opera tomorrow night. I already purchased the tickets, since they were in danger of being all gone."

"Why, that would be lovely." Mrs. Grant turned to Amethyst. "That will give you a chance to show off your new gown, and we don't have anything planned."

"Yes." She nodded to McHenry. "Thank you for the invitation."

"We could have supper here first. I'll ask Cook to make something special. And the evening after that we are having a group here for supper and entertainment. I do hope you'll be able to join us." She paused. "How long will you be in Chicago?"

Amethyst felt his gaze on her. She looked up and caught his smile. *He looks like the Grant whirlwind just caught him up too.*

"I planned on leaving for home again in a week or so. I want to visit some farm machinery stores and a horse-breeding farm. Too many of the local horses perished in the blizzard, and I'm thinking of buying a Morgan stallion."

"So you plan to raise horses?"

"I seem to be leaning that way."

"My son has the family farm south of Chicago. He might know of some good stock for you to look at. If you'd like, I'll send a message out to him."

"That would be most helpful." He stood and nodded to both of the women. "Thank you for the coffee and cookies and your hospitality upon my abrupt appearance on your doorstep."

"You see him to the door, dear," Mrs. Grant said. She smiled up at McHenry. "I should have some information for you by tomorrow night. We'll see you at six, then?"

Amethyst rose and escorted Jeremiah to the door. "Thank you for coming."

"I'm hoping we can go for a drive along the lake while I am here."

"We'll see what the weather is like." She handed him his hat. "And how busy you are. Knowing Mrs. Grant, I believe she'll find plenty of people for you to meet with."

"I'll see you tomorrow night, then." He sketched a bow, and she closed the door behind him. Here she'd thought her new life was gaining some order, and now this.

Amethyst caught herself and returned to finishing the letter.

I thank you again for the journal you brought me and the kid gloves. I wear them often, as the weather has turned colder and we've had frosty nights. The wind blows off the lake, and while nothing compared to the blizzard of last winter, it still eats into one's bones.
Sincerely,
Amethyst Colleen O'Shaunasy

They did have a marvelous time up until he asked if she would be willing to return to Medora in the hopes she would consider allowing him to court her.

Go back to working for Pearl? Having nothing of her own? But she did miss seeing the children, receiving their love and giving hers in return. Would he be different? Would he no longer take her and what she did for granted? "My life is here now, and I owe Mrs. Grant a debt beyond payment," she finally answered. "Besides, we are too busy for me to consider being gone for even a few days right now."

"I see."

But she could tell he didn't see, and at moments she wondered if she did. Was she putting her lotions before her own happiness? But he had not mentioned anything about caring for her. So did he? And she'd not dared to ask if he still drank. Such a personal question. If he'd asked to court her before she left Medora, would things have been different?

If she didn't care for him, why did she find herself waking up from a dream with tears drying on her cheeks? The dream of a certain dashing, one-eyed man with a limp.

No matter how busy she kept herself during the day and how resolutely she refused to allow herself to think of him, at night he came riding into her mind.

It seemed to be getting worse, not better.

CHAPTER THIRTY-EIGHT

"Rand, any chance you could go look at a place with me on Saturday?"

"Of course. What time?"

Jacob thought a moment. "How about nine o'clock or so? I need to finish up some things around the Robertson place before I go."

"Teaching school kind of cuts into the chore time, doesn't it?" Rand tipped his hat back, the better to look up at Jacob on his horse.

"Pa?" Per called from the gate to the porch. "Pa, come, pease."

"Please, eh? That boy knows how to get what he wants." Jacob waved. "Hi there, Per."

Per waved back and jabbered out an answer that made both of the men smile.

"He can talk a blue streak, but we don't understand too well." Rand stepped back. "See you Saturday morning, then."

"Thanks." Jacob turned his horse and headed up the rise. Besides looking at the abandoned ranch, he had something else to discuss with Rand.

"All right, class, put away all your things, and let's talk some more about the Christmas pageant." On Friday afternoon, Jacob had as bad a case of the restless willies as his pupils. He usually finished the day with reading a story, but today that hadn't been enough to settle them. Someone yanked Ada Mae's braid, and she spun around to pay them back and tipped over an ink bottle. Now there was a black splat on the floor and spots on her dress and the Paddock boy's shirt. And he swore he didn't pull her hair.

Knowing that no one would tattle, Jacob put away the book and turned to the Christmas program. "Starting on Monday, Mrs. Hegland is going to be here two days a week to begin practicing the music. I'm sure you've all been memorizing your parts. . . ." The guilty looks on their faces told him that was an impossible dream. "All right, I see that has not happened. Do I need to send a note home with each of you?" Several shrank down in their seats. "Well, starting Tuesday, you'll be reciting. I'll just call on whomever I think should be ready, and that will be everyone beyond the third grade. I suggest you pair up and drill each other before then. Recess would be a good time to do that."

Someone groaned, but he paid no attention. "That's it for today. I'm letting you out fifteen minutes early. Perhaps you could spend that on your memory work." He smiled. "I didn't mean that, about the memory work, that is. God bless you all."

The room emptied immediately just in case he came up with something else. He knew the feeling. He was having as hard a time as his students thinking of Christmas coming. Indian summer had strode across the hills right on the heels of Jack Frost. Sitting in the school was hard when the geese and ducks could be heard singing their way south.

We need a harvest festival, he thought. But when? And what to do? He'd have to set the women on it. They'd come up with good ideas. Of course a barbeque would be wonderful. He'd heard tell of Rand's skill at that. Perhaps they could do a deer or two instead of a steer, since no one had any extra beef. And they'd have dancing. He could dance with Opal again. When would he find time to practice the fiddle? Somewhere between ten and midnight? After he'd finished his lessons for the next day?

He shut the school door behind him with

the same feeling of relief he'd seen on the children's faces.

"So do you think I should go ahead and buy this?" Jacob gestured at the soddy with a log cabin attached. "Or do you know of any other vacant places within an easy ride of the school?"

"Not with land around them. There are houses in town."

"Opal and Joel would not take to that, I'm afraid."

"That's if Opal agrees to marry you."

"Right. That's something else I want to talk with you about, but let's get this ranch thing done first. What is it I need to do?"

"I'd say you check to see if the previous owners ever purchased the land from the railroad. This here is railroad land, or it was until folks started buying it up. De Mores bought up quite a bit."

"In Dickinson?"

"That's where I went a few months ago to file for homestead rights on my place. That wasn't railroad land out there."

"So if I find that someone filed?"

"Then I'd see if they gave a forwarding address. Most people who left didn't. I think the man who lived here worked for the abattoir. Perhaps de Mores let him live here, and this was part of his land. I don't rightly know. But you start at the land office in Dickinson." Rand studied the house. "Going to take some work to get it habitable. Interesting how a house goes to pieces when no one is living there."

"You think I'd do better to just start from the ground up?"

"No. It would be easy to add on to the log section if you want. Just cut a door through that south wall."

"Add some more windows. And a porch."

"You could do a shed like at the schoolhouse for your horses, right off that corral. When would you like to move in?"

"Not until the school year is over. I promised Mrs. Robertson I'd keep on helping her. But I won't be able to stay at the line shack this year."

"Don't worry. We'll find someone."

They turned the horses toward home.

"What else did you have in mind?" Rand asked.

"I wondered if you would give some thought to allowing me to court Opal this winter? I'm not asking for an answer today, but that you pray about this and take into consideration that I can now afford to have a home and a wife, not that you'd said anything about that when we talked before. But

I'm thinking this might be something for her to look forward to, to prepare for. I know she's not as sad and quiet as she was earlier, but she's still not back all the way."

"You gave your word."

"I know. And I've lived by that and will abide by whatever you decide."

"All right. I'll talk it over with Ruby and pray. And I'd ask the same of you. Not that you talk it over with Ruby, but the prayer part." His slight smile said he was teasing.

Jacob grinned back at him. "Oh, I have been. Maybe I'll ask Mrs. Hegland if she would teach in my place for a couple of days while I go to Dickinson."

"Opal could go watch the children for her. Have you seen the plans Carl has been drawing for the church?"

"Not yet. I hope he's including a basement for the Sunday school rooms."

"He's doing it in stages."

"He's one smart man." Jacob waved as Rand headed on down to his own spread and he toward the Robertsons'. If only he could be talking all this over with Opal. And yet he was hesitant to show her the house and tell her his plans. He and Joel would have a home there whether Opal joined them or not. *Please, Lord, let it be so.*

509

CHAPTER THIRTY-NINE

November

"So what do you think?" Jeremiah nodded to the peaked-roofed barn.

"You sure got that finished in a hurry." Rand rubbed his chin. "Looks mighty fine and ready for those horses."

"Thanks to Carl and all of you who helped me." McHenry tipped his hat back with one finger. "I've never hammered so many nails in my life. And the way Joel, Opal, and Ada Mae spent every minute they had splitting shakes for the roof, why, I got to think of something special to do for them."

"You paid them. That's enough." Rand took his leather gloves out of his back pocket. "Getting right chilly again. When do you leave to pick up the horses?"

"Tomorrow. But, Rand, I need some more advice."

"About?"

"What to do about Amethyst."

"Why don't you come on over for supper

tonight, and we'll think about it on a full stomach. I promised Ruby I'd bring home something for supper, so I need to see what I can bag."

"Going up to the beaver pond?"

"Start there. We need more venison too. Got to keep that smokehouse going." Rand mounted and smiled down at his friend.

"All right. I'll see you tonight. And thanks."

When Jeremiah rode up to the Harrison ranch house late that afternoon, Opal was gutting a deer strung up on a bar between two trees out behind the house.

"Hey, Opal. Rand get that or did you?"

"Hey, yourself. I got it on my way home from Pearl's. Rand isn't back yet. Did you finish that last bit of roof?" She set the heart and liver in a pan, tossing the kidneys to Ghost, who sat waiting patiently. With the insides stripped clean, she started on the skinning.

"Sure did. Got an extra knife?"

"In the kitchen. But you don't have to help."

"I know." Jeremiah tied Kentucky to the back hitching post and headed for the porch. When his foot caught on the first step, he gritted his teeth and righted himself. Here he thought that stumbling was gone. He'd not stumbled climbing the ladder for over a week or two. That's what happened when you got cocky.

"Hi, Ruby, you got another skinning knife?" he asked, entering the house.

"Of course." She pulled open a drawer and handed him a slim-bladed knife along with the whetstone.

"Rand tell you he invited me for supper?"

"No, but it's no trouble to put another plate on the table. Good to see you for a change."

"I know. That barn took up my every minute from the time the sun came up until darkness fell." He spit on the whetstone and began sharpening the knife. "Still have more to do inside, but I can do that after the horses come. Old Kentucky will be right glad to have company." After testing the knife against his finger, he handed her the whetstone and headed for the door.

"Tell Opal to be sure to keep the intestines. We need them for sausage."

"Will do." He joined Opal at the deer carcass. When he passed on Ruby's message, Opal made a face. "I hate cleaning the guts." She nodded toward another pan where she had saved the ropey mess.

"Me too. But I do love sausage." They

skinned the deer in silence but for the swishing of the knives.

"So tell me about your new horses."

"You're going to love them. I'm thinking the stallion might make a good cow pony with some training. You up for taking him on?"

"A blooded horse?" She shook her head. "I don't know about that."

"But you'll give him a try? Morgan horses are known for being quick on their feet and highly intelligent, good workhorses."

"If you want."

"And after the foal is born in March, we'll have a baby to train."

"Okay, let's pull." Together they took hold of the hide and striped it down the front legs, like pulling off long johns that had been on a body for months. After cutting off the hooves, she tossed them to Ghost. "Now she'll have bad breath, but she sure loves to chew on those." Opal folded the hide, hair in, and tied the bundle. "I'll save the brains to use for tanning the hide, the way that Little Squirrel taught me." Opal shook her head. "I sure miss her and Linc. Where do you think he went?"

"Wish I knew, and I'd go talk him into coming back."

"I've been praying he is all right. He sure

loved her. He would have done anything for her." She reached up for one end of the bar that fit through the hamstrings on the back legs. "Grab that, would you, please, and we'll carry this over to the springhouse. If it were a bit colder, I'd leave it hanging here."

"Opal, you sure have come a long way from that little pigtailed girl whose only wish was to ride a horse. You're an amazing young woman."

"Thank you."

He chuckled inside at the red flush that bloomed on her cheeks. As they left the springhouse after settling the bar on the hooks Rand had set up, she took the milking pail with her.

"You want me to milk?"

"You know how?" She slanted him a teasing grin.

Ghost left her hoof and ran barking around the house.

"Rand is home."

"How do you know?"

"She has a special bark just for him."

Rand rode around the end of the house. "Hey, I brought in a deer." He patted the feathered bodies slung over Buck's withers. "And two geese. There aren't many left out there now."

"Any excuse will work."

"You weren't there, so quiet. You want to help me dress it out?"

McHenry glanced at Opal. "If she'll let me off the hook. I told her I'd milk — oh, and we just finished hanging Opal's deer in the springhouse."

Opal rolled her eyes. "Let him clean the intestines for sausage. He said that's his favorite job." She strolled off, swinging the milk pail "Hey, Ghost, go get the cow." The dog tore off on command. "She sure minds better than some people I know," she called over her shoulder.

Laughing, Rand dismounted, and the two men went about dressing out the deer, using the same pans that Opal had left on the bench.

"Supper will be ready in a couple of minutes," Ruby called when they were about done with the insides.

"We'll leave it with the hide on. I see Opal plans on taking the hair off hers. Think we'll do this one as a robe. Could have used more robes to cover the windows last winter."

"I have five beautiful coyote pelts and a couple of wolves'. Miracle there are any deer left with the number of scavengers out there. You want the coyote ones to add to Opal's robe?"

"Give them to her yourself." Rand

paused. "Little Squirrel sewed the pelts into the robe she has. She did it the old way. Made holes with her awl and used sinew thread. We don't make sinew thread like that."

"How hard is it?"

Rand shrugged. "Don't know. Never tried it."

"Can you tell me how?"

"I think Ruby knows."

"I'll take any wolf pelts you hear of." The two men finished washing at the bench and carried the pans into the house to be dealt with later.

McHenry took part in the give and take around the supper table, but at the same time he also felt as if he were standing back watching. The teasing between Rand and Ruby, the way she laid her hand on his shoulder when she leaned over to set a platter on the table, Opal making sure Per used his fork, and Ruby giving Mary a strip of bacon rind to gum to help with her teething — all the normal things of family living he envied.

Lord, I've said this before, and I'll say it again. I want this too, and I think Amethyst is the woman for me. Tell me . . . show me what I need to do to win her.

"How about I clean out those intestines

for you?" Rand asked his wife after the meal was finished.

"Thank you. I know how much you love doing that." Ruby smiled up at her husband. "While Opal does the dishes, I'll put the children to bed so we can have coffee and dessert later."

"Or I'll get Per ready for bed, you take care of Mary, and we'll do the dishes together?" Opal nudged her sister. "Sounds fair."

"And here I thought I could get out of doing the dishes." Ruby sighed, which made Opal chuckle, which set Per to giggling, which set off Mary.

"It don't take much to get them going," Rand said as he headed out the door, chuckling at their antics.

And please add the laughter, Lord. My house needs laughter. Jeremiah thought a moment. *And love.*

"You don't have to help me."

"I know."

They carried the pans out to the pump and, dumping out the old water, added new.

"Pew."

"Smells almost as bad as a skunk."

"You got any more advice for me? The last didn't work too well."

"What would you do in the army if a frontal assault didn't work?"

"First I'd have to consider how many men I had still standing."

"I'm talkin' general principles here, McHenry."

Had it been lighter outside, he was sure he would have seen Rand's eyes roll, but the droll tone said it all. "I'd regroup and most likely attempt a flanking movement." He thought a moment. "Or I'd throw my efforts into a siege."

"So?"

"So I don't know. What did you do?"

"I licked my wounds and kept showing up."

"I see." They carried the pans of cleaned intestines up to the house and into the kitchen to set on the counter of the cupboard Carl had made for the house. Rand sprinkled salt into the water and stirred it around so it would melt. "Have a chair." He motioned toward the two rocking chairs nearer to the fireplace.

"So keep showing up, eh? Somehow I think there's more to this than that. And besides, Chicago is a lot farther away than your ranch is to Little Missouri."

"True. But —"

"Right, Rand, that worked so well for

you." Ruby raised her eyebrows as she handed them their coffee cups.

"Now —"

"You two. Jeremiah McHenry, there is one thing a woman loves to hear."

"Really?" He waited, but when she didn't answer, he was forced to ask. "What?"

Ruby's sigh spoke of long-suffering. "Have you told her that you love her?"

Jeremiah pulled on his earlobe. "Umm. Well, sort of — but not exactly."

Now it was Ruby's turn to roll her eyes. She shook her head for added emphasis. "I suppose you said something along the line that you cared for her?" She gave her husband one of those looks, and he studied the coffee in his cup.

"Ah, I guess so." This was worse than being grilled by a general after a rout. Not that he'd had that happen many times, but once was enough.

"You care for your horse. You care for a cup of coffee on a cold day. You care for —"

He raised his hand. "Stop, I understand." *I hope*. He glared at Rand. "And no laughing at my expense." He turned back to Ruby. "And you guarantee this will work?"

"No, but it'll bring you a lot closer than you are now."

"This is getting as bad as trying to find

Geronimo." He chuckled along with them but wasn't too sure he was off the mark.

Since Amethyst had written how much she enjoyed his animal sketches, he had two of them framed and wrapped for her. One was of the doe and two fawns he'd often seen in his pasture, and the other was of the fox that slipped past his house to go drink at her favorite place on the creek. He gave thanks to Carl, who fashioned the frames. This way she'd have something to see to remind her of him. If she put them out, that is. He clutched the package in one hand and dropped the knocker on the front door of Mrs. Grant's home. This time he'd let them know he was coming.

"Good to see you again, Mr. McHenry." The maid ushered him in. "If you'll wait in the parlor, I'll go find Miss O'Shaunasy."

"Thank you." He handed her his coat and hat, which had been welcome on this blustery day. While November was being kind in the badlands, Chicago shivered in a cold, driving rain. He heard the tap of her shoes before she entered the room. Her smile gave him hope.

"Welcome to Chicago, Mr. McHenry. Come with me. It is warmer in the sitting room where we have a fire in the fireplace.

Seemed the perfect thing for a day like today."

He cleared his throat. "You look lovely."

Amethyst stopped and smiled into his eyes. "Thank you."

I've missed you. He hoped his eyes were saying what his tongue would not. Why was it that he could command troops, fight off attacking Indians, but was not able to say what he wanted to this woman? "I brought you something. It's not much, but I hope you like it." *Now you're rambling. Jeremiah McHenry, you're a broken-down, half-blind, stubborn, overbearing dolt. What could she possibly see in you anyway?* He handed her the package.

"Thank you. I'll open it in the sitting room." She tucked her hand in the crook of his arm and led him out a different door than from the entry and across the hall to a room that looked to have the sun shining in. After ringing for the maid, she sat down in a yellow damask chair and motioned him to take the other. Very carefully, to save the paper, she unwrapped the sketches.

"Oh." She turned them both right side up and looked from one to the other. "You did these?" When she found the signature at the lower right corners, she caught her lower lip between her teeth, blinked, and sniffed.

"Thank you. I have so enjoyed your little pictures on your letters. I shall treasure these." She studied them some more. "When did you become an artist?"

He shook his head. "I'm not an artist. I just like to draw. It's a good way to entertain yourself when you're on a post with not enough to do. I'll have to show you those I did in Arizona someday."

"I'd like that."

At the entry of the maid, Amethyst set the frames upright on the table so they could be seen by all. "Please let Mrs. Grant know that our guest has arrived."

"Oh, she knows. She said to tell you to invite the gentleman to dinner, and she will join you in the dining room."

"All right." Amethyst poured out the coffee. "I'm sorry we have nothing stronger to put in that to help warm you up."

"That's all right. I gave up the stronger drinks."

"Did you really?" The words were out of her mouth before she could think.

"I realized I was coming to depend on it, not only to help with the pain, but . . ." He shrugged. "In general."

"The pain in your leg is better, then?"

"Yes, it is." He sipped from the cup and smiled. "This is perfect. Thank you." *This room suits her. All sunshine and bright colors. Even on a bright day, my house is pretty dark.* He trapped a sigh before it grew into being.

Amethyst watched him over the rim of her cup. He seemed different somehow. Uncertain? Perhaps. "Is something wrong, Mr. McHenry?"

"Ah, no, of course not." He made himself smile and sit straighter. But the comparisons roared through his head: the silver service, the maid, or many maids, the cook, windows that looked out to a garden cared for by gardeners, the grand piano — she'd expressed a wish one time to learn to play the piano at the Heglands. "Have you learned to play the piano?"

"No." She shook her head just the slightest. "I haven't had time."

"I'm sorry. You love music."

"Do you still play the mouth organ?"

"In church every Sunday. It's a far cry from the organ and pianos of large churches, but we enjoy singing." He started to tell her about the barbeque but stopped himself. "Tell me about your business. How are the lotions doing?"

"Wonderfully. We are having a hard time keeping the orders filled. Would you like to see my mixing room?" She stopped. "After our coffee, that is. I mean, if you really want to."

"I would be happy to. Would it be possible for me to purchase some things to take back to Medora with me?"

"You haven't seen them yet."

"I know, but . . ." He paused and took a cookie from the plate she offered. "What about the healing lotion you mentioned in your letter?"

"It's good for burns and bugbites, we've learned."

"Bugbites. That ought to do well in Dakotah Territory."

She could feel herself relaxing as she laughed with him. *Love, JM.* That was the way he signed the pictures. Did he mean that or was it just a way of signing?

She showed him around her mixing room and made him try several of her lotions. "Doesn't that feel good on your hands?"

"Yes." He looked up at her in surprise. "It does." He lifted the back of his hand to his nose. "Mint. What else?"

"Lavender, witch hazel, a lot of other things." She held up another bottle. "I thought perhaps this would be good for men. I've distilled pine for it. What do you think?"

I think you are more beautiful than ever

and that you are far, far beyond the woman I first met. And that I made the biggest mistake of my life when I let you leave. He forced a smile back on his mouth and raised his head from sniffing first one hand and then the other. "I think I like the mint best." He sniffed again. "Although I think many men would like the pine. It is very masculine."

"Thank you." *You just took three steps back or closed the door. What happened? I thought for a moment there you . . .* Amethyst straightened her shoulders and lifted her chin. "Would you like to see our showroom? We've taken over part of the carriage house until we need a larger space."

"Dinner is ready, miss."

"All right, Jenny. Thank you." She smiled up at McHenry. "We'll do that later."

But later did not happen because he had an appointment in the afternoon, and that evening they all three attended the theater.

The following day he left to pick up his horses.

"What do you mean, you never told her you loved her?" Rand stared at him as if he'd lost his mind. "I thought you were going to ask her to marry you."

"I was." McHenry shook his head. "But I can't ask her to give all that up. I counted the cost for her. It was too high."

CHAPTER FORTY

December

Jacob looked up from planing a new piece of board to put in the doorframe so that the Robertsons would have a tighter door this winter. He waved at Rand riding up on Buck. The horse snorted and danced, obviously wanting a real run.

"You have a minute?" Rand asked.

"Of course. Can we talk while I keep working on this? I was hoping to get finished here so I could have some time on my house this afternoon."

"You want some help over there?"

"I'd never turn down help." Jacob sighted along the board. It appeared straight now.

Rand dismounted and ground-tied Buck. "I rode by your place. It's good to see the new door and that window fixed."

"I need to get up on the roof next. Lost a lot of shingles during the last storm."

"You have any?"

"The kids have been splitting some, and Jeremiah brought over the ones he had left.

Said he'd need more in the spring but not now."

"Ruby and I have been talking about your request."

Jacob stopped walking toward the house. Here goes. "And you have come to a decision?"

"Yes, we have agreed that you may court Opal if she is willing."

"You've not spoken to her about it." Jacob felt sure of that from the look on Rand's face.

"No. I thought perhaps we could do that together, but then I decided you should be the one. We've been a bit indecisive on this part, I'm afraid." He raised a hand. "I know you've got arguments for telling her, but to us she is still young Opal. Not getting-ready-for-marriage Opal."

"I understand. I have a feeling that if I have a daughter, I shall not be pushing for her to get married and leave home either." Jacob found it easier to smile now that he'd heard the good news.

"You know, there is one thing." Rand shook his head. "I have a hard time picturing Opal as a pastor's wife."

"You mean in that most pastors' wives don't train horses, work cattle, and excel at hunting?"

"Something like that."

"I promise you something. I will never put pressure on Opal to change. I love her just the way she is."

"Don't go making promises you cannot keep, son. No one knows what lies ahead." Rand mounted Buck again. "When do you think you'll be on your way to your place? I'll bring Beans and meet you there."

"Thanks. I'll get the wagon loaded. Give me two hours or so."

So, Lord, how and when do I tell her, or rather ask her? He fitted the board into the frame, marked where the lockset plate should go, took it out again, cut out the plate hole with a keyhole saw, and fitted the board again. After inserting the hardware, he nodded at the satisfactory click. Now that pesky door would not blow open nor let in drafts.

Now to get his own place — what a good sound that was, *my own place* — as weathertight as this house, and he'd be more than pleased. While he planned to continue living in the soddy, he also thought to spend some nights at his own house. Believing it really was his took some doing. The check from the solicitor had paid for the twenty-five acres, the house, and the drilling of the well. Finding the owner had taken some doing, and while he figured some people would say he'd been lucky, he knew his providence came from his heavenly Father. The previous owner had been grateful for the money.

"You want me to help load the wagon, Pa?" Joel called when he'd finished his other chores.

"Please. And add some of the firewood too."

With the three men working and Joel fetching, they had the roof on the log section repaired before dark.

"See you in the morning," Jacob said as they all headed home. Good thing he'd prepared his sermon earlier in the week. Having some sermons to touch up from his previous parish helped when time was tight, like now.

All the way back to the Robertsons', his mind divided between listening to Joel's chatter and trying to figure how to talk with Opal. Never would he have guessed there would come a time when he wished his son didn't like talking to him quite so much.

Later that night he fell asleep rehearsing ways to bring up the subject.

Opal held Per on her lap as the musicians prepared to open the service. Rand, Mr.

McHenry, Daisy, Cimarron, and Pearl on the piano had practiced already and were laughing at something someone said.

Go up there. She ignored the inner voice, wishing she could ignore the music. But something inside her felt different. Ever since the time of terrible sadness, music only made her feel more sad, like the cloud grew heavier and darker. But now that she thought about it, she'd heard music lately in the cries of the birds migrating to warmer quarters and in the wind whirling the last of the maple and cottonwood leaves to their rest on the ground. She'd even caught herself whistling one day.

"Opa?" Per's voice broke into her reverie.

"What?" she whispered into his ear. "You have to be quiet now."

"Why?" His latest word, and already she was wishing he'd not learned it.

"Because church is starting."

"Go to Pa." He pushed away, but she caught him before he could scramble down.

"No, he's busy. You be a good boy and sit here until he comes."

"Good boy."

"You want to switch with me?" Ruby asked.

"No. We're fine." Mary could be as

531

wiggly as her brother these days.

"Good morning, everyone. Let's stand for the first hymn, 'Holy, Holy, Holy.' " Reverend Chandler stood in front of the congregation, his smile far warmer than the weak sun outside.

Opal stood silently, listening to the words as the voices rose in harmony around her. " 'Early in the morning our songs shall rise to thee . . . merciful and mighty.' " She could hear Jacob's voice, rich and harmonizing, Rand's some deeper, a true baritone, Cimarron's a strong alto. Ruby stood on Opal's left, singing the melody. Others sang around her, their voices doing exactly what the hymn said, " '. . . our songs shall rise to thee.' "

The song ended. "Let us pray," intoned Jacob. "Father in heaven, bless our worship service today and please make all of our service an act of worship. In your Son's precious name, amen."

So why don't I sing anymore? The thought interrupted her concentration on the Bible reading. *Is it that I can't sing anymore?* That thought made her blink. *No, I just don't feel like singing. How do you know that you can still sing, then?* What if God had taken away the gift He had given her?

" 'Whatsoever ye do, do all to the glory of God.' "

Opal absently rubbed Per's back as she listened. *I haven't been doing that, have I?* She sighed and caught Ruby glancing at her. Per sighed and leaned against her chest, his weight growing heavier as he slid into sleep.

When they announced the final hymn, she stood carefully, trying to keep from waking him, but "Onward Christian Soldiers" would wake anyone up. He rubbed his eyes and looked up at her. "Opa, sing."

Opal hugged him close, swaying as she joined in the chorus, softly singing into his ear to make him smile. At least her voice still worked.

Ruby glanced her way, smiled, and nodded.

After the benediction conversations picked up around the room as the congregants filed toward the door. Some crowded around the drawing Mr. Hegland had made of the new church, including the layout of the building. Everyone shrugged into their coats and prepared for the ride to the Heglands' boardinghouse, where they'd eat dinner and visit awhile before heading home. Opal helped Per with his coat and turned to find Jacob beside her.

"Good morning."

She nodded, his smile making her feel warm clear to her toes.

"I need to talk with you about something. I was hoping we could go riding this afternoon, but it looks to me like it might snow."

"Can't we talk at Pearl's?" She held on to Per's hand in spite of his leaning to follow his ma and pa.

"Come, Opa."

"Of course. I'll see you then."

All the way there, Opal wondered what must be so important. He certainly looked serious enough.

As all the others filed inside the house, carrying baskets of food, laughing, and teasing one another, Opal hung back until Jacob stood beside her.

"Thank you for waiting."

"Is something wrong?"

"No, no. Something is very right." He sucked in a breath, his smile lighting his whole face. "This is a bit of a story, so be patient, all right?"

"You know me. I'm always patient."

At that he burst out laughing. "Leave it to you, Opal." Shaking his head, he started again. "Opal, I've been wanting to tell you that I care for you."

"Care? Of course. We're friends. Friends

always care for each other. Other than when you were ignoring me and I figured you —"

He held up a hand. "I know that part. And I'm sorry for that, but it came — well, it's a long story, and we'd freeze out here before it is all told but . . ." He sucked in another deep breath, then coughed as the cold hit his lungs. "Pardon me." When he could speak again, he continued, "What I need to say is —"

"You two going to stand out here all day?" Carl Hegland stuck his head out the door, then looked surprised when someone pulled him back in.

Something really strange is going on here, Opal thought. She took a step toward the door but stopped when Jacob put a hand on her arm.

"Please, let me finish."

"We could talk inside, you know, where you could breathe without choking."

"I said it was a long story, but . . ." He could tell she was about to bolt. "Rand gave me permission to ask your permission to allow me to court you."

"What?" Her forehead wrinkled, and she made a face, shaking her head all the while. "Did you say what I thought you said?"

Might as well jump in with both feet.

"Opal, I have been in love with you for months, and when I went to Rand —"

This time it was Opal who held her hand up. "Slow down."

"I can't. We're freezing."

"Let's walk, then. Around the porch if nothing else. I want to get to the bottom of this." She took his arm and pulled him along. "You say you love me?"

"Yes."

"Are you crazy?"

"Not that I know of."

"You're my friend. I was supposed to marry Atticus."

"Good thing he married someone else, or he'd have had a fight on his hands."

"Atticus is not a fighter."

"Neither am I. Not usually, anyway." They turned and walked back the other way.

"This courting thing. How would it be any different than now?"

"Opal, please, just say yes and let's go inside. I think they're waiting for me to say grace."

"Can't they say grace on their own?"

"I'm sure they can, but I think they are waiting."

"All right."

"All right what?" He stopped midstep.

"All right, let's go in."

He groaned, but as he held the door open, she glanced up at him from the corner of her eye.

"And yes."

She said yes. It was all he could do to not shout it for all to hear. *Opal Torvald said I could court her!*

Two days later at Pearl's for her lessons, Opal rubbed her chin with one finger. "Can I ask you a question?"

"Of course."

"This is rather personal."

"I don't mind." Pearl set Joseph in the high chair and tied a dish towel around his middle, then handed him a hunk of hard bread to chew on.

"How did you know that you loved Mr. Hegland?"

"Well, I wanted to be with him all the time, and when he walked into the room, I felt like someone turned up the lamps —"

"Did you have a funny feeling in your middle, like all warm and mushy?"

"I guess that's as good a description as any. I found myself thinking about him all the time, and when I'd see him again, why, my heart would about leap out of my chest. Why?"

Opal could feel her face flaming hot.

"I see. Is it Jacob Chandler?"

"I thought I loved Atticus, but this is as different as the moon and the sun. But . . ." Her pause grew long.

"But what?"

"I don't think I'm ready to be a wife."

"That's what courting is all about. It gives you time to grow into the idea."

"But how do you know when you're ready?" Opal shook her head again. "Can you think of me as the pastor's wife?"

Pearl rolled her lips together. "I'm thinking the women better start on a new quilt or two."

"Why?"

"Because you're going to need household things for your home someday, and the courting time is a good time to begin gathering what you will need."

"Mary Robertson had a hope chest. She was making things for it all the time. I don't really like to sew, and embroidery makes me bleed on whatever I'm making."

"But do you want to be with Jacob?"

Opal nodded.

"Then don't worry about the rest. Leave it all in God's hands, and now let's see the essay I asked you to write."

"Just like that?"

"Just like that."

"Rand said I can't get married until after I turn sixteen in May."

"That's good. Where's your paper?"

Opal handed it to her. "I won't get all moony-eyed like Edith did, will I?"

"I seriously doubt it, but if you do, I'll remind you, so you don't look too silly." Pearl began reading, and Opal returned to diagramming sentences. This courting thing gave her an awful lot to think about.

"So, Jacob, tell me what courting really means. I mean, like what do I do?" She almost said his name again just because it felt good on her tongue.

"Courting is when two people get to know each other —"

"But we already know each other. Why would two strangers be courting?"

Jacob sighed. Sometimes Opal asked questions that pushed him to the limits. "Let me finish."

"All right."

"They get to know each other better so they can decide if they truly want to marry each other."

"I see." She pondered that. "So I've not really said I am going to marry you, then?"

"No, not really. But I sure hope you do — want to marry me, that is."

"But if I already knew that, what would be the sense of courting?" She handed him the board he pointed at. They were working on his house, making shelves for the kitchen. They could hear Joel and Ada Mae arguing in the soddy section over who could spit the farthest. They were splitting shakes at the same time for the new addition to be put up as soon as spring came.

Jacob put a couple of nails in his mouth to have them handy.

"So then . . ."

He mentally shuddered. Here came another question.

"What is the difference between courting and being betrothed like the Bible says that Mary and Joseph were betrothed?"

He motioned to his mouth to say he couldn't answer. When he'd pounded the three nails into the wood, one of which bent right over and had to be straightened, he turned to her.

"Betrothal is a promise to marry, much like an engagement, but legally binding in Biblical times. They didn't court back then. If we were to announce that we planned to marry, then we would be betrothed."

"I see."

He picked up another board and took it to the sawhorses. "Hold that end, will you please?" He measured and marked the place to cut. Once he finished sawing, he glanced up to see her watching him. Warmth flooded from his head to his heels. "Don't do that."

"Do what?"

"Look at me like that."

"But I like to look at you."

"Could you please add more wood to the fire?" *Or open the door and let it cool off in here*. Sometimes the urge to kiss her rose so strongly that he had to pray it gone. So pray he did.

He found himself praying a lot when they were together. But he also laughed more than ever in his life. And rejoiced for the gift he felt God was giving him.

With Christmas drawing near, Opal finally knew what she would give Jacob for a present. She and Pearl practiced together until they were both delighted with the idea and the way it was turning out.

Each day Opal prayed that the good weather would hold, that no blizzard would roar down and cancel the Christmas services. The Sunday before Christmas the congregation gathered for the regular worship service. With a tree in the corner, decorated by the schoolchildren, the schoolroom even smelled like Christmas.

What if I can't do this? Opal swallowed and fought back the butterflies rampaging in her middle. Before the sermon she felt like leaping up and running back out the door. *Jacob, I do hope you like my present. Father in heaven, please let this go right.*

After the sermon Pearl smiled at Opal, and the two made their way to the piano.

"Ah . . ." Jacob started to say something, but when Pearl nodded, he sat back down.

Opal turned to face the people she knew and loved so well, especially the man in the front row. "This is my Christmas present to all of you." She stared right at him.

Pearl let her fingers wander over the keyboard, and when Opal had taken a deep breath and nodded, she smiled back and played the introduction they had composed. Opal sang for Jacob, her voice richer than it had ever been. It soared on the high notes, dropping beauty into the ears of those she loved, drawing forth tears as she sang of God's great gift of love — love so compelling, love divine, a baby in a manger, love for all time. When she finished, Jacob sat with tears in his eyes. He nodded.

She wanted to run to him and throw herself into his arms, but she smiled instead and returned to her seat.

"Opa, sing mo." Per reached for her, and she hugged him as she sat him on her lap.

Ruby reached over and clutched her hand, then wiped the tears from her eyes.

Jacob stood and turned to the congregation. "And with that gift to us all . . ." He paused and raised his arms. "The Lord bless you and keep you; the Lord make his face shine upon you and give you His peace. Amen."

As everyone stood and made ready to leave, he moved to her side. "I've never heard that song before."

"I know. Pearl and I made it up." She touched his hand. "I wanted to give you something special."

"You did. I was afraid you would never sing again."

"You know the verse you read, about the light?"

He nodded.

"Well, I think now the darkness is gone, and the sadness. And I can sing again." She leaned closer. "I think I'll sing for our wedding. What do you think?"

As if there was no one else around, he nodded and took her hand. "When?"

"Oh, I was thinking that May would be a good month for a wedding."

"I agree." His eyes held hers.

"And then I thought when the new church is finished, I would love to be married in it."

"Lord, help us build it quickly."

Opal watched as he turned and greeted the others who were waiting. He might be Reverend or Pastor Chandler, but he was her Jacob. And from the way she was feeling, being married might be just as exciting as training horses or rounding up cattle.

CHAPTER FORTY-ONE

"All right, time for confession." Mrs. Grant laid her hand over the pages of the record book.

Amethyst looked up. "What do you mean?"

"I mean that ever since Mr. McHenry left, you've been like a flower without water, wilting."

"I . . . I thought . . ." Amethyst brushed a tendril of hair back from her cheek. Even her hair no longer stayed up where it belonged, let alone her thoughts. They kept escaping, running west, screaming, *Why, why? What went wrong?* She started again. "Did you notice the way he signed those drawings he'd framed for me?"

"First thing. Love, JM."

"When I said I was sorry we had nothing stronger to put in his coffee, he said he no longer drank anything stronger."

Mrs. Grant raised her eyebrows, eyes wide open. "That is good news. No longer shades of your father."

"True, but when we were out in the

mixing room and he tried both the pine and mint lotions, one on each hand, all of a sudden it was like a heavy shade blotting out the sun. Oh, he was charming and pleasant from then on, but I no longer saw what I thought might be love shining in his eyes. We were never alone for another moment before he left." She rose and went to stand at the window.

"I don't understand."

"Neither do I."

"Do you love the man?"

"I do. It all started because he was nice to me. I know Mr. Hegland and Mr. Harrison were nice to me also, but they are already married, and that makes it different. At first I thought I wasn't good enough for him, but that never stopped the love from growing. I . . . I've never felt this way about a man before. But I guess it is over. I've not had a letter from him since he returned home."

"It's only been about ten days."

"I know. But last time I had a letter right away." Amethyst took in a deep breath and let it all out. "I sent him a thank-you letter for the pictures. We'll see if he answers."

"Let's back up to something you said. You didn't feel you were good enough for him?"

Amethyst nodded. "You know what I

came from, what a sorry sight I was."

"But that has nothing to do with how good you are, how valuable you are. According to God's Word, we are all of immeasurable value."

"You know what I mean — different class of folks, education, experience."

"But now?"

"But now, thanks to you, I am no longer a poor ragamuffin who's afraid to say two words in a row. And I thank God for you every day."

"That is wise, because He is the one who orchestrated all of this. You mentioned going back to Medora to visit for Christmas so you could see Joel in the pageant."

"Yes. I would like to do that."

"I think that would be a very good idea. And if McHenry has any intelligence at all, he will make you very welcome. Write and let him know you are coming."

"No. I want it to be a surprise. If he really doesn't care, then I will know." *And go on with my life.*

"Just remember, he's not the only fish in the sea."

Amethyst smiled and then grinned. The two chuckled together.

"Something else to contemplate. If you are thinking you cannot be married to the man because you will let me down, think again. We could move the whole business to Medora if we wanted. The train goes right through there, and I know how to travel on it. After all, what's a couple of days either way? If Marquis de Mores could build a meat-shipping enterprise there, we could certainly do the same with lotions and soaps."

Three weeks later Amethyst stepped off the train and thanked the conductor for his care for her.

"You are welcome, Miss O'Shaunasy. I hope I am working the car on your return."

She nodded, her hair securely fastened under a bird's-nest hat with a curved feather flipping in the breeze. At least it wasn't as cold as the last time she had arrived in Medora. It was hard to believe an entire year had passed. And such changes had happened.

She glanced down at her rich wool coat, trimmed with a fur collar. The seamstress had chosen the material for her traveling outfit to match her name. Her fitted vest was fashioned of rich purple and amethyst plaid with a matching dark purple skirt and fitted jacket. A fur muff matched the collar of her coat, and the rest of her things filled the two trunks that were being unloaded onto the platform.

"Aunt Colleen!" Joel called from the back of his horse. He flipped the reins over the hitching rail, slid to the ground, and came running to throw his arms around her. "Sorry I'm late."

She hugged him back. "My, I think you've grown a full foot since I left."

"Four inches. Me and Ada Mae are racing. Isn't Big Red a fine horse?"

"He is handsome. A horse of your own — now, that is a wonder." She nodded to the luggage handler. "Yes, someone will come to pick them up. Thank you."

Joel looked nearly straight into her eyes. "You look different."

"I do?"

"You're all dressed up fancy."

"I surely am warmer than when I came last year about this time."

"Our pageant is tomorrow night."

"I know. That is why I came today. Is someone coming to pick me up?"

"Mr. Hegland, but I rode ahead. The train is early. He said that never happens. But when I heard the whistle, I told Big Red he could run. So we did." He stopped talking long enough to look into her eyes, searching for a true answer. "Do you really like living in Chicago?"

"There are many good things about Chicago, and I really enjoy the work that I am doing. Mrs. Grant is so good to me. I owe her a great deal."

"Hmm."

"I really appreciate your letters. Thank you for writing to me."

"I have to tell you that I want you to come back."

"Miss O'Shaunasy." Carl Hegland waved as he stopped his team. "Sorry I'm late."

"No, I think we were early."

"All aboard!" the conductor called as the train blasted a whistle and steam poured from around the wheels. Inch by inch the mighty wheels turned, and the train picked up speed.

"I'll get the dolly so I can load your trunks. Both of those are yours?"

"Yes." *One is full of presents. I couldn't bring presents before, but now I could.* Such fun she had had buying gifts for her friends here in Medora. She had quickly found the perfect gift for everyone but Jeremiah McHenry. That had not been easy. But when she found the book of nature drawings, she'd known it was just right for him.

Last time a carpetbag, this time two

trunks and her valise. She brought all the women samples of her soap and lotions.

"Ah, Mr. Hegland, it is good to be back here. There's not as much snow this time."

"Nor is it as cold. We won't have you nearly dying on our doorstep." Carl clucked his team into a fast trot, and the jingle of harness bells sparkled across the prairie. The big white house wore a snow hat and drifts around its banked sides, and the front door had a big red bow on a cedar swag.

"Oh, it is so beautiful." Amethyst clasped her hands inside her fur muff. There would be no sleeping in the snow this time.

"I'll bring your trunks in the back door. You go in the front. Pearl's orders."

"If you insist." She allowed him to help her from the sleigh and climbed the steps to the front door.

"Bye," Joel called with a wave. "See you at the pageant."

She waved back. "Don't tell anyone."

"I won't." His answer blew over his shoulder as he, on Big Red, loped toward home.

"You are here!" Pearl pulled open the door and threw her arms around Amethyst. "Carly, see who is here." Wearing a red pinafore, Carly peeked out around her mother. She grinned and ducked her head.

"My, just look at you. A fashion plate direct from *Godey's Lady's Book*." Pearl hugged her again.

"Has anyone told Mr. McHenry?"

"No one else knows. That way your secret could be kept." Arm in arm the two women closed the door behind them, and Pearl helped Amethyst out of her coat. "Isn't this lovely?" Pearl stroked the fur collar. "You have done so well. The move has been a good one." She searched Amethyst's face for an answer.

"Our company is doing well. I have learned so much from Mrs. Grant that I cannot begin to tell you, but I have a favor to ask."

"Ask away."

"Could I please help cook in your kitchen? There are so many servants at Mrs. Grant's that I feel as if I am taking their job if I go into the kitchen."

Pearl covered her giggle with one hand. "I remember at my father's house that was the way it was, but back then I had no interest in cooking. My mother and father are still shocked that their daughter is running a boardinghouse."

"Has business picked up any?"

"Not much, but your room is waiting for you. Your first room." She put her arm

552

through Amethyst's, and together they walked up the stairs.

The schoolhouse was filling fast when they drove up to the door, and Amethyst and Pearl took the two children and hurried in out of the cold.

"Do you think he is here yet?" Amethyst whispered.

"He was coming with Rand, and their sleigh is out there. Rand is playing the guitar, and Mr. McHenry will be on the mouth organ. They do this every Sunday for worship. You know we are getting a church building in the spring?"

"Thanks to everyone's letters and Mr. McHenry's visits, I know most of what has gone on around here." Amethyst shrugged out of her coat and hung it on a hook along with all the others.

Chatter slowly died as they stepped into the schoolroom. The three men in the front, who were tuning their instruments, finished and faced the crowd.

She waited, her heart hammering in her throat. Would he be glad to see her? Or had he really shut the door?

"Miss O'Shaunasy." His voice, so used to command, could be heard even in a whisper.

"Mr. McHenry." She tipped her head slightly. Her hat stayed in place, her hair remained firmly secured under it.

"It seems we have an early Christmas present here." Jacob Chandler caught the wink Rand sent him, and the two played a couple lines of "Joy to the World."

Amethyst could feel the heat rise in her neck as Mr. McHenry stared openmouthed at her. What was he thinking? What would he say?

"Welcome, everyone, to the first annual Christmas pageant here at the Medora School. We would have had one last year, but we were blizzarded out. Let us begin with a word of prayer." Jacob waited for the shuffling to cease. "Father God, we come together tonight to tell your story, that of the first Christmas, when your son was born. Thank you for bringing us all together tonight, safely and with great joy. Amen."

Amethyst fought to keep her mind on the pageant, but her eyes kept going to the man sitting in the front row off to the side. She could see his ear, the way the hair waved around the top of it, the black band that held his eye patch in place. She heard the recitations, the songs with the harmonica sometimes soaring on higher notes, and she watched the children act out the old, old story that never grew too old to hear again and to rejoice in it. Joel played Joseph with nary a smile, and Ada Mae sat at the manger with a doll on her lap, the lone sheep right behind her nuzzling her arm. While she pushed it away, it insisted until she rubbed its ears. Then it lay down in the hay, content. When the shepherds came, they took the sheep back out with them.

The angels sang hallelujahs, everyone sang well-loved Christmas carols, and the lights were extinguished but for one candle carried by a little girl walking up the aisle. One candle, that's all it took to banish the darkness. The harmonica led the child forward, and when she turned, the light burnishing her face and hair, Amethyst could barely see for wiping the tears away.

She heard sniffs from around her, and then Emily played her song on the piano, "The Light of the World is Jesus." The musical notes fell on a silent room as if all were indeed waiting for the light to come. The little girl looked up from her gaze on the candle, beamed her smile around the room, and said, "Merry Christmas to you all."

The applause rocked the walls and the lanterns were relit.

Amethyst watched as Mr. McHenry tried to come to her, finally making it to the back of the room where she sat beside Pearl with Carly on her lap.

"You didn't tell me you were coming."

"I wanted to surprise you."

"You did that."

Others gathered around, calling their greetings to Amethyst, and she watched as someone said something to him. He finally turned back to her. "I'll come to the Heglands' after this?"

She smiled and nodded, her back straight, as Mrs. Grant had taught her. *"Sit straight, stand straight, and smile."*

Pearl leaned closer. "I think you caught his attention."

"He's coming to the house."

"I heard him."

After the children received their presents of an orange and a peppermint stick, Carl carried the sleeping Joseph out to the sleigh and, when they'd all scrambled in, covered them with a heavy robe.

"Keep tucked in. We don't want frozen noses, now, do we?"

"Pa say froze nose." Carly giggled and rubbed her button nose.

"She sure talks more now." While keeping up with the conversation, Amethyst could feel Mr. McHenry's presence as he mounted his horse and rode beside them.

She swallowed. What would he say? Did the look of joy on his face when he saw her mean what she hoped it meant?

Her thoughts so consumed her that she was hardly aware they'd arrived home.

"I'll put the children to bed," Pearl said. "Why don't the two of you visit here in the parlor?"

"Thank you."

He hadn't taken his eyes off hers ever since they came in the door. Amethyst's knees shook. Her hands threatened to. *Back straight. Smile*. But somewhere in there she had to breathe too.

A beautiful tree sat in front of the window again, the white candles ready to be lit, and wrapped presents lay under its branches. She had slipped hers there before they left for the schoolhouse.

She sat on the sofa, being careful to tuck her skirt in around her and not crush the small bustle in the back.

When he sat in the chair, she smiled at him. This was much better than both on the sofa. Now she could watch his dear face for all the changes in expression. If the way he'd greeted her was any indication of how he felt . . . *Please, Lord, make this all work out the way you want it to.*

"Mr. McHenry . . ."

"Miss O'Shaunasy . . ." They spoke at the same time, then shared a smile.

"You want to go first?" He asked the same question she was about to.

She hesitated. Did she want to go first, just to get this waiting over with? After all, she'd been waiting since he left Chicago in November. A month can be a long time when you were waiting for something as important as this.

"Shall we flip a coin?"

She shook her head. *I don't want the rest of my life based on the flip of a coin, but now that the moment is here, how do I say what I want?* She took in a deep breath and let it all out. *Calm. That's right. Be calm above all else.*

"Mr. McHenry, do you love me?" That wasn't what she'd planned to say at all. If only she could grab the words back. She watched his face. He swallowed, bit his lip, lips that were spreading wider in a smile. *Say something.*

"I mean . . ." She could go no further. Mortification was a painful thing, starting in the chest, clamping off breathing and suffusing the face. *Flee! Flee!* a voice screamed inside her head.

His smile broke into a chuckle.

She drew herself up, not only straight but

rigid, and took in a deep breath. But when he put his hand over hers, she nearly collapsed.

"Please, forgive me, but that is the exact same question I wanted to ask you."

"Really?" Now she could at least swallow. This time her breath moved in and out without bothersome little hitches. She wet her lips and felt the look he gave her make them warm. Now, that was an interesting phenomenon. "All right, since I asked the question first, you have to answer first." She thought the twinkle in his eye might match that which she was certain lurked in her own.

"Then I shall answer first. Miss O'Shaunasy, I love you with all I know how to love."

"Oh." Tears stung at the back of her eyes and threatened to run out her nose.

"Now it is your turn."

She nodded. It was indeed her turn. "Mr. McHenry, I do love you, and I would call it the greatest honor if I could learn to love you more each day for the rest of my life." Was that a sheen of tears in his eye? She knew the sheen in hers was trickling down her face.

"Are you asking me to marry you?"

"Not exactly, but if you are agreeable, I

would consider that you just asked me."

"And your answer?"

"Yes."

"That's it? Yes?"

"What more do you want?"

"I want to love you as broadly as the Dakotah sky and as deeply as God shows me how."

"Oh." She reached out to smooth her fingertips over his cheek. He turned his head, clasped her hand in his, and pressed a kiss into her palm. She closed her eyes, the better to feel his lips against her skin.

"May I kiss you?"

"You just did." Several other tears followed their cousin down her face. He wiped them away with the tenderness of a mother comforting her child. She looked into his eye and saw nothing but love there, deep and rich. "But I would like it if you did so again."

"My pleasure, my dear Amethyst." He leaned forward and placed his lips over hers, gently, with all the love he knew.

When he pulled back, she sighed. "May I call you Jeremiah now?"

"I think that would be proper."

Hearing approaching footsteps, they pulled back and sat up straight again.

"Sorry to interrupt, but this little one insisted she wanted to say good night." Pearl appeared in the doorway, Carly at her side, dressed in an ankle-length red flannel gown with white eyelet trim, the gown Amethyst had laid on her bed when she'd arrived. She held out her arms, and Carly ran into them, wrapping her arms around Amethyst's neck and squeezing.

"Thank you," she whispered in Amethyst's ear.

"You're welcome."

"Glad you comed home."

"Me too." Amethyst kissed Carly's cheek and hugged her again. " 'Night."

"Sorry to interrupt." Pearl rolled her lips together and gave a little wave as they left.

"I think she knows." Jeremiah nodded toward the retreating pair.

"That will save us telling one person." Amethyst looked down at their clasped hands. "I have to say something else."

"Have to?"

"Yes." She looked into his face. "I will be returning to Chicago to discuss how Mrs. Grant and I will handle our business. I have a lot to do if we are to move it to Medora."

"Move the lotion business to Medora?" Dawn breaking after a stormy night could not have looked more joyous. "You mean I won't have to move to Chicago?"

"Do you want to?"

"No, not at all, but I would if I had to."

Amethyst sighed. "You couldn't have said anything more perfect."

"Well, that's a miracle in its own right." He nodded. "A spring wedding?"

"How soon do you think the church will be finished?"

"Not soon enough." He glanced up to see Carl standing in the arched doorway with a tray in his hands. "How soon can we have the church built?"

"Well, I was thinking about a year, but I guess we can hurry it up some."

Amethyst gazed at her future husband, fairly certain that he would move half the rocks in the badlands if that's what it took to get the building up sooner. After all, he knew how to organize and win army campaigns. What would building a little church be compared to that?

EPILOGUE

June 1888

"Are you going to be all right for this?" Rand asked.

"Of course." Jacob dug his finger into the neckline of his shirt to loosen the fit. "I said I would conduct the wedding for Jeremiah and Miss O'Shaunasy, and I shall."

"Right before your own?"

"No problem." His voice cracked only slightly. One hour and they would begin. The pastor from Dickinson had arrived on the morning train. The women had about stripped the town of flowers to decorate the church, and even though they didn't have all the windows in the walls, they didn't really need them on this glorious end-of-June morning. The breeze spread the fragrance of the lilacs as a welcome to those arriving.

Together the men had set the altar in place the night before, or rather, early in the morning. Very early. Charlie had his crew lining up the benches from the schoolhouse so the guests would have places to sit. After the weddings, they'd take the benches back to the school, where the afternoon's festivities would take place. Beans had started the steer on the spit over hot coals before sunrise.

"How do I look?" Opal glanced over her shoulder to see Ruby wiping away tears. "You can't cry, or I shall, and I don't want to cry on my wedding day." *I've cried enough the past two years to last a lifetime.*

"Tears of happiness are different."

"You didn't answer me." Opal turned back to the mirror and smoothed her palm down the front of the pearlescent silk gown Mrs. Brandon had sent from New York. With a sweetheart neckline, puffed sleeves, and full skirt gathered to the waistline that dipped in front, the gown fit perfectly. They'd sent gloves, fan, and shoes to match, so all she had to do was get dressed.

"You look lovely. I'm just having a hard time believing my little sister is getting married."

"Me too. I can remember thinking I'd never get married." Her smile turned dreamy. "But I found someone as good as Rand, don't you think?"

Ruby hugged her sister. "That you did. Or did he find you?"

Opal shrugged. "Doesn't matter now, does it?"

"Are you ready?" Pearl peeked in the doorway. Both brides were dressing at her house because there was no separate room finished at the church where they could dress. "Oh, Opal honey, you are beautiful." She sniffed and ducked back out.

"You look lovely, my dear Amethyst." Mrs. Grant smoothed the shoulder of the straight-fronted gown in a purple hue. Deep pleats fell from the waistline, giving the skirt plenty of fullness for the dancing to come later. Light shimmered in Amethyst's russet hair, done up in an intricate knot that gave her the look of a queen.

Amethyst stared at the image in the oval mirror. "It's hard to believe that is the same woman who came west to find her nephew. Perhaps she did indeed die in the snow and resurrected as someone else."

"No, I'd say you were born anew in that snow, and you are stepping into all the happiness you so richly deserve."

"You about ready in here?" Pearl asked from the doorway.

"Any time."

Carl helped the two brides and the other

women into the carriage borrowed from the de Mores' house. "I have the best job of all today. I get to bring the two beautiful brides to the church."

"I'm glad you're going first," Opal whispered. "Then I can see how it is done."

"I want to get it over with before I faint from all the excitement." Amethyst used her fan to cool her face. "I'm so thankful it's not blazing hot."

Opal lifted her chin to let the cooling breeze do its job. She clenched her hands in her lap. She was indeed getting married today.

The ride to the church went quickly and, once those first to be married were in place, the wedding service began. Opal stood in the back while Jacob performed the ceremony for Jeremiah and Amethyst. Jeremiah seemed to be having a hard time getting the words out, while Amethyst said her vows with a clear voice.

Please, Lord, let me do this right when it is my turn.

"I now pronounce you husband and wife. You may kiss the bride," Jacob intoned the age-old words.

Amethyst smiled into her husband's face as he leaned toward her. "I love you," she whispered.

"Good thing," Jeremiah whispered back, cupping her cheeks in his hands and kissing her waiting lips.

Pearl set the piano to dancing as the two made their way back down the aisle, smiling and nodding to all those greeting them.

"Your turn." Amethyst gave Opal a hug.

The minister from Dickinson took his place in front of the church, and Jacob moved to the side, turning to watch as Opal on Rand's arm made her way down the aisle.

When they met in front of the minister, Jacob turned and took both her hands in his.

Amethyst locked her hand through her new husband's arm and, looking into each other's eyes, they whispered their vows again as Jacob and Opal said theirs. When they finished, Jeremiah kissed the ring he had placed on her left hand.

"For as long as God gives us together."

She nodded. "I love you, Mr. McHenry."

Pearl continued playing the piano as folks gathered around to congratulate the two new couples.

"I have a question," Joel said as he shook first his father's hand and then Opal's.

"All right. What is it?" Jacob drew Opal closer to his side.

Joel shook his head and made a face as he

looked to Opal. "What do I call you now? I mean . . ."

Opal shrugged. "I guess you can call me whatever you want. Opal sounds good to me. At least I recognize that name."

"Good." Joel started off, then turned back. "I'm glad you two got hitched."

"Hitched?" Jacob and Opal said at the same time and then, shaking their heads, smiled at Mr. and Mrs. McHenry.

"Married surely sounds better than hitched." Amethyst smiled up at her husband. Ah, what a delightful word, *husband*.

"We might want to mosey on over to the schoolhouse. That steer is getting close being to done," Rand suggested after he congratulated the McHenrys and hugged Opal with one arm while shaking Jacob's hand with the other.

"What a way to bless this new church." Jacob smiled as he looked up at the altar that needed more coats of finish and the walls that needed windows set in. He turned to McHenry. "You think this unfinished church is something like a marriage? The wedding is the framework, but all the living and loving to come fills in what's missing?"

"I think we have years to figure all that out." McHenry turned to his wife. "But I know one thing, I don't want to miss out on any of it. And I thank God for the jewel He brought to my life." He smiled into his wife's eyes. "A real Dakotah treasure."

About the Author

Lauraine Snelling is an award-winning author of over fifty books, fiction and non-fiction, for adults and young adults. Besides writing books and articles, she teaches at writers' conferences across the country. She and her husband, Wayne, have two grown sons, a basset named Chewy, and a cockatiel watch bird named Bidley. They make their home in California.

by the same author:

As Jack Higgins
Exocet
Touch the Devil
Luciano's Luck
Solo
Day of Judgment
Storm Warning
The Eagle Has Landed
The Run to Morning

As Harry Patterson
Dillinger
To Catch a King
The Valhalla Exchange

CONFESSIONAL

JACK HIGGINS

STEIN AND DAY / *Publishers* / New York

First published in 1985
Copyright © 1985 by Jack Higgins
All rights reserved, Stein and Day, Incorporated
Designed by Louis A. Ditizio
Printed in the United States of America
STEIN AND DAY/*Publishers*
Scarborough House
Briarcliff Manor, N.Y. 10510

Library of Congress Cataloging in Publication Data

Higgins, Jack, 1929–
  Confessional.

  I. Title.
PR6058.I343C6   1985   823'.914   84-40777
ISBN 0-8128-3025-3

For my children
Sarah, Ruth, Sean, and Hannah

PROLOGUE

1959

---

*W*HEN the Land Rover turned the corner at the end of the street, Kelly was passing the Church of the Holy Name. He moved into the porch quickly, opened the heavy door, and stepped inside, keeping it partially open so that he could see what was happening.

The Land Rover had been stripped down to the bare essentials so that the driver and the two policemen who crouched in the rear were completely exposed. They wore the distinctive dark green uniforms of the Royal Ulster Constabulary, Sterling submachine guns held ready for instant action. They disappeared down the narrow street toward the center of Drumore, and Kelly stayed in the church for a moment in the safety of the half-darkness, conscious of the familiar odor.

"Incense, candles, and the holy water," he said softly, and his finger reacted, dipping into the granite bowl beside the door.

"Is there anything I can do for you, my son?"

The voice was little more than a whisper, and, as Kelly turned, a priest moved out of the darkness, an old man in shabby cassock, his hair very white, gleaming in the candlelight. He carried an umbrella in one hand.

"Just sheltering from the rain is all, Father," Kelly told him.

He stood there, shoulders hunched easily, hands thrust deep into the pockets of the old, tan raincoat. He was small, five foot-five at the most, not much more than a boy, yet the white devil's face on him beneath the brim of the old felt hat and the dark, brooding eyes that seemed to stare through and beyond, hinted at something more.

All this the old priest saw and understood. He smiled gently. "You don't live in Drumore, I think?"

"No, Father, just passing through. I arranged to meet a friend of mine here at a pub called Murphy's."

His voice lacked the distinctive hard accent of the Ulsterman. The priest said, "You're from the Republic?"

"Dublin, Father. Would you know this Murphy's place? It's important. My friend's promised me a lift into Belfast. I've the chance of work there."

The priest nodded. "I'll show you. It's on my way."

Kelly opened the door, the old man went outside. It was raining heavily now, and he put up his umbrella. Kelly fell in beside him, and they walked along the pavement. There was the sound of a brass band playing an old hymn, "Abide with Me," and voices lifted, melancholy in the rain. The old priest and Kelly paused, looking down onto the town square. There was a granite war memorial, wreaths placed at its foot. A small crowd ranged around it, the band on one side. A Church of Ireland minister was conducting the service. Four old men held flags proudly in the rain, although the Union Jack was the only one with which Kelly was familiar.

"What is this?" he demanded.

"Armistice Day, to commemorate the dead of two world wars. That's the local branch of the British Legion down there. Our Protestant friends like to hang on tight to what they call their heritage."

"Is that so?" Kelly said.

12

They carried on down the street. On the corner, a small girl stood, no more than seven or eight. She wore an old beret a couple of sizes too large, like her coat. There were holes in her socks, and her shoes were in poor condition. Her face was pale, skin stretched tightly over prominent cheekbones, yet the brown eyes were alert, intelligent, and she managed a smile in spite of the fact that her hands, holding the cardboard tray in front of her, were blue with cold.

"Hello, Father," she said. "Will you buy a poppy?"

"My poor child, you should be indoors on a day like this." He found a coin in his pocket and slipped it into her collecting tin, helping himself to a scarlet poppy. "To the memory of our glorious dead," he told Kelly.

"Is that a fact?" Kelly turned to find the little girl timidly holding a poppy out to him. "Buy a poppy, sir."

"And why not?"

She pinned the poppy to his raincoat. Kelly gazed down into the strained little face for a moment, eyes dark, then swore softly under his breath. He took a leather wallet from his inside pocket, opened it, extracted two pound notes. She gazed at them, astonished, and he rolled them up and poked them into her collecting tin. Then he gently took the tray of poppies from her hands.

"Go home," he said softly. "Stay warm. You'll find the world cold enough soon enough, little one."

There was puzzlement in her eyes. She didn't understand and, turning, ran away.

The old priest said, "I was on the Somme myself, but this lot over here," he nodded to the crowd at the Cenotaph, "would rather forget about that." He shook his head as they carried on along the pavement. "So many dead. I never had the time to ask whether a man was Catholic or Protestant."

He paused and glanced across the road. A faded sign said *Murphy's Select Bar.* "Here we are, then. What are you going to do with those?"

Kelly glanced down at the tray of poppies. "God knows."

13

"I usually find that He does." The old man took a silver case from his pocket and selected a cigarette without offering one to Kelly. He puffed out smoke, coughing, "When I was a young priest I visited an old Catholic church in Norfolk at Study Constable. There was a remarkable medieval fresco there by some unknown genius or other. Death in a black hood and cloak, come to claim his harvest. I saw him again today in my own church. The only difference was that he was wearing a felt hat and an old raincoat." He shivered suddenly.

"Go home, Father," Kelly said gently. "Too cold for you out here."

"Yes," the old man said. "Far too cold."

He hurried away as the band struck up another hymn, and Kelly turned, went up the steps of the pub, and pushed open the door. He found himself in a long, narrow room, a coal fire burning at one end. There were several cast-iron tables and chairs, a bench along the wall. The bar itself was dark mahogany and marble-topped, a brass rail at foot level. There was the usual array of bottles ranged against a large mirror, gold leaf flaking to reveal cheap plaster. There were no customers, only the barman leaning against the beer pumps, a heavily built man, almost bald, his face seamed with fat, his collarless shirt soiled at the neck.

He glanced up at Kelly, taking in the tray of poppies. "I've got one."

"Haven't we all?" Kelly put the tray on the table and leaned on the bar. "Where is everyone?"

"In the square at the ceremony. This is a Prod town, son."

"How do you know I'm not one?"

"And me a publican for twenty-five years? Come off it. What's your fancy?"

"Bushmills."

The fat man nodded approvingly and reached for a bottle. "A man of taste."

"Are you Murphy?"

"So they tell me." He lit a cigarette. "You're not from these parts."

"No, I was supposed to meet a friend here. Perhaps you know him?"

"What's his name?"

"Cuchulain."

The smile wiped clean from Murphy's face, "Cuchulain," he whispered.

"Last of the dark heroes."

Murphy said, "Christ, but you like your melodrama, you boys. Like a bad play on television on a Saturday night. You were told not to carry a weapon."

"So?" Kelly said.

"There's been a lot of police activity. Body searches. They'd lift you for sure."

"I'm not carrying."

"Good." Murphy took a large brown carrier bag from under the bar. "Straight across the square is the police barracks. The local provision firm's truck is allowed through the gates at exactly twelve noon each day. Sling that in the back of it. Enough there to take out half the barracks." He reached inside the bag. There was an audible click. "There, you've got five minutes."

Kelly picked up the bag and started for the door. As he reached it, Murphy called, "Hey, Cuchulain, dark hero?" Kelly turned, and the fat man raised a glass, toasting him. "You know what they say. May you die in Ireland."

There was something in the eyes, a mockery that sharpened Kelly like a razor's edge as he went outside and started across the square. The band was on another hymn and the crowd sang, showing no disposition to move in spite of the rain. He glanced over his shoulder and saw that Murphy was standing at the top of the steps outside the pub. Strange, that, and then the publican waved several times, as if signaling someone, and with a sudden roar the stripped Land Rover came out of a side street into the square and skidded broadside on.

Kelly started to run, slipped on the damp cobbles, and went down on one knee. The butt of a Sterling drove painfully into his kidneys. As he cried out, the driver, who he now saw was a sergeant, put a foot hard on Kelly's outstretched hand, and picked up the carrier bag. The men turned it upside down and a cheap wooden kitchen clock fell out. He kicked it like a football across the square into the crowd, which scattered.

"No need for that!" the sergeant shouted. "It's a dud!" He leaned down, grabbing Kelly by the long hair at the back of the neck. "You never learn, do you, your bloody lot? You can't trust anybody, my son. They should have taught you that."

Kelly gazed beyond him at Murphy, standing on the steps outside the bar. So—an informer. Still Ireland's curse, not that he was angry. Only cold now—ice cold and the breath slow, in and out of his lungs.

The sergeant had him by the scruff of the neck, up on his knees, crouched like an animal. He leaned, running his hands under the armpits and over the body, searching for a weapon, then rammed Kelly, still on his knees, against the Land Rover.

"All right, hands behind you. You should have stayed back home in the bogs."

Kelly started to get up, his two hands on the butt of the Browning handgun he had taped so carefully to the inside of his leg, right above the left ankle. He tore it free, turned, and shot the sergeant through the heart. The force of the shot lifted the sergeant off his feet, and he slammed into the constable standing nearest to him. The man spun around, trying to keep his balance, and Kelly shot him in the back, the Browning already arcing toward the third policeman, turning in alarm on the other side of the Land Rover, raising his submachine gun too late as Kelly's third bullet caught him in the throat, driving him back against the wall.

16

The crowd was scattering, women screaming, some of the band dropping their instruments. Kelly stood perfectly still, very calm amidst the carnage, and looked across the square at Murphy, who remained, as if frozen, at the top of the steps outside the bar.

The Browning swept up as Kelly took aim, and a voice shouted over a megaphone in Russian, booming in the rain, "No more, Kelly! Enough!"

Kelly turned, lowering his gun. The man with the megaphone advancing down the street wore the uniform of a colonel in the KGB, a military greatcoat slung from his shoulders against the rain. The man at his side was in his early thirties, tall and thin, with stooped shoulders. He wore a leather trenchcoat and had fair hair and steel-rimmed spectacles. Behind them, several squads of Russian soldiers, rifles at the ready, emerged from the side streets and doubled down toward the square. They were in combat fatigues and wore the flashes of the Iron Hammer Brigade of the elite special forces command.

"That's a good boy! Just put the gun down!" the colonel called. Kelly turned, his arm swung up, and he fired once, an amazing shot considering the distance, and most of Murphy's left ear disintegrated. The fat man screamed, his hand going to the side of his head, blood pumping through his fingers.

"No, Mikhail! Enough!" The man in the leather overcoat cried. Kelly turned toward him and smiled. He said in Russian, "Sure, Professor, anything you say," and placed the Browning carefully down on the hood of the Land Rover.

"I thought you said he was trained to do as he was told," the colonel demanded.

An army lieutenant moved forward and saluted. "One of them is still alive, two dead, Colonel Maslovsky. What are your orders?"

Maslovsky ignored him and said to Kelly, "You weren't supposed to carry a gun."

"I know," Kelly said. "On the other hand, according to the

rules of the game, Murphy was not supposed to be an informer. I was told he was IRA."

"So, you always believe what you're told?"

"The Party tells me I should, Comrade Colonel. Maybe you've got a new rule book for me?"

Maslovsky was angry and it showed, for he was not used to such attitudes—not from anyone. He opened his mouth to retort angrily and there was a sudden scream. The little girl who had sold Kelly the poppies pushed her way through the crowd and dropped onto her knees beside the body of the police sergeant.

"Papa," she wailed in Russian. "Papa." She looked up at Kelly, her face pale. "You've killed him! You've murdered my father!"

She was on him like a young tiger, nails reaching for his face, crying hysterically. He held her wrists tight, and suddenly all strength went out of her and she slumped against him. His arms went around her, he held her, stroking her hair, whispering in her ear.

The old priest moved out of the crowd. "I'll take her," he said, his hands gentle on her shoulders.

They moved away, the crowd opening to let them through. Maslovsky called to the lieutenant, "Right, let's have the square cleared." He turned to the man in the leather coat. "I'm tired of this eternal Ukrainian rain. Let's get back inside, and bring your protégé with you. We need to talk."

THE KGB IS the largest and most complex intelligence service in the world, totally controlling the lives of millions in the Soviet Union itself, its tentacles reaching out to every country. The heart of it, its most secret area of all, concerns the work of Department-13, that section responsible for murder, assassination, and sabotage in foreign countries.

Colonel Ivan Maslovsky had commanded D-13 for five years. He was a thickset, rather brutal-looking man whose appearance was at odds with his background. Born in 1919 in Leningrad, the

18

son of a doctor, he had gone to law school in that city, completing his studies only a few months before the German invasion of Russia. He had spent the early part of the war fighting with partisan groups behind the lines. His education and flair for languages had earned him a transfer to the wartime counterintelligence unit known as SMERSH. Such was his success that he had remained in intelligence work after the war and had never returned to the practice of law.

He had been mainly responsible for the setting up of highly original training schools for spies at such places as Gaczyna, where agents were trained to work in English-speaking countries in a replica of an English or American town, living exactly as they would in the West. The extraordinarily successful penetration by the KGB of the French intelligence service at every level had been, in the main, the product of the school he had set up at Grosnia, where the emphasis was on everything French—environment, culture, cooking, and dress—being faithfully replicated.

His superiors had every faith in him and had given him carte blanche to extend the system, which explained the existence of a small Ulster market town called Drumore in the depths of the Ukraine.

THE ROOM MASLOVSKY used as an office when visiting from Moscow was conventional enough. It had a desk and filing cabinets and a large map of Drumore on the wall. A log fire burned brightly on an open hearth, and he stood in front of it enjoying the heat, nursing a mug of strong black coffee laced with vodka. The door opened behind him as the man in the leather coat entered and approached the fire, shivering.

"God, but it's cold out there."

He helped himself to coffee and vodka from the tray on the desk and moved to the fire. Paul Cherny was thirty-four years old, a handsome good-humored man who already had an international reputation in the field of experimental psychology. A considerable achievement for someone born the son of a blacksmith in a village in the Ukraine. As a boy of sixteen, he had fought with a partisan group in the war. His group leader had been a lecturer in English at the University of Moscow and recognized talent when he saw it.

Cherny was enrolled at the university in 1945. He majored in psychology, then spent two years at the University of Dresden in a unit concerned with experimental psychiatry, receiving a doctorate in 1951. His interest in behaviorist psychology took him next to the University of Peking to work with the famous Chinese psychologist Pin Chow, whose speciality was the use of behaviorist techniques in the interrogation and conditioning of British and American prisoners of war in Korea.

By the time Cherny was ready to return to Moscow, his work in the conditioning of human behavior by the use of Pavlovian techniques had brought him to the attention of the KGB and, in particular, of Maslovsky, who had been instrumental in getting him appointed professor of experimental psychology at Moscow University.

"HE'S A MAVERICK," Maslovsky said. "Has no respect for authority. Totally fails to obey orders. He was told not to carry a gun, wasn't he?"

"Yes, Comrade Colonel."

"So, he disobeys his orders and turns a routine exercise into a bloodbath. Not that I'm worried about these damned dissidents we use here. It's one way of forcing them to serve their country. Who were the policemen, by the way?"

"I'm not sure. Give me a moment." Cherny picked up the telephone. "Levin, get in here."

"Who's Levin?" Maslovsky asked.

"He's been here about three months. A Jewish dissident, sentenced to five years for secretly corresponding with relatives in Israel. He runs the office with extreme efficiency."

20

"What was his profession?"

"Physicist . . . structural engineer. He was, I think, involved with aircraft design. I've every reason to believe he's already seen the error of his ways."

"That's what they all say," Maslovsky told him.

There was a knock on the door and the man in question entered. Viktor Levin was a small man who looked larger only because of the quilted jacket and pants he wore. He was forty-eight years old, with iron gray hair, and his steel spectacles had been repaired with tape. He had a rather hunted look about him, as if he expected the KGB to kick open the door at any moment, which, in his situation, was not an unreasonable assumption.

"Who were the three policemen?" Cherny asked.

"The sergeant was a man called Voronin, Comrade," Levin told him. "Formerly an actor with the Moscow Arts Theater. He tried to defect to the West last year, after the death of his wife. Sentence, ten years."

"And the child?"

"Tanya Voroninova, his daughter. I'd have to check on the other two."

"Never mind now. You may go."

Levin went out and Maslovsky said, "Back to Kelly. I can't get over the fact that he shot that man outside the bar. A direct contradiction of my express order. Mind you," he added grudgingly, "an amazing shot."

"Yes, he's good."

"Go over his background for me again."

Maslovsky poured more coffee and vodka and sat down by the fire, and Cherny took a file from the desk and opened it. "Mikhail Kelly, born in a village called Ballygar on Kerry. That's in the Irish Republic. 1938. Father, Sean Kelly, was an IRA activist in the Spanish Civil War when he met the boy's mother in Madrid. Martha Vronsky, Soviet citizen."

"And as I recall, the father was hanged by the British?"

"That's right. He took part in an IRA bombing campaign in the London area during the early months of World War Two. Was caught, tried, and executed."

"Another Irish martyr. They seem to thrive on them, those people."

"Martha Vronsky was entitled to Irish citizenship and continued to live in Dublin, supporting herself as a journalist, and the boy went to a Jesuit school there."

"Raised as a Catholic?"

"Of course. Those rather peculiar circumstances came to the attention of our man in Dublin, who reported to Moscow. The boy's potential was obvious, and the mother was persuaded to return with him to Russia in 1953. She died two years later. Stomach cancer."

"So, he's now twenty-one and intelligent, I understand?"

"Very much so. Has a flair for languages. Simply soaks them up." Cherny glanced at the file again. "But his special talent is for acting. I'd go so far as to say he has a genius for it."

"Highly appropriate in the circumstances."

"If things had been different, he might well have achieved greatness in that field."

"Yes, well, he can forget about that," Maslovsky commented sourly. "His killing instincts seem well developed."

"Thuggery is no problem in this sort of affair," Cherny told him. "As the Comrade Colonel well knows, anyone can be trained to kill, which is why we place the emphasis on brains when recruiting. Kelly does have a very rare aptitude when using a handgun, however. Quite unique."

"So I observed," Maslovsky said. "To kill like that, so ruthlessly. He must have a strong strain of the psychopath in him."

"Not in his case, Comrade Colonel. It's perhaps a little difficult to understand, but as I told you, Kelly is a brilliant actor. Today, he played the role of IRA gunman and he carried it through, just as if he had been playing the part in a film."

"Except that there was no director to call *cut,*" Maslovsky observed, "and the dead man didn't get up and walk away when the camera stopped rolling."

"I know," Cherny said. "But it explains psychologically why he had to shoot the two men and why he fired at Murphy, in spite of orders. Murphy was an informer. He had to be seen publicly to be punished. In the role he was playing, it was impossible for Kelly to act in any other way. That is the purpose of the training."

"All right, I take the point. And you think he's ready to go out into the cold now?"

"I believe so, Comrade Colonel."

"All right, let's have him in."

WITHOUT THE HAT and the raincoat Mikhail Kelly seemed younger than ever. He wore a dark turtlenecked sweater, a jacket of Donegal tweed, and corduroy slacks. He seemed totally composed, almost withdrawn, and Maslovsky was conscious of that vague feeling of irritation again.

"You're pleased with yourself, I suppose, with what happened out there? I told you not to shoot the man Murphy. Why did you disobey my orders?"

"He was an informer, Comrade Colonel. Such people need to be taught a lesson, if men like me are to survive." He shrugged. "The purpose of terrorism is to terrorize. Lenin said that. In the days of the Irish Revolution, it was Michael Collins's favorite quotation."

"It was a game, damn you!" Maslovsky exploded. "Not the real thing."

"If we play the game long enough, Comrade Colonel, it can sometimes end up playing us," Kelly told him calmly.

"Dear God!" Maslovsky said, and it had been many years since he had expressed such a sentiment. "All right, let's get on with it." He sat down at the desk, facing Kelly. "Professor Cherny feels you are ready to go to work. You agree?"

"Yes, Comrade Colonel."

"Your task is easily stated. Our chief antagonists are America and Britain. Britain is the weaker of the two and its capitalist edifice is being eroded. The biggest thorn in Britain's side is the IRA. You are about to become an additional thorn."

The colonel leaned forward and stared straight into Kelly's eyes. "You are, from now on, a maker of disorder."

"In Ireland?"

"Eventually, but you must undergo more training in the outside world first. Let me explain your task further." He stood up and walked to the fire. "In 1956, the IRA Army Council voted to start another campaign in Ulster. It has been singularly unsuccessful. There is little doubt that this campaign will be called off—and sooner rather than later. It has achieved nothing."

"So?" Kelly said.

Maslovsky returned to the desk. "However, our own intelligence sources indicate that, eventually, a conflict will break out in Ireland of a far more serious nature than anything that has gone before. When that day comes, you must be ready for it, in deep and waiting."

"I understand, Comrade."

"I hope you do. However, enough for now. When I've gone, Professor Cherny will fill you in on your more immediate plans. For the moment, you're dismissed."

Kelly went out without a word. Cherny said, "He can do it. I'm certain of it."

"I hope so. He could be as good as any of the native sleepers, and he drinks less."

Maslovsky walked to the window and peered out at the driving rain, suddenly tired, not thinking of Kelly at all, conscious, for no particular reason, of the look on the child's face when she had attacked the Irishman back there in the square.

"That child," he said. "What was her name?"

"Tanya—Tanya Voroninova."

"She's an orphan now? No one to take care of her?"

24

"Not as far as I know."

"She was really quite appealing, and intelligent, wouldn't you say?"

"She certainly seemed so. I haven't had any dealings with her personally. Has the Comrade Colonel a special interest?"

"Possibly. We lost our only daughter last year at the age of six in the influenza epidemic. My wife can't have any more. She's taken a job in some welfare department or other, but she frets, Cherny. She just isn't the same woman. Looking at that child back there in the square made me wonder. She might just fit the bill."

"An excellent idea, Comrade, for everyone concerned, if I may say so."

"Good," Maslovsky said, suddenly brightening. "I'll take her back to Moscow with me and give my Susha a surprise."

He moved to the desk, pulled the cork from the vodka bottle with his teeth, and filled two glasses. "A toast," he said. "To the Irish enterprise and to . . ." He paused, frowning, "What was his code name again?"

"Cuchulain," Cherny told him.

"Right," Maslovsky said. "To Cuchulain," and he swallowed the vodka down and hurled his glass into the fire.

1982

———————

One

WHEN Major Tony Villiers entered the officers' mess of the Grenadier Guards at Chelsea Barracks, there was no one there. It was a place of shadows, the only illumination the candles flickering in the candelabra on the long, polished dining table, the light reflected from the mess silver.

Only one place was set for dinner at the end of the table, which surprised him, but a bottle of champagne waited in a silver ice bucket, Krug 1972, his favorite. He paused, looking down at it, then lifted it up and eased the cork, reaching for one of the tall crystal glasses that stood on the table, pouring slowly and carefully. He moved to the fire and stood there, examining his reflection in the mirror above it.

The scarlet tunic suited him rather well, and the medals made a brave show, particularly the purple and white stripes of his Military Cross with the silver rosette that meant a second award. He was of medium height with good shoulders, the black hair longer than one would have expected in a serving soldier. In spite of the fact that his nose had been broken at some time or other, he was handsome enough.

It was very quiet now. Only the great men of the past gazed solemnly down at him from the portraits, obscured by the shadows. There was an air of unreality to everything and, for some reason, his image seemed to be reflected many times in the mirror, backward into infinity. He was so damned thirsty. He raised the glass, and his voice was very hoarse, seeming to belong to someone else entirely.

"Here's to you, Tony, old son," he said, "and a Happy New Year."

He lifted the crystal glass to his lips, and the champagne was colder than anything he had ever known. He drank it avidly and it seemed to turn to liquid fire in his mouth, burning its way down, and he cried out in agony as the mirror shattered, and then the ground seemed to open between his feet and he was falling.

HE WOKE AND found himself in exactly the same place he had been for a week now, leaning against the wall in the corner of the little room, unable to lie down because of the wooden halter padlocked around his neck that held his wrists at shoulder level.

He wore a green headcloth wound around his head in the manner of the Baluchi tribesmen he had been commanding in the Dhofar high country until his capture ten days previously. His khaki bush shirt and pants were filthy now, torn in many places, and his feet were bare because one of the Rashid had stolen his suede desert boots. And then there was the beard, prickly and uncomfortable, and he didn't like that. Had never been able to get out of the old Guard's habit of a good close shave every day, no matter what the situation. Even the SAS had not been able to change that particular habit.

There was the rattle of a bolt, the door creaked open, and flies rose in a great curtain. Two Rashid entered, small, wiry men in soiled white robes, bandoliers crisscrossed from the shoulders. They eased him up between them without a word and took him outside, put him down roughly against the wall, and walked away.

30

It was a few moments before his eyes became adjusted to the bright glare of the morning sun. Bir el-Gafamo was a poor place, no more than a dozen flat-roofed houses, with the oasis trimmed by palm trees below. A boy herded half a dozen camels down toward the water trough where women in dark robes and black masks were washing clothes.

In the distance, to the right, the mountains of Dhofar, the most southern province of Oman, lifted into the blue sky. Little more than a week before Villiers had been in those mountains leading Baluchi tribesmen on a hunt for Marxist guerrillas. Bir al-Gafani, on the other hand, was enemy territory, the People's Democratic Republic of the South Yemen stretching north to the Empty Quarter.

There was a large earthenware pot of water on his left, with a ladle in it, but he knew better than to try to drink and waited patiently. In the distance, over a rise, a camel appeared, moving briskly toward the oasis, slightly unreal in the shimmering heat.

He closed his eyes for a moment, dropping his head onto his chest to ease the strain on his neck, and was aware of footsteps. He looked up to find Salim bin al-Kaman approaching. He wore a black headcloth, black robes, a holstered Browning automatic on his right hip, a curved dagger pushed into the belt, and carried a Chinese AK assault rifle, the pride of his life. He stood peering down at Villiers, an amiable-looking man with a fringe of graying beard and a skin the color of Spanish leather.

"*Salaam alaikum,* Salim bin al-Kaman," Villiers said formally in Arabic.

"*Alaikum salaam.* Good morning, Villiers Sahib." It was his only English phrase. They continued in Arabic.

Salim propped the AK against the wall, filled the ladle with water, and carefully held it to Villiers' mouth. The Englishman drank greedily. It was a morning ritual between them. Salim filled the ladle again and Villiers raised his face to receive the cooling stream.

"Better?" Salin asked.

"You could say that."

The camel was close now, no more than a hundred yards away. Its rider had a line wound around the pommel of his saddle. A man shambled along on the other end.

"Who've we got here?" Villiers asked.

"Hamid," Salim said.

"And a friend?"

Salim smiled. "This is our country, Major Villiers, Rashid land. People should come here only when invited."

"But in Hauf, the commissars of the People's Republic don't recognize the rights of the Rashid. They don't even recognize Allah. Only Marx."

"In their own place, they can talk as loudly as they please, but in the land of Rashid . . ." Salim shrugged and produced a flat tin. "But enough. You will have a cigarette, my friend?"

The Arab expertly nipped the cardboard tube on the end of the cigarette and placed it in Villiers's mouth and gave him a light.

"Russian?" Villiers observed.

"Fifty miles from here at Fasari there is an air base in the desert. Many Russian planes, trucks, Russian soldiers—everything!"

"Yes, I know," Villiers told him.

"You know, and yet your famous SAS does nothing about it?"

"My country is not at war with the Yemen," Villiers said. "I am on loan from the British army to help train and lead the Sultan of Oman's troops against Marxist guerrillas of the DLF in Dhofar."

"We are not Marxists, Villiers Sahib. We of the Rashid go where we please, and a major of the British SAS is a great prize. Worth many camels, many guns."

"To whom?" Villiers asked.

Salim waved the cigarette at him. "I have sent word to Fasari. The Russians are coming, sometime today. They will pay a great deal for you. They have agreed to meet my price."

"Whatever they offer, my people will pay more," Villiers

assured him. "Deliver me safely in Dhofar and you may have anything you want. English sovereigns of gold, Maria Theresa silver talers."

"But Villiers Sahib, I have given my word," Salim smiled mockingly.

"I know," Villiers said, "Don't tell me. To the Rashid, their word is everything."

"Exactly!"

Salim got to his feet as the camel approached. It dropped to its knees, and Hamid, a young Rashid warrior in robes of ocher, a rifle slung across his back, came forward. He pulled on the line and the man on the other end fell on his hands and knees.

"What have we here?" Salim demanded.

"I found him in the night, walking across the desert." Hamid went back to the camel and returned with a military-style water bottle and knapsack. "He carried these."

There was some bread in the knapsack and slabs of army rations. The labels were in Russian.

Salim held one down for Villiers to see, then said to the man in Arabic, "You are Russian?"

The man was old, with white hair, obviously exhausted, his khaki shirt soaked with sweat. He shook his head. His lips were swollen to twice their size. Salim held out the ladle filled with water. The man drank.

Villiers spoke fair Russian. He said, "He wants to know who you are. Are you from Fasari?"

"Who are you?" the old man croaked.

"I'm a British officer. I was working for the sultan's forces in Dhofar. Their people ambushed my patrol, killed my men, and took me prisoner."

"Does he speak English?"

"About three words. Presumably you have no Arabic?"

"No," said the old man, "but I think my English is probably better than your Russian. My name is Viktor Levin. I'm from Fasari. I was trying to get to Dhofar."

"To defect?" Villiers asked.

"Something like that."

Salim said in Arabic. "So, he speaks English to you. Is he not Russian, then?"

Villiers said quietly to Levin, "No point in lying about you. Your people are turning up here today to pick me up." He turned to Salim, "Yes, Russian, from Fasari."

"And what was he doing in Rashid country?"

"He was trying to reach the Dhofar."

Salim stared at him, eyes narrow, "To escape from his own people?" He laughed out loud and slapped his thigh. "Excellent. They should pay well for him, also. A bonus, my friend. Allah is good to me." He nodded to Hamid. "Put them inside and see that they are fed, then come to me," and he walked away.

LEVIN WAS PLACED in a wooden halter similar to Villiers's. They sat side by side against the wall in the cell. After a while, a woman in a black mask entered, squatted, and fed them in turn from a large wooden bowl containing goat stew. It was impossible to see whether she was young or old. She wiped their mouths carefully, then left, closing the door.

Levin said, "Why the masks? I don't understand that."

"A symbol of the fact that they belong to their husbands. No other man may look."

"A strange country." Levin closed his eyes. "Too hot."

"How old are you?" Villiers asked.

"Sixty-eight."

"Isn't that a little old for the defecting business? I should have thought you'd left it rather late."

Levin opened his eyes and smiled gently. "My wife died last week in Leningrad. I've no children, so no one they can blackmail me with when I reach freedom."

"What do you do?"

"I'm a professor of structural engineering at the University of Leningrad. I've a particular interest in aircraft design. The Soviet Air Force has five MIG-23s at Fasari, ostensibly in a

34

training role, so it's the training version of the plane they are using."

"With modifications?" Villiers suggested.

"Exactly, so that it can be used in a ground-attack role in mountainous country. The changes were made in Russia, but there have been problems, which I was brought in to solve."

"So, you've finally had enough? What were you hoping to do, go to Israel?"

"Not particularly. I'm not a convinced Zionist for one thing. No, England would be a much more attractive proposition. I was over there with a trade delegation in 1939, just before the war started. The best two months of my life."

"I see."

"I was hoping to get out of Russia in 1959. Corresponded secretly with relatives in Israel who were going to help, then I was betrayed by someone I had thought a true friend. An old story. I was sentenced to five years."

"In the Gulag."

"No, somewhere much more interesting. Would you believe a little Ulster town called Drumore?"

Villiers turned, surprise on his face. "I don't understand?"

"A little Ulster town called Drumore in the middle of the Ukraine." The old man smiled at the look of astonishment on Villiers's face. "I think I'd better explain."

WHEN THE OLD man was finished talking, Villiers sat there thinking about what he had heard. Subversion techniques and counterterrorism had been very much his business for several years now, particularly in Ireland, so Levin's story was fascinating, to say the least. "I knew about Gaczyna, where the KGB trains operatives to work in English, but this other stuff is new to me."

"And probably to your Intelligence people, I think!"

"In Rome in the old days," Villiers said, "slaves and prisoners of war were trained as gladiators, to fight in the arena."

"To the death," Levin said.

"With a chance to survive if you were better than the other man. Just like those dissidents at Drumore playing policemen."

"They didn't stand much chance against Kelly," Levin said.

"No, he sounds as if he was a very special item."

The old man closed his eyes. His breathing was hoarse and troubled, but he was obviously asleep within a few moments. Villiers leaned back in the corner, wretchedly uncomfortable. He kept thinking about Levin's strange story. He'd known a lot of Ulster market towns himself—Crossmaglen, for example. A bad place to be. So dangerous that troops had to be taken in and out by helicopter. But Drumore in the Ukraine—that was something else. After a while, his chin dropped onto his chest and he drifted into sleep.

HE CAME AWAKE to find himself being shaken vigorously by one of the Rashid tribesmen. Another was waking Levin. The man pulled Villiers to his feet and sent him stumbling through the door. It was afternoon now, he knew that from the position of the sun. Much more interesting was the half-track armored personnel carrier—a converted BTR. What the Russians called a Sandcruiser, painted in desert camouflage. Half a dozen soldiers stood beside it wearing khaki drill uniforms, each man holding an AK assault rifle at the ready. Two more stood inside the Sandcruiser manning a 12.7 mm heavy machine gun with which they covered the dozen or so Rashid who stood watching, rifles cradled in their arms.

Salim turned as Levin was brought out behind Villiers. "So, Villiers Sahib, we must part. What a pity. I've enjoyed our conversations."

The Russian officer who approached, a sergeant at his side, wore drill uniform like his men's and a peaked cap and desert goggles that gave him an uncanny resemblance to one of Rommel's Afrika Korps officers. He stood looking at them for a while, then pushed up the goggles. He was younger than Villiers would have thought, with a smooth unlined face and very blue eyes.

36

"Professor Levin," he said in Russian. "I'd like to think you lost your way while out walking, but I'm afraid our friends of the KGB will take a rather different point of view."

"They usually do," Levin told him.

The officer turned to Villiers and said calmly, "Yuri Kirov, captain, 21st Specialist Parachute Brigade." His English was excellent. "And you are Major Anthony Villiers, Grenadier Guards, but, rather more important, of the 22nd Special Air Service Regiment."

"You're very well informed," Villiers said, "And allow me to compliment you on your English."

"Thank you," Kirov said. "We're using exactly the same language laboratory techniques pioneered by the SAS at Bradbury Line Barracks in Hereford. You, also, the KGB wil take a very special interest in."

"I'm sure they will," Villiers said amiably.

"So." Kirov turned to Salim. "To business." His Arabic was not as good as his English, but serviceable enough.

He snapped a finger, and the sergeant stepped forward and handed the Arab a canvas pouch. Salim opened it, took out a handful of coins, and gold glinted in the sun. He smiled and handed the pouch to Hamid, who stood behind him.

"And now," Kirov said, "if you will be good enough to unpadlock these two, we'll get moving."

"Ah, but Kirov Sahib is forgetting." Salim smiled. "I was also promised a machine gun and twenty thousand rounds of ammunition."

"Yes, well, my superiors feel that would be putting far too much temptation in the way of the Rashid," Kirov said.

Salim stopped smiling. "This was a firm promise."

Most of his men, sensing trouble, raised their rifles. Kirov snapped fingers and thumb on his right hand, there was a sudden burst of fire from the heavy machine gun, raking the wall above Salim's head. As the echoes died away, Kirov said patiently, "Take the gold. I would earnestly advise it."

Salim smiled and flung his arms wide. "But of course. Friendship is everything. Certainly not worth losing for the sake of a trifling misunderstanding."

He produced a key from a pouch at his belt and unlocked the padlock, first on the wooden halter that held Levin. Then he moved to Villiers. "Sometimes Allah looks down through the clouds and punishes the deceiver," he murmured.

"Is that in the Koran?" Villiers asked as Hamid removed the halter and he stretched his aching arms.

Salim shrugged and there was something in his eyes. "If not, then it should be."

Two soldiers moved forward on the sergeant's command and ranged themselves on either side of Levin and Villiers. They walked to the Sandcruiser. Villiers and Levin climbed inside. The soldiers followed, Kirov bringing up the rear. Villiers and Levin sat down, flanked by armed guards, and Kirov turned and saluted as the engine rumbled into life.

"Nice to do business with you," he called to Salim.

"And you, Kirov Sahib!"

The Sandcruiser moved away in a cloud of dust, and as they went up over the edge of the first sand dune, Villiers looked back and saw that the old Rashid was still standing there watching them go, only now his men had moved in behind him. There was a curious stillness about them, a kind of threat, and then the Sandcruiser went over the ridge and Bir al-Gafani disappeared from view.

THE CONCRETE CELL on the end of the administrative block at Fasari was a distinct improvement over their previous quarters, with whitewashed walls and chemical toilet and two narrow iron cots, each supplied with a mattress and blankets. It was one of half a dozen such cells that Villiers had noticed on the way in, each with a heavy steel door complete with spyhole, and there seemed to be three armed guards constantly on duty.

Through the bars of the window, Villiers looked out at the

airstrip. It was not as large as he had expected. Three prefabricated hangars with a single tarmacadam runway. The five MIG-23s stood wingtip to wingtip in a line in front of the hangars, looking, in the evening light just before dark, like strange primeval creatures, still, brooding. There were two Mi-8 troop-carrying helicopters on the far side of them and trucks and motor vehicles of various kinds.

"Security seems virtually nonexistent," Villiers murmured.

Beside him, Levin nodded. "Little need for it. They are, after all, in friendly territory entirely surrounded by open desert. Even your SAS people would have difficulty with such a target, I suppose."

Behind them, the bolts rattled in the door. It opened and a young corporal stepped in, followed by an Arab carrying a pail and two enamel bowls. "Coffee," the corporal said.

"When do we eat?" Villiers demanded.

"Nine o'clock."

He ushered the Arab out and closed the door. The coffee was surprisingly good and very hot. Villiers said, "So they use some Arab personnel?"

"In the kitchens and for sanitary duties and that sort of thing. Not from the desert tribes. They bring them from Hauf, I believe," Levin explained.

"What do you think will happen now?"

"Well, tomorrow is Thursday and there's a supply plane in. It will probably take us back with it to Aden."

"Moscow next stop?"

There was no answer to that, of course, just as there was no answer to concrete walls, steel doors, and bars. Villiers lay on one bed, Levin on the other.

The old Russian said, "Life is a constant disappointment to me. When I visited England, they took me to Oxford. So beautiful." He sighed. "It was a fantasy of mine to return one day."

"Dreaming Spires," Villiers observed. "Yes, it's quite a place."

"You know it then?"

"My wife was at university there. St. Hughes College. She went there after the Sorbonne. She's half-French."

Levin raised himself on one elbow. "You surprise me. If you'll forgive me for saying so, you don't have the look of a married man."

"I'm not," Villiers told him. "We got divorced a few months ago."

"I'm sorry."

"Don't be. As you said, life is a constant disappointment. We all want something different, that's the trouble with human beings, particularly men and women. In spite of what the feminists say, they are different."

"You still love her, I think?"

"Oh, yes," Villiers said. "Loving is easy. It's the living together that's so damned hard."

"So what was the problem?"

"To put it simply, my work. Borneo, the Oman, Ireland. I was even in Vietnam when we very definitely weren't supposed to be. As she once told me, I'm truly good at only one thing, killing people, and there came a time when she couldn't take that any more."

Levin lay back without a word, and Tony Villiers stared up at the ceiling, head pillowed in his hands, thinking of things that simply would not go away as darkness fell.

HE CAME AWAKE with a start, aware of footsteps in the passageway outside, the murmur of voices. The light in the ceiling must have been turned on while he slept. They hadn't taken his Rolex from him, and he glanced at it quickly, aware of Levin stirring on the other bed.

"What time is it?" the old Russian asked.

"Nine-fifteen. Must be supper."

Villiers got up and moved to the window. There was a half-moon in a sky alive with stars, and the desert was luminous, starkly beautiful, the MIG-23s like black cutouts. *God. There must be a way.* He turned, his stomach tightening.

"What is it?" Levin whispered as the first bolt was drawn.

"I was just thinking," Villiers said, "that to make a run for it at some point, even if it means a bullet in the back, would be infinitely preferable to Moscow and the Lubianka."

The door was flung open and the corporal stepped in, followed by an Arab holding a large wooden tray containing two bowls of stew, black bread, and coffee. His head was down, and yet there was something familiar about him.

"Come on, hurry up!" the corporal said in bad Arabic.

The Arab placed the tray on the small wooden table at the foot of Levin's bed and glanced up, and in the moment that Villiers and Levin realized that he was Salim bin al-Kaman, the corporal turned to the door. Salim took a knife from his left sleeve, his hand went around the corporal's mouth, a knee went up pulling him off balance, the knife slipped under his ribs. He eased the man down on the bed and wiped the knife on his uniform.

He smiled. "I kept thinking about what you said, Villiers Sahib. That your people in the Dhofar would pay a great deal to have you back."

"So, you get paid twice—once by both sides. Sound business sense," Villiers told him.

"Of course, but in any case, the Russians were not honest with me. I have my honor to think of."

"What about the other guards?"

"Gone to supper. All this I discovered from friends in the kitchens. The one whose place I took has suffered a severe bump on the head on the way here, by arrangement, of course. But come, Hamid awaits on the edge of the base with camels."

They went out. Salim bolted the door, and they followed him along the passageway quickly and moved outside. The Fasari air base was very quiet, everything still in the moonlight.

"Look at it," Salim said. "No one cares. Even the sentries are at supper. Peasants in uniform." He reached behind a steel drum that stood against the wall and produced a bundle. "Put these on and follow me."

The two woolen cloaks were of the kind worn by the Bedouin at night in the intense cold of the desert, each with a pointed hood to pull up. They put them on and followed Salim across to the hangars.

"No fence around this place, no wall," Villiers whispered.

"The desert is the only wall they need," Levin said.

Beyond the hangars, the sand dunes lifted on either side of what looked like the mouth of a ravine. Salim said, "The Wadi al-Hara. It empties into the plain a quarter of a mile from here, where Hamid waits."

Villiers said, "Had it occurred to you that Kirov may well put two and two together and come up with Salim bin al-Kaman?"

"But of course. My people are already halfway to the Dhofar border by now."

"Good," Villiers said. "That's all I wanted to know. I'm going to show you something very interesting."

He turned toward the Sandcruiser standing nearby and pulled himself over the side while Salim protested in a hoarse whisper, "Villiers Sahib, this is madness."

As Villiers dropped behind the driving wheel, the Rashid clambered up into the vehicle, followed by Levin. "I've a dreadful feeling that all this is somehow my fault," the old Russian said. "We are, I presume, to see the SAS in action?"

"During the Second World War, the SAS under David Stirling destroyed more Luftwaffe planes on the ground in North Africa than the RAF and Yanks managed in aerial combat. I'll show you the technique," Villiers told him.

"Possibly another version of that bullet in the back you were talking about."

Villiers switched on and, as the engine rumbled into life, said to Salim in Arabic, "Can you manage the machine gun?"

Salim grabbed the handles of the Degtyarev. "Allah, be merciful. There is fire in his brain. He is not as other men."

"Is that in the Koran, too?" Villiers demanded, but the roaring of the 110-horsepower engine as he put his foot down hard drowned out the Arab's reply.

The Sandcruiser thundered across the tarmac. Villiers swung hard and it spun around on its half-tracks and smashed the tailplane of the first MIG, continuing right down the line as he increased speed. The tailplanes of the two helicopters were too high, so he concentrated on the cockpit areas at the front, the Sandcruiser's eight tons of armored steel crumpling the Perspex with ease.

He swung around in a wide loop and called to Salim. "The helicopters. Try for the fuel tanks."

There was the sound of an alarm Klaxon from the main administration block now, voices crying in the night, and shooting started. Salim raked the two helicopters with a continuous burst, and the fuel tank of the one on the left exploded, a ball of fire mushrooming into the night, burning debris cascading everywhere. A moment later, the second helicopter exploded against the MIG next to it, and that also started to burn.

"That's it!" Villiers said. "They'll all go now. Let's get out of here."

As he spun the wheel, Salim swung the machine gun, driving back the soldiers running toward them. Villiers was aware of Kirov standing still as his men went down the other side of the tarmac, firing his pistol very deliberately in a gallant but totally futile gesture. And then they were climbing up the slope of the dunes, tracks churning sand, and entering the mouth of the *wadi*. The dried bed of the old stream was rough with boulders here and there, but visibility in the moonlight was good. Villiers kept his foot down and drove very fast.

He called to Levin. "You okay?"

"I think so," the old Russian told him. "I'll keep checking."

Salim patted the Degtyarev machine gun. "What a darling. Better than any woman. This, I keep, Villiers Sahib."

"You've earned it," Villiers told him. "Now all we have to do is pick up Hamid and drive like hell for the border."

"No helicopters to chase us," Levin shouted.

"Exactly."

Salim said, "You deserve to be Rashid, Villiers Sahib. I have not enjoyed myself so much in many years." He raised an arm. "I have held them in the hollow of my hand and they are as dust."

"The Koran again?" Villiers asked.

"No, my friend," Salim bin al-Kaman told him. "It is from your own Bible this time. The Old Testament," and he laughed out loud exultantly as they emerged from the *wadi* and started down to the plain below, where Hamid waited.

Two

D-15, that branch of the British Secret Intelligence Service that concerns itself with counterespionage as well as the activities of secret agents and subversion within the United Kingdom, does not officially exist, although its offices are to be found in a large white and red-brick building not far from the Hilton Hotel in London. D-15 can only carry out an investigation. It has no powers of arrest. It is the officers of the Special Branch at Scotland Yard who handle that end of things.

But the growth of international terrorism and its effects in Britain, particularly because of the Irish problem, were more than even Scotland Yard could handle. In 1972, the director general of D-15, with the support of 10 Downing Street, created a section known as Group Four, with powers held directly from the prime minister of the day, to coordinate the handling of all cases of terrorism and subversion.

After ten years, Brigadier Charles Ferguson was still in charge. A large, deceptively kind-looking man, his Guards tie was the only hint of a military background. The crumpled gray suits he favored and the half-moon reading glasses combined with the untidy gray hair to give him the look of some minor academic in a provincial university.

Although he had an office at the directorate general, Ferguson preferred to work from his flat in Cavendish Square. His second daughter, Ellie, who was in interior design, had done the place over for him. The Adam fireplace was real and so was the fire. Ferguson was a fire person. The rest of the room was Georgian and everything matched to perfection, including the heavy curtains.

The door opened and his manservant, an ex-Ghurka naik named Kim, came in with a silver tray, which he placed by the fire. "Ah tea," Ferguson said. "Tell Captain Fox to join me."

He poured tea into one of the china cups and picked up the *Times.* The news from the Falklands was not bad. British forces had landed on Pebble Island and destroyed eleven Argentine aircraft plus an ammo dump. Two Sea Harriers had bombed merchant shipping in Falkland Sound.

The green baize door leading to the study opened and Fox came in. He was an elegant man in a blue flannel suit by Huntsman of Savile Row, the Duke of Windsor's old tailors. He also wore a Guards tie, for he had once been an acting captain in the Blues and Royals until an unfortunate incident with a bomb in Belfast, during his third tour of duty, had deprived him of his left hand. He now wore a rather clever replica that, thanks to the miracle of the microchip, served him almost as well as the original. The neat leather glove made it difficult to tell the difference.

"Tea, Harry?"

"Thank you, sir. I see they've got the Pebble Island story."

"Yes, all very colorful and dashing," Ferguson said, as he filled a cup for him, "But frankly, as no one knows better than you, we've got enough on our plate without the Falklands. I mean Ireland's not going to go away and then there's the pope's visit. He's due on the twenty-eighth. That only gives us eleven days. And he makes such a target of himself. You'd think he'd be more careful after the Rome attempt on his life."

"Not that kind of man, is he, sir?" Fox sipped some of his tea. "On the other hand, the way things are going, perhaps he won't come at all. The South American connection is of primary importance to the Catholic church, and they see us as the villain of the piece in this Falklands business. They don't want him to come, and the speech he made in Rome yesterday seemed to hint that he wouldn't."

"I'll be perfectly happy with that situation," Ferguson said. "It would relieve me of the responsibility of making sure some madman or other doesn't try to shoot him while he's in England. On the other hand, several million British Catholics would be bitterly disappointed."

"I understand the archbishops of Liverpool and Glasgow have flown off to the Vatican today to try to persuade him to change his mind," Fox said.

"Yes, well let's hope they fail miserably."

The bleeper sounded on the red telephone on Ferguson's desk, the phone reserved for top-security-rated traffic only.

"See what this is, Harry."

Fox lifted the receiver. "Fox here." He listened for a moment then turned, face grave, and held out the phone. "Ulster, sir. Army headquarters, Lisburn, and it isn't good!"

IT HAD STARTED that morning just before seven o'clock outside the village of Kilgannon some ten miles from London-derry. Patrick Leary had delivered the mail in the area for fifteen years now, and his Royal Mail van was a familiar sight.

His routine was always the same. He reported for work at headquarters in Londonderry promptly at five-thirty, picked up the mail for the first delivery of the day, already sorted by the night staff, filled up his gas tank at the transport pumps, then set off for Kilgannon. And always at half-past six he would pull off the road and park near the trees beside Kilgannon Bridge to read the morning paper, eat his breakfast sandwiches, and have a cup of coffee from his thermos. It was a routine that, unfortunately for Leary, had not gone unnoticed.

Cuchulain watched him for ten minutes, waiting patiently for Leary to finish his sandwiches. Then the man got out, as he always did, and walked a little way into the wood. There was a slight sound behind him of a twig cracking under a foot. As he turned in alarm, Cuchulain slipped out of the trees.

He presented a formidable figure, and Leary was immediately terrified. Cuchulain wore a dark anorak and a black balaclava helmet that left only his eyes, nose, and mouth exposed. He carried a PPK semi-automatic pistol in his left hand, with a Carswell silencer screwed to the end of the barrel.

"Do as you're told and you'll live," Cuchulain said. His voice was soft with a southern Irish accent.

"Anything," Leary croaked. "I've got a family . . . please."

"Take off your cap and the raincoat and lay them down." Leary did as he was told. Cuchulain held out his right hand so that Leary saw the large white capsule nestling in the center of the glove. "Now, swallow that down like a good boy."

"Would you poison me?" Leary was sweating now.

"You'll be out for approximately four hours, that's all," Cuchulain assured him. Better that way." He raised the gun. "Better than this."

Leary took the capsule, hand shaking, and swallowed it down. His legs seemed to turn to rubber. There was an air of unreality to everything, but a hand was on his shoulder pushing him down. The grass was cool against his face, then there was only the darkness.

DR. HANS WOLFGANG Baum was a remarkable man. Born in Berlin in 1950, the son of a prominent industrialist, on his father's death in 1970 he had inherited a fortune equivalent to

48

$10 million, as well as wide business interests. Many people in his position would have been content to live a life of pleasure, which Baum did, with the important distinction that he derived his pleasure from work.

He had a doctorate in engineering science from the University of Berlin, a law degree from the London School of Economics, and a master's degree in business administration from Harvard. And he had put them all to good use, expanding and developing his various factories in West Germany, France, and the United States, so that his personal fortune was now estimated to be in excess of $100 million.

Yet the project closest to his heart was the development of the plant to manufacture tractors and general agricultural machinery outside Londonderry, near Kilgannon. Baum Industries could have gone elsewhere, indeed the director of the board of management had wanted to.

Unfortunately for them and against sound business sense, Baum was a committed Christian and a truly good man, a rare commodity in this world. A member of the German Lutheran Church, he had done everything possible to make the factory a genuine partnership between Catholic and Protestant. He and his wife were totally committed to the local community, and his three children attended local schools.

It was an open secret that Baum had met with the Provisional IRA, some said with the legendary Martin McGuinness himself. Whether true or not, the PIRA had left the Kilgannon factory alone to prosper, as it did, and to provide work for more than a thousand Protestants and Catholics previously unemployed.

BAUM LIKED TO keep in shape. Each morning, he awakened at exactly the same time, six o'clock, slid out of bed without disturbing his wife, pulled on a track suit and running shoes. Eileen Docherty, the young maid, was already up and making tea in the kitchen, although still in her dressing gown.

49

"Breakfast at seven, Eileen," he called. "My usual. Must get an early start this morning. I've a meeting in Derry at eight-thirty with the Works Committee."

He left himself out of the kitchen door, ran across the park land, vaulted a low fence, and turned into the woods. He ran, rather than jogged, at a fast, almost professional pace, following a series of paths, his mind full of the day's planned events.

By six forty-five he had completed his schedule, turned out of the trees, and hammered along the grassy shoulder of the main road toward the house. As usual, he met Pat Leary's mail van coming along the road toward him. It pulled in and waited, and he could see Leary through the windshield in uniform cap and coat sorting a bundle of mail.

Baum leaned down to the open window. "What have you got for me this morning, Patrick?"

The face was the face of a stranger—dark, calm eyes, strong bones, nothing to fear there at all, and yet it was Death come to claim him.

"I'm truly sorry," Cuchulain said. "You're a good man," and the Walther in his left hand extended to touch Baum between the eyes. It coughed once, and the German was hurled back to fall on the side of the road, blood and brains scattering across the grass.

Cuchulain drove away instantly, but within five minutes he was back at the pulloff by the bridge where he'd left Leary. He tore off the cap and coat, dropped them beside the unconscious postman, and ran through the trees, clambering over a wooden fence a few minutes later beside a narrow farm track, very heavily overgrown with grass. A motorcycle waited there, an old 350cc BSA, stripped down as if for hill climbing, with special ribbed tires. It was a machine much used by hill farmers on both sides of the border to herd sheep. He pulled on a battered, old crash helmet with a scratched visor, climbed on, and kick-started expertly. The engine roared into life and he rode away, passing only one vehicle, the local milk cart, just outside the village.

50

Back there on the main road it started to rain, and it was still falling on the upturned face of Hans Wolfgang Baum thirty minutes later when the milk cart pulled up beside him. At that precise moment, fifteen miles away, Cuchulain turned the BSA along a farm track south of Clady and rode across the border into the safety of the Irish Republic.

Ten minutes later, he stopped beside a phone box, dialed the number of the *Belfast Telegraph,* asked for the news desk, and claimed responsibility for the shooting of Hans Wolfgang Baum on behalf of the Provisional IRA.

"IT DOESN'T MAKE sense," Ferguson said. "Baum was well liked by everyone, and the local Catholic community was totally behind him. He fought his own board of directors every inch of the way to locate that factory in Kilgannon. They'll probably pull out now, which leaves over a thousand unemployed and Catholics and Protestants at each others' throats again."

"But isn't that exactly what the Provisionals want, sir?"

"I wouldn't have thought so, Harry. Not this time. This was a dirty one. The callous murder of a thoroughly good man, well respected by the Catholic community. It can do the Provisionals nothing but harm with their own people. That's what I don't understand. It was such a stupid thing to do." He tapped the file on Baum that Fox had brought in. "Baum met Martin McGuinness in secret, and McGuinness assured him of the Provisionals' good will. Whatever else you may think of him, McGuinness is a clever man. Too damned clever, actually, but that isn't the point." He shook his head. "No, it doesn't add up."

The red phone bleeped. He picked it up. "Ferguson here." He listened for a moment. "Very well, Minister." He put the phone down and stood up. "The secretary of state for Northern Ireland, Harry. Wants me right away. Get on to Lisburn again. Army Intelligence—anything you can think of. Find out all you can."

HE WAS BACK just over an hour later. As he was taking off his coat, Fox came in.

51

"That didn't take long, sir."

"Short and sweet. He's not pleased, Harry, and neither is the prime minister. She's good and mad, and you know what that means."

"She wants results, sir?"

"Only she wants them yesterday, Harry. All hell's broken loose over there in Ulster. Protestant politicians having a field day. Paisley saying I told you so, as usual. Oh, the West German chancellor's been on to Downing Street. To be frank, things couldn't be worse."

"I wouldn't be too sure, sir. According to Army Intelligence at Lisburn the PIRA are more than a little annoyed about this one themselves. They insist they had nothing to do with it."

"But they claimed responsibility."

"They run a very tight ship these days, sir, as you know, since the reorganization of their command structure. McGuinness, among other things, is still chief of Northern Command, and the word from Dublin is that he categorically denies involvement of any of his people. In fact, he's as angry as anybody else at the news. It seems he thought a great deal of Baum."

"Do you think its INLA?"

In the past, the Irish National Liberation Front had shown themselves willing to strike more ruthlessly than the Provisionals, when they felt the situation warranted it.

"Intelligence says not, sir. They have a good source close to the top where INLA is concerned."

Ferguson warmed himself at the fire. "Are you suggesting the other side was responsible? The UVF or the Red Hand of Ulster?"

"Again, Lisburn has good sources in both organizations and the word is 'definitely not.' No Protestant organization was involved."

"Not officially."

"It doesn't look as if anyone was involved officially, sir. There are always the cowboys; of course. The madmen who watch too many midnight movies on television and end up willing to kill anybody rather than nobody."

Ferguson lit a cheroot and sat behind his desk. "Do you really believe that, Harry?"

"No, sir," Fox said calmly. "I was just throwing out all the obvious questions that the media crackpots will come up with."

Ferguson sat there staring at him, frowning. "You know something, don't you?"

"Not exactly, sir. There could be an answer to this, a totally preposterous one that you aren't going to like one little bit."

"Tell me."

"All right, sir. The fact that the *Belfast Telegraph* had a phone call claiming responsibility for the Provisionals is going to make the Provisionals look very bad indeed."

"So."

"Let's assume that was the purpose of the exercise."

"Which means a Protestant organization did it with that end in view?"

"Not necessarily, as I think you'll see, if you let me explain. I got the full report on the affair from Lisburn just after you left. The killer is an absolute professional, no doubt about that. Cold, ruthless, highly organized, and yet he doesn't just kill everyone in sight."

"Yes, that had occurred to me, too. He gave the postman, Leary, a capsule. Some sort of knockout drops."

"And that stirred my mind, so I put it through the computer." He had a file tucked under his arm, and now he opened it. "The first five killings on the list all involved a witness being forced at gunpoint to take that sort of capsule. First time it occurs is 1975, in Omagh."

Ferguson examined the list and looked up. "But on two occasions the victims were Catholics. I accept your argument that the same killer was involved, but it makes a nonsense of your theory that the purpose in killing Baum was to make the PIRA look bad."

"Stay with it a little longer, sir, please. Description of the killer in each case is identical. Black balaclava and dark anorak. Always uses a Walther PPK. On three occasions was known to escape by motorcycle from the scene of the crime."

"So?"

"I fed all those details into the computer separately, sir. Any killings where motorcycles were involved. Cross-referencing with use of a Walther, not necessarily the same gun, of course. Also cross-referencing with the description of the individual."

"And you got a result?"

"I got a result all right, sir." Fox produced not one sheet, but two. "At least thirty possible killings since 1975, all linked to the factors I've mentioned. There are another ten possibles."

Ferguson scanned the lists quickly. "Dear God!" he whispered. "Catholic and Protestant alike. I don't understand."

"You might if you consider the victims, sir. In all cases where the Provisionals claimed responsibility, the target was counter-productive, leaving them looking very bad indeed."

"And the same where Protestant extremist organizations were involved?"

"True, sir, although the PIRA are more involved than anyone else. Another thing, if you consider the dates when the killings took place, it's usually when things were either quiet or getting better or when some political initiative was taking place. One of the possible cases when our man might have been involved goes back as far as July 1972, when, as you know, a delegation from the IRA secretly met William Whitelaw here in London."

"That's right," Ferguson said. "There was a ceasefire, a genuine chance for peace."

"Broken because someone started shooting on the Lenadoon estate in Belfast, and that's all it took to start the pot boiling again."

Ferguson sat there, staring down at the lists, his face expressionless. After a while, he said, "So what you're saying is that somewhere over there is one mad individual dedicated to keeping the whole rotten mess turning over."

"Exactly, except that I don't think he's mad. It seems to me that he's simply following sound Marxist-Leninist principles where urban revolution is concerned. Chaos, disorder, fear. All those factors essential to the breakdown of any kind of orderly government."

"With the IRA taking the brunt of the smear campaign?"

"Which makes it less and less likely that the Protestants will ever come to a political agreement with them, or our own government, for that matter."

"And ensures that the struggle continues year after year and a solution always recedes before us." Ferguson nodded slowly. "An interesting theory, Harry, and you believe it?"

He looked up inquiringly. Fox shrugged. "The facts were all there in the computer. We never asked the right questions, that's all. If we had, the pattern would have emerged earlier. It's been there a long time, sir."

"Yes, I think you could very well be right." Ferguson sat there brooding for a little while longer.

Fox said gently, "He exists, sir. He is a fact, I'm sure of it. And there's something else. Something that could go a long way toward explaining the whole thing."

"All right, tell me the worst."

Fox took another sheet from the file. "When you were in Washington the other week, Tony Villiers came back from the Oman."

"Yes, I heard something of his adventures there."

"In his debriefing, Tony tells an interesting story concerning a Russian Jewish dissident named Viktor Levin whom he brought out with him. A fascinating vignette about a rather unusual KGB training center in the Ukraine."

He moved to the fire and lit a cigarette, waiting for Ferguson to finish reading the file. After a while, Ferguson said, "Tony Villiers is in the Falklands now, did you know that?"

"Yes, sir, serving with the SAS behind enemy lines."

"And this man, Levin?"

"A highly gifted engineer. We've arranged for one of the

Oxford colleges to give him a job. He's at a safe house in Hampstead at the moment. I've taken the liberty of sending for him, sir."

"Have you indeed, Harry? What would I do without you?"

"Manage very well, I should say, sir. Ah, and another thing. The psychologist whom Paul Cherny mentioned in that story. He defected in 1975."

"What, to England?" Ferguson demanded.

"No, sir—Ireland. Went there for an international conference in July of that year and asked for political asylum. He's now a professor of experimental psychology at Trinity College, Dublin."

VIKTOR LEVIN LOOKED fit and well, still deeply tanned from his time in the Yemen. He wore a gray tweed suit, soft white shirt, blue tie, and black library spectacles that quite changed his appearance. He talked for quite some time, answering Ferguson's questions patiently.

During a brief pause he said, "Do I presume that you gentlemen believe that the man Kelly, or Cuchulain—to give him his code name, is actually active in Ireland? I mean, it's been twenty-three years."

"But that was the whole idea, wasn't it?" Fox said. "A sleeper to go in deep. To be ready when Ireland exploded. Perhaps he even helped it happen."

"And you would appear to be the only person outside of his own people who has any idea what he looks like, so we'll be asking you to look at some pictures. Lots of pictures," Ferguson told him.

"As I say, it's been a long time," Levin said.

"But he did have a distinctive look to him," Fox suggested.

"That's true enough, God knows. A face like the devil himself, when he killed. But of course, you're not quite right when you say I'm the only one who remembers him. There's Tanya. Tanya Voroninova."

"The young girl whose father played the police inspector whom Kelly shot, sir," Fox explained.

"Not so young now. Thirty years old. A lovely girl, and you should hear her play piano," Levin told them.

"You've seen her since?" Ferguson asked.

"All the time. Let me explain. I made sure they thought I'd seen the error of my ways, so I was rehabilitated and sent to work at the University of Moscow. Tanya was adopted by Maslovsky, the KGB colonel, and his wife. They really took to the child."

"He's a general now, sir," Fox put in.

"She turned out to have great talent for piano. When she was twenty, she won the Tschaikovsky competition in Moscow."

"Just a minute," Ferguson said, for classical music was his special joy. "Tanya Voroninova, the concert pianist. She did rather well at the Leeds Piano Festival two years ago."

"That's right. Mrs. Maslovsky died a month earlier. Tanya tours abroad all the time now. With her foster father a KGB general, she's looked upon as a good risk."

"And you've seen her recently?"

"Six months ago."

"And she spoke of the events you've described as taking place at Drumore?"

"Oh, yes. Let me explain. She's highly intelligent and very well balanced, but she's always had a thing about what happened. It's as if she has to keep turning it over in her mind. I asked her why once."

"And what did she say?"

"That it was Kelly. She could never forget him because he was so kind to her, and in view of what happened, she couldn't understand that. She said she often dreamed of him."

"Yes, well as she's in Russia, that isn't really very much help." Ferguson got to his feet. "Would you mind waiting in the next room a moment, Mr. Levin?"

Fox opened the green baize door, and the Russian passed

through. Ferguson said. "A nice man. I like him." He walked to the window and looked down into the square below. After a while, he said, "We've got to root him out, Harry. I don't think anything we've handled has ever been so vital."

"I agree."

"A strange thing. It would seem to be just as important to the IRA that Cuchulain is exposed as it is to us."

"Yes, sir, the thought had occurred to me."

"Do you think they'd see it that way?"

"Perhaps, sir." Fox's stomach was hollow with excitement, as if he knew what was coming.

"All right," Ferguson said. "God knows, you've given enough to Ireland, Harry. Are you willing to risk the other hand?"

"If you say so, sir."

"Good. Let's see if they're willing to show some sense for once. I want you to go to Dublin to see the PIRA Army Council or anyone they're willing to delegate to see you. I'll make the right phone calls to set it up. Stay at the Westbourne as usual. And I mean today, Harry. I'll see to Levin."

"Right, sir," Fox said calmly. "Then if you'll excuse me, I'll get started," and he went out.

Ferguson went back to the window and looked out at the rain. Crazy, of course, the idea that British Intelligence and the IRA could work together, and yet it made sense this time. The point was, would the wild men in Dublin see it that way.

Behind him, the study door opened and Levin appeared. He coughed apologetically, "Brigadier, do you still need me?"

"But of course, my dear chap," Charles Ferguson said. "I'll take you along to my headquarters now. Pictures—lots of pictures, I'm afraid." He picked up his coat and hat and opened the door to usher Levin out. "But who knows? You might just recognize our man."

In his heart, he did not believe it for a moment, but he didn't tell Levin that, as they went down in the lift.

Three

*I*N Dublin, it was raining, driving across the Liffey River in a soft gray curtain as the cab from the airport turned into a side street just off George's Quay and deposited Fox at his hotel.

The Westbourne was a small, old-fashioned place with only one bar-restaurant. It was a Georgian building and therefore listed against redevelopment. Inside, however, it had been refurbished to a quiet elegance, exactly in period. The clientele, when one saw them at all, were middle-class and distinctly aging, the sort who'd been using it for years when up from the country for a few days. Fox had stayed there on numerous occasions, always under the name of Charles Hunt—profession, wine wholesaler, a subject he was sufficiently expert on to make an eminently suitable cover.

The receptionist, a plain young woman in a black suit, greeted him warmly. "Nice to see you again, Mr. Hunt. I've managed you number three on the first floor. You've stayed there before."

"Fine," Fox said, "Messages?"

"None, sir. How long will you be staying?"

"One night, maybe two. I'll let you know."

The porter was an old man with very white hair and the sad, wrinkled face of the truly disillusioned. His green uniform was a little too large and Fox, as usual, felt slightly embarrassed when he took the bags.

"How are you, Mr. Ryan," he inquired as they went up in the small lift.

"Fine, sir. Never better. I'm retiring next month. They're putting me out to pasture."

He led the way along the small corridor, and Fox said, "That's a pity. You'll miss the Westbourne."

"I will so, sir. Thirty-eight years." He unlocked the bedroom door and led the way in. "Still, it comes to us all."

It was a pleasant room with green damask walls, twin beds, a fake Adam fireplace, and Georgian mahogany furniture. Ryan put the bag down on the bed and adjusted the curtains.

"The bathroom's been done since you were last here, sir. Very nice. Would you like some tea?"

"Not right now, Mr. Ryan." Fox took a five-pound note from his wallet and passed it over. "If there's a message, let me know straightaway. If I'm not here, I'll be in the bar."

There was something in the old man's eyes, just for a moment; then he smiled faintly. "I'll find you, sir, never fear."

That was the thing about Dublin these days, Fox told himself as he dropped his coat on the bed and went to the window. You could never be sure of anyone, and there were sympathizers everywhere, of course. Not necessarily IRA, but thousands of ordinary decent people who hated the violence and the bombing, but approved of the political ideal behind it all.

The phone rang, and when he answered it Ferguson was at the other end.

"It's all set. McGuinness is going to see you."

"When?"

"They'll let you know."

60

The line went dead and Fox replaced the receiver. Martin McGuinness, chief of Northern Command for the PIRA, among other things. At least he would be dealing with one of the more intelligent members of the Army Council.

He could see the Liffey at the far end of the street, and rain rattled against the window. He felt unaccountably depressed. Ireland, of course. Just being here. For a moment he felt a distinct ache in the left hand again, the hand that was no longer there. All in the mind, he told himself and went downstairs to the bar.

It was quite deserted except for a young Italian barman. Fox ordered a Scotch and water and sat in a corner by the window. There was a choice of newspapers on the table and he was working his way through the *Times* when Ryan appeared like a shadow at his shoulder.

"Your cab's here, sir."

Fox glanced up. "My cab? Oh, yes, of course." He frowned, noticing the blue raincoat across Ryan's arm. "Isn't that mine?"

"I took the liberty of getting it for you from your room, sir. You'll be needing it. This rain's with us for a while yet, I think."

Again, there was something in the eyes, almost amusement. Fox allowed him to help him on with the coat and followed him outside and down the steps to where a black taxicab waited.

Ryan opened the door for him and said, as Fox got in, "Have a nice afternoon, sir."

The cab moved away quickly. The driver was a young man with dark, curly hair. He wore a brown leather jacket and white scarf. He didn't say a word, simply turned into the traffic stream at the end of the street and drove along George's Quay. A man in a cloth cap and peacoat stood beside a green telephone box. The cab slid in to the curb, and the man in the peacoat opened the rear door and smoothly got in beside Fox.

"On your way, Michael," he said to the driver and turned to Fox genially. "Jesus and Mary, but I thought I'd drown out there. Arms up, if you please, Captain. Not too much. Just enough." He searched Fox thoroughly and professionally and found nothing. He leaned back and lit a cigarette, then he took a pistol from his pocket and held it on his knees. "Know what this is, Captain?"

"A Ceska, from the look of it," Fox said. "Silenced version the Czechs made a few years back."

"Full marks. Just remember I've got it when you're talking to Mr. McGuinness. As they say in the movies, one false move and you're dead."

They continued to follow the line of the river, the traffic heavy in the rain, and finally pulled in at the curb halfway along Victoria Quay.

"Out!" the man in the peacoat said and Fox folowed him. Rain drove across the river on the wind, and he pulled up his collar against it. The man in the peacoat passed under a tree and nodded toward a small public shelter beside the quay wall. "He doesn't like to be kept waiting. He's a busy man."

He lit another cigarette and leaned against the tree, and Fox moved along the pavement and went up the steps into the shelter. There was a man sitting on the bench in the corner reading a newspaper. He was well-dressed, a fawn raincoat open revealing a well-cut suit of dark blue, white shirt, and a blue-and-red striped tie. He was handsome enough, with a mobile intelligent mouth and blue eyes. Hard to believe that this rather pleasant-looking man had been featured on the British army's "most-wanted" list for almost thirteen years.

"Ah, Captain Fox," Martin McGuinness said affably. "Nice to see you again."

"But we've never met," Fox said.

"Derry, 1972," McGuinness told him. "You were a cornet, isn't that what you call second lieutenants in the Blues and Royals? There was a bomb in a pub in Prior Street. You were on detachment with the military police at the time."

"Good God!" Fox said. "I remember now."

"The whole street was ablaze, and you ran into a house next

62

to the grocer's shop and brought out a woman and two kids. I was on the flat roof opposite with a man with an Armalite rifle who wanted to put a hole in your head. I wouldn't let him. It didn't seem right under the circumstances."

For a moment, Fox felt rather cold. "You were in command in Derry for the IRA at that time."

McGuinness grinned. "A funny old life, isn't it? You shouldn't really be here. Now then, what is it that that old snake Ferguson wants you to discuss with me?"

So Fox told him.

WHEN HE WAS finished McGuinness sat there brooding, hands in the pockets of his raincoat, staring across the Liffey. After a while, he said, "That's Wolfe Tone Quay over there, did you know that?"

"Wasn't he a Protestant?" Fox asked.

"He was so. Also one of the greatest Irish patriots there ever was."

He whistled tunelessly through his teeth. Fox said, "Do you believe me?"

"Oh, yes," McGuinness said softly. "A devious bloody lot, the English, but I believe you all right and for one very simple reason. It fits, Captain, dear. All those hits over the years, the shit that's come our way because of them and sometimes internationally. I know the times we've not been responsible and so does the Army Council. The thing is, one always thought it was the idiots, the cowboys, the wild men." He grinned crookedly. "Or British Intelligence, of course. It never occurred to any of us that it could have been the work of one man. A deliberate plan."

"You've got a few Marxists in your own organization, haven't you?" Fox suggested. "The kind who might see the Soviets as Savior."

"You can forget that one." Anger showed in McGuinness's blue eyes for a moment. "Ireland free and Ireland for the Irish. We don't want any Marxist pap here."

"So, what happens now? Will you go to the Army Council?"

"No, I don't think so. I'll talk to the chief of staff. See what he thinks. After all, he's the one who sent me. Frankly, the fewer people in on this, the better."

"True." Fox stood up. "After all, Cuchulain could be anyone. Maybe somebody close to the Army Council itself."

"The thought had occurred to me." McGuinness waved, and the man in the peacoat moved out from under the tree. "Murphy will take you back to the Westbourne now. Don't go out. I'll be in touch."

Fox walked a few paces away, paused, and turned. "By the way, that's a Guards tie you're wearing."

Martin McGuinness smiled beautifully. "And didn't I know it? Just trying to make you feel at home, Captain Fox."

FOX DIALED FERGUSON from a phone booth in the foyer of the Westbourne so that he didn't have to go through the hotel switchboard. The brigadier wasn't at the flat, so he tried the private line to his office at the directorate-general and got through to him at once.

"I've had my preliminary meeting, sir."

"That was quick. Did they send McGuinness?"

"Yes, sir."

"Did he buy it?"

"Very much so, sir. He'll be back in touch, maybe later tonight."

"Good. I'll be at the flat within the hour. No plans to go out. Phone me the moment you have more news."

Fox showered, then changed and went downstairs to the bar again. He had another small Scotch and water and sat there, thinking about things in general and McGuinness in particular. A clever and dangerous man, no doubt about that. Not just a gunman, although he'd done his share of killing, but one of the most important leaders thrown up by the Troubles. The annoying thing was that Fox realized, with a certain sense of irritation, that he really rather liked the man. That wouldn't do at all, so he went into the restaurant and had an early dinner, sitting in solitary splendor, a copy of the *Irish Press* propped up in front of him.

Afterward, he had to pass through the bar on the way to the lounge. There were a couple of dozen people in there now, obviously other guests from the look of them, except for the driver of the cab who'd taken him to meet McGuinness earlier. He was seated on a stool at the end of the bar, a glass of lager in front of him, the main difference being that he now wore a rather smart gray suit. He showed no sign of recognition and Fox went on into the lounge, where Ryan approached him.

"If I remember correctly, sir, it's tea you prefer after your dinner and not coffee?"

Fox, who had sat down, said, "That's right."

"I've taken the liberty of putting a tray in your room, sir. I thought you might prefer a bit of peace and quiet."

There was that look in the eyes again, and he turned without a word and led the way to the lift. Fox played along, following him, expecting, perhaps, a further message, but the old man said nothing and when they reached the first floor, led the way along the corridor and opened the bedroom door for him.

Martin McGuinness was watching the news on television. Murphy stood by the window. Like the man in the bar, he now wore a rather conservative suit, in his case of navy blue worsted material.

McGuinness switched off the television, using the hand control. "Ah, there you are. Did you try the Duck à l'Orange? It's not bad here."

The tray on the table with the tea things on it carried two cups. "Shall I pour, Mr. McGuinness?" Ryan asked.

"No, we can manage." McGuinness reached for the teapot and said to Fox as Ryan withdrew, "Old Patrick, as you can see, is one of our own. You can wait outside, Michael," he added.

Murphy went out without a word. "They tell me no gentleman would pour his milk in first, but then I suppose no real gentleman would bother about rubbish like that. Isn't that what they teach you at Eton?"

"Something like that." Fox took the profferred cup. "I didn't expect to see you quite so soon."

"A lot to do and not much time to do it in." McGuinness drank some tea and sighed with pleasure. "That's good. Right. I've seen the chief of staff, and he believes, with me, that you and your computer have stumbled onto something that might very well be worth pursuing."

"Together?"

"That depends. In the first place, he's decided not to discuss it with the Army Council, certainly not at this stage, so it stays with just me and himself."

"That seems sensible."

"Another thing, we don't want the Dublin police in on this, so keep Special Branch out of it and no Military Intelligence involvement either."

"I'm sure Brigadier Ferguson will agree."

"He'll bloody well have to, just as he'll have to accept that there's no way we're going to pass across general information about IRA members, past or present. The kind of stuff you could use in other ways."

"All right," Fox said, "I can see that, but it could be a tricky one. How do we cooperate if we don't pool resources?"

"There is a way," McGuinness poured himself another cup of tea. "I've discussed it with the chief of staff and he's agreeable if you are. We use a middleman."

"A middleman?" Fox frowned. "I don't understand?"

"Someone acceptable to both sides. Equally trusted, if you know what I mean."

Fox laughed. "There's no such animal."

"Oh, yes there is," McGuinness said. "Liam Devlin, and don't tell me you don't know who *he* is?"

Harry Fox said slowly, "I know Liam Devlin very well."

"And why wouldn't you. Didn't you and Faulkner have him kidnapped by the SAS back in '79 to help you break Martin Brosnan out of that French prison to hunt down that mad dog Frank Barry?"

"You're extremely well-informed."

"Yes, well, Liam's here in Dublin now, a professor at Trinity College. He has a cottage in a village called Kilrea, about an hour's drive out of town. You go and see him. If he agrees to help, then we'll discuss it further."

"When?"

"I'll let you know, or maybe I'll just turn up unexpected like. The way I kept ahead of the British army all those years up north." He stood up. "There's a lad at the bar downstairs. Maybe you noticed?"

"The cab driver."

"Billy White. Left or right hand, he can still shoot a fly off the wall. He's yours while you're here."

"Not necessary."

"Oh, but it is." McGuinness got up and pulled on his coat. "Number one, I wouldn't like anything to happen to you, and number two, it's a convenience to know where you are." He opened the door, and beyond him, Fox saw Murphy waiting. "I'll be in touch, Captain." McGuinness saluted mockingly, and the door closed behind him.

FERGUSON SAID, "IT makes sense, I suppose, but I'm not sure Devlin will work for us again, not after that Frank Barry affair. He felt we'd used him and Brosnan rather badly."

"As I recall, we did, sir," Fox said. "Very badly indeed."

"All right, Harry, no need to make a meal of it. Phone and see if he's at home. If he is, go and see him."

"Now, sir?"

"Why not? It's only nine-thirty. If he is in, let me know and I'll speak to him myself. Here's his phone number, by the way. Take it down."

FOX WENT ALONG to the bar and changed a five-pound note for 50p coins. Billy White was still sitting there, reading the evening paper. The glass of lager looked untouched.

"May I buy you a drink, Mr. White?" Fox asked.

"Never touch the stuff, Captain." White smiled cheerfully and emptied the glass in one long swallow. "A Bushmills would chase that down fine."

Fox ordered him one. "I may want to go out to a village called Kilrea. Do you know it?"

"No problem," White told him. "I know it well."

Fox went back to the phone booth and closed the door. He sat there for a while thinking, then dialed the number Ferguson had given him. And the voice, when it answered, was instantly recognizable. The voice of perhaps the most remarkable man he had ever met.

"Devlin here."

"Liam? This is Harry Fox."

"Mother of God!" Liam Devlin said. "Where are you?"

"Dublin—the Westbourne Hotel. I'd like to come and see you."

"You mean right now?"

"Sorry if it's inconvenient."

Devlin laughed. "As a matter of fact, at this precise moment in time I'm losing at chess, son, which is something I don't like to do. Your intervention could be looked upon as timely. Is this what you might term a business call?"

"Yes, I'm to ring Ferguson and tell him you're in. He wants to talk to you himself."

"So the old bastard is still going strong? Ah, well, you know where to come?"

"Yes."

"I'll see you in an hour then. Kilrea Cottage, Kilrea. You can't miss it. Next to the convent."

68

When Fox came out of the booth after phoning Ferguson, White was waiting for him. "Are we going out then, Captain?"

"Yes," Fox said. "Kilrea Cottage, Kilrea. Next to a convent, apparently. I'll just get my coat."

White waited until he'd entered the lift, then ducked into the booth and dialed a number. The receiver at the other end was lifted instantly. He said, "We're leaving for Kilrea now. Looks like he's seeing Devlin tonight."

AS THEY DROVE through the rainswept streets, White said casually, "Just so we know where we stand, Captain, I was a lieutenant in the North Tyrone Brigade of the Provisional IRA the year you lost that hand."

"You must have been young."

"Born old, that's me, thanks to the B Specials when I was a wee boy and the sodding Royal Ulster Constabulary." He lit a cigarette with one hand. "You know Liam Devlin well, do you?"

"Why do you ask," Fox demanded warily.

"That's who we're going to see, isn't it? Jesus, Captain, and who wouldn't be knowing Liam Devlin's address?"

"Something of a legend to you, I suppose?"

"A legend, is it? That man wrote the book. Mind you, he won't have any truck with the Movement these days. He's what you might call a moralist. Can't stand the bombing and that kind of stuff."

"And can you?"

"We're at war, aren't we? You bombed the hell out of the Third Reich. We'll bomb the hell out of you, if that's what it takes."

Logical, but depressing, Fox thought, for where did it end? A charnel house with only corpses to walk on. He shivered, face bleak.

"About Devlin," White said as they started to leave the city. "There's a tale I heard about him once. Would you know if it's true, I wonder?"

"Ask me."

69

"The word is, he went to Spain in the '30s, served against Franco, and was taken prisoner. Then the Germans got ahold of him and used him as an agent here during the big war."

"That's right."

"The way I heard it, after that, they sent him to England. Something to do with an attempt by German paratroopers to kidnap Churchill in 1943. Is there any truth in that?"

"Sounds straight out of a paperback novel to me," Fox said.

White sighed and there was regret in his voice. "That's what I thought. Still, one hell of a man for all that," and he sat back and concentrated on his driving.

AN UNDERSTATEMENT AS a description of Liam Devlin, Fox thought, sitting there in the darkness. A brilliant student who had entered Trinity College, Dublin, at the age of sixteen and had taken a first-class honors degree at nineteen. Scholar, writer, poet, and highly dangerous gunman for the IRA in the '30s, even when still a student.

Most of what White had said was true. He had gone to Spain to fight for the antifacists, he had worked for the Abwehr in Ireland. As to the Churchill affair? A story whispered around often enough, but as to the truth of it? Well, it would be years before those classified files were opened.

During the postwar period, Devlin had been a professor at a Catholic Seminary called All Souls just outside of Boston. He'd been involved with the abortive IRA campaign of the late '50s, had returned to Ulster in 1969 as the present troubles had begun. One of the original architects of the Provisional IRA, he had become increasingly disillusioned by the bombing campaign and had withdrawn active support to the Movement. Since 1976, he had held a position on the English faculty at Trinity.

Fox had not seen him since 1979 when he had been coerced, indeed, blackmailed, by Ferguson into giving his active assistance to the hunting down of Frank Barry, ex-IRA activist who had turned international terrorist-for-hire. There had been various reasons why Devlin had gone along with that business, mostly because he had believed Ferguson's lies. So, how would he react now?

They had entered a long village street, and Fox pulled himself together with a start as White said, "Here we are—Kilrea, and there's the convent and that's Devlin cottage, set back from the road behind the wall."

He turned the car into a gravel driveway and cut the engine. "I'll wait for you, Captain, shall I?"

Fox got out and walked up a flagstone path between rose bushes to the green-painted porch. The cottage was pleasantly Victorian, with most of the original woodwork and gable ends. A light glowed behind drawn curtains at a bow window. He pressed the doorbell. There were voices inside, footsteps, and then the door opened and Liam Devlin stood looking out at him.

Four

EVLIN wore a dark blue flannel shirt open at the neck, gray slacks, and a pair of expensive-looking Italian brogues in brown leather. He was a small man, no more than five foot-five or six and, at sixty-four, his dark, wavy hair showed only a light silvering. There was a faded scar on the right side of his forehead, an old bullet wound; his face was pale, the eyes an extraordinarily vivid blue. A slight ironic smile seemed permanently to lift the corner of his mouth—the look of a man who had found life a bad joke and had decided that the only thing to do was laugh about it.

The smile was utterly charming and totally sincere. "Good to see you, Harry." His arms went around Fox in a light embrace.

"And you, Liam."

Devlin looked beyond him at the car and Billy White behind the wheel. "You've got someone with you?"

"Just my driver."

Devlin moved past him, went along the path, and leaned down to the window.

"Mr. Devlin," Billy said.

Devlin turned without a word and came back to Fox. "Driver, is it, Harry? The only place that one will drive you to is straight to hell."

"Have you heard from Ferguson?"

"Yes, but leave it for a moment. Come along in."

The interior of the house was a time capsule of Victoriana. Mahogany paneling and William Morris wallpaper in the hall, with several night scenes by the Victorian painter Atkinson Grimshaw on the walls.

Fox examined them with admiration as he took off his coat and gave it to Devlin. "Strange to see these here, Liam. Grimshaw was a very Yorkshire Englishman."

"Not his fault, Harry, and he painted like an angel."

"Worth a bob or two," Fox said, well aware that ten thousand pounds at auction was not at all out of the way for even quite a small Grimshaw.

"Do you tell me?" Devlin said lightly and opened one half of a double mahogany door and led the way into the sitting room.

Like the hall, it was period Victorian. Green flocked wallpaper stamped with gold, more Grimshaws on the walls, mahogany furniture, and a fire burning brightly in a fireplace that looked as if it was a William Langley original. The man who stood before it was a priest in dark cassock, and he turned from the fire to greet them. He was about Devlin's height with iron gray hair swept back over his ears. A handsome man, particularly at this moment as he smiled a welcome, and there was an eagerness to him, an energy that touched something in Fox. It was not often that one liked another human being so completely and instinctively.

"With apologies to Shakespeare, two little touches of Harry in the night," Devlin said, "Captain Harry Fox, meet Father Harry Cussane."

Cussane shook hands warmly. "A great pleasure, Captain

Fox. Liam was telling me something about you after you rang earlier."

Devlin indicated the chess table beside the sofa. "Any excuse to get away from that. He was beating the pants off me."

"A gross exaggeration, as usual," Cussane said. "But I must get going. Leave you two to your business." His voice was pleasant and rather deep. Irish, yet more than a hint of American there.

"Would you listen to the man?" Devlin had brought three glasses and a bottle of Bushmills from the cabinet in the corner. "Sit down, Harry. Another little snifter before bed won't kill you." He said to Fox. "I've never known anyone so much on the go as this one."

"All right, Liam, I surrender," Cussane said. "Fifteen minutes, that's all, then I must go. I like to make a late round at the hospice as you know, and then there's Danny Malone. Living is a day-to-day business with him right now."

"Heart of corn, Danny," Devlin said. "But I'll drink to him. It comes to us all."

"You said hospice?" Fox inquired.

"Yes. There's a convent next door, the Sacred Heart, run by the Little Sisters of Pity. They started a hospice for terminal patients some years ago."

"Do you work there?"

"Yes, as a sort of administrator cum priest. Nuns aren't supposed to be worldly enough to do the accounts. Absolute rubbish. Sister Anne-Marie, who's in charge over there, knows to every last penny. And this is a small parish, so the local priest doesn't have a curate. I give him a hand."

"In between spending three days a week in charge of the press office at the Catholic secretariat in Dublin," Devlin said. "Not to mention flogging the local youth club through a very average five performances of *South Pacific,* complete with a star cast of ninety-three local school kids."

Cussane smiled. "Guess who was stage manager? We're trying *West Side Story* next. Liam thinks it too ambitious, but I believe it's better to rise to a challenge than go for the easy choice always."

He swallowed a little of his Bushmills. Fox said, "Forgive me for asking, Father, but are you American or Irish? I can't quite tell."

"Most days, neither can he," Devlin laughed.

"My mother was an Irish-American who came back to Connacht in 1938 after her parents died, to seek her roots. All she found was me."

"And your father?"

"I never knew him. Cussane was her name. She was a Protestant, by the way. There are still a few in Connacht, descendants of Cromwell's butchers. Cussane is often called Patterson in that part of the country by pseudotranslation from Casan, which in Irish means 'path.'"

"Which means he's never certain whether he's Harry Patterson or Harry Cussane," Devlin put in.

"Only some of the time." Cussane smiled. "My mother returned to America in 1946, after the war. She died of influenza a year later, and I was taken in by her only relative, an old great-uncle who ran a farm in the Ontario wheat belt. He was a fine man and a good Catholic. It was under his influence that I decided to enter the Church."

"Enter the devil, stage left." Devlin raised his glass.

Fox looked puzzled and Cussane explained. "The seminary that accepted me was All Souls, at Vine Landing outside Boston. Liam was English professor there."

"He was a great trial to me," Devlin said. "Mind like a steel trap. Constantly catching me out in misquoting Eliot in class."

"I served in a couple of Boston parishes and another in New York," Cussane said, "but I always hoped to get back to Ireland. Finally, I got a move to Belfast in 1968. A church on the Falls Road."

76

"Where he promptly got burned out by an Orange mob the following year."

"I tried to keep the parish together, using a school hall," Cussane said.

Fox glanced at Devlin, "While you ran around Belfast adding fuel to the flames?"

"God might forgive you for that," Devlin said piously, "for I cannot."

Cussane emptied his glass. "I'll be off then. Nice to meet you, Harry Fox."

He held out his hand. Fox shook it, and Cussane moved to the French windows and opened them. Fox saw the convent looming up into the night on the other side of the garden wall. Cussane walked across the lawn, opened a gate, and passed through.

"Quite a man," he said as Devlin closed the windows.

"And then some." Devlin turned, no longer smiling. "All right, Harry. Ferguson being his usual mysterious self, it looks as if it's up to you to tell me what all this is about."

IN THE HOSPICE, all was quiet. It was as unlike the conventional idea of a hospital as it was possible to be, and the architect had designed the ward area in a way that gave each occupant of a bed the choice of privacy or intimacy with other patients. The night sister sat at her desk, the only light, a shaded lamp. She didn't hear Cussane approach, yet suddenly he was there, looming out of the darkness.

"How's Malone?"

"The same, Father. Very little pain. We have the drug input just about in balance."

"Is he lucid?"

"Some of the time."

"I'll go and see him."

Danny Malone's bed, divided from the others by bookshelves and cupboards, was angled toward a glass window that gave a view of the grounds and the night sky. The night-light beside the bed brought his face into relief. He was not old, no more than forty, his hair prematurely white, the face like a skull under taut skin, etched in pain caused by the cancer that was slowly and relentlessly taking him from this life to the next.

As Cussane sat down, Malone opened his eyes. He gazed blankly at Cussane, then recognition dawned. "Father, I thought you weren't coming."

"I promised, didn't I? I was having a nightcap with Liam Devlin is all."

"Jesus, Father, you're lucky you got away with just the one with him, but he's big for the Cause, Liam, I'll give him that. There's no man living done more for Ireland."

"What about yourself?" Cussane sat down beside the bed. "No stronger fighter for the Movement than you, Danny."

"But how many did I kill, Father, there's the rub, and for what?" Malone asked him. "Daniel O'Connel once said in a speech that although the ideal of Irish freedom was just, it was not worth a single human life. When I was young, I disputed that. Now that I'm dying, I think I know what he meant." He winced in pain and turned to look at Cussane. "Can we talk some more, Father? It helps get it straight in my own mind."

"Just for a while, then you must get some sleep," Cussane smiled. "One thing a priest is good at is listening, Danny."

Malone smiled contentedly. "Right, where were we? I was telling you about the preparation for the bombing campaign on the English Midlands and London in '72."

"You were saying the papers nicknamed you the Fox," Cussane said, "because you seemed to go backward and forward between England and Ireland at will. All your friends were caught, Danny, but not you. How was that?"

"Simple, Father. The greatest curse on this country of ours is the informer, and the second greatest curse is the inefficiency of the IRA. People full of ideology and revolution blow a lot of wind and are often singularly lacking in good sense. That's why I preferred to go to the professionals."

"Professionals?"

"What you would call the criminal element. For example, there wasn't an IRA safe house in England during the '70s that wasn't on the Special Branch's list at Scotland Yard sooner or later. That's how so many got caught."

"And you?"

"Criminals on the run, or needing a rest when things get too hot, have places they can go, Father. Expensive places, I admit, but safe, and that's what I used. There was one in Scotland south from Glasgow in Galloway run by a couple of brothers called Mungo. What you might call a country retreat. Absolute bastards, mind you."

The pain was suddenly so bad that he had to fight for breath. "I'll get Sister," Cussane told him in alarm.

Malone grabbed him by the front of his cassock. "No, you damn well won't. No more painkillers, Father. They mean well, the sisters, but enough is enough. Let's just keep talking."

"All right," Harry Cussane said. Malone lay back, closed his eyes for a moment, then opened them again. "Anyway, as I was saying, these Mungo brothers, Hector and Angus, were the great original bastards."

DEVLIN PACED UP and down the room restlessly. "Do you believe it?" Fox asked.

"It makes sense and it would explain a great deal," Devlin said. "So let's just say I accept it in principle.

"So, what do we do about it?"

"What do *we* do about it?" Devlin glared at him. "The effrontory of the man. Let me remind you, Harry, that the last time I did a job for Ferguson, the bastard conned me. Lied in his teeth. Used me."

"That was then, this is now, Liam."

"And what is that pearl of wisdom supposed to mean?"

There was a soft tapping at the French window. Devlin opened the desk drawer, took out an old-fashioned Mauser pistol with a bulbous silencer on the end, and cocked it. He nodded to Fox, then Devlin pulled the curtain. Martin McGuinness peered in at them, Murphy at his shoulder.

"Dear God!" Devlin groaned.

He opened the French window, and McGuinness smiled as he stepped in. "God bless all here!" he said mockingly and added to Murphy, "Watch the window, Michael." He closed it and walked over to the fire, holding his hands to the warmth. "Colder as the nights draw in."

"What do you want?" Devlin demanded.

"Has the captain here explained the situation to you yet?"

"He has."

"And what do you think?"

"I don't think at all," Devlin told him. "Especially where the lot of you are concerned."

"'The purpose of terrorism is to terrorize,' that's what Mick Collins used to say," McGuinness told him. "I fight for my country, Liam, with anything that comes to hand. We're at war." He was angry now. "I've got nothing to apologize for."

"If I could say something," Fox put in. "Let's suppose that Cuchulain exists, then surely it isn't a question of taking sides? It's accepting that what he's doing has needlessly protracted the tragic events of the past thirteen years."

McGuinness helped himself to a whisky. "He has a point. When I was O. C. Derry in 1972, I was flown to London with Daithi O'Connell, Seamus Twomes, Ivor Bell, and others to meet Willie Whitelaw to discuss peace."

"And the Lenadoon shooting broke the cease-fire," Fox said, and turned to Devlin. "It doesn't seem to me to be a question of taking sides any more. It would seem that Cuchulain has worked deliberately to keep the whole rotten mess going. I

80

would have thought anything that might have helped stop that would be worth it."

"Morality, is it?" Devlin raised a hand and smiled wickedly. "All right, you win."

"Good," McGuinness said, "then let's get down to brass tacks. This fella Levin, who actually saw Kelly or Cuchulain or whatever his name is, all those years ago. I presume Ferguson is showing him pictures of every known KGB operative?"

"And all known adherents of the IRA, UDA, UVF. Anything and everything," Fox said. "That will include looking at what they have at Special Branch in Dublin, because we swap information."

"The bastards would," McGuinness said bitterly. "Still, I think we've got a few that neither the police in Dublin nor your people in London have ever seen."

"And how do we handle that?" Fox demanded.

"You get Levin over here, and he and Devlin look at what we've got—no one else. Is it agreed?"

Fox glanced at Devlin, who nodded. "Okay," Fox said. "I'll ring the brigadier tonight."

"Fine," McGuinness turned to Devlin. "You're sure your phone's not tapped or anything like that. I'm thinking of those Special Branch bastards."

Devlin opened a drawer in the desk, produced a black metal box that he switched on so that a red light appeared. He approached the telephone and held the box over it. There was no reaction.

"Oh, the wonders of the electronic age," he said and put the box away.

"Fine." McGuinness said. "So, let's see where we start. The only people who know about this besides yourself, Captain, are Ferguson, Liam, the chief of staff, and myself."

"And Professor Paul Cherny," Fox said.

McGuinness nodded. "That's right. We've got to do something about him." He turned to Devlin. "Do you know him?"

"I've seen him at parties at the university. Exchanged a civil word, no more than that. He's well liked. A widower. His wife died before he defected. There's a chance he isn't involved in this, of course."

"And pigs might fly," McGuinness said crisply. "The fact that it was Ireland he defected to is too much of a coincidence for me. A pound to a penny he knows our man, so why don't we pull him in and squeeze it out of him?"

"Simple," Fox told him. "Some men don't squeeze."

"He's right," Devlin said. "Better to try the softly-softly approach first."

"All right," McGuinness said. "I'll have him watched twenty-four hours a day. Put Michael Murphy in charge. He won't be able to go to the bathroom without our knowing it."

Devlin glanced at Fox. "Okay by you?"

"Fine," Fox told him.

"Good." McGuinness buttoned his raincoat. "I'll get off then. I'll leave Billy to look after you, Captain." He opened the French window. "Mind your back, Liam." And then he was gone.

FERGUSON WAS IN bed when Fox phoned, sitting up against the pillows, working his way through a mass of papers, preparing himself for a Defense Committee meeting the following day. He listened patiently to everything Fox had to say. "So far, so good, Harry, as far as I can see. Levin spent the entire day working through everything we had at the Directorate. Didn't come up with a chin."

"It's been a long time, sir. Cuchulain could have changed a lot and not just because he's older. I mean, he could have a beard, for example."

"Negative thinking, Harry. I'll put Levin on the morning flight to Dublin, but Devlin will have to handle him. I need you back here."

"Any particular reason, sir?"

"Lots to do with the Vatican. It really is beginning to look as if the pope won't come. However, he's invited the cardinals of Argentina and Britain to confer with him."

"So the visit could still be on?"

"Perhaps, but more important from our point of view, the war is still on, and there's talk of the Argentinians trying to get ahold of this damned Exocet missile on the European black market. I need you, Harry. Catch the first flight out. By the way, an interesting development. Tanya Voroninova, remember her?"

"Of course, sir."

"She's in Paris to give a series of concerts. Fascinating that she should surface at this particular moment."

"What Jung would call synchroneity, sir?"

"Jung, Harry? What on earth are you babbling about?"

"Carl Jung, sir. Famous psychologist. Synchroneity is a word he coined for events having a coincidence in time, and, because of this, the feeling that some deeper motivation is involved."

"The fact that you're in Ireland is no excuse for acting as if you've gone soft in the head, Harry," Ferguson said testily.

He put down the phone, sat there thinking, then got up, pulled on his robe, and went out. He knocked on the door of the guest room and went in. Levin was sitting up in bed wearing a pair of Ferguson's pajamas and reading a book.

Ferguson sat on the edge of the bed. "I thought you'd be tired after going through so many photos."

Levin smiled. "When you reach my age, Brigadier, sleep eludes you, memory crowds in. You wonder what it has all been about."

Ferguson warmed to the man. "Don't we all, my dear chap? Anyway, how would you feel about running over to Dublin on the morning plane?"

"To see Captain Fox?"

"No, he'll be returning here, but a friend of mine, Professor

Liam Devlin of Trinity College, will take care of you. He'll probably be showing you a few more photos, courtesy of our friends in the IRA. They'd never let me have them, for obvious reasons."

The old Russian shook his head. "Tell me, Brigadier, did the 'war to end all wars' finish in 1945, or am I mistaken?"

"You and a great many other people, my friend." Ferguson got up and went to the door. "I'd get some sleep if I were you. You'll need to be up at six to catch the early morning flight from Heathrow. I'll have Kim serve you breakfast in bed."

He closed the door. Levin sat there for a while, an expression of sadness on his face, then he sighed, closed the book, turned out the light, and went to sleep.

AT KILREA COTTAGE, Fox put down the phone and turned to Devlin. "All fixed. He'll come in on the breakfast plane. Unfortunately, my flight leaves just before. He'll report to the information desk in the main concourse. You can pick him up there."

"No need," Devlin said. "This minder of yours, young White. He'll be dropping you, so he can pick Levin up at the same time and bring him straight here. It's best we do it that way. McGuinness might be in touch early about where I'm supposed to take him."

"Fine," Fox said. "I'd better get moving."

"Good lad."

Devlin got his coat for him and took him out to the car where Billy White waited patiently.

"Back to the Westbourne, Billy," Fox said.

Devlin leaned down at the window. "Book yourself in there for the night, son, and in the morning, do exactly what the captain tells you to. Let him down by a single inch and I'll have your balls, and Martin McGuinness will probably walk all over the rest of you."

Billy White grinned affably. "Sure and on a good day, they tell me I can shoot almost as well as you, Mr. Devlin."

"Go on, be off with you."

The car moved away. Devlin watched it go, then turned and went inside. There was a stirring in the shrubbery, a footfall, only the faintest of sounds, as someone moved away.

THE EAVESDROPPING EQUIPMENT that the KGB had supplied to Cuchulain was the most advanced in the world, developed originally by a Japanese company, the details, as a result of industrial espionage, having reached Moscow four years previously. The directional microphone trained on Kilrea Cottage could pick up every word uttered inside at several hundred yards. Its ultrafrequency secondary function was to catch even the faintest telephone conversation. All this was allied to a sophisticated recording apparatus.

The whole was situated in a small attic concealed behind the loft water tanks just beneath the pantile roof of the house. Cuchulain had listened in on Liam Devlin in this way for a long time now, although it had been some time since anything quite so interesting had come up. He sat in the attic smoking a cigarette, running the tape at top speed through the blank spots and the unimportant bits, paying careful attention to the phone conversation with Ferguson.

Afterward, he sat there thinking about it for a while, then he reset the tape, went downstairs, and let himself out. He went into the phone box at the end of the village street by the pub and dialed a Dublin number. The phone was picked up almost immediately. He could hear voices, a sudden laugh, Mozart playing softly.

"Cherny here."

"It's me. You're not alone?"

Cherny laughed lightly. "Dinner party for a few faculty friends."

"I must see you."

"All right," Cherny said. "Usual time and place tomorrow afternoon."

Cuchulain replaced the receiver, left the booth, and went back up the village street, whistling softly an old Connemara folk song that had all the despair, all the sadness of life in it.

Five

OX had a thoroughly bad night and slept very little, so that he was restless and ill-at-ease as Billy White took the car expertly through the early morning traffic toward the airport. The young Irishman was cheerful enough as he tapped his fingers on the steering wheel in time to the music from the radio.

"Will you be back, Captain?"

"I don't know. Perhaps."

"Ah, well, I don't expect you to be overfond of the ould country." White nodded toward Fox's gloved hand. "Not after what it's cost you."

"Is that so?" Fox said.

Billy lit a cigarette. "The trouble with you Brits is that you never face up to the fact that Ireland's a foreign country. Just because we speak English . . ."

"As a matter of interest, my mother's name was Fitzgerald and she came from County Mayo," Fox told him. "She worked for the Gaelic League, was a lifelong friend of de Valera, and spoke excellent Irish, a rather difficult language I found, when she insisted on teaching it to me when I was a boy. Do you speak Irish, Billy?"

"God save us, but I don't, Captain," White said in astonishment.

"Well, then I suggest you kindly stop prattling on about the English being unable to understand the Irish."

He glanced morosely out at the traffic. A police motorcyclist took up station on the left of them, a sinister figure in goggles and crash helmet and a heavy caped raincoat against the early morning downpour. He glanced sideways at Fox once, anonymous in the dark goggles, and dropped back as they turned into the side road leading to the airport.

Billy left the car in the short-stay park. As they entered the concourse, the flight announcer was already calling Fox's plane. Cuchulain, who had been with them all the way from the hotel, stood at the door by which they had entered and watched Fox book in.

Fox and Billy walked toward the departure gate, and Fox said, "An hour till the British Airways flight lands."

"Time for a big breakfast," Billy grinned. "T'was a fine time we had, Captain."

"I'll be seeing you, Billy."

Fox put out his good hand and Billy White took it with a certain reluctance. "Try to make sure it isn't at the wrong end of some street in Belfast. I'd hate to have you in my sights, Captain."

Fox went through the gate, and Billy made his way across the concourse to stairs leading up to the café terrace. Cuchulain watched him go, then went out, back across the road to the car park, and waited.

An hour later, he was back inside and consulting the nearest arrival screen. The British Airways shuttle from London was just landing, and he saw White approach the central information desk and speak to one of the attendants. There was a pause and then an announcement over the public address system.

"Will Mr. Viktor Levin, a passenger on the London shuttle, please report to the information desk."

A few moments later, the small squat figure of the Russian appeared from the crowd with one of Ferguson's men beside him. Levin carried a small case and wore a rather large brown raincoat and a black trilby hat. Cuchulain sensed that it was his quarry even before Levin spoke to one of the attendants, who indicated White. Levin and White shook hands and after a few words, Levin's English minder turned to go. Cuchulain watched them for a moment longer, then he turned and left.

"SO THIS IS Ireland," Levin said as they drove down toward the city.

"Your first visit?" White asked.

"Oh, yes. I am from Russia. I have not traveled abroad very much."

"Russia?" Billy said. "Jesus, but you'll find it different here."

"And this is Dublin?" Levin inquired as they followed the traffic down into the city.

"Yes, Kilrea, where we're going, is on the other side."

"A city of significant history, I think," Levin observed.

"And that's the understatement of the age," White told him. "I'll take you through Parnell Square, it's on our way. A great patriot in spite of being a bloody Prod. And then O'Connell Street and the General Post Office where the boys held out against the whole bloody British army back in 1916."

"Good. This I would like very much." Levin leaned back in his seat and looked out on the passing scene with interest.

AT KILREA, LIAM Devlin walked across the back lawn of his cottage, let himself through the gate in the wall, and ran for the rear entrance of the hospice as the rain increased into a sudden downpour. Sister Anne-Marie was crossing the hall, accompanied by two young white-coated interns on loan from University College, Dublin.

She was a small, sparse little woman, very fit for her seventy years, and wore a white smock over her nun's robe. She had a doctorate in medicine from the University of London and was a Fellow of the Royal College of Physicians. A lady to be reckoned with. She and Devlin were old adversaries. She had once been French, but that was a long time ago, as he was fond of reminding her.

"And what can we do for you, Professor?" she demanded.

"You say that as if to the devil coming through the door," Devlin told her.

"An observation of stunning accuracy."

They started up the stairs, and Devlin said, "Danny Malone—how is he?"

"Dying," she said calmly. "Peacefully, I hope. He is one of those patients who responds well to our drug program, which means that pain is only intermittent."

They reached the first of the open-plan wards. Devlin said, "When?"

"This afternoon, tomorrow—next week." She shrugged. "He is a fighter, that one."

"That's true," Devlin said. "Big for the Cause all his life, Danny."

"Father Cussane comes in every night," she said, "and sits and lets him talk through this violent past of his. I think it troubles him, now that he nears his end. The IRA, the killing."

"Is it all right if I sit with him for a while?"

"Half-an-hour," she said firmly and moved away, followed by the interns.

Malone seemed to sleep, eyes closed, the skin tight on the facial bones, yellow as parchment. His fingers gripped the edge of a sheet tightly.

Devlin sat down. "Are you there, Danny?"

"Ah, there you are, Father," Malone opened his eyes, focused weakly, and frowned. "Liam, is that you?"

"None other."

"I thought it was Father Cussane. We were just talking."

"Last night, Danny. You must have fallen asleep. Sure and you know he works in Dublin at the secretariat during the day."

Malone licked dry lips. "God, but I could do with a cup of tea."

"Let's see if I can get you one." Devlin got up.

As he did so, there was a sudden commotion on the lower level, voices shouting, drifting up. He frowned and hurried forward to the head of the stairs.

BILLY WHITE TURNED off the main highway onto the narrow road, flanked by fir plantations on either side, that led to Kilrea. "Not long now." He half-turned to speak to Levin behind him and noticed, through the rear window, a *Gardai* motorcyclist turn off the main road behind them.

He started to slow and Levin said, "What is it?"

"Gardai," Billy told him. "Police to you. One mile over the limit and they'll book you, those sods."

The police motorcyclist pulled up alongside and waved them down. With his dark goggles and helmet, White could see nothing of him at all. He pulled in angrily at the side of the road. "And what in hell does this fella want? I wasn't doing an inch over thirty miles an hour."

The animal instinct that had protected his life through many years of violence made him wary enough to have his hand on the butt of the revolver in the left pocket of his raincoat as he got out of the car. The policeman pushed the motorcycle up onto its stand. He took off his gloves and turned, his raincoat very wet.

"And what can we do you for, officer, on this fine morning?" Billy asked insolently.

The policeman's hand came out of the right pocket of his raincoat holding a Walther, a Carswell silencer screwed onto the end of the barrel. White recognized all this in the last moment of his violent life, as he frantically attempted to draw his revolver. The bullet ripped into his heart, knocking him back against the car. He bounced off and fell on his face in the road.

In the rear seat, Levin was paralyzed with horror, yet he was not afraid for there was an inevitability to all this, as if it was somehow ordained. The policeman opened the door and looked in. He paused, then pushed up the goggles.

Levin gazed at him in astonishment. "Dear God in heaven," he whispered in Russian, "It's you."

"Yes," Cuchulain answered in the same language. "I'm afraid it is," and he shot him in the head, the Walther making no more than an angry cough.

He pocketed the weapon, walked back to the bike, pulled it off its stand, and rode away. It was no more than five minutes later that a van making morning deliveries of bread to the village came across the carnage. The driver and his assistant got out of their van and approached the scene with trepidation. The driver leaned down to look at White. There was a slight groan from the rear of the car and he glanced quickly inside.

"My God!" he cried. "There's another in here and he's still alive. Take the van and get down to the village quick as you can and fetch the ambulance from the hospice."

WHEN DEVLIN REACHED the foyer, they were pushing Viktor Levin on a trolley into the receiving room.

"Sister Anne-Marie's on ward three. She'll be right down," he heard one of the ambulancemen tell the young sister in charge. The driver of the bread van stood there helplessly, blood on one sleeve of his overall coat. He was shaking badly. Devlin lit a cigarette and handed it to him. "What happened?"

"God knows. We found this car a couple of miles up the road. One man was dead beside it and him in the back. They're bringing the other in now.

As Devlin, filled with a terrible premonition, turned toward the door, the ambulancemen hurried in with Billy White's body, his face plain to see. The young sister came out of the receiving room and went next door to check White. Devlin stepped in quickly and approached the trolley on which Levin still lay, moaning softly, blood congealing in a terrible head wound.

Devlin leaned down. "Professor Levin, can you hear me?" Levin opened his eyes. "I am Liam Devlin. What happened?"

Levin tried to speak, reached out one hand and got hold of the lapel of Devlin's jacket. "I recognized him. It was Cuchulain. He's here."

His eyes rolled, there was a rattle in his throat and, as his grip slackened, Sister Anne-Marie hurried in. She pushed Devlin to one side and leaned over Levin, searching for a pulse. After awhile, she stepped back. "You know this man?"

"No," Devlin told her, which was true in a sense.

"Not that it would matter if you did," she said. "He's dead. A miracle he didn't die instantly, with a head wound like that."

She brushed past him and went next door where they had taken White. Devlin stood looking down at Levin, thinking of what Fox had told him of the old man. Of the years of waiting to get out. And this was how it had ended. He felt angry, then, at the brutal black humor of life that could allow such a thing to happen.

HARRY FOX HAD only just arrived back at Cavendish Square, had hardly got his coat off, when the phone rang. Ferguson listened, face grave, then placed a hand over the mouthpiece. "Liam Devlin. It seems the car with your man, Billy White, and Levin, was ambushed just outside Kilrea. White was killed instantly, Levin died later in the hospice at Kilrea."

Fox said. "Did Liam get to see him?"

"Yes. Levin told him it was Cuchulain. That he recognized him."

Fox threw his coat on the nearest chair. "I don't understand, sir."

"Neither do I, Harry." Ferguson said into the mouthpiece, "I'll get back to you, Devlin."

He put the receiver down and turned, hands out to the fire. Fox said, "It doesn't make sense. How would he have known?"

"Some sort of leak, Harry, at the IRA end of things. They never keep their mouths shut."

"The thing is, sir, what do we do about it?"

"More important, what do we do about Cuchulain?" Ferguson said. "That gentleman is really beginning to annoy me."

"But there isn't much we can do now, not with Levin gone. After all, he was the only person who had any idea what the bastard looked like."

"Actually, that isn't quite true." Ferguson said. "You're forgetting Tanya Voraninova, who at this precise moment is in Paris. Ten days, four concerts, and that opens up a very interesting possibility."

ABOUT THE SAME time, Harry Cussane was at his desk in the press office of the Catholic secretariat in Dublin talking to Monsignor Halloran, who was responsible for public relations.

From his comfortable chair, Halloran said, "It's a terrible thing that such a significantly historical event as the Holy Father's visit to England should be put in such jeopardy. Just think of it, Harry, His Holiness at Canterbury Cathedral. The first pope in history to visit it. And now . . ."

"You think it won't come off?" Cussane asked.

"Well, they're still talking away in Rome, but that's how it looks to me. Why, do you know something I don't?"

"No," Cussane told him. He pushed up a typed sheet. "I've had this from London—his planned itinerary, so they are still acting as if he's coming." He ran an eye over it. "Arrives on the morning of May 28 at Gatwick Airport. Mass at Westminster

Cathedral in London. Meets the queen at Buckingham Palace in the afternoon."

"And Canterbury?"

"That's the following day—Saturday. He starts early with a meeting with religious at a London college. Mainly monks and nuns from enclosed orders. Then by helicopter to Canterbury, stopping at Stokely Hall on the way. That's unofficial, by the way."

"For what reason?"

"The Stokelys were one of the great Catholic families who managed to survive Henry VIII and hang on to their faith over the centuries. The National Trust owns the house now, but it contains a unique feature. The family's private chapel. The oldest Catholic church of any description in England. His Holiness wishes to pray there. Afterward, Canterbury."

"All of which, at the moment, is on paper only," Halloran said.

The phone rang. Cussane picked it up. "Press office, Cussane here." His face grew grave. He said, "Is there anything I can do?" A pause. "I'll see you later then."

Halloran said, "Problems?"

Cussane replaced the receiver. "A friend from Kilrea. Liam Devlin of Trinity College. It seems there's been a shooting incident outside the village. Two men taken to the hospice. Both dead."

Halloran crossed himself. "Political, is it?"

"One of them was a known member of the IRA."

"Will you be needed? Go if you must."

"Not necessary." Cussane smiled bleakly. "They need a coroner now, Monsignor, not a priest. I've plenty to do here, anyway."

"Yes, of course. Well, I'll leave you to it."

Halloran went out, and Cussane lit a cigarette and went and stood at the window, looking down into the street. Finally, he turned, sat at his desk, and got on with some work.

PAUL CHERNY HAD rooms at Trinity College, which being, as so many people considered, at the very center of Dublin, suited him very well indeed. But then, everything about that extraordinary city commended itself to him.

His defection had been at Maslovsky's express orders. A KGB general was not to be argued with. He was to defect in Ireland, that had been the plan. One of the universities was certain to offer him a post, his international reputation would assure that. He would then be in a perfect position to act as Cuchulain's control. Difficult in the early days with no Soviet embassy in Dublin and the necessity to always work through London, but now that had been taken care of and his KGB contacts at the Dublin embassy gave him a direct link with Moscow.

Yes, the years had been good, and Dublin was the kind of paradise he'd always dreamed of. Intellectual freedom, stimulating company, and the city—the city he had grown to love. He was thinking these things as he left Trinity that afternoon, walked through College Green, and made toward the river.

Michael Murphy followed at a discreet distance, and Cherny, unaware that he was being tailed, walked briskly along beside the Liffey until he reached Usher's Quay. There was a rather ugly Victorian church in red brick, and he moved up the steps and went inside. Murphy paused to examine the board with the peeling gold paint. It said *Our Lady, Queen of the Universe.* Underneath were the times of mass. Confessions were heard at one o'clock and five on weekdays. Murphy pushed open the door and entered.

It was the sort of place that merchant money had been poured into back in the prosperous days of the quays during the nineteenth century. There was lots of Victorian stained glass and fake gargoyles, and the usual smell of candles and incense. Half a dozen people walked by a couple of confessional boxes and Paul Cherny had joined them, seating himself on the end of the bench.

"Jesus!" Murphy muttered in surprise. "The bugger must

have seen the light." He positioned himself behind a pillar and waited.

It was perhaps fifteen or twenty minutes before Cherny's turn came. He slipped into the oaken confessional box, closed the door, and sat down, his head close to the grill.

"Bless me, Father, for I have sinned," he said in Russian.

"Very funny, Paul," the reply came from the other side of the grill in the same language. "Now let's see if you can still smile when you've heard what I've got to say."

When Cuchulain was finished, Cherny said, "What are we going to do?"

"No need to panic. They don't know who I am, and they aren't likely to find out now that I've disposed of Levin."

"But me?" Cherny said. "If Levin told them about Drumore all those years ago, he must have told them of my part in it."

"Of course. You're under surveillance now. IRA variety, not British Intelligence, so I wouldn't worry just yet. Get in touch with Moscow. Maslovsky should know about this. He might want to pull us out. I'll phone you again tonight. And don't start worrying about your tail. I'll take care of it."

Cherny went out and Cuchulain watched through a crack in the door as Michael Murphy slipped from behind the pillar and followed him. There was a bang as the sacristy door opened and shut, and an old cleaning woman came down the aisle as the priest in alb and black cassock, a violet stole around his neck, came out of the confessional box.

"Are you finished, Father?"

"I am so, Ellie." Harry Cussane turned, a smile of great charm on his face as he slipped off the stole and started folding it.

MURPHY, HAVING NO reason to think that Cherny was doing anything other than returning to the college, stayed some distance behind him. Cherny stopped and entered a telephone box. He wasn't in it for long and Murphy, who had paused under a tree as if sheltering from the rain, went after him again.

A car drew into the curb in front of him and the driver, a priest, got out, went around and looked at the nearside front tire. He turned and, catching sight of Murphy, said, "Have you got a minute?"

Murphy slowed, protesting, "I'm sorry, Father, but I've an appointment."

And then the priest's hand was on his arm, and Murphy felt the muzzle of the Walther dig painfully into his side. "Easy does it, there's a lad. Just keep walking."

Cussane pushed him to the top of the stone steps that went down to a decaying wooden jetty below. They moved along its broken planks, footsteps echoing hollowly. There was a boat house with a broken roof, holes in the floor. Murphy wasn't afraid, but ready for action, waiting his chance.

"That'll do," Cussane said.

Murphy stayed, his back toward him, one hand on the butt of the automatic in his raincoat pocket. "Are you a real priest?" he asked.

"Oh, yes," Cussane told him. "Not a very good one, I'm afraid, but real enough."

Murphy turned slowly. His hand came up out of the raincoat, already too late. The Walther coughed, and the first bullet caught Murphy in the shoulder, spinning him around. The second bullet drove him forward headfirst into a ragged hole in the floor, and he plunged down into the dark water below.

DIMITRI LUBOV, WHO was supposedly a commercial attaché at the Soviet embassy, was, in fact, a captain in the KGB. On receiving Cherny's carefully worded message, he left his office and went to a cinema in the city center. It was not only relatively dark in there, but reasonably private, for few people went to the cinema in the afternoon. He sat in the back row and waited, and Cherny joined him twenty minutes later.

"Is it urgent, Paul?" Lubov asked. "Not often we meet between fixed days."

"Urgent enough," Cherny said. "Cuchulain is blown. Maslovsky must be informed as soon as possible. He may want to pull us out."

"Of course," Lubov said, alarmed. "I'll see to it as soon as I get back, but hadn't you better fill me in on the details?"

DEVLIN WAS WORKING in his study at the cottage, marking a thesis on T. S. Eliot submitted by one of his students, when the phone rang.

Ferguson said, "It's a fine bloody mess. Someone must have coughed at your end. Your IRA cronies are not exactly the most reliable people in the world."

"Sticks and stones will get you nowhere," Devlin told him. "What do you want?"

"Tanya Voraninova," Ferguson said. "Harry told you about her?"

"The little girl from Drumore who was adopted by this Maslovsky character. What about her?"

"She's in Paris at the moment to give a series of piano concerts. The thing is, being the foster daughter to a KGB general gives her a lot of leeway. I mean, she's considered an excellent risk. I thought you might go and see her. There's an evening flight from Dublin direct to Paris. Only two and a half hours, Air France."

"And what in the hell am I supposed to do? Get her to defect?"

"You never know. When she hears the whole story, she might want to. See her anyway, Liam. It can't do any harm."

"Well, why not?" Devlin said. "A little breath of French air might do me good."

"I knew you'd see it my way," Ferguson said. "Report to the Air France desk at Dublin Airport. They've got a reservation. When you arrive at Charles de Gaulle, you'll be met by one of my chaps based in Paris. Fella called Hunter—Tony Hunter. He'll see to everything."

"I'm sure he will," Devlin said and rang off.

He packed a bag quickly, feeling unaccountably cheerful, and was just pulling on his trench coat when the phone went again. It was Martin McGuinness. "A bad business, Liam. What exactly happened?"

Devlin told him and when he was finished, McGuinness exploded. "So, he exists, this bastard?"

"It would appear so, but more worrying from your point of view is how did he know Levin was due in? The one man who might be able to identify him."

"Why ask me?"

"Because Ferguson thinks there's been a leak at your end."

"Well, screw Ferguson."

"I wouldn't advise it, Martin. Listen, I've got to go. I've a flight to Paris to catch."

"Paris? What's there, for Christ's sake?"

"A girl called Tanya Voraninova, who might be able to identify Cuchulain. I'll be in touch."

He put down the receiver. As he picked up his bag, there was a tap on the French windows. They opened and Harry Cussane entered.

Devlin said, "Sorry, Harry, I must fly or I'll miss my plane."

"Where on earth are you going?" Cussane demanded.

"Paris." Devlin grinned and opened the front door. "Champagne, loose women, incredible food. Don't you think it's just possible you joined the wrong club, Harry?"

The door banged. Cussane listened to the engine of the car start up, turned, and ran out through the French windows, around to his cottage at the back of the hospice. He hurried upstairs to the secret room behind the water tanks in the roof, where he had the eavesdropping equipment. Quickly, he ran back the tape and listened to the various conversations Devlin had had that day until he came, in the end, to the important one.

By then, of course, it was too late. He cursed softly, went down to use the phone, and rang Paul Cherny's number.

Six

*I*N the sacristy of the village church later as he robed for evening mass, Cussane examined himself in the mirror. Like an actor getting ready for a performance. Next thing, he'd be reaching for the makeup. Who am I, he thought? Who am I, really? Cuchulain, mass murderer, or Harry Cussane, priest. Mikhail Kelly didn't seem to enter into it any more. Only an echo of him now, like a half-forgotten dream.

For more than twenty years he had lived multiple lives, and yet the separate persona had never inhabited his body. They were roles to be played out as the script dictated, then discarded.

He slipped the stole around his neck and whispered to his alter ego in the mirror, "In God's House I am God's priest," and he turned and went out.

Later, standing at the altar with the candles flickering and the organ playing, there was genuine passion in his voice as he cried, "I confess to Almighty God and to you, my brothers and sisters, that I have sinned through my own fault."

And when he struck his breast, asking blessed Mary ever

Virgin to pray for him to the Lord our God, there were sudden hot tears in his eyes.

AT CHARLES DE Gaulle Airport, Tony Hunter waited beside the exit from customs and immigration. He was a tall man in his mid-thirties with stooped shoulders. The soft brown hair was too long, the tan linen suit creased, and he smoked a Gitaines cigarette without once taking it from his mouth as he read *Paris Soir* and kept an eye on the exit. After a while, Devlin appeared. He wore a black Burberry trench coat, an old black felt hat slanted over one ear, and carried one bag.

Hunter, who had pulled Devlin's photo and description off the wire, went to meet him. "Professor Devlin? Tony Hunter. I've got a car waiting." They walked toward the exit. "Was it a good flight?"

"There's no such thing," Devlin told him. "About a thousand years ago, I flew from Germany to Ireland in a Dornier bomber on behalf of England's enemies and jumped by parachute from six thousand feet. I've never got over it."

They reached Hunter's Peugeot in the car park and as they drove away, Hunter said, "You can stay the night with me. I've got an apartment on the Avenue Foch."

"Doing well for yourself, son, if you've living there. I didn't know Ferguson handed out bags of gold."

"You know Paris well?"

"You could say that."

"The apartment's my own, not the department's. My father died last year. Left me rather well off."

"What about the girl? Is she staying at the Soviet embassy?"

"Good God, no. They've got her at the Ritz. She's something of a star, you see. Plays rather well. I heard her do a Mozart concerto the other night. Forgotten which one, but she was excellent."

"They tell me she's free to come and go?"

"Oh, yes, absolutely. The fact that her foster father is General

Maslovsky takes care of that. I followed her all over the place this morning. Luxembourg Gardens, then lunch on one of those boat trips down the Seine. From what I hear, her only commitment tomorrow is a rehearsal at the Conservatoire during the afternoon."

"Which means the morning is the time to make contact?"

"I should have thought so." They were well into Paris by now, just passing the Gare du Nord. Hunter added, "There's a bagman due in from London on the breakfast shuttle with documentation that Ferguson's having rushed through. Forged passport. Stuff like that."

Devlin laughed out loud. "Does he think all I have to do is ask and she'll come?" He shook his head. "Mad, that one."

"All in how it's put to her," Hunter suggested.

"True," Devlin told him. "On the other hand, it would probably be a damned sight easier to slip something into her tea."

It was Hunter's turn to laugh now. "You know, I like you, Professor, and I'd started off by not wanting to."

"And why could that be?" Devlin wondered, interested.

"I was a captain in the Rifle Brigade. Belfast, Derry, South Armagh."

"Ah, I see what you mean."

"Four tours between 1972 and 1978."

"And that was four tours too many."

"Exactly. Frankly, as far as I'm concerned, they can give Ulster back to the Indians."

"The best idea I've heard tonight," Liam Devlin told him cheerfully, and he lit a cigarette and sprawled back in the passenger seat, felt hat tilted over his eyes.

AT THAT MOMENT in his office at KGB headquarters in Dzerhinsky Square, Moscow, Lieutenant General Ivan Maslovsky was seated at his desk, thinking about the Cuchulain affair. Cherny's message, passed on by Lubov, had reached Moscow only a couple of hours earlier. For some reason it made him think back all those years to Drumore in the Ukraine and Kelly in the rain with a gun in his hand, the man who wouldn't do as he was told.

The door opened and his aide, Captain Igor Kurbsky, came in with a cup of coffee for him. Maslovsky drank it slowly. "Well, Igor, what do you think?"

"I think Cuchulain has done a magnificent job, Comrade General, for so very many years. But now . . ."

"I know what you mean," Maslovsky said. "Now that British Intelligence knows he exists, it's only a matter of time until they run him down."

"And Cherny they could pull in at any time."

There was a knock at the door and an orderly appeared with a cable. Kurbsky took it and dismissed him. "It's for you, sir. From Lubov in Dublin."

"Read it!" Maslovsky ordered.

The gist of the message was that Devlin was proceeding to Paris with the intention of meeting with Tanya Voroninova. At the mention of his foster daughter's name, Maslovsky stood up and snatched the cable from Kurbsky's hands. The enormous affection the general felt for his foster daughter was no secret especially since the death of his wife. In some quarters he was known as a butcher, but Tanya Voroninova he truly loved.

"Right," he said to Kurbsky, "who's our best man at the Paris embassy? Belov, isn't it?"

"Yes, Comrade."

"Send a message tonight. Tanya's concert tour is canceled. No arguments. Full security as regards her person until she can be returned safely to Moscow."

"And Cuchulain?"

"Has served his purpose. A great pity."

"Do we pull him in?"

"No, not enough time. This one needs instant action. Cable Lubov at once in Dublin. I want Cuchulain eliminated. Cherny also, and the sooner the better."

"If I might point out, I don't think Lubov has had much experience on the wet side of things."

"He's had the usual training, hasn't he? In any case, they won't be expecting it, which should make the whole thing rather easy."

IN PARIS, THE coding machine in the intelligence section of the Soviet embassy started whirring. The operator waited until the message had passed line-by-line across the screen. She carefully unloaded the magnetic tape that had recorded the message and took it to the night supervisor.

"This is an eyes-only message from KGB, Moscow, for Colonel Belov."

"He's out of town," the supervisor said. "Lyons, I think. Due back tomorrow afternoon. You'll have to hold it anyway. It requires his personal key to decode it."

The operator logged the tape, placed it in her data drawer, and went back to work.

IN DUBLIN, DIMITRI Lubov had been enjoying an evening at the Abbey Theatre, an excellent performance of Brendan Behan's *The Hostage*. Supper afterward at a well-known fish restaurant on the Quays meant that it was past midnight when he returned to the embassy and found the message from Moscow.

Even when he'd read it for the third time, he still couldn't believe it. Within the next twenty-four hours, he was to dispose of not only Cherny, but Cussane too. His hands were sweating, trembling slightly, which was hardly surprising for in spite of his years in the KGB and all that dedicated training, the plain fact was that Dimitri Lubov had never killed anyone in his entire life.

TANYA VORONINOVA CAME out of the bathroom of her suite at the Ritz as the room waiter brought her breakfast tray in.

105

Tea, toast, and honey, which was exactly what she'd asked for. She wore a khaki green jumpsuit and brown boots of soft leather, and the combination gave her a vaguely military appearance. She was a small, dark, intense girl with untidy black hair, which she constantly had to push back from her eyes. She regarded it with disfavor in the gilt mirror above the fireplace and twisted it into a bun at the nape of the neck, then she sat down and started on breakfast.

There was a knock on the door and her tour secretary, Natasha Rubenova, came in. She was a pleasant, gray-haired woman in her mid-forties. "How are you feeling this morning?"

"Fine. I slept very well."

"Good. You're wanted at the Conservatoire at two-thirty. Complete run-through."

"No problem," Tanya said.

"Are you going out this morning?"

"Yes, I'd like to spend some time at the Louvre. We've been so busy during this visit that it might be my last opportunity."

"Do you want me to come with you?"

"No thanks. I'll be fine. I'll see you back here for lunch at one o'clock."

IT WAS A fine soft morning when she left the hotel and went down the steps at the front entrance. Devlin and Hunter were waiting in the Peugeot on the far side of the boulevard.

"Looks as if she's walking," Hunter said.

Devlin nodded, "Follow her for a while, then we'll see."

Tanya carried a canvas bag slung from her left shoulder, and she walked at quite a fast pace, enjoying the exercise. She was playing Rachmaninov's Fourth Piano Concerto that night. The piece was a particular favorite so that she had none of the usual nervous tension that she sometimes experienced, like most artists, before a big concert.

But then, she was something of an old hand at the game now. Since her successes in both the Leeds and Tschaikovsky festivals, she had established an international reputation. There had been very little time for anything else. On the one occasion she had fallen in love, she'd been foolish enough to choose a young military doctor on attachment to an airborne brigade. He'd been killed in action in Afghanistan the year before.

The experience, though harrowing, had not broken her. She had given one of her greatest performances on the night that she had received the news, but she had withdrawn from men, there was no doubt about that. There was too much hurt involved, and it would not have needed a particularly bright psychiatrist to find out why. In spite of success and fame and the privileged life her position brought her; in spite of having constantly at her shoulder the powerful presence of Maslovsky, she was still, in many ways, a little girl on her knees in the rain beside the father so cruelly torn away from her.

ALONG THE CHAMPS Elysées and into la place de la Concorde she went, walking steadily.

"Jesus, but she likes her exercise," Devlin observed.

She turned into the cool peace of the Jardin des Tuileries and Hunter nodded. "I thought she would. My hunch is that she's making for the Louvre. You go after her on foot from here. I'll drive around, park the car, and wait for you at the main entrance."

There was a Henry Moore exhibit in the Tuileries Gardens. She browsed around it for a little while and Devlin stayed back, but it was obvious that nothing there had much appeal for her and she moved on through the gardens to the great Palais du Louvre itself.

Tanya Voroninova was certainly selective. She moved from gallery to gallery, choosing only works of acknowledged genius, and Devlin followed at a discreet distance. From the Victory of Samothrace at the top of the Daru staircase by the main entrance, she moved on to the Venus de Milo. She spent some time in the Rembrandt Gallery on the first floor, then stopped to look at what is possibly the most famous picture in the world—Leonardo da Vinci's *Mona Lisa.*

Devlin moved in close. "Is she smiling, would you say?" he tried in English.

"What do you mean?" she asked in the same language.

"Oh, it's an old superstiton in the Louvre that some mornings she doesn't smile."

She turned to look at him. "That's absurd."

"But you're not smiling, either," Devlin said. "Sweet Jesus, are you worried you'd crack the plate?"

"This is total nonsense," she said, but smiled all the same.

"When you're on your dignity, your mouth turns down at the corners," he said. "It doesn't help."

"My looks, you mean? A matter of indifference to me."

He stood there, hands in the pockets of the Burberry trench coat, the black felt hat slanted over one ear, and the eyes the most vivid blue she had ever seen. There was an air of insolent good humor to him and a kind of self-mockery that was rather attractive, in spite of the fact that he must have been twice her age, at least. There was a sudden aching excitement that was difficult to control, and she took a deep breath to steady herself.

"Excuse me," she said and walked away.

Devlin gave her some room and then followed. A darling girl and frightened, for some reason. Interesting to know why that should be.

She made her way to the Grande Galerie, finally stopped before El Greco's *Christ on the Cross,* and stood there for quite some time gazing up at the gaunt mystical figure, showing no acknowledgment of Devlin's presence when he moved beside her.

"And what does it say to you?" he asked gently. "Is there love there?"

"No," she said. "A rage against dying, I think. Why are you following me?"

"Am I?"

"Since the Tuileries Gardens."

"Really? Well, if I was, I can't be very good at it."

"Not necessarily. You are someone to look at twice," she said simply.

"And you, my love, are heart of corn." Strange how suddenly she felt like crying. Wanted to reach out to the incredible warmth of that voice. He took her arm and said gently, "All the time in the world, girl dear. You still haven't told me what El Greco says to you."

"I was not raised a Christian," she said. "I see no savior on the cross, but a great human being in torment, destroyed by little people. And you?"

"I love your accent," Devlin said. "Reminds me of Garbo in the movies when I was a wee boy, but that was a century or so before your time."

"Garbo is not unknown to me," she said, "and I'm duly flattered. However, you still have not told me what it says for you?"

"A profound question when one considers the day," Devlin told her. "At seven o'clock this morning, they celebrated a rather special mass in St. Peter's Basilica in Rome. The pope together with cardinals from Britain and the Argentine."

"And will this achieve anything?"

"It hasn't stopped the British navy proceeding on it's merry way or Argentine Skyhawks from attacking it."

"Which means?"

"That the Almighty, if He exists at all, is having one hell of a joke at our expense."

Tanya frowned. "Your accent intrigues me. You are not English, I think?"

"Irish, my love."

"But I thought the Irish were supposed to be extremely religious?"

"And that's a fact. My old Aunt Hannah had callouses on her knees from praying. She used to take me to mass three times a week when I was a boy in Drumore."

Tanya Voroninova went very still. "Where did you say?"

"Drumore. That's a little market town in Ulster. The church there was Holy Name. What I remember most are my uncle and his cronies, straight out from mass and down the road to Murphy's Select Bar."

She turned, her face very pale now. "Who are you?"

"Well, one thing's for sure, girl dear." He ran a hand lightly over her dark hair, "I'm not Cuchulain, last of the dark heroes."

Her eyes widened and there was a kind of anger as she plucked at his coat. "Who sent you?"

"In a manner of speaking, Viktor Levin."

"Viktor?" She looked bewildered. "But Viktor is dead. Died somewhere in Arabia a month or so ago. My father told me."

"General Maslovsky? Well, he would, wouldn't he? No, Viktor escaped. Defected, you might say. Ended up in London and then Dublin."

"He's well?"

"Dead," Devlin said brutally. "Murdered by Mikhail Kelly or Cuchulain or the dark bloody hero or whoever you want to call him. The same man who shot your father dead twenty-three years ago in the Ukraine."

She sagged against him. His arm went around her in support, strong and confident. "Lean on me, just put one foot in front of the other, and I'll take you outside and get you some air."

THEY SAT ON a bench in the Tuileries Gardens and Devlin took out his old silver case and offered her a cigarette. "Do you use these things?"

"No."

"Good for you, they'd stunt your growth and you with your green years ahead of you."

Somewhere, he'd said those selfsame words before, a long, long time ago. Another girl very much like this one. Not beautiful, not in any conventional sense, and yet always there would be the compulsion to turn and take a second look. There was pain in that memory that even time had not managed to erase.

"You're a strange man," she said, "for a secret agent. That's what you are, I presume?"

He laughed out loud, the sound clear so that Tony Hunter, reading a newspaper on a bench on the other side of the Henry Moore exhibition, glanced up sharply.

"God save the day." Devlin took out his wallet and extracted a scrap of pasteboard. "My card. Strictly for formal occasions, I assure you."

She read it out loud. "Professor Liam Devlin, Trinity College, Dublin." She looked up. "Of what?"

"English literature. I use the term loosely, as academics do, so it would include Oscar Wilde, Shaw, O'Casey, Brendan Behan, James Joyce, Yeats. A mixed bag there, Catholics and Prods, but all Irish. Could I have the card back, by the way? I'm running short. . . ."

He replaced it in his wallet. She said, "But how would a professor of an ancient and famous university come to be involved in an affair like this?"

"You've heard of the Irish Republican Army?"

"Of course."

"I've been a member of that organization since I was sixteen years old. No longer active, as we call it. I've some heavy reservations about the way the Provisionals have been handling some aspects of the present campaign."

"Don't tell me, let me guess." She smiled. "You are a romantic at heart, I think, Professor Devlin?"

"Is that a fact?"

"Only a romantic could wear anything so absurdly wonderful as that black felt hat. But there is more, of course. No bombs in restaurants to perhaps blow up women and children. You would shoot a man without hesitation. Welcome the hopeless odds of meeting highly trained soldiers face-to-face."

Devlin was beginning to feel distinctly uneasy. "Do you tell me?"

"Oh, I do, Professor Devlin. You see I think I recognize you now. The true revolutionary, the failed romantic who didn't really want it to stop."

"And what would *it* be, exactly?"

"Why, the game, Professor. The mad dangerous wonderful game that alone makes life worth living for a man like you. Oh, you may like the cloistered life of the lecture room or tell yourself that you do, but at the first chance to sniff powder . . ."

"Can I take time to catch my breath?"

"And worst of all," she carried on relentlessly, "is your need to have it both ways. To have all the fun, but to also have a nice clean revolution where no innocent bystanders get hurt."

She sat there, arms folded in front of her in an inimitable gesture as if she would hold herself in, and Devlin said, "Have you left anything out, would you say?"

She smiled tightly. "Sometimes I get very wound up like a clock spring and I hold it until the spring goes."

"And it all bursts out and you're into your imitation of Freud," he told her. "I bet that goes down big over the vodka and strawberries after dinner at old Maslovsky's summer *dacha*."

Her face tightened. "You will not make jokes about him. He has been very good to me. The only father I have known."

"Perhaps," Devlin said. "But it wasn't always so."

She gazed at him angrily. "All right, Professor Devlin, we have fenced enough. Perhaps it is time you told me why you are here."

HE OMITTED NOTHING, starting with Viktor Levin and Tony Villiers in the Yemen and ending with the murder of Billy

White and Levin outside Kilrea. When he was finished, she sat there for a long moment without saying anything.

"Levin said you remembered Drumore and the events surrounding your father's death," Devlin said gently.

"Like a nightmare, it drifts to the surface of consciousness now and then. Strange, but it is as if it's happening to someone else and I'm looking down at the little girl on her knees in the rain beside her father's body."

"And Mikhail Kelly or Cuchulain as they call him? You remember him?"

"Till my dying day," she said flatly. "It was such a strange face, the face of a ravaged young saint and he was so kind to me, so gentle—that was the strangest thing of all."

Devlin took her arm. "Let's walk for a while." They started along the path, and he said, "Has Maslovsky ever discussed those events with you?"

"No."

Her arm under his hand was going rigid. "Easy, girl dear," he said softly, "and tell me the most important thing of all. Have you ever tried to discuss it with him?"

"No, damn you!" She pulled away, turning, her face full of passion.

"But then, you wouldn't want to do that, would you?" he said. "That would be opening a can of worms with a vengeance."

She stood there looking at him, holding herself in again. "What do you want of me, Professor Devlin? You want me to defect like Viktor? Wade through all those thousands of photos in the hope that I might recognize him?"

"That's a reasonable facsimile of the original mad idea."

"Why should I?" She sat on a nearby bench and pulled him down. "Let me tell you something. You make a big mistake, you people in the West, when you assume that all Russians are straining at the leash, anxious only for a chance to get out. I love my country. I like it there. It suits me. I'm a respected artist. I can travel wherever I like. Now, this morning, here in Paris. No KGB—no men in black overcoats watching my every move. I go where I please."

"With a foster father a lieutenant general in the KGB in command of Department-5, among other things, I'd be surprised if you didn't. It used to be called Department-13, by the way. Distinctly unlucky for some and then Maslovsky reorganized it in 1968. It could best be described as an assassination bureau, but then, no well-run organization should be without one."

"Just like your IRA?" She leaned forward. "How many men have you killed for a cause you believed in, Professor?"

He smiled gently and touched her cheek in a strangely intimate gesture. "Point taken, but I can see I'm wasting your time. You might as well have this, though."

He took a largish buff envelope from his pocket, the one that had been delivered by Ferguson's bagman that morning, and placed it in her lap.

"What is it?" she demanded.

"The people in London, being ever hopeful, have made you a present of a British passport with a brand-new identity. Your photo looks smashing. There's cash in there—French francs—and details of alternative ways of getting to London."

"I don't need it."

"Well, you've got it now. And this." He took his card from his wallet and gave it to her. "I'll fly back to Dublin this afternoon. No point in hanging around." Which wasn't strictly true, for the bagman from London had flown in with more than the package containing the false passport. There had also been a message from Ferguson for Devlin personally. McGuinness and the chief of staff were hopping mad. As far as they were concerned, the leak was none of their doing. They wanted out, and Devlin was to mend fences.

She put the packet and the card into her shoulder bag with some reluctance. "I'm sorry. You came a long way for nothing."

"You've got my number," he said. "Call any time." He stood up. "Who knows, you just might start asking questions."

"I think not, Professor Devlin." She held out her hand. "Goodbye."

Devlin held it for a moment, then turned and walked back along the gardens to where Hunter was sitting. "Come on!" he said. "Let's get moving!"

Hunter scrambled to his feet and trailed after him. "What happened?"

"Nothing," Devlin told him as they reached the car. "Not a bloody thing. She didn't want to know. Now let's go back to your place so that I can get my bag, then you can take me up to Charles de Gaulle. With luck, I might make the afternoon flight to Dublin."

"You're going back?"

"Yes, I'm going back," Liam Devlin said, and he sank down in his seat and tipped the back of his black felt hat over his eyes.

Behind them, Tanya Voroninova watched them go, turning out into the traffic of the rue de Rivoli. She stood there thinking about things for a moment, then moved out of the gardens and started to walk along the pavement, considering the extraordinary events of the morning. Liam Devlin was a dangerously attractive man, no doubt about it, but more than that, his story had been terribly disturbing for her, and events from a past perhaps best forgotten were trying to call to her, as if from a great distance.

She was aware of a car pulling into the curb ahead of her, a black Mercedes saloon. As she approached it, the rear door opened and Natasha Rubenova looked out. She seemed agitated. No, more than that—afraid.

"Tanya!"

Tanya turned toward her, "Natasha—what on earth are you doing here? What's happened?"

"Please, Tanya. Get in!"

There was a man sitting beside her, young and with a hard, impacable face. He wore a blue suit, dark blue tie, and white shirt. He also wore black leather gloves. The man in the passenger seat next to the chauffeur could have been his twin. They looked as if they might be employed by a high-class funeral firm, and Tanya felt slightly uneasy.

"What on earth is going on?"

In a second, the young man beside Natasha was out of the car, a hand taking Tanya above the left elbow in a grip, light but strong. "My name is Turkin—Peter Turkin, Comrade. My colleague is Lieutenant Ivan Shepilov. We are officers of GRU and you will come with us."

Soviet Military Intelligence. She was more than uneasy now. She was frightened and tried to pull away.

"Please, Comrade." His grip tightened. "You'll only hurt yourself by struggling and you have a concert tonight. We don't want to disappoint your fans."

There was something in his eyes, a hint of cruelty, of perversity, that was very disturbing. "Leave me alone!" She tried to strike him, and he blocked her blow with ease. "You'll answer for this. Don't you know who my father is?"

"Lieutenant General Ivan Maslovsky of the KGB, under whose direct orders I am acting now, so be a good girl and do as you are told."

She had no will to resist, so great was the shock, and she found herself sitting next to Natasha, who was close to tears. Turkin got in on the other side.

"Back to the embassy!" he told the chauffeur.

As the Mercedes pulled away, Tanya held on to Natasha's hand tightly. For the first time since she was a little girl, she felt really and truly afraid.

Seven

NIKOLAI Belov was in his fifties, a handsome enough man with the slightly fleshy face of someone who enjoyed the good things of life more than was healthful for him. The kind of good Marxist whose dark suit and overcoat had been tailored on London's Savile Row. The silver hair and decadent good looks gave him the air of an aging and rather distinguished actor instead of a colonel in the KGB.

This trip to Lyons could hardly have been classified as essential business, but it had been possible to take his secretary, Irana Vronsky, with him. As she had been his mistress for some years now, it meant that they had enjoyed an extremely pleasurable couple of days, the memory of which had faded rather rapidly when he discovered the situation waiting for him on his return to the Soviet embassy.

He had hardly settled into his office when Irana came in. "There's an urgent communication from KGB Moscow for your-eyes-only."

"Who's it from?"

"General Maslovsky."

The name alone was enough to bring Belov to his feet. He went out and she followed him down to the coding office, where the operator got the relevant tape. Belov keyed in his personal code, the machine whirred, the operator tore off the printout sheet and handed it to him. Belov read it and swore softly. He took Irana by the elbow and hurried her out. "Get me Lieutenant Shepilov and Captain Turkin. Whatever else they're on, they drop."

BELOV WAS SEATED at his desk, working his way through papers, when the door opened and Irana Vronsky ushered in Tanya, Natasha Rubenova, and Shepilov and Turkin. Belov knew Tanya well. His official position at the embassy for some years had been senior cultural attaché, and, in that cover role, he had escorted her to parties on a number of occasions.

He stood up. "It's good to see you."

"I demand to know what's going on here," she told him passionately. "I'm pulled off the pavement by these bullyboys here and . . ."

"I'm sure Captain Turkin was only acting as he saw fit." Belov nodded to Irana. "Get the Moscow call now." He turned to Tanya. "Calm yourself and sit down." She stood there, mutinous, then glanced at Shepilov and Turkin standing against the wall, gloved hands folded in front of them. "Please," Belov said.

She sat and he offered her a cigarette. Such was her agitation that she took it, and Turkin moved in smoothly and lit it for her. His lighter was not only by Cartier, but gold. She coughed as the smoke caught at the back of her throat.

Belov said. "Now tell me what you did this morning."

"I walked to the Tuileries Gardens." The cigarette was helping, calming her down. She had control now, and that meant she could fight.

"And then?"

"I went to the Louvre."

"And whom did you talk to?"

The question was direct and meant to entrap her by causing an automatic response. To her own surprise, she found herself replying calmly, "I was on my own. I didn't go with anyone. Perhaps I didn't make that clear?"

"Yes, I know that," he said patiently. "But did you speak to anyone when you got there? Did anyone approach you?"

She managed a smile. "You mean, did anyone try to pick me up? No such luck. Considering its reputation, Paris can be very disappointing." She stubbed out the cigarette. "Look, what's going on, Nikolai? Can't you tell me?"

Belov had no reason to disbelieve her. In fact he very much wanted to accept what she said. He had, in effect, been absent from duty the night before. If he had not been, he would have received Maslovsky's directive then and Tanya Voroninova would not have been allowed to stir from her suite at the Ritz that morning. Certainly not unaccompanied.

The door opened and Irana entered. "General Maslovsky on line one."

Belov picked up the phone and Tanya tried to snatch it. "Let me speak to him."

Belov pulled away from her. "Belov here, General."

"Ah, Nikolai, she is with you now?"

"Yes, General." It was a measure of length of their friendship that Belov left out the Comrade.

"And she is under guard? She has spoken to no one?"

"Yes to both questions, General."

"And the man Devlin has not attempted to get in touch with her?"

"It would seem not. We've had the computer pull him out of the files for us. Pictures, everything. If he tries to get close, we'll know."

"Fine. Now give me Tanya."

Belov handed her the phone, and she almost snatched it from him. "Papa?"

She had called him so for years and his voice was warm and kind as always. "You are well?"

"Bewildered," she said. "No one will tell me what is happening."

"It is sufficient for you to know that for reasons that are unimportant now, you have become involved in a matter of state security. A very serious business indeed. You must be returned to Moscow as soon as can be."

"But my tour?"

The voice of the man at the other end of the line was suddenly cold, implacable, and detached. "Your tour will be canceled. You will appear at the Conservatoire tonight and fulfill that obligation. The first direct flight to Moscow is not until tomorrow morning, anyway. There will be a suitable press release. The old wrist injury giving problems again. A need for further treatment. That should do nicely."

All her life, or so it seemed, she had done his bidding, allowed him to shape her career, aware of his genuine concern and love, but this was new territory.

She tried again, "But Papa!"

"Enough of argument. You will do as you are told and you will obey Colonel Belov in everything. Put him back on."

She handed the phone to Belov mutely, her hand shaking. Never had he spoken to her like this. Was she no longer his daughter, but merely another Soviet subject to be ordered about at will?

"Belov, General." He listened for a moment or two, then nodded. "No problem." Belov looked at Tanya. "You can rely on me."

He put the phone down and opened a file on his desk. The photo he took from it and held up to her was of Liam Devlin, a few years younger perhaps, but Devlin unmistakably.

"This man is Irish. His name is Liam Devlin. He is a university professor from Dublin with a reputation for a certain Irish charm. It would be a mistake for anyone to take him lightly. He has been a member of the Irish Republican Army for all his adult

120

life. An important leader at one stage. He is also a ruthless and capable gunman who has killed many times. As a young man, he was an official executioner for his people."

Tanya took a deep breath. "And what has he to do with me?"

"That need not concern you. It is sufficient for you to know that he would very much like to talk to you and that we simply can't allow, can we Captain?"

Turkin showed no emotion. "No, Colonel."

"So," Belov told her. "You will return to the Ritz now, you and Comrade Rubenova, with Lieutenant Shepilov and Captain Turkin in attendance. You will not go out again until tonight's performance, when they will escort you to the Conservatoire. I will be there myself because of the reception afterward. The ambassador will be there and the president of the Republic, Monsieur Mitterand, himself. His presence is the only reason we are not canceling tonight's concert. Is there anything you don't understand in all this?"

"No," she said coldly, her face white and strained. "I understand only too well."

"Good," he said. "Then go back to the hotel now and get some rest."

She turned, Turkin opened the door for her, a slight, twisted smile on his mouth. She brushed past him, followed by a thoroughly frightened Natasha Rubenova, and Shepilov and Turkin followed them both.

IN KILREA, DEVLIN had not been long back at the cottage. He didn't have a regular housekeeper, just an old lady who came in twice a week, put the place into shape, and did the laundry, but he preferred it that way. He put the kettle on in the kitchen, went into the living room, and quickly made the fire. He had just put a match to it when there was a rap on the French window, and he turned to find McGuinness there.

Devlin unlocked it quickly. "That was fast. I'm only just back."

"So I was told within five minutes of your landing at the

airport." McGuinness was angry. "What's the score, Liam? What's going on?"

"What do you mean?"

"Levin and Billy, and now Mike Murphy's been pulled out of the Liffey with two bullets in him. It must have been Cuchulain. You know it and I know it. The thing is, how did he know?"

"I don't have any fast answer on that one." Devlin found two glasses and the Bushmills and poured. "Try this for size and calm down."

McGuinness swallowed a little. "A leak is what I think, at the London end. It's a well-known fact that the British Security Service has been heavily infiltrated by the Soviets for years."

"A slight exaggeration, but some truth to it." Devlin said. "As mentioned earlier, I know that Ferguson thinks the leak is from your people."

"To hell with that. I say we pull in Cherny and squeeze him dry."

"Maybe," Devlin said. "I'd have to check on that with Ferguson. Let's give it another day."

"All right," McGuinness said, with obvious reluctance. "I'll be in touch, Liam. Close touch." And he went out through the French windows.

Devlin poured another whisky and sat there savoring it and thinking, then he picked up the phone. He was about to dial, then hesitated. He replaced the receiver, got the black plastic box from the desk and switched it on. There was no positive response from the telephone, nor indeed from anywhere in the room.

"So," he said softly, "Ferguson or McGuinness. It's one or other of the buggers that it's down to."

He dialed the Cavendish Square number and the receiver was picked up at once. "Fox here."

"Is he there, Harry?"

"Not at the moment. How was Paris?"

"A nice girl. I liked her. Pretty confused. Nothing more I could do than present the facts. I gave her the material your bagman brought over. She took it, but I wouldn't be too sanguine."

"I never was," Fox said. "Will you be able to smooth things down in Dublin?"

"McGuinness has already been to see me. He wants to move on Cherny. Try some old-fashioned pressure."

"That might be the best solution."

"Jesus, Harry, but Belfast left its mark on you. Still, you could be right. I've stalled him for a day. If you want me, I'll be here. I gave the girl my card, by the way. She thought I was a failed romantic, Harry. Have you ever heard the like?"

"You give a convincing imitation, but I've never bought it."

Fox laughed and rang off. Devlin sat there for a while, a frown on his face, then there was another tap on the French window, it opened and Cussane entered.

"Harry," Devlin said. "You're sent from heaven. As I've often told you, you make the best scrambled eggs in the world."

"Flattery will get you anywhere." Cussane poured himself a drink. "How was Paris?"

"Paris?" Devlin said. "Sure and I was only joking. I've been to Cork. Some university business to do with the film festival. Had to stay over. I've just driven back, and I'm the original starving man."

"Right," Harry Cussane told him. "You lay the table and I'll scramble the eggs."

"You're a good friend, Harry," Devlin said.

Cussane paused in the door. "And why not, Liam. It's been a long time," and he smiled and went into the kitchen.

TANYA HAD A hot bath, hoping it would relax her. There was a knock at the door and Natasha Rubenova entered. "Coffee?"

"Thank you." Tanya lay back in the warm, foamy water and sipped the coffee gratefully.

Natasha pulled a small stool forward and sat down. "You must be very careful, my love. You understand me?"

"Strange," Tanya said. "No one has ever told me to be careful before."

It occurred to her then that she had always been sheltered from the cold, ever since the nightmare of Drumore, which surfaced only in her dreams. Maslovsky and his wife had been good parents. She had wanted for nothing. In a Marxist society that had been envisaged in the great days of Lenin and the revolution as giving power to the people, power had quickly become the prerogative of the few.

Soviet Russia had become an elitist society in which *who* you were was more important than *what* you were, and she, to all intents and purposes, was Ivan Maslovsky's daughter. The best housing, superior schools, her talent carefully nurtured. When she drove through Moscow to their country house, it was in a chauffeured limousine traveling in the traffic-free lane kept open for the use of the important people in the hierarchy. The delicacies that graced their table, the clothes she wore, all bought on a special card at GUM.

All this she had ignored, just as she had ignored the realities of the state trials of the Gulag. Just as she had turned from the even harsher reality of Drumore, her father dead on the street and Maslovsky in charge.

Natasha said, "You are all right?"

"Of course. Pass me a towel," Tanya wrapped it around herself. "Did you notice the lighter that Turkin used when he lit my cigarette?"

"Not particularly."

"It was by Cartier. Solid gold. Didn't some Western writer say, 'All animals are equal, but some are more equal than others'?"

"Please, darling," Nathasha Rubenova was obviously agitated. "You mustn't say things like that."

"You're right." Tanya smiled. "I'm angry, that's all. Now I think I would like to sleep. I must be fresh for tonight's concert."

They went into the other room and she got into bed, the towel still around her. "They're still out there?"

"Yes."

"I'll sleep now."

Natasha closed the curtains and went out. Tanya lay there in the darkness thinking about things. The events of the past few hours had been a shock in themselves, but strangely enough, the most significant thing had been the way in which she had been treated. Tanya Voroninova, internationally acclaimed artist, she who had received the Medal of Culture from Brezhnev himself, had felt the full weight of the State's hand. The truth was that for most of her life she had been somebody, thanks to Maslovsky. Now it had been made plain that when the chips were down, she was just another cipher.

It was enough. She switched on the bedside lamp, reached for her handbag, and took out the packet that Devlin had given her. The British passport was excellent. Issued, according to the date, three years before. There was an American visa. She had entered that country twice, also Germany, Italy, Spain, and France—one week previously. A nice touch. Her name was Joanna Frank, born in London, professional journalist. The photo, as Devlin had said, was an excellent likeness. There were even one or two personal letters with her London address in Chelsea, an American Express credit card, and a British driver's license. They'd thought of everything.

The alternative routes were clearly outlined. The direct plane flight from Paris to London wasn't on the list. Surprising how cool and calculating she was now. She would have only the slimmest of chances of getting away, if an opportunity presented itself at all, and she would be missed almost at once. They would have the airports covered instantly.

It seemed obvious that the same would be true of the ferry terminals at Calais and Boulougne. But the people in London had indicated another way, one that might possibly be overlooked. There was a train service from Paris to Rennes, changing there for St.-Malo on the Brittany coast. From there, a hydrofoil service to Jersey in the English Channel Islands. And from Jersey, there were several planes a day to London.

She got up quietly, tiptoed into the bathroom, and closed the door. Then she lifted the receiver on the wall telephone and called reception. They were extremely efficient. Yes, there was a night train to Rennes, leaving the Gare du Nord at eleven. In Rennes, there would be a delay, but she could be in St.-Malo for breakfast. Ample time to catch the hydrofoil.

She flushed the toilet and went back into the bedroom, rather pleased with herself for she hadn't quoted a room number or given her name. The inquiry could have come from any one of hundreds of guests.

"They're turning you into a jungle animal, Tanya," she told herself softly.

She got her holdall bag from the wardrobe, the one she used to take all her bits and pieces to the concerts. She couldn't secrete much in there. It would show. She thought about it for a while, then took out a pair of soft suede boots and rolled them up so they fitted neatly in the bottom of the bag. She next took a black cotton jumpsuit from its hanger, folded it, and laid it in the case. She placed the concerto score and the orchestra parts that she had been studying on top.

So, nothing more to be done. She went to the window and peered out. It was raining again and she shivered, suddenly lonely, and remembered Devlin and his strength. For a moment she thought of phoning him, but that was no good. Not from here. They would trace the call in minutes, the moment they started checking. She went back to bed and switched off the lamp. If only she could sleep for an hour or two. Then the face surfaced in her consciousness; Cuchulain's bone white face and dark eyes made sleep impossible.

SHE WORE A gown in black velvet for the concert. It was by

126

Balmain and very striking, with a matching jacket. The pearls at her neck and the earrings were supposed to be lucky, a gift from the Maslovskys before the finals of the Tschaikovsky competition, her greatest triumph.

Natasha came in and stood behind her at the dressing table. "Are you ready? Time's getting short." She put her hands on Tanya's shoulders. "You look lovely."

"Thank you. I've packed my case."

Natasha picked it up. "Have you put a towel in? You always forget." She zipped it open before Tanya could protest, then froze. She looked at the girl, eyes wide.

"Please?" Tanya said softly. "If I ever meant anything to you."

The older woman took a deep breath, went into the bathroom, and returned with a towel. She folded it, placed it in the case, and zipped it up. "So," she said. "We are ready."

"Is it still raining?"

"Yes."

"Then I shan't wear the velvet cape. The trench coat, I think."

Natasha took it from the wardrobe and draped it over her shoulders. Tanya felt her hands tighten for a moment. "Now we must go."

Tanya picked up the case and opened the door and went into the other room where Shepilov and Turkin waited. They both wore dinner jackets, because of the reception after the performance.

"If I may be permitted the observation, you look superb, Comrade." Turkin told her. "A credit to our country."

"Spare me the compliments, Captain," she said frostily. "If you wish to be of use, you may carry my case," and she handed it to him and walked out.

THE CONSERVATOIRE CONCERT hall was packed for this very special occasion. When she walked out on stage, the orchestra stood to greet her, and there was a storm of applause, the audience standing also, following President Mitterand's example.

She sat down, all noise faded. There was complete silence as the conductor waited, baton ready, and then it descended, and as the orchestra started to play, Tanya Voroninova's hands rippled over the keyboard.

She was filled with joy, an ecstasy almost, and she played as she had never played in her life before, with a new, vibrant energy—as if something that had been locked up in her for years was now released. The orchestra responded, trying to match her, so that at the end, in the dramatic finale to Rachmaninov's superb concerto, they fused into a whole that created an experience to be forgotten by few people there that night.

The cry from the audience was different from anything she had experienced in her life before. She stood facing them, the orchestra standing behind her, all clapping, and someone threw a flower on the stage, and more followed as women unpinned their corsages.

She went off to the side and Natasha, waiting, tears streaming down her cheeks, flung her arms around her. "Babushka, you were wonderful. The best I ever heard."

Tanya hugged her fiercely. "I know. My night, Natasha, the one night I can take on the whole world, if need be, and come out ahead of the game," and she turned and went back on stage to an audience that refused to stop applauding.

FRANCOIS MITTERAND, PRESIDENT of the Republic of France, took both her hands and kissed them warmly. "Mademoiselle, I salute you. An extraordinary performance."

"You are more than kind, Monsieur le President," she answered in his own language.

The crowd pressed close as champagne was offered, and cameras flashed as the president toasted her and then introduced her to the minister of culture and others. She was aware of Shepilov and Turkin by the door, Nikolai Belov talking to them, handsome in velvet evening jacket and ruffled shirt. He raised his glass in a toast and moved toward her. She glanced at her watch. It was just after ten. If she was to go, it must be soon.

Belov reached for her right hand and kissed it. "Tremendous stuff. You should get angry more often."

"A point of view." She took another glass of champagne from a waiter. "Everyone who is anyone in the diplomatic corps seems to be here. You must be pleased. Quite a triumph."

"Yes, but then, we Russians have always had a soul for music that is lacking in certain other peoples."

She glanced around. "Where's Natasha?"

"Over there with the press. Shall I get her?"

"Not necessary. I need to go to the dressing room for a moment, but I can manage perfectly well on my own."

"Of course." He nodded to Turkin who came across. "See Comrade Voroninova to her dressing room, Turkin. Wait for her and escort her back." He smiled at Tanya. "We don't want you to get hurt in the crush."

The crowd opened for her, people smiling, raising their glasses, and Turkin followed along the narrow corridor until they came to the dressing room.

She opened the door. "I presume I'm permitted to go to the toilet on my own?"

He smiled mockingly. "If you insist, Comrade."

He took out a cigarette and was lighting it as she closed the door. She didn't lock it, simply kicked off her shoes, pulled off the jacket, and unzipped her lovely dress, allowing it to fall to the floor. She had the jumpsuit out of her case in a moment, was into it within seconds, zipping it up and pulling on the suede boots. She picked up the trench coat and handbag, moved into the toilet, closed the door, and locked it.

She had checked the window earlier. It was large enough to get out of and opened into a small yard on the ground floor of the Conservatoire. She climbed up on the seat and wriggled through. It was raining hard now. She pulled on her trench coat, picked up her shoulder bag, and ran to the gate. It was bolted on the inside and opened easily. A moment later, she was hurrying along the rue de Madrid looking for a taxi.

Eight

EVLIN was watching a late-night movie on television when the phone rang. The line was surprisingly clear, so much so that at first he thought it must be local.

"Professor Devlin?"

"Yes."

"It's Tanya—Tanya Voroninova."

"Where are you?" Devlin demanded.

"The Gare du Nord. Paris. I've only got a couple of minutes. I'm catching the night train to Rennes."

"To Rennes?" Devlin was bewildered. "What in the world would you be going there for?"

"I change trains there for St.-Malo. I'll be there at breakfast time. There's a hydrofoil to Jersey. That's as good as being in England. Once there, I'm safe. I'll catch a plane for London. I only had minutes to give them the slip, so it seemed likely the other routes your people supplied would be blocked."

"So, you changed your mind. Why?"

"Let's just say I've realized I like you and I don't like them. It doesn't mean I hate my country. Only some of the people in it. I must go."

"I'll contact London," Devlin said. "Phone me from Rennes, and good luck."

The line went dead. He stood there, holding the receiver, a slight ironic smile on his face, a kind of wonderment. "Would you look at that now?" he said softly. "A girl to take home to your mother and that's a fact."

He dialed the Cavendish Square number and Ferguson answered it almost at once. "Ferguson here." He sounded cross.

"Would you by any chance be sitting in bed watching the old Bogart movie on the television?" Devlin inquired.

"Dear God, are you going into the clairvoyance business now?"

"Well, you can switch it off and get out of bed, you old bastard. The game's afoot with a vengeance."

Ferguson's voice changed. "What are you saying?"

"That Tanya Voroninova's done a bunk. She's just phoned me from the Gare du Nord. Catching the night train to Rennes. Change for St.-Malo. Hydrofoil to Jersey in the morning. She thought the other routes might be blocked."

"Smart girl," Ferguson said. "They'll pull every trick in the book to get her back."

"She's going to phone me when she gets to Rennes. I presume, at a guess, that would be about three-thirty or maybe four o'clock."

"Good man," Ferguson told him. "Stay by the phone. I'll get back to you."

In his flat, Harry Fox was just about to get into the shower before going to bed when the phone rang. He answered it, cursing. It had been a long day. He needed some sleep.

"Harry?"

He came alert at once at the sound of Ferguson's voice. "Yes, sir?"

"Get yourself over here. We've got work to do."

CUSSANE WAS WORKING in his study on Sunday's sermon when the sensor device linked to the apparatus in the attic was activated. By the time he was up there, Devlin was off the phone. He played the tape back, listening intently. When it was finished, he sat there, thinking about the implications, which were all bad.

He went down to the study and phoned Cherny direct. When the professor answered, he said, "It's me. Are you alone?"

"Yes. Just about to go to bed. Where are you ringing from?"

"My place. We've got bad trouble. Now listen carefully."

When he was finished, Cherny said, "It gets worse. What do you want me to do?"

"Speak to Lubov now. Tell him to make contact with Belov in Paris at once. They may be able to stop her."

"And if not?"

"Then I'll have to handle it myself when she gets here. I'll keep in touch, so stay by the phone."

He poured himself a whisky and stood in front of the fire. Strange, but he still saw her as that scrawny little girl in the rain, all those years ago.

He raised his glass and said softly, "Here's to you, Tanya Voroninova. Now, let's see if you can give those bastards a run for their money."

WITHIN FIVE MINUTES, Turkin had realized something was very badly wrong, had entered the dressing room and discovered the locked toilet door. The silence, which was the only answer to his urgent knocking, made him break down the door. The empty toilet, the window, told all. He clambered through, dropped into the yard, and went into the rue de Madrid. There was no sign of her, and he went around to the front of the Conservatoire and in through the main entrance, black rage in his heart. His career ruined, his very life on the line now because of that damned woman.

Belov was on another glass of champagne, deep in conversation with the minister for culture when Turkin tapped him on the shoulder. "Sorry to interrupt, Colonel, but could I have a word?" He took him into the nearest corner and broke the bad news.

NIKOLAI BELOV HAD always found that adversity brought out the best in him. He had never been one to cry over spilled milk. At his office at the embassy, he sat behind the desk and faced Natasha Rubenova. Shepilov and Turkin stood by the door.

"I ask you again, Comrade," he said to her. "Did she say anything to you? Surely you of all people would have had some idea of her intentions?"

She was distressed and tearful, all quite genuine, and it helped her to lie easily. "I'm as much at a loss as you are, Comrade Colonel."

He sighed and nodded to Turkin, who moved up behind her, shoving her down into a chair. He pulled off his right glove and squeezed her neck, pinching a nerve and sending a wave of the most appalling pain through her.

"I ask you again," Nikolai Belov said gently. "Please be sensible, I hate this kind of thing."

Natasha, filled with pain, rage, and humiliation, did the bravest thing of her life. "Please! Comrade, I swear she told me nothing! Nothing!"

She screamed again as Turkin's finger found the nerve and Belov waved a hand. "Enough. I'm satisfied she's telling the truth. What would her purpose be in lying?"

She sat there, huddled, weeping, and Turkin said, "What now, Comrade?"

"We have the airports fully covered. No possible flight she could have taken yet."

"And Calais and Boulogne?"

"Our people are already on their way by road. The soonest she could leave from both places would be on one of the morning ferries, and they will be there before those leave."

Shepilov, who seldom spoke, said quietly, "Excuse me, Comrade Colonel, but have you considered the fact that she may have sought asylum at the British embassy?"

"Of course," Belov told him. "As it happens, since June of last year, we have a surveillance system operating at the entrance during the hours of darkness for rather obvious reasons. She has certainly not appeared there yet, and if she does so . . ." he shrugged.

The door opened and Irana Vronsky hurried in. "Lubov, direct from Dublin for you, Comrade. Most urgent. The radio room has patched it through. Line one."

Belov picked up the phone and listened. When he finally put it down, he was smiling. "So far so good. She's on the night train to Rennes. Let's have a look at the map." He nodded to Natasha. "Take her out, Irana."

Turkin said, "But why Rennes?"

Belov found it on the map on the wall. "To change trains for St.-Malo. From there she will catch the hydrofoil to Jersey in the Channel Islands."

"British soil?"

"Exactly. Jersey, my dear Turkin, may be small, but it is very possibly the most important off-shore finance base in the world. They have an excellent airport, several flights a day to London and many other places."

"All right," Turkin said. "We must drive to St.-Malo. Get there ahead of her."

"Just a moment. Let's have a look in Michelin." Belov found the Red Guide in the top left-hand drawer of his desk and leafed through.

"Here we are—St.-Malo. Three hundred and seventy-two miles from Paris and a great deal of that through the Brittany countryside. Impossible to get there by car now, not in time. Go along to Bureau-5, Turkin. Let's see if they've got anyone we can use in St.-Malo. And you, Shepilov. Tell Irana that I want all the information she has on Jersey. Airport, harbor, plane and boat schedules, and so on—and hurry."

AT CAVENDISH SQUARE, Kim was making up the fire in the sitting room while Ferguson, in an old terry cloth robe, sat at the desk working his way through a mass of papers.

The Ghurka stood up. "Coffee, Sahib?"

"God, no, Kim. Tea, nice and fresh and keep it coming, and some sort of sandwiches. Leave it to you."

Kim went out and Harry Fox hurried in from the study. "Right, sir, here's the score. She'll have a stopover at Rennes for almost two hours. From there to St.-Malo is seven miles. She'll arrive at seven-thirty."

"And the hydrofoil?"

"Leaves at eight-fifteen. Takes about an hour and a quarter. There's a time change, of course, so it arrives in Jersey at eight-thirty our time. There's a flight from Jersey to London, Heathrow, at ten minutes past ten. She'll have plenty of time to catch that. It's a small island, sir. Only fifteen minutes by cab from the harbor to the airport."

"No, she can't be alone, Harry. I want her met. You'll have to go over first thing. There must be a breakfast plane."

"Unfortunately it doesn't get into Jersey until nine-twenty."

Ferguson said, "Damnation!" and banged his fist on the desk as Kim entered carrying a tray containing tea things and a plate of newly cut sandwiches. They gave off the unmistakable odor of grilled bacon.

"There is a possibility, sir?"

"What's that?"

"My cousin, Alex, sir. Alexander Martin. My second cousin, actually. He lives in Jersey. Something in the finance industry. Married a local girl."

"Martin?" Ferguson frowned. "The name's familiar."

"It would be, sir. We've used him before. When he was working for a merchant banker here in the city, he did a lot of traveling. Geneva, Zurich, Berlin, Rome."

"He isn't on the active list?"

"No, sir. We used him as a bagman mainly, though there was an incident in East Berlin three years ago when things got out of hand, and he behaved rather well."

"I remember now," Ferguson said. "Supposed to pick up documents from a woman contact and when he found she was blown, he brought her out through Checkpoint Charlie in the trunk of his car."

"That's Alex, sir. Short service commission in the Welsh Guards, three tours in Ireland. Quite an accomplished musician. Plays the piano rather well. Mad as a hatter on a good day. Typically Welsh."

"Get him!" Ferguson said. "*Now*, Harry." He had a hunch about Martin and suddenly felt much more cheerful. He helped himself to one of the bacon sandwiches. "I say, these are really rather good."

ALEXANDER MARTIN WAS thirty-seven, a tall, rather handsome man with a deceptively lazy look to him. He was much given to smiling tolerantly, which he needed to do in the profession of investment broker, a career he had taken up on moving to Jersey eighteen months previous. As he had told his wife, Joan, on more than one occasion, the trouble with being in the investment business was that it threw you into the company of the rich, and as a class he disliked them heartily.

Still, life had its compensations. He was an accomplished pianist, if not a great one. If he had been, life might have been rather different. He was seated at the piano in the living room of his pleasant house in St. Aubin overlooking the sea, playing a little Bach—ice-cold, brilliant stuff that required total concentration. He was wearing a dinner jacket, black tie undone at the

137

neck. The phone rang for several moments before it penetrated his consciousness. He frowned, realizing the lateness of the hour, and picked it up.

"Martin here."

"Alex? This is Harry. Harry Fox."

"Dear God!" Alex Martin said.

"How are Joan and the kids?"

"In Germany for a week, staying with her sister. Her husband's a major with your old mob. Detmold."

"So, you're on your own? I thought you'd be in bed."

"Just in from a late function." Martin was very much awake now, all past experience telling him this was not a social call. "Okay, Harry. What is this?"

"We need you, Alex, rather badly, but not like the other times. Right there in Jersey."

Alex Martin laughed in astonishment. "In Jersey? You've got to be joking."

"Girl called Tanya Voroninova. Have you heard of her?"

"Of course, I damn well have." Martin told him. "One of the best concert pianists to come along for years. I saw her perform at the Albert Hall in last season's promenade concerts. My office gets the Paris papers each day. She's there on a concert tour at the moment."

"No, she isn't," Fox said. "By now, she'll be halfway to Rennes on the night train. She's defecting, Alex."

"She's what?"

"With luck, she'll be on the hydrofoil from St.-Malo, arriving Jersey at eight-twenty. She has a British passport in the name of Joanna Frank."

Martin saw it all now. "And you want me to meet her?"

"Exactly. Straight to the airport and bundle her onto the ten-ten to Heathrow, and that's it. We'll meet her this end. Will that give you any problem?"

"Certainly not. I know what she looks like. In fact, I think I've still got the program from her concert at the Proms. There's a photo of her on that."

138

"Fine," Fox told him. "She's phoning a contact of ours when she gets into Rennes. We'll warn her to expect you."

There was a slight pause, then Martin heard, "Ferguson here."

"Hello, sir," Martin said.

"We're very grateful."

"Nothing to it, sir. Just one thing. What about the opposition?"

"Highly unlikely there'll be any. KGB will be waiting at all the obvious bolt holes—Charles de Gaulle, Calais, Boulogne. Highly unlikely they'll be on to this one. I'll hand you back to Harry now."

Fox said, "We'll stay close Alex. I'll give you this number, in case of any problems."

Martin wrote it down. "Should be a piece of cake. Make a nice change from the investment business. I'll be in touch."

He was totally awake now and decidedly cheerful. No hope of sleep. Things were looking up. He poured himself a vodka and tonic and went back to his Bach at the piano.

BUREAU-5 WAS THAT section of the Soviet embassy in Paris that dealt with the French Communist party, infiltration of trade unions, and so on. Turkin spent half an hour with their file on St.-Malo and the immediate area, but came up with nothing.

"The trouble is, Comrade," he told Belov when he returned to the office, "that the French Communist party is extremely unreliable. The French tend to put country before party when the chips are down."

"I know," Belov said. "It comes of an inborn belief in their own superiority." He indicated the papers spread out on his desk. "I've looked Jersey over pretty thoroughly. The solution is simple enough. You know that little airfield outside Paris that we've used before?"

"Croix?" Turkin said. "Lebel Air Taxis?"

"That's right. Jersey Airport opens early. You could land there at seven. Ample time to be down at the harbor to meet her.

You have the usual selection of passports available. You could go as French businessmen."

"But how do we bring her back?" Turkin asked. "We'd have to pass through customs and immigration for the return flight from Jersey Airport. It would be an impossibility. Too easy for her to create a fuss."

"Excuse me, Comrade Colonel," Shepilov put in, "but is it really necessary for us to bring her back at all since all that is needed in this affair is her silence, or have I got the wrong impression?"

"You certainly have," Belov told him coldly. "Whatever the circumstances, however difficult, General Maslovsky wants her back. I'd hate to be in your shoes if you had to report the need to shoot her, Shepilov. I think there is an easy solution. According to the brochures, there is a yachting marina in St. Helier Harbor. Boats for hire. Wasn't sailing always something of a hobby of yours back home, Turkin?"

"Yes, Comrade."

"Good, then I'm sure it's hardly beyond your abilities to sail a motor launch from Jersey to St.-Malo. You can hire a car there and bring her back by road."

"Very well, Colonel."

Irana came in with coffee on a tray. He said, "Excellent. Now all that's needed is for someone to haul Lebel out of bed. The timing should work just nicely."

SURPRISING HERSELF, TANYA managed to sleep for most of the train journey and had to be prodded into wakefulness by two young students who had traveled next to her all the way from Paris. It was three-thirty and very cold on the station platform at Rennes, although it had stopped raining. The students knew of an all-night café outside the station in le boulevard Beaumont and showed her the way. It was warm and inviting in there, not too many people. She ordered coffee and an omelette and went to call Devlin on the public telephone.

140

DEVLIN, WHO HAD been waiting anxiously, said, "Are you all right?"

"Fine," she said. "I even slept on the train. Don't worry. They can't have any idea where I am. When will I see you again?"

"Soon," Devlin told her. "We've got to get you to London safely first. Now listen to me. When the hydrofoil gets into Jersey, you'll be met by a man called Martin. Alexander Martin. Apparently he's a bit of a fan of yours, so he knows what you look like."

"I see. Anything else?"

"Not really."

"Good, then I'll get back to my omelette, Professor."

She rang off and Devlin replaced the receiver. A girl and a half, he told himself as he went into the kitchen. In the cottage, Harry Cussane was already phoning Paul Cherny.

CROIX WAS A small airfield with a control tower, two hangars, and three Nissen huts, headquarters of an aero club, but also used by Pierre Lebel to operate his air-taxi service from. Lebel was a dark, taciturn man who never asked close questions, if the price was right. He had flown for Belov on a number of occasions and knew Turkin and Shepilov well. He hadn't the slightest idea that they were Russian. Something illegal about them, he'd always thought that, but as long as it didn't involve drugs and the price was right, he didn't mind. He was waiting for the two men when they arrived and opened the door of the main hangar so that they could drive inside.

"Which plane?" Turkin asked.

"We'll use the Chieftain. Faster than the Cessna and there's a headwind all the way to Golfe de St.-Malo."

"When do we leave?"

"As soon as you like."

"But I thought the airport at Jersey wasn't open until seven?"

"Whoever told you that got it wrong. It's officially seven-thirty for air taxis. However, the airport is open for the paper plane from five-thirty."

"Paper plane?"

"Newspapers from England. Post and so on. They're usually sympathetic to a request for an early landing, especially if they know you. I did get the impression that there was some urgency on this one?"

"There certainly is," Turkin told him.

"Good, let's go up to the office and settle the business end of things."

The office was up a flight of rickety stairs, small and cluttered, the desk untidy, the whole lit by a single bulb. Turkin handed Lebel an envelope. "Better count it."

"Oh, I will," the Frenchman said, and then the phone rang. He answered it at once, then passed it to Turkin. "For you."

Belov said, "She's made contact with Devlin from Rennes. There's a new complication. She's being met off the hydrofoil in Jersey by an Alexander Martin."

"Is he a pro?" Turkin asked.

"No information on him at all. One wouldn't have thought they'd have any of their people in a place like Jersey. Still . . ."

"No problem," Turkin said. "We'll handle it."

"Good luck."

The line went dead and Turkin turned to Lebel. "All right, my friend. Ready when you are."

IT WAS JUST six o'clock when they landed at Jersey Airport, a fine, blustery morning, the sky already lightening in the east, an orange glow on the horizon as the sun came up. The officer on duty at customs and immigration was pleasant and courteous. No reason not to be, for their papers and French passports were perfectly in order, and Jersey was well used to handling thousands of French visitors each year.

"Stopping over?" he asked Lebel.

"No, straight back to Paris," the Frenchman told him.

"And you gentlemen?"

"Three or four days. Business and pleasure." Turkin said.

"And nothing to declare?" You've read the notice?"

"Not a thing." Turkin offered his holdall.

The officer shook his head. "All right, gentlemen. Have a nice stay."

They shook hands formally with Lebel and passed out into the arrival hall, which at that time of the morning was deserted. There were one or two cars parked outside, but the taxi stand was empty. There was a telephone on the wall, but just as Turkin was moving to use it, Shepilov touched his arm and pointed. A cab was drawing up at the entrance to the airport. Two air hostesses got out and went in. The Russians waited, and the cab pulled up beside them.

"Early start, gentlemen," the driver said.

"Yes, we're just in from Paris," Turkin told him. "Private flight."

"Oh, I see. Where can I take you?"

Turkin, who had spent much of the flight examining the Jersey guidebook Irana had provided, particularly the town map of St. Helier, said. "The Weighbridge, isn't that right? By the harbor."

The taxi drew away. "You don't need a hotel then?"

"We're meeting friends later. They're taking care of that sort of thing; we thought we'd get some breakfast."

"You'll be all right there. There's a café close to the Weighbridge, opens early. I'll show you."

The roads at that time in the morning were far from busy, and the run down to Bel Royal and along the dual carriageway of Victoria Avenue took little more than ten minutes. The sun was coming up now and the view across St. Aubin Bay was rather spectacular, the tide in so that Elizabeth Castle on its rock was surrounded by water. Ahead of them was the town, the harbor breakwater, cranes lifting into the sky in the distance.

The driver turned in by the car park at the end of the esplanade. "Here we are, gentlemen. The Weighbridge. There's the tourist office. Open later, if you need information. The café is just across the road over there around the corner. Let's see, we'll call that three pounds."

Turkin, who had been supplied with several hundred pounds in English bank notes by Irana, took a fiver from his wallet. "Keep it. You've been very kind. Where's the marina from here?"

The driver pointed. "Far end of the harbor. You can walk around."

Turkin nodded to the breakwater stretching out into the bay. "And the boats come in there?"

"That's right. Albert Quay. You can see the car-ferry ramp from here. Hydrofoils berth farther along."

"Good." Turkin said. "Many thanks."

They got out and the cab moved away. There was a public toilet a few yards away and, without a word, Turkin led the way in and Shepilov followed. Turkin opened his holdall and burrowed under the clothing it contained, lifting up the false bottom to reveal two handguns. He slipped one into his pocket and gave Shepilov the other. The weapons were automatics, each gun fitted with a silencer.

Turkin zipped up his holdall. "So far so good. Let's take a look at the marina."

THERE WERE SEVERAL hundred boats moored there of every shape and size. Yachts, motor cruisers, speedboats. They found the office of a boat-for-hire firm easily enough, but it was not open yet.

"Too early," Turkin said. "Let's go down and have a look around."

They walked along one of the swaying pontoons, boats moored on either side, paused, then turned into another. Things had always worked for Turkin. He was a great believer in his destiny. The nonsense over Tanya Voroninova had been an unfortunate hiccup in his career, but soon to be put right, he was confident of that. And now, fate took a hand in the game.

There was a motor cruiser moored at the end of the pontoon, dazzlingly white with a blue band above the watermark. The name on the stern was *L'Alouette,* registered Granville, which he knew was a port along the coast from St.-Malo. A couple came out on deck talking in French, the man, tall and bearded with glasses. He wore a dark reefer coat. The woman wore jeans and a similar coat, a scarf around her head.

As the man helped her over the rail, Turkin heard him say, "We'll walk around to the bus station. Get a taxi from there to the airport. The flight to Guernsey leaves at eight."

"What time are we booked back?" she said.

"Four o'clock. We'll have time for breakfast at the airport."

They walked away. Shepilov said, "What is Guernsey?"

"The next island," Turkin told him. "I read about it in the guidebook. There's an interisland flying service several times a day. It takes only fifteen minutes. A day out for tourists."

"Are you thinking what I am?" Shepilov inquired.

"It's a nice boat," Turkin said. "We could be in St.-Malo and on our way hours before those two get back this afternoon." He took out a pack of French cigarettes and offered one to his companion. "Give them time to move away, then we'll check."

They took a walk around the pontoons, returning in ten minutes and going on board. The door to the companionway that led below was locked. Shepilov produced a spring-blade knife and forced it expertly. There were two cabins neatly furnished, a salon, and a galley down there. They went back on deck and tried the wheelhouse. The door to that was open.

"No ignition key," Shepilov said.

"No problem. Give me your knife." Turkin worked his way up behind the control panel and pulled down several wires. It took only a moment to make the right connection, and when he pressed the starter button, the engine turned over at once. He checked the fuel gauge. "Tank's three-quarters full." He unfastened the wires again. "You know, I think this is our day, Ivan," he said to Shepilov.

They walked back around to the other side of the harbor and turned along the top of the Albert Quay, pausing at the end to look down at the hydrofoil berth.

"Excellent." Turkin looked at his watch. "Now all we have to do is wait. Let's find that café and try some breakfast."

AT ST.-MALO, the Condor hydrofoil moved out of the harbor past the Mole des Noires. It was almost full, mainly French tourists visiting Jersey for the day, to judge from the conversations Tanya overheard. Once out of harbor, the hydrofoil started to lift, increasing speed, and she gazed out into the morning feeling totally exhilarated. She'd done it. Beaten all of them. Once in Jersey, she was as good as in London. She leaned back in the comfortable seat and closed her eyes.

ALEX MARTIN TURNED his big Peugeot onto the Albert Quay and drove along until he found a convenient parking place, which wasn't easy for the car ferry was in from Weymouth and things were rather busy. He had not slept at all and was beginning to feel the effect of that, although a good breakfast and a cold shower had helped. He wore navy blue slacks, a turtleneck sweater in the same color, and a sports jacket in pale blue tweed, by Yves St.-Laurent. Partly this was a desire to make an impression on Tanya Voroninova. His music meant an enormous amount to him and the chance to meet a performer he admired so much was of more importance to him than either Ferguson or Fox could have imagined.

His hair was still a little damp and he ran his fingers through it, suddenly uneasy. He opened the glove compartment of the Peugeot and took out the handgun he found there. It was a .38-caliber Smith and Wesson Special, the Airweight model with the two-inch barrel, a weapon much favored by the CIA. Six years before, he'd taken it from the body of a Protestant terrorist in Belfast, a member of the outlawed UVF. The man had tried to kill Martin, had almost succeeded. Martin had killed him instead. It had never worried him, that was the strange thing. No regrets, no nightmares.

"Come off it, Alex," he said softly. "This is Jersey."

But the feeling wouldn't go away, Belfast all over again, that touch of unease, and remembering an old trick from undercover days, he slipped the gun into the waistband at the small of his back. Frequently, even a body search missed a weapon secreted there.

He sat smoking a cigarette, listening to Radio Jersey on the car radio, until the hydrofoil moved in through the harbor entrance. Even then, he didn't get out. There were the usual formalities to be passed through, customs and so on. He waited until the first passengers emerged from the exit of the passenger terminal, then got out and moved forward. He recognized Tanya at once in her black jumpsuit, the trench coat over her shoulders like a cloak.

He moved to meet her. "Miss Voroninova?" She examined him warily. "Or should I say Miss Frank?"

"Who are you?"

"Alexander Martin. I'm here to see that you get on your plane safely. You're booked on the ten-past-ten to London. Plenty of time."

She put a hand on his arm, relaxing completely, totally unaware of Turkin and Shepilov on the other side of the road against the wall, backs partially turned. "You've no idea how good it is to see a friendly face."

"This way." He guided her to the Peugeot. "I saw you play the *Emperor* at the Proms at Albert Hall last year. You were amazing."

He put her into the passenger seat and went around to the other side and got behind the wheel.

"Do you play yourself?" she asked, as if by instinct.

"Oh, yes." He turned the ignition key. "But not like you."

Behind them, the rear doors opened on each side and the two Russians got in, Turkin behind Tanya. "Don't argue, there's a silenced pistol against your spine and hers. These seats aren't exactly body armor. We can kill you both without a sound and walk away."

Tanya went quite rigid and gasped. Alex Martin said calmly, "You know these men?"

"GRU. Military Intelligence."

"I see. What happens now?" he asked Turkin.

"She goes back if we can take her. If not, she dies. The only important thing is that she doesn't talk to the wrong people. Any nonsense from you and she'll be the first to go. We know our duty."

"I'm sure you do."

"Because we are strong and you are weak, pretty boy," Turkin told him. "That's why we'll win in the end. Walk right up to Buckingham Palace."

"Wrong time of the year, old son," Alex said. "The queen's at Sandringham."

Turkin scowled. "Very amusing. Now get this thing moving around to the marina."

THEY WALKED ALONG the pontoon toward *L'Alouette*, Martin with a hand on the girl's elbow. the two Russians walking behind. Martin helped Tanya over the rail. She was trembling, he could feel it.

Turkin opened the companionway door. "Down below, both of you." He followed close behind, his gun in his hand now. "Stop!" he said to Martin when they reached the salon. "Lean on the table, legs spread, and you—sit down," he told Tanya.

Shepilov stood to one side, gun in hand. Tanya was close to tears. Alex said gently. "Keep smiling. Always pays."

"You English really take the biscuit," Turkin said as he searched him expertly. "You're nothing any more. Yesterday's news. Just wait till the Argentinians blow you out of the water down there in the South Atlantic." He lifted Martin's jacket at the rear and found the Airweight. "Would you look at that?" he said to Shepilov. "Amateur. I noticed some cord in the galley. Get it."

Shepilov was soon back. "And once at sea, it's the deep six?" Martin inquired.

"Something like that." Turkin turned to Shepilov. "Tie him up. We'd better get out of here fast. I'll get the engine started."

He went up the companionway. Tanya had stopped trembling, her face pale, rage in her eyes and desperation. Martin shook his head a fraction, and Shepilov kneed him painfully in the rear. "Up you come, hands behind you." Martin could feel the muzzle of the silencer against his back. The Russian said to Tanya, "Tie his wrists."

Martin thought, "Don't they ever teach you chaps anything? You never stand that close to anyone."

He swung, pivoting to the left, away from the barrel of the gun. It coughed once, drilling a hole in the bulkhead. His right hand caught the Russian's wrist, twisting it up and around, taut as a steel bar. Shepilov grunted and dropped the weapon, and Martin's clenched left fist descended in a hammer blow, snapping the arm.

Shepilov cried out, dropping to one knee. Martin bent down and picked up the gun, and miraculously, the Russian's other hand swung up, the blade of a spring-knife flashing. Martin blocked it, aware of the sudden pain as the blade sliced through his sleeve, drawing blood. He punched Shepilov on the jaw, knuckles extended, and kicked the knife under the seat.

Tanya was on her feet, but already there were hurried steps on deck. "Ivan?" Turkin called.

Martin put a finger to his lips to the girl, brushed past her, and went into the galley. A small ladder led to the forward hatch. He opened it and went out on deck as he heard Turkin start down.

It had begun to rain again, a fine mist drifting in from the sea. He stepped lightly across the deck to the entrance of the companionway. Turkin had reached the bottom and stood there, gun in his right hand as he peered cautiously into the salon. Martin didn't make a sound, gave him no chance at all. He simply extended his pistol and shot him neatly through the right arm. Turkin cried out, dropped his weapon, and staggered into the salon, and Martin went down the companionway.

Tanya moved to join him. Martin picked up Turkin's gun and put it into his pocket. Turkin leaned against the table clutching his arm, glaring at him. Shepilov was just pulling himself up and sank onto the bench with a groan. Martin swung Turkin around and searched his pockets until he found his Smith and Wesson. He turned to Turkin again.

"I was careful with the arm. You aren't going to die—yet. I don't know who owns this boat, but you obviously meant to leave in it, you and chummy here. I'd get on with it if I were you. You'd only be an embarrassment to our people, and I'm sure they'd like you back in Moscow. You ought to be able to manage between you."

"Bastard!" Peter Turkin said in despair.

"Not in front of the lady," Alex Martin told him. He pushed Tanya Voroninova up the companionway and turned. "As a matter of interest, you two wouldn't last one bad Saturday night in Belfast," then he followed the girl up to the deck.

When they reached the Peugeot, he took off his jacket gingerly. There was blood on his shirtsleeve, and he fished out his handkerchief. "Would you mind doing what you can with that?"

She bound it around the slash tightly. "What kind of a man are you?"

"Well, I prefer Mozart myself," Alex Martin said as he pulled on his jacket. "I say, would you look at that?"

Beyond, on the outer edge of the marina, *L'Alouette* was moving out of harbor. "They're leaving," Tanya said.

"Poor sods," Martin told her. "Their next posting will probably be the Gulag, after this." He handed her into the Peugeot and smiled cheerfully as he got behind the wheel. "Now let's get you to the airport, shall we?"

AT HEATHROW AIRPORT'S terminal one, Harry Fox sat in the security office and drank a cup of tea and enjoyed a cigarette with the duty sergeant. The phone rang, the sergeant answered, then passed it across.

"Harry?" Ferguson said.

"Sir."

"She made it. She's on the plane. Just left Jersey."

"No problems, sir?"

"Not if you exclude a couple of GRU bogeymen snatching her and Martin off the Albert Quay."

Fox said. "What happened?"

"He managed, that's what happened. We'll have to use that young man again. You did say he was Guards Brigade?"

"Yes, sir. Welsh."

"Thought so. One can always tell." Ferguson said cheerfully and rang off.

"NO, MADAME, NOTHING to pay," the steward said to Tanya as the one-eleven climbed into the sky away from Jersey. "The bar is free. What would you like. Vodka and tonic, gin and orange? Or we have champagne."

Free champagne. Tanya nodded and took the frosted glass he offered her. To a new life, she thought, and then she said softly, "To you, Alexander Martin," and emptied the glass in a long swallow.

LUCKILY, THE HOUSEKEEPER had the day off. Alex Martin disposed of his shirt, pushing it to the bottom of the garbage in one of the bins, then went to the bathroom and cleaned his arm. It really needed stitching, but that would have meant questions and that would never do. He pulled the edges of the cut together with neat butterflies of tape, an old soldiers' trick, and bandaged it. He put on a bathrobe, poured himself a large Scotch, and went into the sitting room. As he sat down, the phone rang.

His wife said. "Darling, I phoned the office and they said you were taking the day off. Is anything wrong? You haven't been overdoing it again, have you?"

She knew nothing of the work he'd done for Ferguson in the past. No need to alarm her now. He smiled ruefully, noting the slash in the sleeve of the Yves St. Laurent jacket on the chair next to him.

"Certainly not," he said. "You know me? Anything for a quiet life. I'm working at home today, that's all. Now tell me—how are the children?"

Nine

AT Cavendish Square, Ferguson was seated at the desk holding the telephone, face grave, when Harry Fox came in from the study with a telex message. Ferguson made a quick gesture with one hand, then said, "Thank you, Minister," and replaced the receiver.

"Trouble, sir?" Fox asked.

"As far as I'm concerned it is."

"Come on, out with it."

"The foreign office people have just informed me that the pope's visit is definitely on. The Vatican will make an announcement within the next few hours. What have you got?"

"Telex, sir. Information on the task force's progress. The bad news is that H.M.S. *Antelope* has finally sunk. She was bombed by Skyhawks yesterday. The good news is that seven Argentinian jets have been brought down."

"I'd be happier about that if I saw the wreckage, Harry. Probably half that figure in actuality. Battle of Britain all over again."

"Perhaps, sir. Everybody claims a hit in the heat of the moment. It can be confusing."

Ferguson stood up and lit one of his cheroots. "I don't know, sometimes the bloody roof just seems to fall in. I've got the pope coming, which we could well have done without . . . Cuchulain still on the loose over there . . . and now this nonsense about the Argentinians trying to buy Exocet missiles on the black market in Paris. Orders have gone through to pull Tony Villiers from behind enemy lines in the Falklands?"

"No problem, sir. He's being off-loaded by submarine in Uraguay. Flying from Montevideo by Air France direct to Paris. Should be there tomorrow."

"Good. You'll have to go over on the shuttle. Brief him thoroughly, then get straight back here."

"Will that be enough, sir?"

"Good God, yes. You know what Tony's like when he gets moving. Hell on wheels. He'll sort the opposition out over there, no problem. I need you here, Harry. What about the Voroninova girl?"

"As I told you, sir, we stopped off at Harrods on the way in from Heathrow to get her a few things. Only had what she stood up in."

"She'll be broke, of course," Ferguson said. "We'll have to tap the contingency fund."

"As a matter of fact that won't be necessary, sir. It seems she has a very substantial bank account here. Record royalties and so on. She certainly won't have any difficulty in earning her living. They'll be clamoring for her, all the impresarios, when they know she's available."

"That will have to wait. She's very definitely to stay under wraps until I say so. What's she like?"

"Very nice indeed, sir. I settled her into the spare room and she was having a bath."

"Yes, well don't let's make her too comfortable, Harry. We want to get on with this thing. I've heard from Devlin, and it seems another of McGuinness's hatchet men, the one who was supposed to be keeping an eye on Cherny, has turned up in the Liffey. He doesn't waste time, our friend."

"I see, sir," Fox said. "So what are you suggesting?"

"We'll get her over to Dublin now—this afternoon. You can escort her, Harry. Hand her over to Devlin at the airport, then get back here. You can go to Paris on the morning shuttle."

Fox said mildly, "She might just feel like sitting down for a moment. Taking a deep breath. That sort of thing."

"So would we all, Harry, and if that's a subtle way of telling me how you feel, then all I can say is you should have taken that job they offered you at your uncle's merchant bank. Start at ten, finish at four."

"And terribly, terribly boring, sir."

Kim opened the door at that moment and ushered Tanya Voroninova in. Her eyes were slightly hollowed, but she looked surprisingly well, the general effect enhanced by the blue cashmere sweater and neat tweed skirt she had purchased at Harrods. Fox made the introductions.

"Miss Voroninova. A great pleasure," Ferguson said. "You've certainly had an active time of it. Please sit down."

She sat on the couch by the fire. "Have you any idea what's happening in Paris?" she asked.

"Not yet," Fox said. "We'll find out in the end, but if you want an educated guess, the KGB never care for failure at the best of times, and if we consider your foster father's special interest in this case..." He shrugged. "I wouldn't care to be in Turkin's or Shepilov's shoes."

"Even such a shrewd old campaigner as Nikolai Belov will have difficulty surviving this one," Ferguson put in.

"So, what happens now?" she asked. "Do I see Professor Devlin again?"

"Yes, but that means flying over to Dublin. I know your feet have hardly touched the ground, but time is of the essence. I'd like you to go later on this afternoon, if that's all right. Captain

Fox will escort you, and we'll arrange for Devlin to meet you at Dublin Airport."

She was still on a high, and somehow it seemed a part of what had already happened. "When do we leave?" she said.

"THE EARLY EVENING plane," Devlin said. "Sure, I'll be there. No problem."

"You'll make your own arrangements about the necessary meeting with McGuinness so that she can look at whatever photos or other material they want to show her?"

"I'll take care of it," Devlin said.

"Sooner rather than later," Ferguson told him firmly.

"I hear and obey, O Genie of the lamp," Devlin said. "Now let me talk to her."

Ferguson handed her the phone. Tanya said, "Professor Devlin? What is it?"

"I've just heard from Paris. The Mona Lisa is smiling all over her face. See you soon."

AND IN MOSCOW important things had been happening that morning. Events that were to affect the whole of Russia specifically and world politics generally. Yuri Andropov, head of the KGB since 1967, was named secretary of the Communist Party Central Committee. He still inhabited his old office at KGB headquarters at Dzerhinsky Square, and it was there that he summoned Maslovsky, just after noon. The general stood in front of the desk, filled with foreboding, for Andropov was possibly the only man he had ever known of whom he was genuinely afraid. Andropov was writing, his pen scratching the paper. He ignored Maslovsky for a while, then spoke without looking up.

"There is little point in referring to the gross inefficiency shown by your department in the matter of the Cuchulain affair."

"Comrade." Maslovsky didn't attempt to defend himself.

"You have given orders that he is to be eliminated together with Cherny?"

"Yes, Comrade."

"The sooner the better." Andropov paused, removed his glasses and ran a hand over his forehead. "Then there is the matter of your foster daughter. She is now safely in London, due to the bungling of your people."

"Yes, Comrade."

"From which city Brigadier Ferguson is having her flown to Dublin, where the IRA intends to give her any help she needs to identify Cuchulain?"

"That would appear to be the case," Maslovsky said weakly.

"The Provisional IRA is a fascist organization, as far as I am concerned, hopelessly tainted by its links with the Catholic Church, and Tanya Voroninova is a traitor to her country, her party, and her class. You will send an immediate cable to the man Lubov in Dublin. He will eliminate her as well as Cherny and Cuchulain."

He replaced his glasses, picked up his pen, and started to write again. Maslovsky said in a hoarse voice, "Please, Comrade, perhaps . . ."

Andropov glanced up in surprise. "Does my order give you some sort of problem, Comrade General?"

Maslovsky, wilting under those cold eyes, shook his head hurriedly. "No, of course not, Comrade," and he turned and went out, feeling just the slightest tremor in his limbs.

AT THE SOVIET embassy in Dublin, Lubov had already received a message from Paris informing him that Tanya Voroninova had slipped the net. He was still in the radio room digesting this startling piece of news when the second message came through, the one from Maslovsky in Moscow. The operator recorded it, placed the tape in the machine, and Lubov keyed in his personal code. When he read the message, he felt physically sick. He went to his office, locked the door and got a bottle of Scotch from the cupboard. He had one glass and then another. Finally, he phoned Cherny.

"Costello, here." It was the code name he used on such occasions. "Are you busy?"

"Not particularly," Cherny told him.

"We must meet."

"The usual place?"

"Yes, but I must talk to you first. Very important. However, we must also arrange to see our mutual friend this evening. Dun Street, I think. Can you arrange that?"

"It's very unusual."

"As I said, matters of importance. Ring me back to confirm this evening's meeting."

Cherny was very definitely worried. Dun Street was a code name for a disused warehouse on City Quay, which he had leased under a company name some years previously, but that wasn't the point. What was really important was the fact that he and Cussane and Lubov had never all met together in the same place before. He phoned Cussane at the cottage without success, so he tried the Catholic secretariat offices in Dublin. Cussane answered at once.

"Thank God," Cherny said. "I tried the cottage."

"Yes, I've just got in," Cussane told him. "Is there a problem?"

"I'm not sure. I feel uneasy. Can I speak freely?"

"You usually do on this line."

"Our friend Costello has been in touch. Asked me to meet him at three-thirty."

"Usual place?"

"Yes, but he's also asked me to arrange for the three of us to meet at Dun Street tonight."

"That *is* unusual."

"I know. I don't like it."

158

"Perhaps he has instructions for us to pull out," Cussane said. "Did he say anything about the girl?"

"No. Should he have?"

"I just wondered what was happening there, that's all. Tell him I'll see you at Dun Street at six-thirty. Don't worry, Paul. I'll handle things."

He rang off, and Cherny got straight back to Lubov.

"Six-thirty, is that all right?"

"Fine." Lubov told him.

"He asked me if you'd heard anything about the girl in Paris."

"No, not a word," Lubov lied. "I'll see you at three-thirty." He rang off, then poured himself a drink, unlocked the top drawer of his desk, took out a case, and opened it. It contained a Stetchkin semiautomatic pistol and a silencer. Gingerly, he started fitting them together.

IN HIS OFFICE at the secretariat, Harry Cussane stood at the window looking down into the street. He had listened in on Devlin's conversation with Ferguson before leaving the cottage and knew that Tanya Voroninova was due that evening. It was inconceivable that Lubov would not have heard, either from Moscow or Paris, so why hadn't he mentioned it?

The meeting at Dun Street was an unusual enough item in itself, but in view of that meeting, why meet Cherny in the usual back row at the cinema first? What could possibly be the need? It didn't fit, any of it, and every instinct that Cussane possessed, honed by his years in the trenches, told him so. Whatever else Lubov wanted to see them for, it was not conversation.

PAUL CHERNY WAS reaching for his raincoat when there was a knock at the door of his rooms. When he opened it, Harry Cussane was standing outside. He wore a dark trilby hat and raincoat of the kind affected by priests, and he looked agitated.

"Paul, thank God I caught you."

"Why, what is it?" Cherny demanded.

"The IRA man who followed you, the one I disposed of the other day? They've set another one on. This way."

Cherny's rooms were on the first floor of the old graystone college building. Cussane went up the stairs quickly to the next floor and turned at once up another flight of stairs.

"Where are we going?" Cherny called.

"I'll show you."

On the top landing, the tall Georgian window at the end had its bottom half pushed up. Cussane peered out. "Over there," he said. "On the other side of the quad."

Cherny looked down to the flagstones and the green grass of the quadrangle. "Where?" he asked. There was the hand in the small of his back, a sudden violent push. He managed to cry out, but only just as he overbalanced across the low windowsill and plunged head first toward the flagstones eighty-feet below.

Cussane ran along the corridor and descended the backstairs hurriedly. In a sense, he had been telling the truth. McGuinness had indeed replaced Murphy with a new watchdog, in fact two of them this time, sitting in a green Ford Escort near the main entrance. Not that it was going to do them much good now.

LUBOV HAD THE back row to himself. In fact, there were only five or six people in the cinema at all, as far as he could see in the dim light. He was early, but that was by intention, and he fingered the silent Stetchkin in his pocket, his palms damp with sweat. He'd brought a flask with him, and he took it out now and swallowed deep. More Scotch to give him the courage he needed. First Cherny and then Cussane, but that should be easier, if he was at the warehouse first and waiting in ambush. He took another swig at the flask, had just replaced it in his pocket, when there was a movement in the darkness and someone sat down beside him.

"Paul?" he turned his head.

An arm slid around his neck, a hand clamped over his mouth.

In the second that he recognized Cussane's pale face under the brim of the black hat, the needle point of the stiletto that Cussane held in his right hand probed in under his ribs, thrusting up into the heart. There was not even time to struggle. A kind of blinding light, no pain, then only darkness.

Cussane wiped the blade carefully on Lubov's jacket and eased him back in the seat, as if asleep. He found the Stetchkin in the dead man's pocket, took it out, and slipped it into his own. He had been right, as usual. The final proof. He got up, went down the aisle, a shadow only in his black coat, and left through one of the exit doors.

HE WAS BACK at the office in the secretariat within half an hour and had hardly sat down when Monsignor Halloran came in. He was very cheerful and obviously excited.

"Have you heard? Just had the confirmation from the Vatican. The Pope's visit is on."

"So they've decided. You'll be going across?"

"Yes, indeed. Seat booked in Canterbury Cathedral. An historic occasion, Harry. Something for people to tell their grandchildren about."

"For those who have any," Cussane smiled.

Halloran laughed. "Exactly, which hardly applies to us. I must be off. I've got a dozen things to organize."

Cussane sat there thinking about it, then reached for his raincoat where he'd thrown it on a chair, and took out the poniard in it's leather sheath. He put it in one of the desk drawers, then took out the Stetchkin. What a bungling amateur Lubov had been to use a weapon of Russian manufacture. But it was the proof that he had needed. It meant that to his masters, he was not only expendable—he was now a liability.

"So what now, Harry Cussane?" he asked himself softly. "Where do you go?"

Strange that habit, when speaking to himself, of addressing

Cussane by his full name. It was as if he were another person which, in a way, he was. The phone rang and when he answered, Devlin spoke to him.

"There you are."

"Where are you?"

"Dublin airport. I'm picking up a houseguest. A very pretty girl, actually. I think you'll like her. I thought we all might have supper tonight."

"That sounds nice," Cussane said calmly. "I've agreed to take evening mass, though, at the village church. I'll be finished at eight. Is that all right?"

"Fine. We'll look forward to seeing you."

Cussane put the phone down. He could run, of course, but where and to what purpose? In any event, the play had at least one more act to run, all his instincts told him that.

"No place to hide, Harry Cussane," he said softly.

WHEN HARRY FOX and Tanya came through the gate into the arrival hall, Devlin was waiting, leaning against a pillar smoking a cigarette, wearing the black felt hat and trench coat. He came forward, smiling.

"*Cead mile failte,*" he said and took the young woman's hands. "That's Irish for a hundred thousand welcomes."

"*Go raibh maith agat.*" Fox gave him the ritual thanks.

"Stop showing off." Devlin took her bag. "His mother was a decent Irishwoman, thank the Lord."

Her face was shining. "I'm so excited. All this is so—so unbelievable."

Fox said. "Right, you're in safe hands now. I'm off. There's a return flight in an hour. I'd better book in. We'll be in touch, Liam."

He went off through the crowd, and Devlin took her elbow and led her to the main entrance. "A nice man," she said. "His hand? What happened?"

162

"He picked up a bag with a bomb in it in Belfast one bad night and didn't manage to throw it fast enough. He manages with the electronic marvel they've given him."

"You say that so calmly," she said, as they crossed to the car park.

"He wouldn't thank you for the wrong kind of sympathy. Comes of his particular kind of upbringing. Eton, the Guards. They teach you to get on with it, not cry in your beer." He handed her into his old Alfa Romeo sports car. "Harry's a special breed, just like that ould bastard Ferguson. What's known as a gentleman."

"Which you are not?"

"God save us, my ould mother would turn in her grave to hear you even suggest it," he said as he drove away. "So, you decided to give things some more thought after I left Paris? What happened?"

She told him everything. Belov, the phone conversation with Maslovsky, Shepilov and Turkin, and, finally, Alex Martin in Jersey.

Devlin was frowning thoughtfully as she finished. "So they were on to you? Actually waiting in Jersey? How in the hell would they know that?"

"I asked about the train times at the hotel," she told him. "I didn't give my name or room number. I thought that covered it. Perhaps Belov and his people were able to make the right sort of inquiries."

"Maybe. Still, you're here now. You'll be staying with me at my cottage in Kilrea. It isn't far. I've got a call to make when we get in. With luck, we'll be able to set up the right kind of meeting for you tomorrow. Lots of photos for you to plow through."

"I hope something comes of it," she said.

"Don't we all? Anyway, a quiet night. I'll make the supper, and a good friend of mine is joining us."

"Anyone interesting?"

"The kind of man you'd find rather thin on the ground where you come from. A Catholic priest. Father Harry Cussane. I think you'll like him."

HE PHONED MCGUINNESS from his study. "The girl is here. Staying with me at my place. How soon can you set up the right meeting?"

"Never mind that," McGuinness told him. Have you heard about Cherny?"

Devlin was immediately alert. "No."

"Took a very long fall from a very high window at Trinity College this afternoon. The thing is, did he fall, or was he pushed?"

"I suppose one could say his end was fortuitous," Devlin said.

"For one person only," McGuinness told him. "Jesus, I'd like to get my hands on that sod."

"Set up the meeting with the girl then," Devlin said. "Maybe she'll recognize him."

"I'd go to confession again if I thought that could be guaranteed," McGuinness told him. "Okay, leave it with me. I'll get back to you."

CUSSANE ROBED FOR mass in the sacristy, very calm, very cold. It wasn't like a play any longer. More like an improvization in which the actors created a story for themselves. He had no idea what was going to happen.

The four acolytes who waited for him were village boys, clean and neat and rather angelic in their scarlet cassocks and white cottas. He settled the stole around his neck, picked up his prayer book, and turned to them.

"Let's make it special tonight, shall we?"

He pressed the bell button at the door. A moment later, the organ started to play. One of the boys opened the door, and they moved in procession through into the small church.

DEVLIN WAS WORKING in the kitchen preparing steaks. Tanya opened the French windows and was immediately aware of the organ music drifting across the garden from the other side of the wall. She went in to Devlin. "What's that?"

"There's a convent over there and a hospice. Their chapel is the village church. That'll be Harry Cussane celebrating mass. He won't be long."

She went back into the living room and stood listening at the French windows. It was nice and peaceful. The organ playing was really rather good. She crossed the lawn and opened the door in the wall. The chapel, on the end of the convent, looked picturesque and inviting, soft light flooding from the windows. She went up the path and opened the oaken door.

THERE WERE ONLY a handful of villagers, two people in wheelchairs who were obviously patients from the hospice, and several nuns. Sister Anne-Marie played the organ. It was not much of an instrument and the damp atmosphere had a bad effect on the reeds, but she was good. She had spent a year at the Conservatoire in Paris as a young girl before heeding God's call and turning to the religious life.

The lights were very dim, mainly candles, and the church was a place of shadows and calm, the nuns' voices sweet as they sang the offertory, *Domine Jesu Christ, Rex Floriae* . . . At the altar, Harry Cussane prayed for all sinners everywhere whose actions cut them off from the fact of God's infinite mercy and love. Tanya took a seat by herself to one side, moved by the atmosphere. The truth was that she had never attended a church service like this in her life. She couldn't see much of Cussane's face. He was simply the chief figure down there at the altar in the dim light, fascinating to her in his robes, as was the whole business.

The mass continued and most of those in the congregation went forward to the rail to receive the Body and Blood of Christ.

She watched, as the priest moved from one person to the other, his head bending to murmur the ritual words, and she was filled with a strange unease. It was as if she knew this man, as though some trick of physical movement seemed familiar.

When the mass was over, the final absolution given, he paused on the steps to address the congregation. "And in your prayers during the coming days, I would ask each one of you to pray for the Holy Father, soon to visit England at a most difficult time." He moved forward a little, the candlelight falling on his face. "Pray for him that your prayers added to his own grant him the strength to accomplish his mission."

His gaze passed over the entire congregation, and for a moment it was as if he was looking at her directly, then he moved on. Tanya froze in horror, absorbing the shock, the most terrible she had ever known in her life. When he spoke the words of the benediction, it was as if his lips moved with no sound. It was the face—the face that had haunted her dreams for years. Older, of course, kinder even, and yet unmistakably the face of Mikhail Kelly, the man they had named Cuchulain.

WHAT HAPPENED THEN was strange, yet perhaps not so strange, if one considered the circumstances. The shock was so profound that it seemed to drain all strength from her, and she remained in the half-darkness at the back of the church while people moved out and Cussane and the acolytes disappeared into the sacristy. It was very quiet in the church as she sat there trying to make sense of things. Cuchulain was Father Harry Cussane, Devlin's friend, and it explained so many things. Oh, my God, she thought, what am I going to do? And then the sacristy door opened and Cussane stepped out.

THINGS WERE ALMOST ready in the kitchen. Devlin checked the oven, whistling softly to himself, and called, "Have you laid the table in there?"

166

There was no reply. He went into the living room. Not only was the table not laid, but there was no sign of Tanya. Then he noticed the French window ajar, took off his apron, and moved forward.

"Tanya?" he called into the garden and in the same moment saw that the door in the garden wall stood open.

CUSSANE WORE A black suit and clerical collar. He paused for a moment, aware of her presence, although he made no sign. He'd noticed her almost at once during the mass. The fact that she was a stranger would have made her stand out, but in these circumstances it had been obvious who she must be. Knowing that, he saw the ghost of the child there in her face, the child who had struggled as he held her that day in Drumore, all those years ago. Eyes never change and the eyes—he had always remembered.

He turned at the altar rail, dropping to one knee to genuflect, and Tanya, in a panic now and terribly afraid, forced herself to her feet and moved along the aisle. The door to one of the confessional boxes stood partially open and she slipped inside. When she pulled it close, there was a slight creaking. She heard him walk down the aisle, the steps slow, distinct on the flagstone. They came closer. Stopped.

He said softly in Russian. "I know you are there, Tanya Voroninova. You can come out now."

SHE STOOD THERE, shivering, very cold. He was quite calm, his face grave. Still in Russian, he said, "It's been a long time."

She said, "So, do you kill me like you killed my father? As you have killed so many others?"

"I hoped that wouldn't be necessary." He stood there looking at her, his hands in the pockets of his jacket, and then he smiled gently and there was a kind of sadness there. "I've heard you on records. You have a remarkable talent."

"So have you." She felt stronger now. "For death and destruction. They chose you well. My foster father knew what he was doing."

"Not really," he said. "Nothing is ever that simple. I happened to be available. The right tool at the right time."

She took a deep breath. "What happens now?"

"I thought we were supposed to be having dinner together, you, Liam and I," he said.

The porch door banged open and Devlin walked in. "Tanya?" he called and then paused. "Oh, there you are. So you two have met?"

"Yes, Liam, a long, long time ago," Harry Cussane told him. And his hand came out of the right pocket of his jacket holding the Stetchkin pistol he had taken from Lubov.

AT THE COTTAGE, he found cord in the kitchen drawer. "The steaks smell good, Liam. Better turn the oven off."

"Would you look at that?" Devlin said to the girl. "He thinks of everything."

"The only reason I've got this far." Cussane said calmly.

They went into the living room. He didn't tie them up, but motioned them to sit on the sofa by the fire. He stepped onto the hearth and reached up inside the chimney to find the Walther hanging on its nail, the one Devlin always kept there for emergencies.

"Keeping you out of temptation, Liam."

"He knows all my little secrets," Devlin said to Tanya, "but then he would. I mean, we've been friends for twenty years now." The bitterness was there in the voice, the shake of raw anger, and he helped himself to a cigarette from the box on the side table without asking permission and lit it.

Cussane sat some distance away at the dining table and held up the Stetchkin. "These things make very little sound, old friend. No one knows that better than you. No tricks. No foolish Devlin gallantry. I'd hate to have to kill you."

He laid the Stetchkin on the table and lit a cigarette himself.

"Friend, is it?" Devlin said. "About as true a friend as you are priest."

"Friend," Cussane insisted. "And I've been a good priest. Ask anyone who knew me on the Falls Road in Belfast in sixty-nine."

"Fine," Devlin said. "Only even an idiot like me can make two and two make four occasionally. Your masters put you in deep. To become a priest was your cover. Would I be right in thinking that you chose that seminary outside Boston for your training because I was English professor there?"

"Of course. You were an important man in the IRA in those days, Liam. The advantages that the relationship offered for the future were obvious, but friends we became and friends we stayed. You cannot avoid that fact."

"Sweet Jesus!" Devlin shook his head. "Who are you, Harry? Who are you really?"

"My father was Sean Kelly."

Devlin stared at him in astonishment. "But I knew him well. We served in the Lincoln Washington Brigade in the Spanish Civil War. Just a minute. He married a Russian girl he met in Madrid."

"My mother. My parents returned to Ireland, where I was born. My father was hanged in England in 1940 for his part in the IRA bombing campaign of that time. My mother and I lived in Dublin till 1953, then she took me to Russia."

Devlin said. "The KGB must have fastened onto you like leeches."

"Something like that."

"They discovered his special talents," Tanya put in. "Murder for example."

"No," Cussane answered mildly. "When I was first processed by the psychologists, Paul Cherny indicated that my special talent was for the stage."

"An actor, is it?" Devlin said. "Well, you're in the right job for it."

"Not really. No audience, you see." Cussane concentrated on Tanya. "I doubt whether I've killed more than Liam. In what way are we different?"

"He fought for a cause," she told him passionately.

"Exactly. I am a soldier, Tanya. I fight for my country—our country. As a matter of interest, I'm not an officer of the KGB. I am a lieutenant colonel in Military Intelligence." He smiled deprecatingly to Devlin. "They kept promoting me."

"But the things you've done. The killing," she said. "Innocent people."

"There cannot be innocence in this world, not with Man in it. The Church teaches us that. There is always iniquity in this life—life is unfair. We must deal with the world as it is, not as it might have been."

"Jesus!" Devlin said. "One minute you're Cuchulain, the next, you're a priest again. Have you any idea who you really are?"

"When I am priest, then priest I am." Cussane told him. "There is no avoiding that. The Church would be the first to say it, in spite of what I have been. But the other me fights for his country. I have nothing to apologize for. I'm at war."

"Very convenient," Devlin said. "So, the Church gives you your answer, or is it the KGB—or is there a difference?"

"Does it matter?"

"Damn you, Harry, tell me one thing? How did you know we were on to you? How did you know about Tanya? Was it me?" he exploded. "But how could it have been me?"

"You mean you checked your telephone as usual?" Cussane was at the drinks cabinet now, the Stetchkin in his hand. He poured Bushmills into three glasses, carried them on a tray to the table in front of the sofa, took one and stepped back. "I was using special equipment up there in the attic of my place. Directional microphone and other stuff. There wasn't much that went on here that I missed."

170

Devlin took a deep breath, but when he lifted his glass, his hand was steady. "So much for friendship." He swallowed the whisky. "So, what happens now?"

"To you?"

"No, to you, you fool. Where do you go, Harry? Back home to dear old Mother Russia?" He shook his head and turned to Tanya. "Come to think of it, Russia isn't his home."

Cussane didn't feel anger then. There was no despair in his heart. All his life, he had played each part that was required of him, cultivated the kind of professional coolness necessary for a well-judged performance. There had been little room for real emotion in his life. Any actions, even the good ones, had been simply reaction to the given situation, an essential part of the performance. Or so he told himself. And yet he truly liked Devlin, always had. And the girl? He looked at Tanya now. He did not want to harm the girl.

Devlin, as if sensing a great deal of this, said softly, "Where do you run to, Harry? Is there anywhere?"

"No," Harry Cussane said calmly. "Nowhere to go. No place to hide. For what I have done, your IRA friends would dispose of me without hesitation. Ferguson certainly would not want me alive. Nothing to be gained from that. I would only be a liability."

"And your own people? Once back in Moscow, it would be the Gulag for sure. At the end of the day, you're a failure, and they don't like that."

"True," Cussane nodded, "Except in one respect. They don't even want me back, Liam. They just want me dead. They've already tried. To them also I would only be an embarrassment."

There was silence at his words, then Tanya said. "But what happens? What do you do?"

"God knows," he said. "I am a dead man walking, my dear. Liam understands that. He's right. There is no place for me to run. Today, tomorrow, next week. If I stay in Ireland, McGuinness and his men will have my head, wouldn't you agree, Liam?"

"True enough."

Cussane stood up and paced up and down, holding the Stetchkin against his knee. He turned to Tanya. "You think life was cruel to a little girl back there in Drumore in the rain? You know how old I was? Twenty years of age. Life was cruel when they hanged my father. When my mother agreed to take me back to Russia. When Paul Cherny picked me out at the age of fifteen as a specimen with interesting possibilities for the KGB." He sat down again. "If my mother and I had been left alone in Dublin, who knows what might have happened to that one great talent I possessed. The Abbey Theatre, the Old Vic, Stratford?" He shrugged. "Instead . . ."

Devlin was conscious of a great sadness. He forgot everything else for the moment, except that for years he had liked this man more than most.

"That's life," he said. "Always some bugger telling you what to do."

"Living our lives for us, you mean?" Cussane said. "School-teachers, the police, union leaders, politicians, parents?"

"Even priests," Devlin said gently.

"Yes, I think I see now what the anarchists mean when they say 'Shoot an authority figure today.'" The evening paper was on a chair with a headline referring to the pope's visit to England. Cussane picked it up. "The pope, for instance."

Devlin said, "A bad joke, that."

"But why should I be joking?" Cussane asked him. "You know what my brief was all those years ago, Liam? You know what Maslovsky told me my task was? To help create chaos, disorder, fear, and uncertainty in the West. I've helped keep the Irish conflict going, by hitting counterproductive targets, causing great harm on occasion to both Catholic and Protestant causes; IRA, UVF, I've pulled everyone in. But here." He held up the newspaper with the photo of Pope John Paul on the front page. "How about this for the most counterproductive target of all time? Would they like that in Moscow?" He nodded to Tanya,

"You must know Maslovsky well enough by now. Would it please him, do you think?"

"You're mad," she whispered.

"Perhaps." He tossed a length of cord across to her. "Tie his wrists behind his back. No tricks, Liam."

He stood well back, covering them with the Stetchkin. There was little for Devlin to do except submit. The girl tied his hands, awkwardly. Cussane pushed him down on his face beside the fire.

"Lie down beside him," he told Tanya.

He pulled her arms behind her and tied her hands securely, then her ankles. Then he checked Devlin's wrists and tied his ankles also.

"So, you're not going to kill us?" Devlin said.

"Why should I?"

Cussane stood up, walked across the room, and with one swift jerk pulled the telephone wire out of the wall. Devlin turned his head to one side, pillowed against the rug. "Where are you going?"

"Canterbury," Cussane said. "Eventually, that is."

"Canterbury?"

"That's where the pope will be on Saturday. They'll all be there. The cardinals, the archbishop of Canterbury, Prince Charles. I know these things, Liam. I run the press office at the secretariat, remember."

"All right, let's be sensible," Devlin said. "You'll never get near him. The last thing the Brits want is the pope dead on their hands. They'll have security at Canterbury that would make even the Kremlin sit up and take notice."

"A real challenge," Cussane said calmly.

"For God's sake, Harry, shoot the pope? To what end?"

"Why not?" Cussane shrugged. "Because he's there. Because I've nowhere else to go. If I've got to die, I might as well go down doing something spectacular." He smiled down. "And you can always try and stop me, Liam, you and McGuinness and Ferguson and his people in London. Even the KGB would move heaven and earth to stop me, if they could. It would certainly leave them with a lot of explaining to do."

Devlin exploded. "Is that all it is to you, Harry? A game?"

"The only one in town," Cussane said. "For years, I've been manipulated by other people. A regular puppet on a string. This time, I'm in charge. It should be an interesting change."

He moved away, and Devlin heard the French window open and close. There was silence. Tanya said, "He's gone."

Devlin nodded and struggled into a sitting position. He forced his wrists against the cord, but he was wasting his time and knew it.

Tanya said, "Liam, do you think he means it? About the pope?"

"Yes," Devlin said grimly. "I believe he does."

ONCE AT HIS cottage, Cussane worked quickly and methodically. From a small safe hidden behind books in his study he took his Irish passport for his usual identity. There were also two British ones in different names. In one he was still a priest—in another, a journalist. There was also two thousand pounds in notes of varying sizes—English, not Irish.

He got a canvas holdall from his wardrobe, of a type favored by army officers, and opened it. There was a board panel in the bottom, which he pressed open. Inside he placed most of the money, the false passports, and a Walther PPK with a Carswell silencer and several additional clips of ammunition. He put in a block of plastic explosive and a couple of timing pencils. Like the soldier he thought himself to be, he had to be ready for anything, so he got a couple of army field dressing packs from the bathroom cupboard and some morphine ampules and put them in also. He replaced the panel, rolled up one of his black cassocks and placed it in the bottom of the bag. A couple of shirts and what he thought of as civilian ties, socks, toilet articles. His prayer book went in, the Host in the silver pyx, and the holy oils, all as a reflex habit. It had been second nature to travel with them for years now.

He went downstairs to the hall and pulled on his black raincoat, then he took one of the two black felt hats from the hall cupboard and went into the study. Inside the crown of the hat he had sewn two plastic clips. He opened a drawer in his desk and took out a .38 Smith and Wesson revolver with a two-inch barrel. It fitted snugly into the clips, and he put the hat into his holdall. The Stetchkin, he put into the pocket of his raincoat.

So, he was ready. He glanced once around the study of the cottage that had been his home for so long, then turned and went out. He crossed the yard to the garage, opened the door, and switched on the light. His motorcycle stood beside the car, an old 350cc B.S.A. in superb condition. He strapped his holdall onto the rear, took the crash helmet from the peg on the wall, and put it on.

When he kicked the starter, the engine roared into life at once. He sat there for a moment adjusting things, then he crossed himself and rode away. The sound of the engine faded into the distance and after awhile, there was only silence.

IN THE COTTAGE, Devlin had long since given up trying to force his way free from the cords. He and Tanya sat side by side, leaning against the sofa.

"This could get very unfunny," he said. "My cleaning lady is due tomorrow, but not until ten o'clock."

AT THAT MOMENT in Dublin, Martin McGuinness was watching one of his men put the receiver back down on the phone rest.

"There's no busy signal and no dial tone. The line's dead, that's certain."

"That seems more than a bit strange to me, laddie," McGuinness said. "Let's pay Liam a visit, and let's drive fast."

It took McGuinness and a couple of his men forty minutes to

get there. McGuinness stood watching while his men released Devlin and the girl, and he shook his head.

"Christ, Liam, it would be funny seeing the great Liam Devlin trussed up like a chicken if it wasn't so bloody tragic. Tell me what it's about then."

He and Devlin went into the kitchen, and Devlin filled him in on what had happened. When he was finished, McGuinness exploded. "The cunning bastard. On the Falls Road in Belfast City they remember him as a saint, and him a sodding Russian agent pretending to be a priest."

"I shouldn't think the Vatican will be exactly overjoyed," Devlin told him.

"And you know what's worse? What really sticks in my throat? He's no fucking Russian at all. Jesus, Liam, his father died on an English gallows for the Cause." McGuinness was shaking with rage now. "I'm going to have his balls."

"And how do you propose to do that?"

"You leave that to me. The pope at Canterbury, is it? I'll close Ireland up so tight that not even a rat could find a hole to sneak out."

He bustled out, calling to his men, and was gone. Tanya came into the kitchen. She looked pale and tired. "Now what happens?"

"You put on the kettle and we'll have a nice cup of tea. You know, they say that in the old days, a messenger bearing bad news was usually executed. You'll excuse me for a few minutes while I go across the road and ring Ferguson.

Ten

BALLYWALTER on the coast just south of Dundalk Bay near Clogher Head could hardly be described as a port. A pub, a few houses, half-a-dozen fishing boats, and the tiniest of harbors. It was a good hour and a half after Devlin's phone call to Ferguson that Cussane turned his motorcycle into a wood on a hill overlooking the place. He pushed his machine up on its stand and went and looked down at Ballywalter, clear in the moonlight below. Next he went back to the wood, unstrapped his holdall, and took out the black trilby, which he put on his head instead of the crash helmet.

He started down the road, bag in hand. What he intended now was tricky, but clever if it worked. It was like chess, really. Trying to think not just of one move, but three moves ahead. Certainly now was the time to see if all that information so carefully and gently extracted from the dying Danny Malone would prove worthwhile.

SEAN DEEGAN HAD been publican in Ballywalter for eleven

years. It was hardly a full-time occupation in a village that boasted only forty-one men of the legal age to drink, which explained why he was also skipper of the forty-foot motor fishing boat *Mary Murphy*. Added to this, on the illegal side of things, he was not only a member of the IRA, but very much on the active list, having only been released from Long Kesh Prison in Ulster in February. He had been there serving three years imprisonment for possession of illegal weapons. The fact that Deegan had personally killed two British soldiers in Derry had never been traced to him by the authorities.

His wife and two children were away visiting her mother in Galway, and he had closed the bar at eleven, intending fishing early. He was still awake when Cussane came down the street, for the simple reason that he had been awakened from his bed by a phone call from one of McGuinness's men. Deegan offered an illegal way out of the country to the Isle of Man, a useful staging post for England. The description of Cussane was brief and to the point.

Deegan had hardly put the phone down when there was a knock at the door. He opened it and found Cussane standing there. The description he had been given was accurate enough to tell him who his nocturnal caller was, although the clerical collar and black hat and raincoat would have been enough in themselves.

"What can I do for you, Father?" Deegan asked, stepping back so that Cussane might come in.

They went into the small bar and Deegan stirred the fire. "I got your name from a parishioner, Danny Malone," Cussane said. "My name is Daly, by the way."

"Danny, is it?" Deegan said. "I heard he was in a bad way."

"Dying, poor soul. He told me you could do a run to the Isle of Man if the price was right, or the cause."

Deegan went behind the bar and poured a whisky. "Will you join me, Father?"

"No thanks."

"You're in trouble? Political or police?"

"A little of both." Cussane took ten English fifty-pound notes from his pocket and laid them on the bar. "Would this handle it?"

Deegan picked the notes up and weighed them thoughtfully. "And why not, Father? Look, you sit by the fire and keep yourself warm, and I'll make a phone call."

"A phone call?"

"Sure and I can't manage the boat on my own. I need at least one crew and two is better."

He went out, closing the door. Cussane went around the bar to the phone there and waited. There was a slight tinkle from the bell and he lifted the receiver gently.

The man was talking urgently. "Deegan here at Ballywalter. Have you Mr. McGuinness?"

"He's gone to bed."

"Jesus, man, will you get him? He's here at my place now. That fella Cussane your people phoned about."

"Hold right there." There was a delay, then another voice said, "McGuinness. Is it yourself, Sean?"

"And none other. Cussane's here at my pub. Calls himself Daly. He's just given me five hundred quid to take him to the Isle of Man. What do I do, hold him?"

McGuinness said, "I'd like nothing better than to see to him myself, but that's childish. You've got some good men there?"

"Phil Egan and Tadgh McAteer."

"So—he dies, this one, Sean. If I told you what he's done in the past, the harm he's done the Movement, you'd never believe it. Take him in that boat of yours, nice and easy, no fuss, then a bullet in the back of the head three miles out and over the side with him."

"Consider it done," Deegan told him.

He put down the phone, left the living room, went upstairs,

and dressed fully. He went into the bar, pulling on an old pilot coat. "I'll leave you for a while, Father, while I go and get my lads. Help yourself to anything you need."

"That's kind of you," Cussane told him.

He lit a cigarette and read the evening paper for something to do. Deegan was back in half an hour, two men with him. "Phil Egan, Father. Tadgh McAteer."

They all shook hands. Egan was small and wiry, perhaps twenty-five. McAteer was a large man in an old reefer coat with a beer belly heavy over his belt. He was older than Deegan. Fifty-five at least, Cussane would have thought.

"We'll get going then, Father." Cussane picked up his bag and Deegan said, "Not so fast, Father. I like to know what I'm handling."

He put Cussane's bag on the bar, opened it and quickly sifted through the contents. He zipped it up, turned and nodded to McAteer, who ran his hands roughly over the priest and found the Stetchkin. He took it out and placed it on the bar without a word.

Deegan said, "What you need that for is your business. You get it back when we land you in the Isle of Man." He put it in his pocket.

"I understand," Cussane said.

"Good, then let's get going," and Deegan led the way out.

DEVLIN WAS IN bed when McGuinness rang him. "They've got him," he said.

"Where?"

"Ballywalter. One of our own, a man called Sean Deegan. Cussane turned up there saying he was a friend of Danny Malone and needed an undercover run to the Isle of Man. Presumably Danny had told him a thing or two he shouldn't."

"Danny's a dying man. He wouldn't know what he was saying half the time," Devlin said.

180

"Anyway, Cussane, or Father Daly as he's now calling himself, is in for a very unpleasant shock. Three miles out, Deegan and his boys nail the coffin lid on him and over he goes. I told you we'd get the sod."

"So you did."

"I'll be in touch, Liam."

Devlin sat there thinking about it. Too good to be true. Cussane had obviously discovered from Danny Malone that Deegan offered the kind of service he needed. Fair enough, but to turn up as he had done, no attempt at disguise beyond a change of name. It could be argued that he might have assumed that it would be morning before Devlin and Tanya would be found, but even so . . . It didn't make any kind of sense—or did it?

THERE WAS A light mist rolling in from the sea as they moved out, but the sky was clear and the moon touched things with a luminosity that was vaguely unreal. McAteer busied himself on deck, Egan had the hatch to the small engine room off and was down the ladder, and Deegan was at the wheel. Cussane stood beside him peering out through the window.

"A fine night," Deegan observed.

"Indeed it is. How long will it take?"

"Four hours and that's taking it easy. It means we can time it to catch the local fishing boats going back to the Isle of Man with their night catches. We'll land you on the west coast. Little place I know near Peel. You can get a bus across to Douglas, the capital. There's an airport, Ronaldsway. You can get a plane to London from there or just across the water to Blackpool on the English coast."

"Yes, I know," Cussane told him.

"Might as well go below. Get your head down for a while," Deegan suggested.

The cabin had four bunks and a fixed table in the center, a small galley at one end. It was very untidy, but warm and snug, in spite of the smell of diesel oil. Cussane made himself tea in a mug and sat at the table drinking it and smoking a cigarette. Then he lay on one of the bottom bunks, his hat beside him, eyes closed. After a while, McAteer and Egan came down the companionway.

"Are you all right, Father?" McAteer inquired. "Cup of tea or anything?"

"I've had one, thank you," Cussane said. "I think I'll get some sleep."

He lay there, eyes almost closed, one hand negligently reaching under the hat. McAteer smiled at Egan and winked and the other man spooned instant coffee into three mugs and added boiling water and condensed milk. They went out. Cussane could hear their steps on deck, the murmur of conversation, a burst of laughter. He lay there, waiting for what was to come.

IT WAS PERHAPS half an hour later that the engine stopped and they started to drift. Cussane got up and put his feet to the floor.

Deegan called down the companionway, "Would you come up on deck, Father?"

Cussane settled his hat on his head at a neat angle and went up the ladder. Egan sat on the engine hatch, McAteer leaned out of the open wheelhouse window, and Deegan stood at the stern rail, smoking a cigarette and looking back toward the Irish coast two or three miles away.

Cussane said. "What is it? What's happening?"

"The jig's up!" Deegan turned, holding the Stetchkin in his right hand. "You see, we know who you are, old son. All about you."

"And your wicked ways," McAteer called.

Egan rattled a length of heavy chain. Cussane glanced toward him, then turned to Deegan, taking off his hat and holding it across his chest. "There's no way we can discuss this, I suppose?"

182

"Not a chance," Deegan told him.

Cussane shot him in the chest through the hat and Deegan was punched back against the rail. He dropped the Stetchkin on the deck, overbalanced, grabbed for the rail unsuccessfully, and went into the sea. Cussane was already turning, firing up at McAteer in the wheelhouse as he tried to draw back, the bullet catching the big man just above the right eye. Egan lashed out at him with the length of chain. Cussane avoided the awkward blow with ease.

"Bastard!" Egan cried, and Cussane took careful aim and shot him in the heart.

He moved fast now, pocketing the Stetchkin that Deegan had dropped, and launched the inflatable with its outboard motor, which was stowed amidships. He tied it to the rail and went into the wheelhouse where he had left his bag, stepping over Mc-Ateer's body to get it. He opened the false bottom, took out the plastic explosive, and sliced a piece off with his pocketknife. He stuck one of the pencil timers in it, primed to explode in fifteen minutes, and dropped it down the engine hatch, then he got into the inflatable, started the motor, and moved back to shore at speed. Behind him, Sean Deegan, still alive in spite of the bullet in his chest, watched him go and kicked slowly to keep afloat.

Cussane was well on his way when the explosion rent the night, yellow and orange flames flowering like petals. He glanced back only briefly. Things couldn't have worked out better. Now he was dead and McGuinness and Ferguson would call off the hounds. He wondered how Devlin would feel when he finally realized the truth.

He landed on a small beach close to Ballywalter and dragged the inflatable up into the shelter of a clump of gorse bushes. Then he retraced his steps up to the wood where he had left the motorcycle. He strapped his bag onto the rear, put on his crash helmet, and rode away.

IT WAS ANOTHER fishing boat from Ballywater, the *Dublin*

Town, out night fishing, that was first on the scene. The crew, on deck handling their nets about a mile away, had seen the explosion when it occurred. By the time they reached the position where the *Mary Murphy* had gone down, about half an hour had elapsed. There was a considerable amount of wreckage on the surface, and a life jacket with the boat's name stenciled on it told them the worst. The skipper notified the coast guard of the tragedy, by radio, and continued the search for survivors, or at least the bodies of the crew, but had no success. A thickening sea mist made things even more difficult. By five o'clock, a coast guard cutter was there from Dundalk, also several other small fishing craft, and they continued the search as dawn broke.

THE NEWS OF the tragedy was passed on to McGuinness at four o'clock in the morning and he, in turn, phoned Devlin.

"Christ knows what happened," McGuinness said. "She blew up and went down like a stone."

"And no bodies, you say?"

"Probably inside her, or what's left of her on the bottom. And it seems there's a bad riptide in that area. It would carry a body a fair distance. I'd like to know what happened. A good man, Sean Deegan."

"So would I," Devlin said.

"Still, no more Cussane. At least that bastard has met his end. You'll tell Ferguson?"

"Leave it with me."

Devlin put on a dressing gown, went downstairs, and made some tea. Cussane was dead and yet he felt no pain for the man who, whatever else, had been his friend for more than twenty years. No sense of mourning. Instead a feeling of unease, like a lump in the gut that refused to go away.

He rang Cavendish Square number in London. It was picked up after a slight delay and Ferguson's voice answered, still half asleep. Devlin gave him the news and the brigadier came fully awake with some rapidity.

184

"Are you sure about this?"

"That's how it looks. God knows what went wrong on the boat."

"Ah, well," Ferguson said. "At least Cussane's out of our hair for good and all. The last thing I needed was that madman on the rampage." He snorted. "Kill the pope indeed."

"What about Tanya?"

"She can come back tomorrow. Put her on the plane and I'll meet her myself."

"Right." Devlin said. "That's it then."

"You don't sound happy, Liam. What is it?"

"Let's put it this way. With this one, I'd like to see the body," Devlin said and rang off.

THE ULSTER BORDER with the Irish Republic—in spite of road blocks, a considerable police presence, and the British Army—has always been wide open to anyone who knows it. In many cases, farms on both sides have land breeched by the border's imaginary line and the area is crisscrossed by hundreds of narrow country lanes, field paths, and tracks.

Cussane was safely in Ulster by four o'clock. Any kind of a vehicle on the road at that time in the morning was rare enough to make it essential that he drop out of sight for a while, which he did, on the other side of Newry, holing up in a disused barn in a wood just off the main road.

He didn't sleep but sat comfortably against a wall and smoked, the Stetchkin ready at hand, just in case. He left shortly after six, a time when there would be enough early workers on the road to make him inconspicuous, taking the A1 through Banbridge to Lisburn.

It was 7:15 when he rode into the car park at Aldergrove Airport and parked the motorcycle. The Stetchkin joined the Walther in the false bottom of the bag. The holiday season having started, there was a flight to the Isle of Man leaving at 8:15, with flights to Glasgow, Edinburgh, and Newcastle as possible alternatives if there was difficulty in obtaining a seat, all leaving within a period of one hour. The Isle of Man was his choice by preference because it was a soft route, used mainly by holiday-makers. In any event, there was space available, and he had no difficulty in obtaining a ticket.

As regards the items hidden in the bottom of his bag, all hand baggage would be x-rayed, but that was true at most international airports these days. At Belfast, most baggage destined for the hold was x-rayed also, but he knew that this did not always apply to the softer routes during the holiday season. Any difficulty he might have would present itself at customs in the Isle of Man.

IT WAS APPROXIMATELY eight-thirty and Cussane had been airborne for a good ten minutes when the *Dublin Town,* running low on fuel, gave up the fruitless search for survivors from the *Mary Murphy* and turned toward Ballywalter. It was the youngest member of the crew, a fifteen-year-old boy coiling rope in the prow, who noticed the wreckage a couple of yards to starboard and called to the skipper, who altered course at once. A few minutes later, he cut the engines and coasted in beside one of the *Mary Murphy*'s hatches.

Sean Deegan was sprawled across it on his back. His head turned slowly and he managed a ghastly smile. "Took your sweet time about it, didn't you?" he called in a hoarse voice.

AT RONALDSWAY AIRPORT, Cussane had no difficulty at all with customs. He retrieved his bag and joined the large number of people passing through. No one made any attempt to stop him. As with all holiday resorts, the accent was on making things as painless for the tourist as possible. Islander aircraft made the short flight to Blackpool on the English coast numerous times during the day, but they were busy that morning and the earliest flight he could get was at noon. It could have been worse, of course, and he purchased a ticket and went along to the cafeteria to have something to eat.

IT WAS ELEVEN-THIRTY when Ferguson answered the phone and found Devlin on the line. He listened, frowning in horror. "Are you certain?"

"Absolutely. This man Deegan survived the explosion only because Cussane shot him into the water beforehand. It was Cussane who caused the explosion, then took off back to the shore in the fishing boat's inflatable. Almost ran Deegan down."

"But why?" Ferguson demanded.

"The clever bastard has been beating me at chess for years. I know his style. Always three moves ahead of the game. By staging his apparent death last night, he pulled off the hounds. There has been no one looking for him. No need."

Ferguson was filled with a dreadful foreboding. "Are you trying to say what I think you are?"

"What do you think? He's on your side of the water now, not ours, Brigadier."

Ferguson swore softly. "Right, I'll get some official help from Special Branch in Dublin. They can turn over that cottage of his for us. Photos, fingerprints. Anything useful."

"You'll need to inform the Catholic secretariat," Devlin told him. "They're going to love this one at the Vatican."

"The lady at number ten isn't likely to be too ecstatic about it, either. What plane had you booked the Voroninova girl on?"

"Two o'clock."

"Come with her. I need you."

"There is just one item of minor importance, but worth mentioning," Devlin told him. "On your side of the water, I'm still a wanted man, from way back. A member of an illegal organization is the least of it."

"I'll take care of that, for God's sake," Ferguson said. "Just get your backside on that plane," and he hung up.

Tanya Voroninova brought tea in from the kitchen. "What happens now?"

"I'm going with you to London," he said, "and we'll take it from there."

"And Cussane? Where is he, would you say?"

"Anywhere and everywhere." He sipped some of his tea. "He has one problem, however. The pope arrives Friday, according to the morning paper. Visits Canterbury the next day."

"Saturday the twenty-ninth?"

"Exactly, so Cussane has some time to fill. The question is, where does he intend to go and what does he intend to do?"

The phone rang. McGuinness was on the other end. "You've spoken to Ferguson?"

"I have."

"What does he intend to do?"

"God knows. He's asked me to go over."

"And will you?"

"Yes."

"Jesus, Liam, did you hear about this Russian, Lubov, turning up dead in the cinema. He preaches a hell of a sermon, this priest of yours."

"He's developed a slightly different attitude toward the job since he discovered his own people were trying to knock him off," Devlin said. "Interesting to see where it takes him."

"To Canterbury is where it's taking the mad bastard," McGuinness said, "and we can't help with that. It's up to British Intelligence to handle this one. Nothing more the IRA can do for them. Watch your back, Liam."

He rang off and Devlin sat there, frowning thoughtfully. He stood up. "I'm going out for a little while," he said to Tanya. "Shan't be long," and he went out through the French windows.

THE CUSTOMS OFFICERS at Blackpool were just as courteous as they had been at Ronaldsway. Cussane actually paused, smiling as the stream of passengers moved through, and offered his bag.

"Anything to declare, Father?" the officer asked.

Cussane unzipped his bag. "A bottle of Scotch and two hundred cigarettes."

The customs man grinned. "You could have had a liter of wine as well. It isn't your day, Father."

"Obviously not." Cussane zipped up his bag and moved on.

He hesitated outside the entrance of the small airport. There were several taxicabs waiting, but he decided to walk down to the main road instead. He had, after all, all the time in the world. There was a newsstand across the road, and he crossed over and bought a paper. As he came out, a bus pulled in at the stop a few paces away. Its indicator said Morecambe, which he knew was another seaside resort some miles up the coast. On impulse, he ran forward and scrambled on board as it drew away.

He purchased a ticket and went up on the top deck. It was really very pleasant and he felt calm, yet full of energy at the same time. He opened the newspaper and saw that the news from the South Atlantic was not good. H.M.S. *Coventry* had been bombed and a Cunard container ship, the *Atlantic Conveyor,* had been hit by an Exocet missile. He lit a cigarette and settled down to read about it.

WHEN DEVLIN WENT into the ward at the hospice, Sister Anne-Marie was at Danny Malone's bed. Devlin waited and she finally whispered something to the nurse, then turned and noticed him. "And what do you want?"

"To talk to Danny."

"He isn't really up to conversation this morning."

"It's very important."

She frowned in exasperation. "It always is with you. All right. Ten minutes." She started to walk away, then turned. "Father Cussane didn't come in last night. Do you know why?"

"No," Devlin lied. "I haven't seen him."

She walked away and he pulled a chair forward. "Danny, how are you?"

Malone opened his eyes and said hoarsely. "Is it you, Liam? Father Cussane didn't come."

"Tell me, Danny, you talked to him of Sean Deegan of Bally-walter, who handles the Isle of Man run, I understand."

Malone frowned. "Sure, I talked to him about a lot of things."

"But mainly of IRA matters."

"Sure, and he was interested in me telling him how I managed things in the old days."

"Particularly across the water?" Devlin asked.

"Yes. You know how long I lasted without getting caught, Liam. He wanted to know how I did it." He frowned. "What's the problem?"

"You were always the strong one, Danny. Be strong now. He wasn't one of our own."

Malone's eyes widened. "You're having me on, Liam."

"And Sean Deegan in hospital with a bullet in him and two good men dead?"

Danny sat there, staring at him. "Tell me." So Devlin did. When he was finished, Danny Malone said softly, "Bastard!"

"Tell me what you can remember, Danny. Anything that particularly interested him."

Malone frowned, trying to think. "Yes, the business of how I stayed ahead of Special Branch and those Intelligence boys for so long. I explained to him that I never used the IRA network when I was over there. Totally unreliable, you know that, Liam."

"True."

"I always used the underworld myself. Give me an honest crook any day of the week, or a dishonest one—if the price is right. I knew a lot of people like that."

"Tell me about them," Devlin said.

190

CUSSANE LIKED SEASIDE towns, especially the ones that catered to the masses. Honest, working-class people, out for a good time. Lots of cafés, amusement arcades, fairgrounds, and plenty of bracing air. Morecambe certainly had that. The dark waters of the bay were being whipped into whitecaps, and on the far side he could see the mountains of the Lake District.

He walked across the road. It was not the height of the season yet, but there were plenty of tourists about, and he threaded his way through the narrow streets until he found his way to the bus station.

It was possible to travel to most of the major provincial cities by high-speed bus, mainly on the motorways. He consulted the timetables and found what he was looking for, a bus to Glasgow via Carlisle and Dumfries. It left in one hour. He booked a ticket and went in search of something to eat.

Eleven

EORGI Romanov was senior attaché in charge of public relations at the Russian embassy in London. He was a tall, amiable-looking man of fifty, secretly rather proud of his aristocratic name. He had worked for KGB in London for eleven years now, had been promoted to lieutenant colonel the previous year. Ferguson liked him and he liked Ferguson. They got on so that when Ferguson phoned him just after his final telephone conversation with Devlin and suggested a meeting, Romanov agreed at once.

They met in Kensington Gardens by the Round Pond, a rendezvous so convenient to the embassy that Romanov was able to walk. Ferguson sat on a bench reading the *Times*. Romanov joined him.

"Hello, Georgi," Ferguson said.

"Charles. To what do I owe the honor?"

"Straight talking, Georgi. This one is about as bad as it could be. What do you know about a KGB agent, code name Cuchulain, put in deep in Ireland a good twenty years ago?"

"For once I can answer you with complete honesty," Romanov said. "Not a thing."

"Then listen and learn," Ferguson told him.

When he was finished, Romanov's face was grave. "This really is bad."

"You're telling me. The important thing is this. This madman is somewhere in the country, having boasted his intention of shooting the pope at Canterbury on Saturday and frankly, with his track record, we have to take him seriously. He isn't just another nutter."

"So what do you want me to do?"

"Get in touch with Moscow at the highest level. I should imagine the last thing they want is the pope dead at the hands of someone who can be proven to be a KGB agent, especially after the botched attempt in Rome. Warn them that on this one, we'll brook no interference. And if, by some wild chance, he gets in touch with you, Georgi, you tell me. We're going to get this bastard, make no mistake, and he dies, Georgi. No nonsense about a trial or anything like that. There again, I'm sure that's what your people in Moscow will want to hear."

"I'm sure it is." Romanov stood up. "I'd better get back and send a message."

"Take a tip from an old chum," Ferguson told him. "Make sure you go higher than Maslovsky."

IN VIEW OF the importance of the matter, Ferguson had to go to the director general, who in turn spoke to the home secretary. The result was a summons to Downing Street when Ferguson was halfway through his lunch. He rang for his car at once and was there within ten minutes. There was the usual small crowd at the end of the street, behind barriers. The policeman at the door saluted. It was opened the moment Ferguson raised a hand to the knocker.

There was a hum of activity inside, but then there would be, with the Falklands affair beginning to hot up. He was surprised

194

that she was seeing him personally. His guide led the way up the main staircase to the first floor and Ferguson followed. On the top floor, the young man knocked at a door and ushered him in.

"Brigadier Ferguson, Prime Minister."

She looked up from her desk, elegant as always, in a gray tweed dress, the blonde hair groomed to perfection, and laid down her pen. "My time is limited, Brigadier. I'm sure you understand."

"I would have thought that an understatement, Ma'am."

"The home secretary has filled me in on the relevant facts. I simply want an assurance from you that you will stop this man."

"I can give you that without the slightest hesitation, Prime Minister."

"If there was any kind of attempt on the pope's life while he is here, even an unsuccessful one, the consequences in political terms would be disastrous for us."

"I understand."

"As head of Group-4, you have special powers, direct from me. Use them, Brigadier. If there is anything else you need, do not hesitate to ask."

"Prime Minister."

She picked up her pen and returned to work, and Ferguson went out, to find the young man waiting for him outside. As they went downstairs, it occurred to Ferguson, and not for the first time in his career, that it was his own head that was on the block as much as Cussane's.

IN MOSCOW, IVAN Maslovsky received another summons to the office of the minister for state security, still occupied by Yuri Andropov, whom he found sitting at his desk considering a typed report.

He passed it across. "Read it, Comrade."

Maslovsky did so, and his heart seemed to turn to stone. When he was finished he handed it back, hands shaking.

"Your man, Maslovsky, is now at large in England, intent on assassinating the pope, his sole idea apparently being to seriously embarrass us. And there is nothing we can do except sit back and hope that British Intelligence will be 100 percent efficient in this matter."

"Comrade, what can I say?"

"Nothing, Maslovsky. This whole sorry affair was not only ill-advised. It was adventurism of the worst kind." Andropov pressed a button on his desk. The door opened behind Maslovsky, and two young KGB captains in uniform entered. "You will vacate your office, hand over all official keys and files to the person I designate. You will then be taken to the Lubianka to await trial for crimes against the State."

The Lubianka . . . how many people had he sent there himself? Suddenly, Maslovsky found difficulty in breathing and there was a pain in both arms, his chest. He started to fall and clutched at the desk. Andropov jumped back in alarm, and the two KGB officers rushed forward to grab Maslovsky's arms. He didn't bother to struggle, he had no strength, but he tried to speak as the pain got worse, tried to tell Andropov that there would be no cell in the Lubianka, no state trial. Strangely enough, the last thing he thought of was Tanya, his beloved Tanya seated at the piano playing his favorite piece, Debussy's *La Mer,* and then the music faded and there was only darkness.

FERGUSON HAD A meeting with the home secretary, the commander of D-13, Scotland Yard's antiterrorist squad, and the director general of the security services. He was tired when he got back to the flat and found Devlin sitting by the fire reading the *Times.*

"The pope seems to be taking over from the Falklands at the moment," Devlin said and folded the paper.

"Yes, well that's as may be," Ferguson said. "He can't go back fast enough for me. You should have been with me at this meeting I've just attended, Liam. Home secretary himself, Scotland Yard, the director, and you know what?" He warmed himself, back against the fire. "They aren't taking it all that seriously."

"Cussane, you mean?"

"Oh, don't get me wrong. They accept his existence, if you follow me. I showed them the record, and his activities in Dublin during the past few days have been bad enough, God knows. Levin, Lubov, Cherny, two IRA gunmen. The man's a butcher."

"No," Devlin said. "I don't think so. To him, it's just part of the job. Something that has to be done and he gets it over with cleanly and expeditiously. He has frequently spared lives over the years. Tanya and myself were a case in point. He goes for the target, that's all."

"Don't remind me." Ferguson shuddered, and then the door opened and Harry Fox came in.

"Hello, sir. Liam. I believe things have been happening while I've been away."

"I think one could say that," Ferguson told him. "Did things go well in Paris?"

"Yes."

"You can tell me later. I'd better fill you in on the latest events."

Which he did, as quickly as possible, Devlin occasionally making a point. When Ferguson was finished, Harry Fox said, "What a man. Strange." He shook his head.

"What is?"

"When I met him the other day, I rather liked him, sir."

"Not a difficult thing to do," Devlin said.

Ferguson frowned. "Let's have no more of that kind of bloody nonsense." The door opened and Kim entered with tea things on a tray and a plate of toasted crumpets. "Excellent," Ferguson said. "I'm famished."

Fox said, "What about Tanya Voroninova?"

"I've fixed her up with a safe house for the moment."

"Which one, sir?"

"The Chelsea Place apartment. The directorate supplied a woman operative to stay with her till we get sorted out."

He handed them each a cup of tea. "So, what's the next move?" Devlin asked.

"The home secretary and the director, and I must say I agree with them, don't feel we should make too public an issue of this at the moment. The whole purpose of the pope's visit is sweetness and light. A genuine attempt to help bring about the end of the war in the South Atlantic. Imagine how it would look on the front pages of the nationals. The first visit ever of a pope to England and a mad-dog killer on the loose."

"And a priest to boot, sir."

"Yes, well we can discount that, especially as we know what he really is."

Devlin said. "Discount nothing. Let me, as a not very good Catholic, fill you in on a few things. In the eyes of the Church, Harry Cussane was ordained a priest at Vine Landing, Connecticut, twenty-one years ago, and he still is a priest. Haven't you read any Graham Greene lately?"

"All right," Ferguson said testily. "Be that as it may be, the prime minister doesn't see why we should give Cussane front-page publicity. It won't do any of us any good."

"It could catch him quickly, sir," Fox said mildly.

"Yes, well they all expect us to do that anyway. Special Branch in Dublin has lifted his prints for us at his cottage. They've gone into the Dublin computer, which, as you know, is linked with the security services computer at Lisburn, which, in turn, is linked to our computer here and at central records, Scotland Yard."

"I didn't realize you had that kind of hookup." Devlin said.

"Miracle of the microchip," Ferguson said. "Eleven million people in there. Criminal records, schooling, professions, sexual preferences. Personal habits. Where they buy their furniture."

"You've got to be joking."

"No. Caught one of your lot over here from Ulster last year

because he always shopped at the Co-op. Had an excellent cover, but couldn't change the habit of a lifetime. Cussane is in there now and not only his fingerprints, but everything we know about him, and as most of the big provincial police forces have what we call visual display characteristics on their computer system, they can plug in to our central bank and punch out his photo."

"God Almighty!"

"Actually, they can do the same with you. As regards Cussane, I've instructed them to insert a deliberately amended record. No mention of the KGB or anything like that. Poses as a priest, known connections with the IRA. Extremely violent— approach with care. You get the picture."

"Oh, I do."

"To that end, we're releasing his picture to the press and quoting very much the details I've just given you. Some evening papers will manage to get it out, but all the national newspapers will have it in tomorrow's editions."

"And you think that will be enough, sir?" Fox asked.

"Very possibly. We'll have to wait and see, won't we? One thing is certain." Ferguson walked to the window and glanced out. "He's out there somewhere."

"And the thing is," Devlin said. "No one can do a damn thing about it till he surfaces."

"Exactly." Ferguson went back to the tray and picked up the pot. "This tea is really quite delicious. Anyone like another cup?"

A LITTLE LATER that afternoon, His Holiness Pope John Paul II sat at a desk in the small office adjacent to his bedchamber and examined the report that had been just handed to him. The man who stood before him wore the plainest of black habits and, on appearance, might have been a simple priest. He was, in fact, father general of the Society of Jesus, that most illustrious of all orders within the Catholic Church. The Jesuits were proud to be known as Soldiers of Christ, had been responsible, behind the scenes, for the pope's security for centuries now. All of which explained why the father general had hastened from his office at the Collegio di San Roberto Bellarmino on the Via del Seminario to seek audience with His Holiness.

Pope John Paul put the report down and looked up. He spoke in excellent Italian, only a trace of his Polish native tongue coming through. "You received this when?"

"The first report from the secretariat in Dublin three hours ago, then the news from London a little later. I have spoken personally to the British home secretary, who has given me every assurance for your safety and referred me to Brigadier Ferguson, mentioned in the report as being directly responsible."

"But are you worried?"

"Holiness, it is almost impossible to prevent a lone assassin from reaching his target, especially if he does not care about his own safety, and this man Cussane has proved his abilities in the killing area of things on too many occasions in the past."

"Father Cussane." His Holiness got up and paced to the window. "Killer he may have been, may still be, but priest he is and God, my friend, will not allow him to forget that."

The father general looked into that rough-hewn face, the face that might have belonged to any one of a thousand ordinary working men. It was touched with a strange simplicity, a certainty. As had happened on other occasions the father general, for all his intellectual authority, wilted before it.

"You will go to England, Holiness?"

"To Canterbury, my friend, where blessed Thomas Beckett died for God's sake."

The father general reached to kiss the ring on the extended hand. "Then your Holiness will excuse me. There is much to do."

He went out and John Paul stood at the window for a while, then crossed the room, opened a small door, and entered his

200

private chapel. He knelt at the altar, hands clasped, a certain fear in his heart as he remembered the assassin's bullet that had almost ended his life, the months of pain. But he pushed that away from him and concentrated on all that was important. His prayers for the immortal soul of Father Harry Cussane and for all sinners everywhere whose actions cut them off from the infinite blessing of God's love.

FERGUSON PUT DOWN the phone and turned to Devlin and Fox. "That was the director general. His Holiness has been informed in full about Cussane and the threat he poses. It makes no difference."

"Well, it wouldn't, would it?" Devlin said. "You're talking about a man who worked for years in the Polish underground against the Nazis."

"All right," Ferguson said. "Point taken. Anyway, you'd better get going. Take him along to the directorate, Harry. Grade-A security pass. Not just another piece of plastic with your photo on it," he said to Devlin. "Very few people have this particular one. It'll get you in anywhere."

He moved to his desk, and Devlin said, "Will it entitle me to a gun? A Walther wouldn't come amiss. I'm one of nature's pessimists, as you know."

"Out of favor with most of our people since that idiot tried to shoot Princess Anne and her bodyguard's Walther jammed. Revolvers never do. Take my advice."

He picked up some papers and then went into the study and got their coats. "I still prefer a Walther," Fox said.

"One thing's for sure," Devlin said, "whatever it is, it better not jam, not if you're facing Harry Cussane." He opened the door and they went out to the lift.

HARRY CUSSANE HAD a plan of sorts. He knew the end in view on Saturday at Canterbury, but that left the best part of three days and three nights, in which he had to hide out. Danny

Malone had mentioned a number of people in the criminal world who provided the right kind of help at a price. Plenty in London, of course, or Leeds or Manchester, but the Mungo brothers and their farm in Galloway had particularly interested him. It was the very remoteness that appealed. The last place anyone would look for him would be Scotland, and yet the British Airways shuttle from Glasgow to London took only an hour and a quarter.

Time to fill, that was the thing. No need to be in Canterbury until the very last moment. Nothing to organize. That amused him, sitting there in the bus speeding up the motorway to Carlisle. One could imagine the preparation at Canterbury Cathedral, every possible entry point guarded, police marksmen everywhere, probably even the SAS in plain clothes, dispersed among the crowd. And all for nothing. It was like chess, as he used to tell Devlin, the world's worst player. It wasn't the present move that counted. It was the final move. It was rather like a stage magician. You believed what he did with his right hand, but it was what he did with his left that was important.

He slept for quite a while and when he awakened, there was the sea on his left, shining in the afternoon light. He leaned over and spoke to the old woman in front of him. "Where are we?"

"Just past Annan." She had a thick Glasgow accent. "Dumfries next. Are you a Catholic?"

"I'm afraid so," he said warily. The Scottish Lowlands had always been traditionally Protestant.

"That's lovely. I'm Catholic myself. Glasgow-Irish, Father." She took his hand and kissed it. "Bless me, Father. You're from the old country."

"I am indeed."

He thought she might prove a nuisance, but strangely enough, she simply turned her head and settled back in her seat. Outside, the sky was very dark and it started to rain, thunder rumbling ominously, and soon, the rain had increased into a monsoonlike force that drummed loudly on the roof of the bus. They stopped in Dumfries to drop two passengers off and then moved on through streets washed clean of people, out into the country again.

Not long now. No more than fifteen miles to his dropping-off point at Dunhill. From there, a few miles on a side road to a hamlet called Larwick and the Mungos' place, in the hills a mile or two outside.

The driver had been speaking into the mike on his car radio and now he switched over to the coach's loudspeaker system. "Attention ladies and gentlemen. I'm afraid we've got trouble up ahead, just before Dunhill. Bad flooding on the road. A lot of vehicles already stuck in it."

The old woman in front of Cussane called, "What are we supposed to do? Sit in the bus all night?"

"We'll be in Corbridge in a few minutes. Not much of a place, but there's a milk stop there on the railway line. They're making arrangements to stop the next train for Glasgow."

"Three times the fare on the railway," the old woman called.

"The company pays," the driver told her cheerfully. "Don't worry, love."

"Will the train stop at Dunhill?" Cussane asked.

"Perhaps. I'm not sure. We'll have to see."

Lag's Luck, they called it in prison circles. Danny Malone had told him that. No matter how well you planned, it was always something totally unforseeable that caused the problem. No point in wasting energy in dwelling on that. The thing to do was examine alternatives.

A white sign, Corbridge etched on it in black, appeared on the left, and then the first houses loomed out of the heavy rain. There was a general store and a newsstand. The tiny railway station opposite, and the driver turned the coach into the forecourt.

"Best wait in here while I check things out." He jumped down and went into the railway station.

The rain poured down relentlessly. There was a gap between

the pub and the general store, beams stretching between to shore them up. Obviously the building that had stood there had just been demolished and a small crowd had gathered. Cussane watched idly, reached for the packet of cigarettes in his pocket and found it empty. He hesitated, then picked up his bag, got off the coach and ran across the road to the newsstand. He asked the young woman standing in the entrance for a couple of packs of cigarettes and an ordnance survey map of the area if she had it. She did.

"What's going on?" Cussane asked.

"They've been pulling down the old grain store for a week now. Everything was fine until this rain started. They've got trouble in the cellars. A roof fallen or something."

They moved out into the entrance again and watched. At that moment, a police car appeared from the other end of the village and pulled in. There was only one occupant, a large, heavily built man who wore a navy blue anorak with sergeant's stripes on it. He forced his way through the crowd and disappeared.

The young woman said, "The cavalry's arrived."

"Isn't he from around here?" Cussane asked.

"No police station in Corbridge. He's from Dunhill. Sergeant Brodie—Lachlan Brodie." The tone of her voice was enough.

"Not popular?" Cussane asked.

"Lachlan's the kind who likes nothing better than finding three drunks together at the same time on a Saturday night to beat up on. He's built like the rock of ages and likes to prove it. You wouldn't be Catholic, by any chance?"

"I'm afraid so."

"To Lachlan, that means Antichrist. He's the kind of Baptist who thinks music is a sin. A lay preacher as well."

A workman came through the crowd in helmet and orange safety jacket. His face was streaked with mud and water. He leaned against the wall. "It's a sod down there."

"That bad?" the woman said.

"One of my men is trapped. A wall collapsed. We're doing our best, but there isn't much room to work in and the water's rising." He frowned and said to Cussane. "You wouldn't be Catholic by any chance?"

"Yes."

The man grabbed his arm. "My name's Hardy. I'm the foreman. The man down there is as Glaswegian as me, but Italian. Gino Tisini. He thinks he's going to die. Begged me to get him a priest. Will you come, Father?"

"But of course," Cussane said without hesitation and handed his bag to the woman. "Would you look after that for me?"

"Certainly, Father."

He followed Hardy through the crowd and down into the excavation. There was a gaping hole, cellar steps descending. Brodie, the police sergeant, was holding people back. Hardy started down and as Cussane followed, Brodie caught his arm. "What's this?"

"Let him by," Hardy called. "He's a priest."

The hostility was immediate in Brodie's eyes, the dislike plain. It was an old song to Cussane, Belfast all over again. "I don't know you," Brodie said.

"My name's Fallon. I came in on the bus on the way to Glasgow," Cussane told him calmly.

He took the policeman's wrist, loosening the grip on his arm, and Brodie winced at the strength of it as Cussane pushed him to one side and went down the steps. He was at once knee-deep in water. He ducked under a low roof and followed Hardy into what must have been a narrow passageway. There was a certain amount of light from an extension lamp and it illuminated a chaos of jumbled masonry and planking. There was a narrow aperture and as they reached it, two men stumbled out, both soaked to the skin and obviously at exhaustion point.

"It's no good," one of them said. "His head will be under the water in a matter of minutes."

Hardy brushed past them and Cussane went after them. Gino Tisini's white face loomed out of the darkness as they crouched to go forward. Cussane put out a hand to steady himself. A plank fell and several bricks.

"Watch it!" Hardy said. "The whole thing could go like a house of cards."

There was the constant gurgle of water as it poured in. Tisini managed a ghastly smile. "We don't have time for confession, Father."

"We haven't got that long. Let's get you out," Cussane said.

There seemed to be a sudden extra flow of water—it washed over Tisini's face and he panicked. Cussane moved behind him, supporting the man's head above the water, crouching over him protectively.

Hardy felt under the water. "There's a lot that has moved here," he said. "That's where the inflow of water helps. There's just one beam pinning him down now, but it leads into the wall. If I put any kind of force on it, it could bring the whole thing in on us."

"If you don't, he drowns within the next couple of minutes," Cussane said.

"You could be in trouble, too, Father."

"And you," Cussane said. "So get on with it."

"Father!" Tisini cried. "In the name of God, absolve me!"

Cussane said in a firm, clear voice, "May Our Lord Jesus Christ absolve you, and I, by His authority, absolve you from your sins in the name of the Father and the Son and of the Holy Spirit." He nodded to Hardy. "Now!"

The foreman took a breath and dipped under the surface, his hands gripping the edges of the beam. His shoulders seemed to swell, he came up out of the water, the beam with him, and Tisini screamed, floating free into Cussane's hands. The wall started to bulge. Hardy pulled Tisini up and dragged him toward the entrance, Cussane pushing from the rear as the walls crumbled around them. He put an arm up to protect himself, was aware that they were at the steps now, willing hands reaching down to help, and then a brick struck him a glancing blow on the head. He tried to go up the steps, fell on his knees, and there was only darkness.

Twelve

*H*E came awake slowly to find the young woman from the shop crouching over him. He was lying on a rug in front of a coal fire, and she was wiping his face.

"Easy," she said. "You'll be fine. Remember me? I'm Moira McGregor. You're in my shop."

"What about the Italian and that fellow Hardy?"

"They're upstairs. We've sent for a doctor."

"Where's my bag?"

"I've kept it safe in the other room," she said.

The big policeman, Brodie, loomed over them. "Back in the land of the living are we?" There was an edge to his voice. An unpleasantness. "Worth a couple of dozen candles to the Virgin, I suppose."

He went out. Moira McGregor smiled at Cussane. "Take no notice. You saved that man's life, you and Hardy. I'll get you a cup of tea."

She went into the kitchen and found Brodie standing by the table. "I could do with a touch of something stronger myself," he said.

She took a bottle of Scotch and a glass from a cupboard and put them on the table without a word. He reached for a chair and pulled it forward, not noticing Cussane's bag, which fell to the floor. The top being unzipped, several items tumbled out, a couple of shirts and the pyx and the violet stole among them.

"This his bag?" Brodie asked.

She turned from the stove, a kettle in her hand. "That's right."

He dropped to one knee, stuffing the items back into the bag and frowned. "What's this?"

He was holding a British passport. Brody opened it. "He told me his name was Fallon."

"So?" Moira said.

"Then how come he has a passport in the name of Father Sean Daly? Good likeness, too." His hand groped further. The false bottom of the bag had come loose when it fell from the chair. "God Almighty!" Brodie said, and his hand came out holding the Stetchkin.

Moira McGregor felt sick. "What does it mean?"

"We'll soon find out."

Brodie went back into the other room and put the bag down on a chair. Cussane lay quietly, eyes closed. Brodie knelt down beside him, took out a pair of handcuffs and very gently, eased one bracelet over Cussane's left wrist. Cussane opened his eyes and Brodie seized the other wrist and snapped the steel cuff in place. He pulled the priest to his feet, then shoved him down into a chair.

"What are you doing?" Cussane said.

Brodie said, "What's all this then?" He pulled the false bottom up completely and sifted through the contents. "Three handguns, assorted passports, and a sizable sum in cash. Bloody fine priest you are. What's it all about?"

"You're the policeman, not me," Cussane said.

Brodie cuffed him on the side of the head. "Manners, my little man. I can see I'm going to have to chastise you."

Watching from the door, Moira McGregor said, "Don't do that."

Brodie smiled contemptuously. "Women—all the same. Fancy him, do you, just because he played the hero with the Italian?"

He went out. She said to Cussane desperately. "Who are you?"

He smiled. "I wouldn't bother your head about that. I could manage a cigarette, though, before bullyboy gets back."

BRODIE HAD BEEN a policeman for twenty years, after five years in the military police. Twenty undistinguished years. He was a sour and cruel man, whose only real authority was the uniform. And his religion had the same purpose as the uniform. To give him a spurious authority. He could have rung headquarters in Dumfries, but there was something special about this, he felt it in his bones, so instead, he rang police headquarters in Glasgow.

GLASGOW HAD RECEIVED photo and full details on Harry Cussane only one hour previously. The case was marked "priority one," with immediate referral to Group-4 in London. Brodie's telephone call was transferred at once to Special Branch. Within two minutes he found himself talking to a Chief Inspector Trent.

"Tell me all about it again," Trent told him. Brodie did so. When he was finished, Trent said, "I don't know how much time you've got in, but you've just made the biggest collar of your career. This man's called Cussane. A real IRA heavy. You say the passengers on the bus he was on are being transferred to the train?"

"That's right, sir. Flooding on the road. This is only a milk stop, but they're going to stop the Glasgow Express."

"When is it due?"

"About ten minutes, sir."

"Get on it, Brodie, and bring Chummy with you. We'll meet you in Glasgow."

Brodie put down the phone, choking with excitement, then he went into the sitting room.

BRODIE WALKED CUSSANE along the platform, one hand on his arm, the other clutching Cussane's bag. People turned to watch curiously as the priest passed, wrists handcuffed in front of him. They reached the guard's van at the rear of the train, the guard standing on the platform beside the open door.

"What's this?"

"Special prisoner for Glasgow." Brodie pushed Cussane inside. There were some mailbags in the corner, and he shoved him down onto them. "Now you stay quiet like a good boy."

There was a commotion and Hardy appeared at the door, Moira McGregor behind him. "I came as soon as I could," the foreman said. "I just heard."

"You can't come in here," Brodie told him.

Hardy ignored him. "Look, I don't know what this is about, but if there's anything I can do."

On the platform, the guard blew his whistle. Cussane said. "Nothing anyone can do. How is Tisini?"

"Looks like a broken leg."

"Tell him his luck is good."

There was a lurch as the train started. "It suddenly occurs to me that if I hadn't drawn you in to help, you wouldn't be here now," Hardy said.

He moved out to join Moira on the platform as the guard jumped inside. "Luck of the draw," Cussane called. "Don't worry about it."

And then Hardy and the woman were swept away into the past as the guard pulled the sliding door shut and the train surged forward.

TRENT COULDN'T RESIST phoning Ferguson in London and

the directorate general patched him in to the Cavendish Square phone. Fox and Devlin were out and Ferguson answered himself.

"Trent here, sir, chief inspector, Special Branch, Glasgow. We think we've got your man, Cussane."

"Have you, by God?" Ferguson said. "What shape is he in?"

"Well, I haven't actually seen him, sir. He's been apprehended in a village some miles south of here. He's arriving by train in Glasgow within the hour. I'll pick him up myself."

"Pity the bugger didn't turn up dead," Ferguson said. "Still, one can't have everything. I want him down here on the first available plane in the morning, Chief Inspector. Bring him yourself. This one is too important for any slipups."

"Will do, sir," said Trent eagerly.

Ferguson put down the receiver, reached for the red phone, but some innate caution stopped him. Much better to phone the home secretary when the fish was actually in the net.

BRODIE SAT ON a stool, leaning back in the corner watching Cussane and smoking a cigarette. The guard was checking a list on his desk. He totaled it and put his pen away. "I'll make my rounds. See you later."

He went out and Brodie pulled his stool across the baggage car and sat very close to Cussane. "I've never understood it. Men in skirts. It'll never catch on." He leaned forward. "Tell me, you priests—what do you do for it?"

"For what?" Cussane said.

"You know. Is it choirboys? Is that the truth of it?" There were beads of perspiration on the big man's forehead.

"That's a hell of a big moustache you're wearing," Cussane said. "Have you got a weak mouth or something?"

Brodie was angry now. "Cocky bastard. I'll show you."

He reached forward and touched the end of the lighted cigarette to the back of Cussane's hand. Cussane cried out and fell back against the mailbags.

Brodie laughed and leaned over him. "I thought you'd like that," he said and reached to touch the back of the hand again. Cussane kicked him in the crotch. Brodie staggered back clutching at himself, and Cussane sprang to his feet. He kicked out expertly, catching the right kneecap and, as Brodie keeled forward, raising his knee into his face.

The police sergeant lay on his back moaning, and Cussane searched his pockets, found the key, and unlocked his handcuffs. He got his bag, checked that the contents were intact, and slipped the Stetchkin into his pocket. He pulled back the sliding door and rain flooded in.

The guard, entering the baggage car a moment later, caught a brief glimpse of him landing in heather at the side of the track and rolling over and over down the slope. Then there was only mist and rain.

WHEN THE TRAIN coasted into Glasgow Central, Trent and half a dozen uniformed constables were waiting on platform one. The door of the baggage car slid open and the guard appeared.

"In here."

Trent paused at the entrance. There was only Lachlan Brodie sitting on the guard's stool, nursing a bloody and swollen face. Trent's heart sank. "Tell me," he said wearily. Brodie did the best he could. When he was finished, Trent said. "He was handcuffed, you say, and you let him take you?"

"It wasn't as simple as it sounds, sir," Brodie said lamely.

"You stupid, stupid man," Trent said. "By the time I'm finished with you, you'll be lucky if they put you in charge of a public lavatory."

He turned away in disgust and went back along the platform to phone Ferguson.

CUSSANE AT THAT precise moment was halted in the shelter of some rocks on top of a hill north of Dunhill. He had the ordnance survey map open that he'd purchased from Moira McGregor. He found Larwick with no trouble and the Mungos' farm was just outside. Perhaps fifteen miles and most of that over hill country, yet he felt cheerful enough as he pressed on.

The mist curling in on either hand, the heavy rain, gave him a safe enclosed feeling, remote from the world outside—a kind of freedom. He moved on through birch trees and wet bracken that soaked his trouser legs. Occasionally grouse or plover lifted from the heather, disturbed by his passing. He kept on the move, for by now his raincoat was soaked through, and he was experienced enough to know the dangers of being in hill country like this in the wrong clothing.

He came over the edge of an escarpment, perhaps an hour after leaving the train, and looked down into a valley glen below. Darkness was falling, but there was a clearly defined man-made track a few yards away, ending at a cairn of rough stones. It was enough and he hurried on with renewed energy, plunging down the hillside.

FERGUSON WAS LOOKING at a large ordnance survey map of the Scottish Lowlands. "Apparently he got the coach in Morecambe," he said. "We've established that."

"A neat way of getting to Glasgow, sir," Fox said.

"No," Ferguson said. "He took a ticket to a place called Dunhill. What in the hell would he be doing there?"

"Do you know the area?" Devlin asked.

"Had a week's shooting on some chap's estate about twenty years ago. Funny place, the Galloway Hills. High forests, ridgebacks, and secret little lochs everywhere."

"Galloway, you said?" Devlin looked closer at the map. "So that's Galloway?"

Ferguson frowned. "So what?"

"I think that's where he's gone," Devlin said. "I think that's where he was aiming to go all along."

Fox said, "What makes you think that?"

215

He told them about Danny Malone, and when he was finished, Ferguson said, "You could very well have something."

Devlin nodded. "Danny mentioned a number of safe houses used by the underworld in various parts of the country, but the fact that he's in the Galloway area must have some significance for this place run by the Mungo brothers."

"What do we do now, sir?" Fox asked Ferguson. "Get Special Branch, Glasgow, to lay on a raid of this Mungo place?"

"No, to hell with that," Ferguson said. "We've already had a classic example of just how efficient the local police can be. They had him and let him slip through their fingers." He glanced out of the window at the darkness outside. "Too late to do anything tonight. Too late for him as well. He'll still be on foot in those hills."

"Bound to be," Devlin said.

"So—you and Harry fly up to Glasgow tomorrow. You check out this Mungo place personally. I'm invoking special powers. On this one, Special Branch will do what you want."

He went out. Fox gave Devlin a cigarette. "What do you think?"

"They had him, Harry, in handcuffs," Devlin said. "And he got away. That's what I think. Now give me a light."

CUSSANE WENT DOWN through birch trees following the course of a pleasant burn that splashed between a jumble of granite boulders. He was beginning to feel tired now, in spite of the fact that the going was all downhill.

The burn disappeared over an edge of rock, cascading into a deep pool as it had done several times before. He slithered down through birch trees in the gathering dusk, rather faster than he had intended, landing in an untidy heap, still holding onto his bag.

There was a startled gasp and Cussane, coming up on one knee, saw two children crouched at the side of the pool. The girl, on a second look, was older than he had thought, perhaps sixteen; she wore Wellingtons and jeans and an old reefer coat that was too big for her. She had a pointed face, wide dark eyes, and a profusion of black hair, which flowed from beneath a knitted tam-o'-shanter.

The boy was younger, no more than ten. He wore a ragged sweater, cut-down tweed trousers, and rubber-and-canvas running shoes that had seen better days. He was in the act of withdrawing a gaff from the water, a salmon spitted on it.

Cussane smiled. "Where I come from that wouldn't be considered very sporting."

"Run, Morag!" the boy cried and lunged at Cussane with the gaff, the salmon still wriggling on the end.

A section of the bank crumbled under his foot and he fell back into the pool. He surfaced, still clutching the gaff, but in an instant the swift current, swollen by the heavy rain, had him in its grasp and carried him away.

"Donal!" the girl screamed and ran to the edge.

Cussane got a hand to her shoulder and pulled her back just in time as another section of the bank crumbled. "Don't be a fool. You'll go the same way."

She struggled to break free, and he dropped his bag, shoved her out of the way, and ran along the bank, pushing through the birches. At that point the water poured through a narrow slot in the rocks with real force, taking the boy with it.

Cussane plunged on, aware of the girl behind him. He pulled off his raincoat and threw it to one side. He cut out across the rocks, trying to get to the end of the slot before the boy, reaching out to grab one end of the outstretched gaff, which the boy still clutched, minus the salmon now.

He managed it, was aware of the enormous force of the current, and then went in headfirst, a circumstance impossible to avoid. He surfaced in the pool below, the boy a yard or so away, and reached out to secure a grip on his sweater. A moment later, the current took them in to a shingle strand. As the girl ran down the bank, the boy was on his feet, shaking himself like a terrier and scrambling up to meet her.

A sudden eddy brought Cussane's black hat floating in. He picked it up, examined it, and laughed. "Now that will certainly never be the same again," he said, and tossed it out into the pool.

He turned to go up the bank and found himself looking into the muzzle of a sawed-off shotgun held by an old man of at least seventy, who stood at the edge of the birch trees. The girl, Morag, and the young Donal stood beside him. He wore a shabby tweed suit, a tam-o'-shanter that was twin to the girl's, and he badly needed a shave.

"Who is he, Granda?" the girl asked. "No water Baillie."

"With a minister's collar, that would hardly be likely." The old man's speech was tinged with the soft blâs of the highlander. "Are you a man of the cloth?"

"My name is Fallon," Cussane told him. "Father Michael Fallon." He recalled the name of a village in the area from his examination of the ordnance survey map. "I was making for Whitechapel, missed the bus, and thought I'd try a shortcut over the hill."

The girl had walked back to pick up his raincoat. She returned and the old man took it from her. "Away you now, Donal, and get the gentleman's bag."

So, he must have seen everything from the beginning. The boy scampered away and the old man weighed the raincoat in his hand. He felt in a pocket and produced the Stetchkin. "Would you look at that now? No water Baillie, Morag, that's for sure, and a damn strange priest."

"He saved Donal, Granda." The girl touched his sleeve.

He smiled slowly down at her. "And so he did. Away to the camp then, girl. Say that we have company and see that the kettle is on the fire."

He put the Stetchkin back in the raincoat and handed it to Cussane. The girl turned and darted away through the trees, and the boy came back with the bag.

218

"My name is Hamish Finlay and I am in your debt." He rumpled the boy's hair. "You are welcome to share what we have. No man can say more."

They moved up through the trees and started through the plantation. Cussane said, "This is strange country."

The old man took out a pipe and filled it from a worn pouch, the shotgun under his arm. "Aye, the Galloway is that. A man can lose himself here, from other men, if you take my meaning?"

"Oh, I do," Cussane said. "Sometimes we all need to do that."

There was a cry of fear up ahead, the girl's voice raised high. Finlay's gun was in his hands in an instant, and as they moved forward, they saw her struggling in the arms of a tall, heavily built man. Like Finlay, he carried a shotgun and wore an old patched tweed suit. His face was undeniably brutal and badly needed a shave, and yellow hair poked from beneath his cap. He was staring down at the girl as if enjoying her fear, a half-smile on his face. Cussane was conscious of real anger, but it was Finlay who handled it.

"Leave her, Murray!"

The other man scowled, hanging onto her, then pushed her away with a forced smile. "A bit of sport only." The girl turned and ran away behind him. "Who's this?"

"Murray, my dead brother's child you are, and my responsibility, but did I ever tell you there's a stink to you like bad meat on a summer day?"

The shotgun moved slightly in Murray's grasp and there was hot rage in the eyes. Cussane slipped a hand in his raincoat pocket and found the Stetchkin. Calmly, almost contemptuously, the old man lit his pipe, and something went out of Murray. He turned on his heel and walked away.

"My own nephew." Finlay shook his head. "You know what they say. 'Our friends we choose ourselves, but our relations are chosen for us.'"

"True," Cussane said as they started walking again.

"Aye, and you can take your hand off the butt of that pistol. It won't be needed now, Father—or whatever ye are."

THE CAMP IN the hollow was a poor sort of place. The three wagons were old, with patched canvas tilts and the only motor vehicle in view was a jeep of World War II vintage, painted khaki green. A depressing air of poverty hung over everything, from the ragged clothes of the three women who cooked at the open fire, to the bare feet of the children who played tag among the half-dozen horses that grazed beside the stream.

Cussane slept well, deep, dreamless sleep that was totally refreshing, and awakened to find the girl, Morag, sitting on the opposite bunk watching him.

Cussane smiled. "Hello there."

"That's funny," she said. "One minute you were asleep, the next your eyes were open and you were wide awake. How did you learn to do that?"

"The habit of a lifetime." He glanced at his watch. "Only six-thirty."

"We rise early." She nodded outside the wagon. He could hear voices and smell bacon frying.

"I've dried your clothes," she said. "Would you like some tea?"

There was an eagerness to her as if she desperately wanted to please, something infinitely touching. He reached to pull the tam-o'-shanter down more over one ear. "I like that."

"My mother knitted it for me." She pulled it off and looked at it, her face sad.

"That's nice. Is she here?"

"No." Morag put the tam-o'-shanter back on. "She ran away with a man called McTavish last year. They went to Australia."

"And your father?"

"He left her when I was a baby." She shrugged. "But I don't care."

"Is young Donal your brother?"

"No. His father is my cousin, Murray. You saw him earlier."

"Ah, yes. You don't like him, I think."

She shivered. "He makes me feel funny."

Cussane was conscious of the anger again, but controlled it. "That tea would be welcome, plus the chance to get dressed."

Her reply, cynical and far too adult for her age, totally surprised him. "Frightened I might corrupt you, Father?" She grinned. "I'll fetch your tea." And she darted out.

His suit had been thoroughly brushed and dried. He dressed quickly, omitting the vest and clerical collar and pulling a thin black turtleneck sweater over his head instead. He pulled on his raincoat because it was still raining and went out.

Murray Finlay leaned against the side of a wagon smoking a clay pipe, and Donal crouched at his feet.

Cussane said, "Good morning," but Murray could only manage a scowl.

Morag turned from the fire to offer Cussane tea in a chipped enamel mug, and Murray called, "Don't I get one?"

She ignored him, and Cussane said. "Where's your grandfather?"

"Fishing by the loch..I'll show you. Bring your tea."

There was something immensely appealing, a gamin quality that was somehow accentuated by the tam-o'-shanter. It was as if she were putting out her tongue at the whole world, in spite of her ragged clothes. It was not pleasant to think of such a girl brutalized by contact with the likes of Murray and the squalor of the years to come.

They went over the rise and came to a small loch, a pleasant place where heather flowed down to the shoreline. Old Hamish Finlay stood thigh-deep, rod in hand, making one extremely expert cast after another. A wind stirred the water, small black fins appeared, and suddenly a trout came out of the deep beyond the sandbar, leapt in the air, and vanished.

The old man glanced at Cussane and chuckled. "Would you look at that now? Have you noticed how often the good things in life tend to pop up in the wrong places?"

"Frequently."

Finlay gave Morag his rod. "You'll find three fat ones in the basket. Off with you and get the breakfast going."

She turned back to the camp, and Cussane offered the old man a cigarette. "A nice child."

"Aye, you could say that."

Cussane gave him a light. "This life you lead is a strange one, and yet you aren't gypsies, I think?"

"People of the road. Tinkers. People have many names for us and some of them none too kind. The last remnants of a proud clan broken at Culloden. Mind, we have links with other road people on occasion. Morag's mother was an English gypsy."

"No resting place?" Cussane said.

"None. No one will have us for long enough. There's a village constable at Whitechapel who'll be up here no later than tomorrow. Three days—that's all we get and he'll move us on. But what about you?"

"I'll be on my way this morning as soon as I've eaten."

The old man nodded. "I shan't query the collar you wore last night. Your business is your own. Is there nothing I can do for you?"

"Better by far to do nothing," Cussane told him.

"Like that, is it?" Finlay sighed heavily, and somewhere Morag screamed.

CUSSANE CAME THROUGH the trees on the run and found them in a clearing among the birches. The girl was on her back, Murray was crouching on top, pinning her down and there was only lust on his face. He groped for one of her breasts, she cried out again in revulsion, and Cussane arrived. He got a handful of Murray's long yellow hair, twisting it cruelly so that it was the big man's turn to cry out. He came to his feet, and Cussane turned him around, held him for a moment then pushed him away.

"Don't touch her again!"

222

Old Hamish Finlay arrived at that moment, shotgun at the ready. "Murray, I warned you."

But Murray ignored him and advanced on Cussane, glaring ferociously. "I'm going to smash you, you little worm!"

He came in fast, arms raised to destroy. Cussane pivoted to one side and delivered a left to Murray's kidneys as he lurched past. Murray went down on one knee, stayed there for a moment, then got up and swung the wildest of punches. Cussane sank a left under his ribs followed by a right hook to the cheek, splitting flesh.

"Murray, my God is a God of wrath when the occasion warrants it. Now listen to me." He punched the big man in the face a second time. "Touch this girl again and I'll kill you, understand?"

Cussane kicked Murray under the kneecap. The big man went down on his knees and stayed there.

Old Finlay moved in. "I've given you your last warning, you bastard." He prodded Murray with the shotgun. "You'll leave my camp this day and go your own way."

Murray lurched painfully to his feet and turned and hobbled away toward the camp. Finlay said, "By God, man, you don't do things by halves."

"I could never see the point," Cussane told him.

Morag had picked up the rod and fishbasket. She stood looking at him, a kind of wonder in her eyes. And then she backed away. "I'll see to the breakfast," she said in a low voice, turned and ran toward the camp.

There was the sound of the jeep's engine starting up, it moved away. "He hasn't wasted much time," Cussane said.

Finlay said, "Good riddance. Now let's to breakfast."

MURRAY FINLAY PULLED up the jeep in front of the newsstand in Whitechapel and sat there thinking. Young Donal sat beside him, trembling. He hated and feared his father, had not wanted to come, but Murray had given him no option.

"Stay there," Murray told him. "I need tobacco."

He went to the door of the newsstand, which obstinately stayed closed when he tried to push it open. He cursed and started to turn away, then paused. The morning papers were stacked in the shop doorway and his attention was caught by a photo on the front page of one of them. He took out a knife, cut the string that tied the bundle, and picked up the top copy.

"Would you look at that? I've got you now, you bastard." He turned, hurried across the street to the police cottage, and opened the garden gate.

Young Donal, puzzled, got out of the jeep and picked up the next paper. He found himself looking at a reasonably good photo of Cussane. He stood staring for a moment at the photo of the man who had saved his life, then turned and ran up the road as fast as he could.

MORAG WAS STACKING the tin plates after breakfast when Donal arrived on the run.

"What is it?" she cried, for his distress was obvious.

"Where's the Father?"

"Walking in the woods with Granda. What is it?"

There was the sound of the jeep approaching. Donal showed her the paper wildly. "Look at that. It's him."

Which it undeniably was. The description, as Ferguson had indicated, had Cussane only posing as a priest and made him out to be not only IRA, but a thoroughly dangerous man.

The jeep roared into camp, and Murray jumped out holding his shotgun, followed by the village constable. He was in uniform, but obviously had not had time to shave.

"Where is he?" Murray demanded and grabbed the boy by the hair and shook him. "Tell me, you little scut!"

Donal screamed in pain. "In the woods."

Murray pushed him away and nodded to the constable. "Right, let's get him," and he turned and hurried toward the woods.

224

Morag didn't think, simply acted. She ducked into the wagon, found Cussane's bag and threw it into the jeep. Then she climbed behind the wheel and pressed the starter. She had driven it often, knew what she was doing, and took the jeep away, wheels spinning across the rough ground. She turned away to one side of Murray and the constable. Murray spun and she was aware of the rage in his face, the flat bang of the shotgun. She swung the wheel, brushing him to one side, and took the jeep straight into the forest of young birch trees. Cussane and Finlay, alerted by the commotion, were running toward the camp when the jeep came crashing through the trees and stopped.

"What is it, lass?" Finlay cried.

"Murray got the police. Get in! Get in!" she said to Cussane.

He didn't argue, simply vaulted in beside her, and she took the jeep around in a circle, crashing through the trees. Murray came limping toward them, the constable beside him, and the two men dived to one side. The jeep burst out of the trees, bumped across the rough ground past the camp, and turned onto the road.

She braked to a halt. "Whitechapel won't be right. Won't they block the road?"

"They'll block all the bloody roads," he said.

"So where do we go?"

"We?" Cussane said.

"Don't argue, Mr. Cussane. If I stay, they'll arrest me for helping you."

She passed him the newspaper Donal had given her. He looked at his photo and read the salient facts quickly. He smiled wryly. Someone had been on to him a damn sight more quickly than he would ever have imagined.

"So where to?" she asked impatiently.

He made his decision then. "Turn left and keep climbing. We're going to try and reach a farm outside a village called

Larwick, on the other side of those hills. They tell me these things will go anywhere so who needs roads? Can you handle it?"

"Just watch me!" she said and drove away.

Thirteen

THE glen was mainly national forest. They left the road and followed a track through pine trees, climbing higher and higher beside a burn swollen by the heavy rain. Finally, they came up out of the trees at the head of the glen and reached a small plateau.

He touched her arm. "This will do," he called above the roaring of the engine.

She braked to a halt and switched off. Rolling hills stretched on either side, fading into mist and heavy rain. He got out the ordnance survey map and went forward to study the terrain. The map was as highly accurate as only a government survey could make it. He found Larwick with no difficulty. Glendhu, that was where Danny Malone had said the Mungos' farm was, a couple of miles outside the village. The Black Glen, it meant in Gaelic, and there was only one farm marked. It had to be the place. He spent a few more minutes studying the lay of the land below him in conjunction with the map and then went back to the jeep.

Morag looked up from the newspaper. "Is it true, all this stuff about you and the IRA?"

He got in out of the rain. "What do you think?"

"It says here you often pose as a priest. That means you aren't one?"

It was a question as much as anything else, and he smiled. "You know what they say. If it's in the papers it must be true. Why, does it worry you being in the company of such a desperate character?"

She shook her head. "You saved Donal at the burn and you didn't need to. You helped me—saved me from Murray." She folded the paper and tossed it into the back of the jeep, a slight frown of bewilderment on her face. "There's the man in the paper and then there's you. It's like two different people."

"Most of us are at least three people," he said. "There's who I think I am, then the person you think I am."

"Which only leaves who you really are," she cut in.

"True, except that some people can only survive by continuously adapting. They become many people, but for it to work, they must really live the part."

"Like an actor?" she said.

"That's it exactly, except that like any good actor, they must believe in the role they are playing at that particular time."

She leaned back in the seat, half-turned toward him, arms folded, listening intently, and it struck him then that in spite of her background and the sparseness of any formal education in her life, she was obviously highly intelligent.

"I see," she said. "So when you pose as a priest, you actually become a priest."

The directness was disturbing. "Something like that." They sat there in silence for a few moments before he said softly, "You saved my hide back there. If it hadn't been for you, I'd have been in handcuffs again."

"Again?" she said.

"I was picked up by the police yesterday. They were taking me to Glasgow in the train, but I managed to jump for it. Walked over the hill from there and met you."

"Lucky for Donal," she said. "Lucky for me, if it comes to that."

"Murray, you mean? Has he been a problem for long?"

"Since I was about thirteen," she said calmly. "It wasn't so bad while my Mam was still with us. She kept him in check, but after she left . . ." She shrugged. "He's never had his way with me, but lately, it got worse. I'd been thinking of leaving."

"Running away? But where would you go?"

"To my grandma. My mother's mother. She's a true gypsy. Her name's Brana—Brana Smith, but she calls herself Gypsy Rose."

"I seem to have heard a name like that before," Cussane said, smiling.

"She has the gift," Morag told him seriously. "Second sight in all things. With the palm, the crystal, or the tarot cards. She has a house in Wapping in London, on the river, when she isn't working the fairgrounds with the traveling shows."

"And you'd like to go to her?"

"Granda always said I could when I was older." She pushed herself up. "What about you? Do you intend to make for London?"

"Perhaps," he said slowly.

"Then we could go together." This, she said to him calmly and without emotion as if it was the most natural thing in the world.

"No," he said flatly. "I don't think so. For one thing, it would only get you deeper in trouble. For another, I have to travel light. No excess baggage. When I have to run, I have to run fast. No time to think of anyone but me."

There was something in her eyes, a kind of hurt, but she showed no emotion, simply got out of the jeep and stood at the side of the track, hands in pockets. "I understand. You go on from here. I'll walk back down the glen."

He had a momentary vision of the wretched encampment, imagined the slow and inevitable brutalization of the years. And she was worth more than that. Much more.

"Don't be stupid," he said. "Get in!"

"What for?"

"I need you to drive the jeep, don't I, while I follow the map. Down through the glen below and over that center hill. There's a farm in a place called Glendhu outside Larwick."

She got behind the wheel quickly, smiling. "Have you friends there?"

"Not exactly." He reached for his bag, opened it, pulled open the false bottom, and took out the bundle of banknotes. "This is the kind of stuff they like. Most people do, if it comes to that." He pulled two notes off, folded them and put them in the breast pocket of her old reefer coat. That should keep you going till you find your grannie."

Her eyes were round in astonishment. "I can't take that."

"Oh yes you can. Now get this thing moving and let's get to the place as soon as possible."

She selected a low gear and started down the track carefully. "And what happens when we get there? To me, I mean?"

"We'll have to see. Maybe you could catch a train. On your own, you'd probably do very well. I'm the one they're really after, so your only real danger is in being with me."

She didn't say anything to that, and he studied the map in silence. Finally, she spoke again. "The business about me and Murray. Does that disgust you? I mean, the wickedness of it?"

"Wickedness?" He laughed softly. "My dear girl, you have no conception of what true wickedness, real evil, is like, although Murray is probably animal enough to come close. A priest hears more of sin in a week than most people experience in a lifetime."

She glanced at him briefly. "But I thought you said you only posed as a priest."

"Did I?" Cussane lit another cigarette and leaned back in the seat, closing his eyes.

230

AS THE POLICE car turned out of the car park at Glasgow Airport, Chief Inspector Trent said to the driver, "You know where we're going. We've only got thirty-five minutes, so step on it." Devlin and Fox sat in the rear of the car, and Trent turned toward them. "Did you have a good flight?"

"It was fast, that was the main thing," Fox said. "What's the present position?"

"Cussane turned up again, at a gypsy encampment in the Galloway Hills. I got the news on the car radio just before you got in."

"And got away again, I fancy?" Devlin said.

"As a matter of fact, he did."

"Nice, that."

"Anyway, you said you wanted to be in the Dunhill area. We're going straight to Glasgow Central Railway Station now. The main road is still flooded, but I've made arrangements for us to board the Glasgow-to-London Express. They'll drop us at Dunhill. We'll also have the oaf who had Cussane and lost him in the first place, Sergeant Brodie. At least he knows the local area."

"Fine," Devlin said. "That takes care of everything, from the sound of it. You're armed, I hope?"

"Yes. Am I permitted to know where we're going?"

Fox said, "A village called Larwick not far from this Dunhill place. There's a farm outside, which according to our information, operates as a safe house for criminals on the run. We think our man could be there."

"But in that case, you should let me call in reinforcements."

"No," Devlin told him. "We understand the farm in question is in an isolated area. The movement of people in any kind of numbers, never mind men in uniform, would be bound to be spotted. If our man is there, he'd run for it again."

"So we'd catch him," Trent said.

Devlin glanced at Fox, who nodded, and the Irishman turned back to Trent. "The night before last, three gunmen of the

Provisional IRA tried to take him on the other side of the water. He saw them all off."

"Good God!"

"Exactly. He'd see off a few of your chaps, too, before they got to him. Better to try it our way, Chief Inspector," Harry Fox said. "Believe me."

FROM THE CREST of the hill above Glendhu, Cussane and Morag crouched in the wet bracken and looked down. The track had petered out, but in any case, it had seemed politic to Cussane to leave the jeep up there out of sight. There was nothing like an ace in the hole, if anything went sour. Better the Mungos didn't know about that.

"It doesn't look much," Morag said. Which was an understatement, for the farm presented an unlovely picture. One barn without its roof, tiles missing from the roof of the main building. There were potholes in the yard, filled with water, a truck minus its wheels, a decaying tractor, red with rust.

The girl shivered suddenly. "I've got a bad feeling," she breathed. "I don't like that place."

He stood up, picked up his bag, and took the Stetchkin from his pocket. "I've got this. There's no need to worry. Trust me."

"Yes," she said and there was a kind of passion in her voice. "I do trust you."

She took his arm, and together they started down through the bracken toward the farm.

HECTOR MUNGO HAD driven down to Larwick early that morning, mainly because he'd run out of cigarettes. Come to think of it, they'd run out of almost everything. He purchased bacon, eggs, various canned foods, a carton of cigarettes, and a bottle of Scotch, and he told the old lady who ran the general store to "put it on the bill," which she did, because she was afraid of Mungo and his brother. Everyone was afraid of them.

On his way out, Hector helped himself to a morning paper as an afterthought, got into the old van, and drove away.

He was a hard-faced man of sixty-two, looking sullen and morose in an old flying jacket and tweed cap, a gray stubble covering his chin. He turned the van into the yard, pulled up, and got out with the cardboard box filled with his purchases, and ran for the door through the rain, kicking it open.

The kitchen he entered was indescribably filthy, the old stone sink piled high with dirty pots. His brother, Angus, sat at the table, head in hands, staring into space. He was younger than his brother, forty-five, with cropped hair and a coarse and brutal face that was rendered even more ugly by the old scar that had bisected the right eye, leaving it milky white.

"I thought you'd never come." He reached into the box as his brother put it down and found the whisky, opening it and taking a long swallow. Then he found the cigarettes.

"You idle bastard," Hector told him. "You might have put the fire on."

Angus ignored him. Simply took another pull at the bottle, lit a cigarette, and opened the newspaper. Hector moved across to the sink and found a match to light the Calor gas stove beside it. He paused, looking out into the yard as Cussane and Morag appeared and approached the house.

"We've got company," he said.

Angus got up and moved to join him. He stiffened. "Just a minute." He laid the newspaper down on the draining board. "That looks damn like him right there on the front page to me."

Hector examined the newspaper report quickly. "Jesus, Angus, we've got a right one here. Real trouble."

"Just another little Mick straight out of the bogs," Angus said contemptuously. "Plenty of room for him at the bottom of the well, just like the others."

"That's true." Hector nodded solemnly.

"But not the girl." Angus wiped his mouth with the back of

one hand. "I like the look of her. She's mine, you old bastard. Just remember that. Now let them in," he added as there came a knock at the door.

"YOU KNOW THE Mungo brothers then, sergeant?" Fox asked Brodie.

They were in the guards' van at the back of the speeding train, the four of them—Devlin, Fox, Trent, and the big sergeant.

"They're animals," Brodie said. "Everyone in the district is terrified of them. I don't know how they make a living up there. They've both done prison time. Hector for operating an illegal whisky still. He's been inside three times for that. Angus has a string of minor offenses to his name, and then he killed a man in a fist fight some time back. Sentenced to five years, but they let him out in three. Twice, he's been accused of rapes and then the women concerned have dropped the charges. The suggestion that they operate a safe house doesn't surprise me, but I've no knowledge of it and it certainly has never been mentioned in their files."

"How close can we get to their farm without being spotted?" Trent asked.

"About a quarter of a mile. The road up Glendhu only goes to their place."

"No other way out?" Fox asked.

"On foot, I suppose, up the glen, over the hill."

Devlin said, "We've got to allow for one important point. If Cussane did mean to stay with the Mungos, his plans were badly disrupted. Being taken by the sergeant here, jumping from the train, that gypsy encampment, were not on the agenda. That could have changed his plans."

"True," Harry Fox said. "And there's the girl, too."

Trent said, "They could still be back there in the hills. On the other hand, they've got to pass through Larwick to get to the farm if they're in that jeep. In a village that size, somebody must have seen it."

234

"Let's hope so," Devlin said, and the Express started to slow as they came into Dunhill.

"DANNY MALONE." HECTOR Mungo poured strong tea into dirty mugs and added milk. "A long time since we had Danny here, isn't it, Angus?"

"Aye, it is that." Angus sat with a glass in his hand, ignoring the other two and staring at Morag, who did her best to avoid his gaze.

Cussane was already aware that he had made a big mistake. The service the Mungo brothers had offered people like Danny years before must have been very different from what was available now. He ignored the tea and sat there, one hand on the butt of the Stetchkin. He wasn't sure what his next move should be. The script seemed to be writing itself this time.

"Actually, we were reading about you just before you arrived." Hector Mungo shoved the paper across. "No mention of the girl, you see."

Cussane ignored the paper. "There wouldn't be."

"So what can we do for you? You want to hole up here for a while?"

"Just for the day," Cussane said. "Then tonight, when it's dark, one of you can take us south in that old van of yours. Fill it up with stuff from around the farm, hide us in the back."

Hector nodded gravely. "I don't see why not. Where to? Dumfries?"

"How far to Carlisle where the motorway begins?"

"Sixty miles. It'll cost you though."

"How much?"

Hector glanced at Angus and licked dry lips nervously. "A thousand. You're hot, my friend. Very hot."

Cussane opened his case, took out the wad of banknotes and peeled ten off. He laid them on the table. "Five hundred."

"Well, I don't know," Hector began.

"Don't be stupid," Angus said. "That's more money in one

piece than you've seen at any time during the past six months."
He turned to Cussane. "I'll drive you to Carlisle myself."

"That's settled then." Cussane got up. "You've got a room we
can use, I suppose."

"No problem." Hector was all eagerness. "One to spare for the
young lady, too."

"One will do just fine," Cussane said as they followed him out
into the flagstoned corridor and up the rickety stairs.

He opened the first door on the landing and led the way into a
large bedroom. There was a murky, unpleasant smell, and the
flowered wallpaper was stained with damp. There was an old
brass double bed with a mattress that had seen better days,
army surplus blankets stacked on top of it.

"There's a lavatory next door," Hector said. "I'll leave you to
it then."

He went out, closing the door. They heard him go back downstairs. There was an old rusting bolt on the door. Cussane
rammed it home. There was another door on the opposite side of
the room with a key in the lock. He opened it and looked out on a
stone staircase against the side of the house going down to the
yard. He closed the door and locked it again.

He turned to the girl. "All right?"

"The one with the bad eye." She shuddered. "He's worse than
Murray." She hesitated. "Can I call you Harry?"

"Why not?"

He quickly unfolded the blankets and spread them on the
mattress. "What are we going to do?" she asked.

"Rest," he said. "Get a little sleep. No one can get in. Not at the
moment."

"Do you think they'll take us to Carlisle?"

"No, but I don't think they'll try anything until it's dark and
we're ready to leave."

"How can you be sure they will try?"

"Because that's the kind of men they are. Now lie down and
try to get some sleep."

236

He got on the bed without taking off his coat, the Stetchkin in his right hand. She lay down on the other side of the bed. For a while, she stayed there, and then she rolled over and cuddled against him.

"I'm frightened."

"Hush." His arm went around her. "Be still now. I am here. Nothing will touch you in this place."

Her breathing became slow and heavy. He lay there holding here, thinking about things. She was already a liability and how long he could sustain that, he wasn't sure. On the other hand, he owed her. There was a moral debt in that, surely. He looked down at the purity of the young face, still untouched by life. Something good in a bad world. He closed his eyes, thinking of that, and finally slept.

"DID YOU SEE all that cash?" Hector asked.

"Yes," Angus said. "I saw it."

"He's locked the door. I heard him."

"Of course he has. He's no fool. Not that it matters. He's got to come out sooner or later. We'll take him then."

"Good," Hector said.

His brother poured another whisky. "And don't forget. I get the girl."

DEVLIN, FOX, TRENT and Brodie drove up to Larwick from Dunhill in an old blue Ford van, which the police sergeant borrowed from a local garage. He parked it outside the general store in the village and went in while the others waited. He returned five minutes later and got behind the wheel.

"Hector Mungo was in earlier for groceries. The old girl in there runs the saloon bar at the pub in the evenings. She says both of them are around, but no strangers, and they'd stick out like a sore thumb in a place like this."

Devlin looked out one of the rear windows in the van doors. There was really only one street, a row of granite cottages, a

237

pub, the store, and the hills lifting steeply above. "I see what you mean."

Brodie started the engine and drove away, following a narrow road between gray stone walls. "The only road and the farm at the end of it." A few minutes later he said. "Right, this is about as far as we can go without being seen."

He pulled in under some trees and they all got out. "How far?" Trent asked.

"Less than a quarter of a mile. I'll show you."

He led the way up through the trees at the side of the road, scrambling up through the bracken, and paused cautiously on the ridge line. "There you are."

The farm was below in the hollow a few hundred yards away. "Cannery Row," Devlin murmured.

"Yes, it does look a bit like that," Fox replied. "No sign of life."

"What's more important, no sign of the jeep," Devlin said. "Maybe I was wrong after all."

At that moment, both the Mungo brothers came out of the kitchen door and crossed the yard. "That's them, presumably." Fox took a small pair of Zeiss field glasses from his pocket and focused them. "Nasty-looking couple," he added as they went into the barn.

A moment later Morag Finlay came into view on the far side of the house, hesitated, then crossed the yard to the barn.

Trent said excitedly, "It's the girl. Has to be. Reefer coat, tam-o'-shanter. Fits the description exactly."

"Jesus, Mary, and Joseph," Devlin said softly. "I was right. Harry must be in the house."

Trent said, "How are we going to handle this?"

"You've both got personal radios?" Fox asked.

"Sure."

"Right, give me one of them. Devlin and I will go in from the rear of the farm. With any kind of luck, we'll take them by surprise. You go back and wait in the van. The moment I give

238

you the good word, you come up that road like an express train."

"Fine."

Trent and Brodie went back toward the road. Devlin took a Walther PPK from his pocket and cocked it. Fox did the same.

The Irishman smiled. "Just remember one thing. Harry Cussane isn't the kind of man to give any kind of a chance to."

"Don't worry," Fox said grimly. "I shan't." He started down the slope through the wet bracken and Devlin followed.

MORAG CAME AWAKE and lay staring blankly up at the ceiling, and then she remembered where she was and turned to look at Cussane beside her. He slept quietly, his breathing light, the face in repose, very calm. He still clutched the Stretchkin in his right hand. She gently eased her feet to the floor, stood up and stretched, then walked to the window. As she looked out, Hector and Angus Mungo crossed the yard and went into the barn, opposite. She opened the door and stood at the top of the stone stairs and was aware of some sort of engine starting up. She frowned, listening intently, and then quickly went down the steps and crossed the yard.

In the bedroom, Cussane stirred, stretched, then opened his eyes, instantly awake as usual. He was aware of the girl's absence at once, was on his feet in a second, and then he noticed the open door.

THE BARN WAS filled with the sour-sweet smell of mash, for the Mungos operated their still in there. Hector switched on the old gas engine and pump that provided their power supply, then checked the vat.

"We need more sugar," he said.

Angus nodded. "I'll get some."

He opened a door that led into a hut built on the side of the building. There were all the various ingredients of their illegal work in there, including several sacks of sugar. He was about to pick one up when, through a broken plank, he saw Morag Finlay outside, peering in the window at what was going on in the barn. He smiled delightedly, put down the sack, and crept out.

Morag was not even aware of his approach. A hand was clamped over her mouth, stifling her cry, and she was lifted in strong arms and carried, kicking and struggling, into the barn.

Hector turned from stirring the vat. "What's this?"

"A little nosey parker that needs teaching its manners," Angus said.

He put her down and she struck out at him wildly. He slapped her backhanded and then again with enough force to send her sprawling on a pile of sacks.

He stood over her and started to unbuckle his belt. "Manners," he said. "That's what I'm going to teach you."

"Angus," Harry Cussane called from just inside the door. "Are you a bastard by nature or do you really have to work at it?"

He stood there, hands negligently in the pockets of his raincoat, and Angus turned to face him. He bent down to pick up a shovel.

"You little squirt, I'm going to split your skull."

"Something I picked up from the IRA," Cussane said. "A special punishment for special bastards like you."

The Stetchkin came out of his pocket, there was a dull thud, and a bullet splintered Angus Mungo's right kneecap. He screamed, fell back against the gas motor and rolled over, clutching at his knee with both hands, blood pumping between his fingers. Hector Mungo gave a terrible cry of fear, turned, and ran headlong for the side door, arms up in a futile gesture of protection. He burst through and disappeared.

Cussane ignored Angus and pulled Morag to her feet. "Are you all right?"

She turned and looked down at Angus, rage and humiliation on her face. "No thanks to him."

He took her arm and they went out and crossed the yard to the kitchen door. As the girl opened it, Harry Fox called, "Hold it

240

right there, Cussane!" and moved from behind the parked van.

Cussane recognized the voice instantly, sent the girl staggering through the door, turned and fired, all in one smooth motion. Fox fell back against the van, the gun jumping from his hand. In the same moment, Devlin came around the corner and fired twice. The first bullet ripped Cussane's left sleeve, the second caught him in the shoulder, spinning him around. He went through the kitchen door headfirst, kicked it closed behind him, turned, and rammed home the bolt.

"You're hit!" Morag cried.

He shoved her ahead of him. "Never mind that! Let's get out of here!" He pushed her up the stairs toward the bedroom. "You take the bag," he urged her and ran across to the open door and peered out.

The van, with Fox and Devlin, was just around the corner. He put a finger to his lips, nodding to Morag, and went down the stone staircase quietly, the girl following. At the bottom, he led the way around to the back garden, ducked behind the wall, and started along the track through the bracken that led to the head of Glendhu.

DEVLIN OPENED FOX'S shirt and examined the wound just below the breast on the left. Fox's breathing was bad, his eyes full of pain. "You were right," he whispered. "He's hell on wheels."

"Take it easy," Devlin said. "I've called in Trent and Brodie."

He could already hear the Ford approaching. Fox said, "Is he still in the house?"

"I doubt it."

Fox sighed. "We cocked it, Liam. There'll be hell to pay over this. We had him and he got away."

"A bad habit he has," Devlin said, and the Ford entered the farmyard and skidded to a halt.

CUSSANE SAT SIDEWAYS in the passenger seat of the jeep, feet on the ground. He was stripped to the waist. There wasn't a great deal of blood, just the ugly puckered lips of the wound. He knew that was a bad sign, but there was no point in telling her that. She carefully poured onto the wound sulfa powder from his small medical kit, and she affixed one of the field service dressing packs, under his instructions.

"How do you feel?" she asked anxiously.

"Fine." Which was a lie, for now that the initial shock was wearing off, he was in considerable pain. He found one of the morphine ampules. They were of the kind used on the battlefield. He gave himself an injection and the pain started to ease quite quickly.

"Good," he said. "Now pass me a clean shirt. There should still be one left."

She helped him on with it and then with his jacket and raincoat. "You'll be needing a doctor."

"Oh, sure," he said. "Please help me? I've got a bullet in the shoulder. Why, the first thing he'd reach for would be a telephone."

"Then what do we do? They'll really start hunting you now. All the roads will be covered."

"I know," he said. "Let's have a look at the map." After a while, he said. "The Solway Firth between us and England. Only one main route through to Carlisle, via Dumfries and Annan. Not much road to plug."

"So we're trapped?"

"Not necessarily. There's the railway. There might be some sort of chance there. Let's get moving and find out."

FERGUSON SAID, "IT'S a mess. Couldn't be worse. How's Harry Fox?"

"He'll live, as they say. At least that's the local doctor's opinion. They've got him here in Dumfries at the general hospital."

"I'll make arrangements to have him shipped down here to

London as soon as possible. I want him to have the best. Where are you phoning from?"

"Police headquarters in Dumfries. Trent's here with me. They're turning out all the men they can. Roadblocks and so on. The weather isn't helping. Still raining like hell."

"What do you think, Liam?"

"I think he's gone."

"You don't think they are going to net him up there?"

"Not a chance in the wide world."

Ferguson sighed. "Yes, frankly, that's how I feel. Stay for a while with Harry, just to make sure, then come back."

"Now—this evening?"

"Get the night train to London. The pope flies in to Gatwick Airport at eight o'clock tomorrow morning. I want you with me."

CUSSANE AND MORAG left the jeep in a small quarry in a wood above Dunhill and walked down toward the railway line. At that end of the small town, the streets were deserted in the heavy rain, and they crossed the road, passed a ruined warehouse with boarded-up windows, and squeezed through a gap in the fence above the railway line. A freight train stood on the siding. Cussane crouched down and watched as a driver in overalls walked along the track and pulled himself up into the engine.

"But we don't know where it's going?" Morag said.

Cussane smiled. "It's pointing south, isn't it?" He grabbed her arm. "Come on!"

They went down the bank through the gathering dusk, crossed the line as the train started to move. Cussane broke into a trot, reached up, and pushed back a sliding door. He tossed in the bag, pulled himself up, turned and reached for the girl's hand. A moment later and she was with him. The train car was almost filled with packing cases, some of them stenciled with the address of a factory in Penrith.

"Where's that?" Morag asked.

"South of Carlisle. Even if we don't go farther than that, we're on our way."

He sat down, feeling reasonably elated, and lit a cigarette. His left arm worked, but it felt as if it didn't belong to him. Still, the morphine had taken care of the pain. Morag snuggled beside him, and he put an arm around her. A long time since he had felt protective toward anyone. To be even more blunt, a long time since he had cared.

She had closed her eyes and seemed asleep. Thanks to the morphine, the pain had not returned and he could cope when it did. There were several ampules in his kit. Certainly enough to keep him going. With the bullet in him and no proper medical attention, sepsis would only be a matter of time, but all he needed now was thirty-six hours. The Holy Father flew into Gatwick in the morning. And the day after that, Canterbury.

As the train started to coast along the track he leaned back, his good arm around the girl, and drifted into sleep.

Fourteen

MORAG came awake with a start. The train seemed to be skidding to a halt. They were passing through some sort of siding, and light from the occasional lamp drifted in through the slats, picking Cussane's face out of the darkness at intervals. He was asleep, the face wiped clean of any expression. When she gently touched his forehead, it was damp with sweat. He groaned and turned on one side, and his arm swung across his body; she saw that he was clutching the Stetchkin.

She was cold, so turned up the collar of the reefer coat and put her hands into her pockets, and watched him. She was a simple girl, uncomplicated in spite of the life she had known but blessed with a quick mind and a fund of sound common sense.

She had never known anyone like Cussane. It was not just the gun in his hand, the quick, cold violence of the man. She had no fear of him. Whatever else he was, he was not cruel. Most important of all, he had helped her, and that was something she was not used to. Even her grandfather had had difficulty in protecting her from Murray's brutality. Cussane had saved her from that, and she was enough of a woman to realize he'd saved her from far worse. That *she* had helped *him* simply did not occur to her. For the first time in her life, she was filled with a sense of freedom.

The train jolted again. Cussane's eyes opened and he turned quickly, up on one knee, and checked his watch. "One-thirty. I must have slept for a long time."

"You did."

He peered out through the slats and nodded. "We must be moving into the sidings at Penrith. Where's my bag?"

She pushed it across. He rummaged inside, found the medical kit, and gave himself another morphine injection. "How is it?" she asked.

"Fine," he said. "No trouble. I'm just making sure."

He was lying, for the pain on waking had been very real. He slid back the door and peered out. A sign for Penrith loomed out of the dark. "I was right," he said.

"Are we getting out here?"

"No guarantee this train goes any farther, and it's not much of a walk to the motorway."

"Then what?"

"There'll be a service center, a café, shops, parked cars, trucks. Who knows?" The pain had faded again now, and he managed a smile. "An infinite possibility to things. Now give me your hand, wait till we slow right down, and jump."

IT WAS A longer walk than Cussane had anticipated so that it was three o'clock when they turned into the car park of the nearest service center on the M-6 and approached the café. A couple of cars moved in off the motorway and then a truck, a freightliner so massive that Cussane didn't see the police car until the last moment. He pulled Morag down behind a van and the police car stopped, the light on top of it lazily turning.

"What shall we do?" she whispered.

"Wait and see."

The driver stayed behind the wheel and the other policeman got out and went into the café. They could see him clearly through the plate glass windows. There were perhaps twenty or thirty people in there, scattered among the tables. He took a good look around and came out again. He got back in the car and was speaking on the radio as it drove away.

"They were looking for us." Morag said.

"What else?" He took the tam-o'-shanter off her head and stuffed it into a nearby waste bin. "That's better. Too much like advertising." He fumbled in his pocket and found a five-pound note, which he gave to her. "They do takeouts in these places. Get some hot tea and sandwiches. I'll wait here. Safer that way."

She went up the ramp and into the café. He saw her hesitate at the end of the counter, then pick up a tray. He noticed a bench against a low wall nearby, half-hidden by a large van. He sat down and lit a cigarette and waited, thinking about Morag Finlay.

Strange how right it seemed to think of Morag, and it occurred to him wryly, with the usual priest's habit of self-doubt, that he should not be doing so. She was only a child. He had been celibate for more than twenty years and had never found it in the slightest degree difficult to manage without women. How absurd it would be to fall in love at the end of the day with a little sixteen-year-old gypsy girl.

She came around the van with a plastic tray and put it on the bench. "Tea and ham sandwiches, and what do you think of this? We're in the paper. There was a newsstand by the door."

He carefully drank the scalding hot tea from one of the plastic cups and unfolded the paper on his knee, reading it in the dim light that was falling across the car park from the café. The newspaper was a local paper, printed in Carlisle the previous evening. They had Cussane on the front page, a separate picture of Morag beside him.

"You look younger," he said.

"That was a snap my mother took last year. Granda had it on the wall in his caravan. They must have taken it. He'd never have given it to them."

"If a local paper had this last night, I'd say we'll be in every national newspaper's first edition later on this morning," he said.

There was a heavy silence. He lit another cigarette and sat there smoking it, not saying anything.

"You're going to leave me, aren't you?" she said.

He smiled gently. "My God, you're about a thousand years old, aren't you? Yes, I'm going to leave you. We don't have any choice."

"You don't have to explain."

But he did. "Newspaper photos can be meaningless to most people. It's the unusual that stands out, like you and me together. On your own, you'd stand a very good chance of going anywhere you want. You've got the money I gave you?"

"Yes."

"Then go in the café. Sit in the warm and wait. The express buses stop in here. I should know. I came up on one the other day, going the opposite way. You should get one to Birmingham and on to London from there with no trouble."

"And you?"

"Never mind about me. If they do lay their hands on you, tell them I forced you to help me. Enough people will believe that to make it true." He picked up his bag and put a hand to her face. "You're a special person. Don't ever let anyone put you down again. Promise me?"

"I will." She found herself choking, reached up to kiss his cheek, then turned and ran away.

She had learned, in a hard school, not to cry, but there was a hot prickly feeling at the back of her eyes as she went into the café. She brushed past a table, and a hand caught her sleeve. She turned to look down at a couple of youths in motorcyclist's black leathers—hard, vicious-looking young men, with cropped hair. The one who had her sleeve was blond and had a Nazi Iron Cross on his breast.

He said, "What's your problem, darling? Nothing that a ride on the back of my bike wouldn't fix."

She pulled away, not even angry, went and got a cup of tea and sat at a table, hands wrapped around its healing warmth. He had come into her life, he had gone from it, and nothing would ever be the same again. She started to cry, slow bitter tears, the first in years.

CUSSANE HAD TWO choices. To take his chance on thumbing a lift or to steal a car. The second gave him more freedom, more personal control, but it would only work if the vehicle in question wouldn't be missed for some time. There was a motel on the other side of the motorway. Anything parked there would belong to people staying overnight. Three to four hours at least before any of those would be missed, and by then he would be long gone.

He went up the steps to the overpass, thinking about Morag Finlay, wondering what would happen to her, but that wasn't his problem. What he had said to her made perfect sense. Together, they stuck out like a sore thumb. He paused on the bridge, lit another cigarette, trucks swishing past beneath him on the motorway. All perfectly sensible and logical, so why did he feel so rotten about it?

"Dear God, Harry," he said softly, "you're being corrupted by honesty and decency and innocence. It's not possible to soil that girl. She'll always remain untouched by the rottenness of life."

And yet . . .

SOMEONE MOVED UP beside her and a soft voice said, "You okay, kid? Anything I can do?"

He was West Indian, she knew that, with dark, curling hair, a little gray at the edges. He was perhaps forty-five and wore a heavy driving coat with fur collar, all much stained with grease, and carried a plastic sandwich box and a thermos flask. He smiled, the kind of smile that told her instantly that she was okay, and sat down.

"What's the problem?"

"Life," she said.

"Heh, that's really profound for a chick as young as you. Can I do anything?"

"I'm waiting for the bus."

"To where?"

"London."

He shook his head. "It's always London you kids make for when you run away from home."

"My grandmother lives in London," she said wearily. "Wapping."

He nodded and frowned as if considering the matter, then stood up. "Okay, I'm your man."

"What do you mean?"

"I drive a freightliner and London is my home base. The long way around, mind you, 'cause when I hit Manchester, I've got to take the Pennine Motorway to Leeds to drop something off, but we should be in London by the early afternoon."

"I don't know." She hesitated.

"Bus won't be through here for another five hours, so what have you got to lose? If it helps, I've got three girls of my own, all older than you, and my name is Earl Jackson."

"All right," she said, making her decision and went out at his side.

They walked down the ramp and started across the car park. The freightliner also towed a huge trailer. "Here we are," he said. "All the comforts of home."

There was a footstep and as they turned, the blond biker from the café moved around from behind another truck. He came forward and stood there, hands on hips. "Naughty girl," he said. "I told you you'd be better off on the back seat of my bike, and what do I find? You're flying off into the night with Rastus here. Now that's definitely out of order."

"Oh, dear," Earl Jackson said. "It talks and everything. Probably wets if you give it water."

He leaned down to put his sandwich box and thermos on the ground, and the other biker ducked from under the truck and booted him so that he staggered forward, losing his balance, and the blond one lifted a knee in his face. The one behind pulled Jackson to his feet, an arm around his throat, and the other flexed his hands, tightening his gloves.

"Hold him, Sammy. He's my meat now."

Sammy screamed as a fist swung into his kidneys. He jerked in agony, releasing his grip on Jackson, and Cussane hit him again, sending him to his knees.

He slipped past Jackson to confront the other biker. "You really should have stayed under your stone."

The youth's hand came out of his pocket and as Morag cried a warning, there was a click as a blade sprang into view, flashing in the pale light. Cussane dropped his bag, swayed to one side, grabbed for the wrist with both hands, twisted it around and up, locking the arm, and ran him headfirst into the side of the truck. The youth dropped to his knees, blood on his face, and Cussane pulled him up, reaching for the other, who was now standing. He pulled them close.

"I could put you on sticks for a year, but perhaps you'd just rather go?"

They backed off in horror, turned, and stumbled away. Cussane was aware of the pain then, so bad that it made him feel sick. He turned, clutching at the canvas side of the trailer, and Morag ran forward and put an arm around him.

"Harry, are you all right?"

"Sure, don't worry."

Earl Jackson said, "You saved my hide, man. I owe you." He turned to Morag. "I don't think I got the whole story."

"We were together, then we got separated." She glanced at Cussane. "Now we're together again."

Jackson said, "Is his destination London, too?"

She nodded. "Does the offer still hold good?"

He smiled. "Why not. Climb up in the cab. You'll find a sliding panel behind the passenger seat. An improvement of mine. There's a bunk in there, blankets and so on. It means I can sleep in the car park and save on hotel bills."

Morag climbed up. As Cussane made to follow her, Jackson caught his sleeve. "Look, I don't know what gives here, but she's a nice kid."

"You don't need to worry," Cussane told him. "I think so too," and he climbed up into the cab.

IT WAS JUST after eight o'clock on a fine, bright morning when the Alitalia jet that had brought Pope John Paul from Rome landed at Gatwick Airport. The pontiff came down the ladder, waving to the enthusiastic crowd, and his first act was to kneel and kiss English soil.

Devlin and Ferguson stood on the balcony looking down. The brigadier said, "It's at moments like this that I'd welcome my pension."

"Face facts," Devlin said. "If a really determined assassin, the kind who doesn't mind committing suicide, sets his sights on getting the pope, or the queen of England, or whomever, the odds are heavily in his favor."

Below, the pope was welcomed by Cardinal Basil Hume and the Duke of Norfolk on behalf of the queen. The cardinal made a speech of welcome and the pope replied. Then they moved to the waiting cars.

Devlin said, "What happens now?"

"Mass at Westminster Cathedral. After lunch, a visit with

her majesty at Buckingham Palace. Then St. George's Cathedral at Southwark to anoint the sick. It's going to be all go, I can see that." Ferguson was unhappy and it showed. "Dammit, Liam, where is he? Where is that sod, Cussane?"

"Around," Devlin said. "Closer than we think, probably. The only certainty is that he'll surface within the next twenty-four hours."

"And then we get him," Ferguson said as they walked away. "Bound to."

"If you say so," was Liam Devlin's only comment.

THE YARD OF the warehouse in Hunslet, Leeds, quite close to the motorway, was packed with trucks. Cussane had the sliding panel open and Jackson said, "Keep out of sight, man. Passengers are strictly verboten. I could lose my license."

He got out of the truck to see to the disengagement of the trailer, then went into the freight office to get a signature for it.

The clerk looked up from his desk. "Hello, Earl, good run?"

"Not bad."

"I hear they've been having fun over there on the M-6. One of the lads rang in from outside Manchester. Had a breakdown. Said they'd had a lot of police activity."

"I didn't notice anything," Jackson said. "What was it about?"

"Looking for some guy that's mixed up with the IRA. Has a girl with him."

Jackson managed to stay calm and signed the sheets. "Anything else?"

"No, that's fine, Earl. See you next trip."

Jackson moved outside. He hesitated beside the truck, then followed his original intention and went out of the yard across the road to the transport café. He gave the girl behind the counter his thermos to fill, ordered some bacon sandwiches, and bought a newspaper, which he read slowly on the way back to the truck.

He climbed up behind the wheel and passed the thermos and

sandwiches through. "Breakfast and something to read while you eat."

The photos were those that had appeared in the Carlisle paper and the story was roughly the same. The details on the girl were sparse. It simply said she was in his company.

As they entered the slip road leading up to the motorway, Cussane said, "Well?"

Jackson concentrated on the road. "This is heavy stuff, man. Okay, I owe you, but not that much. If you're picked up . . ."

"It would look bad for you."

"I can't afford that," Jackson told him. "I've got a record. Been inside twice. Cars were my game till I got smart. I don't want trouble, and I definitely don't want to see the inside of Pentonville Prison again."

"Then the simplest thing to do is keep driving," Cussane told him. "Once in London, we drop off and you go on about your business. No one will ever know."

It was the only solution and Jackson knew it. "Okay," he sighed. "I guess that's it."

"I'm sorry, Mr. Jackson," Morag told him.

He smiled at her in the mirror. "Never mind, kid. I should have known better. Now keep inside and close that panel," and he turned the freightliner into the motorway.

DEVLIN WAS ON the phone to the hospital in Dumfries when Ferguson came in from the study.

As the Irishman put down the receiver, the brigadier said, "I could do with some good news. Colonel Jones just got killed taking Goose Green in the Falklands. Turned out to be about three times the Argentinian troops there as anticipated."

"What happened?"

"Oh, they won the day, but Jones died, I'm afraid."

"The news on Harry Fox is comforting," Devlin said. "They are flying him down from Glasgow this evening. But he's in fair shape."

"Thank God for that," Ferguson said.

"I spoke to Trent. They can't get a word out of those tinkers. Nothing helpful anyway. According to the old grandfather, he's no idea where the girl might go. Her mother's in New Zealand."

"They're worse than gypsies, tinkers," Ferguson said. "I know. I come from Angus, remember. Funny people. Even when they hate each other, they hate the police more. Wouldn't even tell you the way to the public toilet."

"So what do we do now?"

"We'll go along to St. Georges to see what his holiness is up to, then I think you can take a run down to Canterbury. I'm laying on a police car and driver for you, by the way. I think it will help for you to look as official as possible from now on."

MORAG SAT IN the corner of the bunk, her back against the wall. "Why did you come back at Penrith? You haven't told me."

Cussane shrugged. "I suppose I decided you weren't fit to be out on your own or something like that."

She shook her head. "Why are you so afraid to admit to kindness?"

"Am I?" He lit a cigarette and watched her as she took an old pack of cards from her pocket and shuffled them. They were tarot. "Can you use those things?"

"My grandma showed me how years ago when I was quite young. I'm not sure if I have the gift. It's hard to tell."

She shuffled the cards again. He said, "The police might be waiting at her place."

She paused, surprise on her face. "Why should they? They don't know she exists."

"They must have asked questions at the camp and someone must have told them something. If not your grandad, there's always Murray."

"Never," she said. "Even Murray wouldn't do a thing like that. You were different—an outsider, but me—that's not the same at all."

She turned the first card. It was the Tower, the building struck by lightning, two bodies falling. "The individual suffers through the forces of destiny being worked out in the world," Morag commented.

"That's me. Oh, that's very definitely me," Harry Cussane told her, and he started to laugh helplessly.

SUSAN CALDER WAS twenty-three, a small girl, undeniably attractive in the neat, navy blue, police uniform with the hat with the black and white checks around the brim. She had trained as a schoolteacher, but three terms of that job had definitely been enough. She had volunteered for the Metropolitan Police and had been accepted. She had served for just over one year. Waiting beside the police car outside the Cavendish Square flat, she presented a pleasing picture and Devlin's heart lifted. She was polishing the windshield as he came down the steps.

"Good day to you, *a colleen,* God save the good work."

She took in the black Burberry, the felt hat slanted across the ears, was about to give him a dusty answer, but paused. "You wouldn't be Professor Devlin, would you?"

"As ever was. And you?"

"WPC Susan Calder, sir."

"Have they told you you're mine until tomorrow?"

"Yes, sir. Hotel booked in Canterbury."

"There *will* be talk back at the station. Let's get moving then," and he opened the rear door and got in. She slipped behind the wheel and drove away and Devlin leaned back, watching her. "Have they told you what this is about?"

"You're with Group-4, sir, that's all I know."

"And that is?"

"Antiterrorism—intelligence side of things, as distinct from the Yard's antiterrorist squad."

"Yes, Group-4 can employ people like me and get away with it." He frowned. "The next sixteen hours will see the making or

256

breaking of this affair, and you'll be with me every step of the way."

"If you say so, sir."

"So I think you deserve to know what it's about."

"Should you be telling me, sir?" she asked calmly.

"No, but I'm going to," he said and started to talk, telling her everything there was to know about the whole affair from the beginning and especially about Harry Cussane. It was one way to get it all straight in his own head.

When he was finished, she said, "It's quite a story."

"And that's an understatement."

"There is just one thing, sir."

"And what would that be?"

"My elder brother was killed in Belfast three years ago while serving there as a lieutenant in the marines. A sniper hit him from a place called the Divis flats."

"Does that mean I pose a problem for you?" Devlin asked her.

"Not at all, sir. I just wanted you to know," she said crisply and turned into the main road and drove down toward the river.

CUSSANE AND MORAG stood in the quiet street on the edge of Wapping and watched the freightliner turn the corner and disappear.

"Poor Earl Jackson," Cussane said. "I bet he can't get away fast enough. What's your grandma's address?"

"Cork Street Wharf. It's five or six years since I was there. I'm afraid I can't remember the way."

"We'll find it."

They walked down toward the river, which seemed the obvious thing to do. His arm was hurting again and he had a headache, but he made no sign of any of this to the girl. When they came to a grocery shop on a corner, she went in to make inquiries.

She came out quickly. "It's not far. It's only a couple of streets away."

They walked to the corner and there was the river. A hundred yards farther on, there was a sign on the wall saying, *Cork Street Wharf.*

Cussane said, "All right, off you go. I'll stay back out of the way, just in case she has visitors."

"I shan't be long."

She hurried off down the street, and Cussane stepped back through a broken door into a yard half-filled with rubble and waited. He could smell the river. Not many boats now though. This had once been the greatest port in the world, now it was a graveyard of rusting cranes pointing into the sky like primeval monsters. He felt lousy and when he lit a cigarette, his hand shook. There was the sound of running steps and Morag appeared. "She isn't there. I spoke to the next-door neighbor."

"Where is she?"

"With a touring show. A fairground show. She's in Maidstone this week."

And Maidstone was only sixteen or seventeen miles from Canterbury. There was an inevitability to things. Cussane said, "We'd better get going then."

"You'll take me?"

"Why not?" and he turned and led the way along the street.

HE FOUND WHAT he was looking for within twenty minutes, a pay-and-display parking lot.

"Why is this so important?" she demanded.

"Because people pay in advance for however many hours of parking they want and stick the ticket on the windshield. A wonderful aid to car thieves. You can tell just how long you've got before the car is missed."

She scouted around. "There's one here says six hours."

"And what time was it booked in?" He checked and took out his pocketknife. "That'll do. Four hours to go. Dark then, anyway."

He worked on the vent with the knife, forced it, and unlocked the door, then he reached under the dashboard and pulled the wires down.

"You've done this before," she said.

"That's true." The engine roared into life. "Okay," he said, "let's get out of here." And as she scrambled into the passenger seat, he drove away.

Fifteen

"**O**F course, it's hardly surprising that the pope wants to come here, sir," Susan Calder said to Devlin. "It was St. Augustine who founded the cathedral here. In Saxon times. This is the birthplace of English Christianity."

"Is it now?"

They were standing in the magnificent perpendicular nave of the cathedral, the pillars soaring to the vaulted ceiling high above them. The place was a hive of activity, workmen everywhere.

"It's certainly spectacular," Devlin said.

"It was even bombed in 1942 during the Canterbury blitz. The library was destroyed, but it's been rebuilt. Up here in the northwest transept is where Saint Thomas Beckett was murdered by the three knights eight hundred years ago."

"I believe the pope has a particular affinity for him," Devlin said. "Let's have a look."

They moved up the nave to the place of Beckett's martyrdom. The precise spot where traditionally he was believed to have fallen was marked by a square stone. There was a strange atmosphere. Devlin shivered, suddenly cold.

"The Sword's Point," the girl said simply. "That's what they call it."

"Yes, well they would, wouldn't they? Come on, let's get out of here. I could do with a smoke and I've seen enough."

They went out through the south porch past the police guard. There was plenty of activity outside also, men working on stands, and a considerable police presence. Devlin lit a cigarette, and he and Susan Calder moved out onto the pavement.

"What do you think?" she said. "I mean, not even Cussane could expect to get in there tomorrow. You've seen the security."

Devlin took out his wallet and produced the security card Ferguson had given him. "Have you seen one of these before?"

"I don't think so."

"Very special. Guaranteed to unlock all doors."

"So?"

"Nobody has asked to see it. We were totally accepted when we walked in. Why? Because you are wearing a police uniform. And don't tell me that's what you are. It isn't the point."

"I see what you mean." She was troubled and it showed.

"The best place to hide a tree is in a forest," he said. "Tomorrow, there'll be policemen all over the place and church dignitaries, so what's another policeman or priest."

At that moment, someone called his name and they turned to see Ferguson walking toward them with a man in a dark overcoat. Ferguson wore a greatcoat of the kind favored by Guards officers and carried a smartly rolled umbrella.

"Brigadier Ferguson," Devlin told the girl hastily.

"There you are," the brigadier said. "This your driver?"

"WPC Calder, sir," she saluted smartly.

"This is Superintendant Foster, attached to Scotland Yard's antiterrorist squad," Ferguson said. "I've been going over things with him. Seems pretty watertight to me."

"Even if your man gets as far as Canterbury, there's no way

he'll get into the cathedral tomorrow," Foster said simply. "I'd stake my reputation on it."

"Let's hope you don't have to," Devlin told him.

Ferguson tugged at Foster's sleeve impatiently. "Right, let's get inside before the light fails. I'm staying here tonight myself, Devlin. I'll phone you at your hotel later."

The two men walked up to the great door, a policeman opened it for them, and they went inside. "Do you think he knows them?" Devlin asked her gently.

"God, I don't know. You've got *me* wondering now, sir." She opened the door of the car for him. He got in and she slid behind the wheel and started the engine. "One thing."

"What's that?"

"Even if he did get in and did something, he'd never get out again."

"But that's the whole point," Devlin said. "He doesn't care what happens to him afterward."

"God help us then."

"I wouldn't bank on it. Nothing we can do now, girl dear. We don't control the game any more, it controls us, so get to my hotel in your own good time, and I'll buy you the best dinner the place offers. Did I tell you, by the way, that I have this terrible thing for women in uniform?"

As she turned out into the traffic, she started to laugh.

THE TRAILER WAS large and roomy and extremely well-furnished. The bedroom section was separate in its own small compartment, with twin bunks. When Cussane opened the door and peered in, Morag appeared to be sleeping.

He started to close the door and she called, "Harry?"

"Yes?" He moved back in. "What is it?"

"Is Grandma still working?"

"Yes."

He sat on the edge of the bunk. He was in considerable pain now. It even hurt to breathe. Something was badly wrong, he knew that. She reached up to touch his face, and he drew back a little.

She said, "Remember in Granda's trailer that first day? I asked if you were frightened I might corrupt you?"

"To be precise," he told her, "your actual words were: 'Are you frightened I might corrupt you, *Father.*'"

She went very still. "You are a priest then? A real priest? I think I always knew it."

"Go to sleep," he said.

She reached for his hand. "You wouldn't leave without telling me?"

There was genuine fear in her voice. He said gently. "Now would I do a thing like that to you?" He got up and opened the door. "Like I said, get some sleep. I'll see you in the morning."

He lit a cigarette, opened the door, and went out. The Maidstone fairground was a comparatively small affair—a number of sideshows, various stalls, bingo stands, several carousels. There were still a number of people around, noisy and good-humored, in spite of the late hour, music loud on the night air. At one end of the trailer was the Land Rover that towed it, at the other, the red tent with the illuminated sign that said *Gypsy Rose.* As he watched, a young couple emerged, laughing. Cussane hesitated, then went in.

Brana Smith was at least seventy, a brightly colored scarf drawing back the hair from her brown parchment face. She wore a shawl over her shoulders, a necklace of gold coins around her neck. The table she was seated at had a crystal ball on it.

"You certainly look the part," he said.

"That's the general idea. The public likes a gypsy to look like a gypsy. Put up the closed sign and give me a cigarette." He did as he was told, came back, and sat opposite her like a client, the crystal between them. "Is Morag asleep?"

"Yes." He took a deep breath to control his pain. "You must never let her go back to that camp, you understand me?"

"Don't worry." Her voice was dry and very calm. "We gypsies

264

stick together and we pay our debts. I'll put the word out and one day soon, Murray will pay for what he's done, believe me."

He nodded. "When you saw her picture in the paper today and read the circumstances, you must have been worried. Why didn't you get in touch with the police?"

"The police? You must be joking." She shrugged. "In any case, I knew she was coming, and I knew she would be all right."

"Knew?" Cussane said.

She rested a hand lightly on the crystal. "These are only the trappings, my friend. I have the gift, as my mother did before me and hers before her."

He nodded. "Morag told me. She read the tarot cards for me, but she isn't certain of her powers."

"Oh, she has the gift," the old woman nodded. "As yet unformed." She pushed a pack of cards to him. "Cut them, then hand them back to me with your left hand."

He did as he was told, and she cut them in turn. "The cards mean nothing without the gift. You understand this?"

He felt strangely light-headed. "Yes."

"Three cards, that will tell all." She turned the first. It was the Tower. "He has suffered through the forces of destiny," she said. "Others have controlled his life."

"Morag drew that card," he said. "She told me something like that."

She turned the second card. It showed a young man suspended upside down from a wooden gibbet by his right ankle.

"The Hanged Man. When he strives hardest, it is with his own shadow. He is two people. Himself and yet not himself. Impossible now to go back to the wholeness of youth."

"Too late," he said. "Far too late."

The third card showed Death in traditional form, his scythe mowing a crop of human bodies.

"But whose?" Cussane laughed a little too loud. "Death, I mean? Mine or perhaps somebody else's?"

"The card means far more than its superficial image implies.

265

He comes as a redeemer. In this man's death lies the opportunity for rebirth."

"Yes, but for whom?" Cussane demanded, leaning forward, and the light reflected from the crystal seemed very bright.

She touched his forehead, damp with sweat. "You are ill."

"I'll be all right. I need to lie down, that's all." He got to his feet. "I'll sleep for a while, if that's all right with you, then I'll leave before Morag wakes. That's very important. Do you understand me?"

"Oh, yes," she nodded. "I understand you very well."

He went out into the cool night. Most people had gone home now, and the stalls, the carousels were closing down. His forehead was burning. He went up the steps into the trailer and lay on the bench seat, looking up at the ceiling. Better to take the morphine now than in the morning. He got up, rummaged in the bag and found an ampule. The injection worked quite quickly and after awhile, he slept.

HE CAME AWAKE with a start, his head very clear. It was morning, light was coming in through the windows, and the old woman was seated at the table smoking a cigarette and watching him. When he sat up, the pain was like a living thing. For a moment, he thought he was going to stop breathing.

She pushed a cup across to him. "Hot tea. Drink some."

It tasted good, better than anything he had ever known, and he smiled and helped himself to a cigarette from her packet, hand shaking. "What time is it?"

"Seven o'clock."

"And Morag's still asleep?"

"Yes."

"Good. I'll get going."

She said gravely. "You're ill, Father Harry Cussane. Very ill."

He smiled gently. "You have the gift, so you would know." He took a deep breath. "Things to get straight before I go. Morag's position in all this. Have you got a pencil?"

"Yes."

"Good. Take down this number." She did as she was told. "The man on the other end is called Ferguson, Brigadier Ferguson."

"Is he police?"

"In a way. He'd dearly love to get his hands on me. If he isn't there, they'll know how to contact him wherever he is, which is probably Canterbury."

"Why there?"

"Because I'm going to Canterbury to kill the pope." He produced the Stetchkin from his pocket. "With this."

She seemed to grow small, to withdraw into herself. She believed him, of course, he could see that. "But why?" she whispered. "He's a good man."

"Aren't we all?" he said, "or at least were, at some time or other in our lives. The important thing is this. When I've gone, you phone Ferguson. Tell him I'm going to Canterbury Cathedral. Also tell him I forced Morag to help me. Say she was frightened for her life. Anything." He laughed. "Taking it all in all, that should cover it."

He picked up his bag and walked to the door. She said, "You're dying, don't you know that?"

"Of course I do." He managed a smile. "You said that Death on the tarot cards means redemption. In my death lies the opportunity for rebirth. That child's in there. That's all that's important." He opened the bag, took out the bundle of fifty-pound notes, and tossed them on the table. "The money's for her. I won't be needing it now."

He went out. The door banged. She sat there listening, aware of the sound of the car starting up and moving away. She stayed like that for a very long time, thinking about Harry Cussane. She had liked him more than most men she had known, but there was death in his eyes; she had seen that at the very first meeting. And there was Morag to consider.

There was a sound of movement next door where the girl

slept, a faint stirring. Old Brana checked her watch. It was eight-thirty. Making her decision, she got up, let herself out of the trailer quietly, and hurried across the fairground to the public phone box and dialed Ferguson's number.

DEVLIN WAS HAVING breakfast at the hotel in Canterbury with Susan Calder when he was called to the phone. He was back quite quickly.

"That was Ferguson. Cussane's turned up. Or at least his girlfriend has. Do you know Maidstone?"

"Yes, sir. It can't be more than sixteen or seventeen miles from here. Twenty at the most."

"Then let's get moving," he said. "There really isn't much time for any of us now."

IN LONDON, THE pope had left the Pro-Nunciature very early to visit more than 4,000 religious: nuns, monks, and priests, Catholic and Anglican, at Digby Stuart Training College in London. Many of them were from enclosed orders. This was the first time they had gone into the outside world in many years. It was a highly emotional moment for all when they renewed their vows in the Holy Father's presence. It was after that that he left for Canterbury in the helicopter provided by British Caledonian Airways.

STOKELY HALL WAS bounded by a high wall of red brick, a Victorian addition to the estate when the family still had money. The lodge beside the great iron gates was Victorian also, though the architect had done his best to make it resemble the early Tudor features of the main house. When Cussane drove by on the main road, there were two police cars at the gates, and a police motorcyclist who had been trailing behind him for the past mile, turned in.

Cussane carried on down the road, the wall on his left, fringed by trees. When the gate was out of sight, he scanned the opposite side of the road and finally noticed a five-barred gate and a track leading into a wood. He drove across quickly, got out, opened the gate, then drove some little way into the trees. He went back to the gate, closed it, and returned to the car.

He took off his raincoat, jacket and shirt—awkwardly, because of his bad arm. The smell was immediately apparent, the sickly odor of decay. He laughed foolishly and said softly, "Jesus, Harry, you're falling apart."

He got his black vest and clerical collar from the bag and put them on. Finally, the cassock. It seemed a thousand years since he had rolled it up and put it in the bottom of the bag at Kilrea. He reloaded the Stetchkin with a fresh clip, put it in one pocket and a spare clip in the other, and got into the car, as it started to drizzle. No more morphine. The pain would keep him sharp. He closed his eyes and vowed to stay in control.

BRANA SMITH SAT at the table in the trailer, an arm around Morag, who was crying steadily.

"Just tell me exactly what he said," Liam Devlin told her.

"Grandma . . ." the girl started.

The old woman shook her head. "Hush, child." She turned to Devlin. "He told me he intended to shoot the pope. Showed me the gun. Then he gave me the telephone number to ring in London. The man Ferguson."

"And what did he tell you to say?"

"That he would be at Canterbury Cathedral."

"And that's all?"

"Isn't it enough?"

Devlin turned to Susan Calder standing at the door. "Right, we'd better get back."

She opened the door. Brana Smith said, "What about Morag?"

"That's up to Ferguson," Devlin shrugged. "I'll see what I can do."

He started to go out, and she said, "Mr. Devlin?" He turned. "He's dying."

"Dying?" Devlin said.

"Yes, from a gunshot wound."

He went out, ignoring the curious crowd of fairground workers and got in the front passenger seat beside Susan. As she drove away, he called up Canterbury Police Headquarters on the car radio and asked to be patched through to Ferguson.

"Nothing fresh here," he told the brigadier. "The message was for you and quite plain. He intends to be at Canterbury Cathedral."

"Cheeky bastard!" Ferguson said.

"Another thing. He's dying. It would seem sepsis must be setting in from the bullet he took at the Mungos' farm."

"Your bullet?"

"That's right."

Ferguson took a deep breath. "All right, get back here fast. The pope should be here soon."

THE POPE HAD expressed a desire to pray in Stokely Hall. It was one of the finest Tudor mansions in England and the Stokelys had been one of the handful of English aristocratic families to maintain Catholicism after Henry VIII and the Reformation. The thing that distinguished Stokely was the family chapel, the chapel in the wood, reached by the tunnel from the main house. Regarded by most experts as being, in effect, the oldest Catholic church in England.

Cussane lay back in the passenger seat, thinking it over. The pain was a living thing now, his face ice cold and yet dripping sweat. He managed to find a cigarette and started to light it and then in the distance heard the sound of engines up above. He got out of the car and stood listening. A moment late, the blue-and-white painted helicopter passed overhead.

SUSAN CALDER SAID, "You don't look happy, sir."

"It was Liam last night. And I'm not happy. Cussane's behavior doesn't make sense."

"That was then, this is now. What's worrying you?"

"Harry Cussane, my good friend of more than twenty years. The best chess player I ever knew."

"And what was the most significant thing about him?"

"That he was always three moves ahead. That he had the ability to make you concentrate on his right hand when what was really important was what he was doing with his left. In the present circumstances, what does that suggest to you?"

"That he hasn't any intention of going to Canterbury Cathedral. That's where the action is. That's where everyone is waiting for him."

"So he strikes somewhere else. But how? Where's the schedule?"

"Back seat, sir."

He found it and read it aloud. "Starts off at Digby Stuart College in London, then by helicopter to Canterbury." He frowned. "Wait a minute. He's dropping in at some place called Stokely Hall to visit a Catholic chapel."

"We passed it on the way to Maidstone," she said. "About three miles from here. But that's an unscheduled visit. It's not been mentioned in any of the newspapers that I've seen and everything else has. How would Cussane know?"

"He used to run the press office at the Catholic secretariat in Dublin." Devlin slammed a fist into his thigh. "That's it. Has to be. Get your foot down hard and don't stop for anything."

"What about Ferguson?"

He reached for the mike. "I'll try and contact him, but too late for him to do anything. We'll be there in a matter of minutes. It's up to us now."

He took the Walther from his pocket, cocked it, then put the safety catch on as the car shot forward.

THE ROAD WAS clear when Cussane crossed it, and he moved into the shelter of the trees and walked along the base of the wall. He came to an old iron gate, narrow and rusting, fixed

271

firmly in the wall, and as he tested it, heard voices on the other side. He moved behind a tree and waited. Through the bars he could see a path and rhododendron bushes. A moment later, two nuns walked by.

He gave them time to pass, then went back to where the ground under the trees rose several feet, bringing him almost level with the wall. He reached for a branch that stretched across. It would have been ridiculously easy if it had not been for his shoulder and arm. The pain was appalling, but he hoisted the skirts of his cassock to give him freedom of movement and swung across, pausing on top of the wall for only a moment before dropping to the ground.

He stayed on one knee, fighting for breath, then stood up and ran a hand over his hair. Next he hurried along the path, aware of the nuns' voices up ahead, turned a corner by an old stone fountain, and caught up with them. They turned in surprise. One of them was very old, the other younger.

"Good morning, Sisters," he said briskly. "Isn't it beautiful here? I couldn't resist taking a little walk."

"Neither could we, Father," the older one said.

They walked on side-by-side and emerged from the shrubbery onto an expansive lawn. The helicopter was parked a hundred yards to the right, the crew lounging beside it. There were several limousines in front of the house and two police cars. A couple of policemen crossed the lawn with an Alsatian guard dog on a lead. They passed Cussane and the two nuns without a word and continued down toward the shrubbery.

"Are you from Canterbury, Father?" the old nun inquired.

"No, Sister . . . ?" he paused.

"Agatha—and this is Sister Anne."

"I'm with the secretariat in Dublin. A wonderful thing to be invited over here to see His Holiness. I missed him during his Irish trip."

SUSAN CALDER TURNED in from the road at the front gate

and Devlin showed his security pass as two policemen moved forward. "Has anyone passed through here in the last few minutes?"

"No, sir," one officer said. "A hell of a lot of guests came before the helicopter arrived though."

"Move!" Devlin said.

Susan went up the drive at some speed. "What do you think?"

"He's here!" Devlin said. "I'd stake my life on it."

"HAVE YOU MET His Holiness yet, Father?" Sister Anne inquired.

"No, I've only just arrived from Canterbury with a message for him."

They were crossing the gravel drive now, past the policemen standing beside the cars, up the steps and past the two uniformed security guards, and in through the great oak door. The hall was spacious, a central staircase lifting to a landing. Double doors stood open to the right, disclosing a large reception room filled with visitors, many of them church dignitaries.

Cussane and the two nuns walked toward it. "And where is this famous Stokely chapel?" he asked. "I've never seen it."

"Oh, it's so beautiful," Sister Agatha said. "So many years of prayer. The entrance is just down the hall, see where the Monsignor is standing?"

They paused at the door of the reception and Cussane said, "If you'll excuse me for a moment. I may be able to give my message to His Holiness before he joins the reception."

"We'll wait for you, Father," Sister Agatha said. "I think we'd rather go in with you."

"Of course. I shan't be long."

Cussane went past the bottom of the stairs and moved into the corner of the hall where the monsignor was standing, resplendent in scarlet and black. He was an old man with silver hair and spoke with an Italian accent.

"What do you seek, Father?"

"His Holiness."

"Impossible. He is at prayer."

Cussane put a hand to the old man's face, turned the handle of the door, and forced him through. He closed the door behind him with a foot.

"I'm truly sorry, Father." He chopped the old priest on the side of the neck and gently lowered him to the floor.

A long narrow tunnel stretched ahead of him, dimly lit, steps leading up to an oaken door at the end. The pain was terrible now, all consuming. But that no longer mattered. He fought for breath momentarily, then took the Stetchkin from his pocket and went forward.

SUSAN CALDER SWUNG the car in at the bottom of the steps and as Devlin jumped out, she followed him. His security pass was already in his hand as a police sergeant moved forward.

"Anything out of the way happened? Anyone unusual gone in?"

"No, sir. Lots of visitors before the pope arrived. Couple of nuns and a priest just went in."

Devlin went up the steps on the run past the security guards, Susan Calder at his heels. He paused, taking in the scene, the reception room at the right, the two nuns waiting by the door. *A priest,* the sergeant had said.

He approached Sisters Agatha and Anne. "You've just arrived, Sisters?"

Beyond them, the guests talked animatedly, waiters moving among them.

"That's right," Sister Agatha said.

"Wasn't there a priest with you?"

"Oh, yes, the good father from Dublin."

Devlin's stomach went hollow. "Where is he?"

"He had a message for His Holiness, a message from Canterbury, but I told him the Holy Father was in the chapel so he went to speak to the monsignor on the door." Sister Agatha led the

274

way across the hall and paused, "Oh, the monsignor doesn't seem to be there."

Devlin was running and the Walther was in his hand as he flung open the door and stumbled over the monsignor on the floor. He was aware of Susan Calder behind him, was even more aware of the priest in the black cassock mounting the steps at the end of the tunnel and reaching for the handle of the oak door.

"Harry!" Devlin called.

Cussane turned and fired without the slightest hesitation, the bullet slamming into Devlin's right forearm, punching him back against the wall. Devlin dropped the Walther as he fell, and Susan cried out and flattened herself against the wall.

Cussane stood there, the Stetchkin extended in his right hand, but he did not fire. Instead, he smiled a ghastly smile.

"Stay out of it, Liam," he called. "Last act!" and he turned and opened the chapel door.

Devlin was sick, dizzy from shock. He reached for the Walther with his left hand, fumbled and dropped it as he tried to stand. He glared up at the girl.

"Take it! Stop him! It's up to you now!"

Susan Calder knew nothing of guns beyond a couple of hours of basic handling experience on her training course. She had fired a few rounds from a revolver on the range, that was all. Now, she picked up the Walther without hesitation and ran along the tunnel. Devlin got to his feet and went after her.

THE CHAPEL WAS a place of shadows hallowed by the centuries, the sanctuary lamp the only light, and His Holiness Pope John Paul II knelt in his white robes before the simple altar. The sound of the silenced Stetchkin, muffled by the door, had not alerted him, but the raised voices had. He was on his feet and turning as the door crashed open and Cussane entered.

He stood there, face damp with sweat, strangely medieval in the black cassock, the Stetchkin against his thigh.

John Paul said calmly, "You are Father Harry Cussane."

"You are mistaken. I am Mikhail Kelly." Cussane laughed wildly. "Strolling player of sorts."

"You are Father Harry Cussane," John Paul said relentlessly. "Priest then, priest now, priest eternally. God will not let go."

"No!" Cussane cried in a kind of agony. "I refuse it!"

The Stetchkin swung up, and Susan Calder stumbled in through the door, falling to her knees, skirt riding up, the Walther leveled in both hands. She shot him twice in the back, shattering his spine and Cussane cried out in agony and fell on his knees in front of the pope. He stayed there for a moment then rolled onto his back, still clutching the Stetchkin.

Susan stayed on her knees, lowering the Walther to the floor, watching as the pontiff gently took the Stetchkin from Cussane's hand.

She heard the pope say in English, "I want you to make an act of contrition. Say after me: O my God who art infinitely good in thyself . . ."

"Oh my God . . . ," Harry Cussane said and died.

The pope, on his knees, started to pray, hands clasped.

Behind Susan, Devlin crawled in and sat with his back against the wall, holding his wound, blood on his fingers. She dropped the gun and eased against him as if for warmth.

"Does one always feel like this?" she asked him harshly. "Dirty and ashamed?"

"Join the club, girl dear," Liam Devlin said, and he put his good arm around her.

Epilogue

*I*T was six o'clock on a gray morning, the sky swollen with rain when Susan Calder turned her mini car in through the gate of St. Joseph's Catholic Cemetery, Highgate. It was a poor sort of place with lots of Gothic monuments from an obviously more prosperous past, but now, everything overgrown, nothing but decay.

She was not in uniform and wore a dark headscarf, blue belted coat, and leather boots. She pulled in at the superintendent's lodge and found Devlin standing beside a taxi. He was wearing his usual dark Burberry and black felt hat and his right arm was in a black sling. She got out of the car and he came to meet her.

"Sorry I'm late. The traffic," she said. "Have they started?"

"Yes." He smiled ironically. "I think Harry would have appreciated this. Like a bad set for a second-rate movie. Even the rain makes it another cliché," he said as it started to fall in heavy drops.

He told the taxi driver to wait, and he and the girl went along the path between gravestones. "Not much of a place," she said.

"They had to tuck him away somewhere." He took out a cigarette with his good hand and lit it. "Ferguson and the home office people felt you should have had some sort of gallantry award."

"A medal?" There was genuine distaste on her face. "They can keep it. He had to be stopped, but that doesn't mean I liked doing it."

"They've decided against it, anyway. It would be too public; require an explanation. They can't have that. So much for Harry wanting to leave the KGB with the blame."

They came to the grave and paused some distance away under a tree. There were two gravediggers, a priest, a woman in a black coat, and a girl."

"That Tanya woman?"

"Yes, and the girl is Morag Finlay," Devlin said. "The three women in Harry Cussane's life, together now to see him planted. First, the one he so greatly wronged as a child, then the child he saved. I find that ironic. Harry the redemptionist."

"And then there's me," she said. "His executioner, and I never even met him."

"Only the once," Devlin said. "And that was enough. Strange —the most important people in his life were women and in the end they were the death of him."

The priest sprinkled the grave and the coffin with holy water and incensed them. Morag started to cry, and Tanya Voroninova put an arm around her as the priest's voice rose in prayer:

Lord Jesus Christ, Savior of the world, we commend your servant to you and pray for him.

"Poor Harry," Devlin said. "Final curtain and he still didn't get a full house."

He took her arm and they turned and walked away through the rain.